MORE SCORCHING PRAISE FOR AWARD-WINNING
EMMA HOLLY AND HER NOVELS

"Emma Holly brings a level of sensuality
to her storytelling that may shock the uninitiated."
—*Publishers Weekly*

"Emma Holly is a name to look out for."
—Bestselling author Robin Schone

"A deliciously steamy read. This is how erotica must be written!"
—Michele Hauf, author of *Here Is My Heart*

"Titillating, erotic, and fun."
—*The Best Reviews*

"A sensual feast."
—*Midwest Book Review*

"She creates tantalizing tales."
—*Rendezvous*

"A wonderfully passionate read."
—*Escape to Romance*

"Deeply sensual and emotional."
—*Booklist*

"Holly pens one hot, hot, hot story."
—*Romantic Times*

"Surprisingly erotic."
—Award-winning author Susan Sizemore

"A treat . . . moves seamlessly from one hot and sexy situation to the
next . . . More from Ms. Holly, please." —Elizabeth Coldwell, *Forum*

"A story of sex, romance, and intrigue that goes beyond the norm."
—*Affaire de Coeur*

"I CAN'T WAIT FOR THE NEXT EMMA HOLLY STORY."
—Thea Devine

Beyond Desire

EMMA HOLLY

BERKLEY SENSATION, NEW YORK

THE BERKLEY PUBLISHING GROUP
Published by the Penguin Group
Penguin Group (USA) Inc.
375 Hudson Street, New York, New York 10014, USA
Penguin Group (Canada), 90 Eglinton Avenue East, Suite 700, Toronto, Ontario M4P 2Y3, Canada
(a division of Pearson Penguin Canada Inc.)
Penguin Books Ltd., 80 Strand, London WC2R 0RL, England
Penguin Group Ireland, 25 St. Stephen's Green, Dublin 2, Ireland (a division of Penguin Books Ltd.)
Penguin Group (Australia), 250 Camberwell Road, Camberwell, Victoria 3124, Australia
(a division of Pearson Australia Group Pty. Ltd.)
Penguin Books India Pvt. Ltd., 11 Community Centre, Panchsheel Park, New Delhi—110 017, India
Penguin Group (NZ), Cnr. Airborne and Rosedale Roads, Albany, Auckland 1310, New Zealand
(a division of Pearson New Zealand Ltd.)
Penguin Books (South Africa) (Pty.) Ltd., 24 Sturdee Avenue, Rosebank, Johannesburg 2196,
South Africa

Penguin Books Ltd., Registered Offices: 80 Strand, London WC2R 0RL, England

This is a work of fiction. Names, characters, places, and incidents either are the product of the author's imagination or are used fictitiously, and any resemblance to actual persons, living or dead, business establishments, events, or locales is entirely coincidental. The publisher does not have any control over and does not assume any responsibility for author or third-party websites or their content.

PRINTING HISTORY
Beyond Innocence: Jove mass market edition / July 2001
Beyond Seduction: Jove mass market edition / June 2002
Berkley Sensation trade paperback omnibus edition / January 2006

Library of Congress Cataloging-in-Publication Data

Holly, Emma.
   [Beyond innocence]
   Beyond desire / Emma Holly.
      p. cm.
   Beyond innocence—Beyond seduction.
   ISBN 0-425-20786-2
   1. Holly, Emma. Beyond seduction. II. Title.

PS3608.O4943B49 2006
813'.6—dc22   2005054558

PRINTED IN THE UNITED STATES OF AMERICA

10 9 8 7 6 5 4 3 2 1

CONTENTS

BEYOND INNOCENCE

I

BEYOND SEDUCTION

239

Beyond Innocence

To Laurie,
who taught me a thing or two about older siblings.

You're the best, Sis!

Prologue

"A FOOTMAN!" EDWARD RAGED. "YOU WERE CAUGHT IN YOUR bedroom with a *footman?*"

Anger had pulled him to his feet behind the study desk. Now he gripped the edge of the carved bog oak as if pressure alone could will his brother's confession away.

Freddie was slumped in the red morocco chair, one foot propped on his knee while he examined his well-buffed nails. The nonchalant pose suited his lanky frame. In blazing white shirt and tastefully embroidered waistcoat, he was the golden boy at rest: his graceful limbs asprawl, his beauty a stylish disarray.

His face, however, was patently miserable.

"It's the calves," he said in a weak attempt at humor. "Never could resist a man with a good pair of legs."

Something strained in Edward's chest. He sat, abruptly weak in the knees. "Freddie, if I believed for an instant you meant that, I'd slit my bloody wrists."

Freddie's head came up, clearly startled by his brother's tone. He opened his mouth, then shut it. Alert now, he dropped his boot to the floor and dried his palms on the front of his trousers.

" 'Course I don't mean it," he said. "You know me. Can't pass up a quip. We'll call it temporary insanity. Trying to recapture my schooldays or some such tripe."

Edward covered his face. Freddie's light response could not disguise his inner turmoil. Edward never should have sent him to Eton. Never mind the generations of Burbrooke males who had gone before them. He should have known a sensitive boy like Freddie wouldn't survive that pit of adolescent anarchy. Edward had been seventeen when he made the decision, his parents newly dead, his twelve-year-old brother left solely in his care. He'd thought Freddie needed Eton. He'd thought he couldn't take his rightful place in society without it.

A warm hand settled on the back of his neck. Freddie had perched on the corner of his desk. "Here now," he said, gently squeezing Edward's nape. "It isn't your fault. You weren't even there."

Edward let out his breath and looked up. His face hardened. "Who found you?"

Freddie winced. His finger drew a circle on the shiny black desk. "There's the rub, I'm afraid. It was the local squire, invited to the house party because Farringdon's in debt to him up to his eyeballs."

"What's his name?" Edward persisted, determined to turn to the business of cleaning this up.

"Samuel Stokes."

"The brewing magnate?"

Freddie pulled a face. "The very same. Bought his way into the neighborhood after he got knighted. Bit of a mushroom, according to Farringdon."

"But that just makes it worse! If one of our own set had found you, they might make you the latest *on-dit,* but they wouldn't threaten to inform on you. Do you have any idea what would happen if this went to court? You'd be ruined!"

"Actually"—Freddie cleared his throat—"Stokes did threaten to take me before the magistrate. Said I was setting a bad example for the lower orders."

"Oh, Lord."

"But he backed off when he found out whose brother I was." Freddie wagged his brows. "Seems you're well respected among the manufacturing set, despite being a useless toff."

"Wonderful," Edward groaned. He pushed out of his chair and closed his eyes. His temples throbbed under the weight of Freddie's hopes.

"Maybe you could throw him a sop," Freddie suggested. "Sponsor him to join your club."

"I'll meet him," Edward said, pinning Freddie with his sternest gaze, "and if he's suitable, I'll *consider* putting his name forward at White's."

"But Edward—"

Edward silenced him by laying a hand on his broad young shoulder. Freddie had been a champion rower at school, captain of the team, admired by everyone who met him. He still was admired. Edward knew he'd give his right arm to keep that from changing. His little brother would never be society's laughingstock.

"Freddie," he said, "I'm going to give Stokes my word this won't happen again, and I'm going to rely on you to make it true."

Freddie didn't drop his gaze, didn't in fact say a word. But his lips were pressed so tightly together they'd gone white.

"You can do this," Edward said, letting the love he felt for his brother soften his voice. "You've only to set your mind to it. Remember when you took that first in Maths? Remember when you learned to swim?"

Freddie choked out a laugh. "I learned to swim out of terror."

"Then be afraid," Edward said, softer yet. "People won't overlook this sort of lark, not if you rub their noses in it."

Freddie's sunny blue eyes welled with unshed tears. He bowed his head. "I didn't mean to rub anyone's nose in it, least of all yours."

Edward pulled him into a hug. "I know you didn't. But it's time to put these games behind you." He pushed back and braced Freddie's shoulder. "Why not settle on one of those debutantes who's always mooning in your wake?"

"Don't know who'll have me once this gets around."

Freddie ventured a crooked grin. "The husband-hunting mamas steer clear of me already, me being a younger son and all."

"Idiots," Edward said, echoing Freddie's smile. "They ought to know I'd never see you short of blunt."

Freddie sighed, his expression wistful. Edward had tried to prevent his brother's financial dependence from chafing. Other than a small property their mother had set aside for her younger son, control of the Burbrooke estate was entirely in Edward's hands. He made sure Freddie never had to beg for money and Freddie, while not a pinchpenny, was careful to live within his allowance. That very care told Edward his pride must occasionally sting. But the restrictions of primogeniture were not, apparently, the cause of Freddie's sigh.

"Choosing a wife who's good enough to be your sister-in-law won't be easy," he said.

Edward laughed and slapped his back, but inside, where his love for Freddie lived, he knew the danger had not passed.

Chapter 1

WITH STERN FACE AND TREMBLING HANDS, MISS FLORENCE Fairleigh stepped from the stuffy railway carriage and into a scene from Bedlam. A dizzying population of males—workmen, clerks, and here and there a gentleman in top hat—jostled each other in haste to reach the train she had lately vacated. Above her the roof of Euston Station yawned in two barnlike peaks, its smutted glass filtering a watery species of sunshine more appropriate to dusk than noon. Beneath her . . . well, beneath her the ground did not yet seem quite solid.

Frowning, she smoothed her crumpled black bombazine skirts. None of these observations were to the purpose. Her purpose was her future and her future would not wait on missish fears. She turned to her companion. Lizzie, the Fairleighs' maid-of-all-work, still clung to the carriage door, its grime putting her mistress's best white gloves at risk. Florence's old pink day dress, another loan, hung on Lizzie's slender frame. Though sixteen, and nearly grown, the maid looked all of twelve.

Truly, Florence thought, the only advantage to traveling with a person more timid than oneself was that it served to stiffen up one's spine. She stiffened it now and gestured for Lizzie to come down.

"It is safe," she said with all the firmness she could muster.

Face filled with trepidation, Lizzie tottered down the steps as if the train were a dragon that had momentarily, and perhaps not reliably, agreed to cough her out.

"Oh, miss," she breathed in awestruck tones, "isn't London grand?"

"You must call me Miss Fairleigh," Florence corrected, taking Lizzie's arm to guide her through the crowded train shed. "As is proper for a young lady towards her governess."

This was the fiction they had agreed upon, since Florence could not travel without a chaperone, and a less imposing chaperone than Lizzie Thomas could hardly be imagined. In her dull black gown, Florence thought she looked very much a governess, though not—due to the width of her sleeves and the lumpishness of her bustle—a particularly fashionable one. The ruse had worked well in the dimness of the carriage. When they disembarked at the various watering stations between Lancashire and London, however, Florence had been the subject of interested stares.

Even a governess, it seemed, was not immune to male attention.

"Oh, miss," said Lizzie, calling Florence to the present, "I mean, Miss Fairleigh. However shall we find our way?"

"We shall follow these others," said Florence. "They must be heading towards the street."

A brief argument was required to convince Lizzie she was not to carry Florence's portmanteau. That settled, they soon found themselves under the station's monumental Doric entry arch. To Florence's dismay, the bedlam inside the station merely increased in the out-of-doors. Here the confusion was multiplied by carriages and drays, by costermongers shouting their wares, and by a pungent smell which was half stableyard, half day-old fire. Florence did not have the least idea how to fight through the snarl.

She was swallowing back tears by the time a ragged urchin tugged on the hem of her mantelet. His eyes were huge in his dirty face, but so canny Florence felt a moment's fear. She put her hand on her reticule.

"Need a cab?" he offered. "I'll call one for a penny."

"A penny!" Lizzie exclaimed, her temper restored by this proposed raid on their resources. "You'll do it for a farthing, you scamp."

Florence smiled at her outrage. "A penny is fine," she said, "but we'll pay you after we get in."

This was agreeable to the young man, who proved capable at his task. Within minutes she and Lizzie were climbing into a smart black hansom cab. Florence gave their direction to the driver, which fortunately he knew. After another delay to ease into traffic, they joined the stream of broughams and carts and rumbling double-decked omnibuses. Since the cabbie sat on a high seat at the back of the two-wheeled carriage, his passengers had a clear view of all they passed.

Florence tried to maintain her dignity, but Lizzie was openly agog.

"Look, miss!" she exclaimed, pointing at the distinguished terraces of Bedford Square. "Look at that nursemaid in her apron! Isn't she the grandest thing you've ever seen!"

For her part, Florence took careful note of the classical, columned bulk of the British Museum. If she accomplished nothing else on this terrible trip, she vowed she'd see the Elgin marbles.

The cab continued to the Strand. Florence found the business district crowded and dirty, but strangely exciting nonetheless. Tiny shivers prickled over her scalp as she looked around. Everyone here had an air of purpose. They seemed not to see St. Paul's golden dome, rising behind the sooty haze like a fairy apparition. They were intent on their business, she supposed, and accustomed to the city's marvels. Perhaps someday she would be, too.

At that singular thought, they clopped onto a cobbled side street and stopped before a narrow building with a soot-stained brick face.

"Here you be, miss," said the cabbie.

Florence's heart, which had settled during the ride, resumed its former gallop. She pressed one dampened glove to her stays. This was the moment that would decide her future, the place at which her dreams would be met or dashed. Blowing out a careful breath, she counted a shocking number of coins from her reticule, and helped her supposed mistress to alight.

A small plaque declared the building that of "Mr. Mowbry, Solicitor," so Florence squared her shoulders and tugged the bell. The door was opened by a solid-looking man of middle years who stroked his beard and squinted. His brown tweed frock coat hung open around his belly. From the thick gold fob that gleamed on his matching waistcoat, Florence judged he must be Mr. Mowbry.

"Miss Fairleigh?" he said, peering dubiously from one woman to the other.

Florence flushed, knowing by his expression that they must look quite disreputable.

"I am Miss Fairleigh," she said and offered her hand. The solicitor took it with an air of bemusement. "Please forgive our appearance. We come to you straight from the train. I know such haste is irregular, but we wish to conclude our business quickly."

Her consciousness of the need to obtain a favorable outcome was so great her voice cracked on the final word. At the telltale sound, Mr. Mowbry flashed a kindly smile.

"Of course," he said, ushering her gently before him. "I'm sure I would be pleased to do anything I may for the daughter of my old friend."

Once inside, Florence looked about with interest. Mr. Mowbry's office was small but well kept. The paneling shone with a recent polish, the shelves were filled with heavy vellum tomes, and the dark Turkish carpet showed not the slightest sign of wear—all of which boded well for Florence's hopes. The tightness in her shoulders eased as tea was brought and condolences offered. Lizzie being settled with the charwoman in a little room off the hall, and knowing she should delay no longer, Florence came to the point of her visit.

"As my father's solicitor," she began, "you know he left me a small independence."

Mr. Mowbry nodded. "Indeed. I have been impressed by the conservative manner in which you have drawn upon it. Many young ladies would not have been so sensible."

"Yes," said Florence, and twisted her gloves in her lap. She feared when he heard her plan he would not think her sensible at all. With difficulty, she continued. "I have been careful in the six months since my father's death, but have come to realize the money will not keep me very long. I do not blame my father. He was a genial man and his position as vicar obliged him to entertain. Indeed, not realizing the expense of this little luxury or that, he believed I was able to set something aside from my housekeeping monies. I allowed him to continue in this belief because he was kind and loving and I did not wish him to worry. But now I have forgone everything I can forgo, except for Lizzie, who I dare not discharge even if I would because she is an orphan like myself and I don't know what would become of her!"

"I see," said Mr. Mowbry. The smile that hovered on his lips belied his serious tone. Spreading his arms, he tapped the corners of his desk. "Forgive me for being so bold, Miss Fairleigh, but you are a handsome young woman. Don't you think you might marry before the money runs out?"

"That is my intent," she said, struggling to steady her voice. "Only I should like . . . Perhaps it is selfish of me, but I should like to marry decently. There is only one gentleman at home who could be considered an appropriate suitor, and he wishes me to give Papa's money to a Society and join him on a ministry to Africa. I'm sure this is a worthy occupation and if it were any other man I might consider it, but he is—he is—"

"A sanctimonious prig?" suggested Mr. Mowbry.

"Quite," she agreed, blushing furiously at his frankness but unwilling to contradict him.

"So you have come to London where the gentlemen are many and various."

"Yes," she said and leaned earnestly forward in her chair. "I have heard there are ladies here who, for a fee, will sponsor an unconnected young woman for a Season, who will see she is chaperoned and introduced to respectable men. I would be willing, if you could recommend such an individual, to venture fully half my inheritance upon the enterprise."

Mr. Mowbry opened his mouth to speak, but for the first time in her adult life, Florence cut a gentleman off. This was the crux of the matter and Mr. Mowbry must understand what she wished, before he entered into the scheme.

"I am not aiming high," she assured him. "A younger son will do. Even a tradesman. I know I am not particularly accomplished. A little music and a bit of French is all I claim. But I am, as you say, attractive, and no one has ever complained about my manners. I do not hope for love but only to be treated kindly. Most of all, I wish not to be afraid, to know I shall always have a roof over my head and that it shall be my roof, not that of an indifferent employer or a pitying friend.

"I wish," she concluded, hiding her shaking hands among her skirts, "for a bit of security."

To all this, Mr. Mowbry had listened with an expression of intense concentration. Indeed, it had been so intense Florence had been hard-pressed to hold his gaze.

"Hm," he said now, tapping his lips with folded hands. "I think, Miss Fairleigh, that you underestimate your charms. Of course, your modesty does you credit, as much credit as your looks." Standing, he began to pace back and forth before the glass-fronted bookcase.

His vigor impressed her, as did his obvious seriousness of thought. He was muttering under his breath, saying things like "yes," and "she'd do," and "most delicate, but if it were brought forward in the proper way . . ." Watching him, Florence knew her father had been right to call him Clever Mr. Mowbry. If any man could launch Florence's future, it was this one.

Finally, he stopped in the center of his path and turned to face her. "I believe I have hit upon a solution." He lifted his hands to forestall a question she had not the nerve to pose. "I make no promises, Miss Fairleigh, but if I am able to pull this off—ah, if!—it could make both our fortunes."

"Oh, no, Mr. Mowbry." Florence shook her head emphatically. "I've no need of fortunes, only a small—"

"Hush," ordered the solicitor. "If I am correct in my surmise, you shall have precisely what you wish: an impeccable sponsor, an amiable husband, and the best possible roof above your head. First, however, we must see to your wardrobe. You cannot call upon anyone in that gown."

Though Florence had known this would be necessary, she could not forbear an inward groan. Ladies' dresses were very dear, and her little account could scarcely bear the drain. But she knew she must be brave. She must risk all in order to gain any. If the worst came to pass and her money was wasted, she would find a new position for Lizzie, and herself become a governess. Other women had done it, women gentler bred than she. Surely some had faced fears as great as hers. Florence could do no less. She might be shy but she was not, in the end, a coward.

Thus resolved, her hands were almost steady by the time she accepted a hastily scribbled letter from Mr. Mowbry. The red wax seal was warm beneath her thumb. These days most people used envelopes, but perhaps the old gentlemanly habit was one that appealed to a lawyer. Like vicars' daughters, most were neither here nor there in the eyes of society.

"This is an introduction to a friend of mine," he said. "A talented dressmaker, newly arrived from Paris, who is building her clientele. I have instructed her to put what you need on my account. No." He pressed a quieting finger to his lips. "Do not protest. Your father was good to me at Oxford and stood me many dinners when I had not two shillings to rub together. You must consider this repayment of the debt."

"With interest," Florence said, tears springing to her eyes at his kindness.

"With interest," Mr. Mowbry agreed, and called his clerk to hail a cab.

MR. MOWBRY'S FRIEND, MADAME VICTOIRE, WORKED OUT OF a pretty little house near the fancy shops of Bond Street. Bright red geraniums spilled from the ledges of the windows, all of which were open and one of which revealed the slumbering form of an orange cat.

Florence, who had been known to have difficulties with cats, hoped its nap would be a long one.

A parlormaid in black dress and white apron ushered them into the parlor. Though small, the room was lofty, its ceilings molded in the graceful Georgian style. Such light as there was poured through the casement windows. The furniture was old-fashioned and delicate, a medley of gold and cream—a more pleasant room by far than any Florence had lived in, despite her father's love of comfort. The only sign that the parlor figured in its owner's business was the bare dressmaker's form that stood in a pool of pallid sun, and the ell of purple velvet that lay folded in a chair.

On joining them, Madame Victoire bubbled with excitement. Like many of her countrywomen, she was slender and dark, with twinkling gestures and a wide red mouth.

"Oh, la la," she exclaimed, taking Florence's hands to pull her into the silvery light. "Who have we here come to visit my humble shop?"

Florence had no chance to reply for Madame Victoire immediately turned her around and began clucking over her dress. *"Quelle horreur,"* she said, touching the lumpish bustle. "And black! Mademoiselle, you must never wear black. She is not for you, this color."

"B-but I'm in mourning," Florence stammered.

"I take you out of it," Madame Victoire pronounced. *"Immédiatement.* It is a crime to put such a beautiful woman in such an ugly dress." She gestured to the watching parlormaid. *"Regardez* her bosoms, Marie. Look at her glowing cheeks!" With a gasp of excitement, she removed Florence's worn kid gloves. "Her hands are as small as a child's. They are white and—"

Abruptly, Madame Victoire fixed Florence with a deadly glare. Her fingertips had found the calluses on her palms.

"Mademoiselle," she said in a tone of deep affront, "this must be remedied. No more floor-scrubbing for you. You are too perfect to suffer a single flaw."

"I—" said Florence, but the Frenchwoman did not allow her to explain.

"Such beauty is a grave *responsabilité.* Not only to yourself, but to me. You, mademoiselle, are going to be a walking advertisement for the skills of Madame Victoire. Better than the sandwich board man. Mr. Worth will eat the crow when he hears of my triumph."

"Mr. Worth?" Florence said weakly. If the dressmaker meant who she thought, Florence could not, in good conscience, impose on Mr. Mowbry's generosity.

"Yes, yes," said Madame Victoire. "Mr. Charles Worth, with whom I worked in Paris. That is why you are here, is it not?"

Florence dried her hands on her much-abused dress. "Actually, I am here on the recommendation of Mr. Alastair Mowbry. But I'm afraid I cannot afford the services of an associate of Mr. Worth."

"Pah," said Madame Victoire. "Mr. Worth is no associate of me. And you are a friend of Monsieur Mowbry. We will come to the *arrangement.*"

Florence's cheeks burned with the heat of the blood that rushed beneath them. She feared Madame Victoire had jumped to the wrong conclusion.

"Forgive me, madame," she said, "but I am not that sort of friend to Mr. Mowbry."

To Florence's amazement, Madame Victoire burst into peals of laughter. "But of course you are not, little *chou*. I know this because *I* am 'that sort of friend' to him. Granted, he is a gentleman of great strength, but no man is strong enough to require more woman than Amalie Victoire."

This declaration so astonished Florence she could not frame a response, appropriate or otherwise. The best she could manage was to close her gaping mouth. Happily, the silence was broken by the entrance of a noisy little boy. No more than three and dressed in a navy sailor suit, he thundered across the carpet with what looked like a headless bear.

"Look, *maman*," he cried, seeming more excited than bereaved by the decapitation. "Kitty got him."

He stopped in his tracks when he spotted his mother's guest.

Florence's chest tightened, but once he had seen her, she knew what came next was inevitable. The boy hesitated, staring up at her with round, bedazzled eyes, shyness and interest at war in his face. Then, like a child unable to resist a stranger's toy, his shyness broke and he pounded across the room. For a moment, Florence feared he would actually fling his arms around her legs. Fortunately, he settled for grabbing her hand and tugging it.

"Pretty!" he declared with three-year-old directness. "You come play!"

Florence needed a surprising amount of strength to resist his pull.

"Goodness," said Madame Victoire. "He does not usually behave this way with strangers."

If it had been possible, Florence would have sunk through the floor. She patted the boy's hand in the hope he would loosen his grip. "Children . . . like me," she explained.

"Children and cats," Lizzie qualified, as if this were cause for pride.

"Well," said Madame Victoire, her lips twitching with amusement, "perhaps Marie should lock Kitty in the bedroom before you suffer more attacks."

"Yes," Florence said faintly. "That would probably be wise."

Once Marie had left to secure the cat, Florence gathered herself sufficiently to remember Mr. Mowbry's note. Madame Victoire took longer to read it than she expected, the message being two pages instead of one. Whatever the solicitor had written inspired much raising of the Frenchwoman's brows. When Madame Victoire had finished, she tapped the missive against her chin. She seemed not to hear the distant rumble of thunder outside her home.

"Hm," she said in precisely the tone Mr. Mowbry had used.

Her "hm" troubled Florence even more than the solicitor's.

He had put something in that letter which he meant to keep from Florence, and for a deeper reason than not wanting to raise her hopes. Oh, how she hated trusting her fate to anyone else's hands! Life with her father, dear as he was, had taught her to rely on no one but herself. How could it be otherwise when one's sole guardian was likelier to forget one's name than remember to pay a bill? Short of giving up her dream, however, she did not see what choice she had. She had to trust the lawyer and his friend. She could only pray his hidden agenda was not a danger to her own.

"EDWARD BURBROOKE, EARL OF GREYSTOWE, WAS SPATTERED all over with mud. Too tired to ring the bell, he pushed into his Belgravia town house and collapsed on the marble bench inside the door. For a moment, all he could do was stare at his ruined boots.

He straightened when he heard footsteps: Grimby, no doubt, coming to see who'd entered the hall.

"My lord!" he said, obviously shocked by his master's appearance. "You're wet."

Edward snorted at this statement of the obvious and handed the butler his soggy top hat. He should have turned back when it started raining, but the horse had been eager and the park for once uncrowded and Edward's temper too black to miss his daily ride.

This morning there'd been a limerick in the *Illustrated Times*:

> *There was a young viscount of G———*
> *Who couldn't keep off of his knees.*
> *The footman was there, with his hands in his hair,*
> *And his a———hanging out in the breeze.*

Anyone who knew Freddie would recognize the scandal to which it referred. Edward wished he could strangle the supposed wit who'd sent it in, not to mention the editor who'd printed it. That being impractical, he'd vented his frustration on the turf in Hyde Park.

The plop of water from his hat told Edward the butler was still there.

"Sir?" said Grimby. "Shall I call Mr. Lewis to pull your boots?"

"Yes," said Edward, "and have him draw a hot bath."

The knocker sounded just as Grimby disappeared into the servants' hall. Edward heaved to his feet with a weary laugh. Hell, he thought, I can open a blasted door.

The individual behind it, caught digging in his pocket for a card, was so surprised he could only gawk.

"Mr. Mowbry?" Edward said, recognizing the broad, bearded figure of his London solicitor. The man had been his father's lawyer: then a member of a larger firm, now striking out on his own. He was, so far as Edward knew, utterly reliable. But Edward could not imagine why he was calling on him at home.

"My lord," said Mowbry, recovering his composure. "Forgive me for arriving unannounced, but an opportunity has arisen of which I thought you'd want to be apprised."

"An investment opportunity?"

If a man could squirm without moving, Mowbry did so. "No, your lordship. The opportunity regards Viscount Burbrooke."

A chill joined the water that had run down Edward's neck. After this morning's nastiness in the *Times,* he did not want to think what Mowbry's business might entail. He pushed the door ajar. "Come inside. We'll talk in the library." He was halfway there when he noticed he was tracking mud across the cabbage roses of the Brussels carpet. "Blast," he muttered, and stood where he was while Lewis, his valet, rushed towards him in consternation.

This was not how he'd intended to spend his day.

"A VICAR'S DAUGHTER?" EDWARD SAID.

"Yes," Mowbry confirmed, sipping his tea with quiet relish. He and Edward sat by the fire Lewis had insisted on building, any differences in rank leveled by their mutual enjoyment of the warmth.

Edward propped his slippers on the fender. "Fresh from the country?"

"As fresh as can be, but gently bred and exceedingly good-natured. What novel writers like to call a womanly little soul."

Edward balanced his saucer on his thigh. "How womanly?"

Mowbry's white-flecked whiskers lifted in a smile. "Imagine, my lord, if a dewy English rose were to wear Delilah's form. Miss Fairleigh is poor, it is true, but more than enough of a beauty to be considered a catch. Were young Lord Burbrooke to display a partiality to her, no one would think it amiss. And, sir, if you'll forgive me for speaking frankly, I doubt she'd understand the gossip surrounding your brother even if she heard it."

Edward's brows rose. Such innocence was hard to conceive. More to the point, if she were that innocent, would she be able to bring a skittish stallion like Freddie to stud? Still—he rubbed one finger across his lips—the matter was worth investigating. A girl in Miss Fairleigh's position would have few options beyond marriage. Seamstressing or working as a governess could not match the security of wedded life. Certainly, she could do worse than a kind young man like Freddie, who neither drank nor gambled nor cursed in the presence of ladies. As clever Mr. Mowbry had divined, Edward was determined that Freddie marry. In fairness, however, he could not wish Freddie to be the sole beneficiary of the match.

Of course, if Mowbry had exaggerated Florence Fairleigh's charms, the entire matter might be moot. He came to a decision.

"I shall wish to look her over," he said. "Without her knowledge."

The solicitor set his cup and saucer on the tea table. "If you would be amenable to a short ride, my lord, I believe I could arrange for you to see her today."

Edward narrowed his eyes. The lawyer seemed to have been expecting the request. His expression was mild, and suspiciously complacent. Edward could not be certain, but he thought he'd just been managed.

IF EDWARD HAD KNOWN WHAT HE WAS GOING TO SEE, HE never would have called for his carriage. The oddities began when Mowbry directed him to the servants' entrance of the house. A tiny housemaid, quiet as a nun, glided before him through the basement and up the back stairs, which were so narrow his elbows brushed the walls at every turn. On the second floor, they passed a large, well-lighted room where four women bent over sewing machines. Their feet worked busily on the treadles while their hands fed lengths of cloth beneath the needles. Three more machines stood empty. All were black and painted with yellow roses.

This house, he concluded, must be a dressmaker's establishment.

"Almost there," whispered his diminutive guide.

Her accent was French and very pretty, but Edward had no time to consider why she was whispering because she soon led him into a small room. The presence of a secretaire and settee suggested it was sometimes used as a sitting room, but for now the space was cramped with bolts of cloth.

A spindly chair had been pulled between two towers of jewel-bright satin. By gesture, the maid directed him to sit, then hushed his questions with a finger to her mouth.

Feeling somewhat ridiculous, Edward sat, then stiffened when her arm brushed his shoulder. People simply did not touch the earl of Greystowe without permission.

"Pardon," she murmured and pressed a latch that had been hidden among the birds and foliage of the wallpaper. A small aperture opened in the wall.

"Watch," she said. "You will see all you wish to know."

Edward blinked at the peephole, then at his guide, but the little maid was already slipping out the door. His heart beat hard with shock. Were Mowbry's other clients so jaded they could accept this sort of offer without offense? Just how dissipated did the solicitor think he was, expecting him to spy on a half-dressed woman who might conceivably become his brother's bride?

His face warmed with anger, but then he calmed. He'd said he wanted to look the girl over without her knowledge. What better means than this? Besides, for all he knew, she and the dressmaker were merely talking in the other room, fully clothed, with none of their womanly attributes hanging out.

Despite this assurance, his mouth was dry as he pressed his eye against the wall.

The room into which he gazed was small and bright, the gloom outside cast away by the light of a dozen bull's-eye lamps. A tall cheval glass reflected the figures of two dark-haired women.

Heat flashed over his body. The dressmaker was clothed in a smart gold gown, but Miss Fairleigh wore only her chemise and drawers. She was everything Mowbry claimed: lush and rosy with a mass of shining chestnut hair rolled and braided on the crown of her head. The dressmaker had just peeled away her corset. Even without the restraint, her waist dipped in like an hourglass.

Edward swallowed, but did not pull away. No more than medium height, the woman's legs seemed disproportionately long. He could see the shadow of her bottom through the fine linen drawers. A mended patch rested atop one shapely buttock, an endearing imperfection which could not detract from the charm of her derriere. Her flesh was full and well lifted. A man would find a pleasurable handhold should he coax this paragon beneath him. Indeed, he'd find many pleasurable grips. Her breasts were a bounty, her arms both soft and graceful. Her feet— He tugged a sudden tightness at his collar. Her feet were small and white, feet he'd thought only a painter could create, with tiny curled toes and ankles a man could circle with his hand.

A lucky man.

Edward shifted on the stingy padding of his chair. Mere seconds had passed since he'd first looked in the room, but his cock stretched full within its skin. The tip pulsed tight against the placket of his trousers, heavy and urgent, a creature with a mind of its own. The knowledge that what he was doing was beyond the bounds of all propriety simply made the swollen tissues pulse harder.

When he released his bated breath, he realized he could hear as well as see. What struck his ears first was the rumbling purr of an orange cat that had curled adoringly at Miss Fairleigh's feet. Clever cat, he thought, in total sympathy with its instincts.

"We must order three French corsets," the dressmaker was saying as she stretched a measuring tape around Miss Fairleigh's admirable waist. "Two for ordinary wear and one cut low for evening. With one of the new spoon busks, I think. They are *très élégante*. You will like them very much."

Miss Fairleigh opened her mouth, then blushed as the tape moved to circle her bosom. The dressmaker's fingers met at the center of her cleavage, pressing it slightly together. In the glow of the lamps, Edward watched as hectic color spread enchantingly over her chest.

Miss Fairleigh cleared her throat. "I really think one new corset would be enough—if, as you say, I must have a French one."

"As I say?" tutted the dressmaker, kneeling down to measure the length of Miss Fairleigh's legs. The cat mewed with displeasure as she elbowed it aside. "As I *know,* mademoiselle. You must marshal your weapons. A good set of corsets is a powerful weapon indeed."

"But my finances . . ." said Miss Fairleigh, her voice faint. The dressmaker ignored her.

"Stop wiggling," she ordered. "You would think no one but me had ever seen your ankles." With a sigh of satisfaction, she stood and wiped a single curl from her narrow forehead. "It is good. Your measurements are very close to a dress I have on hand today. A snip here, a tuck there, and you shall at once be decent."

Miss Fairleigh's dovelike hands fluttered to her trembling breast "Oh, no, Madame Victoire. I can't take someone else's dress."

"Nonsense," said Madame. "This customer is late settling her account. Therefore, I will be late with her delivery." And, without giving further heed to Miss Fairleigh's protests, she called for someone named Marie to bring the claret-colored visiting dress.

"Claret?" Miss Fairleigh's tone was rife with dread.

"Non, non," scolded the dressmaker, briskly lacing her into her re-

putedly inferior English corset. "Do not worry yourself. Your father would want you to go on with your life, would he not?"

"Yes, but—"

"There are no buts. You do what you must. A man will not marry a crow!"

The exchange had Edward smiling, despite the pounding weight between his legs. This woman was so shy and self-effacing that Madame Victoire's attempts to exhort her to femme-fatale-dom could only be amusing. Miss Fairleigh was a peach, he decided, a juicy country peach whose sweetness tempted one to bite.

Of course, he reminded himself, his teeth would not be doing the biting.

Unfortunately, this caution did not quell his fascination as the dressmaker arrayed Miss Fairleigh in the frock. Had he ever watched his mistresses being dressed? If he had, he could not recall it. Surely, few sights could be more seductive than that of a woman tying another woman's petticoats, or steadying a bustle, or dropping a rustling silk skirt over two submissively raised white arms.

Miss Fairleigh herself seemed conscious of the erotic charge. Edward doubted she'd ever had a lady's maid; doubted she'd ever been intimately touched by another human being. Her creamy, broad-boned cheeks were once again pink as Madame Victoire hooked the separate bodice. The fit over her breasts was snug, but the dressmaker seemed more satisfied than otherwise when she returned to consider her front.

"With a French corset," she said, "this would lie perfectly." As if in demonstration, she ran her hands from Miss Fairleigh's shoulders to her waist. Her palms swept the tips of her client's breasts. Edward did not think Miss Fairleigh could feel much pressure through the layers of cloth, but what she did feel had her ears turning scarlet.

He experienced a nearly uncontrollable urge to rush into the room and cuddle her against his chest. Madame Victoire should not tease the girl this way. She was an innocent. She deserved protection!

Which did not change the fact that watching the Frenchwoman touch her had aroused him. His hands were fisted on his thighs, sweat prickled his linen, and the wall beneath his cheek was growing damp. He could not recall a desire this urgent. His body shook with the force of it. His breath came in long, hard pulls. If he hadn't known the house was full of people, he'd have opened his trousers and eased himself. He wasn't prone to self-indulgence, but it would have been a business of moments. As it was, he was heartbeats from exploding.

But Madame Victoire had finished arranging the pleated muslin fraise that framed the dress's neckline. She turned her client to face the mirror. Edward's jaw dropped at the same time Miss Fairleigh's did.

In her chemise and drawers, Miss Fairleigh had been a schoolboy's naughty dream. In the elegant claret dress, she stopped the heart.

She looked a grand London lady, every inch, from her stiff stand-up collar to the train of her polonaise. The complicated draping of her bustle seemed to echo the piquant flesh he knew it hid. Only her expression, wondering and unsure, betrayed her country roots.

"There," said Madame Victoire, her hands on Miss Fairleigh's shoulders. "How does that make you feel?"

Miss Fairleigh touched the waist of the figure-hugging gown as if the silk might burn. "I think it frightens me."

Madame smiled and smoothed a fallen lock into her customer's coiffure. Miss Fairleigh's hair was ruler straight and, if the dressmaker's expression was a guide, quite pleasant to touch. Again he felt that dark frisson of the forbidden. The girl did not know what Madame was doing. The girl could not guess what such gestures conveyed.

"You are seeing your feminine power," said the dressmaker, "without that ugly black dress to dim its light."

Miss Fairleigh lifted her chin in the first hint of stubbornness Edward had seen her display. "A woman shouldn't be powerful just because she's pretty."

"Shouldn't she?" The dressmaker clucked in her droll French way. "Why do you worry about 'shouldn't'? This is the way things are, *chérie*. Women walk a hard road in this world. We must use our weapons where we find them. Just as you must use yours, *non*? You must hunt the nice husband. If your beauty brings him close enough to see how nice he is, what is wrong with that?"

"I've never liked being stared at," Miss Fairleigh confessed.

"Oh, la!" Madame trilled out a laugh. "I would tell you to get used to it, but I know your shyness is part of your charm. Like honey to the bee. When you quiver and blush, you make the men feel big and strong."

Without warning, Miss Fairleigh laughed, as if the absurdity of her complaint had just then struck her. The sound was an infectious warble that seemed to come from deep within her chest. "I shall stop!" she declared between the merry bursts. "I shall never blush again."

And the dressmaker laughed, because her client's face was rosy even then.

EDWARD STALKED TO THE CARRIAGE WITHOUT WAITING FOR an escort. He was angry with himself for staying so long, angry for being attracted to the hapless country miss, angry at Alastair Mowbry for putting an innocent in that position. That the man had been right about Miss Fairleigh did not calm him in the least, nor did the thought that, most likely, a wish for her well-being had played some part in the solicitor's scheme.

Worst of all was his sense of violation. Edward was sweating with arousal, still half hard beneath his clothes. The minute Mowbry saw him he would guess what he was feeling—as Madame Victoire must have guessed, and the little maid, and perhaps even the seamstresses down the hall. This, to Edward, was intolerable. As wrong as it had been, his experience in that chamber should have been completely private.

His mood was as thunderous as the sky by the time he ducked into the waiting Greystowe brougham. The coachman did not tarry for instructions, but snapped the horses sharply into motion.

Mowbry sat in the shadows of the opposite seat. Silent. Knowing.

"You will fill that peephole at once," Edward said in his coldest, darkest voice.

If the solicitor's expression changed, Edward did not see it.

"It is only for private use," he said. "A game between myself and Madame Victoire. You are the first outsider to have seen it."

His tone was entirely neutral, free of insinuation or censure. Edward forced his hands to unclench. Obviously, he was in no position to judge this man.

"She is all you said," he admitted gruffly.

Wisely, Mowbry didn't take this as an invitation to repeat his estimation of Miss Fairleigh's charms. Edward didn't think he could have borne that. Instead, the solicitor brushed a bit of lint from the bowler he held in his lap. "Have you a sponsor in mind, my lord?"

"My aunt Hypatia," he said, "the dowager duchess of Carlisle. She can bring her forward as some sort of country cousin."

Mowbry simply nodded. He must have known his approval was neither necessary nor welcome. Despite his fury, Edward's estimation of the lawyer rose. Without question, he had behaved abominably, but he had carried it off with rare aplomb.

"You are a man of hidden depths," Edward said.

A small, dry smile acknowledged the warning in his words. "You may call upon my depths whenever you wish, Lord Greystowe. They are entirely at your disposal."

This man is ambitious, Edward thought, but he could not tell whether that boded ill or well.

Chapter 2

EDWARD DROPPED MOWBRY AT HIS OFFICE, THEN ORDERED the coachman to drive to Lady Hargreave's. The rain continued to fall steadily but not hard, and the wheels made a soft, sticky sound as they rolled through the muddy streets. A mist wreathed the city, muffling the edges of the buildings, slowing traffic and sound until he seemed to ride through a dream. The softness of the air was that of spring, but the color could well have been winter.

He closed his eyes and saw again the delicate slope of Miss Fairleigh's shoulders. How vulnerable were the planes of a woman's back: any woman's, but especially hers, in her mended chemise with the fragile bits of lace around the sleeves.

Warmth crept up his thighs as his blood rushed to his center. He was hardening at the simple memory of her spine. He thought of her buttocks and ached to cup them in his hands. Shaking himself, he turned his gaze to the fog-shrouded window. Should the strength of his reaction worry him? Perhaps he ought to put himself on guard.

But, no. She was a pretty woman; that was all. Any man would have responded. He was glad her powers of attraction were strong. He wanted Freddie happy. He needed Freddie safe.

They reached Regent's Park and the columned marble stretch of Cumberland Terrace, its houses strung end to end so that they looked like a Grecian temple. Edward flipped his watch open. Late teatime. But Lady Hargreave would have no visitors. She'd sent a note that morning, delicately scented, informing him she wouldn't be "at home" to anyone else. Her husband, never the possessive type, was visiting his property in Scotland. Despite the clearness of the field, Edward directed the coachman to a public stable down the street. He preferred not to park his carriage near her house. It was one thing to cuckold a man and quite another to rub his nose in it.

He paused in the act of unfurling his umbrella, caught by a half-conscious thread of memory. Whatever it was, it didn't matter. Nothing mattered but easing the terrible knot of hunger in his groin.

Lady Hargreave awaited in her boudoir. Well aware of how best to display her assets, she was sprawled artistically across an ice-blue chaise longue, with a novel she probably wasn't reading. Her hair, a smooth champagne blonde, spilled like silk down her slender arms. The filmy pink wrap she wore left little to the imagination. He could see the small cones of her breasts beneath it, and the fair thatch of curls that covered her mound.

"Darling!" she cried and, in her usual languid manner, floated to the door to greet him.

His kiss was deeper than was his custom. Rather than let her break it, he gripped her hair to hold her in place. He discovered he wanted to make her melt today; wanted to hear her cry with helpless need.

"My," she said when he finally released her. Her hands slid down his waistcoat to fondle his growing bulge. "Someone's been thinking naughty thoughts."

He did not answer, nor did he want her to speak. He wanted a good hard screw that didn't end for hours. He wanted oblivion and release, and Imogene was damn well going to provide it.

Her hands were clever even through his clothes. She found the tip of his penis and gently pinched it, forcing his linen against the seep of moisture. He gasped as her nails increased the pressure.

"Nice Eddie," she said, and returned to the petting with which she'd begun.

But he wasn't a dog she could cosset to submission. He tore her wrapper down the front and kissed her when she dared to laugh. With inexorable force, he stepped her back to the satin chaise. To hell with adjourning to her bedchamber. He would take her here and now.

"The maid—" she gasped, but her little bosom was heaving up and down. Edward watched it, telling himself he did not wish she were lush instead of lithe, or dark instead of blonde, and that he would not rather she tremble instead of pant.

"Damn the maid." Cupping her breast, he nipped its reddened peak. "Let her get an eyeful."

Imogene laughed and wound her arms behind his neck. "Oh, yes," she purred, crushing her groin to the clothbound arch of his sex. "I like you in this mood."

Their embrace became a skirmish, with Imogene fighting to get on top. Edward used his strength against her, something he had not done in all their times together. She did not seem to mind. In truth, she seemed to like it. Her languor abandoned her. She clutched him as if she could not get enough of his muscle and skin, her hands tearing at his clothes, her throat vibrating with desperate cries.

"Oh, please," she begged when he refused to let her open his trousers. "Please, Edward."

Perversely, he knelt above her, straddling her narrow hips, holding her down with one hand spread between her trembling breasts. With the other, he opened his trouser buttons. As the strain gave way, new blood rushed into tissues already full. He had never been this hard, this needy, and yet he found himself not in the moment but seeing it from a distance. She was lovely, Lady Hargreave, all blonde and pink and eager, her youth wasted on a man twelve years her senior. Edward was what she needed. She had said so many times. Only he could scratch the itch that left her tossing in her bed.

He pushed his trousers to his hips, even that light friction a goad. The air was cool on his fiery skin. Look, he thought. Here's what you want.

Imogene looked, her eyes seeming to glaze as she took in the thick red thrust of his erection. Edward studied it himself: the heavy veins, the nervously jumping sack, the sheen of hunger on the bulbous tip. Why did women want this ugly beast? And why did the sight of it, the feel of it hard and ready, imbue him with a sense of power?

She sighed as she watched it pulse in defiance of gravity's pull. Despite his hold, her hands found him, stroked him, teased him until he ached to drive inside her. He ground his teeth rather than give in. He did not know why, only that something compelled him to delay.

"Fuck me," she whispered, her body writhing between his knees. "I want you inside me."

But he touched her first, because he did not wish to be agreeable. He touched her with his hard male fingers, parting her tangled golden hair. Arousal soaked her delicate folds and plumped her tiny pearl. His fingers slid around the swollen bud. She groaned as he teased it, melting as she never had before, her fair locks clinging to her temples, the pillow rustling as she lashed her head against the chaise. This was what he wanted, to make her helpless, and yet it did not satisfy the formless need inside his soul. With a growl of frustration, he wrenched her legs wide. Enough preliminaries. He would take her and be damned.

He notched her gate and plunged, but found no resistance beyond the stricture of her size.

"Oh, yes," she said, encouraging him to work his engine in. "Oh, yes."

Her knees rose, squeezed the ribs beneath his arms. Back and forth they rocked until her body eased and took him, until his thighs tightened to penetrate the final inch. He stopped and held inside her, his body shaking with desire.

"You're a monster," she breathed, her face white, her pupils huge. "You're the biggest fucking cock I've ever had."

For once he did not doubt this silly claim. He felt like the biggest. He felt as if he could screw the entire world. Her fingers trailed down his spine to grip his straining buttocks.

"Now," she urged. "Do it."

At last, he was willing to comply. With a mutual groan, they thrust in tandem, strongly, smoothly, both selfishly eager to reach their ends. Beyond control, Imogene's nails broke the surface of his skin. Edward grunted and gripped the bottom of the couch to lever deeper, to thrust with greater force. Imogene's neck arched off the cushion, her outward breath a wail.

"Keep going," she gasped, her hips frantically beating his. "Don't stop. Don't stop."

He pounded into her, her flesh tightening around him, his pleasure rising. His cock was steel within her heat, so burstingly hard he could scarcely stand it. He closed his eyes and pressed his brow to the small embroidered pillow beside her head. Images flashed behind his lids: a scrap of lace, a tiny foot, a breast swelling above a corset. The muscles of his belly tensed. He yearned. He ached. And then his partner broke, great shudders of orgasm that milked him to the tooth-grinding edge of release. He pulled out at the very last, coming in heavy, draining spurts against her thigh.

He hung above her on his elbows, shaken by a fear he could not explain.

"Oh, my," she murmured, languidly stroking the scratches on his back. "If people knew how passionate you can be, they'd never call you Edward Coldheart."

He was tempted to inquire who called him that, as this was an insult he'd never heard. In the end, though, he didn't care enough to ask. He looked down at Imogene. Her skin was flushed with satiation, her gray eyes starred. She didn't have the strength to stop him when he pulled away, merely mewled like a disappointed kitten. Too polite to leave outright, he sat by her hip and stroked her arm. Their sexual connection had always been strong, but they'd never shared an encounter this intense. He hadn't spent so fiercely since he'd been a lad of seventeen, nor taken a woman with so little finesse.

Not that Imogene seemed to mind.

"Edward," she sighed, her golden lashes drifting down, "you're enough to make a woman petition for divorce."

He didn't think she meant it, but the declaration rattled him. He didn't feel closer to Imogene. He felt empty. And restless. And weary of the pleasures of life.

He raked his hair back with a sigh. Come to think of it, he felt alone.

HIS MOOD WAS NO BRIGHTER BY THE TIME HE CALLED ON HIS aunt Hypatia. Wednesday was her at-home day and he was forced to sit, hat in hand, while some idiot countess and her two marriageable daughters tried to engage him in predictably pointless conversation. They left much beyond the recommended quarter hour, and reluctantly at that. Edward nodded stiffly at the departing girls, but could not bring himself to rise.

"Edward," said Aunt Hypatia, "if you hadn't obviously come on important business, I would scold you for being rude. You're getting too old to dismiss every girl who bats her eyes at you." She patted the spot beside her on the gold and white settee. "Come closer, dear. You're looking unusually dour, even for you. I trust nothing untoward has befallen my investments."

"No," he said, jerkily taking the seat, still warm from its occupation by the countess. For the last few years, he'd been handling the duchess's money. "Your investments are safe. It's this business with Freddie."

"Ah," said his aunt, her unruffled response easing some of the tightness in his chest. Hypatia was a handsome woman, slim and straight despite her years, with a crown of silver-white hair that was all her own. She had not in her youth been a beauty, but her elegance and pride had made it seem as if she were. Now she folded her hands in the pale lavender satin of her skirts. "I wondered when you'd get around to asking my advice."

"It is more than advice I need." He bent forward over his knees and tapped his hat against his shin. "I'm afraid I require your services as a social fairy."

"Indeed," she said, then grabbed his hat and gloves and rang for her rail-thin footman, John.

"Yes, your Grace?" he said in his distinctive sepulchral tones.

"Take Lord Greystowe's coat," she ordered. "Bring the port and bar the door. I am presently indisposed."

"Very good," he said and glided off with what might have been the ghost of a smile.

She would not let Edward speak until the port arrived and he'd downed one brimming glass. "Now," she said, "I suppose your need of my social clout means you've found some chit foolish enough, or desperate enough, to consider a match with the footman's scourge."

"Is that what they're calling Freddie: the footman's scourge?"

"Well, I can think of one footman who isn't. From what I hear, they were having a lovely time before that wretched beermaker burst in. Oh, don't pull that face with me, Edward. I'm older than you and I've seen things a good deal more shocking than young Freddie's peccadillo. Done them, for that matter."

She patted his shoulder and filled his glass again with wine. Edward frowned into its ruby depths. Then a happier thought struck him. If the duchess could view this scandal with levity, Freddie's position must not be as irretrievable as he'd feared.

"Tell me about this girl," she said. "Just how impossible is she?"

"Not too, I don't think, but green. She's a vicar's daughter. Grew up in Lancashire somewhere. Poor as a church mouse, of course, but *very* pretty."

"Oh, 'very'?" said Aunt Hypatia, with a humorous twist to her mouth.

Edward ignored what his unwitting emphasis might have meant. "She needs polish," he went on, "and someone to sponsor her for the Season."

"What does the Season matter if she's going to marry Freddie?"

"She doesn't know she's going to marry Freddie. I want him to woo her. I want people to believe this is a love match."

"Does Freddie know what you intend?"

"He will," Edward said, "and he will do what I say."

"I've no doubt he'll try, but—" Aunt Hypatia stopped herself midsentence. Lost in thought, she stacked her hands over the cut-glass stopper of the wine decanter. "No," she said slowly. "You're right. Freddie needs to settle. Better he should do it now, before it becomes impossible."

"So you'll help?"

She turned to him with her still brilliant smile. "You know me, darling: my family right or wrong. Besides, how could I not help my favorite nephew out of a bind?"

The sting of hurt pricked him too suddenly to hide it. True, Freddie had the charm of the family; Edward was accustomed to his little brother being everyone's favorite. The only person who'd ever preferred Edward was their father, a compliment he could not prize since the former earl had been a bastard. But of the people Edward himself respected, he'd always thought— He swallowed and clenched his hands. He'd always thought Aunt Hypatia was partial to him.

Reading the involuntary flash of pain, she clasped his face in her cool, papery hands. "Oh, Edward, Freddie is only my favorite because he needs people's approval more than you do. Why, sometimes I think you'd survive the very Flood all by yourself." She lowered her hands to squeeze the conjoined fist he'd made of his own. "Dearest, I love you every bit as much. What's more, you're the one I would turn to were I in need."

The concern in her eyes made Edward aware of how ridiculous he was being. Of course, Freddie ought to come first. Edward put Freddie first himself. Gently, he pulled his hands loose and cleared his throat.

"No need to talk nonsense," he said. "I'm a grown man, not a child."

"We're all children when it comes to love," said his aunt. "When you're my age, I hope you know that as well as I do."

Edward hoped he would not, but only time would tell.

THE DOWAGER DUCHESS OF CARLISLE WAS THE MOST IMPOSing woman Florence had ever met. She was as tall as a man, nearly six foot, and not yet bowed by age. Her clear blue eyes were as sharp as diamonds, and far more penetrating. Her dress was exquisite, a tailored masterpiece of navy and silver stripes with a long basque waist and a bustle so restrained it made one long to burn one's ruffles.

At least, it made Florence long to.

Her knees had begun to knock the moment the ghoulish footman led her up to the drawing room. The ceilings were twice the height of a normal room, with gilded moldings and a teardrop chandelier that no doubt took the servants days to clean. The only thing that saved her from utter terror was an amusing coincidence: the duchess had the same gold and white Louis XV furniture as Madame Victoire. The duchess's, of course, was no papier-mâché imitation.

"Stand up straight," she snapped when a smile threatened to touch Florence's lips. "How can I tell how you look if you slump?"

Florence's eyes widened because she knew she was standing straight. Her cheeks warmed as the duchess stumped around her with an elegant ivory cane. Florence suspected she liked it more for the sound it made than for any support it might provide.

"Hmpf," said the duchess, the awful thumping coming to a halt. She had stopped just behind Florence's shoulder, but Florence didn't dare look around. She felt like an errant soldier on review.

"Who made your dress?" the duchess demanded.

"Madame Victoire of Brook Street, your Grace, a former associate of Mr. Worth."

"Never heard of her." The duchess stumped to Florence's front. She touched her collar, her hands surprisingly gentle on the pleated cloth. "This red is good for you but far too dark for a chit barely out of the schoolroom."

"It was made on short notice," Florence said without a quaver. She'd always found it easier to stand up for others than for herself, and she didn't want the dressmaker's judgment called into question. "It was all she had on hand."

"Hmpf," said the duchess. Her diamond eyes seemed to measure every seam. She began to stump again. "Play the piano?"

"Tolerably well, your Grace."

"Sing?"

"Not for all the tea in China."

The stumping stopped. Florence gasped and held her breath. The duchess's stare seemed to bore holes into her forehead. "Are you trying to be smart with me, girl?"

"No, your Grace, it just popped out."

A noise issued from the duchess's nose which sounded uncommonly like a snort of laughter. "Oh, very well," she said in the tone of someone who had grudgingly conceded an argument. "You'll do. Sit and have some tea. I'm parched even if you aren't. And stop calling me 'your Grace.' To you, I'm Aunt Hypatia."

"Aunt Hypatia?" Florence's knees gave way as she sank into a chair.

"Yes," said the duchess. "After all, I can hardly present a mere vicar's daughter to the queen."

"Oh, your Grace . . . Aunt Hypatia, I wouldn't presume—"

"You had better learn to presume. No protége of mine is going to scuffle through life like a frightened mouse."

"I am not a mouse," Florence said, even as she pressed her knees together to still their trembling.

Aunt Hypatia glared. Florence lifted her chin. She wasn't a mouse. Shy, maybe. Timid, certainly. But not a mouse. Mice didn't run their father's home. Mice didn't get themselves to London. Mice didn't risk everything to build a solid future.

After what seemed like an eternity, the duchess's face softened with satisfaction.

"Well," she said, "at least you've got spine. Not much, but some. Which is just as well. Most people exercise their temper far too often. Then, when they really need to stand firm, they crumble."

Florence bowed her head. "I'll try to remember that, your Grace."

"Aunt," the duchess corrected, and lifted the pot to pour her tea. "In fact . . ." Her expression grew distant. "I think you'll be my goddaughter."

At that moment, the duchess could have knocked Florence over with a feather. She laughed when she saw Florence's face, her eyes twinkling with the mischief of a child.

"I can hardly wait to take you out," she said, actually rubbing her hands with glee. "You're going to cause a sensation, an ab-so-lute sensation. There'll be so many noses out of joint, we'll have to count them by the bushel."

This was not a prediction Florence could welcome. "I really don't care to cause a sensation," she murmured. "Just to meet a nice, eligible man."

"You will, my dear," the duchess assured her. "Cartloads. But first"—she chucked Florence under the chin—"first we're going to have fun!"

AUNT HYPATIA'S GENEROSITY HAD JUST BEGUN. SHE ASsigned Florence a spacious room on the second floor, with windows overlooking the fenced-in park at the center of Grosvenor Square. Lizzie had a cozy closet right beside. The girl was atwitter, for she was to be trained by the duchess's own abigail to be a lady's maid.

"It's a dream," she breathed on hearing the news. "Oh, miss, don't pinch me or I'll wake up!"

Florence wished her own enjoyment were as pure. What sort of paragon, she wondered, accepted a perfect stranger into her home and treated her not like a cousin but like a long-lost daughter? The duchess claimed Mr. Mowbry had done her a favor, but Mr. Mowbry must be quite the solicitor to have a duchess in his debt! Nor did Hypatia seem the type to dedicate her life to charitable causes. Open-

handed she was, but hardly self-sacrificing. Florence could only conclude some benefit for her lay in the arrangement. Perhaps she had a
social rival whose daughter she hoped to put in the shade. That Florence could believe, though she knew the suspicion did her no credit.
Her father had raised her to think the best of people: to say "thank
you" rather than "why." He would tell her to count her good fortune,
not question her rescuer's motives.

When Aunt Hypatia wanted Florence to patronize her dressmaker,
however, a woman who lived *on* Bond Street, not just near it, Florence
had to draw the line.

"I'm paying," the duchess huffed. "The least you can do is let me
have my way."

But even if Madame Victoire was a trifle odd, Florence could not
betray her trust.

"If I marry," she said, "I shall be able to pay you back. Perhaps not at
once," she added, thinking of the possible tradesman, "but eventually."

She held her ground even in the face of the duchess's glare. Finally,
her benefactress gave in with a snort of annoyance. "Next you'll be
wanting to pay room and board."

"If your Grace wishes," Florence agreed.

"Cheek," muttered the duchess. "Don't know what girls are coming to these days."

Happily, when Madame Victoire arrived, the duchess's feathers
were quickly smoothed. Florence had feared the dressmaker's manner
would be too familiar, but her treatment of the duchess was impeccable, almost obsequious—though the duchess didn't seem to mind.

Their taste was in perfect accord. As a result, Florence had no say
whatsoever. She was to have three new corsets, all French, four carriage dresses, six dinner dresses, another six suitable for dancing, and
the Lord only knew how many petticoats, chemises, and shoes. A single pair of satin slippers would have strained Florence's purse, but
Aunt Hypatia did not intend for the madness to stop there.

"If you take, we'll buy more," she said. "Since people will remember what you've worn."

"I feel as if I'm taking enough already," Florence mourned. "I
begin to pity my poor husband. His wife will be shockingly in debt."

Aunt Hypatia laughed and kissed her brow, but Florence had not
spoken in jest.

ON SATURDAY, HER CARDS WENT OUT; OR, RATHER, DUCHESS
Carlisle's cards went out with Florence's name written underneath.

Florence and the duchess did not accompany the cards. One of her more ordinary footmen drove them around on his own.

"I have only sent out thirty," said Aunt Hypatia. "We are being select."

Thirty sounded like a great number to Florence, but she nodded as if she thought it small. It was the peaceful hour before bedtime. She sat at the duchess's feet in her boudoir, with her new muslin skirts spread around her, idly helping to roll a skein of cashmere yarn. It seemed odd to have no chores. The Fairleighs, even at their most flush, had never possessed sufficient servants to excuse Florence from the nightly round of dishes and water-carrying and stoking or banking of fires. Now she had only to listen to Aunt Hypatia's voice, to admire the Oriental carpets and the lovely watercolors and the flicker of a fire someone else had built to keep the cool May night at bay. She was growing comfortable here; too comfortable, truth be told.

"What," she said, picking up the thread of conversation, "are we selecting for?"

"For those who are powerful," said the duchess, "and those who are so interesting we cannot resist. Alas, those circles very seldom overlap."

"Except in your case, Aunt Hypatia."

The duchess rewarded her teasing with a sharp rap from her fan. "I have not taught you to be so flattering."

"No, your Grace," she dared to say. "You have not had the time."

Aunt Hypatia chuckled. "Ah, child, it's good to see you smile. When you are frightened you tend to look very prim."

"That is preferable to showing terror, I believe."

"Yes," said the duchess with a quiet sigh. "It is."

She stroked Florence's cheek where the fire had not warmed it. It was a brief caress and when it ended, the duchess subsided into thought. Florence watched her regal, time-worn face: the nose haughty and sharp, the eyes wise and heavy. She did not know this woman and yet she felt as if she did. Despite her suspicions, she could not hold out against the tugging on her heart. Florence did not remember her mother. Sarah Fairleigh had died too young. She thought, however, that the tender spot beneath her breast must be the shadow of a daughter's love.

In that moment, her resistance wavered. The most hardened cynic—and Florence was hardly that—could not doubt Hypatia's affection. It was offered too wistfully to be shammed. If the duchess wished to use Florence in some fashion, well, so be it. Florence judged her patroness had more than earned it.

*   *   *

ON SUNDAY MORNING, THE DUCHESS THUMPED INTO FLO-
rence's room while Lizzie was struggling with the laces of her corset.
The new ones would not arrive for weeks, but Lizzie was determined
her mistress's waist would come up to London's mark.

"Reach up and grab the bedpost," the duchess instructed, "and let
Lizzie give a heave."

Florence squeaked at how well this succeeded, but the duchess
showed no pity.

"You'll get used to it," she said, "and if you faint, we'll let the
laces out."

Certain she did not welcome the prospect of fainting, Florence
vowed she'd somehow learn to breathe. "Do you require my assistance?" she gasped through the constriction around her ribs. "You
know I'd be happy to help in any way."

"No, I don't require your assistance," the duchess huffed. "I require
your presence at breakfast. In the cream tarlatan with the green velvet
bows. The boys will be joining us. You can have your first dry run."

Florence stepped into the first of many petticoats. " 'The boys'?"

The duchess thumped her cane. "My nephews, and your cousins.
So no 'my lord' this and 'viscount' that. It's Freddie and Edward to
you and don't forget it."

"Oh," said Florence, her heart beating very fast. She was going to
take breakfast with men, titled men, the dowager duchess's relatives.
Her nerves being what they were, she sincerely hoped the meal
wouldn't end up on her dress.

She worried for nothing, though, because the duchess's nephew
Freddie immediately made her comfortable.

"Hullo, cuz," he said, rising as she entered the breakfast parlor. He
was the handsomest man she'd ever seen, like a hero out of a novel,
with wavy, golden brown hair, bright blue eyes, and a smile as sunny
as the day outside.

"How do you do?" Florence responded shyly, unable to resist smiling back.

His brother was a tall broad shadow beside the window. Florence
wouldn't have taken much note of him if her fingers hadn't tingled
strangely in his grip.

"How do you do?" he said, bowing over her hand. His eyes were
the same bright blue as his brother's, but his lashes were black as coal.
Within that brooding frame, his stare was remarkably penetrating. A

peculiar heat curled through Florence's chest. Embarrassment, she thought, but it wasn't precisely that.

"Oh, kiss her knuckles." Impatience incarnate, the duchess waved him on. "The girl needs to get used to gallantry."

With great solemnity, her nephew obeyed. He was graceful but stiff, and when his lips pressed briefly to her skin, she could not suppress a shiver. His mouth had been warm, almost hot. When he straightened, two spots of color flew on his cheeks.

"Enough of that," chuckled his brother. "Edward don't do the pretty like I do."

He took Florence's arm to lead her to the sideboard, where an astonishing array of food was laid out in silver dishes. Florence goggled at the deviled kidneys and eggs, at the kedgeree and kippers, at the porridge and toast and rolls and the pots of jelly that gleamed like jewels. She doubted four people could eat this much in a week, even if two of them were men.

"Shall I serve you, Florence?" Freddie suggested, grinning to soften his use of her Christian name.

"Yes . . . Freddie," she responded and was rewarded with a boyish laugh.

"We'll get on," he said with a friendly wink. "I can see you're a sensible girl."

He could not have picked a better compliment and the meal proceeded with amazing ease. Freddie was a witty raconteur, a bit naughty perhaps, but never over the line.

"My brother," he confided, as that stern fellow cut his kidneys with methodical care, "is the despair of all the mamas in London."

"Is he?" she said, though she wasn't sure she ought to encourage Freddie at his brother's expense. Edward, as she forced herself to think of him, did not seem the type to relish teasing.

"Yes," said Freddie and bumped her shoulder companionably with his own. "They try to snare him for their daughters, but he won't go. Can't even get him to flirt."

Edward frowned at his plate, but did not scold.

"Not all men were born to flirt," Florence said, feeling oddly as if she should defend him. "Perhaps he—I mean you—oh, dear. Forgive me, Lord Greystowe. I ought not speak for you."

"Edward," he said with a chill authority that proved he was Hypatia's nephew.

"Edward," she said, her cheeks aflame beneath his strange, measuring gaze. "I'm sure your reasons for not flirting with the mamas' daughters are very wise."

"Hah!" said Freddie, apparently in no fear of his brother's ire. "He's married to his responsibilities. To his corn and his sheep and his cotton mill in Manchester."

Edward set down his knife and fork. "Now, Freddie," he said with a perfectly sober face, "it isn't nice to say a man is married to his sheep."

Florence almost choked on a piece of toast. One of the footmen had to thump her on the back until she stopped.

"Come, come," Edward chided. "Surely a country girl like yourself is familiar with the animal side of life."

Florence was almost certain he was teasing. Some emotion curled the corner of his surprisingly sensual mouth. His tone, however, was completely serious.

Her nerves in hopeless confusion, she crumpled her napkin in her lap. Whatever this family's reasons for taking her in, she did not want them to think her common, or that her father had not sheltered her as he should. If she'd heard the village lads joking about such things, it was purely by accident! "I know n-nothing of it at all," she stammered. "Why, when Father carved the turkey, he always asked if I'd take a slice of bosom."

She'd meant this to prove the vicar's propriety, but the declaration caused Freddie to cough loudly into his fist. As for Edward, though he did not succumb to humor, a definite glint shone in his eye.

"Very proper," he said. "The white meat is the tenderest."

His head was lowered over his plate, but when he peered up through his lashes, his gaze seemed to rove laughingly across her bodice. She'd never seen a man laugh that way, with nothing but his eyes. It was at once disconcerting and appealing. And it made it utterly impossible not to press her hand to the swell of her breast.

"Edward," Hypatia scolded, "you're making the girl uncomfortable."

The polite thing would have been to deny it, but Florence's mouth wasn't working well enough for that.

"No worries," Freddie said, recovered from his cough. "Old Edward's made his joke for the quarter. You needn't fear he'll try another until August."

"Freddie!" said Hypatia, no happier with his jest.

Despite the duchess's disapproval, Florence felt the heat recede from her cheeks. The brothers' effect on her could not have been more different. Thank goodness for Freddie. His words made her comfortable again: a part of the fun rather than the object of it. When Edward tendered a stiff apology, she was able to accept it with a modicum of dignity.

"See, Edward," Freddie teased, "not just pretty but forgiving."

Florence returned his friendly grin. What an agreeable young man, she thought. If he was a sample of what London had on offer, her quest to find a husband would not be hard at all.

Chapter 3

THE FOLLOWING WEEK WAS SPENT IN GIVING AND RETURNING calls. Florence doubted she was "taking," as Aunt Hypatia put it. The blur of faces and names confused her, and she rarely thought of anything to say. How could she? She did not know the people being discussed, nor any more of fashion than Madame Victoire had laid on her back.

Aunt Hypatia, however, gave every appearance of being pleased.

"Modest and unassuming," she pronounced as the footman handed them into the carriage after a visit in posh Park Lane. With an air of satisfaction, she spread her skirts more comfortably around her, then laughed at Florence's grimace. "You mustn't fear being dull, my dear. You would only seem awkward if you tried to be gay. The important thing is for people to meet you and see how pretty you are, which they could not fail to do if they were blind."

Such claims made Florence uncomfortable but, considering how generous the duchess had been and how little else Florence had to offer, she felt she really ought not to complain.

When she was not engaged with calls, Freddie claimed cousin's privilege to squire her around, taking her riding in the parks or on a boat ride down the Thames. She enjoyed herself immensely, for Freddie was a charming companion, full of witty stories but also drawing her to talk about herself. By the end of the week, he knew more about her than almost anyone alive.

She had to remind herself the duchess could not mean for her to fix her affections on him. Her nephew would marry an heiress, she decided, one of those laughing Americans, perhaps, who would not make him stand on ceremony.

"Do you think so?" he said when she shared her theory. He fixed her with an odd, speaking look which, provokingly, did not speak clearly to her.

They were leaning over the rail of a pleasure boat, chugging westwards from the pool of London. The Victoria Embankment lay ahead, and the bristling brown towers of Parliament. They stood so close they bumped elbows but, as ever, she was comfortable with his touch.

"You don't like Americans?" she probed, expecting some quip in response.

Instead, he turned his gaze to a nearby collier. The heavy ship wallowed under its load of coal and Freddie's expression wasn't much lighter. He looked so sad of a sudden Florence's ribs squeezed tight with pity.

"I'm fond of English lasses" was all he said. "Pretty ones, with straight dark hair and eyes as green as glass."

She did not take the implication seriously, not from a flirt like him. No doubt some foolish American had broken his heart, and that was the source of his pain. But if one had, he did not reveal it. The moment passed and he was soon as bright as ever.

His brother joined a few of their outings, which was not an unmitigated joy. Florence did not know why, but he seemed to have taken her in dislike. Freddie's claim that his sibling would not venture more than one witticism per quarter seemed to be correct. Not that she wanted to hear more foolish sheep jokes. One had been enough. Still, she hardly thought it necessary that he frown every time he looked at her. She would have been tempted to evade him but for Freddie's obvious delight. He adored his older brother and, despite Edward's wooden manner, she could see the sentiment was returned. Nor could she fault Edward's politeness. Everywhere they went, he introduced her as their cousin. Shy as she was, she couldn't help being gratified at being seen with these impressive men.

If only the elder of the two could have been a little warmer!

He was not ugly, she decided. To be sure, his build wasn't as lithe as Freddie's, but he was every bit as tall. His shoulders were broader, his limbs heavier and more powerful. His face was interesting if one looked past his glower. His expression had an intensity and an intelligence which was impossible to ignore. True, his brows overhung his eyes, and his nose was as sharp as Aunt Hypatia's. His forehead, however, was truly noble, his jaw strong, and the most exacting critic of human beauty could not have found fault with the sensual perfection of his mouth.

His hands, she thought with a peculiar inward shiver, were also nice. They were large and careful and capable. She found it hard to imagine the task they could not do.

When they all went riding in Rotten Row, her pride in the brothers' company was so great she felt the glow of it in her cheeks. Freddie's style turned every eye and Edward, who rode a magnificent, deep-chested black stallion, was so imposing the other horses sidled away at his approach. His hands seemed barely to move upon the reins. Freddie's gelding frisked with high spirits, but Edward's horse behaved as if he were too proud to do anything except precisely what Edward asked. Florence found this astonishing. In her experience, stallions were rarely fit for anyone but madmen and braggarts to ride—and Edward was clearly neither. He called the beast Samson, for his long caramel-colored mane.

Florence's bay mare, leased from a local stable, seemed inordinately fond of the big black horse. She was a pretty creature, with a gait as light as a cat's, but if Florence's attention strayed for even a moment, she would shoulder over to Samson and rub her muzzle against his neck.

"She's in love," Freddie teased the dozenth time Florence tried to wrestle the mare away. "Edward, you'll have to bring Buttercup back to Greystowe for Samson's harem."

Florence had heard such talk before, of course. Back home, horses and their breeding were as great a topic of conversation as the weather. Nothing Freddie said should have embarrassed her. For some reason, though, maybe because Edward's eyes were on her, or because the mare chose that moment to press even more amorously into Samson's side, a great wash of heat poured through her limbs. From head to toe, her body pulsed with the fiery tide. Florence had never experienced the like. Sweat prickled between her breasts and where her thigh was jammed against Edward's burned as if his leg were made of coal.

With a soft cry, she thrust out her hand to keep from being crushed between their mounts. Her palm caught Edward's hip, right where his buff-colored breeches stretched across his groin. His leg was harder than she expected. Her fingers curled in reaction and, as a muscle shifted abruptly beneath her touch, the strange throbbing heat intensified inside her.

Edward wrenched away with a curse. "For God's sake," he exclaimed, his color high, "watch where you lay your hand."

"I—I—" said Florence, but before she could get the apology out, he was tearing through the trees towards the Serpentine's banks, clods of turf kicking up beneath Samson's hooves.

Mortified, Florence tried to contain her tears. In all her life no one had spoken to her so coldly. Of course, she could not deny she deserved it. He must think her twice the fool: first for not controlling her horse and second for having the temerity to touch him where no lady should. That she hadn't meant to hardly mattered. Worst of all, there were witnesses to her shame. Two young women in jaunty feathered hats had stopped beside the sandy path, and now were tittering behind their gloves. Florence had the awful feeling she'd met them on one of her calls. The Misses Wainwright, she believed, whose mama had asked so many pointed questions about Freddie and his brother. The woman had been most encroaching and Florence had thought perhaps it was her nose Aunt Hypatia meant to put out of joint by launching her.

Florence certainly hadn't helped that ambition today. They, too, cantered off before she could decide whether she ought to nod.

The only saving grace was that Freddie hadn't seen them cut her. "Don't mind Edward," he said, giving her horse's withers a soothing pat. "God love him, but he's moody."

"He's right," she said, every part of her aquiver. "My failings as a horsewoman are undeniable."

"Pooh." Freddie waved the suggestion away. "Got as fine a seat as anyone. Not your fault Edward chose a horse with a fancy for his."

Her heart picked up strangely at his words. "Edward chose my horse?"

"Didn't he just! Wouldn't trust the job to anyone else. Drove the man at Tattersall's batty. Nothing too slow, he says, but nothing too fast and, no, that one ain't near pretty enough. And what does he get for his pains but this lovelorn creature?"

The mare whickered as if she took offense. Most of Florence's hurt was lost in the laugh she and Freddie shared. Not all of it, though.

Lord Greystowe's disapproval had a powerful sting.

EDWARD RODE FULL OUT UNTIL HE HIT THE QUIET OF KENsington Gardens. Up till then, the necessity of dodging phaetons and buggies had kept his mind from the brand Miss Fairleigh's palm had seared onto his thigh. The girl was too innocent for her own good. Too innocent for *his* good.

With a muttered curse, he dismounted beneath the willows that lined the Long Water's banks. His lingering erection made him awkward but he ignored it. He was used to it by now, or should have been. He had only to think of the girl and his sex began to fill. Worse, he was beginning to like her. Most girls in her position would have been grasping or sly, but she was an amiable little thing, and so tempting to tease. A hundred times a day he thought of some quip to make her blush, then had to remind himself that charming her was Freddie's business. Sighing, he removed his hat and raked his sweaty hair back from his brow. A heron stalked the placid lake before him, its stately progress calming his disordered nerves. As if to remind him how hard he'd been working, Samson blew impatiently in his ear.

"Yes," said Edward, stroking the horse's lathered nose. "You're a good fellow."

A better fellow than his master. Samson hadn't lost control when that mare rubbed up against him. Nor was Samson contemplating another visit to Cumberland Terrace. Three times this week that made, with each encounter more frenzied than the last. Imogene was cooing.

He shook his head in disgust and opened his collar to the breeze. He couldn't keep exorcizing his lust for his brother's intended with his mistress. Even if Imogene didn't know, it wasn't right. No, he had to wrestle this demon to ground himself. Florence wasn't for him. Florence was for Freddie. And they were getting on famously. Per instructions, Freddie was giving a fair imitation of an increasingly besotted man. Nor did his interest seem feigned. He was fond of the girl, genuinely fond. He repeated things she'd said, planned excursions for her pleasure, and, as far as Edward could see, enjoyed their time together.

Just the other day, he told Edward how she'd charmed the duke of Devonshire's horse. "Silly beast tried to eat the girl's hat," he'd laughed. "You know what she said? 'Why, your Grace. I'd no idea that hat had such good straw.' That shows pluck, Edward. Pluck. Especially for a girl who'd jump at her own shadow." Freddie was proud of her, as a man should be proud of his future wife. All in all, Edward's plan could not have been progressing better.

If he hadn't been so attracted to her himself, he was certain he would have been glad.

FREDDIE, FLORENCE, AND THE DUCHESS STOOD IN A COURT-yard behind a big Palladian building on Piccadilly, waiting for Edward to arrive. For the last four years, this brown and white mansion had housed the Royal Academy of the Arts. According to Aunt Hypatia, the private viewing of the spring show, for which they had come, was the first great event of the Season. The look of the crowd upheld her claim. All around them, the cream of London society filed slowly towards the entrance, their clothes exquisite, their demeanor impossibly proud. Always an object of attention, the duchess nodded at many who passed, all of whom seemed pleased to be acknowledged. Surprisingly, many nodded at Florence as well. Florence did her best to smile and bow, but was far too agitated to attempt more greeting than that. To her relief, she did not see the Misses Wainwright.

"Don't fidget," said Aunt Hypatia, softening the order with a pat.

Florence barely heard her. She did not know if she was glad or sorry Edward had chosen to see the show. The duchess could use his arm, of course, and Freddie was always happy to have him, but Florence was finding Edward's company increasingly oppressive to her nerves. She could not seem to catch her breath when he was near. If he should chance to touch her, her hands would begin to shake. The mere sight of his shoulders in one of his conservative black coats caused a peculiar palpitation of her heart.

Today, his top hat did her in. It was perched with perfect straightness on his head, its gleam no richer than that of his wavy hair, which was clipped so close to his neck the locks didn't dare curl over his collar. What drove a man to treat his hair as if it were in danger of running wild? And what, she wondered, would happen if he let it?

The question was nonsensical, of course, and the answer not her concern. Determined not to pursue it, she folded her hands at her waist and composed herself to greet him.

He met them with his usual stiff bow and frown, a frown that deepened as he took in her long-waisted apricot gown. She wore one of her new French corsets beneath it, laced only a little tighter than she was used to. The color was flattering, as was the ecru lace that spilled from its neck and sleeves. The bustle was modest, the sweep of the polonaise no more extravagant than any woman her age might wear. Her hat was a marvel of simplicity: a tilted satin chip with a single white feather in its brim, so small it perched atop her upswept hair like a saucer to a teacup. Freddie had gone into raptures when he saw her; said she'd outshine anything the painters could devise. And Freddie knew fashion. Because of this, Florence refused to believe Edward was frowning at her outfit.

Which meant he had to be frowning at her.

"Florence," he said, no more than that, and turned to escort his aunt.

The deflation she felt once his eyes had left her was completely inexplicable.

"Are you sure he wanted to come?" she whispered to Freddie as they, and the rest of the crowd, crept up the double staircase in the hall. "You didn't bully him into it, did you?"

"Me?" Freddie's eyes widened in surprise. "Lord, no. Couldn't keep him away. Edward's a true patron of the arts. You watch. Everyone else will be gossiping about who's wearing what and who's wooing whom and old Edward will be looking at the pictures."

Freddie, apparently, belonged to the gossiping set. She lost him to a group of laughing men as soon as they entered the hall. He waved at her to join him but she didn't want to go, not only because his companions looked a trifle fast, but because she wanted to see the show. This, to her, was the lure of London. Not parties, not *cartes de visites,* but plunging into the heart of art and culture. When she couldn't spot Edward or the duchess, she resigned herself to touring alone.

Happily, no one paid the least attention as she wandered from room to room. Each wall took a good deal of study, for the paintings were crammed together, one atop the other, all the way to the ceiling. Florence didn't mind the confusion. She loved seeing these works in person, rather than as engravings in a magazine. Even the bad paintings pleased her, for she could see the brush strokes and the colors and imagine the real live painter at his work. How wonderful it must be, she thought, to have the ability to create.

Some of the pictures were very fine. For long minutes, she stood entranced by Mr. Millais's portrait of the grand Mrs. Bischoffshein, her character captured so thoroughly Florence felt as if she knew her. A termagant, she thought, but one with a sense of humor. She stopped as well when she reached Tissot's *Too Early,* which, by luck or design, hung by itself above a lovely marble fireplace. The picture depicted four lovely, but obviously embarrassed, girls, waiting with their escorts in an empty ballroom.

"Do you like it?" said a deep familiar voice.

Florence's heart began to pound. She couldn't recall Edward soliciting her opinion before. She snuck a look at him but, thankfully, his stern blue gaze rested on the painting. She answered as steadily as she could.

"I like it very much," she said. "The artist has so perfectly captured the awkwardness of arriving first one can hardly help but smile."

Edward tugged his lapels. "You like a picture that tells a story?"
"As long as the story is interesting."

"What about that French fellow, Monet, or Mr. Sisley?" For the first time, he looked directly at her, both his gaze and his tone challenging. Florence felt an odd swooping in her stomach. No man should have lashes that thick. For a moment, her face was so hot she thought she'd faint. She had to swallow before she could speak.

"I'm afraid I'm not familiar with their work."

Edward nodded as if her answer was no more than he'd expected. "Come with me," he said. "I have something to show you."

To her amazement, he took her not by the arm but by the hand. Even through her gloves she could feel the warmth of his hold. Her fingers were utterly swallowed in his grip. She could only pray he did not sense the sudden dampness of her palm.

He led her through a maze of arched doorways to the very smallest of the galleries. There he handed her a pair of silver opera glasses and pointed to a painting which hung, as if the Academy were ashamed to have accepted it, in a high, dingy corner near the ceiling.

Florence put the glasses to her eyes. "Am I looking at Mr. Monet or Mr. Sisley?"

"Neither," he said, with the perversity she had come to expect. "This work is Mr. Whistler's."

She could feel him breathing, slowly, steadily. He stood directly behind her, his long legs brushing her skirts, his big hands tilting the binoculars to guide her gaze. Her arms began to tremble. They only stopped when she focused on the painting.

"Oh," she sighed, unable to keep her wonderment inside. The picture showed a bridge just after sunset on a misty night, with the shadow of a solitary boatman punting the current underneath. She'd never seen anything like it. It was a completely new thing, a blur of subtle colors which somehow created a world. She felt her mind open in the strangest way. This, she thought, is a painting of the future.

Edward seemed to share her excitement.

"Isn't it something?" he said, the words a gentle stir beneath her hat.

"It's extraordinary! Why, it's nothing but smears of dark and light blue, but you know exactly what it is. He has it precisely: how the water looks at night, even how it feels, as if the whole world had gone to sleep but you. It makes me want to cry just looking at it and yet it's quite, quite beautiful."

Lost in admiration, she didn't even jump when Edward's hands settled briefly on her shoulders, just a quick, warm squeeze and they were gone.

"I was thinking I would buy it," he said.

Florence couldn't help herself. She lowered the glasses and turned to him. His expression was musing, his exquisite mouth relaxed. For once, he looked as young as Freddie. Oh, I could like him, she thought. If only he behaved this way more often, I'm certain we could be friends.

"Do you know," she said, "I've never known anyone who bought a painting."

He laughed at her admission, a soft, open sound that brushed her ears like a puppy's growl. "Careful, Miss Fairleigh. You betray your origins by such a statement."

His eyes were twinkling so kindly she knew he was teasing. All the same, she found it impossible to hold his gaze. It was too blue, too warm. She looked at her hands instead, still clasped around his opera glasses. "My origins are difficult to hide," she said, smiling a little herself. "Aunt Hypatia says I mustn't even try."

"Well, if Aunt Hypatia says . . ." he agreed, and smoothed back the little white feather which had fallen forward from her hat. It was a gesture his brother might have made, thoughtful and protective. Florence shivered under it as she never had with Freddie.

"Are you cold, Miss Fairleigh?" Edward asked, his voice low and oddly husky. He had bent forward to view her face, an action necessitated by his greater height. She could see the shadow of his whiskers beneath his skin; could smell the woodsy aroma of his cologne. She wouldn't have thought he'd wear scent, a sober man like him. The fact that he did pricked her deep inside. He has secrets, she thought. He is not at all the man he seems.

"Miss Fairleigh?" he said. So lightly she might have dreamt it, his finger brushed the curve of her cheek. Its tip was bare and slightly rough. He must have removed his gloves. Her stomach tightened at the unexpected intimacy.

"I am well," she said, just a shade too loudly. "Quite."

Edward stiffened at her tone and took half a step back. He buttoned his elegant coat and smoothed it down. "Perhaps we ought to rescue Aunt Hypatia from the tea room."

"Yes," she said, both relieved and disappointed.

He offered his arm this time, the elbow held well out from his side. When Florence put her hand through it, his yielding had disappeared. The limb might as well have been a block of wood. A sigh escaped her corseted lungs. She'd thought Freddie's brother was warming to her, and had been foolish enough to welcome the change. She should have known better. Clearly, it would take more than a moment's amity to melt this man of stone.

LEWIS TAPPED ON THE DOOR TO THE DRESSING ROOM JUST AS Edward slid an onyx stud through the front of his stark white shirt. He was planning his strategy for tonight's ball, a strategy that did not include forgetting himself as he had at the Academy. He would be civil to Miss Fairleigh, no more. He would not touch her. He would not smile at her. Most definitely he would not dance with her. Until he found a means to control his disturbingly volatile reactions, he was not going to get close to her again.

He didn't care if her eyes were as green as Irish grass. He didn't care if she did agree that Whistler was a genius, or that her blushes made him want to crush her to his chest and kiss her senseless. From now on, distance would be the lynchpin of their relationship.

"Sir?" said Lewis. Having failed to get a response from his master, the valet stepped just inside the door. "I'm afraid a small problem has arisen."

Edward's mind flew to Freddie, and footmen, but he pushed the thought aside as quickly as he could. Freddie had given his word. That was all Edward needed to know. He fastened the stud beneath his pointed collar. He reached for his white bow tie. "What small problem?"

"It's Miss Fairleigh."

Edward's heart skipped a beat. Damnation. Her name was enough to tighten the muscles of his groin. "Is Miss Fairleigh unwell?"

"Not precisely, my lord." Lewis took the tie from Edward's hands before he mangled it. "Apparently, she's grown so anxious over the prospect of her first formal ball that she is . . . prostrate."

" 'Prostrate'?" Edward lifted his chin for Lewis to tie the bow. An image of Miss Fairleigh fainting drifted disturbingly through his mind. He could almost feel himself catching her.

"A disturbance of the stomach," Lewis elucidated.

In spite of a rush of sympathy, Edward laughed. "You mean she's so frightened she cast up her accounts."

"Yes, sir," said the valet. "Her courage has failed her. She swears she'll return to Keswick tomorrow, rather than make a fool of herself tonight."

"Keswick?" With a frown, Edward submitted to a subtle re-arrangement of his hair.

"Her home village," Lewis explained and Edward experienced an illogical prick of annoyance that his servant knew this when he did not. "Duchess Carlisle is at her wit's end. She sent her footman over to see if young Lord Burbrooke can talk some sense into her, but your brother has already left for his dinner engagement at the Brawleighs'."

"Surely my aunt could—"

"She says it's a job for a man: the voice of authority appealing to the rational in a woman." Lewis looked as if he doubted this quality existed in female form. Then again, for the past year, Lewis had been trying without success to coax the senior chambermaid into his bed.

"I'll speak to her," Edward said, though he knew it flew in the face of his resolutions. "Most likely she only needs to be reassured she won't be left standing through the waltzes."

"Yes, my lord." Lewis held up his waistcoat for him to slip his arms into the sleeves. The design was very plain, black with a smooth shawl collar and a satin back. It fit like a second skin.

Edward ignored the tingle of excitement that warmed his spine. This mission of mercy posed no danger. After all, how appealing could a "prostrate" woman be?

"BRUSH YOUR TEETH," SAID LIZZIE, HOLDING OUT THE TIN of tooth powder.

Florence buried her face in the pillow. She was never leaving this room. The Vances were expecting five hundred people at their ball. Her stomach lurched at the very thought. She'd been brave up till now; she truly had, but this was too much to expect. Five hundred people! And Aunt Hypatia wanted her to dazzle them. She'd be lucky if she survived.

"Already brushed them twice," she mumbled.

"Once more before you go," Lizzie insisted. "Duchess's orders."

"But I'm not going. I'm not, I'm not!" She knew how hysterical she sounded, but she could not stop herself. She couldn't go. She simply couldn't. She might be pretty but she was hopelessly inept. With a groan, she piled the pillow over her head.

"Honestly," Lizzie huffed, and Florence knew she'd put her hands on her skinny hips. "You make me ashamed to know you, Miss Florence."

"And you should be ashamed," said a voice that had her bolting up with the pillow clutched to her chest, though her dressing gown was perfectly modest. Her hair was down. And this was her bedroom. And he was a man. All of which was enough to throw her into a panic.

"Lord Greystowe!" she gasped.

He sat very gently on the edge of the bed, as if she were an invalid. She thought he would take her hand but he only stroked the coverlet beside her hip.

"Now, Florence," he said, "tell me what has frightened you."

He made her feel foolish by simple virtue of asking the question. But she wasn't foolish. No one understood how terrible this was for her, least of all this man, who'd probably never been frightened in his life. She plumped the pillow in her lap and sniffed back a tear. "Aunt Hypatia says five hundred people are coming to the Vances' ball."

"And?" he said, as if five hundred people were nothing. Her tears welled again, but now they were tears of resentment.

"They'll stare," she said, her nails curling into her palms. "They'll stare and they'll titter and they'll talk behind their fans as if I were a cow at a county fair."

"Because you're pretty," he said in that same infuriatingly reasonable tone.

"Yes!" she said, almost shouting it.

Edward smiled and her temper abruptly snapped. How dare he mock her fears? Before she could stop herself, she pounded his chest with both hands. Edward caught them before she could land a second blow.

"Hush," he said, and pressed a gentle kiss to the knuckles of each fist. This procedure so astonished her she didn't think to pull back. His eyes shone with humor and something that in any other man she would have said was fondness. "Allow me to explain the economies of size, Miss Fairleigh. With five hundred attendees, at least half of them women, you can count on, oh, fully twenty being prettier than yourself. A good many will have jewels more dazzling than your own. A fair number will be dressed so inappropriately anyone who sees them will not be able to look away. Add to that those guests who are either the subject or repository of gossip, and you'll find no more than a tenth of those present will stare at you even once."

"And a tenth is only fifty," Lizzie put in, who was proud of her skill at math.

Florence was neither impressed nor reassured.

"All I know are country dances," she said, her voice still quavering. "I don't remember a step Aunt Hypatia's dancing master tried to teach me."

Edward squeezed her hands. "You'll remember. The moment the music starts it will all come back. Come now, Florence. Where's the girl who charmed the duke of Devonshire with her wit? Where's her courage?"

"In the chamberpot," Florence muttered.

"Nonsense," said Edward. "That was only lunch."

"And since it's gone," Lizzie added with country practicality, "you needn't worry about being sick."

Florence's shoulders sagged. She didn't want to be strong. She wanted to be weak and helpless and stay where she was safe. But Lizzie was counting on her and so was Aunt Hypatia, and even Edward, in a way. If his "cousin" proved a coward, it would not reflect well on him.

"I suppose I have no choice."

"No choice at all," Edward agreed. He smiled at her. Florence saw a hint of pride in it and thought perhaps she wouldn't fail after all.

Chapter 4

A BURNING SHIVER SWEPT THE BARE EXPANSE OF FLO-rence's shoulders. Edward was watching her descend Aunt Hypatia's curving stairs. He wore an expression of utter stupefaction.

"Perhaps," he said, in an unusually faint tone, "I have misled you."

Florence didn't know what to make of his reaction—or her own. Edward had never looked at her like this, as other men did, as if she were a meal they wished to devour. Usually this look discomfited her. She couldn't imagine why she welcomed it from him. Certainly, she didn't *desire* his attention. He was the opposite of everything she val-ued in a man: not gentle, not affectionate, and certainly not safe! No, indeed. Most likely her response was merely nerves.

"Misled me?" she said, the question dangerously close to a squeak.

"Yes," he murmured and pressed his hand to his pristine shirt-front. His father's ruby signet gleamed on his smallest finger. "I fear you *shall* be the prettiest woman there."

"Enough," said the duchess, thumping her ivory cane. "Move aside so I can see."

At her instruction, Florence turned slowly before her. She knew she looked her best. Her gown was daffodil satin, cut low off the shoulder and draped at capsleeve and train with dotted tulle. Beneath this ephemeral net, the skirt gathered yard upon yard of fabric, an extravagant expanse from whose folds peeped vines of pink silk roses. More roses decorated her elaborately braided chignon. Around her neck a stunning choker was clasped, formed by thousands of seed pearls strung into the shape of flowers. The gown's waist required such stringent lacing Florence felt as if two large hands were wrapped around her ribs. The sensation was unexpectedly pleasant but, as a result, her breasts were forced so dramatically upward she feared she was overly décolleté.

If she was, Aunt Hypatia did not disapprove. Instead, she touched the necklace with one age-stiffened finger. She nodded brusquely.

"Suits you," she said. "Never did believe in girls wearing ribbons around their necks. Not if they've got something better."

"I'm grateful for the loan," Florence said, knowing the duchess had worn these pearls when she was Florence's age. "I shall take good care of them."

"Know you will," said Aunt Hypatia. The light from a wall sconce caught a sudden glitter in her eye. Was she thinking of her dear departed duke or some other youthful conquest? Assuredly she had had them. The duchess was too self-assured for it to be otherwise. But Florence doubted she would share the tale. Indeed, as soon as Hypatia blinked, the glitter disappeared. Once more in command of herself, the duchess rapped her cane against the footman's calf.

"Well, John," she snapped to the senior man, "have them bring around the carriage."

"Yes, your Grace," he said in his eerily drawn-out voice, as if being struck by his mistress were an everyday occurrence.

It made Florence wonder what she'd gotten into when she let the duchess take her under her wing. If she failed to live up to Hypatia's plans, would her calves be stinging, too?

HER HEART HAD PLENTY OF TIME TO FLUTTER BEFORE THEIR coach crawled its way up the line of carriages to the door. Such dresses she saw as they waited! Such silks and jewels and clouds of expensive perfume! For once, she was glad Madame Victoire had spared no expense on her couture. She would at least look as if she belonged.

When they reached the fancy overhang of the porte cochere, Edward lifted her out of the carriage. The clasp of his hands made her even more breathless than the corset. She hadn't supposed a man could be that strong. She seemed to weigh nothing in his arms. As he set her on the pavement, their eyes locked. Edward's shone like hot blue flames, intense but mysterious, and completely focused on her. Warmth spread over her breasts. Wish though she might, she could not quell the reaction. Embarrassed, she touched the tulle that swathed her bodice. Edward looked away.

"Watch your train," he said, as gruff as ever, and helped the duchess down.

When she was settled, they ventured together up the stairs. Grateful for the distraction, Florence could not contain her curiosity. She'd never been in a house this grand. To her it seemed a palace. A pair of torches shaped like nymphs, with gas globes balanced on their shoulders, lit the reception area inside the door. While the liveried footman announced their names, Florence goggled. The nymphs bore no more covering than a gauzy, scarflike cloth which seemed to have blown across their privy parts. Their breasts were bare and topped with swollen nipples—not stiffly swollen, as if the nymphs were cold, but soft, as if the breeze that blew the scarves had gently kissed their skin.

An irrational yearning pulled her closer. She would have liked to touch that polished bronze. Even more puzzling, she would have liked to stand in the nymphs' place, equally bare, to be kissed by the balmy breeze and admired by passersby. A statue could not be shy, after all. A statue could only be adored. She touched the metal plinth, surprised to find it cold.

"Florence," hissed the duchess.

She hurried after her with a gasp. What was she thinking? Without a doubt, her recent fears had disordered her mind!

IN ITS WAY, THE VANCES' HOME WAS AS CONFUSING AS EUSTON Station. The mansion in Knightsbridge had been designed by Robert Adam in an opulent, classical style. Every public room—and there were many—boasted marble columns and gilt and inlay and magnificent stuccowork ceilings. The paintings were as fine as any she had viewed at the Academy. With difficulty, she tore herself past Gainsboroughs and Reynoldses and followed a female servant up the stairs to the women's cloakroom.

In this bustling boudoir, an obliging lady's maid took her wrap and smoothed her hair and, best of all, showed her a quiet corner where she could sit. There, behind a sheltering screen of potted palms, with the sweet night air flowing in through an open window, Florence shut her eyes and tried to catch her breath.

She told herself she could do this. She would take the evening slowly. She would speak when spoken to, dance when asked, and— above all—pay attention to any nice gentlemen she met. The sooner she settled herself, the sooner she could repay Aunt Hypatia's faith, not to mention her purse.

Her face had begun to cool when a trio of women stopped on the other side of the wall of greenery. To her dismay, two were the Misses Wainwright, in matching white tarlatan gowns. They stood so close she could not possibly leave without them seeing her. But perhaps she would stay where she was a little longer. Discretion was, after all, the better part of valor. Her cowardice thus justified, Florence steeled herself to wait as quietly as she could.

"They say he's smitten," the elder Miss Wainwright was saying. Her name was Greta, Florence recalled, and the younger's name was Minna. Both sisters were handsome, built on Amazonian lines with dark gleaming hair and equally dark and gleaming eyes. Their curls, the likes of which Lizzie despaired of ever coaxing from Florence's hair, hung in perfect corkscrews to their shoulders. They sang charmingly, she had heard, and possessed a wealth of airs and graces. Their only flaw, if it even was one and not a figment of her imagination, was a certain petulance to their mouths. Truthfully, whatever Hypatia's ambitions, Florence could not imagine outshining these lovely girls.

"I can't believe his affections are engaged," said a third woman whom Florence didn't know. "Everyone knows he's an incorrigible flirt. I'm sure he's simply being cousinly."

"Perhaps," drawled Miss Minna in a cool, superior tone. "But one of her cousins doesn't welcome the association. I saw him cut her myself. Galloped off without a word when the hopeless ninny bumped his horse. I thought she'd burst into tears right there."

Heavens, Florence thought, starting up in her chair. They were talking about her, about her and Edward. Heart thundering, she shrank back and willed the women not to see her. Fortunately, they were too caught up in their gossip to look around. Even as Florence held her breath, the third whispered furiously in Minna's ear. When she'd finished, Minna's curls trembled with indignation.

"Now that," she pronounced, "is the grossest slander yet. Freddie Burbrooke adores women. Any female who's met him knows that. In any case"—she snapped her painted fan—"I don't see why we should concern ourselves with such a nobody. Why, if it weren't for that tired old dragon who's carting her about, no one would pay her any mind."

"She *is* pretty," Greta said in the tone of one too sure of her own beauty to be threatened.

"Milkmaid pretty," Minna scorned. "And who among us believes those blushes don't come out of a pot?"

If the trio had seen Florence then, they would have known her blushes were real. Her very ears were hot. With relief, she watched the women moving towards the door. The third, alas, had a final parting shot.

"It's animal magnetism," she said as they rustled off. "She's coarse and fleshy and men are the biggest animals of all. Didn't you hear what Devonshire's horse did to her hat?"

Florence clapped her hands to her cheeks. Were people really talking about that?

A low, musical laugh broke through her shock. Florence looked up. A slim young woman with frizzy gold hair and freckles was parting the fronds beside her ear, like an African hunter who'd found his game.

"I see from your horror," she said, "that you are the infamous Miss Fairleigh."

The woman's words were so mischievous Florence couldn't help but laugh. She rose and dropped a small curtsey. "I am," she said. "Milkmaid blushes and all."

"And I," said the girl, "am Meredith Vance, the plainest deb in London." She gave Florence's hand a brisk, unfeminine shake. "Shall we walk down together and show those silly cats that plain girls and milkmaids know how to behave?"

Florence had not met Miss Vance before, but knew her to be the daughter of their hosts and, therefore, the daughter of a duke. Consequently, she was momentarily flustered by her offer.

"It would be my honor, Miss Vance," she said once she had found her voice.

Miss Vance wrinkled her nose. "Call me Merry," she said, as if Florence herself were the daughter of a peer. "All my friends do and I'm certain we're going to be friends."

Miss Vance's kindness stole her breath. Dear as Keswick was, the village had been home to a great many genteel old ladies. Florence couldn't remember when she'd last had a friend her own age. Of course, she thought more soberly, Miss Vance's generosity meant she couldn't hide in the cloakroom all night.

"My brothers are going to swamp you," her rescuer predicted.

Florence endeavored to look as if this news were good.

*   *   *

EDWARD LEANED AGAINST THE WALL WITH HIS CHAMPAGNE punch, watching an endless succession of males whirl Florence Fairleigh around the floor. She was, as she'd predicted, an awkward dancer. Not surprisingly, none of her partners seemed to mind. Rather, they gazed at her with puppyish eyes, trying to coax her to lift her shyly lowered lashes by telling amusing tales. Even the older men played this game, as if she in her innocence made them remember theirs.

Only Freddie succeeded. He arrived late with a shower of apologies and immediately swept Florence into a waltz. Within minutes, she was shaking her head with laughter, easy in his arms as she was in no one else's. Her smile dazzled Edward all the way across the room. Freddie was good for her. Freddie brought her into her own. Even when he took her to meet his friends, she did not lose her glow. Edward saw her speaking to them and watched them laugh at whatever she'd said. Somehow, Freddie had found a way to share his charm with her.

Her earlier terror might as well have been a dream. Certainly, she didn't need Edward's assistance now.

He thrust his hands into his pockets, glummer than he could ever remember being. He shouldn't stare at her like this. He was only torturing himself. But how could he look away? Peter Vance was dancing with her now, a sprightly polka which could not have shown her stiffness to worse effect. Why did her awkwardness enthrall him? His heart thumped at the way she craned her slender neck to watch her stumbling feet, at the way her skirts caught Vance's legs, at the way— God help him—she blushed when Vance bent to whisper some tease in her shell-like ear.

Edward ground his teeth. He was an idiot. A complete and utter idiot. The obsession he felt for this girl made no sense whatsoever. It did no one any good: not him, not her, not Freddie.

"People are saying you snubbed her," said a throaty, boyish voice.

Caught by surprise, Edward looked down quite a few inches and found himself gazing into the wide freckled smile of their hosts' youngest daughter. He'd met her at Tattersall's, he recalled, a horsemad girl, as plain in speech as she was in appearance.

"Miss Vance," he said, and bowed politely over her hand. "Forgive me for not noticing your approach."

She gave him a rap with her fan that put him more in mind of

Aunt Hypatia than a seventeen-year-old coquette. "Didn't you hear me? People are saying you don't like Florence Fairleigh."

Edward squinted in confusion. "Are you acquainted with Miss Fairleigh?"

"Oh, yes," she said airily. "Your cousin and I are great friends— ever since I heard those Wainwright witches taking cuts at her in the cloakroom."

Edward's spine snapped straight. Someone had hurt Florence? Someone had dared? "What Wainwright witches?"

His unwitting growl made his companion laugh. "The same Wainwright witches whose mama has been stalking you these past two years."

"Oh," he said, unconsciously pursing his mouth in distaste, "Greta and Minna."

"Yes. Greta and Minna. And if you don't dance with your cousin, they'll convince everyone you disapprove of her." Her eyes narrowed and she poked the center of his chest with the end of her fan. "You don't really dislike her, do you? I'd hate to think so. Because she's obviously a nice girl and just as obviously perfect for your brother. If you meant to be cruel, I would be forced to greatly lower my estimation of your character."

Edward was startled to hear Miss Vance had any estimation of him at all. Taken aback, he had only enough presence of mind to blink when she grabbed both his wrists and pulled him onto the crowded floor. What a hellion she was to behave this outrageously in public!

"We'll dance straight to her," she said, lifting his arms into the appropriate position. "My brother Peter has got her now and he's already stood up with her twice. Once more and Mama will fear he means to make a declaration. He'll know he must relinquish her to you."

Contrary to Edward's expectations, Miss Vance, the freckle-faced, horse-mad girl, proved a neat dancer. Almost before he knew it, she'd spun them through the other couples to Florence's side. He wasn't certain, but he suspected Miss Vance had been leading.

FLORENCE'S WORLD SHRANK DOWN TO A SINGLE SOUL. EDWARD stood before her. Tall Edward. Grave Edward. Edward of the burning eyes and the beautiful mouth. Peter Vance faded into insignificance, though he'd stepped a mere foot away. Freddie's older brother was all that she could see. This was not good, she thought, not good at all.

"Oh," she said stupidly, and put one hand to her stays to keep her heart from bursting through. "Edward."

"Florence," he said, with a low, formal bow. How broad his shoulders were, and how well his black tailcoat showed off the trimness of his waist! With customary dignity, he straightened. "Might I have the honor of this dance?"

Florence blinked. "You wish to dance with me?"

He frowned and at once she felt more clearheaded. A scowling Edward she was used to.

"Yes, I wish to dance with you. Have you some objection, cousin?"

"Oh, no," she said. "I—I'd be happy to."

"Well then," he said.

As if on cue, the orchestra struck up a waltz. Her skin tingled as he took her in his arms. At once, she knew this dance was different. Edward held her with complete assurance, born to rule the ballroom. The hand he'd placed on her waist almost lifted her through the steps.

"Stop looking at your feet," he whispered, his cheek for one moment pressed to hers.

At the touch, her limbs turned to honey, liquid and warm, as if she'd been set in the sun. "Oh," she said, enchanted in spite of every scrap of sense that spoke against it. "Oh, my, you dance divinely."

He laughed, the second time she'd heard him do so. She wanted to hear that happy sound again. She wanted to hear it every day. His arm tightened and suddenly her breasts were pressed lightly to his chest. That, she thought dizzily, was even better. His legs, so long, so sure, brushed the front of her skirts. She had only to follow their motion; had only to let him lead.

"It's like flying," she said, helpless to keep her smile inside.

He grinned back at her, his face creasing upward, his bright blue eyes agleam. "It's dancing, Florence, the way it was meant to be."

She caught her breath with pleasure as he spun her even faster. The other couples seemed to part like the sea before them. The music swooped, giddy, magical. She took a firmer grip on his shoulders and closed her eyes.

"You're as lovely as a rose," he murmured, just loudly enough for her to hear.

With a quiet sigh, he gathered her closer still. She felt the warmth of his body, the hardness of his chest. His breath came quickly from his exertions. In. Out. Stirring her hair. Warming her cheek. The sound put a spell on her. Something throbbed inside her: an ache, a nameless want. She thought she heard him whisper her name. *Yes,* she thought, and her lips moved soundlessly on the word. He must have seen her do it. His hand tightened on hers, his fingers strong, sending a message her body could not help but read. Without warning, a flood of heat washed through her flesh. Her knees wobbled and gave and she stumbled over his foot.

Edward caught her before she fell.

"Goodness," she said, mortified by her near collapse. "I'm afraid all that twirling has made me dizzy."

For once, Edward's frown was more worried than disapproving. He put his arm around her waist to steady her. "Come. Let's get you some air."

He would not listen to her demurs, but led her from the stuffy ballroom and down a corridor to a large conservatory. Florence would have liked to see this marvel by daylight. Arched high above their heads, the white iron framework glowed faintly beneath the moon. Perhaps, like the Crystal Palace, the great Paxton had designed it. The structure was certainly grand enough. Small Japanese lanterns shaped like gold and black pagodas lit the winding paths. Ankle boots crunching on the pebbles, Edward guided her past towering palms and banks of ferns and a large lily pond beneath which orange fishes hung in sleep. He stopped at last under a cool dome of glass where roses of every imaginable hue grew in lushly scented profusion.

"Here." He seated her on a pretty cast-iron bench. "Close your eyes and breathe." To her surprise, he sat beside her and patted her hand. "Lizzie laced you too tightly, didn't she?"

"Oh, no," she said, her eyes flying open to find his gaze. "Aunt Hypatia's maid wouldn't let her. It was the dancing, I think. All that swooping around. It was wonderful, of course, but suddenly I felt so hot."

His brows lowered, shading his eyes to blackness. His expression was most peculiar. "You felt hot."

"Yes." She fanned her face at the memory. "Astonishingly hot. As if someone had dropped me in a pot of steam. You don't suppose I've taken ill, do you?"

She knew the words were hopeful. Though the ball had not been as terrifying as she'd feared, she still would have liked to go home.

"No," he said, but he touched her cheek with the back of his hand.

"There it is again!" she gasped.

"Florence," he said, half laugh, half groan. "You cannot be so ignorant you do not know why you are flushed."

"Well, I—" she began and then her gaze caught on his smiling lips. "I'm sure it's not—I've found men appealing before, you know, and they never affected me like this!"

"Didn't they?" His eyes were heavy, his tone a soft, insinuating growl. "Didn't they make you hot from the inside out? Didn't they make you yearn and ache and feel as if you would die unless you held them?"

His head drew closer, lips brushing her cheek like heated satin.

"Edward," she gasped, a shiver supplanting her flush. She wished he wouldn't speak so; wished he wouldn't draw so close. "You can't be meaning to kiss me!"

"Indeed," he said with that same groaning laugh, his mouth sliding along her jaw. "I assure you I don't mean to. Common sense forbids it. And decency. And every drop of affection my brother pulls from my heart."

She didn't know what Freddie had to do with it, but she was certain what he was doing qualified as a kiss. His lips had slid over hers, soft but firm and parted for the rush of his breath. She brought her palms to his chest, meaning to push him away but mysteriously unable to do so. She felt like the victim of a mesmerist, caught in the spell of his magnetic power. His chest was so hard, so warm. Helpless to resist, her fingers curled into the starchy linen of his shirt.

"Stop me, Florence," he whispered, shivering beneath her touch. "Stop me before I hurt us both."

"Stop yourself," she said, though she couldn't imagine where she'd found the wickedness to do so.

At least he was not angry. Chuckling, he nipped her chin, then did what no one had ever done before. First he licked her lower lip, then pressed beyond it with the tip of his tongue, actually breaching the outer reaches of her mouth.

"Sweet," he said, and did it again, more deeply than before.

Florence was shocked beyond fear. The smooth wet curve slid past her teeth before she could gather her wits to stop him. She could taste the champagne punch he'd drunk; could feel the texture of his tongue as it stroked her own. The effect was peculiarly seductive. It made her want to lick him back; made her want to close her eyes and sigh. But it was an unconscionable intimacy, a thing even a husband might not do. And now he was sucking her, pulling at her tongue as if he meant to lure it from her mouth. Her shoulders stiffened and her hands clutched his arms. Her heart beat like a fox chased to ground. A kiss was bad enough, but this . . . this blatantly carnal invasion—she could not allow it, simply couldn't.

"Let me," he whispered when she twisted her head away. "Oh, God, Florence. I'll go mad if I can't kiss you."

A sound broke in her throat, a hopeless whimper. His sweet, husky plea made her tingle from head to toe. He was right. She was attracted to him. That honeyed warmth was pouring through her veins, curling low in her belly and thighs, like a tide no force of will could stop.

"Let me," he said, as if he sensed her weakening. He nibbled her neck, then the lobe of her ear. "One kiss, Florence. One kiss to satisfy us both. No one will see. I'd never let anyone see."

She tried to think of Aunt Hypatia, of the five hundred guests who might take it into their heads to wander out. She tried to think of what she'd come here to find. A nice, safe husband. Not a moody, black-hearted wretch who insulted her one moment and begged for kisses the next.

Sadly her efforts were for naught. "Just one?" she asked in a shameful rush of breath.

He covered her mouth with a sighing moan, his tongue searching, caressing, his arms slowly circling her back. This time she kissed him back. She couldn't help it. He was gentle but unstoppable, like treacle rolling down a heated pan.

"Yes," he praised at her tentative foray. "Kiss me, Florence. Kiss me as deeply as you can." One hand slid up her spine to cup her head. He was tilting her neck: guiding her, she thought with an odd, warm start, so that her vulnerability to his possession would be complete.

And then her neck wasn't the only thing that was tilting. He was tipping her backwards, dizzying her as he laid her down along the bench. Satin rustled and hissed. She had to clutch his back to keep from falling and then she *wanted* to clutch his back. Its breadth was a pleasure she could not resist: its warmth, the slow, shifting strain of its muscles. His mouth lifted for breath, then sank again.

Oh, her head was spinning. His hand gripped her waist, then her hip, then wedged beneath the bulk of her bustle to squeeze her bottom as if he loved the give of the generous flesh. Her moan was not the protest it should have been. His weight felt so right between her legs. This was what men and women were meant to be. His hardness was the match for her softness, his pressure for her yielding. She gave in to the urge to hold him tighter, sliding her arms beneath the cover of his coat.

To her surprise, his shirt clung damply to his skin.

"Florence," he groaned. "You don't know what you're doing."

But then he kissed her even harder, as if his life depended on the total plunder of her mouth. His fingers tightened on her neck, sliding under Aunt Hypatia's pearls. When his father's signet pressed her skin, the metal was fever-warm. His scent surrounded her, not merely cologne but a subtle, animal smell. He began to push his hips against hers, slowly but with force, rubbing up and down the very center of her heat. That heat seemed to double as she realized his manly organ was not soft. Rather, it was thick and thrusting and hard, like a creature that needs to mate.

Abruptly panicked, she struggled to get away, but he only held her tighter. He was groaning her name now, grinding her with his hardness. His body seemed beyond his own control.

Florence could not wait for him to control it; could not stop to think. She did what she'd heard the village lads joke about. She reached around his legs and gave his parts a forceful squeeze. Apparently, she'd done it right. Swallowing a yelp, Edward shoved back as if she'd stabbed him. The blackness of his glare was enough to make her quail. Burning fingers pressed to her mouth, she struggled to sit upright.

"I'm sorry," she said, barely able to get it out. "Did I hurt you?"

"Did you—? Good Lord!" He raked his hair with both hands, then dropped his head back and breathed: long, slow breaths that lifted his belly and chest. The place she'd pinched was still humped between his legs, a rise of black cloth that pulsed like a living heart. Seeing it, she went hot again and knew she'd lost her mind. Surely she couldn't regret calling a halt to his affront!

As if he sensed her stare, Edward opened his eyes. Unlike her, he seemed to have regained his calm.

"You did precisely as you should," he said. "It is I who must beg forgiveness. I drank more champagne than I ought tonight, and took advantage of your inexperience. It was utterly despicable and I promise it shall never happen again."

He was saying he'd only kissed her because he was drunk. The confession should have comforted but it didn't. She wound her hands together in her lap. "What you did wasn't completely terrible."

He laughed, the sound harsh. "I'm glad it wasn't terrible, but it was wrong. You mustn't let other men get you alone where they can try it."

"I'm not so green I don't know that," she snapped, with a salutary hint of anger. "It's just you're, well, you're supposed to be my cousin!"

"Quite." He sighed and dragged his hand through his hair again, causing it to stand up rather comically. He was right to worry about his wavy locks. They could turn wild. But he didn't seem to notice. He nodded towards the path. "Perhaps you should go. I wouldn't want anyone to miss you."

She knew he was right. She stood and smoothed her skirts, perversely reluctant to leave. "Are you sure you're well?"

"Yes," he said sternly. "Now go."

She trudged two steps and turned back. "Your hair."

He furrowed his brows at her.

"It's sticking up. You need to smooth it."

"I shall," he assured her. And then she had no more excuses to stay.

As soon as she'd gone, Edward sagged over his knees. How could he have been so irresponsible? Anyone might have walked in on them. Florence would have been ruined, not to mention his plans for saving Freddie. Edward couldn't imagine what had come over him. All his life he'd known the value of discipline. Even before his parents died and left him alone to care for Freddie, he'd been the master of his passions. Edward didn't cry when he was scolded, or skinned his knees, or was shunned by his schoolmates because he refused to bully the boys in the lower forms. Edward was a Greystowe, an English earl. Edward set his course and followed it.

He certainly didn't drive a vicar's daughter to pinch his balls.

"Damnation," he said, and wished he knew just what he cursed.

With a long, low sigh, he pushed to his feet. He tidied his hair as well as he could and marveled at Florence's consideration in giving him the warning. What she must think of him, he couldn't guess— nor could he afford to lament the loss of her good opinion. If she stayed away from him, all the better. Clearly, he could not be trusted to keep his vows.

Imogene Hargreave cornered him halfway down the corridor to the ballroom. He had no chance to avoid her. Apart from the distant hum of merriment, and a marble cherub with a mass of roses in its arms, they were alone.

"There you are," she cooed, tiptoeing her fingers up his chest. "Charles is staying at his club tonight. I thought you might whirl me around the floor."

He caught her hand and held it away. Her hair gleamed like flax in the flickering gaslight, her skin like ivory. She was as seductive as ever, as beautiful and as skilled, but she moved him no more than a statue.

"I'm on my way out."

"Are you?" Imogene chuckled. "I'll admit the Vances' parties are a bit tame, but your aunt and her little charge seem to be enjoying themselves. Quite the sensation, that one. You'd better take care or you'll have more than a cousin on your hands. Your brother is acting smitten."

Edward stiffened at her tone. "Florence Fairleigh is a perfectly respectable young woman. If my brother chooses to pursue her, the duchess and I would hardly disapprove."

Imogene's eyes widened. "Well, of course. I'm sure she's everything that's agreeable."

"She is," Edward insisted.

Imogene cocked her head, then shook off her puzzlement. She stroked his arm. "Come, darling, let's not talk about your relatives. Let me give you a ride home." Her brows rose suggestively. "To my home, if you like."

Edward hesitated. He had no doubt Imogene intended the journey to end in her bed, a place he'd vowed not to visit again. On the other hand, if he took the carriage he came in, he'd have to send it back for Hypatia. Going with Imogene would save the coachman an extra trip. Besides which, he'd put off talking to her longer than he should.

"I'll be going to my home," he said, "but if the offer stands, I'd be happy for it."

"Of course it stands," said Imogene, playfully swatting his shoulder.

As he'd suspected, she was planning to change his mind. The carriage hadn't left the Vances' drive before she'd slid over to his seat and pulled the shades. The lantern that swayed from the hook above the door made a glowing nest of the interior. The coach's upholstery was blue, a sleek, pale satin that echoed Imogene's eyes.

"There," she said, giving him a deep, practiced kiss. "This is more like it."

He did not stop her. He was waiting—hoping, he suspected—to see if her kiss could do to him what Florence's had. But the truth was as he'd feared. The memory of Florence's touch, innocent as it was, was more exciting than the reality of Imogene's. That pleasure had been fresher, sharper—more right, God help him. Kissing Imogene was wrong in ways he hadn't the courage to examine.

After a moment, he eased back. "We need to talk."

"Oh, dear," she said with a high, brittle laugh. "I'm sure I don't like the sound of that."

He covered her hand where it lay soft and supple on her thigh. "You know I admire you, Imogene. You're one of the most beautiful, vibrant women I've ever known. You can't imagine how grateful I am for the time you've given me."

"Edward." She pulled her hand away, a flush staining her cheeks. "I don't want your gratitude. Why are you doing this? We're good together. The passion we share is special."

Edward watched her hand where it clutched her satin skirts. There was no way to say this without hurting her, but perhaps that was best. Perhaps the gentlemanly thing would be to let her hate him. "It doesn't feel special to me," he said as gently as he could.

She shook her head as if she couldn't believe what she was hearing. "My aunt was right about you. You are a cold-hearted bastard. Just like all the Greystowes. Unless there's another woman?" She narrowed her smoky eyes. "Tell me it's not Millicent Parminster. That two-faced bitch. I'll rip her bloody hair out."

"It's no one," he said, wondering when he'd met her aunt. "I just can't do this anymore."

She snorted. "I'll believe you can't do it when someone tells me your stones have fallen off."

"It's over, Imogene," he said. "I'm tired of feeling dirty."

He was sorry he'd said it the instant it left his mouth. Her lips moved to repeat his final word. Then she covered them with her hands. "It's your cousin, isn't it? The blushing miss who's been batting her eyes at your brother. She's a clean one, all right. Clean enough to squeak!"

"It's no one," he repeated, the denial a threatening growl.

Imogene wasn't fooled. "Bloody hell," she laughed, the sound like glass. "The mighty Edward Burbrooke has fallen for his brother's country mouse!"

He caught her arm. "You breathe that to a soul and I'll see you ruined."

In that moment, he meant the threat, unfair as it was. Fortunately, Imogene seemed to believe him. "Oh, I won't repeat it," she sneered. "That timorous twit is going to dish out all the revenge I need. I hope you stew without me, Edward. I hope you spend your whole bloody life dreaming of a woman you can't have."

Then she rapped the roof with her fan, ordering the coachman to set him down by the side of the road. He was miles from home, but Edward didn't protest. He knew the walk would not be as bad as the memory of her curse.

Chapter 5

THE PICNIC WAS FREDDIE'S IDEA. A REWARD, HE SAID, FOR Florence's having braved three balls in one week—not to mention a presentation to the queen. Curtseying to the monarch had been by far the easier ordeal, despite having to practice walking backward in a train. Not the least bit terrifying, Queen Victoria had reminded Florence of the plump, kindly widows back in Keswick. All the same, she was grateful the business was over.

Momentarily free of obligations, they spread their blanket across the grass in Aunt Hypatia's town house garden, a small stretch of ground enclosed by a tall brick wall. A sundial shaded Freddie's shoulder and a picturesque urn spilled ivy down a pedestal of stone. Florence's relaxation had as much to do with Freddie's presence, and the lack of anyone else's, as it did with the glass of currant wine he'd pressed into her hand. At peace for the first time since Edward had taken leave of his senses at the Vances' ball, she sat in the circle of her dark chintz skirts—housecleaning clothes from Keswick—and watched Freddie pick idly at the remains of their cold repast.

He lay sprawled on his belly, his jacket discarded, his sleeves rolled to his elbows. Florence knew she could stare at him for hours. His profile was that of a Greek coin; his physique, a young athlete's. More than either of these things, however, his visible good nature drew her eye. He had, she thought, the most agreeable face she'd ever seen.

He'd been quiet today. More than once, she'd caught him gazing at her in a deeply considering manner. He didn't appear to be smitten. Fond, yes, but not smitten. Spiteful or not, the Wainwrights' friend seemed to have been correct. But that was fine with Florence. She hadn't the least desire to threaten Freddie's heart.

"Penny for your thoughts," he said and batted her sunhat with a tasseled blade of grass.

"I'm happy," she said, "because I'm sitting in the sun without my corset."

He hid his smile by drawing circles on the blanket. "As a gentleman, I'll pretend I didn't hear that."

Florence grinned back and wondered if she'd ever find a suitor she felt as comfortable with as him. She touched his shoulder with the tip of her finger. "May I ask you a question?"

He rolled onto his back. "Ask away, dearest."

"It's a personal question," she cautioned, "one that might inspire sad thoughts."

"I shall not renege my permission because of that."

She set her wine in the grass. "I know you lost your parents when you were young, but I don't know how they died."

"Ah," he said, and closed his eyes. To her relief, he was not offended. "They took a trip to Egypt to see the pyramids. On the journey back, one of the passengers brought the yellow fever onto the ship. It was a bad outbreak. Twenty-two died before they were able to contain it, my parents among them. My mother was one of those who nursed the sick. She saved a few, they say, and died a heroine. I imagine Father was proud of her in the end."

Here, at last, was a hint of sadness. Florence wanted to comfort him, but wasn't sure she should. Had his father been ashamed of his wife? Had he reason? The question seemed too prying. Rather than ask it, she pleated the worn flowered cotton of her dress. "That was when Edward became your guardian."

She could not forestall a blush at speaking his name, but Freddie did not notice.

"Actually, Aunt Hypatia became our guardian. Edward was only seventeen, and I was twelve. But he fathered me from then on, if that's what you mean."

"Was it difficult?"

"To let Edward have charge of me? Not in the least, for he'd been doing it all along. Even as a boy, he took his duty as elder brother seriously." His face softened with memory. "Our father was strict. A hard man, you'd say, to the point where he sometimes seemed cruel. His father had been the same. According to family lore, our great-grandfather was a wastrel. Nearly gambled Greystowe into the poorhouse. Perhaps the generations left to repair the damage were right to run a tight ship. Whatever the reason, many times Edward stood between my father's rod and me."

He rolled onto his elbow and covered the hand that was crumpling her skirt. "Shall I tell you the best Edward story?"

Ignoring the sudden skipping of her heart—for why should she care about Edward's part in the tale?—she smiled into his boyish face. "Of course you should tell me."

He composed himself by propping his jaw on his hand. "You may not know this, but Greystowe is built above a lake with an island in its center and a family of proud black swans who return each year to raise their brood."

"*Black* swans?"

"None other. Nasty, noisy things, if you want to know the truth, but handsome enough to look at. At any rate, when Edward was seven, our father decided he ought to learn to swim. He rowed him to the deepest end of Greystowe Lake and pushed him over the side of the boat. Edward, of course, immediately flailed around and went under. When my father judged he had swallowed enough water, he hauled him out, let him catch his breath, and did it again."

"Heavens!" said Florence, her hand to her breast.

"I told you my father was stern. I imagine his father did the same to him. He liked to say Greystowe men were made of iron."

"But Edward might have drowned!"

"He learned not to soon enough," Freddie assured her, and soothingly patted her hand. "Edward being who he was, when it came my turn to learn, he insisted *he* be allowed to teach me. Told my father the responsibility would prepare him to be a leader. He always was better at getting around the earl than I was."

Florence shook her head against a dawning horror. "You can't mean to tell me Edward dumped you in that lake!"

"Indeed, no." Freddie laughed and her shoulders unwound in relief. "But he did take it into his head that I had to learn in a single day or Father would do it instead. We stayed in that lake till midnight, a shivering pair of prunes."

"And did you learn to swim?"

"Enough to satisfy Father. And better over the course of the summer. Edward was so pleased he gave me lessons every day. Two years later, I won a swimming prize at school. Edward doesn't know I know this but, to this day, he keeps that medal in a cabinet by his bed."

Florence blinked her stinging eyes. "What a wonderful story. It makes me wish I really were your cousin, so I could have been there to cheer you on."

"I should have liked that." He touched her cheek where a single tear had slipped away. "Now you must let me ask you a question."

"Oh, Freddie, you know I can't tell stories like you."

"It's not a question that requires a story. At least, I don't think it is."

"Very well," she said, and smoothed her simple skirt. "Ask me anything you like."

He cocked his head at her answer, eyes twinkling, but all he said was, "What do you think of Peter Vance?"

"The duke of Monmouth's son?" She sat straighter in surprise.

"Yes. Aunt Hypatia tells me he sent you violets this morning and invited you to the opera with his family."

She squirmed at the memory of the card that had accompanied his bouquet. Something about the "violet hiding in the shade" and the "sweet and simple beauty" that its perfume betrayed. The sentiment was flattering, even poetic, but Florence had felt supremely uncomfortable when she'd read it.

"I'm sure he only sent them to please his sister," she said. "And even if he didn't, he's the son of a duke."

"The youngest son," Freddie interposed.

"Yes, but I don't think he is someone I should consider. I am only a vicar's daughter."

"You may consider anyone you please. You're a sweet and pretty girl. The question is, does Peter Vance please you?"

Florence gazed at the sky, at the sheer white clouds and the swallow that soared above them towards the greensward in Grosvenor Square. Did Peter Vance please her? He didn't have half Freddie's sense of humor, but he was handsome and ardent and undeniably better than a simple girl like her deserved. Instinct told her he'd be kind to his wife and take a mistress in half a year. Which did not rule him out as husband material—at least, not the sort of husband she'd told Mr. Mowbry she was seeking.

If her thoughts had been haunted of late by a taller, darker, and infinitely more dangerous figure, that was a foolish romantic notion she would do her best to quash.

"I suppose he pleases me," she said. "But how can I tell? I have danced with him and talked of nothing. He has brought me punch and paid compliments to my hair. All I really know is that he likes horses, is pleasant to look at, and has an agreeable sister."

"Agreeable sisters are important."

He seemed to be teasing, but Florence couldn't smile. "You must think me terribly cold-blooded."

"You, Florence? Never."

"But to hunt for a husband this way, as if he were a bit of beef, rather than a living human being who would be yoked to me for a lifetime."

"What a horror that would be!"

She shoved his muscular shoulder. "Scoundrel. You always make me laugh. I must confess, I halfway wish I could marry you."

This stilled him.

"Do you?" he said, eyes hooded from her gaze. She wondered if she'd alarmed him.

"I'm afraid so," she admitted as lightly as she could. "But please don't tell your aunt. She'd be aghast."

"I don't know about that. From what I've seen, she's very fond of you."

"Not fond enough to invite a silly nobody into her family!"

He peered at her from under his brows, the same measuring look he'd been turning on her all day. "You might be surprised." He smoothed the blanket beside her knee. "Florence, would you really want to marry someone like me?"

"How can you doubt it? You're quite the nicest man I've met. You're funny and you're kind and when I'm with you, I almost feel brave."

He pressed his hand to his heart. "Goodness. I am a paragon."

She clucked her tongue at him in scold. Though his eyes shone with more than laughter, she should have known he couldn't be serious.

But then he cleared his throat. "Florence?"

"Yes, Freddie."

He drew a breath and let the words out in a rush. "Would you marry me? Would you really? I know I'm not as good as I could be, but I'm not as bad as some. I don't drink or gamble or curse. I don't often work hard, but I can, and I'd always do my best to keep you happy."

Her eyes felt as round as saucers. He wanted her to marry him, the man she'd made a model for her ideal. She should have been elated—indeed, part of her was—but behind the elation, a sensation uncommonly like panic was expanding in her chest.

"You can't be serious," she said, half of her wanting him to admit he was teasing.

"Yes, Florence, I am." He sat up and took her hands. "I'd very much like to marry you. That is, if you think you'd enjoy yoking us together."

Her heart was pounding like a drum. She told herself only the thought of Edward kept her from jumping into Freddie's arms, because he'd kissed her, because he'd made her pulse race and her skin tingle from head to toe.

But Edward wouldn't marry her. Even if he would, he wasn't what she needed. Peter Vance might disappoint her, but Edward would break her heart. She knew that as surely as she knew her name. She'd promised herself she wouldn't end up like her father, half her soul lost to mourning a love she could never find again. Florence was not some hearts-and-flowers ninny. Florence was a sensible girl. Despite which, she couldn't quite make herself accept.

"I don't know what to say," she said.

"Say yes," Freddie urged.

"Oh, Freddie. How can I? Your aunt will think I've betrayed her trust."

"I assure you she won't, but I'd face even that if you feel certain you'd like to have me."

She searched his dear, kind eyes, eyes that for once seemed as shy and unsure as her own. She could make him happy, she thought. They were not in love, but there was fondness between them, and respect. She could make a home he would be pleased to call his own. She could ease the sadness she sometimes saw behind his smile. As for her . . .

She would be safe, as safe as she'd ever dreamed. Freddie was a good man: young in some ways, but decent to the core.

"Yes," she said, squeezing his hands. "I'd be honored to be your wife."

She was not sure whose palms were colder: Freddie's or her own.

"CONGRATULATIONS," EDWARD SAID, HIS JAW ALMOST TOO stiff to force out the word. His brother had broken the news in Hypatia's private parlor, amidst the comfortable chairs and the thick pile rugs and the knitting work she loved to nod over by the fire. "You'll want a quick wedding, of course."

Florence furrowed her brow and looked to Freddie, who pressed a kiss to the back of her hand. The gesture was given and taken so naturally Edward's heart twisted in his chest.

"Yes," Aunt Hypatia agreed. "A small, quiet wedding, so as not to break your mourning too badly. The vicar at St. Peter's is a friend of mine. I'm sure he can fit you in."

"I don't understand." Florence looked from Edward to his aunt. "You aren't upset. You seem pleased. I don't mean to insult you, your Grace, but I honestly thought you'd agreed to sponsor me because you hoped I'd upstage Greta and Minna Wainwright."

"And you think this won't do that?" Hypatia barked out a laugh. "No, no, my dear, while I admit the thought of foiling their mother's ambitions lends this match an extra savor, I assure you I had no such ulterior motive. I'm fond of you, Florence. More so now than ever. You've made my nephew a happy man."

"But I'm only—"

"Only my goddaughter," said Edward's cheerfully mendacious aunt as she leaned forward to kiss her cheek. "We're not snobs. I'm sure you'll be a credit to the Burbrooke name."

Florence began to cry, slow fat tears she tried to hide behind her hands. With a fond smile, Freddie pulled her into his shoulder and stroked her hair. She looked as if she belonged there, as if they were married already.

"There, there," he said. "It's nothing to cry over."

"You've been so kind," she said, with a teary hiccup. "I don't know how I shall repay you."

"You can repay us by being happy," Freddie said. "That's really all we ask."

His gaze met Edward's over her shoulder. His expression held a grief Edward could scarcely bear to face, a grief not so much for himself as for Florence—as if, between them, they were committing some terrible sin against the girl.

But they weren't. Edward tugged his lapels and set his jaw. They were saving her. They were making her happy. Any idiot could see she and Freddie were meant to be. This would not be a marriage like his parents', with one partner cold and the other miserable. This would be as near to a love match as Edward had ever seen. If a deception made that possible, well, so be it.

"We all want you happy," he said, his voice gentler than he'd intended.

She looked around at him, her cheek still pressed to Freddie's chest. Her eyes dazzled him, soft with emotion, green as the buds of spring. With no more weapon than that, she speared him to the floor.

Good Lord, he thought, chill with horror. I love her.

"Thank you," she said, as if his approval meant the world. "I'd be proud to join your family."

She held out her hand to him, her small, soft hand.

He thought the hardest thing he'd ever done was clasp it and let it go.

Chapter 6

EDWARD'S IDEA OF A QUICK WEDDING WAS NOT THE SAME AS his aunt's. He saw no reason to wait beyond the obtainment of a special license. She, however, cautioned against the appearance of undue haste.

"It won't do," she said. "Anything less than six months is simply vulgar."

But that was before Imogene Hargreave extended her claws.

Hypatia heard the news before he did. He was sitting down to breakfast when her carriage dropped her at his door. She didn't wait for Grimby to announce her, but strode straight through. Edward looked up from his plate, too stunned by his aunt's appearance to venture a greeting. Her skirts swished loudly with her haste, then released a cloud of lavender as she flung herself into a chair. Her hat was askew, her yellow gloves an offense against her purple dress. Her cane was nowhere in sight.

"We have trouble," she said, yanking off the gloves as if she wished to do them harm. Her hat followed with equal force.

Edward swallowed his final bite of toast. A hank of silver hair was standing up from Hypatia's head. Suspecting she needed bracing more than he did, he slid his steaming cup of tea in front of her. "What trouble?"

Her face twisted with anger. Edward hadn't seen her in such a fury since the one and only time his father had struck him. Freddie had been six, as he recalled, and the earl had decided to take him cub hunting, it being common practice for inexperienced riders to be set after the younger foxes before the season. Freddie hadn't understood what would happen until it came time to "blood" him with the kill. He'd turned hysterical then, refusing to let their father smear his forehead—no surprise, since the boy still slept with a stuffed rabbit. Only Edward's intervention had stopped the earl from shouting his younger son deaf, for which act Edward had earned a black eye.

He'd known at once his father regretted lashing out. The earl had

grown very quiet; actually picked Freddie up and carried him back to
the house—gently, too, as if he meant to comfort him. When Aunt
Hypatia discovered what had happened and slapped her elder brother
across the face, the earl accepted her judgment without a word.

She looked as if she wanted to slap someone now, but her fingers
merely tightened on the teacup. "It's that bastard Charles Hargreave,"
she said. "He's telling people he saw someone who looked 'uncommonly like Freddie Burbrooke' coming out of an introducing house
on Fitzroy Street."

Edward sagged back in his chair. Despite his fears, the news
caught him completely unprepared. An introducing house was a ho-
mosexual brothel that specialized in underage boys. If it was true . . .

"I don't believe it," he said, breathless and hot with shock. "Freddie gave me his word. Even if he hadn't, he would never do anything
to take advantage of the young."

He wouldn't, he told himself, the possibility unbearable. Not
Freddie. Not the brother he loved. His hands clenched so tightly the
skin over his knuckles stretched white.

"I'm inclined to agree with you," said his aunt. "Whatever his
faults, Freddie has never been a bully." Her mouth pursed with distaste. "To do what one would rather no one did, with those too young
to give permission, to even understand what they risk, isn't something I want to think he would consider. But it hardly matters
whether the story is true. If people believe it, the damage will be great
enough."

Edward smashed his fist into his thigh. "It's Imogene. That bloody
bitch put her husband up to it."

Hypatia stared at him, one thin brow raised in judgment. That
she'd indulged in similar language did not seem to matter. Edward
rubbed the ache in the center of his forehead.

"Sorry," he said. "Shouldn't have lost my temper."

"Of course you should have. Hargreave's behavior is despicable,
even if his wife is behind it." Calm now, she turned the blue and white
teacup in a circle. She reminded him of merchants he knew, planners,
men of business. Her gaze was as cool as theirs. "I won't ask why Lady
Hargreave might have a grievance against this family. I simply trust
that no one in it will have anything further to do with her."

Edward's laugh was brief and bitter. "You can rest easy on that."

"Good." With a brisk rustle, the duchess rearranged her skirts.
"Now all we have to do is decide how to get Florence to Greystowe."

He blinked at this change of tack. "To Greystowe?"

"Well, we can't let her stay in London. She's bound to hear the gossip. And we can't send her anywhere alone. She's half in love with Freddie already. If we throw the two of them together, she'll be committed to him by summer's end."

Without quite realizing he'd done it, Edward pressed a hand over his stomach. *Summer's end.* Was that all it would take? "They'll need a chaperone," he said, his voice strangely distant to his ears. "Are you willing to accompany them?"

"More than. But I think you'd better come, too."

"Me?" The ache in his belly increased.

"I trust Freddie," said the duchess. "But I trust him more when he knows your eyes are on him."

Edward wished he could close those eyes and shake his head. Florence. In his house. With Freddie. Leaving her scent in the hall. Her laugh. Her twinkling footsteps. His aunt had no idea what she was asking.

Which was good news, really, even if it meant he'd be living out Imogene's curse. She'd kept her word, damn her; she seemed not to have told anyone that Florence had enamored him. She'd found a better way to hurt him: through Freddie, through the brother who was his heart. But at least they'd be taking Florence beyond her reach. He didn't trust his former mistress to hold her tongue should the two meet face-to-face.

EDWARD'S CHANCE TO SPEAK TO FREDDIE CAME THAT AFTERnoon. He found him in the study, slumped in a chair with the curtains drawn, a bottle and glass close to hand. A single lamp burned on the table by his elbow. The low yellow light turned his wavy brown hair to gold. From the rumpled state of his clothes, it appeared he'd been sitting—and drinking—for some time. His collar was open, his tie a draggle around his neck. He looked a fallen angel, one who mourned his former state of grace. Where had he heard the news? At his club? On the street? At a loss as to how to begin, he walked to Freddie's side and looked down. His brother did not look up.

"Join me?" he said, his voice slurred but steady. "We can drink to the end of Freddie Burbrooke as we know him."

Edward's breath came faster. "I know you didn't do what they're saying."

Freddie finished his drink and poured another. The decanter clinked against the cut-glass rim, but the liquor did not spill. "How do you know?" he said, eerily calm. "I'm a deviate, aren't I? The victim of unnatural urges. Who can say where my depravity ends?"

Edward grabbed his shoulders and shook him. The glass tumbled down Freddie's shirtfront, spraying whiskey over them both on its way to the floor. Freddie's head rolled back and forth like a rag doll's, but Edward could not stop.

"I know you didn't do it," he said, almost shouting. "I know!"

With a sudden burst of energy, Freddie pushed him off. He wasn't as strong as Edward but he was strong enough. He stood and put the chair between them. "You don't know, damn you. I can see how afraid you are. I can hear it in your voice." He raked his hair back with a curse, then pointed in accusation. "You can't know because you don't know anything about that side of me. You don't know how it works. You don't know how it thinks. I don't blame you for doubting me, Edward, but I swear to you, I'd rather die than do a thing like that."

Edward stepped to the front of the chair and laid his hand on Freddie's shoulder. His brother was shaking, his teeth chattering with the force of his distress. His eyes were red but dry. They seemed to burn as they met Edward's gaze.

"Never," Freddie said, tight and low. "Never with anyone but an equal. Never with anyone who didn't want it as much as I did."

The terrible doubt inside him eased. He knew Freddie was telling the truth and yet, as grateful as he was, he didn't want to hear this; didn't want to know there had been others besides the footman, besides the boys at school. He looked down at the empty chair, at the drying liquor stain on its seat. "Aunt Hypatia and I have decided we need to go to Greystowe: you, me, the duchess, and Florence."

"Florence?" Freddie's brow lifted in astonishment. "Edward. You can't mean to go through with this engagement. Florence is bound to hear."

"That's why we're going to Greystowe."

"For the rest of our natural lives?"

Edward stooped to retrieve the fallen glass. "Just for the summer. Memories are short. The next scandal will push this one from people's minds."

"And if it doesn't? Good Lord, Edward, think of Florence. It's hardly fair to—"

"Why not? You're the same man who proposed to her. The same man she clung to with joy. The same man who'll keep a roof over her head and a meal on her plate."

"There's more to life than roofs and meals."

"You are more than a meal to her, Freddie. You're her friend." Edward knew he spoke the truth, just as he knew this was the way things had to be, for all their sakes. Maybe Florence did deserve to marry more than a friend. Maybe she deserved the world. That didn't mean she wouldn't be perfectly content as Freddie's wife. And Freddie would be content as Florence's husband: content and safe. In this sorry old world, who had the right to ask more than that? Throat tight, Edward opened the decanter and poured. Freddie watched wide-eyed as his brother tossed back the drink. The fine Irish whiskey hit his belly like a punch. He coughed before he spoke. "I'm telling Lewis we leave tomorrow."

"Tomorrow?"

"Tomorrow," he rasped, and prayed the decision would not destroy them all.

FLORENCE WAS EXITING THE LIBRARY WITH A BOOK WHEN the senior footman informed her that her cousins were in the drawing room.

"My cousins?"

"Lord Greystowe and Viscount Burbrooke."

"Of course," she said, nervously smoothing her skirts. "Thank you, John. I'll go right up."

She wondered what they wanted, as it was past the hour for calls. Business involving the engagement, perhaps? But it seemed unlikely they would discuss that without the duchess, and she was spending the evening with friends.

"Gentlemen," she said, striving to present a calm exterior as she entered the elegant room.

The men rose and bowed. To her consternation, both wore matching sober faces. Indeed, Florence had never seen Freddie so serious. Heavens, she thought, her heart giving the oddest leap. They must be calling off the betrothal.

"Is something wrong?" she said aloud, her hand pressed to her throat. "Aunt Hypatia hasn't met with misfortune, has she?"

"No, no," said Edward. His smile seemed forced even for him. "Freddie here"—he slung his arm around his brother's shoulder—"has a surprise for you."

Freddie looked a bit green around the gills but he nodded in agreement. "Thought you might fancy a trip to Greystowe. See my boyhood haunts and all."

Florence blinked at him, then broke into a grin. "I'd love to, Freddie. Absolutely love to." She skipped across the room to squeeze his hands. "How did you know I'd been longing for the country?"

"You don't have to go," he said. "Only if you really want to."

There was something in his eyes she didn't understand, some inexplicable discomfort, as if he were making this offer under duress. Edward cleared his throat.

"What's the matter?" she asked, her hands slipping to Freddie's lapels. "Don't *you* want to go?"

" 'Course I want to go. Just thought you might regret missing the rest of the Season."

Florence had to laugh at that. "I'd pay to miss the rest of the Season. But are you well, Freddie? You look pale."

"Drank too much at my club," he confessed, pulling away and giving his coat a tug. "Think I'd better see if Aunt Hypatia's footman has a cure."

With that, he hastened from the drawing room as if he were being chased. Florence stared after him. "How peculiar," she said. "It's not like Freddie to overindulge."

"I imagine his friends wanted to toast his engagement."

The explanation rang false, but she shrugged the mystery off. No doubt Edward was hoping to keep some prank from Florence's ears. She could not worry about it now. Freddie's abrupt departure had left the two of them alone. As always, Edward's presence, and all the unsettling feelings it inspired, was quite enough to occupy her mind.

"Shall I ring for refreshment?" she asked even as she hoped he would refuse.

"No," he said, and turned his black silk hat between his hands. She thought he'd make his excuses then, but he remained where he was, as if rooted to the Axminster carpet.

"Brandy?" she offered.

Again he shook his head, then seemed to gather his will. "You are happy, aren't you?"

The question was more accusatory than concerned, and more personal than he had any right to ask. Her temper rose. "Of course I'm happy. Why wouldn't I be? Freddie is a wonderful man. A true gentleman."

Edward flushed at her barb, then tightened his jaw. "Glad to hear it," he said in a patently scornful drawl. "I'd always hoped my brother's wife would appreciate the noble virtues."

"More than you can," she said, and matched him glare for glare. She didn't know when they'd drawn so close but they were nose to nose now, each vibrating with fury. His scent threatened to seep into her skin, musk and salt, heating her blood against her will. Damn him, she thought, for being so blasted masculine.

"If you hurt him . . ." he warned.

"*I?* I hurt him? You're the one who—" But she snapped her mouth shut on the rest. A real lady would pretend their encounter in the Vances' conservatory had never happened.

Not that Edward would let her be a lady. "No, no," he urged. "Finish what you were saying. I'm the one who what?"

She drew herself up and turned her face away. "It could not be of less importance."

"Oh, it couldn't, could it?"

When he gripped her jaw and forced it back, she felt as if she'd been waiting all night for him to do this very thing. Her body thrummed with excitement even as her heart sped up with fear. Her lungs were working like a bellows.

"Florence," he growled, his nostrils flaring as if he, too, could scent her secret flesh. His mouth crashed over hers, all searing male power. He invaded her, drew on her, his hand like iron around her jaw. He kissed her until her knees began to wobble, until her hands fluttered to grab his coat. He kissed her until she whimpered, until every shred of rational thought escaped her brain. The sinews of his neck were damp beneath her palm, his breathing ragged on her cheek. He pulled her up against him, his hold crushing her dress, his thighs hard and hot through the fragile cloth. With one forearm banded beneath her buttocks, his hips began to rock like that night at the ball. The ridge between them was extravagantly large. He seemed to want to brand her with it, to force her to take its measure against her skin. She could not get away; could barely even squirm, but the long, grinding press did not frighten her as before. Instead, to her dismay, she wished she could explore him with her hands; wished she could see the shape of his desire. Here was a passion a woman could drown in. Willingly. Recklessly. Until she begged her seducer to do with her what he pleased.

Of course, she should have known what Edward pleased had nothing to do with her.

Just as she was ready to add her own hunger to the kiss, he tore his mouth away and held her off from him by the shoulder. "Now *that,*" he rasped, "could not be less important."

He strode from the room without another word. *Beast,* she fumed. Horrible, arrogant beast. She couldn't be attracted to a man like that.

Simply couldn't. What was he trying to prove? That she liked his kisses? That she wasn't enough of a lady for his brother?

"I am," she swore to the silent room. "I am."

She released a long, tremulous breath, then smoothed her hair into its coiffure. She was not a heroine from a penny weekly, tripping blithely down the road to ruin. She was a vicar's daughter, a gentle-woman born. This . . . anomaly in her feelings would not sway her. So long as Freddie Burbrooke wished to marry her, she was more than happy to marry him.

Whether she was more than happy to be Edward's sister-in-law, however, was a very different matter.

BLOODY INSANE, HE THOUGHT, SAGGING BACK AGAINST THE drawing room's heavy door. He'd kissed her. Again. For no better rea-son than her implication that his kisses didn't matter. What did he expect her to say? That she was secretly in love with him and that Freddie, "the perfect gentleman," could go hang? As if that would help. He covered his eyes and wagged his head. Better he should pray she hated him.

Of course, after tonight's fiasco, chances were good she did.

THE JOURNEY TO GREYSTOWE WAS AS DIFFERENT AS NIGHT and day from the one she'd made to London. Edward, it seemed, owned a railway carriage.

"The spoils of dirtying one's hands in industry," Freddie teased as he handed a gaping Florence up the stairs.

Inside, the car was as fancy as the duchess's drawing room. The walls were lined in bird's-eye maple, the couches and chairs uphol-stered in dark green satin. Quilted black silk covered the arch of the ceiling and a rich Chinese rug, intricately patterned in red and gold, muffled the floor. The effect was one of sumptuous, masculine splen-dor, so sumptuous Florence blushed to see it. She couldn't help imag-ining Edward stretching some eager maiden across that couch, kissing her perhaps as he'd kissed Florence. How smooth that silk would feel beneath one's skin; how it would whisper when one moved. With a tiny shudder, she pushed the senseless image aside.

That way lay disaster.

"Heavens," she exclaimed, then lowered her voice because Edward was climbing in. "He doesn't own the whole train, does he?"

Freddie laughed and turned to his brother. "Florence wants to know if you own the train."

"No," he said, with his customary curtness. He reached for the duchess's hands. "That honor belongs to the Midland Railway."

His tone suggested Florence had been foolish to ask. She sighed and turned away. Moody, Freddie had called his brother, but no one seemed to bring out the worst of his moods as well as she. Fortunately, she had one of Mr. Dickens's novels to while away the ride. As luxurious as it was, this carriage was not big enough for her and Edward's moods.

He seemed to feel the same. First he buried himself in the *London Times,* and then in a pile of correspondence. She told herself she did not care, could not possibly care. She'd enjoy the trip, just as she'd enjoy their stay at Greystowe.

She had plenty of time to test her vow, for the journey was not a short one. Greystowe, Freddie informed her, was in the East Midlands, not far from the Peak District. As they clattered and chuffed towards the heart of England, they passed picturesque villages and thriving market towns. To her relief, the stench of London quickly cleared the air. The building stone turned gold and soft, and the landscape took on a pleasing roll. Sheep grazed the slopes, but crops had been planted as well. They shimmered low and green beneath the clear June sky.

The country girl inside her drank it in like a healing balm.

At last, as the sun began to sink behind the hills, they entered a sheltered valley. Its fields were fed by the Derwent River and separated not by hedgerows, but by weatherworn walls of stone. Ox-eye daisies waved at her from the side of the track. The grass was wonderfully green. After her stay in London, the color almost hurt her eyes.

The station bordered the village of Greystowe, a handsome tumble of half-timbered Tudor shops. Edward's car was unhooked from the rest and towed onto a private siding.

"Thank God," Freddie said, stretching until his spine cracked.

Florence echoed his sentiment with a smile, but saved her stretch for later. Aunt Hypatia would not have approved, even if she had been sleeping for hours. With a tenderness that belied his surly mood, Edward touched his aunt's shoulder. His face was achingly beautiful in its kindness.

The duchess awoke with a start. "Goodness," she said. "Must have dropped off for a minute."

No one was rude enough to contradict her, but even Edward joined the exchange of grins.

A big old-fashioned coach awaited them on the road, accompanied by a much plainer wagon into which half a dozen liveried servants were loading their luggage. Their silent efficiency was impressive to behold. Clearly, Edward's arrival had whipped them to their best.

"Not far now," said Freddie, and draped his arm around her back. His warmth was twice as welcome after all those hours of Edward's chill. She had to admit, though, she was surprised to find him eager to resume his rural life. If ever a man had been made for the city, it was Freddie. He loved people and parties and gossiping till dawn.

"Tell me Cook has a big dinner waiting," he called to the coachman, obviously an old retainer.

"Could be, sir," said that large, grizzled fellow. "Did think I smelled a Yorkshire pudding afore I left."

Florence's stomach growled at the mention of food. They'd had a light tea on the train, but that was all. Freddie, of course, could not ignore the unladylike sound.

"Roast beef," he said, rubbing his hands in exaggerated glee. "Horseradish sauce and gravy."

She laughed and pushed his shoulder to make him stop. "You'd think you'd been fasting for days!"

Beside her, Edward rediscovered his frown.

The church was farther into town, with a handsome stone school beside it. The town fathers—here she glanced at Edward—had not stinted on the windows, all of which would be taxed. She smiled when she remembered her father bullying the council to put in his windows. *Children need light,* he'd exhorted. *Light and air and a place for little eyes to wander.* As always, the thought of him brought a touch of sadness. Poor Papa. So much love in that big, warm heart and no one to spend it on but his daughter and his flock. They hadn't been enough. Hard as he tried to hide it, she'd always known a part of him had broken with her mother's death.

Freddie noted what had drawn her attention. "You'll have to visit when school starts up."

"Yes," she said and shyly squeezed his hand. Would they be here then? Did Freddie mean for them to live at Greystowe? Would he allow her to teach? Florence had done so at home. As the vicar's daughter, it was expected. When she married Freddie she'd be a lady but, oh, how little she'd like that honor if it meant she had to sit home all day and stitch!

These questions massed inside her as they rolled through the pretty town, but Edward's presence compelled her to hold them back.

She didn't know if Freddie had spoken to his brother about the future. Would they have a small place of their own? Would Freddie want one? She could have burst with all she wished to ask. Even not knowing, the thought that this might be her home added interest to every soul they passed.

People called out to Freddie, she noticed, and tipped their caps to the earl.

All thoughts of the future faded with her first glimpse of the estate. The railway carriage should have warned her, and the mention of the cotton mill. Despite these hints, the sheer size of the place took her aback.

Greystowe sprawled across its grassy rise like a small Gothic town: a fortress town. Though of relatively modern construction, with all the attendant tracery and windows and archwork, the house was topped by battlements of stone. The lake reflected its blocks and towers, not so much in vanity as in emphasis. Swans aside, Florence couldn't help being reminded of a moat. This house made no bones about its intent. It was built to impress, to dominate, to hearken back to a time when lords were lords and everyone else was not.

Her lips twitched as she snuck a look at Edward's stern, feudal visage. She bet he'd have liked clumping about in armor, or galloping off on Samson to terrorize England's foes. What a step down he must feel it, to be reduced to terrorizing country mice!

"Home, sweet home," said Freddie, and Florence's burst of humor faded. Anything less like a home she could not imagine. The setting sun flamed across a numberless march of windows: rose on the lower stories, lime on the upper.

It would take a miracle, she thought, to make a girl like her feel comfortable here.

Even as she pondered this impossibility, the front door—a great ironbound arch that required two brawny footmen to prop it open—released a long double line of servants. They filed down the wide granite steps, crisp as you please, like a regiment forming ranks. Their livery was black and fawn, with shining brass buttons on the coats. Edward waited for them to assemble, precisely as if he intended to review them. When they'd finished, one man and one woman stepped forward.

The man was tall and elegant, with salted black hair and pale gray eyes. The woman, a bit older, was round and merry. Good humor notwithstanding, she held herself with authority. Florence suspected she was the housekeeper.

"Welcome home, your lordship," said the man. "We received your telegram and everything is in readiness."

"I've prepared the best upstairs apartment for the young lady," the woman added, "and the duchess"—here she dropped a curtsey—"shall have her usual rooms on the ground floor."

"Very good," said Edward. He turned to Florence, his eyes strangely wary. If she hadn't known better, she'd have said he was worried about her reaction. "Florence, this is our steward, Nigel West, and our housekeeper, Mrs. Forster. They've both been with us for years. Should you require anything at all, one or the other of them will be happy to oblige."

"And may we say," Mrs. Forster put in, "that we're very pleased to meet young Lord Burbrooke's intended?"

"I believe you have said it," Freddie cried, and pulled the older woman into a hug.

The woman laughed as he spun her around, her dignity forgotten. Florence smiled at the spectacle. Leave it to Freddie to put everyone at their ease. Edward, naturally, called a halt to the merriment. "We should go in," he said. "I'm sure the ladies would like to freshen up."

Mrs. Forster immediately squirmed down and sobered. "At once, my lord. If the ladies would follow me?"

He's an ogre, Florence thought as the housekeeper led her up the main stair. He's an old sourpuss who can't bear to see anyone happy. The thought steadied her, as if it were a shield against confusion. But when she stepped into the blue and white splendor of her rooms, something awaited that put her to shame. It wasn't the huge tester bed, or the breathtaking view of the lake, or even the gorgeous carving on the fireplace. It was the picture that hung above it: Mr. Whistler's blue bridge, even more beautiful than when it had hung in that poor dingy corner of the Academy.

"Oh, my," she breathed, hands to her mouth. He'd remembered her admiration for this painting, and deigned to share the pleasure of owning it with her. That the same horrid creature who'd used his kisses to insult her could be so thoughtful was beyond her power to fathom.

Mrs. Forster was a step behind her. "Funny sort of mess," she said. "Lord Greystowe claims it's art, but if you don't like it, I'll take it somewhere else."

"Oh, no," said Florence. "There isn't another picture I'd like to look at more."

She hadn't been fair, she thought as the housekeeper withdrew.

Perhaps he had some reason for his behavior, perverse as it was, which she did not comprehend. Perhaps, in fact, he meant this as an apology.

And perhaps pigs will fly in Hades, her more practical self put in. But if there was even a chance he wasn't set against her, that he was only concerned she would let his brother down, she had to do her best to win him over. And that's all I want, she promised herself: to be friends, to turn the other cheek as her father would have wished. For the sake of her and Freddie's happiness, she knew she had to try.

DINNER, WHICH HAD BEEN BLISSFULLY QUIET APART FROM Florence's attempt to thank him for hanging that blasted painting in her room, was followed by a stroll through the back garden. Edward didn't see why he had to go along, but when his aunt took his arm he couldn't find a mannerly way to refuse. In spite of his annoyance, Florence's pleasure was a joy to see. He knew the house had shocked her. Greystowe was far too grand to welcome a simple vicar's daughter. She loved his gardens, though. Her eyes shone with it. Her cheeks flushed. When they passed the tangled grape arbor, she actually clapped her hands.

Like his father, Edward favored simple landscaping. Greystowe shunned Frenchified bedding arrangements for a more natural, parklike effect. Nothing was allowed to run wild, of course; the thickets and glades were strictly planned. But in appearance, at least, the grounds might have been dropped from God's hand. Even the rose garden, his mother's special project, bore an admirably spontaneous air.

Florence had just stepped onto its crushed oyster shell walk when a sudden belling from the hounds warned Edward that one segment of the household's population had yet to welcome them home. The pack raced across the lawn in full cry, their tails wagging madly, their keeper in hot pursuit. "Hoy," yelled that hapless fellow. "Hoy there, lads. Hold up!"

Edward braced himself for an embarrassing scene. He was not disappointed. In a matter of heartbeats, the wolfhound's paws struck his shoulders. Nor was he the last of the assault. Between barks and whines of joy, a dozen tongues lashed his hands, and a dozen noses snuffled whatever they pleased.

"Enough," he said, thrusting the worst of them away. To his amazement, he was obeyed.

Then he saw why.

Every one of the smaller dogs was groveling furiously at Florence's feet. True, she had knelt down to pet them, but even so, the division of attention was unprecedented. Even Freddie, whom the dogs knew, didn't warrant such a greeting.

Florence looked up from the tangle of wriggling bodies. Her eyes, both laughing and sheepish, found his. The moment hung. To save his life, he could not look away. Her gaze flushed him hot and cold. He hardened, abruptly, fiercely, but his body's reaction was a distant thing. Looking at her, he felt a sense of union he could not reason away, as if the affection of the dogs had mysteriously linked them together. *This one is the same,* their favor seemed to say. *This one is the same as the one we love.*

Ridiculous, he thought. Totally ridiculous.

"Well," Aunt Hypatia observed, "people are right to speak of your animal magnetism."

Florence's head came up in alarm, the pink of her cheeks rivaling his mother's roses. "Oh, no," she said. "I never have this effect on dogs. Only cats and . . . and small children. I'm sure I simply smell of dinner."

That, Edward thought, did not explain the effect she had on him. Even now, in front of his family, in front of the gamekeeper and God, he couldn't control his lust for his brother's future bride. His palms itched to hold her, to touch her in any way. Even to stroke the soft curves of her face, to kiss the tip of her nose, would have brought him satisfaction. Never had he yearned like this for a woman. Aunt Hypatia had spoken true. He was an animal. And Florence, apparently, was the magnet he couldn't resist.

FLORENCE HAD SURVIVED THE DAY: THE TRAIN RIDE AND THE silent dinner and Edward's obvious disapproval over that stupid business with the dogs. As if she'd wanted them to make a cake of her! Now she stood by the window in her darkened sitting room, quiet but for the sound of Lizzie's snores from the room next door. The maid was understandably tired. She'd ridden to Greystowe on the public part of the train, along with the duchess's maid, Edward's valet, and a few of the footmen who weren't needed to keep the London house. Lizzie had been sorry to leave the city until she'd discovered they weren't trading it for a drafty, antiquated heap.

"They've got running water," she'd imparted in a breathless tone. "Hot and cold. And baths in the servants' wing. It's a right palace, Miss Florence. Why, the ground floor has gas!"

This last pleased her most. Lizzie had never relished the messy chore of trimming lamps. Not that she would have been asked to do it here. Thanks to Aunt Hypatia, Lizzie had climbed to the top of the servants' heap. Only the steward and the housekeeper had the right to order her about, a fact that was only beginning to sink in. "I've never been so happy," she said. "Never."

Florence should have been able to say the same. Freddie was a wonderful man. Her future was nearly assured. But instead of enjoying the accomplishment of her dream, she stood sleepless, restless, her forehead pressed to the glass, her mind on a single thorn. Sighing, she gazed out at the grounds. The window overlooked the moonlit lake at the front of the house, the selfsame lake in which Freddie had learned to swim. An arched stone bridge connected its bank to the island in its center. Between the tops of the trees poked a pointed Moorish roof. She wondered what the building beneath it was used for, if it were simply a folly or a place one could shelter from a storm. It seemed large, its architecture unlike anything on the grounds. Florence shivered and rubbed the curtain's gauzy liner against her cheek. The building was exotic, Eastern, a place for self-indulgence and assignations: a man's place.

How easily she could picture Edward there, despite his stuffy manner. He'd furnished his train car, hadn't he? He must harbor a streak of the sybaritic. He'd smoke cigars in that hideaway, she mused, and drink expensive wine. And meet women, of course. The local widows. The saucy laundry maids. They'd know more than his kisses. They wouldn't be too frightened to unwrap the mystery that hung between his legs. They'd touch it bare and feel it harden. They wouldn't fear, not them, not with Edward to guide the way. Edward would know how to protect a woman from the consequences of indiscretion.

With a soft cry of annoyance, Florence banished her foolish thoughts. Indistinct as they were, her imaginings disturbed her. Her heart was beating too fast and a heavy velvet warmth had settled under her belly. The reaction was pointless. What did it matter what Edward did with other women? It was nothing to her. Nothing.

Then, just as she was about to turn away, she saw a figure on a horse, cantering smoothly around the lake. Edward. And Samson. They seemed a creature out of myth, one being. As she watched, Edward slowed the stallion to walk him through a patch of stones.

He cares for that horse, she thought, far more than he'll ever care for me.

Then it came to her: what she could do to win his respect.

Her hand tightened on the drapes and her body tingled with a different sort of thrill. This was the answer. She was sure of it. I must learn to ride, she thought, as well as a lady born.

HEART POUNDING WITH RESOLVE, FLORENCE FOUND FREDDIE in the billiard room after breakfast. Appropriately enough, he was dressed to ride, though, at the moment, he was merely knocking balls around the table. When he looked up from his shot, his eyes glowed with approval.

"Well," he said, "don't you look smart!"

Uncustomarily nervous, at least for an interview with Freddie, she smoothed the front of her teal-colored habit.

With a smile, Freddie set down his stick. "What would you like to do today? We could go into town and meet the shopkeepers, who—believe me—will be delighted to hear there's a lady in residence. Or we could visit the canal. We're not too far from the lock, and the boats hereabouts are the sort of works of art a Philistine like me can appreciate. The owners paint them, stem to stern, like gypsy wagons. They're very pretty. Plus, I'm sure the Quack and Waddle would be happy to have us for lunch."

His enthusiasm was catching, but Florence resisted it. "Sometime I'd like to do that. Especially the Quack and Waddle. For today, though, if you wouldn't mind, I'd simply like to ride. I never got much chance at home. We couldn't afford a lady's horse. I've been thinking I ought learn to do it better."

Freddie cocked his head at her. "You don't ride badly."

"Not riding badly isn't the same as riding well. You and I are . . . are going to be married. I don't want you to be ashamed of me."

"I couldn't be ashamed of you if you rode like a sack of potatoes."

Florence looked down at her hands, folded now across her waist. She was uncomfortably aware that she wasn't being honest with him; that it wasn't Freddie's judgment she hoped to improve. Still, his brother's opinion mattered to him as well. If Florence won Edward over, Freddie would be happier, too.

"I'd like to ride better," she said, and forced herself to meet his eye. "You don't have to teach me yourself. One of the grooms could if you'd rather. Anyone who knows more than me would be a help. Please, Freddie. I'd really like to learn."

"I see that," he said. He seemed perplexed by her persistence. The lift of his golden brows wrinkled the skin of his forehead. "Very well. I'd be happy to teach you what I can."

"Are you sure you don't mind?"

"Not at all." He rolled a green ball into the corner of the table, then grinned. "It will be fun. You have a nice enough seat already. You'll be a nonpareil in no time."

"Oh, Freddie. I don't—"

"I know." He laughed. "You don't want to attract attention. We'll turn you into a quiet nonpareil, a perfectly unobjectionable equestrienne."

Florence was so grateful she rose on tiptoe to kiss his cheek. "That," she said, blushing for her boldness, "would be marvelous."

Chapter 7

THE DAY WAS PERFECT FOR A RIDE: WARM WITH A LIGHT, rose-scented breeze and a flood of sparkling sunshine. She and Freddie crossed the back grounds to reach the stable, a longer walk than she'd expected. Greystowe's servant wing took up fully half of the sprawling house, and the stable was no smaller in scale. Like the main structure, it was built of stone. Blue slate protected its barrel roof and tall arching windows opened onto each horse's stall. The horses were cleaner and better fed than many of the people she'd seen in London. Even the cats looked sleek and fat.

They, thank heavens, took a few twists around her ankles and let her be.

With the efficiency that characterized all of Greystowe's workings, Freddie was mounted on a dappled gray and Florence on a nervous brown mare with the unpromising name of Nitwit.

"She'll settle," the groom assured her when the horse shifted from side to side. "It's the stable she don't like. Once you're in the open, she goes as pretty as you please."

Since they were already in the yard, Florence wasn't certain she believed this. Nitwit had her swaying like a tipsy sailor. Happily, the mare did calm as they left the home paddock behind.

"Watch your footing," the groom called after them. "We've had badgers."

Freddie smiled and waved and clicked his horse to a brisker pace.

"We'll take you across the downs," he said, "and get a look at your form."

The downs were an expanse of low, grassy hills, dotted with sheep and crossed by a narrow stream. After a short ride, Freddie pulled up at a flat, clover-strewn stretch of grass. "Here's a likely spot. 'Course, you probably shouldn't gallop a horse you've never ridden. Would you mind if Sooty and I shake the bugs out while you wait? I can tell he wants to run."

The dappled horse blew noisily in agreement. Florence laughed. "By all means, shake out all the bugs you please. Nitwit and I will enjoy the view."

In truth, Nitwit enjoyed the clover more than the view, but Florence was admiring enough for them both. Freddie rode as well as his brother, though his style was different: more full out, as if the horse's spirit drove that rolling gallop, rather than Freddie's driving the horse. He crouched low over Sooty's neck, his seat rising out of the saddle, his golden hair streaking like a second mane. He was tall for a jockey, but Florence had never seen one with more dash.

He was free out there. She'd never thought of him as less than free, not like his brother, but seeing him today she knew that he, too, had constraints he needed to leave behind.

Horse and rider slowed to a canter, quartering back the way they'd come. Sooty's gait was smooth as butter, a joy to watch. As if to share the pleasure, Freddie hooted and waved his arm.

Until Sooty found the hole.

It caught his right foreleg. She heard the horse scream and saw him fall. Freddie went down with him. He let out a yell, and then she heard nothing. Sensing her alarm, Nitwit began to sidle but Florence dug in her heels and forced her across the field.

"Come on," she urged, her skin all over sweat. "Come on!"

Ten feet from the fall, Nitwit refused to budge.

Even that close, Florence couldn't see Freddie, just the thrashing horse. Lord, she thought, Freddie must be underneath. She jumped from the saddle. The break was bad. Sooty's right cannon bone stuck out beyond his skin, the edges showing ragged through the blood. The horse was rolling his eyes, moaning low in his throat for help. She wished she could stop but she couldn't until she'd seen to Freddie.

As she feared, he lay under the horse, legs trapped by its weight, eyes wide and staring.

"Freddie!" she cried, kneeling beside him. He was pale as parchment.

And he wasn't breathing.

Her moan echoed the horse's. He couldn't be dead. He couldn't. What would Edward do? Edward would die himself. She touched Freddie's throat. A pulse. She felt a pulse. She had to do something. She couldn't move him, but she had to wake him. She had to make him breathe. God, she thought, praying this time. Please, please tell me what to do.

She didn't know if He answered but she drew back her arm and slapped his face. "Freddie! Freddie, wake up!"

His body shuddered so she slapped the other cheek. This time he gasped, his chest lurching upward in a pull for air. His eyes jerked wildly as if he didn't know where he was. A second later, he tried to sit up. His groan was almost too low to hear.

"Don't move," she ordered, pushing him back. She gasped for air herself, so relieved she could barely speak. "You've had a bad fall. I think you got the wind knocked out of you, but you might have hurt your spine."

"Fall?" Then he saw what was lying across his legs. "Bloody hell," he said, the first time she'd heard him curse. "He told me. He told me about the bloody badgers and I forgot." He pressed his arm across his eyes. "God damn it, I've killed my horse."

His fist pounded the grass. Florence caught it before he could hurt himself any more. "Freddie, it was an accident."

"An accident no one but an idiot would have had, a stupid, worthless— Everything I touch goes wrong. I should be shot. I should be drawn and quartered. Edward's never going to forgive me."

Florence stroked his bone-white, clammy face. More than his language shocked her. "Freddie. Edward might be disappointed, but the only thing he'd never forgive is if you'd killed yourself."

Freddie lowered his arm. Tears streaked his face, but she saw her words had calmed him. "You have to ride to the house and get him. Tell him to bring some footmen. And a rifle." Florence looked at him, then at the panting horse. He covered his eyes again. "Hurry, Florence. I don't want Sooty to suffer."

She hurried as well as she could on a horse who tried to skitter sideways every time she saw the house. She had to lash the mare hard before she'd gallop, and then it was only will that kept her in the saddle. Sliding off at the rose garden, she picked up her skirts and ran.

"Edward!" she shouted with the last of her breath. "Edward!"

He appeared, with Nigel West, on the first floor landing. She thought she'd never been so grateful to see anyone in her life.

Edward paled when he saw her. "Florence, what's wrong?"

"It's Freddie. He fell. The horse." She held her stomach and gasped for air. "You need to bring some servants and a rifle."

Both men had run down the stairs in the time it took her to say this. Now Edward grabbed her arms hard enough to bruise. "Is Freddie all right?"

"Yes, I think so. But he's trapped under the horse and the horse has a bad break. Freddie thinks he needs to be put down."

Edward emptied his lungs. Then, visibly in control again, he addressed his companion. "Nigel, you get the men and the gun. We'll meet at the stables and Florence will lead us to where it happened."

The steward pulled himself straighter. "We should bring Jenkyns, too. He can patch Freddie up if he needs it."

"Good," said Edward. "Do it."

He hustled her into the garden before her brain had finished following what he'd said. Fortunately, she'd remembered to loop Nitwit's reins around a bench, though she didn't remember how she'd gotten onto the horse's back without a mounting block. Now Edward tossed her up so quickly, she nearly slid off the other side.

He shook his head, took the reins from her hands, and led her to the stable as if she were a child. His anger was a cold, palpable force. The mare minced after him like a beaten dog. Florence wasn't beaten, though, not when it came to protecting those she loved.

"Freddie's sorry," she said, her jaw tight from steadying her voice. "He's sorrier than you could make him if you tried. There's nothing I can do to stop you from yelling at him, but I really don't think that's what he needs."

Edward stopped. He stared at her as if she'd grown a second head. When he turned away, he quickened his pace. "I've no intention of yelling at my brother."

"What about glowering at him? What about making him feel as if that horse means more to you than he does?"

A muscle bunched in Edward's cheek. "My brother knows better than that."

"Not right now, he doesn't."

Edward walked faster still. Florence knew she had no right to dictate his behavior, but she refused to withdraw a single word. Freddie thought he was worthless. Freddie thought everything he touched went wrong.

"You have to be nice to him," she insisted, though her heart was pounding in her throat.

Edward snorted. "I'll shower him with the milk of human kindness."

His tone was as dry as she'd ever heard it. She could only hope she'd made her point.

SHE THOUGHT HE WAS A MONSTER.

Even as Edward issued orders, Florence's scold played through his mind. Even as he waited for Jenkyns to gather his supplies, even as they rode like thunder across the downs, her estimation of his character made him grind his teeth.

She thought he was a monster.

But when they reached Freddie every worry but his brother left his mind. The horse lay over him from the waist down. This couldn't be good. In a single motion, Edward swung off Samson and tossed his reins to someone else. His knees hit the turf by Freddie's side.

Freddie's eyes fluttered open. His face was the bluish white of too-thin milk. It glistened with perspiration. He was in pain, Edward knew. Bad pain.

"Eddie," he said, a name he hadn't used since they were children. His voice was thready. "Tried to move, but my leg—" He grimaced. "Think I broke it. Only fair, I guess, since I broke the damn horse's."

"Sh," Edward soothed, brushing the hair from Freddie's brow. Freddie's tone alarmed him. Was Florence right? Did his brother think the horse meant more to him than he did?

"Stupid," Freddie said, rolling his head from side to side. "The groom warned me."

By this time, the stablemaster was kneeling by Freddie's other side. He touched Edward's arm. "I'd like to get a look at his eyes, my lord. See how bad a thump he took. Then the men can hoist up the horse and we'll slide him out."

Edward nodded. Jenkyns was the best doctor Greystowe had, a man of sense and experience, with people and horses. Not knowing what else to do, Edward moved to Sooty's head and held his tossing muzzle. "There," he said, over the horse's ragged pants. "You'll be out of this soon."

Sooty's great, liquid eyes held such pleas, and such faith in Edward's ability to grant them, that he felt as if a vise were tightening around his ribs. "You're a good fellow," he said, the words like gravel in his throat. "You've been a good friend to my brother."

"Your lordship?" said Nigel. The steward stood one polite step be-hind him. "Jenkyns is ready to move him. We need your help to lift the horse."

"Of course." Edward gave Sooty a last pat and got to his feet.

To his surprise, Florence moved in as well. Though he couldn't imagine what help she'd be in lifting a horse, some corner of his mind was pleased she wasn't hysterical.

"She's to steady Lord Burbrooke's legs," Jenkyns explained. "We don't want them jostled when we slide him out." The wiry stable-master had positioned himself behind Freddie's shoulders, ready to pull the moment Edward gave the signal.

"All right," Edward said to the other men. "On three."

They got him out on the second try. Both Freddie and the horse cried out at being moved.

"Stand back, Florence," Edward said once his brother was free. He could tell from Freddie's pallor that he was about to be sick. Florence seemed to reach the same conclusion. Despite the warning, she rubbed his back while Jenkyns rolled him gently to his side. She didn't cluck or fuss, just stroked him the way a mother would a weary child.

When his sickness passed, they immobilized Freddie's leg and laid him on a canvas stretcher. Nigel took one end and Jenkyns the other. Woozy with pain, Freddie still reached for Edward before they could carry him off.

"You take care of Sooty," he said, his grip surprisingly strong on Edward's wrist. "He knows you. I don't want him to go without a friend."

"I will" was all he managed to get out.

To Edward's surprise, Florence did not leave with her fiancé.

"I'm staying with you," she said, her face tear-stained but deter-mined.

"With me?"

She glanced at the footman who'd carried the gun, then lowered her voice. "I wronged you, Edward. I should have known you wouldn't treat Freddie harshly. And I want to make sure you're all right."

His mouth fished open and shut. Protests streaked like quicksilver through his head: that he might have yelled at Freddie if she hadn't been there, that a man like himself did not require coddling, that Freddie needed her more and that her continued presence was hardly proper. She was the gentler sex. She was the one who shouldn't see this. Instead, he gazed into her sweet, stubborn eyes and knew he could not refuse her gesture.

"As you wish," he said. Though he'd meant the words to come out cool, they were as low and caressing as a lover's midnight sigh. Embarrassed, he shouldered the rifle and cleared his throat. He pressed the muzzle to the gelding's skull. As if he knew what was coming, Sooty calmed.

"Stand back," he said. "I don't want you spattered."

Florence made a half-swallowed sound, more concern than horror. Edward didn't mean to look at her again, but their eyes locked just as they had over the hounds. A strange, drawing sensation pulled at his breastbone, a thin, painful tug, as if his soul were trying to reach her.

You ought to be mine, he thought. Only I can make you happy. But that was pointless. She belonged to Freddie. She was Freddie's saving grace.

He squinted down the barrel of the gun and blinked to clear his vision. The horse gave one last sigh. Edward gritted his teeth and pulled the trigger.

The recoil knocked him back a step, but the kill was clean: just a pool of blood that soaked quickly into the ground. When he lowered the gun, his arms were shaking as if he had the ague. He didn't resist when Florence tugged him away.

EDWARD DID NOT MAKE IT FROM THE STABLE TO THE HOUSE. Even though he must have been anxious to check on his brother, his legs refused to carry him. Florence watched him go paler and paler until finally, in front of a big oak with a rustic bench beneath, he tightened his hold on her arm and forced her to a stop.

"I have to sit," he said, his voice a ghost. "I can't let Freddie see me like this."

He dropped to the bench and propped his head on shaking hands. Florence sat beside him, her knees turned towards him in worry. He was sweating, and not from exertion. She pulled off her gloves and reached between his arms to unfasten his collar. As she did, he looked at her, his expression naked, his eyes pleading for something deeper than understanding.

"It's all right," she said, laying her hand behind his shoulder. "Breathe slowly. I'm sure you'll feel better soon."

She kept to herself the certainty that his brother would not think ill of his reaction. This was not about Freddie's opinion of Edward, but about Edward's opinion of himself. Gradually, as he breathed in a measure of control, the color returned to his face.

"Father wouldn't have turned a hair at this," he said, his head still lowered. "He'd have put down that horse and called for lunch."

Though Florence knew he was jesting, she did not laugh. "Forgive me for saying so, Edward, but—your father's strength of character aside—I think you're entitled to turn more than a hair. And not over the horse."

"No," he agreed with a grimacing shake of his head. "Not over the horse." He pushed himself upright and let the tree's breeze-blown leaves dapple his face with sun. Florence had never seen him so weary. She longed to hold him, to cradle his head against her breast. Her hands curled with the intensity of the urge and she blushed for fear he might look at her and read the forbidden desire. She sat in agonized silence, not knowing what to say but unable to leave. At last, he sighed and twisted his father's signet around his smallest finger. The cabochon ruby flashed in the dancing light.

"I always got on better with the earl than Freddie did," he said. "Father . . . respected me."

She lifted her gaze to his face, an intimacy that was possible only because he was staring out across the grounds. "Is that a bad thing?"

His lips twisted in a smile. "My father gave me my first horse when I was nine, to ride when I wished without the company of a groom. Freddie never earned that privilege, though he was twelve when Father died. Whatever he did, he came up short. According to Father, he was always too soft or too flighty or too much a mama's boy. My mother—" Edward pinched the bridge of his nose. "My mother was delicate, easily upset, but very sweet-natured. She needed the kind of love Freddie gave her. Unqualified. Unquestioning. But Father couldn't see that. If Freddie wanted to ride alone, he had to sneak a horse out of the stables. He had to break my father's rules and risk getting whipped."

"Are you saying that if your father had let him have his own horse, this accident wouldn't have happened?"

"No. Freddie was born to ride. More than I was, to tell the truth." His hand moved towards her face. With the pad of his thumb, he swept a windblown lock from the corner of her mouth. "I suppose I'm trying to confess I liked it."

His touch befuddled her. Enchanted and confused, she sat frozen while he traced the curve of her lower lip. His expression was musing, almost absentminded. Did he know what he was doing? Could he possibly? Only when his hand fell could she speak. "You liked what?"

"Being first," he said. "Being Father's favorite."

"Surely that's natural. You were just a boy."

"I don't know. Sometimes I think I shouldn't have—well, I admired him, you know. I knew he was a bastard but I wanted his approval."

"He was your father."

"Freddie was my brother, and a far truer soul." Edward turned his body towards her, his forearm on his knee. "You were right to scold me today. Sometimes I'm too much like him. He hurt Freddie. Made him feel the lesser son. But he wasn't less. He simply couldn't be molded into the shape my father thought appropriate for a Greystowe male. In that, Freddie was stronger than I was."

"If Freddie was stronger than you, why did you have to protect him?"

Edward brushed her knee, restlessly smoothing the folds of her riding habit. Her body tensed deep inside and she willed her reaction not to show. Fortunately, he watched his hand rather than her, his extravagant lashes shielding his eyes. His mouth held a soft, ironic curve. "I liked protecting Freddie. I liked that better than if my father had treated us as equals."

This, Florence saw, was the true confession. This was what had tightened his jaw and set that subtle tremor in his hands. But what a thing to feel guilty for, and for so many years! Aching for him, she gave in to the urge to stroke his rich dark hair. Even as she tried to soothe him, she reveled in the feel of that silk sliding through her fingers. She was shamefully glad she'd removed her gloves.

"A thought has consequences," she said carefully, gently. "My father taught me that. But a thought is not a deed. Your enjoyment of protecting Freddie did not cause your father to be cruel. Nor do I think you should worry overmuch about the possible disloyalty of your emotions. Children need to be loved by their parents. Freddie was your mother's favorite, wasn't he? You may as well blame her for what happened—though I know you will not."

Edward was silent for a moment. When he spoke, his response was low and heartfelt. "You are a wise young woman. And a kind one."

"You are easy to be kind to." Moved by his tone, she dared to pet his cheek. He turned his head, pressing his cheekbone to her fingers, brushing his mouth across her palm.

Then, as if he'd done something he devoutly wished he hadn't, he jerked away and stood. Briskly, he tugged the bottom of his waistcoat.

"I must consult with Jenkyns," he said. "Please stay until you are ready to go in."

He did not wait for her to follow. Indeed, his words made following impossible. Instead, she watched him stride stiffly towards the house, once again himself, while she—

She no longer knew who she was.

FLORENCE PACED THE HALL OUTSIDE FREDDIE'S ROOM. SHE was waiting for Edward's steward to finish settling him. The stablemaster had given Freddie a dose of morphine, but he wasn't yet asleep. Though Florence knew she ought to wait till morning to see him, she felt too restless, so restless she was wringing her hands like a heroine in a play.

She couldn't push Edward's expression from her mind. When he'd looked at her as they sat on that little bench, she'd thought—she'd wished—

She wrung her hands and paced the other way. For once, his heart had been in his gaze. When she met it, she seemed to know his every thought: his regret for the horse, his fear for Freddie. Most of all, she'd sensed his hope that no one would guess how weak he was. But Florence didn't think him weak. Instead, she thought him the strongest man she'd ever known.

Was that the real Edward: the man whose heart could break for a wounded horse? Who could torture himself over the tangled motivations of his childhood? Who could worry that his love had not been perfect? And if this was the real Edward, what did that mean for her? Attraction was one thing. Even infatuation could be dismissed. But the pull he exerted when he bared his soul would not be easy to evade. She wasn't even sure she wanted to.

The dilemma seemed destined to remain unsolved. Nigel West stepped out of Freddie's room and carefully shut the door. As befitted his position—the steward ran Greystowe when Edward could not—he was a dignified man of middle years, slender, his temples lightly shot with white. He would have appeared as serious as his master but for his extraordinary gray eyes. They were kind and quiet and crinkled pleasantly at the corners when he smiled. He smiled now at Florence.

"I'm afraid he's dropped off, Miss Fairleigh. Didn't even wait for me to finish plumping the pillows. You can go in, of course, but I doubt he'll wake."

"Oh," she said, feeling as if an escape route had been blocked. "I wouldn't want to disturb him." She started to go, then turned back.

"Will you be looking after him, Mr. West? I know the housekeeper or one of the maids could do it, but he'd probably be more comfortable with a man."

Nigel's brow puckered as if her words held some significance she didn't understand. She wondered if she'd overstepped her place. She had no authority here, nor would she have much more as Freddie's wife. Greystowe was Edward's to arrange. Just as she was about to withdraw the request, Nigel shook himself.

"I imagine I shall be looking after him. With Edward home, I'm rather at loose ends."

Relieved she hadn't put her foot wrong, Florence smiled. "You've been at Greystowe a long time, haven't you?"

"Since his lordship's father paid for my schooling." Nigel grinned at her shocked expression. "You've heard the stories then. All true. The old earl was a devil. But he did believe in fostering potential. I owe this family more than I can say."

Eyes abruptly pricking, Florence gazed past him down the hall. She owed this family a good deal herself, too much to think of betraying their trust. They'd welcomed her, a simple country girl, as Freddie's bride. And Freddie . . . Freddie was the dearest man she'd ever known. "They're complicated, aren't they?" she said. "Even Freddie."

"Yes," Nigel agreed, the gentleness of his tone forcing her to blink back tears. "But steadfast every one. You couldn't want for truer friends."

Friends, she thought. If only her wishes were that simple.

SHORTLY AFTER MIDNIGHT, EDWARD CROSSED THE HALL TO his brother's room. He had no intention of waking Freddie. He simply wanted to stand in the dark and listen to him breathe. The leg with the splint made a funny shape under the sheets, as if a mummy were sharing his bed. Edward was still too shaken to be amused. He didn't know what he'd do if he lost his brother; didn't know who he'd be. He'd built his life around protecting him. Without Freddie alive and well and happy, none of his accomplishments meant a damn.

He turned to the window, hands clenched, muscles tight. Florence, he thought. Oh, Florence. Why do I have to care about you, too? The night could not answer. With dreamlike slowness, the draperies belled in the breeze that cooled the room. Their sheer white hems whispered across the carpet. Edward looked back at the bed. The night was mild, but Freddie could not afford a chill. One good leg had been enough to kick off half the covers. Smiling wryly, Edward pulled them up his chest.

Disturbed by the movement, Freddie snuffled in his sleep and rolled partway onto his side. His arm flopped out, hitting Edward's leg. His eyes opened. "Nigel?"

Edward hunkered beside the bed. "It's Edward. I just came to check on you."

Freddie smiled, his eyes sliding shut again. "You haven't checked on me since Mummy and Daddy died."

"I didn't know you saw me do that."

Covers rustled as Freddie shrugged. "I figured you wanted reassurance that you weren't alone. I didn't mind. It made me feel safe."

"You are safe. I'll always keep you safe."

Freddie laughed under his breath. "Can't promise that, old man. You ain't God yet, though I know you'll try."

His singsong tone told Edward he still felt the morphine. He'd have to warn Jenkyns to watch the dose. He didn't want Freddie getting used to it.

"She did it for you," Freddie said, his fingers plucking idly at the sheet.

"Who did what for me?"

"Florence," he said. "Asked me for riding lessons. She didn't say so, but I know it was you she wanted to impress."

Edward's breath caught. Was it true? Did Florence value his opinion? He'd thought today, when she stroked his face, that she must hold him in some esteem. But how could he know? She was a sympathetic soul. Perhaps she'd have touched anyone as tenderly. Surely after all he'd done she couldn't still care what he thought.

Freddie laughed again. "Thinks you don't like her. Big old grouch."

"Florence called me a big old grouch?"

But Freddie's drug-fogged mind had already wandered on. "You'll have to take over for me. Teach her yourself." He smacked his lips and burrowed deeper in the pillows. "Be like when you taught me how to swim."

Alarmed by the suggestion, Edward stood. Be alone with Florence? Teach Florence? Not on his life. Not unless he wanted his brother to marry a ravaged bride.

Chapter 8

ACCORDING TO JENKYNS, FREDDIE COULDN'T BE MOVED until his bones had a chance to set. Nigel was seeing to his meal when Florence knocked.

"I don't want your blasted broth," she heard Freddie snap. "My leg is broken, not my stomach." Clearly, his pain had made him peevish. Despite his discomfort, he brightened when he saw her. "At last. A kindly nursemaid. Tell this loathsome bully to take his nursery food away."

Florence kissed his brow without a blush. "I'm sure Mr. West is only following doctor's orders."

"Bloody horse doctor," Freddie muttered, then squeezed her hand in apology. "You should go, sweetheart. Have your own breakfast. I'm a bad invalid. Always have been. I'm afraid if you stay, you'll throw me over for a banker."

Florence clucked her tongue and roundly denied the charge. She did as Freddie asked, though, for he was obviously not in a humor to see her. He and Nigel were squabbling again as soon as she shut the door.

Poor Nigel, she thought. She was glad the steward had taken him in hand. Freddie would have talked his way around any of the maids. She proceeded to the breakfast parlor, a pretty yellow room with a view of the breeze-ruffled lake. To her dismay, only Edward sat inside.

"Is Aunt Hypatia—?"

"Sleeping," he said, as short-tempered as ever.

So, she thought, the grumpy earl returns. She filled her plate at the sideboard: eggs, sausage, a freshly baked roll, and strawberries. Refusing to give in to fear, she took the seat around the corner from his. For long minutes, the only sound was the clink of china and the rasp of a snore issuing from the ground floor bedroom next door. Never an early riser, Edward's aunt must have been exhausted by the previous day's excitement.

Florence wanted to smile, but she doubted Edward would appreciate the jest. His mood was blacker than Freddie's—and both his legs were sound. She was beginning to think she'd dreamed the man she'd seen the day before.

"Do you think we ought to call a real doctor?" she asked, perversely wanting him to look at her. Even his scowl was preferable to being ignored.

Edward set down his knife and fork. When the morning sun struck his eyes, they glowed like clear blue gems. His riding coat was for once not black, but a soft brown tweed. His shirt was white and collarless. He looked wonderful: big and broad-shouldered and country-squirish. Not relaxed though. She couldn't imagine Edward ever being relaxed. A short, deep line appeared between his heavy brows. For him, the expression was friendly.

"I'm afraid the doctor in town is a bit decrepit. Jenkyns knows more about broken bones than he does. If we encounter complications, I'll send to London for my physician."

His gaze remained on Florence even after he finished speaking. She'd wanted him to look at her but now that he was, she could barely sit still. His regard, steady and inscrutable, inspired a powerful urge to squirm. When he tipped his coffee to his mouth, his lips drew her eyes like a magnet. Those sensual lips, so at odds with his forbidding face, stirred memories better left alone. He licked them as he set down the cup.

Those lips had kissed her, and those hands, those big, sundarkened hands had held her head, had run down her spine and cupped her bottom. The last time they'd done it he hadn't had drink to excuse him. He did desire her, even if he didn't like her. Perhaps, she thought, he remembered their kisses as vividly as she did. Perhaps he wanted to kiss her now. The possibility made her shiver. She did squirm then, just a little.

"Florence," he said, his voice deeper than usual.

Startled, she glanced guiltily back at his face. "Yes, Edward?"

"I'm arranging for Merry Vance to visit Greystowe, so you won't be bored while Freddie's laid up."

"Oh," she said, surprised he would concern himself with her comfort. "That's very kind, but won't she mind leaving London during the Season?"

His laugh was dry. "She's only seventeen. I suspect she wouldn't be out at all if she hadn't wrapped her father around her finger. I thought she could take over training you from Freddie. By all accounts, she's quite the horsewoman."

"Oh," said Florence, the only word she could think of. Her tea and sausages sat like stones in her belly. Suddenly, the reason for Edward's consideration was clear.

He didn't want to teach her himself.

She looked at her lap, where her traitorous hands were twisting her napkin into a ball. She swallowed. She was being ridiculous. She shouldn't let him hurt her. It wasn't as if having him teach her would be fun. More often than not, he wasn't nice to her at all. Against her will, she thought of Freddie's swimming trophy, the one Edward kept in the cabinet by his bed. She knew then; couldn't deny it any longer. She wanted more than Edward's respect. She wanted him to like her, to care as deeply for her as he did for his brother.

"I'm sure you'll do well," he said, the assurance uncustomarily soft. She had the impression he was leaning towards her, though she didn't dare lift her head. "I'm sure Freddie will be proud."

"Thank you," she managed to say. "I liked Merry Vance very much. It was kind of you to think of her."

"You are easy to be kind to."

Florence couldn't help widening her eyes. Did he mean to remind her of her words to him in the garden? He'd behaved as if he wanted to forget his confidences, and expected her to do the same. But perhaps the reminder was unintentional, or some obscure setdown she was simply too thick to fathom. Oh, she would never understand him, never!

Unfortunately, knowing that did not keep her from wanting to try.

THE ROSE GARDEN BUZZED WITH DRAGONFLIES AND BEES. Two days had passed since Freddie's accident and Florence was taking tea with Aunt Hypatia. According to the duchess, Florence's simple flowered cotton gown—one of her own—was woefully inadequate.

"You look like a farmgirl," she complained.

Florence did not take offense. The duchess liked complaining as much as cats liked cream. She hid her smile behind the gold-plated rim of her cup. "I thought tea dress was meant to be more comfortable."

"It is, but in a picturesque and romantic manner. Here." With the agility she displayed when she chose, she pushed from her chair and snipped two budded yellow roses. The small silver scissors that hung from a cord at her waist made quick work of the thorns. That done, she removed one of her hat pins and fastened the flowers, leaves and all, to Florence's bodice. "There. Marginally better. We won't always be taking tea alone, you know. I do have acquaintances here."

"I'd forgotten that," Florence admitted. "You were born in this house, weren't you? With Freddie's father."

"Wonder is, I survived it," the duchess grumped, though the sparkle in her eye led Florence to believe her memories weren't all unpleasant. "My brother, the thirteenth earl, was the worst scamp you could imagine. The trouble that boy got me into!"

"I thought he was very stern."

"Not until he got the title. Then he had to be a 'Greystowe man.' " She pulled a face Florence suspected was an imitation of the haughty earl. "The peerage ruined him. Destroyed every shred of humor and humanity he had. After that, nothing mattered but the family honor. He threw over a girl he'd been seeing for well on seven years. Everyone assumed they'd marry. But a baron's daughter wasn't good enough for him. He had to take up with the boys' mother and make her miserable, too." She shook her head. "Suzanne was as sweet as spun sugar and about as tough. I doubt anyone had raised their voice to her before her marriage. As for me, when Stephen gained an earldom, I lost a friend. Didn't so much as pat my back until the day I married my duke. That earned me a brother's embrace. That made him love me again."

Florence reached past the tea things to clasp her hand. With a fond smile, the duchess returned the pressure. "No, dear. You mustn't pity a rich old lady. All that happened long ago."

But it wasn't the duchess who worried Florence most.

"Aunt Hypatia," she said, "you don't think Edward is in danger of . . ."

"Becoming like his father?" Aunt Hypatia laughed. "It's good of you to concern yourself, but there's not much chance of that. Sometimes—I fear this will sound callous, but sometimes I think it's better my brother died young. Certainly better for Freddie." Her face softened as people's tended to at his name. "Freddie was raised with love. He'll be a good father someday because Edward was everything my brother should have been. Edward still has his heart."

Did he? Sometimes Florence thought so. Other times, she doubted it very much. She would have liked to sit quietly then, to mull over what she'd heard. Her wish was not to be, however, because Mrs. Forster, the housekeeper, chose that moment to announce the arrival of Merry Vance. When she stepped onto the terrace she looked a different creature from the impeccably dressed young lady Florence had known in London. Her hair was disheveled, her color high, her smart yellow gown wrinkled and dulled by the dust of travel. Her grin, however, was as wide and engaging as ever.

"Yes, yes, I'm early," she said in her happy, breathless way. Holding both gloves in one hand she leaned down to kiss Florence's cheek. "London has been as dull as dishwater without you. I simply couldn't wait to say hello." Her eyes twinkled as she bobbed a curtsey to the duchess. "Please forgive my informality, your Grace. I assure you it isn't personal. Anyone you ask will tell you I'm a hellion."

"Will they indeed?" intoned the duchess.

"Miss Vance," Edward said, appearing at the edge of the grass. His nod was grave but his face creased upward as if he were about to laugh. No doubt he'd caught the duchess's frosty response. "I trust you and Buttercup survived the train from London."

Buttercup? Florence thought. Her cat-light mare from London? Was it possible Edward had bought the horse for her? It would have been an extravagant gesture, and one she really shouldn't accept, but, oh, if he had! But Merry Vance dashed her irrational hope almost before it had time to form.

"I can't thank you enough," she said, "for arranging her as my ride. Teaching is so much easier when you have a good mount."

Edward looked down. This, of all things, seemed to embarrass him. He glanced uncomfortably at Florence, his gaze catching for an instant on the roses the duchess had pinned to her bosom. With an air of distraction, he shook his head and returned his attention to Merry. "Ah, well, pleased I could oblige. I had to buy her in any case. My stallion was moping."

Merry laughed, a surprisingly feminine sound. "How grand! A romance among the stalls. I shall have to keep on top of developments while I'm here."

She smiled at Edward as she said it, as if her words held a meaning known only to the two of them. She wasn't plain then, not with that gleam in her eyes and the sunshine blazing in her cloud of golden hair. She was a little Valkyrie, lithe and strong, if not quite up to a large breastplate. The realization that Edward might find her attractive made Florence distinctly ill at ease.

He doesn't want her, she assured herself. His manner was too casual, too matter of fact.

Even if he had given Merry her horse.

"You'll want to freshen up," Edward said, though not as disapprovingly as the duchess would have.

Merry trilled at the gentle suggestion. "Indeed," she cooed, tapping Edward's chest with the tip of her finger. "Fresh is my middle name."

Florence experienced a nearly uncontrollable urge to pinch her, but Edward was not put off. "Shall we hold tea for you?" he asked.

"Oh, no." Merry tossed her golden hair and turned towards the house. "I'm sure I can cozen something out of the kitchen when I get back. You three enjoy. I'll find my poor old maid and the next time you see me, I'll be free of dust and decent."

"Not too decent," Edward said, perfectly straight-faced.

"My, no." Merry threw a wink over her shoulder. "What fun would. that be?"

Florence could barely lift her jaw. As Merry sauntered across the terrace, her little bottom twitched beneath her dusty bustle. She'd been flirting with Edward. And Edward had flirted back.

"Hm," said Aunt Hypatia once Merry was out of earshot. "That girl bears watching."

Florence didn't know if she meant this as an insult or a compliment, nor was her nephew's demeanor any clue. Still facing the direction Merry had taken, Edward clasped his hands behind his back. Florence sincerely hoped he wasn't watching Merry twitch.

"She's Monmouth's daughter," he said.

"Yes." The duchess stirred her tea. "In a year or two, she'll make some man a fine wife."

"You mean she'll make some man a fine handful."

"That, too," said Aunt Hypatia.

Florence pushed her cucumber sandwich to the farthest edge of her plate. Her appetite had fled, along with her enjoyment of the afternoon. A fine handful indeed! She might not have the right to mind it, but she knew she didn't like the sound of that.

Chapter 9

To FLORENCE'S DISMAY, NITWIT HAD BECOME "HER" HORSE.

"Today you'll groom her," Merry announced as they entered the busy stable. To Florence's amazement, Merry wore breeches. For once, another woman drew more stares than she did. She didn't know whether to blush for her friend or admire her brazen style. Merry behaved as if she were dressed to meet the queen and, while no one so much as whistled, Florence suspected Greystowe's grooms would be talking of this for years. Everywhere they passed, jaws dropped. Apparently, the only males immune to the shock of visible female legs were a trio of school-age boys who were forking soiled hay into barrows.

Grateful for their efforts, Florence picked her way across the hard-packed floor. She sighed when they reached Nitwit's box. The top of the stall door was covered in equine tooth marks, mute testimony to the mare's restless habits. Equally unimpressed with Florence, Nitwit curled her lip and made a rude noise.

They eyed each other while Merry went to Jenkyns for supplies.

"It wasn't my choice," Florence said as the mare deigned to swivel her ears. "We'll simply have to make the best of it."

Merry caught the tail end of the exchange. "Good. You're getting acquainted. You can't ride well if you and the horse aren't comfortable with each other."

As if to prove the unlikelihood of this happening, Nitwit kicked the back of her box.

"We'll have to lead her into the yard," Florence said. "Being inside makes her snappish."

"Nonsense," said Merry. "She only needs settling."

With a sense of resignation, Florence followed her into the stall. Ten minutes later, after Nitwit had clipped Merry twice on the boot, they trooped out.

"Maybe we should ask Jenkyns for another mount," Merry said.

"No, no. She'll be fine once we get her into the paddock." Florence was reluctant to admit it, even to herself, but she was feeling more kindly towards the mare since she'd tried to kick her teacher. Merry's good-humored air of competence was wearing on her nerves. It didn't seem right that someone younger than herself should be so skilled, or so fearless.

Or that someone who obviously didn't need a nice horse should be given one like Buttercup.

She bit her lip at her unkind thoughts. Her father used to say envy was a bitter pill. Now she knew how true those words were. She could barely choke her resentment down. It wasn't justified, of course. Merry was a nice girl, a generous girl to come and teach her this way. And still Florence exulted when Nitwit proved her right. The mare did like being brushed in the open air. She barely twitched when Florence curried her sensitive underbelly.

"Now lift her feet," Merry said. "Let's see if she'll let you check her shoes."

Florence did as she asked, too annoyed to feel a moment's fear.

"Good," Merry exclaimed when Nitwit did not protest. "Horses are flight animals. When they let you hold their feet, that means they trust you."

Florence was tempted to tell her most animals trusted her, but managed to hold her tongue. Merry didn't know about the cats. Merry was only trying to be encouraging. The least Florence could do was pretend to be grateful.

I am grateful, she thought. I am.

But she had to struggle not to grind her teeth.

After they checked Nitwit's shoes for stones, Merry had Florence saddle her and mount. Then, instead of watching Florence ride, she took the halter and told Florence to release the reins.

"Hold your arms out from your sides," she instructed. "And don't put your foot in the stirrup or hook your knee around the head. Sit face front and tuck your leg behind the horn. I'll hold Nitwit steady. You concentrate on centering your weight over the horse's back. That's how you develop a sense of balance."

As far as Florence could tell, she wasn't developing anything but a sense of embarrassment. Her arms shook from lifting the heavy saddle over Nitwit's back. The smallest movement felt as if it would send her sliding. Even worse, the three stableboys had perched on the paddock wall to watch the show.

Either that, or they weren't too young after all to notice the fit of Merry's breeches.

"Doing fine, miss," the tallest one called. The shortest, a round, straw-headed elf, decided to play tightrope on the stones.

Oh, Lord, thought Florence, his antics making her dizzy. She hardly dared breathe for fear of falling off. Nitwit was taller than Buttercup and the ground seemed a long way down.

"Are you ready for me to lead you around?" Merry asked.

Florence's "no" was almost a shout. Merry laughed and patted Nitwit's neck.

"Never mind," she said. "You just sit today. We'll save walking for tomorrow."

Tomorrow, Florence thought, and wished she were enough of a coward to give up.

To FLORENCE'S IMMENSE RELIEF, THE NEXT DAY WAS BETTER, and the next better still. On the fourth day of lessons, Merry put Nitwit on a long leather lead called a lunge line and had her circle the paddock with Florence on her back. First they walked slowly, then swiftly, and then they tried a gentle trot. Merry let her hook her leg around the head for this, but Florence fell off all the same. She was determined, though, especially with her trio of fans. She didn't know if Jenkyns had given them permission or if they'd simply sneaked away, but the three muddy boys managed to watch her every day.

"No worries," they'd call each time she hit the dirt. "You'll get it next time."

Despite her embarrassment, and the fact that her bottom was all over bruises, Florence was glad they were rooting for her. These boys were too old to be the victims of her peculiar charms, and too young to be interested in her ordinary ones. They had to be there by choice. They had to be there because they liked her.

"Forget posting," Merry said when she tried to raise up and down. "Posting is for ninnies. You want to rock back and forth from the hips. With the horse's movements. Easy. Feel how your weight shifts with the horse's steps."

"Woo-hoo," hooted the boys at Merry's suggestive demonstration. Merry merely laughed.

"With the horse," she coaxed. "*With* the horse."

Finally, on the seventh day, Florence got it. Nitwit snorted and pranced as if Florence had performed a miracle. Truth be told, she felt as if she had. How easy this was! How right! It was just the way her body had been wanting to go all along.

Then Merry let her put her foot into the stirrup.

The security Florence felt astounded her—and she had yet to use her hands. Merry was a genius. Even a canter didn't shake her. Oh, her heart was pounding, but her seat was as steady as a rock. When they tried a gallop, Florence thought her soul had taken wing. The rhythm of the gait made the most of Merry's lessons and Nitwit, bless her, flew over the ground as if her legs were pistons and her hooves set on tracks. For the first time in her life, Florence knew what people meant by horse and rider being one. Nitwit might not be as light on her feet as Buttercup, or as even-tempered, but she was strong and fast and as sure as a mountain goat.

"What a goer!" Merry exclaimed and Florence was proud for her mount's sake, too.

As luck would have it, Edward was the first person to meet them coming out of the stable. Florence was too elated to mind her manners. "I did it!" she said, grabbing his hands and bouncing up and down. "I galloped on Nitwit without the reins."

Edward smiled at her. His grip was firm. It even swung a little. "I saw," he said. "That was very brave. I suppose next you'll be wanting to join the circus."

The warmth in his eyes made her shy. "Not the circus. Not me."

"She's a trooper," Merry put in. "A mouse with the heart of a lion."

Her words seemed to remind Edward that he was holding Florence's hands. He dropped them as if they burned and turned to Merry. "You've done a good job, Miss Vance. My stablemaster has been singing your praises."

"She's a wonderful teacher," Florence agreed, too exhilarated to be jealous. "I never believed I could ride a horse like that."

"A girl can ride anything she puts her mind to," Merry said, her eyes laughing suggestively at Edward's. "That's what we're built for."

Even Florence could not fail to catch that double meaning. Edward's lips thinned wryly as he shook his finger. "Your father would wash your mouth, Miss Vance."

"It's Merry," she said, but he was already walking off. Her sigh as she watched him go spoke volumes. "Lord above. Did you ever see such a pair of shoulders?"

Florence looked at them, then at Merry. Merry's hand was pressed to her bosom and her gaze was soft with yearning. Knowledge dawned with a sinking of her stomach. Merry hadn't come to Greystowe because she liked Florence, or because she liked teaching, or even because she was still too young to take the Season seriously. All those

things might be true, but Merry had come to Greystowe because its
earl made her swoon.

When Merry looked back at her, her awareness must have shown.
Her teacher smiled, crookedly, ruefully. Florence's heart squeezed with
sympathy. Merry might not know it but, in this, they were two of a
kind.

"The first time I saw him at Tattersall's," Merry confessed, "my
toes curled in my boots. If only I were bold enough, I think I could
have him. I'm not too terribly ugly. And he does think I'm funny.
Men have been known to fall for less."

Florence supposed they had. She drew breath to assure the girl she
wasn't ugly, then thought better of it. "Maybe you should be careful.
You are young, and he is a grown man."

Merry made a sound halfway between a gurgle and a moan. To Florence's dismay, she knew precisely what it meant. Edward was more
than a grown man. Edward was the epitome of all that was male and,
as such, he called to the most primitive urges a woman had. A man
like Edward made a woman want to forget everything: promises, propriety, even common sense. But perhaps she ought to be glad he had
the same effect on Merry. Perhaps Florence's feelings were nothing to
be concerned over. A natural human temptation. Vicar's daughter or
no, Florence had always known she was human.

"I hope you don't think I'm awful," Merry said, her hand on Florence's arm. "My friends in London say silly things or scoff. You, at
least, know how I feel. After all, you and Freddie must have stolen a
few kisses. Freddie's a handsome young man in his prime." Confidence recovering, she wagged her strawberry brows. "A man with
needs, Florence. A man who's practically chained to his bed. Believe
me, were I in your place and Edward in Freddie's, I know what sort of
nursemaid I'd be."

Her words painted a picture Florence could not thrust away. She
saw Edward wrapped in chains, his chest as bare as a marble statue.
And her hand. She saw her own hand reaching for the secrets she'd
been too timid to explore. That thickness, that shifting, swelling
shape . . . Her body clenched, low and tight. She was liquid inside,
and hot. But she couldn't let Merry guess how she felt. She couldn't
let Merry think what she was planning was appropriate. She eased her
arm from Merry's hold.

"Freddie is a perfect gentleman," she said in her most repressive
schoolteacher tone. "Freddie would never do anything to compromise
a lady's honor."

"Of course not," Merry said, obviously unconvinced.

And Florence knew nothing she'd said had sunk in.

SHE WATCHED THEM TOGETHER AFTER THAT; WATCHED HOW easy Edward was with Merry, how he laughed at her jokes, how his eyes sparked when they debated the merits of various equine traits. Merry would not back down when she thought she was right. Merry would rise out of her seat and pound the table.

And Edward didn't seem to mind.

Was Merry right? Did Edward merely need a push? He didn't act like a besotted man. At least, not the besotted men she knew. But Edward was a creature apart, so perhaps he felt more than he showed.

She watched to see if he touched her, measured his smiles, compared his stares to those he'd shared with her. They weren't the same. They weren't hot and riveting and as sharp as a whetted blade. She could see the difference and she was dreadfully wrong to care. She even watched his hidden flesh to see if it grew large when he and Merry were together. He caught her at it once and gave her the strangest look. Her face had burned like flame. Other things, too. Other things she didn't have names for caught fire between her legs.

She told herself Edward's amours were not her concern.

She told herself if only she knew the truth about his feelings for Merry, she could face them.

But the truth was the last thing she could face. The truth was pressing up inside her, dark and restless, as if Pandora's box were striving to open itself. At her wit's end, she sat on the lid and shut her eyes. She did not know how close the secret was to breaking free.

FLORENCE CONVINCED THE HOUSEKEEPER TO LET HER TAKE Freddie's lunch tray. She'd allowed Nigel to shoulder too much of her intended's care. That was going to change. She couldn't do everything, but she could fluff pillows. She could smooth brows and banish boredom. She could let Freddie know she would never, ever neglect him.

With that resolve, Florence shifted the tray to her hip and rapped lightly on his door.

"You do *not* want to do this," she heard Nigel saying sharply through the wood. When he opened the door a moment later, his face was flushed. He and Freddie must have been fighting again. She'd come just in time, she decided. The poor man must be desperate for a break.

"Sweetheart!" Freddie exclaimed. He had a pillow on his lap and his hair was mussed as if he'd been running his fingers through it. As always, he put on his best face for her. His smile was brilliant. "Your timing is perfect. My warden here was about to thrash me."

"I'll leave you two alone," Nigel said, sounding as stiff as the earl.

Florence clucked at Freddie as soon as the steward was gone. "You shouldn't bait him."

Freddie helped her slide the tray over his lap. "Bait him?"

"I know it's hard on you being shut up like this, but it's hard on him, too. Mr. West wasn't trained to be a nursemaid. Now and then you could squabble with me instead—if only to give the poor man a rest."

Freddie blinked as if he hadn't understood a word. Florence uncovered the beef and barley stew Cook had made to keep his strength up. She knew better than to believe his innocent air. "I know you two were arguing. Mr. West's face was as red as a beet when he opened the door."

For some reason, this made Freddie red, too. He toyed with his fork. "Ah, um, that. We were, um, arguing the merits of a Bath chair. I say I'm ready to go out in one. He says I'm not. Hence our contretemps."

Florence offered him a napkin to tuck into his shirt. His embarrassment spoke well for his conscience, but she couldn't drop the matter yet. It wouldn't be fair to Mr. West. "I'm sure Mr. Jenkyns can decide if you're ready to be wheeled around."

"Of course," he said. "Of course."

He lifted a bite of stew, then set it down. His gaze met hers. His arm rose and, with almost alarming tenderness, he cupped her cheek. He murmured her name, his fingertips stroking the edge of her hair. All her affection for him came rushing back. With relief, she knew she did love him. She might not yearn for him as she yearned for Edward, but she loved him in a good, steady way. A way that would last. She smiled at him and covered his hand with her own.

"You're the dearest woman I know," he said. "Even when you're scolding me."

His tone was oddly wistful.

"I've made you sad," she said, "and I don't even know how."

He shook his head. His hand dropped, its warmth fading quickly from her skin. "I'm only sad for you, Florence, for agreeing to marry a ridiculous creature like me."

"You're not ridiculous. Merely a bad invalid. My father was the same. But I shall pay more attention to you now, and make sure your spirits do not sink."

"If only everything were sinking," he said, with a laugh she did not understand.

"I'm sure Mr. West would help cheer you up if you would let him."

He laughed again, a brief, sharp sound. "Mr. West disapproves of too much 'help.' Considers it a betrayal of the family trust. In which belief he is perfectly correct."

Florence expected such acerbity from his brother, but not from him. Before she could ask what he meant, he shook off whatever had troubled him. He took her hand and pressed a soft kiss to its palm. Her toes did not curl in her boots, but that was because she was a sensible vicar's daughter, not a headstrong girl of seventeen. She and Freddie would be happy. That was all she needed to know.

Or so she told herself as the darkness inside her grew.

NIGEL WASN'T IN HIS OFFICE. EDWARD WANTED TO ASK HIM about the history of some correspondence with the mill, but Freddie must have needed his assistance. He frowned, annoyed that he'd have to put the matter off. Though it probably wasn't urgent, he'd wanted, needed actually, to bury himself in work.

He couldn't stop thinking of Florence. His feelings had escalated beyond control since their talk in the garden. He didn't know why he'd confessed those things about his father. Shock, he supposed, or simply the presence of a sympathetic ear.

Her sympathetic ear.

He'd known she was sweet, but hearing her words—so simple and wise and kind—made his yearning that much worse. He could still feel her small, warm hand against his cheek, the memory of that gentle touch as inflaming as a kiss. She was an ache in his bones, a fierce, impossible desire.

The devil whispered to his conscience. She cares for you, Edward. You could make her happy; could love her like no other man. Let Freddie fend for himself. Don't you deserve to be selfish just this once?

Disgusted by his own weakness, he stalked down the hall with a growl. A scullery maid jumped at the sound, nearly dropping the tray she was carrying to the servants' midday meal. He helped her steady it, which made her tremble all the more.

"I am not an ogre," he snapped.

"Of course not, my lord," she said, eyes showing white as she backed away. "Not at all."

Blast, he thought, his fist thumping a door frame. Nothing brought him ease. He could have taken every woman between Lancashire and London. He could have humped a stone. He could have spilled a river of seed and still come up for more.

The only woman he wanted was her.

He wanted to lock her in his rooms for a fortnight. Wanted to chain her to his bed and slide inside her from dusk till dawn. He wanted her heat, her touch, her gasp when she saw the rigid evidence of his lust. He wanted her silky hair across his chest. He wanted her tender rose-red mouth. He wanted her hips, her breasts. He wanted to wrap his hands around her knees and spread them wide.

He wanted to make her his.

He leaned straight-armed on the wall and hung his head, breathing hard, trying to pull himself together. A line of boots sat inside the room where he'd stopped, clearly awaiting a polish. One of the pairs was smaller than the rest: soft gray kid with matching laces. Before he could stop himself he picked them up. The ankles were soft and supple against his palm. The leather was new yet, the stitching on the toe a series of fancy, twining curls. He ran the tip of his finger over the pattern, knowing the boot belonged to Florence. There wasn't a woman in the house who had a foot as neat. An image formed in his mind, as unstoppable as the tide, of Florence at the dressmaker's, standing barefoot in her chemise and drawers. She'd had such tiny white feet, such adorable toes. Kissable toes. Suckable toes.

The sound of his rumbling groan restored him to his senses. He dropped the boots like a pair of coals. What an arse he was, mooning over a woman's shoes. They'd be carting him off to Bedlam next.

He closed his eyes and clenched his hands. This had to stop. He needed her out of his mind before he lost it. Just an hour, he prayed. Just an hour without this torment. His breath sighed from him as he slowly relaxed his fists. Samson might not know it, but he was about to save his master's life.

THE STABLE WAS GENERALLY CLEAR AT MIDDAY, WHILE THE servants took their meal. Edward was glad for that today. He could saddle Samson as quickly as any groom. Even if he couldn't have, a stretch of solitude was worth the inconvenience. His sex was heavy with longing, his skin a forest of prickling nerves. Mindless, he thought. I need a hard, mindless ride.

Samson whickered at his approach. Regrettably, the big black stallion was not alone.

"Miss Vance," he said.

She turned and smiled—nervously, he thought. He wondered if his temper were that obvious and tried to school his face. She swiped her hand down the outrageous breeches she liked to wear. He would have asked why her maid let her out in that state, except the poor old creature was so nearsighted she probably didn't know.

"Won't you call me Merry?" she said, more serious than was her wont. "I know I'd rather call you Edward."

Since he wasn't sure how to answer this question, he evaded it. "Are you going riding?"

If she was going riding, he wasn't. Edward liked Merry Vance. She was plucky and she amused him, but he wasn't in the mood for her company now: a girl barely out of the schoolroom who didn't know better than to play with fire. Alas, she didn't know better now.

"I'd rather *be* ridden," she said, her voice husky, her freckles lost in a sea of pink. "Maybe you'd care to help me out."

He was not as quick as he should have been. Her words didn't fit together until she stepped to him, wound her arms behind his neck, and pulled his head down for a kiss. His body responded without thought. He was primed for a woman, any woman. His mouth yielded to her pressure. His heart thudded, his cock surged, and before he knew it his shirt was pulled out and pushed up and ten short nails were raking through the hair on his chest.

"Oh," she gasped, pushing back to admire the skin she'd bared. "I knew you'd be like this: too, too perfect for words."

Her head swooped in, catching one of his nipples between her teeth. He yelped. He meant to push her off, but her hands had snaked round his back and were scratching his spine in a manner that made his knees much weaker than he wished. Waves of heat rolled through his body. She was squirming against him like a cat. Her little breasts were soft and bare beneath her cotton shirt. Her nipples were sharp. Her thighs—well, he didn't want to think about her thighs. Those breeches didn't hide the half of what they should.

"Merry," he warned, wondering precisely where it was safe to grab her. "Merry, stop."

"I know I'm not pretty," she said between dangerously descending bites, "or experienced like your usual women, but oh—" Her knees hit the ground as her mouth sucked the skin of his belly. "I'm willing, Edward. Willing to do anything you please."

Her words were whiskey poured on flame. He gasped as her hands found his balls. Where on earth did a girl as young as Merry learn to be so bold? With a muttered curse, he pulled her wrists away. "I said stop, Merry, and I meant it."

Her expression was priceless: part anger, part two-year-old's pout. Any other day, he would have chuckled inside to see it. But she was also hurt, and he knew too well what it was to want what you could not have.

"You like me," she said, stubborn to the last. "I know you do."

"I like you very much, but that doesn't mean I want to sleep with you."

"You want to a little." Hands still trapped, she leaned forward far enough to nudge his erection with her chin.

He rasped out a laugh and moved his hips from harm's way. "Yes, I want you, but you're too young and too well born to be playing this sort of game."

"It's because I'm plain," she huffed. "You're disgusted by the thought of seeing me naked."

"Oh, Lord." Rolling his eyes, he lifted her to her feet. "You're a perfectly nice-looking girl and I'm sure any number of men, myself included, would in many circumstances be delighted to see you without your clothes. However, I've no intention of paying the price for that delight." He held up his hand when she started to speak, no doubt about to swear no one would know but her. "Save that privilege for a man who loves you, Merry. To him you'll be beautiful. And with him what you're proposing to do will be beautiful, too."

She made a sound of disgust much truer to her age than her recent actions. "You sound like my father."

"Good," he said. "I'd much prefer that's how you thought of me."

Her hands were planted on her hips and her gaze traveled over him from neck to groin. It was an ogle whose frankness Imogene would have struggled to match. To his amazement, Edward flushed.

"I could never," she declared, "think of you as my father."

He had to laugh then. Merry Vance wouldn't be a handful; she'd be a plague.

FLORENCE COLLAPSED AGAINST THE OUTER WALL OF THE stable with Nitwit's apple clutched to her heart.

She'd peered in the window to make sure the place was empty. She preferred giving the mare her treats alone, with no witnesses to the silly things she said or the kisses she dropped on her nose. The mare, too, seemed to behave better without an audience, as if she were ashamed to admit she'd grown to like her awkward rider.

She hadn't expected to see Merry and Edward embracing, much less in that fashion! Merry had been on her knees, her arms pushing up Edward's shirt, her mouth nuzzling his belly.

His bare belly.

Muscles had rippled like cobbles at his stomach. Smooth and powerful, they'd tensed as Merry circled his navel with her tongue. A line of ink-black hair rose from the curving indentation, then spread outward over his chest. More muscle swelled there: broad and sunbrowned with fans of tendon at the side.

And he had nipples. Florence had never thought about men having nipples. Who could have guessed they'd be so fascinating? They were small and coppery and the tips poked through that cloud of hair in tiny rose-kissed peaks.

She pressed the apple to her throat, the tips of her own breasts tightening until they ached. She curled her tongue over her lip. She wanted to kiss his nipples. She wanted to rub her face in his hair. She wanted to run her hands up the long, hard curve of his thighs and cup his secret flesh.

He'd been aroused. His organ had swelled into the space between Merry's chin and neck, distorting the cloth of his trousers just as it had that night at the ball. The light from the stall window had limned the arcing shape. The end was round, ridged at the bottom. Big, she thought, with a deep, hot shudder. Big as a summer pippin. Perhaps it hurt to have one's body part grow so large. His expression might have been pained. His eyes had been closed, his face taut with the longing Merry stirred.

Florence's nails pierced the skin of Nitwit's treat.

The longing Merry stirred.

It was true, then. He did want the duke's daughter. Florence hadn't been special. That night in the Vances' conservatory, when he'd kissed her and changed her life, she'd merely been convenient.

Merry served as easily as she.

Her eyes burned but she did not cry. She pushed away from the stable and walked in stiff, measured steps towards the distant grove. When she'd gotten far enough not to be seen, she ran. When she'd disappeared deep enough into the trees, she stopped. She braced her hands on her knees and panted, her bodice soaked with sweat, her head swimming with exertion.

If she'd been wearing one of her Paris corsets, she'd have fainted. As it was, she had to sit, heedless of the dirt and the bugs and the crackle of last year's leaves. The roots of a gnarled old oak formed the arms of her chair, its trunk her back's support. She shut her eyes and everything she'd seen was there, seared into her memory. With a low cry, she pressed her hands to the damp, hot skin of her face, but even that could not shut the visions out.

Pandora's box had spilled its awful secret.

Bad enough she lusted after the brother of the man she meant to wed. She should have been grateful Merry had made pursuing him impossible.

But she wasn't.

She was sick with envy, sicker than she'd been at the loss of Buttercup. Her stomach was cramped, her throat tight, and her heart ached with the truth she'd feared to face. Her affection for Freddie had not saved her, nor her memory of her father's broken heart, nor the many hurts Edward had inflicted without her having done a thing to earn them. Nothing had saved her. Florence was lost.

Florence was in love with Greystowe's earl.

Chapter 10

MRS. FORSTER HAD JUST HELPED FREDDIE WITH HIS BED bath. According to the housekeeper, his morning tiff with Nigel had been of a severity to make the steward reluctant to offer aid.

"Grown men," she clucked as she gathered basins and towels. "Tussling like boys."

Freddie had the decency to look abashed. He sat by the window in a purple throne-backed chair, perhaps an indication that he had won the morning's fight. One leg of his silk pyjamas was slit to make room for his cast. A fine lawn shirt hung open at his chest. It was a nice chest, every bit as nice as Edward's. It was paler and not as broad but it had just as many muscles.

When Mrs. Forster saw who'd come in, she moved to button Freddie up.

"Oh, leave it," he said with a languid wave. "It's warm today and it's only Florence. I doubt my betrothed will faint at the sight of my manly glory."

The housekeeper muttered about "modern morals," but Florence could tell she wasn't truly angry. Freddie's voice stopped her at the door.

"Thank you, Mrs. Forster," he said, gentle and serious. "You've been an angel."

Mrs. Forster had saved her parting shot. "Guess I won't faint at the sight of your manly glory, either."

Freddie grinned at her broad, departing bustle, then offered his hand to Florence. "Good morning, sweetheart. To what do I owe this honor? I thought you'd be at your lessons."

Florence obeyed his urging to perch on the arm of his chair. Unwilling to meet his eyes, she stared at his chest where his breastbone divided two smooth curves of muscle. "Merry is gone. She and her maid left at dawn. I think she and Edward had a disagreement."

"Not over you, surely?"

"No," Florence conceded, but couldn't bring herself to explain. She could still see Edward's strained expression as Merry's mouth teased his belly; could still feel the emotions that stormed inside her when Lizzie broke the news. Merry was gone. She had tried to seduce the earl and the earl had sent her away. For too many reasons to count Florence should have been sorry to see her go. To her dismay, she was exultant. None of which she was about to tell Freddie.

Good-natured as ever, he stroked her cheek with the back of his fingers. "Very well. Never mind telling me why. I can guess. Edward must be kicking himself for not discouraging her sooner. I'm sure he didn't enjoy disappointing you."

"I . . . I'm all right," she said, and deliberately trailed her hand down his resting arm.

Freddie inhaled sharply in surprise. Their eyes met. His were wary, but he masked his caution with a smile. "What is it, Florence? What's troubling you?"

She played with the edge of the cotton that draped his chest. "Would you mind if I kissed you, Freddie?"

His jaw dropped. "Of . . . of course not, sweetheart. But—"

She leaned in before he could blather about innocence and honor and what her father would think if he knew. He fell silent as she braced her hand on the violet seatback beside his head. The fabric brought out the blue in his eyes, eyes as lovely as any she'd ever seen. His face was a pleasing arrangement of strong, smooth bones, his lips well cut and sensitive, his brows perfect winging arches. He was more than handsome: he was as comely as a poet's knight.

"Florence," he whispered as his golden lashes drifted down. Gathering her courage, she pressed her lips to his.

His mouth was soft. Remembering Edward, remembering Merry, she touched its seam with the tip of her tongue. Thankfully, Freddie guessed what she was about. He sighed and opened for her and met her wet, gentle stroke with his own. He knew this game better than she did. She was happy to let him take the lead. His arms gathered her closer, turned her, and pulled her onto his lap. Her breasts rested on his chest, her bottom on the top of his thighs. Despite his cast, she fit easily against him.

His kiss was delicate; careful, as if the least bit of force might break her. An angel might have been rocking her in warmth and kindness. The turmoil she'd felt when kissing Edward was absent, but so was the excitement. Nonetheless, the feelings Freddie stirred were pleasant. Her body relaxed as his fingers trailed down her neck, playing over her collarbones in long figure eights, as if he relished the texture of her skin.

Heartened by her progress, she slipped her fingers under the open edge of his shirt. When she brushed her thumb over the point of his nipple, he stiffened and pulled back. His face showed none of the tautness she'd seen in Edward's, only a brotherly sort of calm. Apparently, she did not have Merry's skill at rousing men.

"I'm sorry," she said, hanging her head. "I know I'm not good at this."

He smiled at her, pulled her hand from his chest, and kissed its knuckles. She felt uncomfortably like a child who was being humored.

"You did nothing wrong. But I think these are not matters we should rush. A woman's honor, once lost, can never be regained. What would your father think?"

"I knew you'd say that."

"You see? You don't feel comfortable, either." He stroked her hair with a warm cupped hand. "Don't be glum, sweetheart. Five months is not so long to wait."

Not for him, perhaps. But a lot could happen in five months. Rather than say so, she snuggled closer. Her movements seemed not to affect him. His manly part did not rise, nor did his heart beat wildly in his chest. Freddie remained what he'd always been: a perfect gentleman.

She wondered what he'd do if he knew his betrothed was not a perfect lady.

*   *   *

AUNT HYPATIA'S INVITATION COULD NOT HAVE COME AT A better time. Florence was desperate for distraction from her failure to seduce her fiancé, if only the distraction of a visit to one of the duchess's childhood friends. Oddly enough, the impending reunion seemed to make the duchess nervous. She fidgeted with her skirts and gloves, then draped her lace-ruffled elbow over the side of the open carriage. Her sigh was soft but audible.

"Is something wrong?" Florence asked.

Aunt Hypatia drummed her fingers on the victoria's curving door. "Just an old woman's memories. When you're my age I suspect you, too, will have the dubious pleasure of seeing the changes time can inflict on those one cares for."

"You're not old," Florence assured her.

Aunt Hypatia laughed, a soft, dry echo of her eldest nephew. "It's not the years, my dear. It's the bruises. But the friends of our childhood are the friends we treasure most. They're our link to the past. No one knows us so well or forgives us so much."

With those provocative words, the carriage pulled into a narrow, rutted lane. Low stone walls girded the road, along with pretty two-storied houses. The one at which they stopped stood out from the others by its fresh-scrubbed air. Half-timbered, with a clean thatch roof, it was not much larger than the vicarage in which Florence had grown up. A small garden surrounded the white limed walls. The gravel path to the door was perfectly straight, as were the low, blooming flowerbeds. Marigolds marched like soldiers down its length, in alternating stripes of orange and gold. The compulsively tidy display made Florence smile.

To her surprise, Aunt Hypatia touched her sleeve to stay her.

"Sit for a moment, dear. I believe I should tell you something of the woman you're about to meet. Catherine and I were girls together. Very dear friends. I have never known a creature so loyal, nor so protective of those she loves."

"But?" Florence prompted when the duchess paused.

"But she was disappointed young, by a man, as it happens. It has made her bitter and perhaps a trifle strange. I know you will not judge her. You're a kindly soul. But it might be best if you did not speak too much of your engagement to Freddie, even if she asks. She worries that other women will make the same mistake she did."

"I shall guard my words," Florence promised, her heart going out to this woman she'd never met. How easily might she step into those painful shoes herself! With more than her usual care, she helped the duchess from the carriage. She was the loyal one, Florence thought, to remain this true to a childhood friend.

A servant in brown twill and apron answered their rap on the door. She was as plain a woman as Florence had ever seen: young, but as stolid as a dockworker. Her eyes were dull in her weary face, her arms thick with muscle. Considering Aunt Hypatia's warning, Florence wondered if she'd been hired for her lack of male-attracting traits.

Inside the little house, the comical tidiness of the garden turned oppressive. The servant, probably a maid-of-all-work like Lizzie had been, led them to a small front parlor. The furniture was spotless and plain and completely unwelcoming, in the style of the days before the queen. Modern taste appeared only in the profusion of gewgaws that covered the polished surfaces of the room. The effect would have been friendly but for the regimental precision with which each item had been aligned. The candlesticks and doilies, the gilt-framed photographs and ceramic memento art seemed an army against the forces of disorder. Even the sunbeams that poured through the broad bow window could not diminish the effect of rigidly imposed control.

Interestingly enough, upon entering, their hostess strode briskly to the window and closed the drapes. "The carpets," she murmured over her shoulder, a gentle, mournful scold.

The hulking servant hung her head. "Sorry, ma'am. I thought your guests might like the light."

Her employer's sad little smile did not alter. Since she wasn't looking at them, Florence studied her with interest. Her figure was not as trim as Aunt Hypatia's, but it had not thickened much. Her hair retained a touch of blonde among its gray and her face, now seamed with age, must once have been very pretty. Her features still conveyed a sense of delicacy, like a fine bisque doll. Her house dress, neither fashionable nor noticeably the opposite, was of well-pressed and slightly faded black silk, as if she'd spent much of her life as a widow.

Hypatia's description of her as a woman disappointed by love hadn't struck her as widowlike. Could losing one's spouse to an early death sour one on the institution of marriage? Her father hadn't been that way, but perhaps Florence hadn't seen enough of life to know the forms that grief could take.

She composed herself on the hard green sofa, expecting the duchess's friend to turn and greet them. The woman, however, was not yet finished with her servant.

"Bertha," she said in a voice even softer than before. "Was that the butcher's boy I saw hanging about the back door this morning?"

A dull flush crept up the lowered face. "Jeb was only dropping off the meat."

"You know how I feel about my servants having followers."

"Yes, ma'am. I wouldn't do that to you. Not never."

By this time, Florence was feeling sorry for the embarrassed girl. When her eyes darted towards her mistress's guests, Florence offered a tiny smile. If the maid saw it, it did not abate her misery. "Shall I bring the tea now, ma'am?"

Their hostess patted the slump of the maid's big shoulder. "You know I'm only thinking of you, Bertha. A woman can so easily be led astray."

"Yes, ma'am. The tea?"

"Of course, Bertha. And use the tongs to arrange the cakes. You know I can't abide finger marks." With that, their hostess finally turned. Her smile was lovely; peaceful even, like a nun who had spent her life in prayer. Florence found herself warming to her, despite her peculiar treatment of her servant. She rose from the couch and offered as graceful a curtsey as she could. The woman seemed to appreciate the effort. Her smile curled more deeply into her cheeks.

"You must be Florence Fairleigh. Hypatia has written me of your many virtues. I am Catherine Exeter, the Honorable Miss Exeter until my father died. But that is ancient history. I hope you will call me Catherine, as my dear old friend Hypatia does. From all she has said, I feel as if I know you already."

"It . . . it would be my honor," Florence stammered, darting a startled look at Aunt Hypatia. Just how much had the duchess told her friend? She felt distinctly off balance as she settled back into her seat.

"You're engaged to Freddie Burbrooke, are you not?" Catherine asked, perching like a bird on the edge of a delicate green and white chair. Her demeanor spoke only of interest, polite but genuine.

"Yes," Florence answered, fighting her impulse to turn to the duchess for guidance. She knew she must not appear overly enthusiastic. "I think we shall suit. He is a kind man."

"I'm certain he seems so," Catherine said. "But a woman can never be too careful. The kindest face can hide a heart of stone, especially when that face belongs to a Burbrooke."

This extraordinary speech robbed Florence of hers.

"Catherine," said the duchess in almost as gentle a scold as her friend's.

As if it were a joke, Catherine released a musical laugh, one that must have charmed her suitors when she was young. "You're right, of course. I must not forget that nest of vipers is your family." Her eyes sparkled with humor as she patted the arm of the couch beside Hypatia. "The Burbrookes brought me you. For that I will always give thanks."

"We can both give thanks," said Hypatia, answering Catherine's smile with one of her own. "Now tell me, old friend, what gossip have I missed since I last stopped at Greystowe?"

The pair had much to catch up on and Florence was happy to relinquish the burden of conversation. Their speech was filled with exclamations like "no" and "indeed, it's true" and "who'd have thought she'd do such a thing?" Florence could tell they were enjoying themselves. As soon as the tea and cakes were comfortably dispersed, she rose to wander the room, taking care not to brush its ornaments.

A lovely fruitwood spinet sat in the farthest corner, with an old Church of England hymn spread open on its stand. She was tempted to sit and play, despite her indifferent skill. Instead, she touched the ornate silver frame of the single photograph on its top. An elegant young woman in rich modern dress gazed serenely out at Florence. The resemblance between her and Catherine Exeter was striking. She had the same sleek fair hair, the same doll-like perfection to her face. The photographer had captured not only her beauty but her confidence. Here was a female secure in her womanly charms. If Catherine Exeter had looked like this when she was young, Florence had a hard time imagining the man who could disappoint her.

"Ah," said Catherine now, "I see you've found the picture of my niece. Pretty, isn't she?"

"Beautiful," Florence agreed.

Her hostess crossed the threadbare carpet to stand behind her. With the tip of her finger, she made an infinitesimal adjustment to the picture Florence had just released. "She writes me every week, you know. Keeps me apprised of the doings of society. Foolishness, most of it. But my Imogene is a sensible girl. Married as well as a woman can, with her head and not her heart. Her husband gives her everything she wants."

"How . . . fortunate," Florence said, not sure how to respond. Despite her words, Catherine Exeter was frowning, as if the beautiful image did not completely satisfy.

"Yes," she said musingly, her lips turned down. "Fortunate. Keeps him wrapped around her finger. Only safe place for a man. My Imogene would never be so foolish as to fall for a Burbrooke."

Florence squinted at her hostess, perplexed by the strangeness of her tone. She seemed to be trying to convince herself of something she knew to be untrue. And what grievance could she have against the Burbrookes? Twice now she had mentioned them disparagingly.

"Catherine," Hypatia warned, but this time her friend did not let the dangerous topic drop.

"No, Hypatia," she said, her eyes remaining on Florence. "The girl has a right to know what she's getting into. Oh, I don't say Freddie is the worst of the Greystowe males. I leave that honor to his brother. But the blood is bad. It chills their hearts and forks their tongues. No one can hold them, neither with beauty nor with charm. By all means, take what you need from them, but do not give them your trust; do not give them your love. If you do, you'll spend your life ruing the day."

Florence's heart beat unevenly in her throat. The woman's claims struck a chord she could not silence. She had given Edward her love and she did indeed rue the day. And Freddie—could he be cold? Was that why he didn't respond to her kisses? But no. She shook herself free of her fear. Freddie liked her; that could not be feigned. As for Edward, if he broke her heart, it would be her fault, not his. He had never promised her anything. He might be moody and brusque, but she'd wager her soul that he was honest.

"I'm sure you must be mistaken," she said, somewhat breathless beneath the intensity of Catherine's gaze. "Edward and . . . and Freddie are very good men."

"The best," Hypatia seconded. She had risen as well and now laid a soothing hand on Catherine's back. "Neither of them are anything like their father."

Catherine gave a little shudder before her expression cleared.

"Perhaps," she said. "But you must promise me"—she captured Florence's hands—"should they ever hurt you, should you ever need help, you'll do me the honor of turning to me."

Florence hadn't the faintest notion what to say. Luckily, Aunt Hypatia loosened Catherine's grip on her hands. "I'm sure that won't be necessary," she said. "My goddaughter is a sensible girl."

Her friend blinked. "Good. Good. I am gratified to hear it. But should you need me do not hesitate to ask."

The duchess stroked the back of Catherine's neck where it rose above the ruffled black silk of her collar. It was, for her, a gesture of uncommon tenderness. "Perhaps we should be going, my dear. We don't wish to overstay our welcome."

"Never," said her friend with a warm, staunch smile. "You are always welcome here. But I know you must have other calls. Letty Cowles will never forgive me if I keep you to myself. She has two new grandchildren, you know. Boys."

Hypatia's laugh was comfortable. "Indeed, we must not rob her of her chance to crow."

The two women clasped shoulders and exchanged affectionate kisses. Florence could see the shadow of their youth in their smiles; the ease of their lifelong friendship. Abruptly, she regretted the departure of Merry Vance. Would she ever be known by anyone as Catherine and Hypatia knew each other: her flaws forgiven, her foibles understood?

She waited until the coachman flicked the reins across the horses' backs to ask the question that had been pressing on her mind. "Catherine is the woman Edward's father jilted, isn't she?"

"Yes," Hypatia admitted, twisting her palm over the head of her ivory cane. "Just one of his many sins. The odd thing is, I think Stephen truly loved her. He always treated Edward's mother coolly, as if it were her fault she'd been born the daughter of a duke. Poor thing never knew what she'd done wrong. Always fluttering about trying to make it up to him."

Florence shivered in spite of the heat. She prayed she'd never know that kind of pain.

EDWARD COULD TELL FLORENCE WASN'T WELL. OFF HER feed, Jenkyns would have said. She didn't ride, didn't laugh, didn't sneak off to the kennel to spoil the dogs. Without a hint of her old anxiety, she followed the duchess on her round of local calls, taking tea with the old ladies as if life held nothing more interesting than grandchildren's antics or the beadle's wife trying to pretend a ten-year-old dress was new. They even went to visit that loony old bat, Catherine Exeter, the one whose door the boys in the village made a dare of touching. Considering her history, Edward knew he ought to make allowances, but she had once pelted three-year-old Freddie with a brace of windfall apples. Called him a spawn of the devil, simply because he'd tumbled over her wall during a game of hide-and-seek. She'd apologized later, and their mother had accepted, but Edward had never been able to forgive her. He didn't care how many socks she knitted for the poor or what a God-fearing Christian she was.

If Florence could visit a woman like that without complaint, there was definitely something wrong.

Even Aunt Hypatia noted her loss of verve.

"Missing your friend?" she probed one night at dinner. "It's a shame she had to leave, but Edward could take over your lessons."

Florence shook her head. "I'm just a bit homesick. Your friends remind me of the ladies I knew in Keswick."

"Hmpf," said Aunt Hypatia.

Edward longed to echo her skepticism. A bit of homesickness didn't put circles under a girl's eyes or cause her to pick at her food like a bird. He couldn't remember the last time Florence had looked directly at him. As uncomfortable as that intimacy could be, he found he missed it. And what did she mean by shaking her head at the suggestion that he help her with her horsemanship? He knew such an arrangement was inadvisable, but that she would dismiss it out of hand pricked him like a nettle. Irritating chit. Did she think he'd sent Merry Vance away to spite her?

His fingers tightened on the stem of his wineglass. Given his behavior in the past, she might believe just that.

"You'll ride with me tomorrow," he announced. "You mustn't forget what you've learned."

She shot him a startled look, her eyes like polished beryl in the rain. He'd forgotten what her gaze could do to him, how it seemed to reach inside and tug directly on his groin. Beneath the shadows of the table, he felt himself start to fill. The head of his cock stretched down his trouser leg. A tide of heat that had nothing to do with the Mulligatawny soup rose threateningly up his neck. He looked away before it could reach his face.

"If you truly wish it," she said, quiet and deferential, "I'd be happy to ride with you."

The deference broke his temper.

"If I didn't wish it, I wouldn't have asked," he snapped.

His aunt lifted her brows but Edward ignored their unspoken question. He'd be damned if he'd explain himself. After a moment, the duchess returned her attention to the curried broth.

"Good," she said her voice both mild and dry. "We wouldn't want Freddie's intended growing bored."

EDWARD REFUSED TO CONSIDER WHAT HE WAS DOING, though he suspected his restless night had been due to dreams of having Florence to himself. He ignored the quickening of his pulse as he boosted her into the saddle. Nothing was going to happen today. Nothing. This prickle of excitement he felt was mere wishful thinking. But the wishes grew deeper as he noted how flatteringly she had dressed. She wore the same form-fitting blue habit that had dried his throat in London, the one that made her breast look provokingly like a pigeon's and her waist a circle a man could span in his hands. Her boots were black and laced to the bottom of her calves. He tried not to hold them any longer than it took to place her left foot in the stirrup.

He couldn't say if he was grateful or annoyed that she did not speak except to thank him.

Clicking Samson to a trot, he headed for the northern border of the estate, to the ruins of the original Greystowe Hall. Under the depredations of the eleventh earl, their land had shrunk to a few surrounding acres. When Edward's grandfather restored the family fortunes and rebuilt, he'd raided the tumbled fortress for its stone. Now only its outlines could be seen between the weeds. Edward's father had brought him here many times. *This is the fruit of demon drink,* he'd say. *Succumb to liquor and games of chance and your destruction will be as sure.*

His father would have shuddered to know how romantic young Edward found the site. Oh, the earl's lessons had found their mark but, to Edward, this was a place where fairies might dance or dragons breathe their last breath. No doubt he shouldn't have brought Florence to a spot so meaningful to him, or so isolated, but at present he found it difficult to be sensible.

"My," she marveled in her soft, country voice, "what a wonderful place. I can just picture you and Freddie here, having imaginary sword fights with a pair of sticks."

"Broom handles," he confessed, and swung off his blowing horse. Many women would have dismissed the ruin as a useless pile of rocks. He was gratified by her reaction. He would admit it, he decided. He would enjoy it. This day was a harmless pleasure. For once he would not spoil the delight of her company with thoughts of all he must not do. When he helped her down from Nitwit, he allowed himself to relish the brief, gloved clasp of her hands. His body was alive in every cell, pulsing, humming. The air was sweeter, the ground springier.

He only wished Florence could share a portion of his joy.

She followed his lead as they walked the horses side by side along the old foundation. She'd kept up with him on the ride. He'd barely had to hold Samson back. He wondered if he ought to compliment her on her skill, but that seemed too great a divulgence. No doubt

Merry had told her how much she had improved. No doubt she knew it herself.

They stopped before a long vista: checkerboard fields and sheep pasture and, in the misty, rolling distance, the first blue rise of the Peaks. Edward removed the horses' bridles. Samson wouldn't wander far and Nitwit would not leave him. The stallion was the master of the stable, certainly the master of the mares. Like two old friends, the horses began tearing grass from the same patch of ground. Florence watched them bump shoulders as if her thoughts were far away, her expression not so much sad as blank. Consequences be damned, Edward thought. He couldn't stand to see her spirits quashed.

"Won't you tell me what's wrong?" he said. "I know more has been bothering you than missing home."

If his concern surprised her, she did not show it. Instead, she fixed him with as level a gaze as he'd ever seen her use. Florence tended to wear her emotions on her sleeve, but he could not read them now.

"I've been wondering about women," she said. "Women's feelings."

Edward coughed, not sure he was prepared to discover where this led. "Women's feelings?"

"Yes." She folded her hands over her waist, the pose perversely prim. "I've been wondering if they are supposed to have the same needs that men do, or if such feelings are exclusive to the male sex."

The flush Edward had managed to avoid the night before blazed like fire across his skin. Of all the things to ask him! He didn't want to think what had inspired the question, but he could not ignore it, not when it so plainly distressed her. Lord, though—what had she and Freddie been getting up to? Stalling for time, he raked his hair back with his hand.

"Of course women have feelings," he said. "I can't swear they're the same as men's, but from the evidence I've seen, they're very similar."

Florence's eyes did not leave his. "And they were ordinary, decent women who provided this evidence? Not—" She waved her arm, reluctant to give a name to women who were otherwise.

This sign of her old diffidence reassured him. He put his hand to her shoulder. "Yes. Ordinary, decent women. Well born. Gently bred. Neither depraved in spirit nor sick in their minds. I assure you, it's quite natural for a woman to feel physical desire."

She pressed her lips together and her gaze evaded his. From chin to brow, her face was as pink as a budded rose.

"Florence." Giving in to temptation, he stroked the velvet warmth of her cheek. The sensation made him want to cry with pleasure, but he did nothing to intensify the caress. He gentled his voice. That was his caress. That was the secret expression of his love. "Has someone been telling you decent women don't feel desire?"

She shook her head, quick and definite, but he wasn't sure he believed her. He'd seen tracts himself, written by doctors, claiming that well-bred ladies did not like the marriage bed.

"It's perfectly natural," he repeated. "What's more, a woman is entitled to the same pleasure as a man in the act of love."

The color in her cheeks heightened from rose to scarlet. For a moment, she did nothing but bite her bottom lip. Then her eyes lifted again to his, bravely, determinedly, but with such uncertainty he wished he had the right to embrace her.

"I'm afraid I don't know what you mean," she said. "Oh, not about the act of love. I grew up in the country, after all. But the other, the pleasure part. I don't—I'm not certain I understand."

Edward's groan would have tumbled a few more stones if he'd dared let it out. Any other woman he would have sent to her fiancé. Such matters were best sorted out between man and wife. Unfortunately, Florence's fiancé was Freddie. For all his brother's popularity with the fairer sex, his actual experience with women was a mystery Edward didn't care to plumb. Would Freddie know how to answer Florence's question? Would he wish to if he could? Edward didn't want to think his brother too selfish to enlighten his betrothed, but he was forced to acknowledge he might be too embarrassed.

Oh, Lord, he thought, I shouldn't do this. I shouldn't even consider it.

But it was more than possible he'd be doing Freddie a favor. Freddie cared for Florence. If she came to her conjugal bed with a few hints as to what went on, her wedding night might not be the catastrophe Edward feared. Moreover, Florence deserved to know the answer.

Sighing, he pulled her trembling form against his chest. The way she snuggled against him, trusting and soft, made him want to hold her there forever.

"I'll show you," he said, his throat tight. "But only so you'll know and only if you promise this stays between us."

At last, he had succeeded in shocking her. She tipped her head back to see his face, her eyes round, her rosy mouth agape. "You'll show me?"

He could not help himself. He had wanted her too long, with more than his body, with more even than his heart. She called to the part of him that could not change, that would love her forever, no matter what life brought them both. With a groan of agonized pleasure, he dipped his head and kissed her.

She did not resist. Indeed, she seemed to melt against him: her mouth, her body, all her softness pressing the parts of him that needed pressing most. The unexpected capitulation drove everything but hunger from his mind. He couldn't remember the difference between what he'd intended and what he hadn't. He could only want; could only seize the moment and hold it tight.

He gripped her bottom and lifted her into his groin. The added pressure made his erection throb intensely enough to hurt. He drove deep into her mouth, needing to taste, to claim, to assuage every instant of longing since he'd held her last. When he suckled her tongue she made a sound like a startled dove. His head spun. She was holding him. Her arms clung to his back, her hands to his shoulders. He wanted to rip off her gloves and bite the tips of her fingers. He wanted to toss her habit over her head and sink forever into her sex. Instead, he hugged her so fiercely she gasped.

He could not bring himself to release her mouth, not even to apologize for being rough. Impatient beyond bearing, and knowing they could not stand here in the open, he swept her off her feet and carried her like a child to the half-ruined hulk of the old hearth.

"Wh-what are you doing?" she said as he set her down. Blood burned in her cheeks, in her bee-stung lips. Her hair had fallen, a shining chestnut gleam across her heaving breasts. Her eyes blazed with wants he doubted she could have named. She looked a perfect wanton. An innocent wanton.

He could not answer her question. He didn't know what he was doing. Instead, he kissed her again, deeply, working his mouth into hers until she moaned and went limp. Only his weight held her up against the chimney, his knees bent to align their heights, his hips grinding slowly over hers. His cock was so hard, so sensitive, he seemed to feel each fold of cloth between them. Florence felt it, too: the pressure of his rigid penis against her mons. The flesh between her legs was very warm. It would be wet, he thought. It would be weeping now for him.

With a groan, he burrowed harder. Her nails pricked his nape. Something shifted inside him, dark and forbidden. He pulled her arms away and pressed them, wide and straight, to the sun-warmed stones above her head. He held her wrists as if his hands were shackles, as if she were the prisoner of his desires. The image whipped him like a lash. His body clamored for him to take her, here, like this, until this terrible desire was sated.

"What are you doing?" she said again, tremulous, her breath panting against his jaw.

He eased his head away, still holding her by the wrists. When he spoke, he scarcely recognized his voice. "I'm showing you."

"Sh-showing me?"

"What desire is."

"But—" She bit her lower lip, swollen now from his kisses. "I already know that."

He could have cried from the bolt of lust that speared his loins. He had to ease his hips away from hers for fear of spilling like the greenest boy. He did not, however, give her a chance to escape. Not that she showed any signs of wanting to. Despite her obvious misgivings, she remained as he'd positioned her: her thighs slightly spread, her arms lifted obediently above her head. Her submission, even her fear, was an aphrodisiac he was reluctant to acknowledge. But he could not deny its allure, nor pull himself away. The best he could do was try to gentle the harshness of his voice.

"Desire comes first," he said, the words hoarser than he wished. "Then pleasure. One builds on the other. Depends on the other." He released one wrist to cup the heated fullness of her breast. Its nipple pressed discernibly through her bodice. He turned his palm and it hardened even more. "Do you feel it? The ache of wanting? In your breasts? Between your legs?"

She nodded, shakily, and he kissed her in reward; kissed her until his head pounded in time with his cock, until his passion burst from his chest in a primitive, animal growl. He kneaded her breast, pinching the sensitive tip, raking the swollen areola with his nails. She began to squirm against the trap of his body, not to get away but to get more. He knew how she felt; oh, did he know. He lowered his head to her breast and bit its peak.

"Edward," she gasped, pushing weakly at his shoulders. "I think I understand this part well enough."

He lifted his head to meet her eyes. He could barely catch his breath. "I'll need to touch you to show you what pleasure is. I'll need to put my fingers between your legs and stroke your little pussy."

"M-my pussy?"

In spite of himself, he smiled. What an innocent she was. He nipped the curve of her chin. "I could call it your love garden, if you prefer. Or Cupid's alley. Or perhaps your buttered crumpet?" She pleased him with a giggle. "In any case, you'll know what it is soon enough . . . if you choose to let me go on."

She thought for a moment, then squared her shoulders. "I do. I do choose to let you."

His tension sighed from him. What a brave little darling she was, what a sweet, untouched, juicy plum. He played his lips over hers, letting their breath mingle in increasingly urgent gusts, letting her taste just the tip of his tongue. When she whimpered, he gave her more. When she moaned, he gave her all. Her fears thus distracted, he gathered up her skirts, slowly, taking the petticoats, too, warming her thinly clad legs with his own. When the mass of cloth reached her waist, she broke free of the kiss.

"Shall I hold my skirts?" she whispered.

"Yes," he said, just as softly. "I may want both my hands."

"If you do, you'll have to let go of my other wrist."

He laughed without sound. Even now, Florence could be practical. He pulled her still trapped hand to his mouth. Sweeping his tongue under the edge of her glove, he bit the plump flesh beneath her thumb. When she shuddered, his body did as well, hardening until the pain of wanting her stung in his eyes like tears. When he released her, his hand shook as badly as hers. Gritting his teeth, he took one step back to look at what he'd bared. Her legs, covered by the fine, lacy drawers, were as long and curvy as he remembered, her hands small against the bundle of sea-struck blue. Her boots—he shut his eyes at a spasm of longing—clung to her ankles with loverlike devotion. He hadn't planned on going to his knees, but his legs would not hold him. He fell and she drew a startled breath. A second later his hands wrapped the ankle of her shoes.

"Oh," she said as his fingers kneaded the bone beneath the kid. "Oh, my."

He smiled when he saw her toes curl, then slid his hands higher. She was sensitive, his Florence: a well-tuned violin. He pressed his temple to her hip and blew softly through the lawn that covered her mons. Her shiver delighted him more than another's full-fledged moan.

"Just a little more," he said, drawing a teasing circle on her calf. "Just a little further and you'll know."

Her thighs trembled when he stroked them. He could scent her now, musky and sweet. Heart pounding, he nuzzled the open slit of her drawers. His hands followed, parting the sheer cotton, finding the crisp, tightly gathered curls. She tensed but did not move away. He sensed her waiting with bated breath. He combed her thatch to pet her mound. How wonderful were these secrets, and what a marvel that

she would share them with him! Gently, he rubbed the tender cushion, gently, until the soothing strokes convinced her to relax. Then he
drew one thumb, light as goosedown, over the shy, warm furrow of
her lips. Tense or no, she was wet. Moisture painted his skin and hers,
rich and fragrant and slick. That he had the power to call it from her
both humbled and aroused.

"This is your pussy," he said, low and husky. "This and the secrets
that lay within. I'd like to touch them if you'd let me. I'd like to show
you the magic they can do."

"This is the pleasure part?"

He smiled and kissed her tangled curls. "Yes. This is the pleasure
part." Hearing no protest, he parted her with his thumbs, rubbing
into and up her folds. Her skin was sleek as satin here, oiled with desire. She jumped when he brushed her clitoris. Smiling again, he
pressed it lightly, the pad of each thumb compressing either side. This
time his reward was a violent shiver. She dropped one hand over his
as if to stop him, then just as nervously withdrew.

"Are you sure this is where you're supposed to be?" she asked.

"I'm sure," he laughed, and squeezed more firmly. This time she
moaned. "This is the secret to a woman's pleasure. This little pink bud
of flesh."

"But it feels so strange. It—oh!" she gasped as his mouth covered
the bundle of nerves. Her hips canted forward, innocently eager. Edward's blood roared in his ears. He hadn't known he was going to do
this until he did. She tasted of the sea, of spice and heaven. His tongue
stroked. His lips suckled. His fingers spread and rubbed her plumping sex.

"Oh," she cried, her head falling back against the ruined wall. "It
almost hurts."

He did not heed the words, only the tone, only the hand that fluttered to his hair to press him closer. He drove her up the slope to climax, savoring every gasp of surprise, every moan of longing. He
craved her pleasure as a starving man craves food. This was Florence.
This was the woman he loved. He used everything his lovers had
taught him: when to push, when to tease, when to murmur things he
wished to do. Most of all, he listened to her body. Her tremors told
him what she liked, the tensing of her thighs, her ever-tightening
grip on his head. For that, no other woman could guide him. This act
was for her alone. When she died the little death, his soul exulted at
her cry. He slid the tip of his finger into her passage, feeling the con-
tractions at her barrier as his mouth swept her over once again. He

didn't need to do this. He'd shown her what he promised. But he couldn't let her go. This was all he would have of her. This first knowledge of her body. This first introduction to her bliss.

He wanted to make it as memorable as he could.

At the fifth orgasm, her knees gave way. She fell against him, taking him by surprise and tumbling them both to the grass. His body surged at the pleasant shock of her weight, remembering all at once that it had needs as powerful as hers.

More powerful, he thought, fighting an urge to do more than run his hands down the length of her back. Unlike her, he'd tasted the joys his cock could know. He knew what it was to slide into a woman's warmth when he was hard enough to scream.

Of course, he'd never known what it was to do it with a heart wound tight by love.

He'd thought she would lay there. He'd thought he would hold her as she calmed. Apparently, Florence did not wish to calm. She squirmed up his body and mouthed the bend of his jaw. Her lips brushed a runaway pulse.

"Show me," she said. "Show me how I can pleasure you."

It was a demand he dared not meet. He made a noise, a low, threatening rumble in his chest.

"Show me," she insisted, her hair hanging round them in a lemon-scented fall.

He didn't know how it had happened, but her wrists were in his hands again. He had manacled them; stretched them out from her sides. He knew he ought to release her. He knew, but he could not. His legs were splayed beneath her. Her thighs lay over his sex. He wanted to imprison them as well, to make his legs a second trap.

"Don't ask that of me," he said through gritted teeth.

She kissed his mouth, a girlish press with an intoxicating hint of tongue. "It's only fair, Edward."

The way she said his name undid him: low and throbbing, as if it held a meaning for her heart. He rolled her beneath him, pressing her into the ground with his greater size and weight. Now he had her. Now she could not get away. He cupped her head between his hands and fed his passion through their mouths.

"Oh," she moaned, gasping for air. "It hurts again."

He nearly came. He had to lift his hips and when he did her hand slipped into the space between them. Before he could stop her, she cupped his straining sex. His body flinched, a great, nerve-jolting shock. He could not speak for the effort it took to hold his climax back. Sweat broke out all over his body.

"Does it hurt for you?" she whispered, gently rubbing him up and down. "Does it hurt when you get big like this?"

"Take it out," he rasped. "Jesus-Mary. Open my trousers and take it out."

But he did it before she could, fumbling with the fastenings, nearly ripping his crumpled linen. His cock fell into her hand as if it knew its rightful home. He was thick, hot, pulsing with ungovernable desire. She clasped him lightly. Her hand was damp and warm and so small her fingers barely met around his shaft.

"Florence," he groaned, muscles jumping uncontrollably in his thighs. She was killing him with that light, curious grasp, sliding over him from balls to crown. The caress was almost too much but he was dying for more. She seemed to sense it. She held him harder. She squeezed him in her tender hand and pushed her tightened fist along his length.

The top of his head seemed to lift from his skull. Pressure built in his groin, swelling in his stones, in his shaft. Instinct took over. He cursed, thrust his hand inside her drawers to clear his path. He pushed forward. His crest touched her parted lips. She was at his mercy and he was huge. Desperate. A single stroke from coming. He groaned and squeezed his tip inside her. Nerves fired and screamed. She was wet. Hot. For him. The earth seemed to tremble at her body's silken clasp.

"Edward," she gasped.

There was fear in the sound. He hovered, trembling, yearning to break the fragile barrier and make her his. She would accept him, he knew. Her fluid heat told him that. He wanted to show her the joy men and women could share more than he wanted his next breath. But he could not do it. He could not soil his brother's bride. Not even out of love.

With a tortured groan, he tore himself away. He wrapped his arms around his shins and pressed his forehead to his knees. Only by holding himself could he keep from taking her where she lay. He cursed until he thought he must be frightening her.

She was slower to sit up. When she did she laid her hand on the back of his head.

"Go," he said, stiffening under the touch. "Go now before I hurt you."

No doubt he had already. No doubt the words were bad enough.

She pulled away and rose. Heart aching, he listened to her shaking down her skirts. For a moment she stood at his side. She did not argue, merely brushed his hair behind his ear, the gesture sweeter than he deserved. He thought she would speak then, but she walked away in silence and left him to his regrets.

OHGOD, OHGOD, THOUGHT FLORENCE, THE REFRAIN UNCON-trollable. She had to pull Nitwit up before she reached the house, so shattered were her nerves. She straightened her hair as well as she could, securing it with what pins she could find among the strands. Her lips burned from Edward's kisses, her breasts from his touch. Indeed, her whole body seemed to vibrate with the pleasure he had shown her.

And when she'd touched him—

His blood had drummed beneath his skin. His organ had length-ened and swelled. And he'd pressed its silken head against her flesh as if it would die without a home.

She cupped the place he'd put his mouth. Her pussy, he'd called it. It was still warm, still pulsing and liquid, as if pleasure were a sound that could echo down the years.

Oh, God, what had she done? Certainly nothing a respectable fi-ancée should do.

The thought chilled her. Was she wrong to marry Freddie when she had these feelings for his brother and not for him? But Freddie didn't seem to want a wife who had those feelings. No matter what Edward said about them being normal, surely Freddie was a better guide to what a gentlewoman ought to be?

Overcome by confusion, she clutched her hands before her mouth. Her body and, yes, her heart had felt lighter with Edward than they ever had before. Which didn't mean she ought to listen to them. Ed-ward didn't offer her safety or affection or anything like a future. Ed-ward only offered heartache. Even if, by some miracle, he were to think of her as a wife, he couldn't be what she needed in a husband, what she'd known she needed since the time she'd found her big, jovial father weeping over a pair of her mother's gloves.

Freddie was what she needed: Freddie's friendship, Freddie's quiet, steady love. He would never break her heart; would never leave her bereft of all that made life worthwhile. And she could be what he needed. She knew she could.

She only had to push these feelings for his brother from her soul.

Chapter 11

"YOU'RE TREATING HER LIKE A NUN," EDWARD SAID.

Propped against a mound of pillows in his bed, Freddie was trying to scratch beneath his bandages with a billiard cue. On the table beside him two novels lay open, along with a deck of playing cards, a decanter of port, a half-written letter, and a slowly bruising bowl of fruit. Edward recognized the signs of boredom but was not inclined to sympathize. Bored or not, Freddie had responsibilities. Edward intended to see that he upheld them.

If some of his anger was self-directed, that did not lessen Freddie's obligation.

Seemingly unimpressed by Edward's outrage, Freddie squinted at his sibling. "Did Florence tell you she felt like a nun?"

"Never mind what she told me. It's got to stop."

Freddie set down the stick. "Does it, now?"

"Yes, damn it!"

"You know, Edward"—Freddie cocked his head—"when you get angry, there's a big blue vein that ticks at the side of your neck."

Edward swore, then shoved his hands into his pockets. He could feel the vein ticking himself. "You need to take this seriously, Freddie. Florence is a grown woman. Healthy. Affectionate. With all that implies. She has a right to be treated with a certain warmth."

"If I understand what you mean by 'a certain warmth,' I'd rather not."

Edward blinked. "You'd rather not."

Freddie swung his legs over the side of his bed, grimacing when the injured limb took a moment to settle comfortably. "I'd rather not push Florence into a physical relationship. I want her to be able to back out of this wedding if she changes her mind."

Edward was so overcome with objections he pressed his fist to the furrow above his brows. If Freddie didn't do something about Florence, Edward doubted he'd survive the summer with his sanity intact. Seeing her was too painful: knowing she had needs Freddie wasn't satisfying, needs Edward would be all too happy to satisfy himself. At least once they were married, his oversight would not be necessary. He could leave the newly weds to themselves.

He was still shaking his head when Freddie hobbled over to take his arm. "I can't force her. It wouldn't be fair."

"Nobody's talking about force. Florence is fond of you, as I assume you are of her. She doesn't disgust you, does she?"

Freddie looked away. "Of course she doesn't."

"Are you reluctant because you think she'll make you miserable?"

"No one could think that."

"Then do it, Freddie. Treat her like a woman. You have to face it someday. You'd like children, wouldn't you?"

"You know I would." Freddie's voice was rough. He drew a ragged breath and let it out. "Very well. I'll do it. I'll treat her . . . warmly. But I won't compromise her virtue. You mustn't ask that."

"I don't," Edward said, his stomach tightening in contradiction to his relief. This was good. Freddie was agreeing. "Just stop treating her like a brother."

"I shall be a perfect Casanova." Freddie's face twisted. He turned his back. "You can leave now. You've made your point—though I doubt it's what you really want."

This last was muttered so far beneath Freddie's breath Edward wasn't certain he'd heard. Doubt stopped him at the door. "Of course it's what I want. Your happiness is important to me."

"And hers?"

"And hers," Edward agreed, forcing a lightness he did not feel.

Freddie said nothing to that, simply stood in a shaft of sun, balanced on his one sound leg. A breeze fluttered his shirt around his broad rower's back. Despite his injury, he looked strong: a graceful young man in his prime. His head, however, was bowed in defeat.

Edward gritted his teeth. This arrangement was best for all of them. He could not allow himself to doubt it. Whatever value he personally put on the pleasures of the flesh, by most people's standards, Freddie would make the better husband. Without even straining, Edward could name half a dozen women who'd jump at the chance to marry him, no matter that he was the younger son. Attentive, amusing, even-tempered, were it not for the unfortunate propensities of his past, Freddie would be a paragon. Once he gave Florence's charms a chance to act on him, Edward was certain those other needs would fade. Freddie had no reason to act defeated; this match was the saving of all their dreams.

All their dreams but his.

The thought slipped past his defenses like a thief. Sternly, grimly, he paid it no mind. The earl of Greystowe could not afford to be chasing dreams.

FREDDIE INVITED HER TO DINE IN THE ORANGERY, SAYING they were due a nice evening alone. Florence was both glad and anxious at the prospect. She welcomed the chance to prove she could put her feelings for Edward behind her, but her guilt interfered with her intention to focus on her betrothed. She'd never done anything as terrible as what she'd done with Edward in the ruins, much less tried to keep it a secret. Her father always said a marriage could not be founded on a lie, but he'd also said one should consider how deeply a truth would wound. If Freddie knew this particular truth, would it shatter his love for his brother? And if it did, what would that do to Edward? Did Freddie have to be told if she promised in her heart it would never happen again?

She could not sort out the right of it, no matter how she tried, and Freddie's arrival did not help. Considering his stated purpose, his mood was decidedly odd. He sniped at Nigel as the steward wheeled him into the small conservatory. The argument was nothing new, but the genuine edge to his anger was. As always, Nigel bore it stoically, wishing Florence a pleasant evening as he withdrew.

"Freddie—" Florence began to chide.

Freddie grimaced, then swatted the air in front of his face as if that would disperse his temper. "I know. I'm a beast. But from now on, I'll behave."

"You always behave with me."

"At least there's that. Ah, sweetheart. Let's forget how we've begun and try to enjoy the night." He surveyed the cloth-covered table that sat among the fruiting trees. A trio of candles scattered light off the crystal and plate, while a centerpiece of deep pink peonies added their perfume to the citrus-scented air. Freddie touched a waxen petal. "How prettily Mrs. Forster has arranged this. We shall dine as if we lived in the land of faerie."

"It was Lizzie," Florence said. "My maid. I'm afraid she has a romantic streak."

Freddie smiled. "Nothing wrong with romance. I could do with more of it myself."

But the meal was not romantic at all. Silence reigned over the lobster bisque and stretched through the pigeon pie. Freddie rallied over the lemon sorbet, sharing an amusing anecdote about a friend who accidentally locked himself in his father's icehouse.

"He was a good fellow," he finished with a wistful sigh. "Had his second child last year."

Florence patted his hand. "You'll be a good father."

Her claim seemed to disturb him. He rubbed a spot between his brows. Behind him, the orangery's glass was a mist-sheened mirror. Darkness had fallen while they ate. The night hummed with insects, as nights must have hummed since the dawn of time. Florence had the sudden, strange sensation that she and Freddie were alone in all the world. She could not hear the life of Greystowe from where she sat: the hiss of the gaslights, the servants' footsteps going to and fro. Only the crickets kept them company.

Their imaginary solitude weighed on her with a portent she did not understand.

Would she feel this way when they were married? Would she be lonely then, too? Disconcerted, she watched Freddie and his reflection turn a silver spoon through the remains of his melted ice.

"You look tired," she said. "Shall I call Nigel to wheel you back to your room?"

"No!" he said, more sharply than she'd expected. He seemed to hear the sharpness, too, and regret it. "Forgive me, Florence. I didn't mean for our dinner to turn out like this. I meant—" He made a face in which she could decipher only frustration. "I meant something quite different, but it seems I cannot do what I intended."

He wrapped his hands around the edge of the table, fingers on the top, thumbs on the bottom. The pose was that of a man bracing for trouble, and Florence found herself bracing, too.

"Florence," he began. "I've been thinking about yesterday. About our kiss."

Dread fluttered in her breast. Was he angry? Would he berate her for what she'd done?

"I know I shouldn't have been so forward," she said to the napkin in her lap. "I promise it won't happen again."

Freddie touched the side of her lowered head. "Don't apologize. What you did wasn't wrong. Not for a couple who care about each other, who are engaged."

"Then what have I done to upset you?" She did not plan for the question to be a cry, but it came out as it would. "If you'd only tell me, I would stop."

"Oh, Florence." He cupped her chin to press a gentle kiss to her trembling lips. "You are too good, my dear. That's why I have to tell you this."

"Tell me what?"

"That you must not expect— That I'm not—" He filled his lungs with air and began again. "I'm not a greatly physical man. Please believe me when I say I care for you, even love you, and wish you all the happiness in the world. But if what you want from marriage is a close physical relationship, I fear you're doomed to disappointment with me. I fear you'd be better crying off."

Florence felt as if he'd struck her. He wanted her to cry off? To give up everything she'd dreamed of? A home, a family, a little security and a good, kind man to share it with? To be rejected by Edward was one thing. For that she blamed her own stupidity. But to be hurt here, where she'd believed herself safe, where she'd laid her modest hopes in perfect confidence that they'd be met was something she'd never prepared for. Her mind could not encompass her shock, not to mention her shame. Again. Again she was cast aside.

It must be a punishment for what she'd done. She'd made her vow to be true to him too late. Her napkin fell to the floor as she pushed stiffly to her feet. "You don't want to marry me."

"No." He caught her hands and squeezed. "That's not what I meant at all. I'd be honored to marry you. You've no idea how deeply I value your affection. But I've been thinking, perhaps, you should not want to marry me."

Her blood was ice, her eyes searing hot. She knew he was being kind. It was his way: a gentleman to the last. She did not deserve to marry a man like him.

"If you wish it," she said, blinking back tears, "I shall release you from your promise."

Instead, he released her hands. "It's not what *I* wish, Florence."

She could not bear his gentle lies. "Please leave," she said with what dignity she could pull around her. "I wish to be alone."

"Are you sure, sweetheart? I could—"

"Please," she repeated, cutting him off.

She barely noticed the trouble it caused him to turn the chair. It was an unwieldy thing, meant to be pushed by another. With an effort, he forced the contraption across the threshold. "I'll speak to you in the morning. Please, Florence, don't decide anything without me."

She nodded, unable to trust her voice.

She did not cry until the crickets drowned out his wheels.

*   *   *

EDWARD REMAINED IN THE LIBRARY LONG AFTER HIS INTER-
est in its contents had palled. His private suite was in the family wing
and the passage outside it led directly past the orangery. He hadn't
wanted to hear Freddie and Florence, nor remind them of his exis-
tence. As a result, here he stayed, a specter by the high French windows, nursing his second glass of brandy for the night.

He'd ordered the servants not to linger near the courting pair.

Stomach knotting, he turned his head towards the spot where the
glassed-in structure angled into his line of sight. He could distinguish
nothing through the foliage but a faint candle glow. They'd been in
there an hour. Was Freddie kissing her? Whispering sweet nothings
in her ear? To be sure, Edward ought to hope he was. He ought to
hope Freddie had swept her completely off her feet.

Needless to say, he did not.

He finished his brandy in a single swallow, then glanced behind
him at the long, book-lined room. He could pace as he'd done earlier.
Past the herbals and the Greeks. Up around the gallery and down the
spiral stair. He could glare at the busts of Plato and Pliny that dignified the doorway to the drawing room. He could even flip through the
duchess's silly Gothic novels and give himself a laugh.

He did none of these things. Fool that he was, he stood, nose vir-
tually pressed to glass, watching a distant, flickering glow that told
him absolutely nothing, yet managed to torture him all the same.

Suddenly he straightened, every muscle tensing to alert. The outer
door to the orangery had opened. A figure was emerging. It was Florence. She was alone.

Anyone else would have thought she was taking a meditative
stroll. Her pace was measured. Her skirts swept negligently behind
her on the grass. Only eyes sharpened by love could perceive the stiffness in her steps, as if a puppet were being tugged by unkind strings.

When she dragged her sleeve across her eyes, he knew she had been
crying.

He did not stop to think, not even to wonder what his brother
had done. He flung through the French door and across the
columned portico. When he gained the lawn, he peered wildly past
the reach of the gaslight. She was moving towards the front of the
house, towards the lake.

Shorter of breath than his brief exertions should have made him,
he hastened in her wake. She was walking faster now. She'd gotten farther ahead of him than he liked. He was aware, in the dimmer recesses

of his mind, that he was being ridiculous. A weeping woman didn't necessarily want or need rescuing, nor would many have chosen his services if they'd shared Florence's experience of him. But he couldn't take the chance that she might want his comfort and he wouldn't be there to give it. He had to be there if she needed him. Had to.

He slowed as he saw her step onto the footbridge that connected to lakeshore to the island. His neck tightened. Where was she going? What did she intend? Surely she wouldn't throw herself off the bridge. Whatever had happened couldn't be as bad as that. In spite of this logic, his shoulders did not relax until she crossed the midpoint of the arch. One of the slumbering swans ruffled its wings in complaint. Cursing too quietly to be heard, Edward followed.

He almost lost her on the other side. She must have had the eyes of a cat. If he hadn't been so familiar with the island's paths, he would have missed his way. As it was, twice he had to strain his ears for the drag of her skirt on the gravel before he knew which turn she'd taken. The beeches began to close in, tall dark shapes in the country night. Florence never faltered. He realized she was heading for the summer house, as if drawn there by a beacon he could not see.

Now more curious than alarmed, he drew to the side of the path as she tried the handle of the heavy Moorish door. It didn't budge. She tried again, then pounded the wood beneath the fanciful crescent of glass. This failing to achieve any effect, she slid sobbing to the stoop. That was more than enough to make Edward admit to his presence.

He stepped out of the shadows. Florence didn't seem at all surprised to see him.

"It's locked," she accused, as angry as a thwarted child.

"It's not locked. It's heavy. And the hinges are probably stuck."

"Well, open it, damn you." The curse sounded comical on her lips and he struggled not to smile. She'd pushed to her feet and was loudly sniffing back tears. Edward wondered if she were going to hit him the way she had that night before the Vances' ball. She certainly looked tempted.

So much for offering comfort, he thought, but did as she asked— though he had to brace his foot on the wall and heave. Finally, with a loud squeal of protest, the stubborn door gave way.

A cloud of dust set them both to coughing. This building had been his and Freddie's grandfather's retreat from family life and their father's after him. It was a place of illicit rendezvous, a smoking room, a bastion of male vices. Edward and Freddie had played Crusades in it when they were young, but that had been long ago. Thankfully, a flint and taper still lay on the shelf inside the door. Edward lit the candle, then made a circuit of the large round room.

The oil in the sconces smelled stale, but burned well enough. Soon a buttery glow lit heaps of satin cushions and silk wool carpets and twisted Oriental columns. No thicker than a man's arm, and ornamented with flowers that never grew, the cast-iron pillars had been painted to resemble stone. Low octagonal tables with mirrors set into their wood spoke of meals served lounging on the floor. A greasy hookah sat atop one, its hose wrapped like a sleeping snake around the cylinder of glass. The colors of the room were rich and dark. Sapphire. Crimson. The green of shadowed pine. Dust cloaked the decadent display, dimming the exotic wood and furring the polished green stone that peeped between the rugs. The dust did not, however, inhibit the rounding of Florence's eyes.

Mouth open, cheeks stained with drying tears, she gaped at the filigreed arch above her head. He could almost see visions of harems running through her mind. Before they could run through his, he cleared his throat. "Might I ask why you were so determined to get in here?"

She turned to finger a musty crimson drape. He suspected she was embarrassed. "I suppose I thought I'd spend the night here."

"Because—?"

"Don't take that tone with me," she said, her anger tinged with fatigue, "as if I were a child sniveling over a broken doll."

He couldn't answer at first. He was too taken by the sight of her in his father's old trysting place, her profile glowing in the lamplight, her figure enough to fuel the dreams of a dozen generations. He felt oddly close to her, despite his obviously having put his foot in it.

I even relish her rebukes, he thought, a laugh for his foolishness caught in his throat.

"Forgive me," he said, all humor hidden. "I didn't mean to belittle your troubles. Please tell me what's wrong. Did Freddie do something to offend you?"

The nearest sconce lit the involuntary pursing of her lips. "Freddie doesn't want to marry me."

The answer caught him by surprise. He took a step closer. "He couldn't have said that. He wouldn't."

"Of course he wouldn't. What he actually said was I shouldn't want to marry him. 'Doomed to disappointment' was how he put it." She turned to face him, her back pressing the velvet drapery to the wall. As if her confession refreshed her horror, she covered her face with her hands. A moment later, she dropped them in resignation.

"I don't know what I shall do," she said. "I'd hoped . . . too much, clearly. I'm sinking in debt. I can't afford to hunt another husband, even supposing anyone would want discarded goods. I suppose I can find some sort of position, but that begs the question of what to do for Lizzie." Her lower lip trembled and she caught it in her teeth. "She's been so pleased, Edward. Since Freddie proposed, she's begun to believe she'll have a happy life."

A single tear spilled down her dove-soft cheek. Edward found this more wrenching than a storm of sobs. He knew it was Florence who'd begun to hope for a happy life. Without stopping to count the cost, he opened his arms.

"Come here," he said. As if she'd been waiting a lifetime for the offer, she ran to him with a hiccuping little cry. Her arms clung tightly to his back. Her body shook but it was warm. She fit the harbor of his chest as if God had made her for his hold. Happier than he had any right to be, he rubbed his cheek against her hair. "You'll work it out. I know Freddie didn't mean what you believe."

"He did," she insisted, her face pressed to the front of his shirt. "I know he did. He didn't want me, either. When I kissed him, he— well, let's just say he wasn't looking forward to having me in his bed. Oh, blast it anyway!"

With a furious shove, she pushed back from his hold. "What's wrong with me?" she demanded, arms flung wide to indicate her person. "What fatal flaw do the Greystowe men find so repulsive? Am I too fat? Too thin? Or perhaps my character's too dull? It can't be my boldness because I'm not very and, in any case, you liked when Merry Vance was bold. By God, you even gave her my horse!"

Edward had to smile at this. That had bothered her, had it? Seeing the smile, Florence crossed her arms and looked as dangerous as a peach-sweet vicar's daughter could. He knew it was time to smooth her ruffled pride. "I didn't give her your horse; I allowed her to ride it. Mostly because she assumed I intended to, and I could not for the life of me explain why I'd made such an extravagant purchase for my brother's fiancée."

This, at last, was the right thing to say. Florence hung her head and scuffed her slipper through the dust. "You truly did buy Buttercup for me?"

"Yes, I truly did."

"And you hung that painting in my room, the one you knew I loved."

"Yes."

"I suppose you really aren't an ogre." Her head ducked lower, muffling the admission. "I suppose I'll miss you, too."

She was crying again. His own eyes stung as he folded her against him. No doubt it was reckless, but he didn't care. "Hush." He pressed his lips to her hair. "No one's going to miss anyone. You're going to marry Freddie and stay right here."

She shook her head against his dampened shirt. "I can't make him marry me. Not if he doesn't want to."

"I'm sure he wants to." Of their own will, his lips found the baby-smooth skin of her temple. Florence's arms clutched his back.

"He doesn't. You liked kissing me better than he did."

"I'm sure that's not true," he murmured, though he wasn't certain what he denied. His mouth had drifted to the tender pink lobe of her ear. He tried to convince himself not to bite it.

"It is true," she insisted. "I know he's a gentleman, Edward, but could something be wrong with Freddie?"

That focused his attention. He straightened and drew back in their embrace. "There's nothing wrong with Freddie. Absolutely nothing."

"Then it has to be me. I'm not woman enough to make him want me."

"Oh, Lord," Edward groaned. "You're woman enough and then some."

She narrowed her eyes. "You didn't want me. Not at the very end."

"I wanted you. Just as I've wanted you since we met."

"But you stopped!"

"And nearly killed myself in the process." He pulled her hips to his, to the shocking thrust of his arousal. "Feel that, Florence. Feel how hard I am. How long and thick. You do that to me. Just by breathing. Just by slipping into my mind. I'm a bloody stag in rut, sweetheart, so don't you tell me you're not woman enough."

A new flush joined the blotches from her tears. The tip of her nose was pink and her lashes stuck together. Even so, he thought her the most delectable creature he'd ever seen. Her hips wriggled in his hold, a devastating little squirm. If she needed further proof of his claims, she certainly got it. His cock leapt like a spawning salmon and his breath rushed from his lungs. His fingers tightened on her bottom, whether to stop her movement or squeeze her closer he couldn't have said. Whatever his intent, she stilled at the increasingly forceful pulsing of his sex. Her gaze met his.

"I want to know," she said, the words all breath and fire. "I know it's wrong of me, but it can't hurt Freddie now. If I'm not going to have a husband, I want to know how it feels to be desired."

For a moment, she thought he would faint. The color drained from his face and he closed his eyes. When he opened them, their blue blazed like flame. She expected an argument, or a polite evasion such as Freddie had offered. Instead he stared at her, blinked, then crashed his mouth down over hers.

After that, it was her turn to feel weak.

"Oh, Florence," he said between deep, devouring kisses. "Don't make me do this."

But she couldn't think of one good reason to stop him. She'd lost everything: her dreams, her future, even her reputation would be ruined when the news of her broken engagement spread. Why shouldn't she, just once, reach for what she truly wanted? Not that she could have stopped Edward. His embrace overwhelmed her, not merely his strength or his size but the blatant ownership of his touch. His hands slid over her, squeezing, rubbing, as if every inch of her were his to claim. He gave no thought to what might embarrass her. He touched her everywhere he wished.

With a low groan, he lifted her off her feet and pressed her back to the wall. Her legs had no place to go but around his waist. He pushed his body between them, eager to rub the hardest part of him against the neediest part of her.

"Wait," she said when he finally let her draw breath.

Panting hard, he dropped his forehead to hers. "Forgive me. I shouldn't have moved so quickly. Or been so rough."

He had misunderstood her. Ignoring the apology, she found the pearl studs that fastened his shirtfront and began to slip them through their holes. His breathing changed course. "What," he asked, "are you doing?"

"I'm touching you the way you wouldn't let me before. I need proof of what I do to you. I need it in my hands."

"You need proof?" The question was strangled. She nodded shyly and hoped he wouldn't stop her. He shuddered. "Proof." He allowed her legs to slide down his sides. He took one step back from her, then another, and then his hands took over the task of divesting his clothes. "Allow me," he said, low and strained.

With a curse of impatience, he shrugged off his satin waistcoat.

Anticipation curled through her like the smoke that hookah must have trailed so long ago. She felt as if more than his body were about to be unveiled. His eyes glittered in the lamplight, color staining his cheeks, brightening his full seducer's lips. He looked beautiful and strange, the victim of a thrall: her thrall. She had asked and he complied. Under his big, capable hands, his shirtfront parted over his chest. He pulled the crisp white garment over his head, his muscles shifting under smooth, sun-browned skin. Her breath seemed trapped in her throat. His shoulders were broad, his nipples two sharp-tipped bronze coins. His build was half laborer, half marble David. But he was so much more exciting than a statue. The sheer cloud of sable hair that trailed invitingly down his center, the warmth of his skin, the way his ribs expanded with his breaths made her feel as if she'd give her very soul to touch his flesh.

"More?" he asked, his fingers resting lightly at the top of his trousers. The swell beneath made a prisoner of her gaze. It was a living, pulsing thing: the object of her unending fascination.

And he obviously feared she might not want to see it.

"Please," she said, the word choked. "May I do it? I've been wanting to touch you ever since I lost my nerve at the Vances' ball."

His laugh was half gasp. "And here I was thinking I'd scared the wits out of you."

"No," she murmured. "Not even when I wished you would."

His arms fell to his sides. She reached. Stepped closer. How extraordinary it was to know that all this time they'd been thinking of each other, and that he, too, had desired her touch. His belly moved in and out as she struggled with the metal clasp. The buttons were easier. The pressure behind them nearly pushed them free. Mindful of his rigidly swollen organ, she eased his linens around its jut. His head dropped back as she pulled the gathered cloth to his ankles. Her fingers brushed the hair on his legs, a prickle of goose-bumps sweeping in their wake.

"Florence," he moaned, the sound beating like his heart.

She looked up at him from the floor: at his hairy chest and his beautiful limbs, at his towering maleness and the odd little sack that dangled underneath. It had pulled up higher than before and she wondered what that meant. He was watching her reaction now, his gaze searingly intense. Despite the attention, she could not drag her eyes from the part of him that was so changed, so gloriously upright. She remembered how smooth it had felt and yet the veins that twined its pulsing girth did not look smooth at all. Its head reared almost to his waist, seeming to loom in threat above her, as if angry at her presumption.

"What do I call it?" she whispered.

"This?" He gripped the column in his fist, pulling slowly towards the gleaming crimson tip. The flesh that sheathed it moved, looser than she'd expected. Her body jumped inside as if his hand were touching her. His longest finger curled over the tiny slit. "This is my penis. My cock."

"Cock," she whispered, trying the hard, crisp word. The thing leapt as if it recognized its name. Her hand ventured towards the hanging sack. "And this?"

"Ballocks," he said, and released his grip.

She scooted closer, steadying her balance by holding his knees. She was not going to let fear get the better of her tonight. "May I kiss them? May I kiss all of you as you kissed me?"

For the space of a breath, he did not answer. She feared she had once again overstepped the bounds of what was done. Then his fingertip stroked gently down her cheek. "You may kiss whatever you like. I said you could have proof."

But she did not kiss him first. First she simply pressed her face to his groin, turning her cheeks back and forth, taking his textures through her skin, his scent, his vital, leaping pulse. He sighed at the slow, catlike caress, then tensed when her tongue came out to taste.

"Yes," he gasped. "Lick me. Lick me as if I were sweet."

"You are sweet." She found a spot that made him shiver. "And big."

He lengthened at the words, noticeably, as if the claim were darkly magic.

"Not too big," he whispered. "Not too."

His words tempted her to laugh. He wanted to be big. He liked that she thought he was. She knew this with an instinct that was born into her sex. The bigger the sword, the more powerful the man who wielded it. The more powerful the man, the safer the people he loved.

"I don't know." She touched the strange papery skin of his sack. "I think perhaps I ought to be afraid."

He could only gasp at that because she'd slid her mouth around the ripe, ruddy head. It was sweet, and smooth, the smoothest of all. She curled her tongue over the satiny curve and sucked, a peculiarly childish delight. The little slit was interesting, too. He had touched it himself and she thought it must feel good. When she tried it, he moaned, pain and pleasure mixing in the sound. His hips flexed and the hot blunt tip strove against the pressure of her tongue. Faintly, deliciously, she tasted salt.

His fingers tangled in her hair, then lifted her away.

"Enough." He pulled her to her feet. "You don't know what you're doing."

For an instant, his words stung. "Then teach me," she said.

But he kissed her instead, a slow, thorough plunder. Her knees failed and she was carried, floating really, to be set on a soft pile of pillows that smelled of old perfume. Her clothes peeled away beneath his expert hands: dress, petticoats, corset. She was embarrassed to be so bare before his eyes, as if he'd stripped away her armor.

"No," he said when she tried to cover her secrets. "Don't deny me the pleasure you wanted for yourself."

He certainly seemed to like her naked body. His hands slid over her, his mouth. The tips of her breasts earned kisses that made her moan. When he saw the marks left by her stays, he rubbed them until the red began to fade.

But he did not remove her boots.

"Are you afraid to see my naked feet?" she teased, her confidence restored by his admiration.

"Perhaps," he said, with a small, shuttered smile.

The shock as he pressed their naked fronts together drove the question from her mind.

"Oh," she said, squirming rapturously against him. "Oh, my!"

He laughed, then growled against her neck. "You were made for this, Florence. Made for love."

She liked the sound of that: made for love. Grinning back, she craned upward for his kiss. Her joy was all the giddier for having begun in pain. She gave herself over to it, over to him, as if she'd never in her life known fear.

"Sweetness," he murmured, sensing her surrender.

He slipped his hand down her belly and through her curls, then moaned at the heat that greeted his caress. Clearly seeking more, his fingers slid between her folds. She felt the delightful ache she'd known before and writhed beneath him, wanting what she knew he could give, thrusting with her hips when she could no longer be still.

This time he watched her climb until she had to close her eyes.

"Yes," he praised, rough and heated by her ear. "Come for me, sweetness, come."

The pleasure broke more sharply than before. She cried out at the startling liquid tremor, and again when his fingers worked her harder still. Lovely wavelets rolled over one another, ebbing and building, lapping deep inside her core. When he finally let her go she was boneless, heated through and through with satiation. As if it were a dream, she felt him stretch against her side. His arm jerked quickly, wildly, until he gasped and stiffened and a burst of something warm splashed her hip.

He sighed heavily when the wetness finished spurting, like a man who'd set down a burden.

He spilled his seed, she thought. He brought himself to pleasure with his fist. She touched the sweaty arm he'd draped across her waist.

"Why did you do that?" she asked. "Why didn't you let me?"

Still breathing hard, he nuzzled the crook of her neck. "I'm sorry, Florence. I wasn't sure you'd want to and I couldn't wait. Watching you was too much. I had to come."

"Then you'll have to teach me to do it quicker."

He rose over her on his elbow. Crinkles spread out from his smiling eyes, warm and reassuring, as if he saw every insecurity she'd tried to hide behind her matter-of-fact tone.

"No," he said, his lips whispering incitingly over hers. "I want you to do it slow."

He showed her how, his organ beginning to grow as soon as he wrapped her fingers around it. He showed her the places he liked to be touched: how a lick of the tongue made her palm slide more deliciously; how his cock rooted deep inside him and could be rubbed behind his sack; how a gentle squeeze at the proper moment left him gasping with delight.

She did all he showed her and gloried in his groans. They excited her more than she could have dreamed: the wild chuffing of his breath, the tight, pained twist of his face as he tried to make the pleasure last. The climactic burst of seed was a revelation, not its quantity so much as the suddenness of its appearance. What a marvel men were. She did not protest when he pressed his mouth between her legs, though her nakedness made the act stranger than before, and the climb to pleasure tired her so greatly she could not stay awake.

"Sweet as honey," she heard him murmur as she drifted off. He held her to his warmth, his arms wrapped protectively around her back. In spite of all she'd been through, she slept as peacefully as a child.

HE HELD HER AS SHE SLEPT, HIS HEART SLOWING, HIS BODY blissfully at ease, his mind held from the press of reality by force of will. One night, he thought, one night until the dawn. Then he would do what he must. Then he would return her to his brother. He knew it was wrong, maybe even impossible, for this night to be forgotten. But what choice did he have? Marry Florence himself and abandon Freddie to the wolves? The lure of doing precisely that was almost stronger than he could stand. But even if marrying him might make Florence happier, that path was primarily selfish: abominably selfish, in fact. How could he live with himself, knowing he'd destroyed his brother's last chance to be saved?

He could still make this work. He could. None of them would have precisely what they wished, but neither would any of them be ruined. And in the meantime, he would have his night.

What could one night matter when the damage already was done? *Done but not compounded,* said his conscience.

He ignored the nagging voice, easing out from under his love to find the bath. He would not regret this night no matter what.

He pushed aside three dusty velvet curtains before he found the hidden door. The marble floor was cool beneath his feet as he looked around, taking in the memories. It was a rich room, shining with Moorish tile and gilt, the crowning luxury of the pavilion. Spiders scuttled in the plunge bath, but water still flowed from the taps. He did his business quickly, splashed his face, then hesitated as his gaze struck an Indian prayer cabinet. The wood was covered in statuettes, each carved to represent the positions of love. Some were only possible for contortionists. Others he and Florence had done tonight. He and Freddie had sniggered over this cabinet when they were boys, but now Edward remembered what it contained: velvet ties, rolls of long velvet ties.

He glanced over his shoulder to the room where Florence slept. He'd said he wanted memories. Why not a memory of the fantasy that had been haunting him since that day at the ruins? He opened the cabinet's folding door. Inside, beneath a smiling cedar Buddha, was a chest he'd never seen. The baroque French coffer was gold, encrusted with ornamental flowers. It was locked, but the key lay beside it. Curious, he opened the lid.

The contents included a collection of brittle letters, the packets bound with red satin cords. Next to these lay a chased gold locket, big enough to fill his palm. Opening it gave him a start. The portrait inside was the spitting image of Imogene Hargreave. For a moment, he suspected someone of playing a nasty joke. Then he realized the picture couldn't be Imogene. For one thing, the clothes were too old-fashioned. The subject's flaxen hair was scraped close to her head, then coaxed into shining coils. Though the face was familiar, the eyes were different from Imogene's: softer, easier to hurt.

How peculiar, he thought, shaken by the coincidence. He teased one yellowed letter from its stack. He opened the final flap. "Yours forever, Catherine," said the girlish signature.

Catherine, he mouthed, his mind working out the puzzle. The writer could only be Catherine Exeter. The letters were not old enough to be his grandfather's and if his father had courted any other Catherine, the people of Greystowe would have known. Old gossip died hard in a town like this.

But what should he make of her curious resemblance to Imogene? They must be related. That was the only reasonable explanation. Perhaps Catherine Exeter was the aunt Imogene spoke of, the one who had warned her about his cold heart. His mouth twisted in a humorless smile. He could guess what Catherine Exeter had to say about Greystowe men. If that bitter old crone were any indication of how Imogene would age, he was lucky to be quit of her.

He didn't feel lucky, though. He felt as if a goose had walked across his grave. The chill trickled unpleasantly down his spine. Maybe he had more in common with his father than he'd thought.

No. He pushed the possibility away. He was his own man with his own sins, one of whom was curled in sleep on a mound of satin pillows. He should not waste this night in dwelling on someone else's dusty past. The present was all that mattered, the present and the memories it could bring. He reached for a more familiar item, a roll of night-black velvet. When he undid the circling ribbon, eight soft quilted ties unfurled across his palm. His breathing quickened. Should he do this? Would Florence mind? Would she even know she ought to?

He didn't think she would and that aroused him most of all. With no mother to guide her, and no married friend her age, she was a stranger to the shapes love could take. She would not know what was ordinary and what was not. Her questions about women's "feelings" had proved that.

But would she enjoy being made his prisoner?

He closed his eyes, picturing the stark black ties against her blushing skin. He could make her enjoy it. If he were gentle and reassuring. If he showed her there was nothing to fear.

He laughed ironically through his nose. Nothing to fear but the overflowing passions of his heart. He was the one who should have been afraid. If she trusted him enough to allow this, he knew it would mark him forever hers.

SHE WOKE TO A SENSE OF SOMETHING OUT OF PLACE. SOME-one . . . someone was kissing her naked feet. She curled her toes against the tickling mouth and smiled without opening her eyes.

"Florence," said a low, beloved voice. "Wake up and see how beautiful you are, how every part of you is a dream of what a woman should be." The voice drew nearer and the heat of a large male body hovered over her where she lay. "You are my dream of what a woman should be, love, my dream of beauty."

She opened her eyes and thought all the beauty his. His face was close, his cheeks flushed with what she'd come to recognize as desire. His blue eyes burned in their satiny fringe of black. His lips were a curve of heaven. She did not mark his glowering brows or the harshness of his jaw. His haughty nose was perfect. Her love, it seemed, had turned all his flaws to virtues.

"I'm glad I please you," she said, her cheeks heating at the admission. "You are the first man I ever wanted to admire me."

"The first, eh?" He hid a boyish smile by trailing kisses up the stretch of her arm. "I hope you're still pleased when you realize what I've done."

"What you've done?" She tried to sit up and look around, but her arms would not leave their place. They were fastened by the wrist to a pair of columns, spread outward like an X. Her legs were tied as well, not to anything but to each other, at ankle and at knee. The ties did not hurt but they were strong. Goodness, how could she have slept through such an alteration?

"Why have you done this?" she asked, abruptly feeling panicked. "Why am I tied?"

"Hush," he said. He laid one hand atop her breast, cupping it in his warmth. "I will not hurt you."

The way he bit his lip belied his sureness. His eyes, always proud and stern, pleaded for acceptance, but acceptance of what, she didn't know.

"Why?" she said, even as she calmed beneath his touch.

"Because I wish it. Because I have dreamed of doing it. Because"—his finger trailed down the midline of her belly—"because it will make me feel safer."

She had to smile at this admission. "How could I frighten you?"

He lowered his face and rubbed it slowly against her own. The scrape of his whiskers made her shiver. "You threaten my control, Florence. When you touch me, you push me to the edge. I could love you as I pleased if I knew you would not tempt me past what can be done." His mouth opened near the bend of her jaw, his breath beating warmth against her neck, his tongue slipping out to test her pulse.

" 'What can be done?' " she repeated.

His lips whispered over her brow. "There are limits. Things we must not do. But if you let me love you this once, this way, we will share every drop of pleasure we can know."

What limits? she wanted to cry. What things? But something stopped her, a quiver of superstition. She was the princess in the ogre's castle, free to open any door but one. If she made her prince explain, would she break the magic spell?

"You truly wish this?" she said, nodding at the ties.

He pulled back and straddled her waist on his knees. The long shadow of his sex flickered against his stomach. It seemed immense in the lamplight, almost grotesque, and yet she found it as beautiful as the rest of him. Too big to hold. Too perfect not to. His palms rubbed up and down his muscled thighs, itching perhaps to touch her. His gaze slid from her left wrist to her right, lingering on the velvet ties. His chest rose and fell as if the mere sight of her bonds excited him. When his eyes met hers, they gleamed like jewels, the pupils huge but steady.

"I wish this more than you could know," he said.

"Then I'm sure I shall enjoy it."

He smiled with a fondness that warmed her heart. "I'll do my utmost not to make you a liar."

"See that you do," she teased.

He laughed and pulled her to her velvet-bound knees.

He had not lied. His kisses were different now, freer, lusher, as if her constraints had loosened his own. His moans were louder, his skin more fevered. He rubbed their bodies together with the enthusiasm of a much less civilized being. "Do you like that?" he whispered. "Do you like my cock against your skin?"

She could not deny it. "It's wet," she gasped as he dragged the throbbing crest across her belly.

"It's crying for you, Florence. It wants to fuck your sweet little pussy." He laughed, low and dark, at her involuntary shiver. "Poor little Florence. I don't mean to frighten you with my words."

"I'm not f-frightened."

He laughed again and squeezed her so tightly his penis seemed to burn between their bodies. "I'll tell you a secret, love. I don't mind if you're a little frightened, so long as you enjoy how I make you feel."

He kissed her before she could respond, deep and possessive, driving every thought from her mind but the sweet, drugging bliss of his touch. His hands were her salvation, his cock the brand that made her his. And she was his, entirely, without a scrap of her soul withheld. Willingly, she surrendered to his wishes, loving that what he wanted was hers to give, loving even the tiny spark of fear. He could do anything to her. Anything.

But he would not hurt her. She knew he would not. The trust she felt was a pleasure in itself. That she, who had so long feared her shadow, could trust a man with not only her body but her body's satisfaction filled her with a hot, sharp streak of pride. Even to Freddie she would not have granted this. Only Edward could be trusted to know her deepest need.

Indeed, even as she tensed with a shadow of self-consciousness, he moved behind her. She sighed at the heady rush the change of positions inspired. She could not see him now, and he could not see her face. She was freed to feel, to react, with that small bit of modesty preserved.

"Cat," he teased at her tiny, purring moan.

As if to underscore the words, his nails raked gently up her back, from the curve of her buttocks to the base of her neck. She rolled her spine and stretched her arms against the limits of her bonds. Despite the unorthodox situation, she had never been so easy in her body. Her wrists were tied to the bottom of the columns, pulled out from her sides but not raised. Such a simple containment, but what a difference it wrought in her mind! I am lucky to be beautiful, she thought, if it makes me the woman this man desires.

"I'm moving closer," he warned. "I'm going to rub us together like the butler and his favorite plate."

He planted his knees outside her calves and slipped his arms around her waist. His chin fit neatly over her head. True to his word, he buffed his front to her back, slowly, firmly, the heavy press of muscle and skin a deep, bone-heating pleasure.

Her enjoyment escaped in a long, melodious sigh.

"Like that?" he said, his fingers drawing circles on her breasts.

"It makes me feel drunk."

"And this?" One big hand covered her belly, pressing her bottom to the thick hot thrust of his sex. Her head fell back against his shoulder.

"Yes," she said. "That, too."

He pleasured her as slowly as she'd pleasured him, hands brushing feather-light against the parts of her that felt it most: her nipples, her mouth, the sensitive stretch of bone between her shoulders. He teased the triangle of curls between her legs and drew patterns over the rise of her hips. He touched her until her skin seemed to hum beneath his hands: burning, yearning, straining harder and harder for the next caress. When he finally slipped one finger between the tightly pressed folds of her mound, the contact made her nerves all leap at once.

But even these enticements could not dull her awareness of what he was doing with his cock. He was rubbing it over her: her bottom, the small of her back, the crease where each cheek met her legs. He squeezed it into the tightly bound clasp of her thighs, just far enough to touch her nether lips before he drew it out. She sensed he was exploring her with it, as if his organ were another hand. She could feel the wet, foreign press of the little eye, warm and slick. He was stretched within his skin, hardening like iron as their play drew out.

"Ready?" he said, his voice harsh but still controlled. "Ready to fly over the edge?"

She could barely move for the waves of longing that weighted her limbs. She managed a feeble nod. For him it was enough. Gone was his teasing then, gone the luxuriant rub of skin on skin. Strength replaced it, and determination. The swiftness of her rise was dizzying. In seconds, her body tensed, coiled with heartstopping pleasure, and sprung free with blinding force. He must have known what was happening to her. His hips jerked faster, pressed harder, and an instant later he joined her in the sweet convulsion. Growling softly, his teeth scored her shoulder as his seed jetted hard against her back.

It was a singular experience, feeling him soften as he held her, knowing they had shared that spasm of joy. He sat back and spooned her against him. This is nakedness, she thought. Letting someone see you lose yourself to the madness of your flesh.

He kissed the place he'd set his teeth, then licked it. Her skin tingled beneath his tongue.

"You bit me," she said, as surprised by his action as she was by her own flutters of intrigue. Obviously, she had much to learn about the secrets of the bedchamber.

Misunderstanding her words, he murmured an apology and bent to release her ties. He checked her wrists to make sure they weren't chafed. The right bore a mark where she'd unwittingly tugged it at the end. He kissed the fading redness, then cradled her hand against his chest. "All right, love?" he said, his pretty eyes concerned.

She'd always be all right when he called her that.

"Just tired," she said, her gratification smothered by a yawn.

The response amused him. "Come then," he said. "I'll get us settled for the night."

AFTER WHAT SEEMED LIKE MINUTES OF FITFUL SLEEP, HE woke to a patter of rain on the domed wooden roof. A necklace of small round windows circled its gilded rim. They bled a pale silver light that did nothing to lift his heart. He was stiff from sleeping on the floor, stiff and cold. He had turned away from Florence in the night, leaving her to hug the pillows for warmth. He knew he should not linger but he watched her just a little longer: her downy, sleep-flushed skin, her shining spill of chestnut hair.

She was a chick barely out of its shell, a child-woman with her hands curled together beneath her cheek. Could anyone who saw her not wish to protect her sweetness?

He thought of the way she'd taken him in her mouth, all curiosity and accidental skill. He thought of the way she'd let him bind her, the way she'd squirmed and sighed in his arms. Her lust was as clean as the brook that fed the downs. No act could sully her; at least, not the woman she was today.

Lips thinned by a rueful smile, he smoothed the gold satin sheet across her back. Life would change her: disappointments, disillusions, the narrow-minded judgments of the world. One day she'd know enough to be embarrassed by what they'd done. For now, though, she was innocent in the one way that mattered. Freddie Burbrooke would take a virgin to his bed.

Edward didn't credit her tale about Freddie not wanting to marry her. That was just a foolish pang of conscience. In the end, his brother would act as wisdom required. He would marry Florence Fairleigh. He would safeguard his future and the future of the Greystowe name.

With eyes gone hot, Edward turned from his brother's bride-to-be. He told himself Freddie would take care of her. Freddie would be kinder than a thousand husbands he could name. He swallowed against the painful thickness in his throat.

One thing only Freddie would not do.

He would not cherish the pure, bright flame that burned within her flesh.

Chapter 12

FLORENCE CUDDLED HER PILLOW, HUGGING THE LAST OF HER dreams to her breast. She felt quite happily a fool. All this time she'd been afraid of Edward. Perhaps he *was* intimidating, even now when she knew he must care for her. It was a good kind of intimidating, though, an exciting kind.

What an adventure being married to him would be! She was a little sorry to be breaking her promise to Freddie, but it wasn't as if he wanted to marry her himself. She was sure a charming man like him would have no trouble finding a more suitable, less passionate bride.

Poor Freddie, she thought. He had no idea what he was missing. Then again, who was she to judge his nature? No doubt he thought her the unfortunate one.

She extended her arms in a supremely satisfied stretch. Despite her moments of anguish, everything had turned out for the best. She could hardly wait to start making Edward happy.

She would have to wait, though, because her lover was nowhere in sight.

He must have left early to preserve her reputation. It wouldn't do for the servants to witness their licentiousness. Never mind that servants could be as bad; Florence understood what was expected. Why force people to know what would make them uncomfortable, even if they did the same themselves? She nodded in agreement to the empty room. Yes, Edward had demonstrated great discretion in leaving the pavilion first.

And, look! He had left her a token. Eyes caught by something shiny, she retrieved his gold signet from between a pair of pillows. It must have rolled off the cushion while she slept.

The ring fit tolerably well on her forefinger, its ruby winking darkly in the rain-dimmed light. Freddie had not given her an engagement ring, an omission she had not thought about till now. Moved to the edge of tears, she brought the gem to her lips and kissed it.

"I love you," she whispered, trying out the words. "I love you, Edward Burbrooke."

She shivered suddenly, chilled by an errant draft. The room seemed empty with only herself to warm it, as much a ruin as the former Greystowe Hall.

I should dress, she told herself, and return to the house. If Edward could be discreet, then so could she.

WHEN SHE ARRIVED, MORE OR LESS DRY THANKS TO AN UM-brella she'd found in a big brass pot beside the door, the front hall was empty. Her pulse beat frantically in her throat as she managed to slip back to her room without encountering any servants, though they had, of course, begun the day's work already. Relieved though she was, sneaking around gave her a sense of wrongdoing she did not like. She wished she could simply declare the truth to everyone.

She and Edward were going to be together. The thought was miraculous to the point of being frightening. Even as she longed to get the announcement over with, she dreaded telling Edward's family. She'd been intimate with him, after all, hardly a cause for pride—especially when she hadn't officially broken off with Freddie.

But, oh, it had been worth any amount of awkwardness to share that night! Her cheeks warmed with a particularly potent memory and suddenly she had to see him, immediately and alone, if only to reassure herself she hadn't dreamed it all.

Her heart tripped thrillingly against her ribs as she slipped down the corridor to his office, darting to the shadows whenever she thought she heard a maid. Thankfully, the carpets muffled her eager footsteps. The day was so dark even gaslight could not dispel the gloom. One of the doors she passed—giving access to the cellar, she imagined—was actually seeping curls of mist beneath its planks. She felt as if she'd stepped into another time; or perhaps a fairy tale, where she was the intrepid princess and Edward the dark, enchanted prince. She almost giggled as she passed a niche with a suit of armor.

Edward was prince and dragon both, but she had just the spell to soothe him. Inside her pocket, coiled like a nesting mouse, were four quilted velvet ties. She could hardly wait to see how Edward liked them; how they'd look twining his strong, masculine wrists.

The door to his office was open a crack. A golden glow spilled out, lamplight rather than gas. Body humming with excitement, she peeped inside. She smiled. Edward was sound asleep, stretched on a leather sofa, his long legs propped and crossed on the brass-studded end. One hand rested on his chest while the other dangled limply to the floor. Last night must have tired him. She considered leaving him to rest, but temptation had her in its grip. That dangling arm was perfectly positioned. If she snuck in now, she could tie him the same way he'd tied her.

To her dismay, he was a much lighter sleeper than she was. He snorted and bolted up before she'd finished the first wrist. He looked at where she'd bound it to the sofa's central leg. "What the hell do you think you're doing?"

Florence trembled. This was not the reaction she'd expected. "I'm s-sorry. Did I make a mistake? Is this something a woman shouldn't do?"

"It's certainly something no woman should do to me."

She backed away, leaving him to wrench the tie loose. "I'm sorry. I shouldn't have woken you. You're in a bad mood."

"There's nothing wrong with my mood!" He glared at her until her cheeks felt boiled, then blew out his breath. "Look, Florence, I'm sorry for growling at you, but you seem to have misunderstood what happened last night."

"Misunderstood?" she said, the word small and cracked.

"I'm not saying it's your fault. I take full responsibility. You're in-experienced and I, well, I needed a woman. I'm aware that's no excuse. It's just the way life is." He spread his hands, a clearer denial of re-sponsibility than his words. Florence watched the gesture with a sense of unreality. He seemed to mean what he was saying. His tone was quite businesslike. "The important thing is," he continued coolly, "I've spoken to Freddie. As I suspected, he didn't mean to give the im-pression that he'd lost interest in marrying you. On the contrary, he's fully prepared to go through with the wedding."

To go through with it, Florence thought. There's a flattering con-struction. But Edward wasn't done.

"I'm leaving tomorrow," he said. "I have business at the mill. I trust you and Freddie will use this time to sort matters out between you. By the time I get back, I expect you'll have forgotten all about, well, everything." Lowering his brows, he gave her his steeliest look. "What happened last night must never happen again."

The finger he shook in her face broke through her shock.

"Then what," she said, thrusting out her hand in accusation, "did you mean by giving me this?"

He stared at his father's ring as if he'd never laid eyes on it before. "Where did you get that?"

"You left it on my pillow."

"Why would I do that? Hell." He scrubbed his face with both hands. "It must have fallen off during the night. It does that when I get cold."

"Then I marvel it ever stays on."

The scrubbing stopped. He peered at her between his fingers, then dropped his hands. He looked so weary she wanted to call back her words. How could he be so cruel, yet look as if he were the one whose heart was breaking?

Stupid Florence, she thought, feeling as weary as he looked. Stupid, gullible Florence. She squared her shoulders and clenched her hands. "You're telling me last night meant nothing to you. Nothing at all."

He hung his hands over his knees, his fingers limp, his shoulders bowed by an invisible weight. "I enjoyed what we did," he said, "but it meant no more than that."

She stared at his face, trying to find the mark of evil, the sign she should have read. All she found was what she'd grown to love: the proud, sharp nose, the scowling brows, the eyes like a summer sky.

"You didn't deserve to enjoy it," she said, her voice shaking with anger. "Men like you don't deserve to enjoy anything."

He dropped his gaze but did not speak; did not try to explain or beg forgiveness or say any of the things she was praying with all her might to hear. It's a mistake, she wanted to cry. You love me. I know you do. She watched a vein tick unevenly in his neck.

And then she turned away.

FLORENCE TROD THE SECOND FLOOR CORRIDOR LIKE A SLEEP-walker, blind to the fading portraits, deaf to the quiet passage of a maid. She'd wanted so badly to believe Edward loved her she'd convinced herself it was true. Catherine Exeter was right. Women were easy to lead astray. With the slightest encouragement, they stuck their necks in the bridle and handed the men they loved a whip.

Lord. Her steps faltered as she pressed her jumping heart. What was she going to do now?

Part of her, the weak part, wanted to throw herself on Freddie's mercy. Marry me, the weak part whimpered. Keep me safe.

But no matter what Edward said, she knew Freddie didn't want her for his wife. She'd seen it in his eyes. She'd read it in his kiss. No doubt, he'd said he did want her because Edward was too forceful to defy.

She knew from experience how difficult opposing him could be.

Continuing her journey, she dragged her fingers along the smooth curry-gold wall. She'd have to speak to Freddie. She wasn't sure what she ought to tell him. That his brother had compromised her virtue, then treated her like something he'd stepped in at the stable? Freddie looked up to his brother. It didn't seem fair to undermine his love. But she had to tell him something to explain why she couldn't spend another minute in this house.

Lost in thought, her hand skimmed the gleaming mahogany rail that marked the turn of the grand stairway towards the ground floor. She descended the first tread. Would Freddie take her back to Keswick? London was out of the question. Even if Florence could have faced it, she couldn't afford to return. Aunt Hypatia certainly didn't owe her more support. Plus, she doubted even the duchess could repair the damage a broken engagement would do to her reputation.

It was all too much to decide. She would put it to Freddie as delicately as she could. He was clever. And he did care for her. Perhaps he would see some solution she could not.

Her panic eased as she drew closer to his rooms. The thought of being held with affection, if only for a while, was a ray of sunshine in a storm. She quickened her step, hurrying through the billiard room to the family's private wing. She rapped lightly on his door, then opened it, too impatient to wait for his acknowledgment.

At first she didn't understand what she was seeing. Oh, she knew the two tall figures by the window were kissing. Their mouths were plastered together, after all, and their hands gripped each others' backsides. One of the figure's shirts had all three buttons undone, with the ensuing V fallen over his shoulder. The cloth hung to his elbow, baring a strong upper arm and a beautifully muscled wedge of back. Her brain took a moment to admit that the back belonged to Freddie, and an even longer one to identify his partner as Nigel West.

Edward's steward was moaning into Freddie's mouth as if he'd rather die than stop. And Freddie was kissing him back with all the hunger he'd claimed he couldn't feel. She saw tongues and teeth. She saw whitened knuckles and sweat-streaked necks. They were grinding their hips together like cats in heat. From what she glimpsed between those hips, both were thoroughly aroused.

She gasped for air as if a huge hand had been holding her underwater and had just then let her up. At the sound, the two men sprang guiltily apart. Freddie hissed out a curse. Nigel went white.

"Florence," Freddie said, raking back his wildly tousled hair.

Florence couldn't meet his eyes. He looked just like Edward had after she'd taken him in her mouth, lust pouring off him in waves. Her mind turned in a stupefied circle. Freddie and Nigel. Nigel and Freddie. It was too extraordinary to comprehend.

"Forgive me," she said, beginning to retreat. "I should have waited until you answered my knock."

Freddie and Nigel exchanged glances. "Knock?" Freddie said. "We didn't hear— Hell. Don't go, Florence. We need to talk. Please."

The sharpness of the plea stopped her. She pressed her hands together beneath her breast, as if she could by that means protect herself from further wounds. "I don't know what there is to say, except that now I think I understand why you don't want to marry me."

"You couldn't understand. Not all of it." With a growl of annoyance that reminded her painfully of his brother, Freddie tugged his shirt back over his shoulder. "Damn Edward and his tidy little plans."

"Edward?" Her heart stalled. "What does Edward have to do with this?"

Freddie lowered himself to the edge of his bed, his legs stretched gingerly out, his face filled with a compassion so deep it scared her. "Come in, Florence. I'll tell you everything."

"I should go," said Nigel.

Freddie nodded at him and in that nod lay a secret history. For one odd moment, despite everything that had passed, Florence experienced a pang of envy. These two shared a bond no one else could know.

"Don't do anything," Freddie said.

"No," Nigel agreed, his voice calm but heavy. "I won't do anything until I speak to you again." His step hesitated in front of Florence, then stopped. "I can't say how sorry I am about all this, Miss Fairleigh. Neither of us meant to—well, let's just say I'm aware that what I did was a profound betrayal of your trust. If there's anything I can do to help, anything at all, I would gladly make the attempt."

He might as well have been speaking Sanskrit. Seeming to realize this, he continued to the door. Florence watched him go, her brain refusing to do anything but spin. She watched his long elegant legs, the proud set of his shoulders and head. It was a small head, beautifully shaped beneath its clipped silvering hair. The hand with which he closed the door had graceful, tapered fingers. When it disappeared, she turned back to Freddie.

"He is a man, isn't he?" she asked, more confused than she'd been in her life.

Freddie laughed, a dry brush of sound. "Yes, he's a man. If he weren't, I wouldn't have been kissing him that way."

"You only like to kiss men?"

Freddie's smile was sad. He brushed back a lock that had fallen from her chignon. "I didn't mind kissing you, sweetheart, but I'm afraid it's true. I only really like kissing men. Born that way, as far as I know."

"But how could you know?"

He shrugged. "Edward thinks Eton did it to me. Blames himself for sending me. There's a tradition there of older boys bullying the younger. Making them personal servants. Giving them forty whacks for imaginary infractions. Part of the servitude sometimes involves more intimate favors."

"Kissing," she said, trying to face it.

Freddie held her gaze. "More than kissing. Boys learn to take their pleasures young, and some don't mind who offers a helping hand. A few, like me, like a male hand best. The first time a boy asked me to do him, I felt as if a pair of blinders had fallen from my eyes. Suddenly what I'd wanted all along was clear."

He took her hands and squeezed them, his eyes filled with a bright, glimmering fire. "I know people say it's unnatural, Florence. I know they say it's a sin. But it doesn't feel like a sin to me. It feels like the way God made me."

"I don't think you're a sinner," she said. The words came slowly as she searched through the tangle of her emotions. "Maybe if I didn't know you, I would, but I've always thought you a good, kind man. My father used to say God weighs each man's sins in private. We can't presume to know what's on the scales."

"Your father sounds wise."

A smile of memory touched her lips. "When it came to other people's hearts, he was."

"So I can hope for forgiveness from the vicar's daughter?"

"I'm not sure you need my forgiveness."

Sighing, he lifted her hands to his mouth. "I'm afraid there's more, Florence, more you deserve to know."

Given what she'd just seen, the story of the footman did not shock her. More disturbing was discovering that Mr. Mowbry was also Edward's solicitor. That her father's old friend would help Edward save Freddie's reputation by engineering a match with her quite stole her breath. Then, when she thought she couldn't bear another blow, Freddie revealed how Aunt Hypatia agreed to help.

"They knew?" she said, her face going hot and cold by turns. Amazement warred with fury in her breast. "Aunt Hypatia *and* Edward? They knew what you were and they still wanted me to marry you?"

"They didn't think of it that way. They thought I'd get over it. They knew you needed a husband, and thought I'd be as good to you as anyone."

"But they tricked me! They let me believe you truly cared."

He cupped her face. "I do care. That's never been a lie. If Nigel and I hadn't—that is, if we hadn't—"

"Oh, go ahead," she snapped with a temper worthy of the duchess. "If you and Nigel hadn't fallen in love, you could have spent a lifetime deceiving me."

Freddie blanched as if she'd told him a truth he wasn't ready to acknowledge. He dropped his arm. "Florence—"

She didn't care what he meant to say. "You're liars, all of you. Liars and cheats. And Edward's the worst of the lot. By God!" Her voice rose out of control and her hands fisted in her skirts as if she meant to rip them from her legs. "I can't believe I actually worried what he thought of me. I can't believe I tried to earn his respect. He's a bug. An insect who isn't worth the energy it would take to squash him!"

"Florence," Freddie chided, a smile flirting with the corners of his mouth.

She jabbed her forefinger into his chest. "He's a slimy, slithering fiend!"

Freddie grabbed her hand and tried to soothe it. To her dismay, she saw she still wore Edward's signet. Before he could see it, she yanked her hand away. Her chin quivered but she positively refused to cry.

"Don't judge him too harshly," Freddie said, the flash of amusement gone. "I don't say his methods were perfect, but he did what he did out of love. He'd protect anyone he cared about that way. Including you."

"Hah!" Florence barked. She swiped her eyes with her sleeve before they could overflow. "There's a pretty bedtime story. Edward protect me? He'd be the first to hammer in the nail."

Freddie protested, but she'd already heard enough. Half blinded by emotion, she spun and left the room. She didn't have to run. Freddie's injury prevented him from following.

Snake, she thought, her skirts kicking fore and aft. What an idiot she'd been to imagine he had a heart. She took the stairs two at a time, panting for breath through her anger and her shame.

They'd all made fools of her, but only Edward had made her a fool for love.

Chapter 13

"I DON'T SEE WHY WE HAVE TO LEAVE," LIZZIE MUTTERED for the umpteenth time since Florence had told her to pack. " 'Least not right away. If your heart is set on going back to Keswick, Viscount Burbrooke will see you get there."

Deliberately ignoring her, Florence frowned at the contents of her wardrobe. Per the duchess's orders, most of her old clothes had been destroyed. Too few remained to pack only what she'd brought with her to London. With a grimace, she pulled out the simplest of her new dresses. If worse came to worst, she could sell them for the price of a railway ticket. Not that she was comfortable with the idea. Strictly speaking, these gowns belonged to Aunt Hypatia.

Lizzie accepted the first, a pale yellow muslin. She smoothed it flat across the bed, then folded it carefully around a length of tissue. Florence had already warned her they'd be taking no trunks; only what the two of them could carry in their portmanteaus.

"Don't know what you think you're going to do in Keswick," Lizzie grumped, her annoyance still sharp.

"I shall hire out as a companion," Florence said with more confidence than she felt.

"Hah." Lizzie fussed over the lay of a hem. "Those old biddies don't have any more money than we do."

"Then I must convince more than one of them to hire me. I shall collect a perfect harem of old biddies."

Taken by surprise, Lizzie puffed out a laugh. But she turned serious quickly enough. "It isn't right: you and Master Freddie parting ways. Whatever you fought about, I'm sure you can work it out. Besides—" Her look grew dark. "I don't like the idea of us going to stay with that friend of the duchess. I've heard the servants talk about her. They say she's barmy."

"She's not barmy," Florence said, fighting for patience. "She's a woman who's seen her share of trouble. Just like us."

"But—"

Guilt at forcing Lizzie to leave her comfortable place, and anguish at having to leave it herself, shortened Florence's temper. "Stay then," she said. "I'm sure the earl will find a position for you. There's always openings in the scullery."

All the blood drained from Lizzie's face. Florence was instantly contrite.

"Blast," she said. "I didn't mean that. Edward wouldn't set you to scrubbing pots. I'm sure if you asked he'd seek out another lady's maid position among his friends."

"B-but—" Lizzie was weeping now. "I don't want to be anyone's lady's maid but yours."

"Well," said Florence, with a humor she thought she'd lost, "it doesn't look as if I'm going to be a lady now."

"You will!" Lizzie declared, flinging herself into her arms. "I know you will."

Florence patted her back. She took a peculiar comfort in consoling the little maid. Poor Lizzie. Deprived of her gaslights and her running water. She resolved that, however events fell out for herself, she would request that Edward help her. She was certain he would, though she couldn't have said from whence that certainty came.

"Maybe you could marry the earl instead," Lizzie mumbled wetly against her neck.

Oh, Lord, thought Florence. God save her from such a fate.

THE DOOR TO CATHERINE'S HOUSE WAS OPENED BY A VISION in lavender silk and ecru lace. Coolly blonde, flawlessly feminine, Catherine's niece was even lovelier in person than in her picture. "My, my," she said with slumberous eyes and curving lips, "if it isn't the fabulous Florence Fairleigh."

In Florence's shaken state, this condescending greeting was more than enough to cow her. "I'm sorry," she said, backing away. "I've come at a bad time."

At once, Imogene sprang into motion. "Nonsense," she said, catching Florence's arm. "My aunt would never forgive me if I let you get away. Clearly, you're in distress. If you could see your way to forgiving my atrocious manners, I'd be happy to help however I may."

With this pretty speech, she drew her guest inside. Florence hardly knew what to make of this changeable creature and her dulcet exclamations of concern. Whatever Imogene's motives, Florence had not the will to resist her welcome. Somewhat less happily, Lizzie shuffled in behind.

Catherine came into the hall at the sound of their entrance. As soon as she saw Florence, she folded her into her arms. "Poor dear," she said, her tone so maternal it tightened Florence's throat. "I feared this would happen. No woman who loved a Greystowe ever failed to come to grief."

"Surely *Freddie* didn't jilt you?" Imogene murmured. Briefly, Florence wondered at the familiarity of the question, but it was hard to take offense. Imogene's curiosity was as delicate as the rest of her. It hung in the air like spider's silk, barely there at all.

She pulled back from Catherine's embrace and wiped her eyes. The two women peered at her in gentle inquiry, their brows—one set gold, one silver—raised in identical slender arches. Despite their kindness, Florence could not answer. Even now, she could not bring herself to speak harshly of the Burbrookes.

"No," Imogene mused, her lambent gray eyes taking the measure of her expression. "Freddie Burbrooke is no heart-breaker, but perhaps the elder . . . ?"

"Tush," scolded Catherine before Florence could do more than bite her lip. "The girl is clearly grieving. We must not pester her with questions. It is enough that you are here, my dear. We ask no more than that."

She would not hear of Florence leaving, though her presence, on top of Imogene's, would make more work for the tiny household. "Your girl can stay with mine in the attic. I'm sure they'll find it perfectly cozy."

Florence would have preferred to keep Lizzie with her but, bereft of support—even her own, it seemed—she hadn't the nerve to object to the arrangement. "You're too kind," she said, her vision shimmering with tears.

Continuing to cluck, Catherine led her to a guest room on the second floor. More grateful than she could express, Florence relinquished her rain-dampened clothes and allowed herself to be bundled into bed.

"Rest," Catherine said, her cool hand stroking Florence's brow. "Sleep is the best remedy for a broken heart."

The hour wasn't even noon, but Florence was exhausted. Bertha, the big, sad-faced maid, brought a beautiful white quilt to tuck around her. She glanced back over her shoulder before she spoke. "Things might look better in the morning," she said in a low, hurried tone, as if she were afraid of being heard. "Men aren't as bad as . . . as some people like to make out."

Florence smiled, touched by her advice. She only wished it were true. She waved at the maid as she left. Then, with a weary sigh, she curled around her starchy pillow like a wounded animal in a burrow. She was safe, at least for now. More than that a woman in her position could not ask.

FOR THE FIRST TIME IN TOO MANY YEARS TO REMEMBER, Edward drank with the intention of getting drunk. The library's shelves stretched around him, above him, the wisdom of centuries held within their tomes. None seemed likely to help him—no more than the liquor. By the fourth whiskey, his head was spinning, his mouth tasted foul, and he could still remember every damn word he'd said.

I enjoyed what we did, but it meant no more than that.

Bloody bastard, he thought, nerves stretched by memory and by the infernal droning of the rain. He had half a mind to shatter the decanter against the wall, just to interrupt the noise. His fingers curled to do it. Fortunately, though—or unfortunately—Edward wasn't a man who easily lost control. With exaggerated care, he pressed the cut-glass stopper into the bottle's throat.

He knew as soon as Florence left that he'd made a terrible mistake: the worst of his life, one that would stain his soul until he died. He'd convinced himself it was better all around that she cease to care for him. In the end, though, all he'd done was wound them both. His heart tore from his chest with each step she took. His brain screamed for him to follow, to tell her something, anything, that would bring back the adoration he'd seen the night before.

He wanted to go after her so badly his body ached in its bones.

But he couldn't do it. He couldn't abandon Freddie. Edward didn't delude himself. Florence was Freddie's last chance for respectability. Only marriage to her could restore his place in their world. Even if some people doubted the sincerity of his brother's vows, they'd know he meant to maintain—at least on the surface—the image society strove to project. If Freddie refused to toe the line, they'd push him forever beyond the pale.

Oh, God, he thought, his head falling back in the wing-backed chair. He could still see Florence's expression as she thrust out his father's ring. *What did you mean by giving me this?* she'd demanded, and all he could think was how right that circle of gold looked on her finger. If only he had given it to her! If only he could have loved her as he wished.

His hands gripped the arms of the chair until the wood creaked with the strain.

He couldn't leave it like this. Whatever the cost, he couldn't let her hate him.

He pushed to his feet, groaning as if his limbs were leaden weights. Unsteadily, he wove through the empty corridors to his rooms. He would change the clothes he'd been wearing since last night. He would brush his teeth and tame his hair. Then he'd speak to Florence. He didn't know what he'd say, only that he ought to look human first.

His valet, Lewis, was waiting in his chamber. He appeared both grim and worried.

"What?" said Edward, already pulling off his collar.

Lewis drew himself up with military straightness. "Your brother has left, my lord. Along with Nigel West."

"Left?" Edward's hands paused.

"Yes, your lordship. They've gone to settle the workers' dispute at the mill."

"But I was going to take care of that. I wanted Freddie and Florence to—" He stopped himself and dropped a cufflink onto the top of his chest of drawers. The onyx gleamed dully in the murky light. "You say Nigel went with him?"

"Yes, sir. Your brother left this note for you. Said I was to place it in your hands." Lewis looked as if he disapproved. Edward barely noticed. If Nigel was with Freddie, perhaps he needn't worry. Edward had known his steward for donkey's years, ever since the old earl had taken him under his wing. Nigel, the son of Greystowe's gamekeeper, had been the brightest of the lads at the village school. Too smart for the army, the old earl had declared, then sent him off to Oxford. He and Edward hadn't been close, of course; Nigel was older and of common birth, but Edward knew him to be a paragon of rectitude, punctilious in his sense of right and wrong, and nearly as loyal to the family as Edward was himself. With him along, at least Freddie wouldn't stumble into another scandal.

Then he broke the old-fashioned wafer seal.

"Good Lord!" he exploded as part of the contents caught his eye.

"Sir?" said Lewis.

Edward waved him off and sank onto the edge of the bed. Heart thundering in his chest, hands shaking, he read Freddie's note from the start.

"Dear Edward," it began. "I've come to realize you aren't likely to relinquish your plan to have me marry Florence unless you are forced to do so. I suspect this ambition lies behind your sudden desire to hie off to Manchester. Consequently, Nigel and I have decided to settle the 'crisis' ourselves. We have become friends during my convalescence, perhaps— as Florence was kind enough to remark—more than friends."

"Florence!" Edward exclaimed, letting the letter slap his thigh. What had his brother been telling Florence? And since when were Nigel and Freddie friends? Whenever Edward saw them, they were snapping at each like mongrels over a bone. Muttering to himself, he lifted the page and continued to read.

"In any case," Freddie wrote, "only time will tell what we can be to each other." (*Be* to each other, Edward snorted.) "Meanwhile, I beg you, be good to Florence. I know you have feelings for her and that she has them for you. It may be that all our happiness rests on taking chances you have thus far refused to consider."

"All our happiness!" Edward spluttered. "He's insane!"

He sprang to his feet but did not move except to press the fist that held the note between his eyes. Damn him. *Damn* him for a misbegotten fool. So. He and Nigel were taking some lovebirds' journey to Manchester. Did Freddie think no one would notice? Was he determined to throw his life into the gutter? No matter what Edward did? No matter what he sacrificed?

Well, fuck it, Edward thought, the whiskey stoking his rage. He was done trying to rescue his little brother. Done, done, done.

"Bloody hell," he swore, and smashed his fist into the wall.

The plaster split, along with the skin over three of his knuckles.

"Sir!" Lewis protested, still hovering nearby.

Edward allowed him to wrap a strip of cotton around the wound.

"Where's Florence?" he said once the cut had been dressed. Seeing her was suddenly all he could think of. Something must be salvaged from this day.

"Miss Fairleigh?" said Lewis, clearly startled by his tone. "I don't know. In her rooms, I imagine."

But Florence wasn't in her rooms. She was gone, along with half her clothes. Her little maid, Lizzie, had also cleared out her belongings. Edward stood, as if rooted, among the scattered signs of their departure: boots left lying on the carpet, a sprinkling of silver hairpins, a small pink glove. His blood beat through his body as if it were a death knell.

She was gone. Too hastily to say good-bye. While he'd been drinking himself stupid, she'd been slipping out the door.

He'd driven her away. He'd driven them both away.

Edward threw back his head and roared.

BY THE FOLLOWING MORNING, THE RAIN HAD SETTLED TO A surly drizzle. Though Edward had discovered where Florence was, any triumph he felt at the success of his detective work was obliterated by the nature of her refuge.

The odds were even as to whether he'd have preferred her to run to the devil.

But the obstacle had to be faced. Florence could not be allowed to remain in such uncaring hands. The witch must be bearded in her den—or whatever the metaphor was for bitter old spinster crones.

He dressed carefully in riding clothes and freshly polished boots. His linen was immaculate, his demeanor as cool as he could make it. Perhaps it was his imagination, but Samson seemed reluctant to stop at Catherine Exeter's house. While the stallion shook his head up and down, Edward threaded his reins through the hitching post ring.

"Wise horse," he muttered, patting his glossy neck.

Lucky horse, in fact, to be able to remain out here.

With a dour smile, Edward strode decisively up the pebbled path. Catherine Exeter herself answered the door. She didn't pretend not to know him, though they hadn't exchanged two words since the incident with Freddie and the apples. Edward's animosity towards the woman seethed in his veins. Only Florence could have brought him within her sphere.

His nemesis stood firmly between the entry way and him. "Little early for a call," she said.

"You know why I'm here."

"Actually"—Catherine smiled like an evil seraph—"if you were Freddie, I would know why you were here. Oh, but I must have forgotten. My niece told me you'd developed a tendre for your brother's fiancée. Tut, tut. Quite incautious of you, Lord Greystowe."

Edward was grinding his teeth so hard his jaw ached. He relaxed it enough to speak. "I want to see her."

"I'm sure you do. She, however, doesn't want to see you. That's what happens when you treat a woman like a dog. She develops an aversion to being kicked."

"I did not treat—" he began, but a movement on the narrow stairs drove the thread of argument from his mind. Florence was coming down in one of her old gowns, this one a medley of pink and yellow flowers. The cotton was faded, the sleeves too wide for fashion, but to him the dress was as joyous a sight as the finest silk. He ran his eyes to her hem and back. How lovely she was, how womanly in every way.

"It's all right, Catherine," she said, her voice calm and soft. "I'll speak to him."

"But dearest—"

Florence squeezed Catherine's small bony shoulder. "Best to get it over with."

After a slight hesitation, Catherine agreed. "As you wish. I'll be in the parlor should you need me."

Florence took her place at the door. Apparently, neither woman intended to let him in. But that was fine with Edward. He had no desire to enter Catherine Exeter's home—as long as Florence returned to his.

For a few slow breaths, he simply looked at her, taking in the soft flushed curve of her cheeks, the sheen of her upswept hair, the uncustomary pallor of her brow. Her lashes dipped, shadowing her grass-green eyes with glistening sable fans. Her mouth was a curve of cherry blossom pink, infinitely sweet. When she bit her lower lip, a shiver of pleasure touched his nape. If it weren't for Catherine, he'd have kissed her then and there.

"You don't know who you've run to," he said.

She lifted her head. "I do. And I've no intention of listening to you malign her. Tell me what you want and be done with it."

With an effort, Edward uncurled his fists. "I want you to return to Greystowe."

"Why?" She crossed her arms beneath her breasts. "So I can marry your brother?"

He thought he knew what she wished him to say, but he could not form the words. He wanted to, but then he thought of Freddie: of Freddie's future as an outcast. Even now he could not claim her as his own.

"I don't want you to hate me," he said, the statement sounding inadequate even to him.

"I don't hate you," she said. "I pity you."

But what he heard in her voice wasn't pity, just as what he saw in Catherine Exeter's eyes wasn't the milk of human kindness.

"I care for you," he said. "I know that's hard for you to believe, but—"

"For pity's sake." Clearly scornful, she cut him off. "If you care for me, I'd hate to see how you'd treat someone you hate. You took my innocence, Edward, and you trampled it in the mud."

"I didn't take your innocence," he hissed, low enough to frustrate listening ears. "You're still a virgin."

"Yes, indeed," she said. "We couldn't have your brother taking a fallen woman to his bed."

Her thrust struck so directly home a tide of shame crept up his neck. Naturally, Florence saw it. "You're despicable," she said, spitting out the words. "If I never see you again, it will be too soon."

Before he could devise an answer, she slammed the door in his face. If Catherine Exeter had done it, he probably would have broken the barrier down. But Florence—Florence's rejection left him gasping for air. He swayed on his feet, his ears ringing from the thud of the heavy wood.

She did hate him. She hated him just as Catherine Exeter had hated his father.

He couldn't handle this. He had to think. He stumbled twice on his way back down the path, his very muscles thrown into shock. Samson lipped his hand as he fumbled with the reins, then stood patiently while he mounted. Secure in the saddle, Edward turned one last time towards the house.

At first he thought he was seeing things: some nightmarish projection of his guilt. When he blinked, however, the image refused to disappear. Imogene Hargreave was gazing out the parlor window, her pale eyes lit by the darkest sort of glee. Oh, Lord, he thought. Florence was in more danger than he'd dreamed.

FLORENCE HAD REMOVED HIS RING. IT LAY NOW IN THE pocket of her skirt. Over and over she turned the circle of gold— seeing his face, hearing his words—while Catherine knitted stockings for the poor. Her niece carried the burden of conversation, chattering amusingly of her many London conquests. Half the city had fallen at her feet, it seemed, a claim Florence could not doubt with her wit and her elegance and her cat-sleek beauty spread like a feast before her miserable country self.

I care for you, Edward had said. *I don't want you to hate me.*

Why had he said those things? Was this a game for him? To see how cruelly he could treat her and still keep her dangling on his string?

I care for you, Florence.

Even now she wanted to believe him. She clucked her tongue in self-disgust. If she wasn't careful, Edward's string would choke her.

Catherine looked up at the tiny exclamation. She sat in her plain

green chair like a roosting sparrow, the click of her needles as famil-
iar to Florence as the beating of her heart. Just so did the ladies of
Keswick occupy their time. "Are you sure you wouldn't like to help?
It might take your mind from your troubles."

She removed her hand from her pocket and straightened her skirt.
"I'm afraid I can't keep my mind on anything today."

"As you wish," Catherine said in her soothing way. The needles
clicked pensively before she spoke again. "You may not believe this,
dear, but once upon a time I had more than socks to offer. When Papa
was alive, before my loathsome cousin, if you'll pardon the expression,
took over the Grange—nothing so fancy as Greystowe, mind, but a
good thriving property—ah, then we carried such riches to the poor!
Smoked hams and preserves and, oh, my, all manner of lovely things,
some of which you may believe I'd be grateful to have today. But such
is life. The Lord gives and the Lord takes, though why He had to give
so much to silly old Jeffrey I'm sure I couldn't say. *He* had money from
his father. But this is how men arrange the world. A girl may not in-
herit her father's home but must be kicked out willy-nilly to fend as
best she can. And if she doesn't find a husband—well! But I'm sure
it's for the best. Women are stronger than men, you know. We can
carry these burdens. And far better to scrimp beneath one's own roof
than to share one with a bully."

"Indeed," Imogene agreed, her tapering fingers stroking her swan-
like neck. "One must teach a man his place or avoid him altogether.
A man one hasn't the ability to control is a danger too great to suffer."

Since Florence had heard much on these themes already, she knew
she needn't answer, only nod occasionally and hum. Humming now,
she turned sideways on the couch and propped her chin against its
back. Ever since she'd left Greystowe, she'd felt as if she were dragging a ball and chain behind her. Heavy. Hopeless. All her dreams
come to grief. Catherine's gentle litany of complaints seemed a vision
of her future, as dreary as the day outside. She'd seen a wider world
now and she would miss it. With the tips of her fingers, she touched
one of the window's rippled panes. The lane beyond was cloaked in
swirling gray. As bad as London. And the interior was no brighter.
Catherine couldn't afford to waste pennies burning candles.

And here she was wasting pennies feeding Florence.

"I'm sorry Freddie left," Florence said, a bit of intelligence Lizzie
had managed to ferret out. "I know he would have escorted me back
to Keswick."

"You mustn't worry about that," said Catherine. "A spot of company is a treat for an old woman like me. And for Imogene as well. As kind as she is to visit me, I know you—who have so lately been to London—are a better audience for her tales."

Imogene murmured something agreeable and untrue. Florence had never been a part of society the way Imogene was. Florence was not that sort of woman. Florence was simple and dull and pitifully forgettable. She sighed, a soft, mournful sound she could not repress.

"Now, now," Catherine chided. "Hold firm, dear. Time heals. Before you know it, you'll be free of the Burbrooke curse."

Would she, though? It seemed to her as if her heart would never be light again.

Chapter 14

EDWARD HALTED A CAUTIOUS DISTANCE FROM THE SHEP-herd's hut. The construction was simple stone and thatch but it was sound. The garden was groomed, the flowers bright, and a flock of fat white chickens pecked the ground outside their coop. Edward wasn't sure the inhabitants of the house would appreciate being the object of charity, but Lizzie had informed him of Catherine Exeter's intent to visit them today.

"If you're interested like," she'd said in a secretive tone, though no one but he was near.

She'd accosted him on the terrace on his way to his morning ride. Despite the heat, she'd pulled her hood over her face like a character in a sensation novel. The market basket dangling from her arm told the excuse she'd used to slip away from the Exeter home. Edward would have chuckled at her melodrama if he hadn't been desperate for word of Florence. Three days running he'd been turned away without a chance to see her. He was beginning to fear he'd have to abduct her to say hello.

Somehow, he didn't think that would improve Florence's opinion of his character.

Now, however, he had another chance because of Lizzie.

"That servant of hers, that Bertha, don't like her one bit," she'd confided. "She told me Miss Exeter flutters in and out when she plays

the grand patroness. And that Lady Hargreave won't go at all. Too
busy with her beauty sleep. I know Florence, though. She'll stay to
dandle the babies. She pretends to be embarrassed when they like her,
but she won't be able to resist. Then you can talk to her."

Edward hoped this would be the case. At least the damn rain had
stopped. He felt a fool lurking behind a thicket while he waited for
Catherine to leave. When she did leave, though, and alone, he knew
the wait had been worthwhile. He straightened his collar, smoothed
his hair, and told himself not to act like a schoolboy with a crush. The
lecture didn't help. His palms were clammy as he knocked on the
weather-grayed planks of the door.

Bartle's wife blinked to find him behind it, then smiled, slow and
broad, as if she knew precisely why he was there.

Perhaps she did. Perhaps his lovesick yearning was written large
across his face.

"Lord Greystowe," she exclaimed, pushing the door wider in welcome. "How kind of you to come. I was just making tea."

Edward stepped inside, his hat in hand. The Bartles' cottage consisted of three rooms: a large main room where the family cooked and
lived and washed, a larder for storage, and a small curtained nook
where Mr. and Mrs. Bartle slept. The floor was well-swept paving
stone, the walls age-yellowed plaster. Wooden pegs for hanging
clothes made an orderly circuit around the room. The clothing ranged
in size from infant to adult, much of it displaying Mrs. Bartle's gift
with needle and yarn. Her husband took part of his pay in wool and
Mrs. Bartle spun it into gold.

Shining her own sort of gold, Florence sat in a sunny corner with
a chubby baby in her lap. A young girl, no more than six, carded wool
at her feet, her shoulder brushing Florence's knee as if she'd known
her all her life. Edward was careful not to look directly at the reason
for his visit.

"I, uh, came to see how your husband is faring," he said. "I heard
he caught a bad cough."

He had indeed heard this, though it had been weeks ago.

"Oh, he's much better," said Mrs. Bartle. "Please thank Mrs.
Forster for her tea."

"I will," he said and, for the life of him, could not think of anything further to say. Florence's presence was a weight behind his back.
He was afraid to turn and meet the censure in her eyes, but even more
afraid of being asked to leave.

Thankfully, Mrs. Bartle took pity on him. She was a fine, fair woman, as Angus Bartle liked to say; broad and blonde, though not as blonde as her four young offspring. She had the calm, capable air some women gain as their families grow.

"I'm sure you know your cousin," she said, turning him gently to face her.

"Florence," he said, eyes drinking her in. She looked a madonna with that child in her lap. His madonna. At that moment, he would have given his right arm for that baby to be theirs.

Her gaze remained on the bundled infant. "Edward," she answered, his name a mere whisper. Her face was pink, her breathing quick. Both could have been the effect of embarrassment, but Edward's body came so swiftly to attention his linens should have caught fire. That he had touched her most intimate parts, that he had heard her sigh with pleasure and could no more seemed utterly intolerable.

He barely heard Mrs. Bartle murmur something about the tea. He was crossing the room towards Florence. He was sitting in the pool of sunshine by her side. The window seat was just big enough for the two of them. Florence's leg pressed his through her flowered skirts. At the contact he felt not an increase in lust, but a comfort so deep it scared him.

He wanted to sit in the sun with her all his life.

The baby fussed as Florence tensed.

"Let me have him." Wanting only to calm her, Edward eased the heavy bundle from her arms. The baby widened his eyes at him, then tried to bat his face. Charmed by his energy, Edward pretended to eat the dimpled fist.

"How's little Ivan?" he growled. "As terrible as ever?"

Ivan wriggled excitedly at the teasing, his baby-chuckle throaty and full out.

"You know him?" Florence said, her gaze finally on him.

"Of course I know Ivan. The Bartles are my tenants."

"And a fine landlord he is," Mrs. Bartle put in, approaching with two steaming dishes of tea. "You couldn't wish for better." The tea dispensed, she handed her daughter a small sweet biscuit. Still leaning into Florence's knee, the girl looked curiously up at Edward.

"Did you bring socks?" she said.

"No-o," Edward answered, the question confusing him.

"Good," said the girl. " 'Cause nobody's socks are as nice as Mama's."

"Hush," scolded Mrs. Bartle, though Edward could tell she was fighting a smile.

He wasn't sure he should ask for an explanation. Instead, he hitched young Ivan to a sitting position and anchored him to his chest with the bend of his arm. "Now I've got you, little man. We'll see if you can get at my tea from there."

The baby squealed with pleasure and flapped his pudgy hands. His little feet pummeled Edward's thigh. He was strong, this boy, strong and full of life.

"What a bruiser." Edward chuckled.

"Like his father," Mrs. Bartle agreed, seeming pleased not to have to wrestle for once with her youngest child. She smiled cagily over the rim of her cup. "You're good with babies, your lordship. Almost as good as Miss Fairleigh."

"I suppose I remember when Freddie was this age." He set his cup on the floor so he could mop a bit of drool from Ivan's chin. "He was better than a new pony to me. A happy baby, just like this fellow."

Florence popped up from the seat as if something had bitten her. "I really should be going," she said, her voice strained. "Catherine will wonder what happened to me."

"I'll walk you back," Edward said, rising just as quickly.

"Oh, yes," Mrs. Bartle agreed, already reaching for her son. "You shouldn't go unescorted."

Florence didn't look happy with this arrangement but, as he'd hoped, she was too polite to put up a fight with Mrs. Bartle looking on. After assuring the shepherd's wife he'd need "the lads" at harvest just like always, he and Florence took their leave. Side by side, they trod the grassy, rock-strewn land, Edward with his hands clasped behind him, Florence with them folded at her waist.

"Are you well?" he asked when she maintained her stubborn silence.

She pressed her lips together and walked faster. Edward was amazed a little thing like her could cover the ground so quickly. Apparently, country living had done more than pink her cheeks. In what seemed like no time at all, they reached the edge of the copse of beeches that led to Catherine Exeter's lane. Edward racked his brains. He had to say something. He didn't know when he'd get another chance.

He cleared his throat. "That's a handsome family Mrs. Bartle has."

Florence came to a standstill. "Stop," she said, as if he'd covered her in curses. "You're not being fair."

"How am I not being fair?" he asked, glad they'd halted but confused.

"You were dandling that baby as if you liked it, as if it were your own."

"I do like it . . . him. Ivan is a nice baby and I've known Angus Bartle since I was small."

This explanation did not satisfy Florence. She brushed impatiently at a fallen wisp of hair. "I know what you're thinking," she said. "You're thinking I can marry Freddie and have babies with you. Well, I won't do it. I won't!"

Edward hadn't been thinking anything of the sort. That she would accuse him of it intrigued him. Despite her fierce denial, Florence didn't sound as sure as she might have liked. Heartened, he ventured to stroke her arm. She yanked her hand away before his fingers could catch it up.

"Don't," she said, and pressed her fist to her mouth. Her eyes glittered with pent emotion, their color richer than the summer trees.

The glitter told him she was weakening; told him she yearned for the comfort he could give. Breath held, he stepped closer and coaxed her head against his chest. His heart sighed with silent pleasure as she yielded, as her hands tightened on the sides of his back. The subtle motion of her fingers on his ribs, a soft, catlike kneading, sent a shiver of sensual enjoyment to his groin. His sex lifted, helplessly, deliciously, as he let his own arms circle her back—not tightly, just enough to hold her near.

"Don't be angry, Florence," he whispered. "I'm only trying to make amends."

"There are no amends for what you've done."

Her words were muffled, hovering on the edge of tears. He murmured her name and pressed his lips to the smooth warm skin of her temple. Longing shot through him like a knife: longing and a pleasure too deep for words. He wanted to take her mouth with his until the wanting melted like wax and drowned them both. Unfortunately, the kiss he did take, gentle though it was, seemed to remind her of what had gone before. With a cry of impatience, she pushed at his chest until he freed her.

"Stay away from me," she said, the warning shaking like a leaf. She backed away, her skirts swishing in the bracken beside the path. She put the length of two men between them before she turned. Edward wanted to follow, but instinct told him to let her go. He watched until she disappeared among the dancing shadows of the trees. He remained where he was, rooted to the damp earth-scented ground.

Something was happening inside him, a subtle shifting, like the changing of a tide. Her accusation had turned his imagination down a frightening path.

Florence thought he wanted her to marry Freddie but sleep with him.

He didn't understand how she could let such an arrangement cross her mind. Couldn't she see it would make a travesty of what they felt? They had cared for each other; still did, he was certain, not just with their bodies but with their hearts. Florence would never have been intimate with him if that were not the case. She was no jaded daughter of the peerage. She was a vicar's child, and a good, sweet woman in her own right. That she could consider a duplicity of this magnitude, even for a moment, meant she must love him very much.

Perhaps as much as he loved her.

The possibility sent a tingle of shock across his scalp. If it was true . . . If he had become as necessary to her happiness as she was to his, how could he offer her less than his all? How could he *not* marry her?

The question dizzied him, rocking foundations he'd thought were granite firm. Marrying Florence would mean putting her first, ahead of Freddie. He'd never set a woman ahead of his brother. He'd never even set one ahead of his holdings. The thought of taking a wife had always made him feel impatient, boxed in. But Florence . . .

He couldn't live without her, not with any ease of heart or mind.

And he no longer believed Freddie would make her happy.

But perhaps Edward could. Perhaps, of all the men in the world, only Edward could. Her tears said she thought so, even if she wasn't willing to admit it.

Freddie wanted to be free to love where he pleased. Maybe Edward should finally let him. Maybe, in spite of all the arguments against it, Freddie knew what was best for him. Edward's heart thudded his ribs as if he'd run a race. Fear was part of what drove its swift percussion, fear and something he thought was hope.

"I will," he whispered to the cloud-flecked sky, to the wind-ruffled leaves and the birds that chittered busily in the trees. "I will marry her."

A whoosh of lightness swept his body. Once he'd made the decision, it seemed inevitable, as if he'd been moving towards it from the moment he saw her at Madame Victoire's. He would marry Florence. He, Edward Arthur Burbrooke, earl of Greystowe, would take the vicar's daughter for his bride. He remembered the way the Bartles' girl had leaned against her knee. The vision made him grin. He and Florence would have beautiful children together.

And all he had to do was bring her to the same conclusion.

FLORENCE HURRIED UP THE NARROW STAIRS AS IF SHE WERE being chased. Her room was a snug little nest on the second floor, small but bright. It had a bed, a chair, a chest of drawers, and a washstand and basin so like the one she'd had at home it might have been its twin. Simple things for a simple life. Her shoulders did not relax until she shut herself among them.

She'd been wrong to want to escape this, to aim any higher than what she had. A simple girl like her could not navigate the snares of the upper class.

It was just as Catherine said. The Burbrookes had a fatal charm.

She sagged back against the door, her hands pressed flat to the wood as if to bar her fears from entry. It was far too late for that. The danger lurked within. Seeing Edward had brought it back: not just the erotic things he'd done, but the sweet ones.

She remembered how protective he was of Freddie. How he'd pulled her by the hand through the Royal Academy of Art, flaunting propriety just to show her a picture he admired. She remembered his rare smiles. His common frowns. The way he'd held her tucked against him in the night. The way they'd danced at the Vances' ball like angels twirling on a cloud. She missed his company with an intensity that made her ache.

Disgusted, she thumped the wood behind her with her fists. Those memories were lies. The real Edward had ice water in his veins. The real Edward cared for nothing except his family name. He was a devil in noble clothes.

But the baby, her torn heart cried. A devil couldn't make a baby laugh!

She swallowed hard and pushed herself from the door. Edward wasn't a devil. He was a man, a man who might well find entertainment in bouncing a baby and still not give a fig for her. He wouldn't have been dreaming of having a child himself. He wouldn't have thought: what a good mother she'd be, or how I'd love to have a daughter with her eyes. No. His only concern had been tricking her into saving his brother, a brother who—quite obviously—didn't want to be saved.

Be firm, she thought, taking Catherine's advice for her own. Be firm, be firm, be firm.

When her legs crumpled beneath her, Edward's ring, still hidden in her pocket, hit the floor with a fateful clink.

THOUGH LIZZIE KEPT EDWARD INFORMED OF FLORENCE'S schedule, he hadn't been able to catch her alone since that day at the Bartles' cottage. She clung to Catherine Exeter as if the woman were a lifeline in a storm.

From what Edward could see, she was the opposite. Day by day, the duchess's friend was sucking the life from his beloved: stealing her glow, her smiles, her very spirit. And who knew what tales Imogene had been telling? Each time he engineered the crossing of their paths, Florence looked paler and thinner. Haunted, he would have said if he'd had a romantic turn of mind.

He worried for her. He would have done anything to help and yet he could do nothing. Nothing but wait, that is, for another chance to speak, to touch, to somehow convince her of his care.

He began to wonder if it was he, by his pursuit, who had put those shadows beneath her eyes. The thought hurt but did not sway him. If it were true, it was only because Catherine Bloody Exeter and her viper of a niece were dripping poison in Florence's ear. He could cleanse her of it, if only she'd give him a chance.

Assuming he didn't lose his mind before he got one.

For the first time in years he attended Sunday service at the village church. He sat in the last row, watching the dip of Florence's hat over the prayer book, feeling his throat tighten as the child behind her tried to climb the wooden pew. The parents scolded and Catherine Exeter shooed, but Florence reached back to brush the little nose with her thumb. Her sheepish smile for the parents nearly broke his heart.

Edward wished it were as easy to make her smile at him.

He positioned himself carefully as the congregation filed out. People whispered when they saw him. Greystowe was not so large they didn't know him by sight. A few of the men nodded and a few of the women smiled, but mostly they were curious. If the earl felt a need to worship, he had a chapel on his land. They couldn't imagine what he was doing here. With them. In the back of their simple church.

Edward didn't care what they thought. Florence was drawing closer, her head averted in a manner that suggested she had seen him. Her arm tightened on Catherine Exeter's and then she was there, in front of him. Gently, he caught her elbow. She yanked away as if he'd burned her.

"Florence," he said, fighting through hurt for calm, "you must speak to me."

"She must do nothing of the kind," said Catherine Exeter.

Edward ignored her. The crowd had bottled up in front of them at the door. He had a few precious seconds before Catherine hastened her away.

"Florence, please." He stroked one finger around her down-turned cheek, the soft still heat of her causing his eyes to sting. "You're breaking my heart, Florence."

"You have no heart to break," snapped Catherine Exeter, but Florence lifted her head. Tears streaked her skin in glistening crisscrossed trails. Her face had hollows he'd never seen before.

"Leave me alone," she said. "I can't bear this anymore."

He fell back, shocked by her appearance, by the dull misery in her voice. Had he done that to her? Had he? Before he could gather his wits, Catherine pulled her briskly through the door and down the steps. Edward could only stare and catch his breath.

"There, there," said a plump older woman, giving his arm a pat. "She'll come around, your lordship. Girls that age don't know what's good for 'em."

It was proof of his distress that he took comfort in a stranger's touch.

HE RETREATED TO GREYSTOWE, TO PACE HIS STUDY AND write a thousand letters in his head. Finally he sent one, then half a dozen in quick succession. They all came back in pieces and he honestly didn't know whether Florence had torn them up herself. He imagined Imogene reading them, and laughing, and couldn't even bring himself to care. No one's opinion mattered except for Florence's.

He missed Freddie, then was glad his brother could not see him in this state. Hypatia he avoided like the plague. He grew disheveled. He did not drink, but looked as though he had. His eyes were red from lack of sleep, his jaw shadowed with the beard he could not be troubled to let Lewis shave. He could not read; he could not sit; he could not follow a train of thought for more than a minute. At night, he walked to town and stood in the lane beneath her darkened window, yearning for her with all his blood and bone.

A different man would have climbed the trellis and carried her away. Edward wished he were that man; wished he didn't fear Florence would scream for help. And what if she were right to do so? What if he were the danger Catherine claimed? He didn't know who he was anymore. All the rules by which he'd lived were gone.

He only knew he loved her to the point of madness.

One sultry gray morning, when the clouds hung as heavy as his spirit, Lewis and his aunt came together to his study. Lewis thumped a mug of cider on his desk, Hypatia a platter of roast and bread. Edward doubted she'd carried anyone a meal before in her life.

"Enough of this self-pitying nonsense," she said. "I'm not leaving until you eat."

"And I'm not leaving until you shave."

Edward looked at them, his aunt and his valet. Worry and anger mixed in their expressions; a bit of fear as to how he'd react, but even more concern. They knew, he thought, his own eyes burning. Everyone knew he loved her.

"You can't go on this way," said the duchess. "You've done that girl wrong. We all have. But you won't begin to undo it unless you pull yourself together."

Edward stared at his hands, spread wide across his desk, and tried to breathe.

"She's just skittish," Lewis added. "Women get that way. You wouldn't let a horse hide in the brambles if it was scared. You'd catch it and you'd gentle it and then you'd lead it home."

"I don't know how," he said, the words a gasp. "She won't—she won't let me."

"Eat," said his aunt, nudging the plate within reach. "Nobody thinks well on an empty stomach."

He stared at the meat, red and glistening with juice, just the way he liked it. Cook had outdone herself. His mouth watered. He cut a piece and took a bite. Amazingly, it tasted good. After the second bite, his head began to clear. "You don't have to stay," he said. "I'll be all right."

His aunt narrowed her eyes. "I want that plate cleaned, Edward. I am not going to tolerate two idiots in one family."

To his surprise, he smiled. "This was very kind," he said. "Thank you."

"Hmpf," said the duchess. "You can thank me when that girl is back where she belongs."

"There's still the matter of a shave," said Lewis, and Edward smiled at him, too.

He wasn't any wiser than he'd been before, but at least he didn't feel alone.

*   *   *

FED AND SHAVED AND BATHED, EDWARD PUT HIS MIND TO work. He had to find the key to coaxing Florence back. He had to remember everything he knew of her. Then he'd be able to formulate a plan. Hoping for inspiration, he returned to her rooms. He touched her remaining dresses, recalling how she'd looked and what she'd done in every one. He took her novels and read them. He dipped his handkerchief in her perfume. He visited her favorite corners of the garden and drank her favorite tea. He steeped himself in memories, letting himself miss her until it hurt. He took a perverse but definite pleasure in the pain.

He'd made up his mind. Nothing and no one could stop him.

Not even her.

Finally, he returned to the pavilion. There he relived their one forbidden night: her kisses and her sighs, her trust and her bravery. Again, he tied her between the columns. Again, he took his pleasure against her velvet curves. His lips remembered, and his sex. He took the lingering scent of her arousal through his skin. He opened himself to feeling as he never had before. Even the last he faced: the moment of his shame when he slipped from her sleeping hold and crept out like a thief. Loving her had not been his error. His error had been letting her go.

Drained but calm, he padded to the bath. As he'd done before, he opened the carved Indian cabinet and removed his father's letters from the chest. One by one he read them and bit by bit he found a compassion for Catherine Exeter he'd never thought to know. She'd loved the former earl, foolishly, recklessly, with the wholehearted innocence of youth. Then, halfway through the second stack, he discovered something unexpected. He groaned when he realized what it was.

Poor bastard, he thought, both awed and aghast. Poor stupid, selfish bastard.

Stephen Burbrooke had loved Catherine Exeter. He hadn't shoved her in a box and forgotten her. He'd written her, every year, on the anniversary of their parting. He'd poured out his heart, expressing a depth of emotion Edward had never glimpsed. He said he was lost without her; said he felt like half a man. She was his soul. She was all of him that had been true and good.

But he never sent the letters. Not one. He'd made his choice. He married Edward's mother, the daughter of the duke. He raised two sons and polished the family name. He suffered in rancorous silence, keeping everyone at arm's length, hoarding his love for a woman who thought he'd ripped it from his chest. How many lives had he damaged when he put his honor above his heart? His wife's, certainly. His sons, without a doubt. Hypatia's, he suspected. Catherine's. His own. Who knew how long the list had grown? And for what? A nod from a duke? A yearly invitation to court?

Edward shuddered, the cold slithering down his spine.

His father's sins could so easily have been his.

Chapter 15

BELIEVING HE'D FOUND THE KEY DIDN'T MAKE EDWARD eager to turn it. Catherine and her niece had done his family too much harm for that. He toyed with his breakfast while possible outcomes ran through his mind. Finally, too nervous to eat, he readied himself to go. He felt as if his future rested on this day; one wrong step and his life would crumble.

The sky stretched clear and blue over the familiar paths to town. Edward swung his leg over low stone walls and vaulted stiles, the exertion a necessity to nerves stretched taut by dread. Fields ripened in the distance, watered by the rains, their growth so vigorous they must have been eager to fall to the harvester's blade. Willing the warmth to calm his nerves, he turned his face to the sun. His father's letters lay in the pocket of his summer coat, a crumpled garment he wore when he lent a hand at calving or in the stables. The cloth was the color of bleached tobacco, so old he couldn't remember when he'd bought it. His shirt was plain and collarless, his trousers nearly out at the knees.

He intended to present his suit as humbly as he could, as man and not as earl.

When he reached the cottage, Catherine was in the garden weeding. Unlike Florence, the marigolds seemed to be thriving in her care.

She looked up from under the brim of a battered straw hat, her mouth pursed with disapproval, her skin showing its years in the brilliant light. He fought a surge of old dislike. Those lines were not all Catherine's making. She'd had cause for bitterness—at least at first.

When she chose to nurture her resentment, the responsibility for its effects became hers.

"Well?" she said, her gaze traveling scornfully over his clothes. "You're certainly dressed to shovel shit. Not that Florence needs to hear any more of that."

With an effort, he held his temper. "It's you I came to speak to. About my father."

"Your father." She chocked her trowel in the dirt and stood with the stiffness of age. Both her gloves and her apron were stained with soil. "There's nothing you could tell me about Stephen Burbrooke that I would care to hear."

"What if I could prove he'd never forgotten you? That he loved you all his life?"

Catherine's face tightened. "That would be a clever trick, but patently untrue. Now, if you'll excuse me, my lord, I have laundry to see to."

In two bounding strides he put himself between her and the door.

"I have proof," he said. "I have letters he wrote to you every year until he died. Love letters, Catherine. He wasn't the man you thought he was. His heart was never cold."

Her eyes narrowed to slits of cloudy ice. "I've no doubt you've concocted some fiction you think will convince me to let you have another go at Florence. The fact remains, however, that she has no desire to speak to you and neither do I. Now step aside or I shall be forced to call the watch."

Since Greystowe's constabulary was funded in large part by its earl, the threat was not a good one. Paying it no mind, Edward withdrew one of the letters and spread it, facing Catherine, across his chest. "You'll recognize his hand, I wager. And perhaps his pet name for you: 'Dearest Angel'?"

"Lies," she spat. Her face turned from the letter as if it were Medusa's hair. "Your tongue is as forked as your father's."

"Perhaps you'd like me to read it?" he suggested. From the way she flinched, he knew his offer was no kindness. It did not matter. However worthy of being discarded he might feel her, and however comfortable she may have grown with her beliefs about his family, he could not allow her misconceptions to survive. They stood between him and Florence. They would have to be destroyed. He turned the letter around to read, hearing in every flowery phrase the ghost of a father he'd never known.

" 'Yesterday,' " he began, " 'I walked to the well—remember our well?—and thought of you; how you scratched our initials in the stone when we were twelve. You were an elfin creature, beauty and mischief, like sunlight dancing on the water far below. My heart barely knew desire and yet, for you, I felt it. I wanted to wrap myself around you, to carry you inside me through the dark. Dearest Angel, I fear you have forgotten those days, but I never shall. That innocent time was all I have ever known of joy.' "

As he read, Catherine drew her hands to her breast and curved her shoulders forward, as if shielding from a blow. He thought his words were getting through, but as soon as he lowered the letter, she exploded.

"Bastard!" she cried, hands lashing at his face. "I won't let you have her. I won't!"

The attack surprised him so much he stumbled back into a boxwood hedge. In a flash, she was in the door. He leapt to push in behind her but her body slammed it shut before he could. He heard the frantic turning of a key, then the dropping of a bolt.

Bloody hell, he thought. He was not going to be bested, not by her, not this time.

Without stopping to think, he ran to the parlor window and drove his elbow through the pane. The glass shattered on the first try. He heard a female shriek, then running feet: Catherine, trying to escape his rage.

Let her run, he thought, his will like fresh-forged iron. Removing his boot, he used the sole to widen the hole. More glass broke, and wood. The truth would find her if he had to shove it down her throat.

Grim as death, elbow throbbing, he shoved his foot back in his boot, wrapped his coat around his hand, and climbed through the broken window. Then, tossing the coat impatiently before him, he stepped onto an ugly puce-green settee, not the least bit sorry to be muddying it as he went. A second shriek greeted his entrance. This voice did not belong to Catherine. As his eyes adjusted to the dimness of the curtained room, he saw a large pale maid huddled like a frightened calf behind the chancy shelter of a spinet.

"Where's Florence?" he said, his tolerance for feminine vapors gone.

The terrified girl pointed towards the ceiling. "Sh-she didn't come down from her room this morning. Nor yesterday, neither."

Edward gritted his teeth and stumped up the stairs. Yet another sin to lay at Catherine's feet: that she had undone Florence's hard-won quest for courage.

"Florence!" he roared, not knowing which door to pound. "Florence, get out here now!"

She appeared with a strangled gasp. He'd obviously caught her combing her hair. The rich brown locks lay over her shoulders and back, falling clear to her waist, as smooth as burnished silk. Her face was pale and puffy, but she was dressed.

"Edward," she said. The hand that held the brush drew inward to cover the skin above her collar. "What are you doing?"

He didn't waste time, but immediately cupped her pallid cheeks between his palms. Her skin was cold. Worried anew, he pressed his lips to the curve of one brow.

"Florence," he said, her name made gruff by the intensity of his feelings. "I love you so much it shames me. I want you to come home. I want to make you happy."

Her brow puckered. She drew a breath to speak, but doubt seemed to silence her. Aching for her confusion, Edward stroked her baby-soft face with his thumbs. Trust me, love, he thought. Trust me.

"Well, well, well," interrupted a voice he'd been praying to avoid. "Look who's come to claim his latest prize." Flushed with sleep and slyness, his former mistress emerged from the second bedroom, draped in a nightdress of filmy, glacier pink.

Edward growled at her. "You stay out of this, Imogene."

"You know her?" Florence gasped.

He cursed his incautious tongue. He'd assumed Imogene had already revealed their sordid past. Apparently, she'd been saving the disclosure for a special occasion: one that had arrived. She folded her arms and smiled.

"Edward knows lots of women," she said, her eyes half closed with pleasure. "Strictly in the biblical sense, mind you. Go all night if you let him. Yes, indeed. Quite the cocksman, our Edward. Knows how to whisper those sweet nothings, then fuck a lady till she screams."

"Hold your tongue," he warned, though he knew she would ignore him. Florence was staring from one to the other with rounded eyes. Noting this, and obviously enjoying it, Imogene flashed her teeth at her.

"Has he gotten masterful yet?" she asked, one long nail brushing Florence's trembling sleeve. "He's good at that. Very top wolf." She assumed a mocking, masculine voice. " 'I must have you, darling. Don't even think of resisting me!' "

It was a canny guess, considering Edward had only behaved that way with her once. She must have added up the dates and realized he was thinking of Florence when he did it. None of which Florence knew, of course. Her face looked as hot as his felt. Nervously, she rubbed her wrists and he knew she was remembering the velvet ties. Damn Imogene for making her think of that as anything but special.

"No," he said. "Never with anyone but you. You're the only woman I've ever loved."

Imogene's laugh was lemon sharp. "My goodness, darling. You must be randy to say a thing like that! The thrill of stealing a march on your little brother must be more seductive than I'd thought."

Edward refused to acknowledge the implication. Instead, he took Florence's shoulders in his hands. He didn't care who heard him or what they thought. He'd get through to Florence if he had to beg her on his knees.

"I love you," he said, low and rough. "I want to marry you if you'll have me. I want us to share the future side by side."

"M-marry me?" Florence stammered just as Catherine came up the stairs. Edward tensed. The old bat must have recovered from the shock of him breaking in. Or perhaps she thought her niece needed reinforcement.

"You see," she said, stealing Florence's gaze from his. "You see what he is? My Imogene is clever. A diamond on a heap of coal. Men turn to puppies when she walks into a room. If he could lie to her— to *her*—why wouldn't he lie to you?"

Even as he consigned her to perdition in his head, Edward struggled to rein in his temper. Abusing an elderly lady would not aid his cause.

"I never lied to Imogene," he said. "And I'm not lying to you. Read the letters, Catherine. My father loved you. Just as I love Florence. The only difference is I'm not fool enough to let her slip away."

The hall fell silent then, the three of them gathering their wits for the next sally in the war for Florence's trust. To everyone's surprise, she was the first to speak.

"You lied to me," she said. "And you started the day we met."

SHE WATCHED EDWARD BLANCH AT HER QUAVERING WORDS and wondered where she'd found the strength to speak them. Her heart was a tumult of anger and confusion. Despite her accusation, she did believe he loved her. He was not the sort of man to expose his feelings unless he meant them, certainly not in public. Even if she'd doubted that, his obvious misery would have convinced her.

But she also believed he'd slept with Imogene: beautiful, polished Imogene, whose charms she could not match in a thousand years.

Maybe Edward *would* marry her, but Florence didn't delude herself that she could keep him. One day, sooner or later, another Imogene would slink into his bed.

Her heart felt as if it were breaking already.

"Florence," he whispered, his expression tortured, "I wish I could take it back. I didn't know how much my lies would hurt you. I swear, though, swear on my mother's grave that I'll do everything I can to make it up to you."

The words were as sweet as a poppy-smoker's dream.

"What—" she croaked, then swallowed and tried again. "What about Freddie?"

At that, his lashes lowered, as if this were a source of shame. "Freddie will have to find his own way. You were meant for me. We both know that."

Before she could respond, Imogene clapped, slow and scornful. "Bravo, darling. You should have been on the stage."

"Pure nonsense," snapped her aunt. "Come away, Florence. You don't have to listen to this scoundrel's lies. We can protect you. We know what's best."

Florence looked at her, then at Imogene, and a veil seemed to fall away from her vision. Neither of them cared about protecting her; they only cared about hurting Edward. Catherine wanted revenge for Edward's father and Imogene for the breakup of their affair. Of the pair, Catherine might possess a modicum of sincerity but, truth be told, they were two of a kind: both preferred to see the world through bitter eyes.

If Florence accepted Catherine's offer of protection, would she end up as cynical as her niece? Would she refuse to believe in love when it was staring her in the face?

"Florence," Edward begged, calling her back, "all I ask is a chance."

A chance. A chance to love and lose like the man who raised her. She closed her eyes. She knew what her father would have chosen; knew he wouldn't have given up the happiness to avoid the pain. For all his sadness, he had loved his life, loved his work, loved her with all his soul. Before her stood the price of living safely, of guarding oneself with vitriol and mistrust. Catherine and Imogene had half the life they might and less than half the joy. Her father would have wanted better for his daughter, even at the risk of being hurt.

She looked at Edward, her heart beating harder, her faith struggling to rise.

"Yes," she said, sliding her arms around his neck. "Yes, please take me home."

He hugged her hard enough to squeak, hard enough to warm her through and through.

"Yea," cheered a little voice from the bottom of the stairs. Florence peeked over Edward's shoulder. Lizzie had been eavesdropping, along with Catherine's servant, Bertha.

"I'll start packing," Lizzie said, scurrying eagerly up the stairs.

"I'll help," Bertha seconded, thumping up behind her. Her eyes held a glint Florence had never seen in them, a rather defiant glint. Florence hid her smile against Edward's neck and hoped Greystowe had room for an extra maid. She suspected Bertha would soon require another post.

"You'll be sorry," Catherine predicted as the four of them trooped down with their belongings. "And next time I won't be here to take you in."

A cooler shadow of her aunt, Imogene watched from the door of her room. "Give my regards to Freddie," she purred.

Florence could not help but shudder at the sweetness of the threat.

EDWARD DIDN'T REMEMBER HIS FATHER'S LETTERS UNTIL they'd walked a score of paces down the lane. The bundle was still in his jacket, which lay in a scatter of glass on the parlor floor. He hesitated a moment, then continued doggedly on. He'd brought those letters for Catherine. They might as well stay where they were. Maybe she'd read them. Maybe she'd throw them on the fire. He didn't give a damn as long as he never saw her again.

Not that he counted on being so lucky.

He looked around at his companions. Considering what they'd escaped, they were surprisingly subdued, blinking in the sunshine like a bunch of prisoners let out from the Tower. Shock, he supposed. It wasn't every day the underside of human nature got exposed. For her part, Florence walked a wagon's rut apart from him, not far enough to insult, but not close enough to touch. The two maids trailed behind, whispering furiously behind their hands, as mismatched a pair as Edward had ever seen, though they seemed to be bosom friends.

"Yes, Bertha can work for me," he called over his shoulder.

The whispering dissolved into giggles. Edward smiled. That was more like it.

"Thank you, Lord Greystowe," chorused the girls.

Buoyed by the change in mood, he reached for Florence's hand. She jumped at his touch but let him hold it. Her warmth was sweeter than sunshine, her closeness a tonic for his soul. He wondered that anyone could take such joys for granted. But Florence wasn't quite as happy as he.

"I feel horribly foolish," she said, low and shamed. "I didn't believe you when you warned me about Catherine Exeter."

"You had no reason to believe me," he said. "And quite a few reasons not to."

"But I should have seen—"

"What her oldest friend could not? Hypatia is no one's fool, you know." Knowing she needed reassurance, he led her across the ditch to sit on a low stone wall. Pasture spread around them, and sheep grazed in huddles. Fields of grain rippled like water in the summer breeze. The girls exchanged knowing grins as Edward waved them on. When Florence was settled beside him, he stroked the full length of her unbound hair: a husband's privilege, one he hoped would soon be his.

"Was it true?" she asked. "About the letters from your father?"

"Yes."

She folded her hands between her knees. "How very sad."

"Mm," he said dryly. "A cautionary tale."

Florence did not smile. "Do you suppose she'll ever read them?"

He wondered why this worried her but he answered. "I don't know. She might not be able to face the truth. Her hatred for my father may be all that gives her life its shape."

"She taught Imogene to hate men, too, you know. Or at least to think she's better than they are."

Edward smiled. "I imagine that's a lesson Imogene's vanity predisposed her to believe." He smoothed Florence's hair behind her ear. "Must we talk about them? I'd far rather talk about us. For instance, you haven't said whether you'll marry me."

"I want to," she whispered, her gaze evading his.

"But?" he said as gently as he could. When he tried to look into her face, she hunched her shoulders. "You can't tell me you don't love me, Florence. I've seen it in your eyes."

"I do," she said. "I do love you."

His heart swelled to hear her say it even though he'd known it to be true. "But?" he repeated.

"But it's so new. So much has happened in the last few months. Leaving Keswick and Freddie and Catherine and, well, it's hard to sort everything out. I believe you when you say you love me, but I wonder—" She drew breath to gather her courage. "I have to wonder just how long that will be true."

"I see," said Edward. And he did see all too well. It was going to take more than pretty words and promises to undo the damage he had done.

Aware that she'd pricked his feelings, Florence wound her fingers into a knot between her knees. She didn't like hurting him but she couldn't call back the words. She would not lie anymore, not to herself and not to him. Imogene might have stretched the truth, but Florence knew she'd told a part of it. Edward was a man accustomed to taking his pleasures. Florence had seen that for herself. Given that she'd done the same, she could not judge him for it. She could, however, fear.

They sat in silence while a wagon full of chickens plodded past them towards the town. The horse wore a hat on its nodding head, its balding owner none. The driver offered a hail which Edward returned with a lift of his hand. From the ease of the exchange, Florence knew the man had not recognized his earl. Not seeming the least insulted, Edward rested his forearms on his knees.

"Florence," he said once the last squawk and rumble had disappeared, "I know I haven't been what I should to you, neither as brother-in-law nor as lover. I lied when I should have been honest. I was a storm when I should have been a shield. If you'll let me, though, from now on I should like to be your friend. I should like the chance to win your trust."

Without turning his head, he extended his hand to her, palm up, fingers gently curved. She knew he did not make this offer lightly. His arm was tense and he watched her from the corner of his eye. She suspected if she turned him down, he might not try again.

She held her breath even as he held his. She was almost certain she could give him what he wished. She knew she couldn't refuse to try, not when he asked so humbly for her pardon. With the sense of leaping into a gulf, she placed her small hand in his large one. His fingers curled around her own, warm and sure and slightly damp. His grip spoke of both strength and vulnerability. An honest hold. A loving hold. The sensations it inspired were so powerful she had to close her eyes. Slowly, as if she might shy, Edward pulled her hand onto his knee.

"So small," he murmured, reverently stroking its back. "And yet within this little hand she holds my heart."

The words startled her, as did the sentiment behind them. Her eyes blinked open to search his face, but he merely smiled and looked away. He seemed no more able than she to get used to this kinder earl.

"Come," he said, gently tugging her to her feet. "I want to take you home."

What to expect when she got there, she had not the faintest clue.

Chapter 16

THE GRANDFATHER CLOCK TICKED IN THE CORNER OF THE dining room, measuring out the silence a second at a time. With nerves as tight as the pendulum's spring, Edward watched Florence push her lamb and peas around her plate. Though her head was studiously lowered, he doubted she'd taken a dozen bites. He wasn't particularly hungry himself. He forced himself to swallow to set a good example.

She was pale yet from her ordeal. If Edward had his way—indeed, if Mrs. Forster had hers—she would have taken this meal in bed. Florence had resisted with the stubborn lift of her chin he'd come to admire as well as dread. "I'm not completely spineless," she'd said. "I think I can manage to dress and come down for dinner."

None of his assurances that he didn't think her spineless had turned her from her intent. Her attitude alarmed him. He was afraid that, in her desire to redeem herself for taking refuge with Catherine Exeter, she might refuse to take refuge with him.

He'd already spoken to Aunt Hypatia; consulted her, actually, on the grounds that she must know more about women than he did. She'd smiled and patted his hand as if she did possess a secret. "It isn't merely you she doesn't trust," she said. "It's herself, her own judgment. If you want her to feel less vulnerable, you have to make yourself more so."

But Edward didn't know how a man could be more vulnerable than to ask the woman he loved to marry him.

"Give it time," his aunt soothed. "You'll think of something."

Because of this exchange, he and Florence sat alone at the long mahogany table—his aunt having developed a convenient headache.

Their plates were set properly at either end, so as not to make Florence feel pressed. Despite the distance between them, he'd never been more aware of her. Every flutter of her lashes stirred a ripple in his heart. The motions of her hands were more erotic than a naked *tableau vivant*. She wore one of the dresses Aunt Hypatia had bought, a pale blue silk with ruffles of ivory lace. The candles in the huge epergne sent shadows dancing across her cleavage, shadows that filled the aching tissues of his groin.

He wished he knew what caused that quick rise and fall of creamy flesh. Nerves? Fear? Or was she, too, thinking of the night to come?

He'd declared his love. He'd asked her to marry him. Those things ought not to have sent her back into her shell. They ought to have set their relationship right. They ought to have brought them closer.

Impatient with their impasse, Edward rose. Florence looked up. As always, her beauty squeezed his heart, more so now because she looked so thin and breakable. Gritting his teeth, he held his wineglass and plate before him.

"I'm coming down there," he said, more aggressively than he'd intended.

Florence merely nodded and continued chasing peas with the tines of her fork.

Muttering under his breath, he took the chair beside her. He gestured to her laden plate. "Cook will be upset if you don't eat."

Florence grimaced and took a single bite. Edward was not satisfied. "You need to build your strength," he insisted. "You don't look well at all."

For some reason, this made her smile. To his surprise, she reached out to smooth his hair, one finger combing it gently around his ear. Edward could count on his hand the times she'd touched him on her own. His body tensed, his breath caught in his lungs. A tingle shivered outward from the passage of her hand. The effect of the simple caress was devastating. He wanted to tip her across the table, to toss up her skirts and shove his aching prick between her legs. He wanted to sink his teeth into her flesh. He wanted to possess her.

But if he did, he'd surely scare her off.

"There's my Edward," she said, light and wry. "Always diplomatic."

Her hand fell from his head to his shoulder, then patted his forearm through the sleeve of his coat. He caught her fingers before she could completely pull away. Her arm stiffened, but he didn't let go. Desire beat at him from inside, so insistent he knew he could not court her as he should. He had touched her secrets; had tasted the honey of her need. He could not remain a gentleman, not when he remembered the pleasures they could share.

"I want you," he said, the words husky. When her lashes rose, her eyes were starred and wide. Fearing what he'd read within them, he shifted his gaze to the satiny curve of her lower lip. A pulse beat in his temple, almost as strong as the throbbing in his groin. He wasn't sure he ought to make this confession, but the words seemed to press out on their own. "There's an ache inside me, Florence. A hunger no one but you can ease. I'm not sure how long I can wait for you to accept my suit."

He could have cursed himself when he saw his words sink in. Her mouth drew up in a troubled little pucker.

"You don't have to marry me," she said, "just to get me into bed."

He sat back in his chair, still holding her hand, his mind working furiously to clear. This was the last response he'd expected. Hadn't she run away because he *wouldn't* marry her?

"Florence," he said, "I wouldn't do that to you. I would like us to marry quickly, yes, as quickly as possible, but I wouldn't treat you like a lightskirt. I mean, I know we—" His voice dropped as he recalled their night in the pavilion. "I know we've shared experiences that perhaps we shouldn't, but things are different now."

She was shaking her head. "You don't understand."

"Then tell me, love." He brushed a kiss across her knuckles. "Tell me."

As if she couldn't both answer and meet his eye, she stared at the hand that lay in her lap. Her breasts rose enticingly with her breath.

"That night," she said, "when you ran after me, when we showed each other pleasure, I told myself I only wanted to know how it felt to be desired. I hoped—" She gave herself a little shake. "Afterwards, I hoped I'd become more to you, that you would ask me to be your wife."

"You weren't wrong to think that. I should have asked."

"No." The hand that lay in her lap rose to join the one he held. Her fingers stroked the tiny hairs on the back of his wrist, raising goose bumps and stilling further words. Then she pulled both hands away. "That isn't what I'm trying to say. I'm trying to say that before we . . . did what we did, I wasn't thinking of what was proper. I genuinely didn't care. I've seen the harm that living up to society's expectations can do: to Freddie, to your father. Then I was too timid to break the rules. Now I'm no longer sure they matter."

Edward cupped the side of her neck and tipped her chin up with his thumb. "They matter, love. Those rules are the way we honor each other. The way we show respect."

Her chin evaded his hold. "You said you were ashamed of loving me."

For a moment, her words robbed him of the power to speak. "I didn't say that. I couldn't have."

"You did. When you came to get me at Catherine's, you said you loved me so much it shamed you." When her eyes met his, they brimmed with tears, like emeralds in the flickering light. "I'm still the vicar's daughter, Edward. Not glamorous. Not rich. Just simple and shy and poor. Marrying me won't polish the Burbrooke name. Marrying me won't earn you anyone's respect. I know you want me tonight, but once you tire of me, wouldn't you rather not be married?"

"Good Lord," he exclaimed, completely thrown aback. "Didn't you hear me today? Do you think I've learned nothing from my father's mistakes?"

Her eyes flashed fire. "I think you want to sleep with me, and your blasted sense of honor demands we be man and wife."

"My blasted sense of honor has nothing to do with it. Lord, Florence, a few days ago you thought I wanted you to marry Freddie and sleep with me."

"Well," she said grudgingly, "I admit I was wrong about that."

"You're wrong about this, as well." He clasped her shoulders, tempted to shake some sense into her. "I want to marry you because I love you. Because you fill a space inside me I didn't know was empty. You make me happy. Holding your hand. Watching you charm a puppy or a little boy. Those things bring me the greatest satisfaction I've ever known. I can't imagine my life without them. I don't *want* to imagine my life without them. What's more, I'm not going to stop loving you. You can get that nonsense out of your head right now."

Her face flushed, but the way she bit her lip told him she still resisted. "Those words are beautiful," she said. "But it's hard for me to believe you really mean them."

Frustration curled inside him in a tight, despairing snarl. "You don't believe me because I lied to you before."

"Maybe I don't believe you because I'm really no one special."

"Oh, Florence." He released her shoulders to stroke her face. "You're incredibly special."

Her chin wobbled, then firmed with challenge. "I'm a pretty country girl is all. A brief, animal attraction. I'm no diamond. I couldn't wrap a man around my finger if I tried."

Edward cursed Catherine's adder tongue, then pressed a kiss to her furrowed brow. "Catherine twisted the facts to suit herself. The truth is I left Imogene because she wasn't you, because I knew she would never move my heart as you have. There's nothing brief about what I feel. And if anyone has me wrapped around her finger, that person is you."

A tear clung to the spikes of her lower lashes. "I want to believe you," she whispered. "I want to so badly it hurts."

"Then do," he said. "Do believe me." Spurred by a sudden impulse, he rose and coaxed her from her seat. "Come with me."

Her confusion was evident, but she complied. "Where are we going?"

He barely knew himself. An idea was forming, rash and nebulous, one act that might prove how committed he was to sharing his life with her. *Make yourself vulnerable,* Hypatia had said, and now he'd thought of a way to do it. He tugged her backward across the parquet floor.

"I asked you to trust me before," he said. "Now I'm going to show you how much I trust you."

She resisted, her arms stretched taut. "You don't have to—"

"Yes, I do, my love. Yes, I truly do."

Walking backwards with both her hands in his, Edward pulled her past the grand stairway in the hall, past ancestral portraits and busts and faded tapestries that smelled of must and spice. Florence knew these objects must have been saved from the old Greystowe Hall, tangible symbols of his family's ancient power.

I don't belong here, she thought, but the words were more habit than conviction. Edward made it easier to believe she might belong, with his iron grip and his eyes like burning flames. Those eyes were willing her to follow, willing her to do everything he asked.

When they reached the arch that led to the billiard room, he turned, releasing her hands to drape his arm around her back. Florence found herself trembling with anticipation. His arm was heavy, knotted with muscle. Its strength made her feel feminine and small.

He guided her down the family hall. Here the carpet was new and soft, a swirl of navy and cream. They passed Freddie's suite, empty now, since he and Nigel had not yet returned from their business at the mill. Finally, two doors from the orangery, he stopped. This close to the greenhouse, the air was citrus sweet.

"These are my rooms," he said, and opened the door to admit her.

She waited just inside while he struck a match and lit a twisting silver branch of candles. The drapes were tied back, the French doors gapped to admit a velvety evening breeze. The doors opened onto the front lawn. Outside, the sky swept from star-dotted sapphire at its peak, to glowing lime, to a glimmer of crimson beyond the ruffled lake. The colors melted into each other as if the heavens were an exotic cordial. Florence could practically taste the last of the sunset, as if it, too, were a scent that hung in the air.

She had an unexpected urge to peel off her clothes and bathe in the vibrant light.

"This way," Edward said, preceding her through the sitting room to another door.

This led to his bedroom. He lit a second branch of candles and set both on tables beside a massive four-poster bed. Her body tightened, helpless to resist the connotations of her surroundings. This was Edward's private chamber, where he slept, where he dressed, where he dreamed whatever it was he dreamed. The bed's carved posts were thick and twisting, the hangings fit for a king. Their bloodred damask folds glittered with gold embroidery, old but well preserved. The rest of the room was equally dark and rich: glossy wood, heavy, overstuffed chairs, and here and there the glint of precious metal. The walls were painted the same earthy red as the bed.

Above the brown marble mantel hung a small icon of a madonna, her halo thick with gold leaf, her robes so realistically rendered Florence almost reached up to touch them. The Mary was plump and smiling and kind, curiously human, despite the painter's mannered Russian style. The mere sight of her brought tears to Florence's eyes.

She turned to Edward, knowing her awe shone in her face.

"No," he laughed, reading her expression. "She isn't what I brought you here to see."

Turning, he crouched to open one of the low teak cabinets beside his bed. Fighting a sigh, Florence watched the seams of his elegant frock coat strain across his shoulders. Only Edward could make this lavish room seem small.

He rose with something in his hand, a ball of black cloth. He extended it towards her, his face serious and perhaps a bit unsure.

"I believe you wanted to use these," he said. "On me."

Curiosity rose from her chest to flutter softly in her throat. She tiptoed across the Oriental carpet, then gasped when she saw what he held: the ties, the black velvet ties he'd used to bind her that night in the pavilion.

Her hand flew back to her breast before she could touch them. "I thought women weren't supposed to—that you didn't like—"

Edward saved her from her confusion. "It's because I trust you. I'm giving you the power to put me at your mercy. You still want it, don't you?"

Her mouth watered at the thought of him stripped and bound. All that male strength hers to explore, to command. Her body went heavy and soft, as if her sex were a ripening plum. She swallowed hard.

"I—" she said, then had to start again. "I wouldn't want to do it if I thought it would displease you."

His laugh was not entirely steady. "Look at me," he said. "I'm as hard as my great-great-grandfather's pike. I'm not sure anything you do could displease me."

The bulge that pressed his trousers forward argued on his behalf. It was indeed large; forceful, with a throbbing shimmer of movement that must have echoed his beating heart. His bemusement urged her to believe him, but before she proceeded she had to understand precisely what he was offering. She couldn't bear to mistake him again.

"I could do anything I wished?" she asked. "Give or take any pleasure I desired?"

Blood climbed his face in a swarthy tide. "Any pleasure at all." The confirmation was rough, as if her question had aroused him. "My will would be yours to command."

She smiled, helpless to conceal her amusement. That the earl of Greystowe, the dour, stone-faced grump, would cede this power to her was almost too much to credit. Amusement, of course, was not the half of what she felt. Her body burned to accept his offer. She dropped her lashes, shielding the fire she knew must glow within her eyes.

"I believe I should like that," she said.

Edward shuddered, then thrust out the hand that held the ties. "Take them, then," he ordered. "Before I change my mind."

She took them, carefully unrolling each quilted strip and laying it on the bed, one for each of the big posts. Edward would reach, she thought, with a shiver for the picture in her mind. Edward was large enough to reach. When she returned to him, he was watching her like a hawk. She touched the lapels of his coat, then stopped.

"I would like to remove your clothes," she said.

This time the shiver moved through him. "You don't have to ask permission, love. Not tonight. Tonight you may do with me as you please."

At last, she began to trust.

EDWARD THOUGHT HE'D DIE OF LUST BEFORE SHE FINISHED stripping off his clothes. Piece by piece, she disrobed him. His frock coat and his vest. His cuff links and his gray silk necktie. The removal of his shoes and socks was mysteriously—almost unbearably—intimate. When, they were gone, she skimmed the tops his feet with the pads of her fingers, sending strange, sensual chills along his legs.

"My, what big long toes you have," she said with a fey, half-hidden smile.

His cock nearly burst through his trousers at her words. He felt like the wolf in the story: a beast with a primitive urge to claim its mate. He trembled under the onslaught of instinctive need, but did not move. She had chained him with the metal of his love. He had to bow his will to hers until he knew she was reassured.

As he did, her confidence grew. He could see it in the way she tossed her hair, in the taunting sway of her hips as she circled his increasingly unclothed body. He loved watching the change; loved the way she ran her hands over his back and shoulders, greedily, leaving fire in her wake, seeming to measure every muscle and bead of sweat. When her fingers drifted lower, over his trousered rump, his buttocks tightened without his will.

"You're hard here," she said, her touch roaming unchecked over tensing curves.

His jaw clenched in an agony of desire. "I'm harder than that in front."

It was a hint she could not miss. She laughed, a womanly sound, sweet and sultry. Her arms wrapped him from behind, hands shaping the heavy muscles of his chest. When they slipped still lower, he gasped. Her fingers had dipped beneath his waistband, teasing the smooth, sweat-dewed skin of his upper belly. His shaft strained upward, outward, desperate for its share of her caresses.

"If I finish undressing you," she said, her face brushing back and forth across his spine, "if I take your hardness in my hand, will you still do as I ask?"

He hesitated, then rasped his answer. "Yes, love. Tonight the power is yours."

She kissed the center of his back, then carefully opened his trousers. Because she stood behind him, her hands moved almost as his would have. He watched them work the buttons, her fingers slim and white. He felt deliciously unmanned, rousingly unmanned, in a way he would not have thought possible. His organ surged at the release of the cloth that constrained it, and at the peculiar sense that it belonged to her now, not to him.

When she pushed his remaining garments to his ankles, her cheek rested lightly on his haunch. Her skin was hot, a flush he could not help but feel. She was excited. This aroused her. A growl threatened to rumble from his chest. His self-control was a thread stretched to breaking.

"Florence," he said, the sound choked, "perhaps you ought to tie me now."

To his complete astonishment, he felt her teeth nip the meat of his buttock. Before he could stop himself, he yelped.

"Oh!" she gasped. "I'm ever so sorry. Did I hurt you?"

"No." His muscles clenched even tighter at the way her hand was rubbing the injured flesh. "You just surprised me."

"I don't know what came over me," she said, still rubbing, still contrite. "You're just so pretty back here. So small compared to the rest of you. Your . . . your bottom is like an apple. I had to take a bite."

He was caught between a laugh and a groan. Her thumbs had curled a little way between his cheeks and now drew arcs towards his tailbone in a manner that was not the least bit soothing—assuming that soothing him was her intent.

"It's all right," he said. "You didn't hurt me." His voice sank. "Actually, what you did was rather sexy."

"Oh," she said, breathless now. "Well . . . good. I'm glad."

He fought the laugh until she slipped around him to his front. Then he could not even smile. He was too busy trying not to groan. Her fingers scratched lightly through his chest hair, then teased the beaded coppery nipples she found within. New sensations sang along his nerves, incendiary twinges that arrowed through his body to his sex. They pulsed in its tip, tapping the sensitive skin like drops of oil. Her fingers had a power no other woman's had possessed. He was drowning in lust, fighting with all his strength to keep control, to keep from frightening her with his need. She bit her lip as she watched his penis bob and darken.

"You like this," she said, still feathering her thumbs across his nipples.

What breath he might have used to admit it disappeared when she sank to her knees. Unable to resist, his hands moved to spear her shining upswept hair.

"Don't touch me," she said. "I want to do this by myself."

"Tie me, then," he groaned. "Because if you take me in your mouth, I'll have to touch you. I won't be able to stop."

After a moment's hesitation, she pushed to her feet. She looked at his straining shaft, then at the bed. "I've changed my mind," she said.

His heart lurched, the reaction violent and confused. Did she mean she released him from his promise to let her do with him as she pleased? He wanted to take her, it was true. He wanted to drag her to the floor, to rip her clothes from her silky skin and drive so deep and hard between her legs she would feel him pounding there for days. He craved that triumph with everything that made him male. And yet, despite his compulsion to conquer and subdue, part of him wanted her to take him first.

He waited for her to explain, his contrary longings at war within his breast. She pressed two fingers to her lips in contemplation, unwittingly drawing the tension out.

"Yes," she finally said, the word decisive. "I want to tie you standing up."

His heart gave a second galvanic pump, this one unmistakably excited.

"If you're lying down," she explained. "I won't be able to touch as much of you."

"Perfectly all right," he rasped. "I quite understand."

She grinned, a sudden flash of humor. "Do you?" Her tone was knowing, seductive. She put one hand on her hip and pointed with the other to the end of the bed. He could see the teacher in her then, the little general who expected to be obeyed. "Please stand in front of those posts so I can tie you."

His skin heated as he complied. His reach was just sufficient to grip the polished turns of wood. She bound his wrists with endearing concentration, more firmly than he expected, and with a great many knots. She would never make a sailor but they would hold.

"That isn't too tight, is it?" she said. He shook his head and she patted the center of his chest. "Just tell me if you want them taken off."

But he didn't. To his amazement, he liked being at her mercy, liked wondering what she'd do next. Whatever she chose would be her idea: no coaxing, no intimidation, just precisely what she wished. He would know what she wanted to give. He would learn what she enjoyed. He looked from the hand that pressed his breastbone to her eyes. They shone with the same excitement that was building in his bones. He didn't want to shatter the magic with a word.

She smiled and took a long step back.

"I'm going to remove my clothes," she said, wonderingly, as if the announcement surprised her, too. "And you're going to watch. You're going to be the first man I ever wanted to see."

His breath rushed out, hollowing his ribs. He couldn't have spoken to save his life. He had an inkling what this meant. Florence had never been comfortable with people's admiration of her looks; she'd always been too shy. But if she wanted him to watch . . .

She must love him, must truly, truly care.

She removed her dress without posturing or flirtation, merely the caution a woman of modest means would use with a valuable garment. She laughed as she struggled with some of the hooks, a little nervously, but not as if she wished to stop. She wore no corset. He supposed the weight she'd lost made it unnecessary. The removal of her gown left her in chemise and drawers, a pretty concoction of lace and tucks and sheer, sheer lawn. He could see her budded nipples through the top, and the triangle of sable curls between her legs. The image drew him back to the day he'd seen her at Madame Victoire's. The arousal he'd felt then was nothing to the yearning that gripped him now. His body trembled with it, and his heart. More than his cock craved her body's tight embrace.

Florence didn't see the tremor that swept his limbs. She was too caught up in squirming out of her underthings before she lost her nerve. The chemise had tugged her chignon halfway off her head. She had to hop on one foot to remove the second leg of her drawers. She seemed the perfect opposite of a coquette and Edward had never loved her more.

"There," she said with nervous, breathless pride as she threw the drawers into a corner.

His grin threatened to split his face. Another woman would have stroked those creamy breasts or palmed that luscious swatch of curls.

Florence merely stood, biting her lip and smiling, looking as if she wished she could wring the lovely hands she'd clasped before her belly. He suspected those hands were shaking more than his.

Her courage moved him beyond belief.

"You," he said, "are the most beautiful woman I've ever seen."

She smiled and ducked her head. "Now you're being foolish."

"No," he said, perfectly serious. "No one has ever seemed more beautiful to me."

"Oh. Well . . . well, thank you," she said, her chin still tucked. "You're rather beautiful yourself."

He laughed at that, but then she set out to prove it.

She kissed every part of him her lips could reach, standing on tiptoe to mouth the arch of his neck, kneeling down to kiss his curling toes. Her hands were pure seduction, feathering touches from his legs to his hips to the curves of his supposedly apple-like arse.

"Oh, Edward," she sighed as she tickled the hair beneath his outstretched arms. "Everything about you is so interesting."

Apparently, she thought his sex was interesting, too. She cupped and jiggled and stroked and squeezed until his every exhalation became a groan.

When she bent to taste, he gripped the posts so hard, his fingers went briefly numb.

Her mouth was heaven, sheer soft, warm, wet, silky heaven. Steadying his shaft with one hand, she cupped his testicles with the other and sucked him to the brink of climax. Her tongue laved the cluster of nerves beneath his crown. Her lips pulled his foreskin over the head. She sucked him as if she loved his taste and feel, as if there was nothing about him she couldn't accept.

He felt himself swell to bursting; felt the sweet, throbbing ache gather at his base. "Florence," he moaned, knowing he should stop her. Instead, his hips thrust towards the strong, clinging heat of her mouth.

One more, he thought, his nails scoring the bedposts. One more heavenly drag and he would stop.

She seemed to sense what his body wanted. Her hands tightened, then her mouth, cajoling him to succumb to the killing urge. Sparks danced before his eyes and reddened and then his cock turned inside out. He bent forward at the waist as if someone had punched him, hips jamming forward, muscles convulsing all at once. The orgasm was a tight, throbbing blaze of feeling, endless, intense. He gasped with shock as the pleasure poured from him into her. He couldn't even groan until it finished, until his stolen breath returned. His legs sagged back onto the mattress, no longer able to hold his weight.

"Florence," he panted. "My God."

She giggled against his chest and he discovered he was holding her. His hands were free. He hadn't even felt her untie him. Still breathing hard, he spread her glorious hair across her shoulders. One last pin scattered to the floor.

"That," she said, hugging him back, "was wonderfully entertaining. I can't imagine why women aren't supposed to do that."

He tipped her head to kiss her, deeply, wetly, his cock going weighty as he realized he could taste himself in her mouth. His seed was salty, bittersweet. That they were sharing it was alarmingly erotic. A sound broke in his throat, helpless and sharp. The noise did something to Florence. Her hands clutched the back of his neck and her soft bare breasts wriggled deliciously against his chest. Abruptly short of breath, he broke the kiss. Her weight was nestled against him, between his legs. From the way she squirmed, he knew she was hoping for a quick recovery.

With a low, easy laugh, he swung her into his arms and tossed her on the bed. She shrieked as she landed, then smiled through tousled hair. To see her naked, in his bed, was a pleasure he had not thought to know.

He crawled up after her, slowly, predatorily, feeling very much the animal he sometimes feared he was. He loomed above her on all fours, his shaft hanging, beginning to thicken even as it swayed.

"Edward?" Florence said, tentatively touching his belly with the back of her hand. Her voice shook as if she were afraid, but her face was deeply flushed.

Edward bared his big sharp teeth with great enjoyment.

"Now, Little Red Riding Hood," he said, "let's see how entertaining *you* can be."

As it happened, she was quite.

Chapter 17

FLORENCE TREMBLED ON THE VERGE OF AN ALMOST TERRI-fying happiness. Edward loved her. Edward trusted her. Edward smiled each time his eyes met hers.

Like children, they had raided the kitchen for a midnight snack. "I need my strength," he'd said, goosing her through the shirt—his shirt—which was all he'd let her wear.

This playful Edward delighted her: the softness of his smiles, the ease of his wolfish chuckles. He seized on any excuse to touch her, playing with her fingers and her hair, squeezing her knee, touching his mouth to the tip of her nose. Having restrained himself so long, he could not seem to keep his hands to himself.

Now they sat cross-legged in the shelter of his bed, the hangings pulled around them, picking at their pilfered tray of fruit and cheese and honey-slathered bread. Edward fed her a slice of apple, eyes glowing as he eased it past her lips. "I have a sudden hunger," he said, "to know everything about you."

She blushed at his tone and let her teeth scrape gently, daringly, down his thumb. "Everything?"

His lashes drifted a fraction lower.

"Everything," he insisted, his hands sliding languorously down her neck. "First word. Favorite color. The name of your very best friend when you were twelve."

The warmth of his touch was wine pouring through her veins. He seemed to like the look of her swimming in his shirt. He clasped her upper arms, forcing the starched white cloth to bunch around his fingers. She had to struggle to think past the pleasure of his nearness.

"My first word was kitty," she said. "Blue is my favorite color. And Papa was always my best friend. He had the silliest sense of humor. Puns and practical jokes. No one could make me laugh the way he did."

Edward's mouth twitched as if the mention of her laughter called to his. "Ball," he said. "Cherry red. And Freddie, though Plunket my pony came close."

"Plunket?"

"Named him myself. Looked just like one of our tutors." He smiled at her then, his eyes as kind as the icon on his wall. "Would you mind, Florence, if I asked how you lost your mother?"

"I was three," she said, covering his hand to reassure him the question had not hurt. "She died in childbed and the baby, too. It would have been a boy. I don't remember her except for Papa's stories. They were born in the same little town. Never loved anyone else, either one. Papa said she was the sweetest, wisest woman he'd ever known and she could never get anywhere on time. He never really recovered when she died. He didn't say so, but sometimes—when he thought I wasn't watching—his eyes grew terribly sad." She looked away, not wanting to dwell on that now, not with Edward so near and dear. She forced a smile. "When I met Freddie, I thought, 'Here's the brother I never got a chance to have.'"

It occurred to her then, and perhaps to Edward, that if she accepted his proposal, she could have Freddie for a brother. Whatever his thoughts, Edward gathered her hands into the dip of silk and skin where his ankles crossed. His fingers rubbed comfort into the hollows of her palms. "I'm sorry you lost your mother so young."

"I was sorry, too," she said as the furrow between his brows melted what was left of her heart. "But Papa was good to me. Our parishioners used to call him Father Fairleigh: the mother hen. He was forever fussing over his flock, making sure the little old ladies had someone to look out for them."

"Little old ladies?"

"We had quite a few in Keswick. Papa liked to call them our first, best crop." The memory warmed her, her father's voice suddenly as clear in her mind as Edward's. How could she have forgotten how optimistic he was, and how little of his life was lost to mourning? "He was a kind man," she said firmly, "and a wonderful father, just not very clever with money."

"Thought God would provide?"

"Well, He did!" she said, laughing at the quirk of Edward's mouth. "He simply didn't provide extra."

"And this attraction you hold for animals—"

"Just cats," she interposed.

"Oh, yes, just cats," he agreed, an entirely unexpected dimple appearing in his cheek. "You always had that effect? Even as a girl?"

"I'm afraid so. The children at school used to call me Little Miss Sardine because, well, sometimes the village cats would follow me home en masse."

"A great embarrassment, I presume."

"Quite. When the local toddlers took to trailing after me as well, I nearly refused to leave the house."

Edward was unable to keep his mirth inside. It escaped in snorts from his aristocratic nose. "Poor Florence!" he cried. "What a trial! Unable to walk down the street without her retinue of small, adoring subjects."

"It was a trial," she protested even as she grinned. She hadn't felt this easy telling a story since she'd had Freddie for a listener. "You can't imagine how mortifying it was."

Edward reached out to tweak her nose. "You're a dear, Florence, but I must admit my sympathies lie with the cats and toddlers."

He grew contemplative then, his smile fading to a gentle curve as he ran his hand along her lower leg. The gesture was absentminded but oddly comforting. Possessive. His hand belonged there, she thought: close and easy and warm.

"Your childhood sounds very rich," he said, his expression hidden from her gaze. She knew his own must have been different. A cold father, a fragile mother, and probably more servants than friends, at least while he lived at Greystowe. She knew he wouldn't want her to feel sorry for him and yet she did. One person to love you unconditionally was more important than any amount of privilege. Of course, Freddie had loved Edward that way but, being much younger, he could not have made Edward feel safe.

She stroked the silky top of his head. "What about your childhood? Freddie told me a little, but not everything."

He shrugged one shoulder. "There's not much to tell. Freddie was the best thing about growing up. Tormenting our tutors—"

"Teaching him to swim."

"He told you about that, then." He squeezed her ankle. "Yes, that's a happy memory. At the time, of course, we were both quite miserable. Not to mention half drowned. Here." With unconscious grace, he rolled from the bed. "I think I still have his first trophy."

He rummaged in the bedside cabinet, then emerged with a triumphant "Ha!" He handed her a round medal, most of the gold worn off, which hung from a frayed blue ribbon. Florence ran her finger around the burnished laurel wreath, wishing—as she had with Freddie— that she could have known Edward then, not as a girl but as a woman. She would have liked to protect the boy he'd been from a father who could only love a memory.

"You really kept it," she said, her eyes filling. "All this time."

Edward had returned to his seat on the bed. He laid his fingertip next to hers. "Yes. Young as I was, I knew that was a day I would want to remember."

"You were a good brother."

A shadow crossed his face, but he covered it with a smile. "Freddie was a good brother." He brushed her hair behind her shoulder. "I imagine our upbringing was different from yours, but Father made sure we never lacked for anything. Anything material, at least." He paused to gather his thoughts, his gaze distant but calm. "I suppose that was the only way he knew to show he cared. He kept the estate together. Made sure we'd never have to struggle to get out of debt, the way his father had to."

"You needn't feel guilty for admiring what was good in him."

Again, one shoulder lifted. "He taught me the value of responsibility. And discipline." His mouth slanted with sudden humor. "Though I fear I've shown precious little of that with you."

"Perhaps not tonight," she said, and they exchanged a smile.

"Oh, Florence." Impulsively, he clasped her hands. "I love you so much. I'm sorry I ever gave you reason to doubt me."

"I love you, too," she said, the words new enough to call a flush to the surface of her skin.

He made a sound, low and hungry, then leaned forward to brush his lips across that building warmth. "I want to finish what we've begun," he said against her cheek. "I want to lie with you, to come inside you, to make our bodies one."

Heat spread through her in a pulsing wave, pooling in her breasts and belly. The reaction was so intense she had to drop her eyes.

"Please," he said, his grip tightening on her shoulders. "Tell me you want that, too."

She slid her own hands up his chest, over his robe, feeling through silk and muscle the hard, swift beat of his heart. It pounded as if he feared what she would say, as if her agreement were a matter of grave importance. Her fingers curled into the cloth.

The answer hung in her mind like an apple about to drop.

She knew if she accepted, she'd be giving herself to him in every sense of the word: all she was and all she would be, till death did them part. Yes, he'd asked her to marry him, but a promise was not a deed. He could change his mind or fall tomorrow for the butcher's daughter.

And Florence would be left with nothing but the memory of this night.

It was enough. She wanted the risk; wanted to leap into the void. Her heart was his already. She had no wish to take it back.

She might be afraid, but she would not be a coward.

"Yes," she said, her answer almost steady. "I should like that very much."

His breath sighed from him. He cupped her jaw, his fingers stroking her neck beneath her hair. "I hope you like it," he said, with a tinge of wryness. "But the only promise I can make is to be careful."

Her hand moved beyond her control, sliding beneath the lapel of his robe to find the warm, hard curve of his ribs. "I don't mind when you're a little wild."

He laughed, the sound all breath. "Not this time, love. I might hurt you. But perhaps you're not familiar with the logistics?"

Her smile curled into his neck. He'd forgotten how much a simple country girl could learn. "I'm familiar with them, though I doubt I've sufficient experience to conduct myself very well after we, er, after we . . ."

"Achieve the desired union of our parts?" he said, saving her from her sudden loss of nerve. His chuckle rumbled in her ear and she knew he liked her shyness. "You needn't worry about the after. After has a way of taking care of itself and, as I said, I'll be careful."

Something in his voice caught her attention, a deeper arousal, a tension that was more anticipation than concern. Wondering what had triggered it, her hand slipped down his gaping robe, over skin and bone and muscle. His stomach tightened as her thumb crossed his navel and then she found him, rising thick and hard from the tight black nest of curls. The base of his cock more than filled the circle her fingers made. He cradled her forearm, gently encouraging her touch.

"I'll be careful," he whispered, the words shaking. "I won't hurt you."

She smiled where he could not see and vowed she'd never let him know she'd guessed his secret. Part of him, the part that would have made a fine Crusader, relished the thought of deflowering her with his symbolic sword. Marauder and protector. Primitive beast and courtly knight. Both were part of Edward's soul. Relaxing her grip, she trailed her fingers lightly up his shaft. The mighty column quivered at her touch. Like a puppy, she thought as she traced the net of swollen veins, wriggling for a treat.

"There is the matter of size," she said as seriously as she could. To her delight, the quiver grew violent.

"Sh." He covered her hand, molding it to his silky, pulsing skin. "I am convinced you shall take me." His second hand slipped beneath her shirt to stroke the lush curve of her hip. "You were made to take me."

"It's true, I'm not delicate, but you must admit your equipment is formidable."

His palm gripped hers, a brief, involuntary spasm. His shaft lengthened in their mutual hold. Oh, how she enjoyed this. What power people's secret wishes had! When he spoke, his voice was whiskey rough. "I know you can't truly be afraid. You aren't even shaking."

"No, but perhaps in my ignorance, I haven't fully appreciated the challenge of—"

He silenced her with a kiss that drove from her mind her intent to tease him. Abruptly urgent, he rolled her beneath him, pressing her down with his weight. The kiss stole her breath and fired her blood. He released her long enough to pant for air, then ripped the shirt she wore down her front. With a whispered curse, he tore off his robe and sank back over her, fitting his hardness to her curves, rubbing them together until every inch of her thrummed with excitement. For long minutes, her mind was filled with nothing but the feel of him under her roving hands, the rush of his breath, the wet, greedy tug of his mouth. She could not get close enough to him, nor he, it seemed, to her. They grappled and writhed and clutched each other's backs. His erection was a brand against her thigh, her hip, her belly. She spread her legs to wrap them around him, and even that embrace was not enough. She wanted him: all his size, all his passion, all his hidden desires.

"You'll have to tell me," she said, gasping as his kiss moved towards her breast. "You'll have to tell me what to do."

"I'll show you," he said, and captured her nipple with lips and tongue. He pulled her into his mouth with shocking strength. Feeling speared through her, turning molten in her sex. She was melting, desire running from her like liquid gold. He turned to the other breast and drew that just as hungrily against his tongue.

Florence groaned and arched her back. "I wish you would show me soon."

He chuckled and cupped his hand around her curls, squeezing the soft, aching cushion within his palm. She groaned again, louder than before. His fingers—so strong, so hard—pressed between her plumping lips but did nothing to ease her need. She whimpered when he let go.

"Put your hand on my cock," he said, the words a smoky rasp. "Take me up against you. Put me where you want me to be."

Now she did shake, though she did not think she shook with fear. She slid her hand down his back, around his hip, her breath coming quick and shallow. They both jumped when she touched him. His organ was heat in her hands, hard, throbbing fire. She drew it closer to her sexual heart.

"Lift your knees," he said, coaxing one leg into position with his hand. He balanced his weight on the other elbow, his hips canting forward as she guided his approach. He had to bow his back to look into her face, and suddenly the disparity in their sizes was very real. He overshadowed her, overwhelmed her, and yet she did not wish him any other way. She knew he would be careful with her. She knew she would be safe.

His eyes squeezed shut for a moment when the crown of him slipped between her lips. He was big and eager, dripping with it as he tried to find his place. She wasn't quite sure how to manage, but his fingers soon joined hers, adjusting, easing, with an intimacy that made her blush. A second later, the hot round tip was pressed inside her, the sensation of pulsing, stretching heat making her sigh and fight a squirm. When he opened his eyes, his pupils had nearly swallowed up the blue.

"There," he whispered. "How does that feel?"

It felt like her soul was tearing down the middle, not with pain but gladness. With this act, her whole being made room for him.

"Silky," she said, afraid to push but wanting to immensely. "And hot. And very, very good." His cock bucked at the words. She could not quell her body's reaction. Her longing flowed out against him. "Oh, Edward, I'm all awash."

He growled against her neck and nipped her lightly with his teeth. "I like you all awash. It tells me you're ready to take me."

But he did not move, not even when she locked her arms behind his waist and urged him in. Instead, he stroked her hair from her brow and kissed it. His lips were hot, his breath harried. She didn't understand his inaction. Didn't he want to take her? Didn't he want to make them one? A niggle of worry began to rise.

"You came this far before," she said, "that first time at the ruins."

"Yes." His face tightened as if the memory hurt. "I did."

"You're not going to pull back this time, are you?"

He shuddered and his hips moved, pressing a tormenting fraction deeper. "You're the only person who could make me."

"I don't want to make you. I want you to—" She bit her lip.

"Tell me," he said and ran his tongue across the place her teeth had sunk.

She let go with a gasp. "I want you to push. I want you all the way inside me."

"Even if it hurts?"

"I don't care." She squeezed his hips with her thighs. "It hurts too much to wait."

"Oh, Florence," he said, her name a moan. "Brave, sweet Florence."

He kissed her, deeply, and began to press gently forward and back against her barrier, nudge and release, nudge and release, until her fingers curled into claws behind his shoulders. What he was doing felt terribly good, but not quite good enough.

"Please, Edward," she breathed, unable to bear it. "Please, please take me now."

She felt him gather; felt a sting of pressure. Then, with a quick forward thrust and a helpless grunt of pleasure, he rent the obstacle between them. He pushed once more, sighed, and forced himself to stop. His shoulders were suddenly slick beneath her hands, his head bowed on his neck. Already, the pain of his entry was fading; was melting into need. She knew she had not taken much of him, not even half. A distance remained between their hips.

"I'm all right," she said, kissing the ball of his shoulder, stroking the clenched and quivering muscle of his rear. "I want the rest."

"Florence." He raised his head, his voice so deep it was nearly hollow. "I want to watch your face when I make you mine."

Their eyes locked. She'd never seen such vulnerability—or such love. He slid one big warm hand beneath her hips, his fingers spread from the small of her back to the lowest swell of her bottom. At last he pushed, slowly, firmly, forcing the walls of her sheath to part for his penetration. Nothing stopped him. She experienced no pain, no fear, no limitation of flesh that would not ease. She *was* made for him. Her body gave before his slow, sleek drive, oiling his way, hugging his pounding length. She sighed when his hips pressed hers, filled to satiation, joined to him by that hot tensile shaft and by the luxuriant pleasure of a close and perfect fit.

He moaned her name, dropping kisses across her face. "Oh, Lord," he breathed. "That's good."

Now that he was seated, he drew her hands from his waist and pressed them above her head, twining their fingers in a tight, sweaty grip. She didn't mind. If she was captured, so was he. Both of them were trembling, both smiling into each other's eyes.

"Love," he said, and began to draw and thrust. Nothing moved except his hips and his expression: like a man seeing a vision he did not want to end. Straight in he stroked. Straight out he pulled. Thick and strong and simple. The way it made her feel, however, was anything but simple. She was conquered and powerful, needy and generous, a pauper and queen of the world. He was making her a woman in the most primitive sense of the word.

He whispered of his pleasure: hot, forbidden words that made her tighten deep inside. He was on fire, he said. Ablaze to feel her spend. He murmured praise to her breasts, to her small, white feet, to the damp, dimpled backs of her knees. He told her how hard he was, how badly he ached. He urged her to rock with him, then swore when she obeyed. It seemed a blessing when he slid like satin inside her, strong as a bull, gentle as a lamb.

Each thrust drove him to his limit, hard but slow, so slow she could scarcely bear his long withdrawals. He seemed to be entering her anew each time, ravishing her anew, as if his cock adored that claiming stroke.

"Don't rush," he pleaded when her body grew impatient. "We'll only have one first time."

He released her hands and curled his thumb between their hips. She shattered at his touch, her body clenching uncontrollably, her throat burning with a helpless cry.

He laughed when she apologized. "Again," he demanded. "Quick, love, do it again."

She couldn't have resisted if she'd tried. He seemed to know what her body wanted before she did; when it needed a pinch, or a stroke, or a greedy, grinding push. She came until her body was limp with joy. At last, though, his own needs rode him too hard to be denied.

"I can still pull out," he said, his arms trembling, his body dripping sweat. "You don't have to take my seed."

Her head rolled back and forth against the bed. "I want it," she said, hands urging his hips. "I want everything."

He winced. His movements were heavier now, less controlled. He was not drawing out as far. He could not seem to bear to.

"If you take it," he growled, "you'd better consider yourself my wife. If I spill inside you, this will be our wedding night."

She smiled, amazed he could doubt she'd already surrendered. "You're the husband of my heart. There will never be another."

He paused long enough to search her eyes. His were narrowed, searching for the truth. She grinned at his seriousness, unable to help herself: he had filled her so with bliss. He must have seen this because he finally nodded, the same curt acknowledgment that had piqued her in the past.

"Good," he said briskly, all Edward, all beloved. "There will never be anyone else for me."

"Come then." Still grinning, she dragged her nails down the long, sweaty curve of his spine. "Make me yours."

He flinched, then darkened, then exploded into motion between her legs. She had unleashed something even he could not control; his release had waited too long on hers. Now he would not take his pleasure, it would take him. His body jolted hers, harder, faster, his sex a piston of throbbing need. She grabbed the side of the bed to keep from sliding and even with this, he'd soon thrust her up against the headboard.

"Hold on," he ordered, bracing his arm on the polished wood. "Hold . . . on . . . to . . . me."

She held, curling her hands behind his shoulders, keening at the pounding wonder of his wildness. He was grunting as he thrust: broken phrases, endearments. *Deeper,* he begged. *Oh, God, sweetheart, deeper.* She tried to help but his skin slipped under her hands. She dug her heels into the mattress. She pushed. The added force unraveled him. He cursed and swelled and drove so far he seemed to breach her womb. His body held, trembled, then shuddered with the first unstoppable wave of climax. His fists were clenched, his eyes screwed tightly shut. Veins stood out on his neck as he strove to hold his place while his cock gushed hot and hard. He gasped at the end, and moaned and then, as his muscles relaxed, her peak unfurled like the petals of a flower. Still couched inside her, his penis twitched at the fluttering pulses, in perfect sympathy with her pleasure.

She was glad her body had waited. She wouldn't have wanted to miss the drama of his peak.

"My," she sighed, stroking his hair as he collapsed onto her breast. "That was wonderful. I can't wait to do it again."

His shoulders shook and she realized he was laughing, silently, but he was. His shaft slipped from her with the motion, heavy and limp and wet, an effect she found peculiarly erotic.

"Florence," he groaned, nuzzling the bend of her neck. "I'm afraid you'll have to wait a bit."

HE FELT AS IF THE EARTH HAD STOPPED TURNING. FOR THE first time in his life, his spirit was at peace. The air was hushed and fragrant, and his heart so full of love he thought it must overflow.

Florence lay against him, nestled in the curve of his arm. She was drowsy and soft and her hand played gently up and down his side. She was easy with him now—as well she should be. This night had been one in a million. Nothing could have prepared him for the ecstasy they'd shared, for the closeness, the profound sense of change he felt within his soul.

She'd called him the husband of her heart.

She'd given herself to him, without reserve.

And this was only the beginning. A lifetime of pleasures opened in his mind, holding her, loving her. She would be his bride. They would walk into the future hand in hand.

He thought he could live on this happiness for years. As it happened, though, he only had a day.

Chapter 18

THEY BATHED TOGETHER IN EDWARD'S PRIVATE PLUNGE bath. The tile was garnet and gold, the tub white-veined black marble. The water flowed hot from the silver tap in a seemingly endless stream. The tub was so deep Florence could sink in it to her neck. She had never seen a marvel like it and yet the greatest luxury of all was the freedom to touch the man she loved. He seemed to feel the same for he teased her and tickled her, whispering foolish endearments as he drew the soapy sponge along her skin. Florence purred under the attention, so weak with pleasure she could barely caress him back.

"You are the queen of the cats," he whispered as he slid inside her once again.

As breath-stopping as their first time had been, this wet, languorous coupling was even better. He taught her what a truly clever cock could do. How it could probe and rub. How it could weep with desire and find tender, hidden places that made her want to weep herself.

"That's the way," he praised as she cried out and clung. "Teach me what you like."

That an organ so inherently selfish could be made so generous she found amazing, almost as amazing as the pleasure she took in its gratification. Awed by the magic they could make together, she cradled him gently in her palm.

"When you touch me like this," he said, his hand lightly stroking hers. "I know how weak a man can be."

Such weakness she could learn to love.

He followed when she slipped back to her room to change. He insisted on dressing her himself, instructing Lizzie through the closed door to take the day off. Far from being scandalized, the maid giggled and pattered off. Florence was certain Edward's sword had reached the limits of its strength but somehow, during the process of lacing her new French corset, it found the wherewithal to rise again.

His fingertips roved the stays that bound her, the lace and satin, the nip of her waist and the swell of her lifted breasts. "Jesus," he said as if the awe of it overwhelmed him. "I can't get enough of you."

As if there weren't a second to lose, he turned her, bending her forward over the end of the bed and tearing her drawers out of the way. His actions were so frantic she could hardly believe they'd been making love for hours. His fingers spread her, his chest cupped her and, with a long, heartfelt groan of relief, he drove into her from behind. He felt huge from that angle, a stranger almost. He did not wait but began thrusting like a man possessed, his expression hidden, his grip desperate on her hips. In seconds his erection stretched to bursting inside her, fevered and thick as he begged her to open, to let him all the way in. *Let me,* he moaned, *let me* with strokes so long and fierce she could only stand and brace. He came so quickly she barely had time to follow, despite the knowing motions of his hands. His hoarse cry of completion pushed her over the trembling edge. When they'd both settled, he apologized for his roughness, but Florence had never found him more exciting.

Shaking her head, she stroked his sweat-sheened face between her palms. "It doesn't matter what you do. Your touch will always move me because it's yours."

He flushed at that and muttered something like "Only time will tell." Florence was prepared to prove her claim, more than prepared. First, however—she stifled a prodigious yawn—she really had to rest. They tumbled together into her bed, fully intending to sleep till dinner.

A low, persistent knocking woke them both.

"Miss Florence," Lizzie called through the door, "Lord Greystowe. Viscount Burbrooke has returned."

Edward bolted up so quickly her head bounced from his chest. In the dying daylight, his face was as pale as the sheets. "Freddie," he panted, his fist pressed to his heart.

It seemed a part of him was not at peace with what they'd done.

*   *   *

FREDDIE HAD CHANGED. EDWARD NOTICED IT THE MOMENT his brother answered his summons to the library. His cast had been removed, for one thing, but the difference ran deeper than that. Though his eyes held the same amusement at the world, their gleam was happier. He seemed more self-possessed; taller, if that were possible. Most of all, despite a slight limp, he had the loose-limbed, loose-hipped stride of a man who'd spent the last few weeks with someone very skilled at exorcizing lust.

Not that Edward wanted to dwell on that.

He turned his attention to the whiskey decanter and the finger of Irish gold he'd poured into Freddie's glass.

"Heavens," said his brother, strolling across the room to where he stood. "This must be serious if you're breaking out the single malt."

"Serious enough," said Edward. He handed Freddie the crystal tumbler, then looked out the window through the colonnade. Torches lit the grounds as if there were going to be a party. Edward had a feeling Lizzie had spread the news about him and Florence to the staff. No doubt this was Mrs. Forster's idea of encouraging romantic midnight walks. Under other circumstances, he would have appreciated the hint. Tonight, however, the reminder of the news he had to break to his little brother made his stomach sink. The fact that Freddie was likely to welcome it did not help.

Unaware of what was coming, Freddie sipped the whiskey and peered at him with half-lidded, ironic eyes. "If you intend to scold me," he said, "you may as well save your breath."

Edward's hand tightened on his glass. "It's not you who needs scolding."

"Do tell," said Freddie in a rakish, mocking drawl.

Unfortunately, what Edward had to say was no laughing matter. He tossed back the drink and set it deliberately down. When he turned, his brother was waiting with one raised brow.

"I'm marrying Florence," Edward said.

The announcement was clipped and challenging. He knew he was glaring, but couldn't quite make himself stop. Freddie was not going to change his mind, not for anything. To be sure, the chance that Freddie would want to was very slim. But rationality had no part in Edward's behavior. Florence was his. He was going to stake his claim.

Given Edward's manner, Freddie's response was mild. He toyed with the edge of the ebony console table where Grimby had left the liquor, then looked up with a smile.

"Well," he said, "as this is something I know you've wanted since before you knew you wanted it, I have to wonder why you're so dour. If you're feeling guilty, I assure you it's misplaced. Any idiot could see your marrying Florence will make us both much happier."

"Will it?" Edward studied his brother. Freddie was dressed casually in a crisp white shirt and summer trousers. His vest was a subtle medley of ivory silk and gold embroidery, colors that called attention to the sun he must have gotten since he'd left. He was the flower of English manhood: kind, witty, brimming with health and life and far handsomer than Edward would ever be. A man with Freddie's gifts could make anything he chose of his life, any dazzling thing at all. He wondered if his brother understood what he was giving up.

"Freddie," he said, "do you realize how cruel the world can be? Imogene Hargreave, for one, will never let this pass. When news of my marriage gets out and the inevitable conclusions are drawn, a great many of your friends will no longer be your friends. Whether they empathize or not, their sense of propriety will oblige them to drop you. You won't be welcome in their homes. They'll cut you on the street. Your life as you've known it will cease to exist."

"Do you believe that's all I care about?" Freddie said. "The cut of my coat and the social round? Unpleasant as becoming a pariah may be, I suspect my fall from grace will mean more to you and the duchess than it will to me."

Edward strove for a reasonable tone. "Hypatia can weather any storm. She's been a social force too long for that to change. As for me, if people cut me, so be it. But you . . . You can't deny you've enjoyed being society's darling, because I know you have. Look." He undid the button that seemed to be choking his neck. "Maybe we could find another woman to marry you. Someone older. A widow, perhaps."

Freddie lifted his hands but not in surrender. "No," he said, with a steeliness Edward had never heard from him before. "No more lies. Nigel and I have discussed this at length and we've both made up our minds."

"Nigel and you."

"Nigel and I," Freddie said, as if to make Edward acknowledge their pairing by force of repetition. "Whether you believe it or not, Nigel and I are in love."

The declaration held an unmistakable tinge of pride; wonder, too, and the same gratitude any new-minted lover might feel. Struggling to understand, to accept, Edward sagged back against the table. He pressed the heel of his palm to the megrim blooming slowly behind his eyes. "This is going to be so hard for you, Freddie. So very, very hard."

"We know that," Freddie said, the softness of his voice clearly meant to reassure. "Perhaps we know it better than you. You love me more than anyone. More than Nigel, I expect, for his is a sentiment only time will prove. In any case, I can hardly harbor illusions as to how the rest of the world will react when you, who love me best, cannot accept me as I am."

"I'm trying," Edward said. "Truly, I am."

"You're trying to protect me. But you can't choose my path this time. You have to let me run ahead and stumble. Otherwise, I'll never have any sort of life at all."

Edward found it difficult to swallow. His stomach had tightened into a knot and his hands were trembling with distress. Every instinct he possessed urged him not to let Freddie do this. There must be some argument he'd neglected, some way he could compel his brother to show some sense.

Alas, he doubted Freddie would forgive him if he found it.

"Do you—do you know what you'll do?" he said, forcing the question past the resistance in his throat.

"We're leaving for France," his brother responded, his gentlest announcement yet. "Probably very soon."

"France. Well." Edward shoved his shaking hands into his pockets. "I know the provinces are beautiful and the political situation does seem to be settling down. I suppose you could reopen the property Mother left you."

"That was our plan. It's in Bordeaux, you know. Nigel and I thought we'd try our hand at growing grapes."

"That . . . well, that sounds . . . Freddie, France is very far away."

"A train to Dover and a ferry to Calais."

"You know what I mean. It's a different country. A different continent. You don't know anyone. You don't even speak French."

"Nigel does," said Freddie with a crooked smile of understanding. "And I shall learn. This is what we need, Eddie. A clean break. A place where no one knows us, where we can live as we please so long as we're discreet."

The knot in Edward's stomach seemed to grow. "You'll tell me if you need anything? Money, letters of introduction?"

"We'll let you know. I suspect we'll be fine." His mouth quirked a little higher. "As you know, Nigel's business skills are formidable."

Edward did know it, but the comfort the knowledge might have brought was tempered by dismay. He and Freddie had spent the better part of their lives together. Freddie was more than a brother; he was the goodness that leavened Edward's soul.

"France," he said, unable to let it go. "I don't know what to say."

"Say you wish me happy."

"I do, Freddie! With all my heart."

Freddie must have heard his reservations. He reached out to clasp Edward's neck, his thumb on the bend of his jaw, his fingers curling warmly behind. It was a gesture of support, a gesture a father might have made. Edward's throat constricted at the strange reversal of their roles.

"I'll miss you," he said, not even trying to hide his pain. "And Florence! I don't know how I'll break the news to her. She was looking forward to being your sister."

Freddie laughed, a soft, bright sound. "Wherever I am, I shall always cherish her as such."

He hugged Edward then, a tight embrace that said far more than words. Edward slapped his back and held tight, wishing Freddie were small again, wishing he could keep him safe. When they let go, they both had to wipe their eyes.

"I love you," Edward said, and there was more in the words than the emotion.

Freddie nodded and backed away, his eyes dazzling bright. He must have known that if he stayed Edward would feel obliged to make another plea.

His retreat left the library very quiet. A clock ticked on one of the mantels. The gas hissed within its painted globes, a breath more even than Edward's own. Exhausted, he tipped back his head and stared at the shadow-haunted gloom of the vaulted ceiling. Angels flew across its mural, their wings as muscular as their limbs. Tonight, in the weak yellow light, they looked to Edward as if they were flying straight to hell.

His little brother was in love with Nigel West. He was leaving the country, leaving everything and everyone he knew.

And Edward was letting him do it.

He clenched his hands to sweating fists, but his stomach had made up its mind. Heat rising queasily in his throat, he ran for the terrace. The air outside was sweet, the breeze a cooling ribbon. Nonetheless, as soon as he gained the lawn, he was violently, miserably ill. Only his hold on the marble column kept him from falling to his knees.

Florence found him after the sickness had passed. He was rocking back and forth at the edge of the colonnade, his boots in the dewy grass, his head pressed to his knees. He did not have to look up to know who sat beside him.

"I don't know how to let him go," he said. "I've tried but it's so hard."

Florence wrapped herself around him. "You're not letting him go. You're letting him be himself."

"The world will do its best to hurt him."

Florence soothed his head with a stroke of her hand. "Maybe losing Nigel would hurt him more. He deserves a chance to be happy, to love and be loved like anyone else. Maybe this is the only way."

"*Maybe,*" Edward moaned. "I'm supposed to let him risk everything for a maybe?"

"Maybe is all anyone has. You have to let him make the choice."

Edward knew she was right, but knowing didn't make it easy. He turned in her arms and clung. He felt utterly helpless, more helpless than he'd been since the days he'd tried to protect his rambunctious little brother from their father's ire. Florence petted his hair and rocked him—the way any woman might comfort a man she loved. Her words, however, were not those of any woman.

"Love him as he is," she said. "That will give him the strength he needs to face the world."

THOUGH AUNT HYPATIA HAD BEEN SUSPICIOUSLY SCARCE OF late, soon after Freddie's return she sent for Florence to meet her in the drawing room. She nodded as Florence entered but did not speak until she'd poured them both a cup of tea.

"I have put this discussion off," she began, "because I felt I owed you the chance to concentrate on working things out with Edward. Since you have obviously done so"—her brows rose with worldly humor—"I feel the two of us should clear the air. First"—she lifted her hand to stall Florence's speech—"I should like to apologize, both for my part in deceiving you and for failing to realize Catherine Exeter was so vindictive. I had no idea she would use you in that fashion. I consider it most unfortunate, and entirely my fault, that you did not feel you could turn to me in your distress."

"It . . . it turned out for the best," Florence said, her hands clutched nervously on her cup.

"Liked having Edward rescue you, eh?"

"Yes, your Grace."

"Hmpf, well." The duchess shot her a knowing glance. "Good for him to have to rouse himself. That boy has always been too stolid. You, at any rate, will keep his blood pumping."

At her blush, Hypatia unbent enough to pat her knee. Then, with a sigh of resignation, she dug her walking stick into the carpet and pushed to her feet. The drawing room windows overlooked the rose garden, now a riot of late-summer blooms. In the bright gold light, the seams of her face showed the struggles she had passed through in her time.

"The Burbrookes have much to answer for," she said. "I wonder you are able to forgive any of us."

"My own actions have hardly been above reproach," Florence cried, distress bringing her off the couch. "I would not blame you for thinking me the worst sort of fortune hunter."

"Piffle," said Hypatia. "I know very well Edward's fortune had nothing to do with it. The point is we lied to you, deliberately and with intent to deceive. The only argument I can offer in my defense is that I honestly thought Freddie would change for you. I thought you would make each other happy."

"We might have," Florence said, "if we hadn't fallen in love with other people."

The duchess sighed and turned her gaze to the garden. "As much as I've seen of life, as much as I've done, you'd think this wouldn't bother me. You'd think I'd say Freddie was entitled to love where he pleased. But I suppose everything's different when it affects your family." She hunched her shoulders, then forced them down. "We should be grateful he didn't fall for that footman, I suppose. At least this Nigel person will know which fork to use. Decent manners and all that."

"Perfectly decent," Florence assured her.

"France, though," said the duchess, shaking her head. "Filthy people. Spend all their time lopping off each other's heads or pinching women's bottoms."

Florence could not stifle a giggle.

"Yes," Hypatia agreed, her face lifting naughtily. "At least Freddie and Nigel won't be compounding that problem!"

She thumped her stick on the floor in enjoyment of her own wit. Florence's heart eased as she laughed along. If the duchess was making jokes about pinching bottoms, Florence knew the worst was past.

*   *   *

Edward prowled the library late into the night. His brother was leaving in the morning. His brother and his lover. He simply couldn't get used to the idea, though he'd never seen Freddie this content. A weight had been lifted from his spirit, a weight Edward hadn't known was there.

Nigel had convinced Freddie to stay through harvest, so as not to deprive Edward of his steward at the busiest time of year. He even coaxed him into helping get the corn into the ricks, a back-breaking, filthy job. "If you're going to be a farmer," Nigel had teased, "you have to be willing to sweat."

The harvest home party they'd held for the laborers was the finest Greystowe had ever seen, a true fête, according to Mrs. Forster, it being in addition to the celebration of Edward and Florence's betrothal. The revels had stretched well into the wee hours. Every man in the county had begged Florence for a dance, including Freddie and Nigel. For once her shyness was forgotten. She read stories to the workers' children, and served up slices of pie she'd baked herself. With every smile, she proved she was at home here, among his people, literally laughing until she cried.

Edward had never known joy could be bittersweet.

He was pacing towards the bust of Plato when the object of his ruminations poked her head past the double door. She was wearing her nightshift and robe, a filmy, flowy combination that sent an immediate surge of heat to his neglected sex. Ever since Freddie's return, he and Florence had observed the proprieties. Edward meant the premarital abstinence as a demonstration of respect, both for his aunt and for Florence. Not so much as a kiss had been stolen behind a door. No doubt that, as much as anything else, was contributing to the foulness of his mood.

"Don't come in here," he warned, his resolve pushed to the limit, "unless you want your skirts tossed over your head."

"I'm not wearing skirts," she said as she padded softly in. Her pretty white feet were bare, twinkling toes and all. Clearly the woman had no sense. As if to prove it, she cocked her head at him and smiled. "I came to make sure you didn't pace straight through the carpet."

"You're playing with fire," he warned, but she ran to him as if fire was what she most desired.

His good intentions disintegrated on the spot. He had his trousers open before she reached him; had her down on the floor before her first laughing kiss brushed his lips. He cursed at the tangle of her gown, and again at the eager encouragement of her hands.

"I'm trying to behave," he protested as she spread her legs beneath his weight.

She muttered something that sounded very much like "To hell with behaving" and then the folds of lawn and lace seemed magically to give way. His nerves spangled like shooting stars. He felt her body's welcome against his crown and entered her before he could think of stopping. The first stroke was pure, tooth-grinding bliss. She was hot and tight and wet, and her tiny cry of pleasure made him groan like a dying man.

"I missed this," she said, hugging him close with arms and thighs. "I missed this so much."

Edward had no control at all. Their coupling was so fast and hard it had both of them gasping for air. He was thumping her into the carpet and she was drumming him deeper with her heels. Nothing mattered but racing to the finish, but reaffirming his ownership of her sex. His climax broke like glittering golden fire, explosively good, blinding him to everything but the long, gushing convulsion. He wouldn't have known she followed but for her sharp orgasmic cry.

Once he'd rolled her above him, he never wanted to move again.

"Now," she said as she sprawled atop his chest with his shaft still pulsing lightly in her sheath. "Tell me what you and Nigel discussed at your oh-so-serious talk."

Edward's breath came out on a sigh. Leave it to Florence to guess what had upset him, and to make it easier for him to share it.

"He apologized for abusing the family's trust," he said. "As if that mattered at this point. He advised me on replacements, gave me the key to his files. Ah, and he assured me he'd take the 'best possible care' of my brother. I felt like the bloody father of the bride."

"Mm," said Florence. "And what did you say in return?"

"Gave him a bank draft," he muttered. "Just in case."

He could feel her smiling against his skin. "I'm sure he appreciated that."

"Of course he did. Unlike Freddie, Nigel is a practical man."

Florence rubbed her face across his chest. At some point during their encounter, she had opened his waistcoat and pulled up his shirt. Now her arm slid under the hem to hug his ribs.

"I'm proud of you," she said, kissing the tender spot above his heart.

"Don't be proud until tomorrow," he huffed. "They'll be lucky if I don't stop the bloody train."

THE TRAIN SAT AT GREYSTOWE STATION, A DUSTY BLACK denizen of the modern world. Steam puffed from its stack as it took on water and coal. Every now and then its whistle sounded a mournful double toot. *Good-bye,* it seemed to say. *Good-bye. Good-bye.* Florence longed most heartily for it to stop.

"I still wish you'd stay for the wedding," she said, hugging Freddie so tightly he pretended to choke. Edward waited a few steps behind her, giving them room for their farewells.

"I know you wouldn't mind," Freddie said. "I, however, shouldn't like the scandal of my presence to distract from your day."

"But I'd far rather you gave me away—instead of my father's old lawyer."

Freddie pushed her back by the shoulders. "Now, now. Mr. Mowbry brought you and Edward together. What could be more appropriate?"

"But I'll miss you," she said, feeling his absence already. Freddie hushed her with two fingers of his neatly gloved hand. He smiled affectionately at her pout.

"Remember what I told you, dearest. You and Edward must get to the business of siring heirs. I expect no less than half a dozen named after me."

"Half a dozen!"

"Oh, yes," he said airily. "Freddie, Frederica, Fredwina, Fredward—and I'll leave the other two to you."

"You are too foolish for words," she said, smiling past her heavy heart.

He straightened the brim of her feathered hat. "I'm counting on you to be foolish in my stead. My brother mustn't be allowed to sink into dourness while I'm gone. Of course, since his sense of humor is extremely primitive, that shouldn't prove too great a trial."

Edward snorted behind her, but neither Florence nor Freddie paid him any mind.

"I shall do my best to cultivate some silliness," she said.

"Good," Freddie responded, his eyes abruptly brimming. Rather than let himself spill over, he blinked hard and squared his shoulders like a soldier on review. "I shall look forward to hearing of your progress. If you like, I'll send explicit instructions on filling his slippers with jam."

This was enough for Edward.

"You're filling her head with nonsense," he said, his voice gruff, his arm dropping warmly around her shoulders.

Freddie chucked her chin before turning to him. "Take care of her," he said. "Remember, she was my sweetheart first."

The brothers exchanged a long, memorizing look. Edward's eyes were serious and Freddie's twinkled, but Florence knew each was recalling what the other had meant to his life. Finally, Edward thrust his hand into his pocket.

"I have something for you," he said, and brought out a familiar disk of gold. "Your first swimming prize. I've kept it all this time. I thought you might like to have it."

Freddie opened both hands so that Edward could lay the medal and ribbon across his palms. "Edward!" he exclaimed, caught between shock and laughter. "If I weren't already, your gift would completely unman me."

"You'll always be a man," Edward said in his gravest voice. "You've proved that more times than I can count."

Freddie covered his eyes and shook his head, more than male enough not to want to cry in front of his sibling. Obviously embarrassed, Edward squeezed his shoulder and stepped back to make room for Aunt Hypatia. Her farewell was punctuated by hugs and barks of laughter. At last, Freddie tore himself away and joined Nigel on the steps of the first-class carriage.

Edward shook hands with his former steward and again with his brother, and then the train chuffed slowly away.

Florence broke into a run before the car could leave the platform. "Winifred!" she shouted, waving her handkerchief wildly at Freddie's window.

"Fredalia," he countered, waving wildly back.

At that, she gave in to tears. She cried all the way home, cuddled close to Edward's chest. She cried at dinner at the sight of Freddie's empty place. She cried when she found the rose he'd left on her pillow, and again when Edward snuck into her room in the middle of the night.

"What a watering pot!" he declared, gathering her in his arms. "Keep this up and I shall leave you in the garden for the flowers."

But Florence knew better than to believe he was annoyed. Freddie was worth the tears. Besides which, she suspected comforting her kept Edward from crying himself. Throwing himself into this very important duty, he rocked her in his lap and crooned under his breath and finally kissed the last tears from her eyes.

"We've been given a gift," he said. "One few people are privileged to know. Freddie wouldn't want us to be sad."

"No," she agreed, dabbing her nose with his best silk handkerchief, the one that had mere minutes ago peeped neatly from the pocket of his robe. The sentiment was so sweet, and the mention of gifts so unwittingly apropos, she almost welled over again.

Edward laughed at her sniffle and hugged her closer. "Florence, Florence, Florence. Where would I be without you to melt my heart?"

Florence didn't know, nor did she care to find out. With an extra flutter to her pulse, she pressed her hand to her belly and lifted her gaze to his. What she found there made her smile even more than the secret she'd been cradling to herself all week.

"Edward," she said, her grin breaking free, "I've been wondering if you'd mind very much if we'd started a little Frederica already."

He blinked at her, then let out a whoop that probably jolted half the staff out of their beds. "Mind?" he said, tossing her into the air until she shrieked herself. "No, I don't mind, Florence. Not at all."

She hadn't caught her breath from landing before he was kissing her senseless, murmuring love words and stroking her belly with a reverence that made her think motherhood might be very nice indeed.

She had taken the greatest risk a woman could and was now facing the consequences, despite which she had not felt a shred of fear since the day the possibility had crept into her mind. She had hoped, she had bubbled with suppressed excitement, but she had not feared what would become of her. Married or not, no woman would be as cosseted as the woman who bore Edward's child. Add to that the love that glowed so steadily in his eyes, and Florence knew this baby would be infinitely more than a seven-month surprise.

This baby would be a gift, a gift they gave and a gift they received; full no doubt of mystery, but wrapped in adoration.

"Are you well?" Edward asked, suddenly stiffening with concern. His big warm hand spread protectively across her womb. "No sickness? No fatigue?"

"I was only sick once," she said with a quiet laugh for his alarm. "Which gave me the notion I might want to start counting days."

"And your tears," he eagerly put in. "They say women are more emotional when they're with child."

"That they do."

He didn't see her amusement. He was too busy examining the unchanged curves of her body. Or almost unchanged. When he cupped her breast, a deeper pang of sweetness streaked through her flesh.

"Just imagine," he mused, his fingers strumming the sensitive peak. "A little Frederica we can cradle in our arms."

Florence's toes curled pleasantly at his caress.

"I don't know," she said, her own hand beginning to wander. "For myself, I'm rather partial to Fredward. . . ."

Epilogue

TRAVELING WITH THE EARL WAS AN EDUCATION. FLORENCE knew her husband possessed many admirable traits, but she'd never guessed he had the patience of a saint. One of them certainly needed it, for Frederica was their companion on the trip. At two, she had her mother's green eyes, her uncle's charm, and her father's stubbornness of mind. Today she seemed convinced she could hasten the horses by bouncing more vigorously on her father's knees. Edward winced but grinned, as if nothing could be more delightful than a pummeling by one's child.

"Settle down," Florence urged, stroking her daughter's wispy golden hair. "Your papa needs his knees for later on."

"Papa, Papa, Papa!" Fredi shrieked, not calming in the least. This chortle was followed by a new bit of intelligence. "Gween," she announced, pointing out the window of their big rented coach. "Look, Mama. Pwetty gween!"

"Yes," said Florence. "Very pretty green."

Her daughter was correct in her judgment, if not her pronunciation. This area of Bordeaux was indeed beautiful: lush in its late spring growth, picturesque in its rambling village, and pure magic in its old châteaux. The coach's high wheels rumbled down a sandy road where glimpses of the Garonne River alternated with crumbling stone gates and workers moving slowly down rows of vines. The scene was timeless and peaceful. With a sigh of pleasure, Florence pulled her daughter back into her lap.

"Soon?" said Frederica, cuddling close in one of her quicksilver changes of moods. "Soon we see Uncle Fweddie?"

"Yes," Florence assured her, kissing her warm, round cheek. "And then you, Madame Stickyfingers, will get a good wash."

"Stickyfinga," Fredi giggled, then subsided with a yawn.

"Why," Edward demanded, "does she always sleep for you?"

"Because I am smart enough to let you wear her out."

Edward returned her grin with a smile so warm it could still bring tears to her eyes. Their life had been rich in warmth since their marriage, an event that caused less comment than she'd feared, due to the timely exposure of Charles Hargreave's affair with Millicent Parminster and his subsequent abandonment of his wife to a castle in Scotland. Poetic justice, according to Hypatia. Florence was simply glad her husband's old mistress chose to take her aunt along for company.

With scandals like this to entertain the peerage, the surprise evoked by Florence Fairleigh marrying the older rather than the younger Burbrooke was mild—especially when the newly weds proceeded to live so quietly. A pair of stay-at-homes, society clucked, little imagining what the earl and his countess were getting up to.

Florence smiled at the memory of those days. Despite society's disapproval of their domesticity, Freddie's absence was mourned more deeply than theirs. Those few who guessed why he'd left kept quiet out of respect for—or, in some cases, fear of—the formidable earl and his equally formidable aunt. The consensus seemed to be that Freddie could do what he pleased, as long as they were not forced to know about it. Society being what it was, she expected this was the best reaction they could hope for.

Out of all of it, the loss of Merry Vance's friendship was her only regret. The two women saw each other, of course. Edward was close to Merry's father; the duke and he shared a number of political interests. As a result, Monmouth's invitations were among the few the couple accepted. Merry always welcomed Florence warmly but Florence could tell her spirits were not what they'd been. She suspected Merry wasn't quite over her infatuation with the earl.

Her husband broke into her thoughts by stroking the curve of her cheek. "Something wrong?" he asked with the gentleness he reserved for those he loved.

She shook her head. "Just wondering if Merry Vance will be happy with that fellow her father seems to be grooming up to marry her."

"Why wouldn't she be? Solid man. They've known each other from the cradle. Plus, his positions on finance are impeccable."

She stifled a smile at this recipe for romance.

"Here's the turn," her husband said, pointing to the bell-towered church that marked it. He tugged at his collar, a sure sign that he was nervous. Florence patted his thigh, but knew there was little she could do to soothe him. Three years was a long time to go without seeing one's brother.

A short avenue of plane trees led to Freddie and Nigel's villa. The house was charming: soft gray stone with ash blue shutters and a roof of red clay tiles. White jasmine trailed from the windows, and the path to the door was paved with ocher brick. Everything was beautiful, but slightly unkempt, as if the people who lived here wanted the humblest visitor to feel at home.

The driver, a big, red-faced Frenchman, climbed down from the box and began untying their luggage. Since Fredi still slept, Florence handed her to Edward to carry out. Her long-awaited uncle bounded around the corner of the house just as Edward was lifting the knocker. Freddie was obviously dressed for gardening, in muddy boots and trousers and a simple peasant shirt. His skin was rosy brown, his hair bleached nearly blond. He'd gained weight since leaving England and it suited him immensely. He was solid now—no boyish rake but a man with his feet planted firmly on the ground. He grinned and covered his mouth when he saw his niece curled in sleep on her father's shoulder. Her ruffled pink dress, once quite fetching, was a hopeless mass of wrinkles from the ride.

"Oh, look at the little princess," he whispered.

"Wait till she wakes up," Edward warned.

Freddie merely laughed and gathered the sleeping bundle into his arms. "You made good time," he whispered over his shoulder. "We weren't expecting you until tonight."

"The princess wakes at dawn," Edward said. "Her subjects have no option but to follow."

Freddie grinned and swept his arm before him. "Welcome to Château Burbrooke."

His garden was a bower of daffodils and roses, with an ancient tinkling fountain and a table Nigel was frantically trying to cover with a cloth. Piles of clippings attested to Freddie's attempt to tidy up. More promising were two bottles of wine left cooling in a bucket of water. In the course of their journey, Florence was certain she'd swallowed half the dust of France.

"Oh, hell," said Nigel. "I mean, welcome to our home. How nice you could come straight back before you'd even seen your rooms."

The look he shot Freddie made it obvious this was not the sequence on which they'd agreed.

"Oops," said Freddie with a sheepishness so endearing Florence had to grin.

"Here," she said, reaching for the other edge of the cloth. "Let me help. I take it we're having a picnic lunch?"

"Yes," said Nigel. "That is, I'd planned a nice dinner but, well, at the moment we have bread and fruit and a wonderful foie gras they sell at a shop in town."

"Perfect," she said. "We very much like picnics and Fredi adores pâté."

"Like a pig in truffles," Edward muttered.

"Oh." Nigel looked looked slightly alarmed. "I hope I have enough."

"Don't worry," said Edward. "We won't wake the little beast till we've had ours."

This unparentlike declaration seemed to startle Nigel but also to calm him. Before he could assure Florence he could manage on his own, she followed him into the cool dark house, keeping up a friendly chatter that rather amazed her. She'd come a long way since her tongue-tied arrival in London. As they progressed through the hall, she gathered an impression of old polished wood and big simple furniture—a bachelor house, designed for comfort and ease. She knew just by walking through it that they'd all enjoy their stay.

By the time they emerged with the food, the brothers had their heads together over the table, where Freddie was sketching something on the back of a crumpled envelope. Like a trusting puppy, Frederica was curled in sleep on Edward's coat in a patch of sun.

"It's ten acres," Freddie was saying, "along the river. We had to re-plant where parts of the vineyard had grown bare, and some drainage needed relaying, but the soil is good and the rootstock is still productive. Right now, we're selling most of our harvest to Château Roudelle but we're thinking that, with the help of a local widow, we could develop a little label of our own."

"We're reeling her in," Nigel said with a laugh as boyish as Freddie's. "We've convinced her to take us under her wing. Teach the bumbling *Anglais* how to save their poor, neglected vines."

The ensuing merriment woke Frederica. Rubbing her eyes, she tottered over to the table and announced that she was hungry.

"Lord," said Edward. "Here comes the bottomless pit."

Despite his words, the facility with which he fixed his daughter a plate of precisely what she liked was a wonder to behold.

"Mm," she said, mouth full of bread and goose liver. "Fwance is good."

"I'll drink to that," said Freddie, and pulled one of the cooling bottles from the bucket by his feet. The dark green glass bore a hand-written label that said "Burbrooke-West, 1875 Bordeaux."

Florence clapped her hands. "It's yours? Oh, Freddie, how marvelous!"

"Merely a *vin ordinaire*," he said with a deprecating grin. "Most of our plants are young. The widow insists, however, that you can taste the shadow of future greatness."

He poured with great skill for a bumbling *Anglais,* tilting the bottle gently so that its contents would not be disturbed on the journey to the small tapered glasses.

"The interesting thing about grapes," he said, continuing this pretty ritual, "is that they thrive on struggle. The soil here is almost entirely gravel for several meters down. Water runs straight through it, along with the minerals the plants need to grow. So the roots"—he finished the last glass with a flourishing twist—"must dig deep if they want to drink. This makes the vine strong and the grapes sweet. Only through hardship can you get a true *grand vin.*"

With a teasing smile, he handed the glasses around, none more than half full, and Fredi's a good deal less. The two-year-old clutched it in chubby hands, as intently as if she held the holy grail. Edward made a sound of concern at this, but Florence shook her head. "Don't worry," she said. "Knowing our little sprout, most of it will end up on her dress."

"We should have a toast," Nigel said, his eyes shy but aglow. "To . . . to family, because the richest grapes grow closest to the root."

"To family," Edward agreed, clinking rims with his brother. Then he turned to Nigel. "And to love, because that is the best vintage of all."

To a one, the men turned red, though Edward did his best to cover it with a frown.

"To love," Florence seconded, loudly, before they could start shuffling their feet.

With a clearing of throats, the toast rang out. The cool new wine was tart and fruity, a burst of sunshine on the tongue. They smiled at each other as they swallowed and everyone there, even Frederica, knew that life was very sweet.

Beyond Seduction

❧❧❧

To my fantabulous editor,
Christine Zika,
for asking me to go beyond.

To my never-say-die agent,
Roberta Brown,
for her humor and her steely nerve.

I am grateful, ladies, more than I can say!

Prologue

"YOUR DAUGHTER *WILL* MARRY MY SON," SAID ALTHORP.

He stood by the parlor window, stout and sure, his chill gaze betraying the ruthless nature at his core. Despite the thickening of his figure, he was as handsome as he'd been at twenty-nine. The cut of his morning coat was impeccable, his posture both casual and assured.

Few would guess he was an object of scorn among the circle to which he had always aspired.

The sight of him in her home—in her life—made Lavinia Vance, celebrated duchess to the duke of Monmouth, want to rake her nails down his cultured face. Instead, she smoothed the skirt of her tightly laced brocade gown. Her skin glowed beside the *terre D'Egypte* red and the long cuirass bodice made her curves seem more imperial than ever. She looked her fashionable best, but rather than experiencing her usual satisfaction at the fact, she found herself wishing she felt as confident as she looked.

Judging by the amusement in his eyes, Althorp was aware of her emotions. He stepped closer, lifting his arm as if to touch her cheek. When she shrank instinctively back, he merely smiled. His hand fell to her arm.

At the touch, a memory came: her own fingers stroking the dunbrown birthmark on his back as they lay in a rumpled hotel bed. He'd been magnetic then, strong and attentive, and so much more intelligent than most of her husband's friends. It had seemed the height of injustice that they snubbed him simply because his father had been in trade. A baronetcy bought with coal, they sneered, the ink on the title barely dry. Hurting back then herself, she'd wanted to kiss his wounds and make them better, never dreaming how coldly he'd use her sympathy to control her—in bed and out. She could not believe the things she'd done, the things she had enjoyed.

Repelled, she turned her head away. If only she could erase that much-regretted time!

Too close to evade, Allhorp's breath stirred her hair. "I remember when you welcomed my caress, when you could not do enough to please me."

"That"—she lifted her chin—"was a lapse of judgment of which I am not proud."

"Tut-tut, Lavinia. Insults gain you nothing. You know you have more to lose than I should our former relationship be exposed."

She shook free of him, part of her wondering as always if he were bluffing. Exposing himself as an adulterer would hardly further his son's ambitions—or, rather, his ambitions for his son; Lavinia doubted Ernest himself aspired so high.

But the doubt remained unspoken. She did not dare test Althorp's determination. Given the paucity of the baronet's support among the peerage, if Lavinia's husband didn't help Ernest stand for the House of Commons, chances were no one with leverage would. If her enemy's dreams of paternal grandeur were dashed, would he hesitate to return the favor?

She could not deny she had more to lose than he did. Her position in society was the culmination of her every hope. If the truth became known, at the very least her husband would banish her to Scotland. For his wife to have had an affair with a man he believed to be his friend . . . Geoffrey's pride would not allow that to go unpunished.

Satisfied he'd made his point, Althorp folded his arms and regarded her from under heavy, half-lidded eyes. Still in his hand, the brim of his black silk top hat rested against his side. It was an exquisite creation, neither too high nor too low, with a crisp, curving rim. The duke did not own one so fine.

"My son is going to be prime minister," he said with the sureness she'd come to loathe. "And your husband, his future father-in-law, is going to start him on that road. He'll have to if he doesn't want people to think his precious Merry has married down. All you have to do is push your idiot daughter into my son's arms."

Lavinia laughed at his claim, an edge of hysteria in the sound. She *had* pushed, to an extent that shamed her. Moreover, she'd made certain her daughter would have no other suitors for her hand. As plain as she was, as outspoken as she was, Merry herself had sabotaged her prospects well enough. Thanks to Lavinia, however, every mother with a son knew what a hellion she was and how she'd be certain to shame any family she married into. Lavinia had disguised her purpose with mournful sighs—no one would think her an unnatural mother—but the few men who had shown a glimmer of interest had thus been scared away.

If only manipulating Merry were as easy.

"I don't dare push her any harder," she said, her fingers twined into an involuntary knot. "She'll only dig her heels in if she feels cornered."

Her plea fell on deaf ears. Althorp dropped his arms and tapped his hat against his trouser leg. The flutter of the paler cloth was a telling sign of his impatience.

"I've given you a year," he said, "and twice she has refused him. For God's sake, my son is not a monster. He is a good-looking, intelligent, well-mannered young man. Your husband approves. And from what I can see, your daughter does not despise him."

"She thinks he'll try to control her."

"She needs controlling!" Althorp exclaimed, then lowered his voice. "Put your foot down, Lavinia. And have your husband put down his. The girl has to marry someone. You and I both know it had better be my son."

Lavinia sensed he was in earnest. She looked down at the hands she'd clutched together in unconscious prayer. Her gloves were creased, and damp inside with fear. With all her heart, she wished she weren't a coward. Surely nothing was more despicable than pandering one's daughter for the selfish preservation of one's place.

"I need more time," she said.

Althorp caught her chin and raised it in an iron grip. The squeeze of his bare fingers was intimate and hot. "One month," he said. "My son is planning to ask her again on New Year's Eve. By New Year's Day I want to hear they are betrothed."

He released her and turned, not saying good-bye or even nodding. He simply pulled on his gloves and strode from the room.

He knew she had no choice but to do precisely as he asked.

Alone once more, an unladylike sweat prickled beneath her breasts. Her heart beat against her stays as if it longed to escape the bonds of flesh. For a moment, she allowed the dark deliverance to whisper its temptations in her ear. But what sort of haven would Death be to a sinner like herself? No haven at all, she thought. And why should she surrender when much of her life was still so sweet? She was the duchess of Monmouth: a social force. She had her house and her clothes and her handsome sons. Her husband had in later years become if not a lover, at least a friend. These were precious gifts she would not willingly leave behind.

Her hands curled into fists. Somehow she had to change her daughter's mind. Then they could all go on with their lives. But how to do it—how?—when the foolish chit would rather be a spinster than a bride.

Chapter 1

NICOLAS CRAVEN, FAMOUS ARTIST AND INFAMOUS LIBERTINE, slouched in the wing-backed leather chair as if he did not ever intend to rise. His paisley brown robe of flowing silk was tied at his trim, hard waist. Beneath this he was naked. In the interest of warmth, a snifter of brandy, mostly full, lay cradled against his chest. A coal fire burned behind the grate on which his slippered feet were propped. Its steady glow lit keen, saturnine features. His eyes were smoke, his jaw as sharp as steel. A pianist would not have scorned his hands. His voice was another matter. In contrast to this lean, dark elegance, it was as hoarse and graveled as if he spent his days shouting on the docks.

That impression was misleading. Nicolas Craven barely had to whisper to draw attention. He was a genius, people said, better than Leighton or Alma-Tadema, not that either of those luminaries would have conceded their position. In any case, people listened when Nic spoke, whether out of respect for his talent or fear of his occasionally cutting wit he did not care. He only cared that they leave him alone when he was tired.

As he was tonight.

He'd completed his latest commission. The bursts of manic activity—elation, frustration, nights spent with brushes clamped between his teeth and paint-stained fingers plunged in his hair—had ceased as if he'd grabbed the clapper of a big bronze bell. His body rang with the echoes of his exertion, emptied out and exhausted. But he would rest now. The portrait was done. Monmouth had come to collect it that morning and pronounced himself pleased, though Nic doubted the duke saw more than a fraction of what the painting said.

He had caught the man.

Hell, he'd caught half the British peerage: their befuddlement at the changing times, their pomposity and self-indulgence, their earnest belief in their ability to save the world . . . as long as the world wanted to be saved in a manner they approved of.

His mouth curled in ironic self-disgust. No point looking down his nose at them. No matter how Nic lived, his blood was just as blue.

Not that he could blame his sins on that.

He turned his gaze to the window, to the jungle of foliage that hid his cozy home in St. John's Wood. A winter fog, thick as cat's fur, had crept out from London to swallow this artist's enclave to the north. He could barely make out the ivy that grew across the glass, obscured as it was by the ashy haze. The mix of chocolate and silver was extraordinary, soft as velvet. If Nic hadn't been too lazy to move he'd have reached for his pastels. That something so foul could be so beautiful he could only marvel.

He was actually considering getting up when a tap on the library door saved him from the effort. At his grunt, his butler, Farnham, entered with a tray of food and coffee. As always, Nic had dismissed the servants in the emotional low water that followed his painting fits. Since this particular low water had come during the holidays, Nic was a popular man. Holiday or no, per usual, Farnham had not hied himself away. The older man had been a sergeant in the Crimea. His sense of duty was stronger than that of the other staff—stronger, in fact, than his employer's.

"Your dinner, sir," he said, just as if Nic had ordered it. He removed the brandy decanter in order to place the meal on the little table at Nic's side. Then he waited. Nic knew the butler wouldn't leave until he saw him eat.

He lifted the hefty beef-and-pickle sandwich and took a bite. "There," he said. "Satisfied?"

Without comment Farnham poured a steaming cup of coffee and set it on a saucer. The smell alone was enough to clear Nic's head—at least until Farnham slid a fat white envelope between the dishes.

"You'll be wanting your mail, sir."

Nic snorted, his mouth full of savory bread and beef. Farnham knew that for a lie as well as he did. This particular letter had been following him around the house all week, appearing beside his plate at breakfast, peeping from the pocket of his coat. Nic had ignored it with a determination honed by years of practice. Unfortunately, unlike Nic, Farnham didn't believe in putting off till tomorrow what one would rather not face today.

With a grimace, Nic put down his coffee and took the envelope. It *had* been a week. His commission was finished, his mind as serene as it ever was. Surely he was ready to open the damn thing now. What was there to fear, after all? The contents of his mother's correspondence were invariably the same.

"I'll leave you to it then," said Farnham as Nic's thumb slid under the flap.

The letter was as he'd expected. A brief expression of hope for Nic's well-being—omitting, of course, any mention of his work—then straight to a summary of the myriad tasks she had undertaken since her last report. The sheep, the fields, the drainage in the village ditch: all had been seen to with his mother's trademark efficiency. She was the strongest, most managing person he knew, and yet behind each proof of competence lay an unspoken accusation. *These responsibilities are yours, Nicolas. Yours.* Never mind she would resent the mildest interference, she still behaved as if his failure to bestir himself were an affront. "What's more," she continued, "the boy needs the steadying influence of a male. He's nearly fifteen. I can no longer guide him as I should."

Guide him. Nic snorted. More like *rule.* Skimming to the end, he crumpled the page and tossed it into the fire. A smaller note remained, which had been tucked inside the other.

Nic opened it. Against his will, his heart began to rap more swiftly against his ribs. The note was from the boy, the usual update on his progress at school. The tone was formal. The boy always called him "sir." Never volunteered more than the impersonal, nor asked questions he'd learned would not be answered. Unlike the dowager marchioness, the boy was far too sharp to inquire when Nic would visit. Nic had seen him twice in his life: once shortly after his birth and again when he was four. At the time, the boy's resemblance to Bess had been too wrenching to make Nic eager to repeat the experience.

Some memories were better left to lie.

He ran one finger over the spiky loops of ink. Despite the stiff language, he fancied he could read the boy's character in the scrawl. Bright. Impatient. True to his friends. Fonder of sport than he was of schooling but, apparently, from one comment he let slip, a budding admirer of Trollope.

Nic smiled at that. With an impulsive movement at odds with his former languor, he opened the drawer in the table at his side. As he'd expected, Farnham had stocked it with writing materials. Using the arm of the chair as a desk, he scribbled a response.

Dear Cristopher,
Am doing well, though busy with work. Should you need anything for which you would prefer not to ask the marchioness, feel free to write my man of business.

He bit the end of his pen and reread what he'd written. His eyes strayed to the nearest rank of shelving. A small flutter of satisfaction warmed his breast. Yes, he did have a leather-bound set of *The Eustace Diamonds*. The pages, bright with gold leaf, hadn't yet been cut. The boy might have read the novel, of course, but not in such handsome form. Rising, he pulled out the first volume and opened it to the frontispiece. The pen was still in his hand. He should write something, shouldn't he? Otherwise, the gift would seem too cold even for him.

He pondered a moment.

"Thought you might like this," he wrote, then hesitated over what to sign. "Your father" would probably please the boy, but Nic wasn't sure he could force that appellation through the nib. He could sign himself "Northwick" he supposed, but that, too, seemed insufferable. In the end, he simply wrote "Nicolas" and, just in case, added a twenty-pound note. Warm, it was not. He had no wish, however, to promise more than he could give.

THE MANSION IN KNIGHTSBRIDGE HUMMED WITH THE pleasure of its guests. The holidays had never come so grandly as they did to these lofty rooms. Hundreds of beeswax tapers lit them, all banded with crimson bows. Every door was a faerie forest of fresh-cut pine. The scent of sugared negus and French perfume drifted like incense through the heated air. Bosoms glowed, jewels glittered, and trains like satiny peacock's tails swept inlaid marble floors. The sweet melancholy of a Chopin nocturne was nearly drowned by laughter.

When the clock in the hall struck midnight, no one showed the least desire to leave.

One reveler stood apart from the cries of "Happy New Year." In the relative quiet of the blue salon, a slender, freckled woman with hair like a scrub brush of red-gold wire stared intently at a portrait of the host. The picture had been hung that morning above the mantel, and ever since Merry Vance, only daughter of the duke of Monmouth, had been haunted by what it said.

Mind, there was nothing wrong with the thing. The likeness was exacting, the execution skilled. The artist had posed her father standing behind the desk in his study, with one hand resting on a globe and the other steepled lightly over a well-thumbed copy of the London *Times*. A soft golden light, like the end of an autumn day, angled down from a nearby window to diffuse over the rich black wool of his coat sleeve. At the very limit of the wedge of slanting sun, a small felt lion lay toppled on its side. The lion was a toy from Merry's childhood, treasured by a father who had four sons and just one daughter. The sight of it lying there, half in the light, half out, struck her with the force of a strange and uncomfortable portent. Indeed, the whole picture made her squirm.

Her father appeared vigorous, his stance confident, his jaw firm. But there was something in his eyes: a look Merry had never noticed and now could not imagine how she'd missed.

How did I get here? the look said, and, *What has happened to the world I used to know?*

In that moment, for the first time in all her twenty years, she thought of her father not as Her Father but as a person like herself. Despite his title and his wealth, despite being a citizen of the mightiest empire on earth, he, too, was capable of doubt. In one way, the realization scared her but, in another, it made her even more determined to control her destiny.

When she was her father's age, she did not want to know regret.

Ten more years and I'll be free, she thought. That's when the estate left in trust to her by her grandmother would be handed into her care. She could live as she pleased then, answerable to no one but herself—but only if she managed to stay unwed.

A husband, she knew, would not support her secret plans.

A whisper of orange-scented silk warned Merry she had company. Her best friend, Isabel Beckett, now Lady Hyde, laid a delicate, white-gloved hand upon her shoulder. Both girls were fair, but where Merry was as wiry as a jockey, Isabel was pleasingly plump. Pretty, too, with fashionably wavy hair and skin as smooth as cream. They'd attended the same finishing school, two incorrigible pranksters. Merry couldn't count the times her friend's batting golden lashes had gotten them out of trouble. As Isabel joined her in gazing at the portrait, her expression was one of amusement.

"They say he spent three months seducing Lady Piggot."

"What!" gasped Merry, far from ready to face this news.

Isabel giggled. "Not your father, silly. Nicolas Craven. The artist. Did you get to meet him while he was here?"

Merry shook her head. "I only caught a glimpse of him in the hall. He was all over paint and wild-eyed—like a refugee from Bedlam. I don't think he even noticed I was there."

"Probably caught up in his Art," said Isabel, nodding sagely. "Mother claims he's a terrible rake. Says no decent woman would sit for him."

"Well," Merry retorted, "he is not a very efficient rake if it took him three months to seduce Lady Piggot."

"No one says she wasn't willing to give in sooner. Apparently, he likes to savor his conquests." The newly married Isabel licked her upper lip. "Morsel by morsel, as it were."

"Hmpf." Merry ignored a rush of warmth through her inner regions. "Likes them panting after him, I'll bet."

"I wouldn't mind panting. My husband is almost as boring as your fiancé."

"Ernest is not my fiancé."

"Good as," Isabel countered. "You know your parents have their hearts set on the match."

Merry did know this, and had known it long before he began proposing. Ernest Althorp was the son of a neighboring landowner, now employed as her father's secretary. Growing up, he'd been her refuge from her brothers: calm when they were impetuous, sympathetic when they teased.

Not that she had ever considered marrying Ernest. He was like a brother to her, and a stuffy brother at that. Besides which, his father's baronetcy was hardly a match for her father's dukedom. Merry cared less for such matters than her friends, but if one had to be legshackled, one did not want to sink! Her father, however, thought him "sound." Her mother just plain adored him. Whenever Merry spent time with her, thankfully not often, she found an excuse to sing Ernest's praises. Merry was beginning to think the duchess had a *tendre* for him herself. Most of all, though, her parents thought Ernest was precisely the steadying influence their wild young daughter needed. *Time you settled,* her father liked to say. *Trade those horses of yours for a husband.*

Merry shuddered. Trade her freedom for a yoke, more like. Ernest was as conservative as he was steady.

"At least he isn't fat," said Isabel, whose own husband was portly. "And at least you like him."

But liking him made it worse. Merry knew she didn't have the meanness to defy him the way she would a bully. Nor did she like him enough. Once upon a time, Merry had been in love. She'd been young, and it hadn't ended well, but the experience had taught her how deeply her passions could be stirred.

Stymied, she stared at Nicolas Craven's painting as if it held the secret to her fate. The candlelight caught a hairline crack in the gilded frame. That will be my life, she thought, if I can't fend Ernest off.

"Nothing has been decided," she said aloud.

"Will be soon," warned her friend. "I'd be surprised if old Ernest doesn't propose again tonight. Your brothers have been winking at him all evening."

"Argh," said Merry, suspecting she was right.

Isabel laughed and squeezed her waist. "Shall I hide you in the broom cabinet the way I used to do at school?"

"No," Merry sighed. "It's time I let them all know where I stand."

MERRY'S ELDEST BROTHER, EVELYN, HIS WIFE INDISPOSED BY her latest pregnancy, had the dubious honor of ensuring his little sister did not languish by the wall. Even at a family party Merry wasn't one to gather beaus—though her following had not always been so sparse.

When she first came out, she'd had her share of admirers, enough to feel a flush of anticipatory pleasure before a ball. At one point, after Ernest's first proposal, she'd thought she might someday say yes to someone else—until she'd realized no one else would ever ask.

Apparently, when males reached a certain age, they lost their tolerance for female frankness. Overnight it seemed her opinions were not as valid as their own. They forgot she'd been raised by a respected member of Parliament and, what's more, had a brain. Where once they'd marveled at her ability to take a fence, now they held her horsemanship in disgust. What they'd praised in a girl, it seemed they could not stomach in a woman.

Beauty might have saved her, or charm, but she had neither. She'd lived too much of her life in the footsteps of her brothers. Even if she'd wanted to simper, she wouldn't have known how.

And now men her age cut their eyes away when she passed, as if to see her was to be tainted. To hell with them, she'd think each time it happened. To hell with them all.

Only her love of dancing induced her to suffer the indignity of being partnered by her brothers.

On this evening, contrary to his usual custom of chattering her ear off, Evelyn maintained a grinning silence through the waltz. When the last strains faded, he led her off the ballroom floor to the palm-lined alcove that held the punch tables. There, two more of her brothers waited with matching smirks. Merry's heart sank to her stomach. Isabel was right. Ernest was planning to propose. Obviously, the man didn't know better than to share his secrets with her siblings.

She sighed in exasperation. Her brothers were three handsome peas in a pod. Like her, they had light-brown eyes, fair, freckled skin, and Grandmother Vance's kinky red-gold hair—though only Merry had to wear it long enough to turn into a bird's nest by itself. True, Evelyn had, since the birth of his second child, cultivated an unfortunate pair of side whiskers, but the less said on that the better.

"So," she said, nonchalantly ladling herself a cup of heated wine, "come to roast me?"

"Nothing of the sort," said James, her second married brother. She hadn't seen him in months, not since his wedding. Like Evelyn, he glowed like a horse who'd been eating rich. His wife, too, was newly breeding.

Neither brother had wasted a moment ensuring their brides would be trapped at home.

"We like Althorp," he added. "We're happy for you."

She sipped her sugared port and tried not to wish it were a whiskey. "I've no idea why you'd be happy, since I'm determined to turn him down just like before."

"Seriously," said James.

"Seriously," echoed Evelyn. "Why won't you marry him? He can ride—"

"And shoot—"

"And he's always good for a loan."

Peter's contribution to the chorus dashed her last hope for support. Still unmarried and a mere two years older than herself, he'd helped her into and out of more scrapes than the others put together. Admittedly, her debut had put a distance between them—she'd had to be a bit of a lady at least—but lately, with the older boys gone from the house to start their families, she and Peter had grown close again.

Unfortunately, her repeated refusal of Ernest Althorp, who'd never been anything but kind to Peter, exceeded even his patience. "Come on, Mer," he said, "haven't you humiliated him enough?"

The accusation stung but she fought to keep a steady voice.

"I'm glad you like Ernest," she said. "I like him myself. But I hold the firm opinion we should not suit as man and wife."

Her brothers goggled at her, clearly unable to comprehend what she was saying.

"Is it because he isn't as rich as we are?" Evelyn asked.

"Of course it isn't. How could you think that!"

"Then it's got to be that his father hasn't got a proper title—which shouldn't worry you, by the by, because you know if you two marry, Father will sponsor him for the Commons, no matter if he does think Ernest isn't cut-throat enough to play top-drawer politics. He'd have more standing as an MP."

"I don't care about Ernest's standing. At least, I wouldn't if I loved him."

Evelyn pulled a face. "Don't tell me you're still in love with Greystowe. That was ages ago and he's a married man."

"I'm not in love with anyone," she assured him through gritted teeth, though she wasn't certain that was true. Edward Burbrooke, the earl of Greystowe, was a political ally of her father. She still blushed when she remembered how she'd thrown herself at him as a chit of seventeen. He'd fallen for Florence Fairleigh: sweet, pretty, womanly Florence Fairleigh. No one since had stirred Merry the way he had, which was probably just as well. Her reckless streak hadn't abated much in the intervening years.

"Good," said Evelyn, his voice gruff. "Didn't like seeing my sis down in the doldrums."

Touched, Merry squeezed his arm. This was why she loved the big, overprotective dolt; why she loved all her oafish brothers. Evelyn, of course, could not quit while he was ahead.

"Althorp would never lift a hand to you, you know. Not even if you deserved it."

Merry let this implication pass. "It's not me I'm worried about. It's Ernest."

"Well, you can start worrying now," James warned, "because that's him coming through the crowd."

Merry turned and pasted on what was probably a sickly smile. Oblivious to the undercurrents surrounding his approach, Ernest beamed at her and waved, a tall, solid figure with a head of smooth blond hair. As usual, his evening clothes didn't quite fit his muscular form. Despite his lack of sartorial splendor, he was attractive: country healthy, country clean. Women turned when he passed, but Ernest never saw. He was a man without mystery, his strides sure, his eyes just a trifle shy.

"Merry," he said, clasping her hands with a fervor he did not usually display.

"Ernest," she answered.

His eyes crinkled happily at her tone. He couldn't have known the softness was born of pity.

As it happened, saying no to Ernest was not as harrowing as she'd feared. Apart from stiffening like a man before a firing squad, her friend took her refusal as he took everything: with good grace and a minimum of fuss.

"Are you certain?" he said. They sat alone in the conservatory, beneath the lantern-lit shadows of the palms. "Your mother led me to
believe you might accept."

Merry wrinkled her nose. Did the duchess actually think Merry
had heeded her gushing praise? "Er, no," she said. "Nothing's changed
my mind. I care for you, Ernest, but I'm convinced we wouldn't pull
well together. You know how I am: always wanting my own way. I'd
drive you to drink within the year."

A muscle bunched in Ernest's jaw. "You could try to change."

"And you"—she nudged his shoulder with her own—"could try to
meet another girl. I'm like an old shoe for you. I might pinch, but
you're used to me. You'd rather not stir yourself to find a better fit."

"I like you," he insisted, "and I know I'd be good for you."

This, of course, was the problem. Like everyone else, he thought
he could fix her, and thought she ought to be grateful for the help.
Frowning, she kicked her heels within her skirts.

"You can do better," she said.

"If it's about the rumors, I don't believe a one of them."

"Rumors?" Merry blinked in surprise.

"I heard someone say—" he began, then pressed his lips together.
"Never mind. It's nonsense. I know what you would and wouldn't do.
So if you're trying to be noble by refusing me . . ."

"No." She covered his hand. "I'm refusing because I truly don't
wish to marry you, because I don't wish to marry anyone. That's not
going to change, no matter how many times you ask."

He pursed his mouth as if he wanted to argue, but all he said was,
"Very well. If you're certain that's what you want."

She was certain, more than ever. Despite her regret at the hurt
she might have caused, she left him with a sense of profound relief.
Even Ernest could not mistake her this time. Her pride might
prick at being left with no suitors at all, but if that earned her the
right to live as she pleased, she would swallow every drop of pride
she had.

And all she had to do was convince her parents they ought to let her.

AS SOON AS THE DUCHESS SAW ERNEST, AN ICY DREAD
spread through her chest. She'd been so hopeful this time, so careful,
even enlisting Peter to plead his case. Ernest had been good to Peter
at school, his protector in the first years, his financial savior in the
last. Were it not for his guidance, Peter might never have learned to
stay out of debt. More than anyone, Merry's favorite brother knew

Ernest's strengths. If his endorsement could not sway her, Lavinia did not know what voice of reason could.

"I'm sorry," Ernest said with a resignation that made her want to slap him. "I wish I had better news."

She swallowed against the panicked pounding of her heart. "I'm sure you did your best, dear. We'll simply have to try harder next time."

Ernest wagged his golden head. "She doesn't want there to be a next time."

"Of course she does." Hands clenched, Lavinia fell one of her nails snap inside her glove. "She's simply being stubborn. You and I both know marrying you is the best thing that could happen."

"I can't force her."

"Force her!" Lavinia's laugh was as sharp as cracking ice. "Darling, the girl doesn't know what's good for her. Come now." She patted his slumping back. "If you love her, she's worth a fight."

He stared at her, mute and miserable, as different from his father as he could be. Normally, she was glad for this; Ernest's decency eased her guilt. Tonight, though, she wished he had a fraction of his sire's Machiavellian spine.

"I'll speak to my husband," she said. "I'm sure between the two of us we can sort our daughter out."

As she returned along the passage to her guests, Lavinia spotted Althorp in the smoking room with her husband and a circle of other men. Behind the clouds of tobacco they were laughing, deep and rough, the way men will when women are not around. To her eyes Althorp stood out like a wolf among sheep, sleeker, slyer, more dangerously focused in his will. A second burst of laughter swelled. The resentment she felt at their ability to enjoy themselves was sharp.

No doubt Althorp had told one of his vaguely mean-spirited jokes. He had a gift for that: making one laugh when one should not.

She couldn't help seeing that the other men, while amused, regarded Althorp more coolly than did her husband.

Geoffrey looked up just then and flashed her a happy grin.

Fool, she thought—though how could he know to distrust this friend and country neighbor? Her husband was not stupid but neither was he suspicious. The depths of Althorp's deceit were beyond his capacity to imagine.

Seeing his expression falter, she forced herself to smile and mime regret that she could not stop. In truth, she had not the nerve. She didn't want Althorp to read her most recent failure in her eyes.

As she left, her enemy's gaze fell like a weight upon her back.

*   *   *

THE STRENGTH OF HER FATHER'S FURY TOOK MERRY BY
surprise. She was so used to her mother's scolds she barely heard them.
And why should she, when time and again her doting papa took her
side? Alas, he did not take her side tonight, the measure of his anger
being that he could not wait till morning to upbraid her, but must
burst into her sitting room while old Ginny was combing out her
hair.

"Merry," he said, his barrel chest swelling with indignation,
"Lavinia tells me you refused Ernest's suit. Again."

To Merry's dismay, her mother swished stiffly in behind him. Her
father wore his old quilted smoking jacket, but the duchess had not
changed from her formal gown. The bodice hugged her in a daring
plunge of blood-red silk.

"Ginny," said the duchess, with a nod for the startled maid.

Ginny had once been her mother's nurse and was now so arthritic
her chores took twice as long as they should. Despite this, she was too
attached to the family to accept their offers to pension her off. Merry
feared if her parents ever pressed the issue, Ginny would go into a
decline.

As might she. After all, a nearly blind, nearly deaf maid could be
quite convenient.

Accustomed to ignoring the elderly servant, her father spoke as if
she were not there.

"Well," he said, "is it true? Did you turn Ernest down?"

"Yes, Papa," she admitted and looked meekly at her hands. She
meant to disarm him, but the appearance of humility seemed to anger
him even more.

Or perhaps the presence of his wife made him want to look too
strong to bend.

"Don't 'yes, Papa' me," he snapped. "Who else do you think will
offer for you? Even the fortune hunters will give up. You're a hellion
and everyone knows it. And don't think I haven't heard about that
stunt you pulled last week. Riding hell-for-leather in Hyde Park. In
breeches no less!"

"It was a dare, Papa," she explained, wishing she could speak to
him alone. "None of your sons would have declined it."

"You're not one of my sons! You're my daughter. I've indulged
you, no doubt. Given you too much rein. But, by God, I'm putting
my foot down now. You'll marry Ernest Althorp or I'll know the reason why!"

"But I don't love him," she said, a tremor in her voice.

Her father's face turned the color of a brick. "Love has nothing to do with it. You simply can't stand the thought of a man having the right to tell you what to do. It's unnatural, Meredith, for a woman to be so willful. Do you want to end up a spinster? Do you want to die alone?"

"I'm only twenty."

"Twenty and impossible!" He threw up his hands and addressed the coffered ceiling. "I thought your moping after Greystowe was bad, but this! This is the limit, to refuse Ernest Althorp, a good, solid man who positively dotes on you."

"Does he, though, Papa?" Merry couldn't help but ask. "Everyone says he adores me, but I think he's more interested in pleasing his father than marrying me. When I turned him down, he hardly even argued."

"Good Lord, Merry. Allow the man some pride. Just because he doesn't turn your idiocy into a scene from the opera doesn't mean he doesn't care."

Merry swallowed, vaguely aware that Ginny's gnarled old hands had settled sympathetically on her shoulders. "I don't want a scene from the opera. I just—I just want—"

"Yes?" prompted her father with a sarcasm he'd never turned on her before. "I'd dearly love to hear what my fastidious daughter wants."

She tried to remind herself of what she'd seen in his portrait: the insecurity, the sense of being powerless in the face of change. He only wanted to protect her. That was the reason for his ire. She squared her shoulders and forced herself to meet his glare. She would speak to him as if they were alone, as if her mother weren't standing there, judging every word.

"I want a husband who'll let me be myself," she said, for once speaking nothing but the truth. "I don't want to be a bird in a cage; I want to be a woman in the world. Free to come and go. Free to read and think and speak just as I please. Dear as Ernest is, he wouldn't let me do that. You said it yourself, Papa. He has his pride. I know it sounds terrible to you, but I'd rather never marry than have to live as a proper wife."

Her declaration seemed to stun him. "What about children? Don't you want a family of your own?"

"I don't know that I do. Maybe with the right man. But until I find him"—she ventured a coaxing smile—"I can always borrow James's and Evelyn's. Their wives seem to pop out new ones every year."

"Merry," he said and shook his head from side to side.

Despite his concern, she sensed a weakening of his will. Praying inside, she clasped his big, broad hands: hands that had tossed her in the air and always caught her, hands that had paddled her when she misbehaved and ruffled her awful hair when she made him laugh. He had spoiled her and she loved him for it.

But her mother was determined not to let him spoil her now.

"Darling," she said to Merry, her hand on her husband's coat. The duke shook himself as if her touch had woken him from a dream. "You know this decision does not affect you alone. Think of the scandal to the family, to your brothers and their wives should their youngest sister stay on the shelf. Really, dear, if we thought you'd find the paragon you describe we might allow it, but it's time we all faced facts. If you don't marry Ernest, you will not marry anyone."

Merry had known everyone thought this, but no one had said it to her face. How much it hurt was hard to believe.

"I'm sorry for the inconvenience to my siblings," she said, with a quaver she could not overcome. "But I'm not afraid to be alone. Better a spinster than a slave."

"A slave," repeated her father. He eased his hands from her pleading grip. "Is that what you think I've made your mother? Is that what you call your brothers' wives?"

"Of course not, Papa." She flushed at the truth of the accusation. "I only meant—"

"Your father and I have discussed this," her mother broke in, her palm still bracing her husband's back. "For your own good, we are determined to save you from yourself."

"But—"

"For your own good," she repeated, her jaw as firm as iron. "We're giving you a week, Meredith, to reconsider your position. At the end of that week, if you have not come to your senses, we shall put your horses on the block."

"No," Merry protested, the shock like a kick to her gut. Not her horses. Not Flick and Sergei and her new Arabian mare. She tried to catch her father's gaze but he would not meet her eye.

"That's not all," her mother added, her voice so low Merry knew old Ginny could not hear. "Once your horses are gone, we're going to make some changes in the staff. We're going to hire a real lady's maid, one who can keep you on a lead."

"No," she said, a whisper this time. The thought that they'd find her a keeper didn't bother her half as much as the thought of losing Ginny. "You can't, Papa. I don't believe it."

Her father cleared his throat. "You know what you have to do if you want to stop it."

Still not looking at her, he strode to the threshold and paused. "A week," he said, and pulled the door shut behind him.

The fire crackled in the silence as his footsteps faded down the hall. Merry's face was hot and a pulse beat raggedly in her neck. Tears burgeoned behind her eyes but she fought them back. She was not going to cry. She was not.

But she almost did when her mother stroked her cheek. Merry's senses must have been more disordered than she thought, because her mother's fingers seemed to shake. Her tone was caressing. "It's for your own good, darling. Truly, it is."

Merry pressed her lips together. She could not speak for fear of saying the unforgivable. As if she sensed her turmoil, Ginny's brush resumed its careful stroking of her hair.

"Perhaps you should leave now, Lavi," the maid said with the familiarity and the tenderness of one who knew the family well. "Give everyone a chance to settle down."

Lavinia started at the sound of her voice, but did not disagree. "Yes," she said dazedly, "perhaps I should."

Merry did not release her tears until her mother had left the room. Even then, she struggled to contain her angry sobs. She had never liked crying, not even as a child.

"Don't you worry," said Ginny, her strokes as steady as a stable lad currying a horse he meant to soothe. "Sometimes a creature has to follow its heart. Sometimes its nature doesn't give it a choice."

Her words made Merry's tears fall all the harder. Her own mother didn't understand her as well as her dear old nurse. She couldn't believe her father would really let Ginny go. Simply couldn't. Not if she lived a hundred years.

Which left her with one conclusion.

Her mother was the evil genius behind her father's stand.

Chapter 2

A NIGHT OF RESTLESS SLEEP HADN'T SHAKEN MERRY'S CON-
viction. Her father hated punishing her, even when she deserved it. So
now she had no choice. She had to change her mother's mind before
she could change her father's. No matter how long the odds, this was
a challenge from which she could not shrink.

Not surprisingly, she found the duchess closeted with her dresser.
The changing tides of fashion were the chief concern of her mother's
life. When Merry proved not only indifferent but a poor frame on
which to hang an elegant gown, Lavinia had lost most of her interest
in her daughter. *She's a fencepost,* she'd lament to anyone who'd listen.
Gets it from her father's side. And then she'd run her hands down her own
more generous curves, as if anyone could possibly doubt her claim.

Merry didn't think her mother did this to be cruel. She simply
could not conceive of a life where anything mattered more than being
perfectly turned out. To be fair, were it not for the duchess's efforts,
Merry knew she'd be considered even plainer than she was. And her
mother could be affectionate, in her absentminded way, though Merry
was tempted to forget that now.

When she entered the suite, Lavinia was standing before a cheval
glass. Her dresser, a woman even more ancient than Ginny, was
known only as Madame. She rarely spoke, English or French, but was,
despite her age, a genius with a needle. Merry's mother would order
her gowns cut by Worth in Paris, then have them stitched at home.
This was not for economy's sake; Lavinia scorned such schemes. She
had Madame sew her clothes because the woman could fit a dress like
a second skin.

At the moment, she and the seamstress were draping lengths of
cloth across her bosom, apparently seeking the ideal color for a gown.

"The emerald plaid camel hair, I think," said Lavinia, "with the
matching silk for the bodice and underskirt."

"The color is good," Madame agreed with an inscrutable pursing
of her lips.

"Mother?" said Merry, before the two could continue what was sure to be a long discussion.

Lavinia spied her in the mirror. "If you're here to ask me to intercede with your father, there's nothing I can do. He is the head of this household. Besides, I agree with him. Remember how glum you were when James and Evelyn wed? Imagine how you'll feel when Peter marries and all your friends have families, too. Women need occupation. And don't tell me you want to be one of those female postal clerks. Even you couldn't be that mad."

Merry hoped her mother couldn't hear her grind her teeth. "I have a plan," she said, struggling to sound pleasant and self-assured. "I've had one for years."

Her mother raised her brows, but before she could respond the butler knocked on the open door. "Pardon, Your Grace. Sir Patrick Althorp has just sent up his card."

Her mother went so pale Merry feared that she would faint. She recovered with a toss of her well-coifed head.

"For goodness sake!" she exclaimed, her cheeks now brightly pink. "Can't you see I am not at home to visitors? Tell the baronet I'll see him later."

And she dismissed the butler with a wave of her elegant hand.

"Is something wrong?" Merry asked, surprised by her response. Lately, the duchess and Ernest's father had been as thick as thieves. The duke didn't seem to mind, but sometimes Merry wondered at his unconcern. She herself did not like the man. He was too watchful, she thought, like a serpent about to strike. "Have you and Sir Patrick fallen out?"

Her mother exhaled loudly but did not confirm this budding hope. Instead, she swapped the green plaid she'd been holding for a deep magenta satin. The color looked fine to Merry, but both Lavinia and Madame immediately shook their heads. Once the offending bolt was set aside, her mother's reflection met her eyes. "You were speaking of a plan?"

"Yes," Merry said, trying to gather her powers of persuasion. "Once I come into Grandmama's money, I want to breed Arabians. I'm sure I can make a go of it. You have to admit I have every qualification I could need."

"Every qualification but one," said her mother. "As far as I know, you have yet to grow a penis."

The shock of this blunt speech tied Merry's tongue. "I don't . . . I don't need a penis to . . ."

"Merry." Her mother silenced her spluttering retort. "Be reason-able. First of all, you won't receive that trust for ages. And second, what man would marry a woman who ran a stud?"

"But I don't want to marry. That's what I've been saying all along."

"You *think* you don't want to marry, but believe me—"

Merry covered her face and fought a scream.

"Believe me," her mother continued, "you'll feel differently when you're thirty and all alone."

Merry sensed this was not the moment to mention her plan to have affairs. Being unmarried did not, after all, mean living like a nun. "I won't feel differently," was all she said as she let her hands drop to her sides. "I know you and Papa only want me to be happy, but I'm sure I wouldn't be happy as Ernest's wife."

"Nonsense," her mother scoffed. "Ernest Althorp is a perfectly nice boy. And far from repulsive. Good manners. Good teeth. Strong as an ox. Plus, I've always liked blond men."

Then why don't you marry him, she thought, but was shrewd enough to keep the words inside.

"Come now," said her mother, her tone light, her expression strangely hard. "You're being overly romantic, which I never thought of as one of your faults. Trust me, a love match is not the least bit like a novel."

"I don't care about a love match. I care about being free."

"Free?" Her mother's laugh was anything but joyful. "Dearest, only whores and rich widows are truly free."

"You don't understand," Merry said.

"I do," her mother insisted. "I simply don't agree."

After that, there was nothing to say.

UNDER LEADEN SKIES, MERRY GALLOPED HER MARE FLAT out across the Knightsbridge grounds, pushing the horse until steam rose from her flanks and clods of turf flew out from her pounding hooves. Even this did not soothe her. How could it, when Flick, the horse she'd bottle-fed as a foal, might soon be carrying a stranger?

There had to be a way to get her father to retreat. She couldn't sur-render, not when surrendering meant making both herself and Ernest wretched.

On the other hand, could she really forego the greatest pleasure of her life? Give up her horses? Let them pass out of her care? Worse, could she risk old Ginny's future?

Damnation. If only her mother weren't so immovable! Merry wasn't sure she had the right to make her father choose between his daughter and his wife. Nor—which was worse, if she was honest—was she certain his decision would come down on her side.

She slowed Flick to a walk, her breath coming as heavily as the mare's. Clearly exhilarated, the horse frisked underneath her. What spirit she had! And how horribly Merry would miss her! She wished Evelyn and James hadn't left for the country, though she knew they did not support her position. Her whole family was against her, every one.

Without their help, she didn't know what she could do.

ISABEL AT LEAST PROVIDED A DISTRACTION. SHE WAS FULL of news when Merry saw her that afternoon. Her father-in-law had died unexpectedly and her husband was now an earl.

"Which makes me a countess," she said, sounding strangely wistful. Sprawled on her back on Merry's four-poster bed, she wore a gray and black bias-striped walking dress. The hem of the overskirt, fetchingly draped and piled, was trimmed with tasseled braid. Even Lavinia had clucked in appreciation as she passed. Isabel's current pose would not do the outfit good, but at the moment she did not care.

Merry sat beside her on the bed. "You're not happy about being a countess?"

"Oh, I suppose I'm happy. I didn't really know Andrew's father, so I can't pretend I'll miss him. But we'll be in mourning just forever. As it is, I barely snuck out of the house wearing this. It's as gloomy as a crypt, Mer. All the mirrors covered. All the drives muffled in straw." Wrinkling her nose, she plucked at her handsome gown. "I'm too young to wear crape."

"I don't know, I think black makes you look ethereal."

Isabel grinned and covered Merry's hand. A moment later, she remembered her complaints. "We're leaving for the estate the day after tomorrow. It's in Wales, Merry. Wales! Some unpronounceable, godforsaken place. Lord knows how long we'll be there. According to Andrew, his father was a cheeseparing old goat who let the place go to ruin. It'll take ages to put things in order the way he wants."

"But surely *you* don't have to stay all that time."

Isabel blushed and busied herself straightening the tassels on her sleeve. "Andrew says he doesn't sleep well anymore unless I'm with him." Her color deepened at Merry's snort. "Yes, I know. I said he was fat and boring, and he is, except . . ."

"Except?"

"Except it is rather comforting to have him close at night, holding me, you know."

Merry could imagine few things less comforting than being held all night by a controlling prig like Andrew Beckett. With an effort, she held her tongue. "Well," she said resignedly. "It looks as if we'll both be prisoners of rectitude for a while."

Isabel hummed in sympathy, then wagged the tips of her black kid shoes. "Merry, I was wondering, are you certain you don't want to marry Ernest Althorp?"

"Not you, too," she groaned. "I'm glad you're content, Isabel, but surely you know that wouldn't be the case for me. Or for Ernest. Can you imagine him trying to put me on a check-rein? We'd be at each other's throats."

"I suppose," Isabel conceded and rolled up onto her elbow. "I simply don't see how you're going to get your parents off your back. Of course, you could keep me company at Caerna-whatsis. Nothing much to do there, you understand, but Andrew's father kept a decent stable and at least you'd have a respite from your mother's scolds."

"You didn't see her face. She's never going to let this go, no matter how long I stay away. What I should do is pretend to go with you, then run off to join the music hall. After that, even Mother would have to give up on marrying me."

"Ha ha," said Isabel, "as if you could even sing."

Merry had meant the idea as a joke, but now it sparked a thought. "Wait," she said. "I know what we need, what both of us deserve."

"I'm sure I don't want to know," said her friend, but her eyes were immediately alight. She was not, apparently, a proper countess yet.

"A prank," said Merry, her blood beginning to hum with anticipation, "like we used to play at school. One last hurrah before our families skewer us on the stake of respectability."

Both she and Isabel were sitting up now, clasping each other's hands. "Nothing too dangerous," Isabel cautioned, "and nothing we'll be caught at."

"Cross my heart," Merry assured her. "No one will know but you and I."

THE ESCAPADE COULD NOT HAVE GONE BETTER. THE MUSIC hall in Soho had held a number of middle-class families, even a few un-attended females like themselves, all outfitted respectably—including the ones they suspected of being women of ill repute. Indeed, Merry and Isabel were underdressed, clad as they were in clothes borrowed from their maids.

The program, too, was all they could desire: a humorous *pose plas-*

tique with men dressed as Greek goddesses reenacting the Judgment of Paris, a bawdy but not indelicate skit called "The Spare Bed," and a number of surprisingly talented singers, the last of whom had pretended to search the audience for a husband.

Merry hummed the refrain about *single young gentlemen, how do you do* as the hired hansom cab dropped them off before Merry's house. Happily, its high brick wall shielded them from sight. The hour was late, the streets nearly empty. Wanting to make sure her friend was safe, she escorted Isabel to her carriage.

The smart five-glass landau waited in the narrow lane between the Knightsbridge house and its nearest neighbor. Once inside, Isabel would pull the shades and change into her own dress, now completely black, while hiding any irregularities of fastening beneath her coat. Then she'd return home to her unsuspecting husband. He, bless him, was under the impression she'd been visiting an ailing friend.

As she invariably did at the end of a prank, Isabel grew fearful. "Be careful," she begged as Merry handed her up the carriage step. "Don't linger in the lane. It's foggy tonight. I want you to go straight to your door."

"I will," Merry promised, and kissed her friend's cheek.

Chuckling to herself at Isabel's nerves—for what could go wrong now?—she pressed a gold sovereign into the coachman's palm. "Take care of her," she said, though the driver and she both knew she meant *take care not to tell.*

With a nod and a grin, he flicked the reins across the horses' backs. Merry watched them pull away. From the sound of it, the leader needed his shoes picked, but that was nothing the Beckett's groom couldn't handle when they got home.

Shrugging off the concern, she followed the long brick wall to the servant's sidegate.

The man must have been waiting in the shadows. She neither saw nor heard him when he grabbed her from behind, hooking her neck and waist to drag her forcibly off the footpath.

A second of frozen shock delayed her scream. That was enough for the man to get his palm across her mouth. She struggled then, violently, but her strength was no match for his. He cursed under his breath when she kicked his shin, but other than that he did not speak.

He seemed quite focused on what he meant to do.

Whatever that was, it involved pulling her around the corner toward the street. He must have a vehicle there, she thought, or perhaps he intended to knock her out and stuff her in a cab. She'd look like a drunken maid out with her gent. No one would give them a second glance, especially here, where the houses were spread out and set back on their grounds.

Her heart hammered in her chest, her mind racing, her nose filled with the stench of tobacco and rank male sweat. She flailed for a hitching ring in the wall, but the man didn't give her a chance to grab it. Then she spied the golden circle of a streetlamp up ahead. If she screamed there and struggled very hard, someone would have to look out and see.

At least, she prayed they would. Oh, if only she'd left right away, or had the carriage wait somewhere else. She didn't know what this man wanted but she could guess. And maybe what he wanted was worse than what she guessed.

She could die tonight.

Sickness rose in her belly. She had to swallow to keep it down. His silence, his intentness was unnerving. She would have felt better if he'd threatened her, but the only noise he made was the heavy sough-ing of his breath.

She tried kicking him again but her legs were tangled in her skirts. Bloody things, she thought. Bloody, bloody stupid things.

He had her off her feet now. Her heels didn't even drag. The hand he'd clamped around her waist was making it hard to breathe. Or maybe the effect was simply fear. She felt like a doll as he carried her, not a person at all. But she couldn't think about that now. Not about slit throats and bloody knives. They had almost reached the lamppost. She had to take her chance.

She pretended to sag in her captor's arms, then bucked wildly as they hit the edge of misty light.

She managed a shriek, short and high, before the man slammed her scarf-wrapped skull against the brick. The cheap wool was no shield. Spots bloomed before her eyes, but she knew she could not af-ford to swoon. Frantically, she blinked her vision clear.

Then she saw it, a second figure running toward them down the street, a man in an Inverness coat. He shouted as he ran: "Hey! Hey there!"

The man who held her shoved her aside. He turned to escape but the second man grabbed him. They scuffled with their coats flapping—her captor's short, her rescuer's long. Their arms grappled for purchase like wrestlers at a fair. With a boarlike grunt, her attacker smashed his forehead into Long Coat's. Long Coat let go and drove his fist into the other's belly.

The uppercut was a prize winner. Merry could hear the *oof* from where she huddled against the wall. Her attacker dropped to his knees, gasping, then scrambled to his feet and ran away. The gaslight caught a slice of his face, coarse and unfamiliar. Then he disappeared into the murky night.

The whole fight hadn't lasted more than a minute.

"You all right, miss?" asked a kind, breathless voice.

Merry forced her chin away from the spot where it was tucked into her chest. The voice belonged to Long Coat, her rescuer. She was shaking too much to answer, almost too much to nod.

How odd that was: now that she was safe she could not move.

"I'm afraid he got away," the man said. Gingerly, he touched his bloodied forehead. "Stunned me a bit. Guess his head was harder than mine."

His grin was wide and slightly wry. Merry's lips twitched, but couldn't quite form a smile. Her rescuer seemed to understand. "There," he said comfortingly, crouching down beside her. "Had a scare, didn't you?"

"Y-yes," she said, the answer shaken by the chattering of her teeth.

"Only natural. You sit a minute and catch your breath. Then I'll see you safely to where you're going."

He smelled different from the other, clean and soapy and faintly of—she wrinkled her nose—yes, he smelled faintly of linseed oil.

Just as she realized who he must be, he offered an ungloved hand. She laid hers in its palm, where he covered it very gently. His hands weren't the largest she'd ever seen but they were graceful and they felt strong. The strangest sensation rippled through her, perhaps the strangest of the night, as if her whole being wanted to yield itself to his care. Nothing could have been further from her nature, and yet she could not deny the intensity of the response.

This, she thought, is how other women feel about their men.

"I'm Nicolas Craven," he said, calling her back from her distraction, "at your very humble service."

"Merry," she replied dazedly, then shook herself. "Mary, er, Colfax."

"Well, Mary Colfax, do you think your legs are steady enough for me to escort you home?"

She nodded, but they weren't because when he helped her up, she almost fell back down. She would have, in fact, if he hadn't caught her against his chest.

"Hm," he said with a gravelly chuckle, "perhaps we were a bit too optimistic."

His hold wasn't what she expected from a supposedly notorious rake. Under the circumstances, it was as polite as it could be. As soon as she found her footing, his hands moved from her back to her elbows. They stood in the outermost arc of the lamplight, his gaze quiet and considering on her face.

"Was it someone you knew?" he asked softly.

Her eyes widened. "No," she said, shocked by the suggestion that she'd know someone who would hurt her. "No, I've never seen that man in my life. He just grabbed me and—" She shuddered. "I don't think he knew who I was, either. I was simply there at the wrong time."

The painter's lips formed a thin, harsh line. "That makes me sorrier then."

"Sorrier?"

"That I let him get away."

"Oh," she said, her shudder returning.

Seeing it, he chafed her shoulders through her coat. His eyes twinkled reassuringly. "There. I've gone and spooked you, which I never meant to do to such a pretty spark of gold."

Merry's hand flew to her disordered hair. Gold it might be, but hardly pretty. In spite of herself, she had to squelch a tiny flare of female pride. Surely he was only being kind.

But he wasn't. The tip of his index finger drew a line across her brow and down her cheek, the touch a shimmer along her nerves. Without warning, her face prickled with sensitivity: her lips, the tip of her nose, the delicate skin around her eyes. She tried to recall if she'd ever felt the like, then stopped when she realized her mouth was hanging open.

Amazingly, her rescuer seemed lost in admiration.

"Look at these bones," he murmured, his gaze following the path of his featherlight caress. "Look at this gorgeous skin. I'd pay a guinea a day to paint you, love, and consider the coin well spent."

"Paint me!" She almost choked on the words. "You want to paint *me?*"

He lugged a curl from beneath her scarf, testing it between his thumb and finger. His mouth curved in a smile. "Yes," he said. "Do you think your employers would give you time away?"

But look at me, she wanted to say. I'm plain as a pikestaff. What idiot would want to paint me? The obvious hope in his eyes was all that kept the words inside.

Well, that and her ludicrous longing to believe him.

"I assure you," he said, misinterpreting her silence, "I am who I say. I just came from that house over there, to change a broken frame. Here." He rummaged inside the caped woolen sweep of his winter coat. "Here's my card."

Somewhat befuddled, Merry peered at it in the lamplight. "Nicolas Craven, Artist," said the tiny black letters, followed by an address in St. John's Wood.

"I believe you are who you say," she admitted, not yet ready to accept the rest.

"Then you'll ask your employers' permission to pose?"

She shook her head, more in wonder than refusal. A thought was beginning to form: what it would mean if she said yes, how it might change her value on the marriage mart. What had Isabel's mother said? *No decent woman would sit for him.*

As if sensing her hesitation, Mr. Craven jerked his chin toward her parents' house, a rise of Georgian marble behind the wall. "Is this where you work? For the Vances? I could speak to them, if you like. Make sure the job wouldn't endanger your position."

The offer, kindly as it was meant, restored her common sense. Even supposing she had been a maid, her mother would never tolerate the presence of a servant who'd sat for the infamous Nic Craven—no more than she'd tolerate one with followers. That his manner held nothing of lechery would not matter; his reputation would be sufficient to condemn her.

All the more reason to agree, hissed the little devil in her ear. You'd ruin yourself but good if you let him paint you. Besides which, if he's as much a gentleman as he seems, you might not have to ruin yourself in truth.

Caught by indecision, she looked at him, really looked, for the first time since her rescue. From her glimpse of him in the house, she knew he was slender and untidy. Now she saw he was also handsome. Never had she seen a man with eyes so wonderfully expressive. One moment they twinkled boyishly. The next they were ironic. The humorous stretch of his mouth made her want to smile along. His bones were as fine as he'd claimed hers were. His nose, narrow and aquiline, was entirely without flaw. His jaw might have been too sharp for beauty, but it lent his face a strength it would otherwise have lacked. All of which came together to form a visage both individual and attractive.

And knowing. That most of all. She could see it in his eyes. This man had plumbed the secrets she'd always wanted to explore. This man had tasted freedoms she could only dream of. A face like Nicolas Craven's promised things.

Merry could imagine how it might make a woman weak.

"I can't," she said with true regret. The devil on her shoulder groaned, but she could not accept his offer, not even if she could devise a way to keep it secret from her parents. A daughter's reputation reflected on her family. No matter how angry Merry was, hers didn't deserve to be treated with so little consideration.

"Don't say you can't," coaxed Mr. Craven, the plea a sweet temptation. "Say you'll think about it. An artist doesn't find such inspiration every day."

Oh, how she wanted to believe him! Her hand clenched around his card, the pull to accept a palpable force. Her chest ached with it, and something deeper, something only one man had ever called from her before.

"I can't," she said again, then slipped inside the gate before his charm, and her foolish susceptibility, could make her turn around.

"I WANT PROGRESS," ALTHORP INTONED, "NOT PROMISES." Like dragon's breath, his words formed puffs of white in the misty predawn air. He'd instructed Lavinia to meet him in Rotten Row, inside the Albert Gate. The Serpentine was frozen, of course, but they were spared the hordes of skaters by the earliness of the hour. Only the groundskeepers threatened their less than splendid isolation.

Lavinia didn't know if Althorp thought he'd been seen too often in her house or if he simply wanted to prove his power to order her about. Either way, the furtive, solitary trip to get here had done nothing to calm her nerves. She hadn't dared use their carriage and had been forced to go on foot. No doubt her reckless daughter would have thought nothing of the walk, but every shadow, every sound had Lavinia jumping in her skin. Fighting to steady herself, she clutched her hands inside her sealskin muff.

"I've put events into motion," she said. "It's only a matter of time."

"You've threatened," corrected Althorp, his voice like curdled scorn. "You've pleaded, you've lied, and you've spread a fair amount of gossip. Beyond that, I have yet to see you act."

"I shall act. I had to warn her. To give her a chance."

"A chance to do what: talk your husband round? Even I know your daughter better than to think a warning will suffice. Dismiss the maid, Lavinia. Only that will teach her you mean what you say."

His arm rose and his large gloved hand formed a V against her neck. His hold was so firm she could barely swallow.

"You're hurting me," she whispered.

"Am I?" His eyes glittered strangely in the fog, watching her mouth, watching his hand. His color was suddenly higher, his breath more swift. "You used to like when I did this; used to melt like butter in July."

"Patrick." His Christian name wrenched from her. She hadn't meant to use it, not ever, not again. The slip seemed to satisfy his urge to shame her. He smiled and dropped his arm.

He was gone before she could protest, before she could plead with him to escort her safely home.

Coward, she thought, her chin quivering on the verge of tears. She had never hated herself more than when she knew she would obey his every word.

ALWAYS AN EARLY RISER, MERRY WAS HALF DRESSED BY THE time the maid came in with a tray of tea and biscuits. She was young; new, Merry thought without surprise. In a household like theirs, the staff was subject to frequent change. This, to Merry's mind, was all the more reason to cherish an old retainer like . . .

The thought ground to a halt as an awful suspicion formed. She closed the book she'd been reading and rose from her chair.

"Where's Ginny?" she demanded, the words as sharp as striking hooves.

She willed the maid to tell her Ginny was in bed with an ache or a creaky knee. Instead, the girl cut her eyes away like someone who does not want to break bad news. She fussed with the arrangement of the tray. "Er, I'm not sure who you mean, Lady Merry."

"Don't lie to me," Merry snapped, her hand flashing out to catch the maid's retreating arm. The girl trembled, her eyes showing white. Merry forced her voice to soften. "I'm not mad at you. I understand why you don't want to tell me. But I really need to know where Ginny is."

"I—" said the maid, then cleared the nervousness from her throat. "I heard she's been let go, sent off to her sister in Devon."

"What? This morning?"

"Yes, Lady Merry. Mr. Leeds put her on the first train out of St. Pancras. Your mother—begging your pardon—didn't even give her time to pack. Said her things'd be sent after."

Merry released the maid's wrist and thrust both hands through her tousled hair. Ginny was gone. Shoved on a train like a sack of bad potatoes.

She stood and paced to the window, needing air, no matter how cold.

Her mother had fired Ginny.

And Papa had let her do it.

This changed everything.

If her parents could do this to an innocent, to an elderly woman who'd never done anything but serve them faithfully and well . . .

They didn't deserve her consideration, didn't deserve the love that even now twisted painfully in her heart.

A rip sounded as Merry inadvertently tore her green satin drapes.

The maid gulped back a frightened whimper. "Shall I— Will you be wanting my help to finish dressing?"

For a moment, Merry could not answer: she was so caught up in what this meant. When her mind cleared and she once again saw the agitated maid, her decision was already firm.

"Yes," she said. "Please lay out the dark-brown habit with the velvet trim."

The maid bobbed a shaky curtsey and withdrew. Merry scarcely noticed. She knew what she had to do, down to the smallest detail, as if she'd been planning it all along.

First, though, she was going to give the best performance of her life. Otherwise, the duchess would not believe she meant to visit Isabel in Wales, where—so Merry would claim—she intended to contemplate the error of her ways. She'd protest and she'd plead, but mostly she'd be shaken. She'd imply she might well marry Ernest Althorp on her return.

Once that ground was laid, she'd give Isabel a stack of letters to mail on her behalf, carefully composed to demonstrate the progressive weakening of her will. Thankfully, her mother was an incurious correspondent. In her supreme self-absorption, she wouldn't think to ask for details about either her daughter or her supposed hosts. A mention of the weather or some dull specific regarding the earl's assumption of his duties would have her eyes glazing with indifference. Only signs of remorse would catch the duchess's attention, only hints of capitulation. And if her mother should make demands or probe, Isabel could fake Merry's hand well enough to dash an appropriately evasive postscript.

Add to this a trunk full of clothes "for Wales" and her mother would be convinced her daughter was where she said.

Merry knew her friend would love the scheme, if only for the spice it would add to her long, dull days in mourning black.

Her sole regret was that Ernest, even more than her mother, was sure to believe the lie.

Chapter 3

FARNHAM LET NIC SLEEP TILL NOON, AT WHICH POINT HE must have lost patience with his master's sloth. The evening before had been bad enough: having to pry him from his bed just to change that broken frame for the duke of Monmouth. Nic hadn't wanted to go, but he supposed he was glad Farnham forced him, even if he had sat for an hour afterward at the police station, waiting to give a description he sincerely doubted anyone wanted to follow up. London's bobbies couldn't be bothered investigating crimes that hadn't happened. Nor had they been pleased by his refusal to reveal the victim's name. Why they expected him to, he couldn't guess. They knew as well as he a servant could be dismissed for sillier reasons than having the misfortune to be attacked.

Nic wondered if Farnham would let him sleep if he knew his master had been a hero.

Deciding it wasn't worth finding out, he shaded his eyes as the butler threw open the drapes. Sadly, the precaution was unnecessary. The fog lingered, curling against the windows.

Nic groaned at the gloom that enfolded him at the sight. He hated winter in London. Hanging would be better than waking up to this.

"I've brought coffee," said Farnham, "and the paper."

Nic pushed himself blearily upright. "What? No more letters from my mother?"

Farnham denied this as solemnly as if he didn't know what sarcasm was.

"What about a caller? A young lady on the small side. Fair curly hair. Might have been interested in sitting?" Though Nic didn't really expect the girl to change her mind, Farnham's answer still disappointed.

"No, sir," he said. "But a young man did come by looking for employment."

From the carefully uninflected tone of Farnham's voice, Nic could tell he'd wanted to help. Spit and polish notwithstanding, his butler was a soft touch.

"Can we use him?" he asked, straightening the covers across his lap.

Farnham settled the tray before he answered. "The gardener is getting on in years, and Mrs. Choate could keep him busy in the kitchen for the winter."

"Seem likely to steal the plate?"

"No, sir. He was surprisingly well spoken. Must have gone to one of the national schools. He said his parents work at the gasworks near Regent's Park."

Nic pulled a face. The two great chimneys across the park did their bit to add another layer of foulness to the pall now smothering London. The working conditions were atrocious. No one who'd seen Doré's engraving of the works in South Lambeth could doubt it. Like one of the circles of Hell. Twelve hours a day. Seven days a week. He didn't wonder a boy would rather scrub pots than follow his parents there.

Pushing this disagreeable thought aside, he took a sip of Farnham's varnish-peeling coffee. The powerful brew inspired a pleasure no depression could obscure. Mrs. Choate had her virtues—an excellent pickle being among them—but Farnham made coffee fit for a man.

"Shall I hire him then, sir?"

"Mm?" said Nic, still wallowing in the drink.

"The boy. Would you like me to hire him?"

Nic shrugged. "Don't see why not. When Mrs. Choate returns from her sister's, I imagine she'll enjoy having someone new to boss around."

"Very good," said Farnham, and handed him the freshly ironed paper. Since the butler continued to hover, Nic suspected he was in for another of that worthy's lectures.

"Yes?" he said, not bothering to hide his annoyance.

"If you wouldn't mind my saying, sir—"

"And if I would?" Nic muttered.

"It has been my experience," Farnham pressed on, "that some light physical activity, or perhaps a visit to a friend, would do far more to lighten your mood than this . . . this torpor."

Nic narrowed his eyes. "I happen to like this torpor. As for my moods, they're an unavoidable outgrowth of my gift."

"I'm sure it's comfortable for you to think so, sir, but—"

"Farnham," said Nic, the warning razor sharp.

Like any old campaigner, the butler knew when to retreat. "Very well, sir," he said. "I'll be in my pantry should you need me."

As soon as he'd closed the door, Nic moved the tray and threw off the covers. Sparring with his butler might not be the twenty laps around the house Farnham had in mind, but it had put a bit of heat in his veins.

He finished his coffee as he dressed: trousers today rather than a robe. He thrust his arms into a clean, starched shirt, then frowned at the line of garish waistcoats that hung in his cedar wardrobe. Bother that. And bother shoes as well. He wasn't going anywhere, and no one was coming here.

He might, however, have just enough energy to send a note to his man of business. See if any new commissions had come in. What Nic wouldn't give for a trip to Paris! Not tomorrow, perhaps, but in a week or so—once he was back to his old self.

Too lazy to button his shirt, he clumped down the stairs with the tails flapping around his hips. "More coal!" he called as his bare feet hit the chilly marble inlay in the hall.

From the corner of his eye he saw a shadow flit in the direction of the kitchen. It couldn't have been Farnham because it didn't stop.

"You there," he said. "New boy."

The shadow froze, then reluctantly turned without coming closer. The boy's gangly shape inspired a nostalgic humor. Nic remembered being that age, all legs and elbows and fits of shyness. If it was shyness. The way the boy hunched into his shoulders made Nic wonder if he were expecting some sort of scold.

"Settling in all right?" he asked more gently.

The shadow mumbled something that probably meant yes.

"You don't have to be afraid of us," Nic assured him. "I know Farnham seems a bit regimental, but as long as you try your best, he'll more than do right by you."

"Yes, sir," said the boy, then started edging farther off. "I'll just fetch that coal you wanted."

The sudden rapping of the doorknocker did nothing to call him back.

Bloody hell, thought Nic. Can't train anyone these days.

Fortunately for his mood, the figure on the stoop called forth an immediate smile.

It was the maid from the night before. The single spot of color in the mist, she wore a hideous tweed coat over an even more hideous orange dress. Its skirt was stained and the ruffles around its hem draggled as if they'd been stepped on. Indeed, they might have been. Both coat and gown hung on their wearer like a sack. Last night she had not seemed this small. Now he saw she was a slip of a thing, not merely short, but tiny. Nor was her size the only trait he'd failed to appreciate by gaslight. He could not have missed her freckles, but her eyes, an interesting sunstruck umber hue, were as bright as the day was not.

Her hair, what he could see beneath her muddy brown knitted scarf, was quite remarkable. He'd guessed it was fair but hadn't expected this blazing mix of red and gold. Kinked by the weather, it was so curly and thick it seemed alive. Like faerie dew, beads of moisture clung to its rippling waves.

In spite of his ennui, his fingers itched for his paints.

"Don't tell me," he said, verging on a laugh, "Farnham tracked you down to jolly me from my gloom."

"I beg your pardon," said his visitor, drawing herself up. Nic had never seen a woman stand that straight. She looked like a little soldier with her shoulders thrust back and her jaw stuck out. Her nose, he noticed, had a funny turned-up ball on the end, like a forgotten bit of clay. Retroussé, a Frenchman would have said, but the word could not convey its winsome humor. A smudge of ash marred the skin of her freckled cheek. What a face, he thought. What a wonderfully unforgettable face.

Too bad he couldn't say as much for her name.

"Forgive me," he said as he racked his brains. "Obviously, you are here on your own initiative. Won't you come in and state your business? I shouldn't like a young lady to stand on my doorstep growing chilled."

Calling her a lady might be a stretch, for no true lady came to a gentleman's home alone. Nic had found, however, that most females, no matter how humble, liked to be spoken to as ladies. Unless they *were* ladies, he thought wryly, recalling how titillated Amanda Piggot had been by his supposedly common touch. But he had no desire to offend this young woman, not when she had most likely come to grant his dearest wish.

Despite his cordiality, his invitation seemed to unnerve her. Perhaps she wasn't as worldly as he'd thought. After a slight hesitation, she stepped past him into the relative warmth of his foyer.

"It is rather cold," she conceded. Her voice was low in pitch, boyish almost: a tinge of stable mixed with a hint of manor. This one, he thought with amusement, had aspirations. Clearly, his furnishings caught her eye. She strolled the circumference beneath the dome, pausing to study a statue of a sleek Egyptian cat. The treasure was carved in basalt and bore a gold-and-lapis collar around its neck. Her hand, gloved in coarse green wool, touched the smooth front paws.

She turned and, for one brief moment, looked as regal as the puss. Little duchess, he thought, his smile too broad to keep inside.

"I wish to know," she said, with that same self-possession, "if you're still looking for a model."

"I might be," he said, then broke into a laugh.

Unable to resist, he began to circle her. His hand caught the end of her scarf and unwrapped it as he went. She uttered a startled sound, but did not fight him, her eyes on his face as he slowly revealed her glory. Three long pins held her hair to her head in a messy lump. Feeling like a naughty schoolboy, he pulled them free. Curls fell, masses of them. Her hair was magic beneath the watery illumination of the skylight, the ends dancing with static, the color indescribable. Past her waist it tumbled, past her hips, a blanket behind which Lady Godiva could easily have hidden. His hands curled into fists. He wanted to paint her like that, naked on a horse, riding proud through the heart of town, making a triumph of what her husband had meant to be a shame.

Come to think of it, Nic needed a centerpiece for his next show. Something provocative. Something the jaded art world could not ignore.

"Take off your coat," he said, his voice hoarse with his urge to see the rest of her.

A wash of peony pink crept up her cheek. "I am not a whore," she said. "Just because my . . . my employer cast me off doesn't mean I'm anyone's for the taking."

"Cast you off?" Her words were a dash of cold reality. "Because of what happened to you last night?"

Hanging her head, she put the toe of one boot atop the other.

"Idiot," he said, and her head jerked in alarm. "Not you, love. Your employer." He cupped the side of her face, pitying her trouble with all his heart. Just once, why couldn't the men of his class respect the women in their care? "Did he try to force himself on you?"

Her mouth dropped and she blinked so rapidly he feared she was about to cry.

"Never mind," he said hastily, reluctant to face a scene. "You don't have to tell me. I just want you to know that no woman is less than a lady to me, no matter how she's been mistreated, no matter if she's worn ruts down the paths of Covent Garden. I have never forced a woman and I never shall."

With the pad of his thumb, he touched her trembling lower lip. She had a plain mouth but a pleasant one, its surface soft and pink. Naturally, now was not the time, but he wouldn't have minded kissing it. He'd do it slowly, he mused, and very, very gently. As if she read his thoughts, she shivered and pulled away.

Her eyes locked warily onto his. "Do you still want to paint me?"

"I do," he said. Deciding a casual tack was best, he examined his paint-stained nails. "I'd want you to board with me, of course."

"Of course," she agreed, a little too quickly. When he peered at her, she squared her shoulders in the way he'd already identified as her habit. "I'm not some quivering miss. I know what's expected of a model."

He smiled at her mixture of innocence and bravado—not that it was amusing, when one thought about it. Despite his assurance that he'd never force a woman, this poor girl was obviously prepared to bed him if she must. He touched her face again, following the hollow of her cheekbone toward her jaw. The artist in him look over from the man. Gripping her chin, he turned her head to catch the light from a different angle. She really was surprisingly dramatic.

"I'll pay you to pose," he said softly. "Whatever else you choose to give is just that: a choice. Unless you understand that very clearly, we can't go on."

She blinked as if he'd spoke in Chinese. "I do understand," she said, "and I thank you."

"Well, then." Suddenly buoyant, he tweaked the tip of her nose between two fingers. "Perhaps you'd be willing to take off your coat and let me see what we've got to work with." Her name returned in a tardy flash. "Mary, isn't it?"

"Yes," she said, fighting with her buttons. "Mary Colfax."

The name pleased him. Simple. Straightforward. Perfect for a woman who'd be a challenge but not a trial.

Taking pity on her struggle, he reached in to remove her awkward gloves. Though she swore under her breath, she let him take them. Curious, he turned her hands between his own. Her fingers were delicate, their nails clipped short, their bases as callused as if she'd shoveled out the stable that seemed to have supplied her original speech patterns. Oddly enough, he liked her better for the roughness. This girl was no layabout. When her coat was off as well, she thrust it at him as if she loathed the very sight. Nic draped the worn tweed over his arm.

"Now then, Mary Colfax," he said, feeling more satisfied with the world, "why don't we drink some tea and discuss your fee."

WITH A HEIGHTENED SENSE OF UNREALITY, MERRY WATCHED him hang the ugly coat as she pressed her fingertips to her palms. They tingled from the way he'd probed them with his thumb. How oddly he treated her: half woman, half object. She could scarcely say which manner disturbed her more. And of all things, he thought her father—*her father*—had despoiled her. The duke of Monmouth was not that sort of man, and yet her tongue cleaved to her mouth before she could push the words out to defend him.

True or not, it was a convincing explanation of why a maid might have been fired.

And it did seem to make Mr. Craven, who obviously had a protective streak, more eager to take her in. Heavens, he'd invited her to board with him! A stroke of luck, that, since she hadn't known where she'd stay if he did not. Given how conveniently everything was falling into place, it hardly behooved her to correct his erroneous impression of her sire.

She couldn't reveal her true identity, after all. No matter how debauched he was, Nicolas Craven would never compromise the daughter of a duke—at least, not an unmarried one.

She had thought her plan through most carefully. Not only was she going to accept his offer to paint her, she was going to let him paint her nude. That would be a scandal even her father could not suppress. She'd be utterly unmanageable then, not just to Ernest but to any respectable man.

Yes, her father would be furious, but Nicolas Craven was wealthy and well known. Beyond a bit of unpleasantness, she suspected the man could defend himself. Certainly, if his swift disposal of her attacker were an indication, her brothers would pose no threat. In truth, they might have to worry about themselves. Still—she waved a mental hand—no mere artist would dare do serious injury to a peer.

Best of all, even if the duke decided to marry her to a commoner, a confirmed bachelor like Mr. Craven was certain to dig his heels in.

When the dust settled, Merry would have her freedom and Mr. Craven would have his art. His reputation might be a touch more notorious, but surely no harm lay in that. Artists like him thrived on notoriety.

The plan was, as far as she could see, without a single flaw.

Or almost without a flaw, she mused, as he led her down a narrow hall. The previous night's encounter had not prepared her for Nicolas Craven in the daylight. He wasn't just good-looking, he was gorgeous. Devilishly so, as if beauty could be a sin. His hair, which she'd simply thought untidy, was poetically long, a dark, smooth spill across his brow. The eyes she'd judged expressive downright smoldered in the light. They were gray and shining, like diamonds filled with smoke. And he was tall, almost as tall as her brothers, his shoulders as lean and broad as a statue from ancient Rome.

The fact that half his chest was showing did nothing to calm her pulse. Even as he walked before her, the sight was emblazoned in her mind. His shirt was in the American style, the kind that buttoned all the way down the tails. Naturally, with four not particularly modest brothers, she'd seen her share of bare male chests. But this male chest was different. For one thing, Mr. Craven could have posed for an anatomy manual. His muscles looked as if they'd been laid in sculptor's clay directly on his frame. He had little chest hair, a mere smattering between his nipples, which—from the glimpses she caught beneath his shirt—were small and sharp. His feet were bare as well: long, strangely graceful feet. Merry was certain she'd never noticed a man's feet before. She found it disconcerting to notice them now, not to mention very personal.

Seemingly unaware of the flutter he had caused, Mr. Craven ushered her into a crowded Chinese parlor, where he rang for tea and savories. The servant who answered, a man he called Farnham, had a crooked nose and brush-cut iron-gray hair. A nasty scar slashed diagonally across his chin between the ends of his long mustache. Its skin puckered as if it had healed without medical care. Since he looked like an old pugilist, she wondered if he'd taught Nic the art of subduing strangers in the street. Happily, his manners were unobjectionable. The man glanced at her, no more than mildly curious. Beyond that, he seemed to make no judgment about her presence.

Of course, as an infamous artist's butler, he must have served more than his share of female guests.

As soon as the servant left, Mr. Craven lounged back in his chair, his chin propped on two fingers and a thumb, his legs sprawled out until his long, naked toes nearly touched her boot.

Unlike most men she knew, he seemed to feel no need to speak.

She forced herself to look down at her hands. Returning his gaze struck her as incautious. She didn't want to spoil her progress by giving him the wrong idea. It was one thing to hint she might welcome his advances, which, to judge by his behavior, required no more than showing up on his doorstep and being female. Actually giving in to those advances, however, was more than she wished to do. To her mind, the less real damage she did to her person the better. She didn't dismiss the possibility of one day having an affair, but she'd learned her lesson from Edward Burbrooke. The next time she offered herself, it would be to a man who wanted her as much as she wanted him.

She couldn't imagine that happening with Nicolas Craven.

"So," he said, crinkling his eyes in a manner that was, despite its urbanity, surprisingly sympathetic, "your life is about to start anew."

Had her story been true, Merry thought this was a very kind way to put it.

"I hope so," she said. "I've always wanted to have adventures."

"Good for you," he responded, his smile curling into his cheeks. His lips, she noticed, were thin and mobile. Their color was rich, as if they'd been stained by wine. Despite its gravelly timbre, his voice was soft. "Couldn't go home to your folks?"

"Dead," she lied, crossing her fingers in her skirt. "For a number of years."

"I'm sorry." To her surprise, he reached forward to squeeze the muscle between her shoulder and her neck. His grip was comforting, despite her lack of any need for comfort. "Don't worry, Mary. I'll make sure you have sufficient funds to keep you when we're done."

"That's very kind of you, Mr.—"

"For God's sake, call me Nic," he said. "And it's not kind, merely good business. I want the best models champing at the bit to work with me."

Merry grinned at the brass-bound edge of the Chinese table. "I imagine plenty of women would be eager to work with you, no matter what you paid."

He laughed, his thumb sliding past her collar to the sensitive skin along her neck. "Lord, I can't wait to get you in my studio."

His enthusiasm surprised her, though he'd said as much the night before. He genuinely seemed to want to paint her, plain old Merry Vance. She didn't know what to make of him, with his lingering touches and his smoldering stares and his "for God's sake, call me Nic." Merry's own manners were hardly priggish, but she had no clue how she ought to respond to his.

He treated her as if she'd been in his bed already.

Was this what Isabel meant by savoring his conquests bit by bit?

"Have I frightened you?" he asked, leaning so close she could smell the bergamot soap in which he washed.

"No," she said staunchly, though she could not suppress a shiver. "I'm looking forward to posing in your studio, Mr. Craven. I'm a great admirer of your work."

He sat back with a chuckle. "A great admirer, eh? Well, Lord willing, you'll have more reason to admire me before long. Maybe you'll even learn to call me Nic."

His implication was as clear as his wagging brows and yet she found she could not take offense. He was so good-naturedly rakish. More a wolf pup than a wolf. Her resistance to his charm began to melt like chocolate in the sun.

This man is dangerous, she thought.

Perhaps to her misfortune, the knowledge did not incline her to turn and run.

THE SAVORIES NIC HAD CALLED FOR TURNED OUT TO BE A meal of sausage and bread and cheese; hardly the dainty tidbits she was used to, but welcome all the same. Her nerves had for once gotten the better of her appetite, and this was the first solid food she'd eaten since the day before.

When Farnham returned to clear their plates—apparently, the other servants were on holiday—Nic showed her to her room.

It was tinier than her maid's chamber at home, with a single window overlooking the back garden, now a tangle of winter brown. The bed was narrow, the washstand chipped, and the Persian rug had seen better days. Dust grimed the painted baseboard, though the floor had at some recent time been swept.

Nic seemed to see nothing wrong in offering these amenities to her.

And why should he? she scolded herself. He had no reason to think she'd known better.

"It's very cozy," she said, forcing a smile.

"Well, the fireplace draws. And we never stint on coal. You're welcome to use as much as you like."

Hm, she thought, squinting at the loaded bucket. Was she expected to stoke the fire herself? She supposed she could manage. She'd seen housemaids do it often enough. To hide her consternation, she moved to the mantel. A painting hung above it, a nice one. If she recalled her "finishing" in art, it was a copy of Correggio's *Jupiter and Io.* The cloudlike god was as sooty and thick as London fog, which didn't stop the nymph he held from swooning in his misty arms.

Merry could imagine all too easily why Nic liked it.

"The water closet is across the hall," he was saying. "Nothing fancy, but you'll have it to yourself."

"I'm sure that will be fine," she said, though she wasn't sure at all. She nodded at the painting. "Did you copy this?"

He smiled and joined her. "Yes, I did. You have a good eye." He tapped the simple wooden frame. "I began my studies in Vienna. My master had a habit of tossing his students' paintings in the fire. This was the first of my efforts to escape the blaze. Ever since, I've had a fondness for Correggio."

"I suppose you studied all over Europe."

His expression grew distant. "I've seen a fair amount of it. Geneva.

Florence. And Paris, of course, when politics allowed. It's good to know the world is bigger than the place you live."

"I've never been out of England."

He looked down at her, his gaze warming as he wound one of her curls around his finger. Those eyes of his . . . They were like molten silver, made even brighter by their short, dark fringe of lashes. She didn't know which moved her more: the kindness they held, or the banked erotic fire.

"Where would you travel if you could?" he asked.

She struggled to think with the heat blooming thick inside her. "The Forbidden City," she said. "Or maybe Rome."

He allowed her hair to spring free of his hold. "Rome might be more practical than China, but I suppose you can go anywhere in your dreams."

His tone was so smoky, so suggestive, she felt compelled to step back. Here again was his persuasion, the sensual charm no woman could resist.

His mouth curled knowingly at her retreat, his eyes half-lidded with enjoyment. "I'll let you freshen up and rest then, shall I? We serve dinner at eight. You can eat with me, or Farnham can bring you a tray, whichever you prefer. It'll be simple fare until my cook returns, but I'm sure we'll manage."

"I'm sure," she agreed, her response embarrassingly ragged. She cleared her throat. "Thank you for showing me to my room. And thank you for taking me on."

His smile deepened, lending his eyes a glow that said the pleasure was all his. He stepped backward to the threshold, then laid his finger beside his nose.

"I'll see you later, Mary Colfax," he said, and closed the door behind him.

Reality struck like a cartload of bricks as soon as she was alone. She, who had never left the bosom of her family except to visit female friends, now shared a roof with a man she barely knew, a man who clearly considered her fair game for his amorous wiles.

"My-y," she said, the word sighing out on a long, low breath. Even she could scarcely credit she'd had the nerve.

She hadn't permitted herself to consider how she'd feel, not when she handed Isabel her packet of bogus letters to send back to Merry's mother, not when she snuck out of the mansion in her stolen dress and hired a cab to St. John's Wood.

She was alone with Nicolas Craven, alone but for a butler who probably saw more depravity in a week than she could imagine in a year. Knees weak, she dropped into a faded fan-backed chair. She felt as if she were galloping toward an unfamiliar jump on a half-broke horse, the hazards untested, the outcome wholly dependent on her and the creature's skill.

The intensity of her terror was a pleasure in itself.

DESPITE HER RESOLVE TO EMBRACE ALL CHALLENGES, MERRY was dismayed to discover she had not planned as well as she'd thought. She went down to dinner at five to eight, still wearing her pitiful maid's dress.

She stopped in her tracks at the entrance to the dining room, barely noticing when Nic rose. This room, a small but perfect oval, was done up like a French salon from the era of the Sun King. Soft, pastoral murals—not Nic's, she thought—filled curlicued medallions on the walls. Gilt and ormolu encrusted the furniture to the extent that she wondered if it was safe to sit. Everything looked antique, even the ivory damask that draped the table.

She'd known Nic Craven was successful, but this eclectic jewel of a home was more than she'd foreseen.

"Is something wrong?" he asked, standing beside his chair.

Recalling herself, she touched the skirt of her orange gown. "I have no clothes," she said.

She lied, of course. She had a steamer trunk full of clothes sitting in the cellar of Isabel's town house. This trunk was supposed to be on its way to Wales as part of her ruse to convince her mother she had gone. Since Nic didn't know this, he looked her up and down, his eyes slanting, his lips curled slightly at the corners.

She didn't understand how an expression so subtle could be so predatory, or what he imagined lay under this baggy gown. Certainly, nothing like what was there, or he wouldn't have been grinning.

"We'll have to see what we can do about that," he said, and offered her the chair across from his. When she took it, he slid it under her with the ease of a gentleman born and bred. "I have gowns I keep on hand for models, but I doubt they'd fit you. You're a good deal slighter than most of the women I paint. If you can survive till Monday, I know a dressmaker we can visit. Very reasonable and discreet."

I'll bet, Merry thought, especially the discreet part.

Nic's eyes gleamed as if he'd read her mind. "I, of course, would never force you to wear a stitch. Speaking as an artist, I think the un-adorned female form is a lovely thing."

Merry shot a repressive look from beneath her brows, but it only made Nic laugh.

"Little cold for that," she said.

Nic put his elbow on the table and tweaked her nose.

"You forget," he said, "in my house, we stoke the fires."

Chapter 4

NIC LED MARY TO THE STUDIO AFTER DINNER. HE PREFERRED his models relaxed and, over the years, he'd learned only one activity ensured that better than a hearty meal.

Mary looked as if she hadn't seen her share of those. Apparently, Nic could add "pinchpenny" to the duke of Monmouth's sins. Feeding his servants was evidently not his priority. She was skin and bones, poor thing, and had eaten every scrap Farnham set before her. Considering her appetite, her ladylike manners made him smile. This was a woman who had striven to improve herself.

The thought of helping her take the next step intrigued him. He suspected she would not waste the coin he paid her, though perhaps even she didn't know what sort of life she'd build.

At the moment, her mind did not appear to be on the future. He watched her circle his work space, her gaze wide and alert, her fingers stopping to touch whatever objects caught her eye. The sight caused an unexpected tightening in his groin. He wouldn't have minded having that attention, and those rough little hands, exploring him.

Until such time as that was possible, there was plenty for her to see. His studio was the largest structure in the house. Rising two stories, it was topped by a tin-lined dome that, during the summer, filled the space with golden light. Tonight, tall candelabra stood in for the sun, their iron branches vaguely medieval. His props ranged around the edges of the room, a mix of period furniture, exotic artifacts, and casts of classic statues. History was popular these days, preferably history that allowed one's models to go about lightly clad. Some might call it pandering, but Nic preferred to think of his choices as pragmatic. He had his say within the limits of what would sell. More often than not, as was the case tonight, what he thought would sell was also what pleased him.

Ignorant of the role she played in his musings, Mary trailed her hand along the edge of the big, stained sink where he washed his brushes. Out of the blue, as if some carnal switch had tripped inside his head, he pictured her sprawled inside the basin. The image was shockingly vivid. She was naked, wet, her legs dangling over the sides while he soaped her curly mound. He could nearly feel the softness of her secret skin; nearly hear the pop of the iridescent foam. A flush swept out like a fever from his loins. In seconds he was stiff, achingly so, just from watching her touch his things.

Who'd have thought a chit like this could rock him on his heels? Generally speaking, Nic's desire for a woman took time to build. His interest rose as he stirred their interest in him. Mary felt his pull, he knew, but had hardly reached the panting desperation he preferred.

Discreetly, before she turned around, he adjusted the sudden rearing of his cock. He'd rather she didn't know what she'd done to him just yet. Unfortunately, no rearrangement could hide the change. Swollen and tight, his shaft felt thicker around than her slender wrist. The thought of comparing the two, side by side, made him want to groan. Cursing the inconvenience of the male physique, he pulled out his shirt and let it hang. Better she think him a sloven than a satyr.

She came to a halt before the stage. "Do you want me to pose here?"

"Yes," he said, wondering if she could hear the bated hunger in his voice.

If she did, it didn't show. She lifted her ugly ruffled skirt, stepped up, and waded through a heap of tasseled cushions. Her ankles were as neat as he'd ever seen, and clad in unexpectedly nice boots. When she turned, he schooled his face to blandness.

"Who," she asked, "do you want me to be?"

A hoyden, he thought, his erection reaching the point of pain. A brazen debauchee.

"Just yourself," he said aloud. "I'm only sketching you tonight. I want to familiarize myself with your features."

She made a face at that and he realized she had no concept of her appeal.

"Sit," he said gruffly, "and make yourself comfortable."

Rather than watch her, which didn't seem wise in his current state, he retrieved his supplies from the cabinet by the sink, wincing a bit as his trousers pinched him on squatting down. Luckily, a block of sketching paper and charcoal was all he'd need. Her coloring was a challenge he preferred to tackle on its own. For tonight, gaining a knowledge of her form would be enough. Then he'd know how he wanted to use her.

As if there were any doubt of that.

Rolling his eyes at himself, he positioned a stool, then lugged one of the candelabra to the stage. Each of its tapers was backed by polished mirror. The gas was also lit, but the room was so large the sconces did not illuminate all he wished. He wanted bones tonight, bones and planes and shadows thrown by curves.

By the time he'd adjusted the light to his satisfaction, Mary sat cross-legged on a cushion with her weight propped on her arms. She'd been watching him. Her face was as curious as a child's.

"How old are you?" he demanded, suddenly suspicious.

"Twenty," she said, adding cheekily: "How old are you?"

"Thirty-one," he muttered.

She forgot her borrowed manners long enough to snort. "Practically decrepit."

"Baggage," he said.

She grinned as if his insult pleased her.

He almost lost his breath. Her grin was wide and infectious. Open and ageless, it did not increase her beauty so much as make him want to laugh. A precious gift, that, one few people had. Ignoring how much he'd like to see her grinning in his bed, he settled onto the stool. Luckily, his attraction ebbed in the oblivion of work. She squirmed more than an experienced model, but at least she did not sulk. With swift, sure strokes, he filled page after page and tossed each one aside. Finally, when his neck began to crick, he told her to stand and have a stretch.

"Are we done?" she asked, locking her hands before her chest.

Something about the way she pushed them caught his eye. She had muscle with her skin and bone, possibly interesting muscle, muscle he could barely see beneath that sacklike gown. He longed to rip it off, but suspected he'd scare her silly.

"Nic?" she said.

He shook himself. "Whether we're done is up to you. Are you too tired to sit any longer?"

She shrugged and again he sensed that hidden, fluid strength. He made up his mind. "That dress is driving me mad," he said and quickly undid the buttons of his shirt.

She gaped at him. "What are you doing?"

"Giving you my shirt. You can put it on behind that screen."

She peered dubiously at the wall of painted Chinese silk, but took the shirt when he thrust it at her. As she walked around the barrier, she held it gingerly by the collar.

"Mary," he said, forcing her to look at him, "wear the shirt *instead* of your chemise, not over it."

Pink crept up her cheeks. "I knew that."

Nic did not believe her for a minute. In spite of all she'd been through, Mary glowed with innocence like a girl fresh from her bath. He hoped she wasn't sorry to be here, that posing for him didn't feel like another step on the road to ruin. For many women, the slide from model to whore would seem a short one. Not that Mary had many options, especially if Monmouth had been too mean to give her a good character. No. She hadn't much choice but to come to him.

An old anger rose, as dark and bitter as the dregs of Farnham's coffee, even deeper for being turned partly against himself. He shoved his vexation away, but couldn't help thinking her former employer a bloody sod. He wondered if Monmouth had forced her or if he simply hadn't been very skilled. Mary certainly didn't act like a happily bedded woman. Perhaps the duke had a problem with performance. Some men preferred to blame that on their partners. Maybe that was the reason the bastard had let her go.

By the time she emerged with his shirt hanging over her drawers, he was fuming at the arrogance of his kind. A woman was not a handkerchief to be discarded once it was torn. Nic couldn't deny he'd parted ways with his share of partners, but never since his youth, never, had he left some poor young innocent to the mercy of the Fates!

Fortunately, Mary's reappearance dispersed his anger like a wind. Those drawers must have cost her a good month's pay. They were frilly and foolish, hanging to her knees in a lavish cascade of lace. Beneath her stockings, her calves were a ruddy marvel: tight and round and strong.

"Turn," he ordered, demonstrating with his hand.

She turned and his breath caught in his throat, part artist's pleasure, part man's. His shirt was loose, of course, but with the candles shining through it, at last he could see her shape. As he'd suspected, she was as slim as a wand. Her bottom demanded cupping, her shoulders a reverent sigh. She looked an athlete: a young Greek girl maybe, and very nearly a young Greek boy. She had breasts, though, small and unbound and perched so high on her ribs he doubted they'd hold his lightest paintbrush in their lee. She wore no corset. Indeed, it would have been a crime against nature if she had. If ever a body defied the need for crushing, it was hers.

"Beautiful," he breathed, and she blushed to the roots of her marvelous red-gold hair.

He had to chuckle at her expression.

"Ah, Mary," he said, "you'll believe me before we're through."

MERRY WRIGGLED IN HER UNFAMILIAR BED, UNABLE TO PUSH the image of the shirtless painter from her mind. She'd been flushed the whole time she posed—and not with embarrassment. Nic was an eyeful: his tightly muscled chest, his long, sinewy arms, the sloping curve at the small of his back where his trousers hung on his narrow hips. He made her mouth water and her hands itch to touch.

Dangerous or not, Nicolas Craven left her stunned.

Naturally, she knew the cure for her condition. Merry's parents had never succeeded in sheltering her, hadn't even tried too hard with three rowdy boys to worry about. She knew the functions of the human body as well as, or better than, many matrons. The infamous Dr. Acton would never convince her women did not feel desire, or that easing it would harm her. She'd heard too many strapping stable boys brag of their addiction to the "solitary vice" to believe it diminished one's vigor in any way.

But to touch herself tonight seemed ill-advised.

She would think of him if she did, would dream she held that long, bare back and gazed into those smoky eyes. She could not afford the fantasy, not if she wished to emerge from this enterprise intact.

Merry wanted more than to be a notch on someone's bedpost.

With a groan of frustration, she rolled onto her back. Though the narrow mattress was piled with covers, her nose and toes were chips of ice. A steady gray sleet spit against the single window and a draft whistled heartlessly through its chinks. She'd tried to start the fire before retiring but her only reward had been a sickly puff of smoke.

Never having been further from assistance than the nearest bellpull, these discomforts were outside her experience. Up till now, she hadn't realized how spoiled she was.

This, she told herself, was the stupidest prank she'd ever pulled.

Loneliness ached inside her like the fading clang of Sunday bells. She missed her motherly old maid and her brothers and her horses and the sweet smell of herbs that scented all her sheets. Lord, what her father would say if he could see her now! Tears welled in her eyes but almost before she'd pressed her arm across them, she threw the self-pity off.

Merry Vance was not a quitter.

Just because her plan proved difficult didn't mean she ought to give it up.

"I won't give up," she muttered, forcing herself to leave her nest of blankets. She nearly crawled straight back. Her chemise and drawers were no match for the icy air. Goose bumps sprang up along her skin, marching from ankle to neck and back again. Her breath was misting in the moonlight. Something suspiciously like a whimper left her throat.

Pretending she hadn't heard it, she stomped determinedly to the grate and knelt before it. This fire was going to catch whether it wanted to or not. Just as she'd seen the housemaids do, she twisted screws of paper between the coals. Match after match was sacrificed to her vow to see them light. When the coals began to smoke, she simply coughed and waved her arm.

She didn't realize how thick the air had gotten until the door banged open behind her.

"Jesus," said Nic, his candle blurred by the haze.

Goodness, Merry thought. That's a lot of smoke.

As soon as he saw she was all right, he strode to the window and heaved it open. She inhaled in protest at the blast of frigid air and caught an unfortunate lungful of floating soot.

Nic crouched down and held her shoulders while she coughed. "What were you trying to do? Burn the bloody house down?"

Merry's teeth chattered. "I was c-cold. I was trying to light the fire."

"Well, it might help if you'd opened the flue!"

"Oh," she said, mortified. "I, uh, guess I forgot. How silly of me."

"I'll say. Why didn't you give up when it started to smoke? And what is all this paper doing in here? You're smothering the fire."

Merry could only hunch her shoulders in a shrug. She could hardly admit she wasn't sure what a flue was, much less how one opened it. Something in the chimney, she thought, and stifled another cough. Despite her embarrassment, she couldn't help noticing Nic was bare from the waist up. The side he'd pulled her to during her coughing fit was smooth-skinned and toasty warm. As if he knew how good he felt, he snuggled her closer. His ribs pressed her arm, moving evenly as he breathed.

She knew the moment his awareness of her shifted, because the rhythm of that movement changed. Apparently, being alone with a scantily clad woman affected even a jaded rogue like him.

"Here." He moved to his knees behind her, his long, lean body spooning hers. "Let me show you how to find it."

He took her hand, cupping its back with his palm and guiding it up the chimney's maw. Merry's heart began to pound. He was so close his jaw brushed hers, its bone sharp, its skin appreciably smoother than her brothers'. When he nudged her hair back with his nose, a shiver skittered deliciously down her spine.

"Here's the handle," he said, his lips next to her ear. His fingers wrapped hers around a rusty metal hoop. He pulled and jiggled and she heard a muffled thunk. Air rushed down the shaft. Like magic, a tiny flame sprang up from one of the coals.

"There," he said, "now the fire can breathe."

Too bad Merry couldn't say the same.

Though he drew their arms back out, he remained on his knees behind her. His sleeping trousers were something a native of India might wear, silk with a twisted cord to tie them at the waist. Feeling her shiver again, he chafed her arms, then hummed low in his throat. The sound of his pleasure was sweet as honey.

"I never had to light the fires," she said, wanting to distract him. "I always worked in the laundry."

Nic smiled against her cheek. "No woman should have to light her own fire unless she enjoys it."

Heat washed Merry's body. She knew he wasn't talking about a fire you built with coal. He was talking about the pleasure she'd refused to give herself before.

The concept rocked a place inside her that had never moved before. That a man might know, and approve, and perhaps even want to watch what women did . . . She couldn't catch her breath. It came in shallow, ragged gasps. She knew he must hear, must guess what his words had done. He made a sound, low and rumbling, and rubbed his front against her like a cat. At once, her spine lost all its starch. His narrow, silk-clad hips slid slowly behind her own. Tiny hairs stood on her arms. He was aroused. His erection strafed her bottom, the friction light but unmistakable, as if he meant to tease them both. The ridge of his sex pulsed behind the silk, its motion enticingly erratic, its heat as humid as a summer day.

Merry struggled for control.

"I've always—" She drew a startled breath as he dragged the rounded tip along the parting of her cheeks. "I've always thought a woman should cultivate independence."

Nic chuckled, the sound a seduction by itself. "To be sure, independence is an admirable trait, but when a man has the strength and the will to offer a woman aid, why shouldn't she accept?"

As he spoke, his longest finger drew a circle on her hip, a deft, suggestive circle that made her want to move his hand a few more inches to the left. With all her strength, she fought a groan. Nic didn't make it easy. The tip of his tongue curled out to flick her ear. "Wouldn't you like my aid, Mary? Wouldn't you like me to ease your needs?"

"I told you, I'm not a wh—"

"Sh," he soothed, before she could say the word. "I remember what you told me and you know what I answered. Nothing will happen between us that you don't wish."

He was rocking her now, hugging her gently with arms and thighs and chest—even the arch of his graceful neck. She wanted to turn in his arms and lift her mouth to his. She remembered the night he'd rescued her and the urge she'd felt to put herself in his hands. Then her longing had been for safety. Now it was for risk. She knew his kiss would be sweet, knew it would sweep her into a mindless joy. Only the thought of all the women who'd succumbed to his charms before gave her the strength to draw away.

"At the moment," she said, pushing to her feet as steadily as she could, "I wish you would leave my room."

He laughed at her tartness and got to his feet as well. Meaning to appear stern, she crossed her arms beneath her breasts. To her dismay, this simply drew attention to the painful tightness of their peaks, pulsing against the muslin, hardened by more than cold. *Look at me,* they seemed to say. *Look at what you've done.* No doubt the part of him that had teased her bottom was shouting the same refrain, but Merry refused to heed its seductive call. Nic smiled, sleepy-eyed, and licked his index finger's pad.

Now what, she wondered, does he mean to do with that? His arm reached toward her, the dampened finger aiming for her breast. Knowledge welled with molten heat. He meant to touch her nipple. He wanted the cloth to cling to her skin.

With a muffled gasp, she shrank out of reach. If Nic was contrite, it did not show.

"Are you sure you want me to leave?" he purred. "I could warm you until the fire takes hold."

He slid the hand she'd evaded down his front, over his breastbone and muscled belly, over the cord that tied his sleeping trousers. They were gray, she saw, with a tiny figure in russet red. She bit her lip as his hand slid lower still, palming the arrogant jut of his erection. To save her life, she could not have looked away. Her breath stalled as he cupped himself and rubbed, a strong, voluptuous motion that pushed the whole of his sex against his front.

Lord, he was . . . it was . . . impressive the way he handled himself so frankly. His fingers squeezed his sack while his thumb worked a lazy circle beneath the crown. He'd grown so long his tip was caught under the cord. The silk clung damply there, outlining the flaring shape. She was staring so hard her eyes were burning. He did not appear to care; in truth, he seemed to savor her attention. He also seemed to know just how mesmerized she was.

"If you don't want me to touch you, you could watch," he suggested, his voice even rougher than before. "See if you like the way my body works."

In that instant, she wanted to watch more than she wanted to guard her pride. This man was beyond any rule she'd ever known. Free of inhibition. Ignorant of shame. She knew instinctively he'd take her places she'd never dreamed.

She spun to face the mantel. "I'm sure you'll manage fine without me."

He did not take her retreat as a rebuff. How could he when her voice was choked with lust? His hands found her upper arms, his thumbs sliding under the puffy sleeves of her chemise. It was her own garment, cut close to her figure to fit the season's narrow gowns. Usually grateful for its lightness, now she felt unbearably exposed. Tingles spread outward from his caress as his chin nudged her hair from the nape of her neck. His lips whispered like satin there, his breath like silent steam. Her very vertebrae were shivering with delight.

"Everything feels better when you watch," he said, his gravelly voice enough to melt her by itself. "You've no idea how hard you make me with a look."

The claim was nonsense, but that didn't stop her from yearning to believe. "You promised," she gasped. "You said you'd do as I asked."

"I said I'd do as you wished," he corrected. He lapped her shoulder with the flat of his tongue, catching a traitorous drop of sweat. "I think you wish this very much."

"Please."

Nic seemed to sense the sincerity of her plea. He hesitated, then withdrew, pausing only to close the window on his way. It was an odd kindness, one that unsettled her as much as his honeyed words.

She suspected he knew just how tempted she'd been to let him stay.

WITH THE CANDLE TO LIGHT HIS WAY, NIC PADDED TO HIS room, down the gold, Morris-papered hall and the narrow stairs, past the still lifes and empty chairs. With one idle corner of his brain, he noticed the boots he'd set out for cleaning had disappeared. He couldn't imagine why anyone would collect them in the middle of the night—unless the new boy was trying to avoid him.

Strange, he thought, shaking the mystery off as he sat down on his bed. His gaze wandered inexorably to the ceiling.

Mary's chamber sat directly above that ornate plaster rose. When he'd woken to the smell of smoke, he'd experienced a wrench as terrible as the one he'd felt when he'd learned of Bess's passing. Not another, he'd thought. Not another death he could have prevented.

The relief of discovering she was safe must have unhinged his mind. It wasn't like him to push a woman. Entice her, yes. Push her, no.

He wanted her more than he could explain.

She was spirited, true, and he liked the thought of teaching her to see her beauty. He had no doubt she'd be a firecracker once he overcame her past experience. But why did he want her enough to risk frightening her off? What did his body read in hers, and obviously crave from hers, that his mind could not perceive?

He didn't for an instant believe the cause romantic. He'd learned long ago he was capable of affection, even attachment, but love? Not Nic Craven. Not for him the scourge of poets.

Rather than dwell on the puzzle, he slid back into bed. His body pulsed beneath the weight of the winter bedclothes but he resisted the urge to ease his discomfort.

Maybe his body wanted him to change his modus operandi. Maybe that was the message behind his reaction to Mary Colfax.

Let yourself want, his body might be saying. *Let yourself wait.*

Nic, after all, made his women wait. They seemed to like the end result. Perhaps he, too, ought to sample the joys of panting for release.

He shifted on the pillow and closed his eyes, but his mind would not behave. He could feel the skin of her neck beneath his lips, the cool, electric crackle of her hair. Despite his resolution, he hoped he wouldn't be waiting long.

MERRY WANTED TO SEE THE SKETCHES, BUT NIC WAS BEING vexing. He held them above his head and made her jump like her brothers used to when she was small.

"Bastard," she fumed while he laughed at her. He wasn't quite as tall as her siblings but he was quicker.

"Tut-tut," he said, switching hands. "You'll never pass for a lady with that filthy mouth."

When Merry ran the other way, he dodged behind a fake Egyptian chair.

"You can't have known many ladies," she panted, "if you think they never curse."

"Now, now, Duchess. I've known a few more ladies than you."

The nickname startled her. She hid her reaction with a huff. "Just give me the pictures, Nic. I know they're only sketches. I promise I won't use them to cast aspersions on your genius."

"My genius?" His eyes danced with laughter. "Oh, I like the sound of that. Almost as much as I like having you chase me around my studio."

She called him another dirty name. He grinned and wagged the pages just out of reach. "What will you give me for them, Mary?"

That stopped her. Merry liked to bargain. She put her hands on her hips. "What do you want for them?"

He tilted his head and raked her with a gaze of lascivious speculation. If chasing him around hadn't warmed her, this look certainly would have. A fresh prickle of perspiration heated the shallow valley between her breasts. He'd loaned her another shirt today and she knew it did little to hide her reaction. His eyes darkened, then lifted reluctantly to her face.

"I should demand a kiss," he said, "a slow, wet, steal-your-breath-till-sunset sort of kiss."

He licked his upper lip and Merry clenched her fists against a shudder of arousal. She'd be damned if she'd let him see how well she could imagine what he described. Her efforts were futile. Nic grinned as smugly as if she'd moaned.

"Alas," he continued, "a kiss might be considered a violation of our agreement. So I'll simply suggest that you pose nude."

"Nude!" she exclaimed, forgetting this was what she'd been hired for. For that matter, it was what she'd counted on having to do.

Nic examined his nails. The sky outside still glowered, but the fog had cleared and the studio windows cast a silvery aura around his form. He cut an elegant silhouette, his hair glossy, his profile sharp and fine. His dress might be Bohemian, but no one could fault its make. The slashing hollows of his cheeks gave him an air of tragedy. Here was a figure for a portrait, a Hamlet perhaps, or an ancient elven king.

His words, however, were anything but tragic.

"I could throw in a veil," he offered slyly.

"I'll give up the shirt," she countered. "And *I* get to arrange my hair."

"Done," he agreed and held out his hand to seal the deal.

Rather than shake it, Merry snatched the pile of sketches from his hold. Considering how quickly he'd done them, their detail quite amazed.

"Hm," she said, studying them. In some of the images, a few swift lines had caught the shape of her shoulder or her hand. In others, interlocking smudges of black and gray brought her features into the round. All the drawings were magical, and all were unmistakably almost her. This was more than the self she saw in the mirror; this was the self Nic saw: slightly foreign, plainer in a way but much more interesting. His simplest scribble had a mysterious vitality. She touched a glimmering profile, half expecting the girl in the sketch to wink.

He's brilliant, she thought, but what she said was: "Does my nose really look like that?"

He came to stand behind her. "Precisely like that."

She looked up at him in surprise.

"I never lie," he said. "Soften perhaps, but not lie."

She narrowed her eyes. "Not with the tools of your trade, you mean."

"Not with anything." He pressed his hand to his well-formed chest. "I am an honest Casanova."

"Hmpf," she said, because she didn't know what to make of this curious claim. Could an honest man succeed as a seducer?

He touched the tip of her nose with something like affection. "Don't let it worry you, Duchess. Just strip off that shirt and we'll get to the business of the day."

He laughed when she slipped behind the changing screen, but Merry would not disrobe in front of him. Even with the concealment, her fingers shook as she opened his baggy shirt. She'd never bared her breasts for a man, not even on a dare. She hadn't expected to feel so vulnerable. For once in her life, she was grateful for her horrible hair. As thick as it was, she had no trouble covering most of her front behind its curls.

"You still there?" he called, as she huddled behind the screen.

She squeaked in alarm when his chin appeared over the top.

His smile was as kind as she'd ever seen it. "If you're not ready to do this, it can wait for another day. I know you've never modeled without your clothes."

"I can do it," she said and tried to square her shoulders. Despite her best efforts, they remained where they were, hunched protectively into her hair. Her eyes sent him a plea she didn't mean to make. Nic read it as easily as he did her fear.

"You know," he said, "I've seen plenty of naked women."

She nodded and blinked hard. "Hundreds," she agreed. "Maybe thousands."

"And you know I won't attack you just because you've taken off your shirt."

She nodded at that as well.

"Nor will I say insulting things. Or even think insulting things. For one thing, you're my model. For another, I like women. And for a third, you're very pretty. Neat as a pin," he added when she grimaced with disbelief. "Like a greyhound or a well-bred filly." His teeth flashed in a brilliant grin. "What do the Americans call those spotted horses?"

"Appaloosas," she said.

"Yes," he mused. "You're a pretty Appaloosa, and I'd be honored if you'd let me capture you in paint."

This comparison, at least, she could swallow.

"Oh, all right," she muttered, and stumped gracelessly around the screen.

Nic made no comment on her appearance, merely directed her to climb onto the sawhorse he'd erected in the middle of the stage. A rug draped the crossbar with a man's jumping saddle slung over that. Merry clutched her hair to her bosom as she clambered on. Silly, she knew—her breasts weren't anything to go barmy over—but she couldn't help herself. Though the stirrups were too long, she refused to bend over to adjust them.

"Your horse is too skinny," she said, unimpressed with his substitute, "and if you paint me astride, you're going to scandalize your critics."

Too late, she remembered that a scandal was to her benefit.

Nic looked up from squeezing blobs of paint onto his palette. She wished he ground his own colors. She would have liked to watch. But she supposed a modern artist didn't bother with romantic fancies, not when he could buy those convenient collapsible tubes. Besides which, Nic was romantic enough. Any more romantic and she might slither out of this saddle in a heap.

His eyes gleamed as if he knew the tenor of her thoughts. "Are you certain Lady Godiva didn't ride astride? And on a skinny horse?"

"A horse would have to be dead to be this skinny." She cocked her head at him, belatedly registering what he'd said. "I'm supposed to be Lady Godiva?"

Her skepticism fed his amusement. "You have to admit you've got the hair for it."

"The hair maybe, but—"

"Hush," he said, one Prussian blue finger to his lips. "I'm the genius here."

Some genius. Even she knew Lady Godiva was supposed to be a siren. Made a bargain with her husband, as she recalled. He'd lower local taxes if she'd ride naked through the street. He thought she'd never dare but he was wrong. The townspeople were so grateful they all closed their shutters while she rode, except for a tailor who became the original Peeping Tom, for which impudence he was blinded. Merry had a hard time imagining her body blinding anyone, but she did feel daring, dressed in nothing but her hair and a pair of lacy drawers. And who knew? Maybe the real Godiva had been plain. Maybe the painters made her pretty.

She shifted in the saddle, uncomfortably conscious of her presence inside her skin. Her hair lay thick and warm across her breasts, brushing their tightened tips with every breath. Her thighs began to sweat where they gripped the saddle. Could Nic see? Could he possibly guess how oddly arousing she found her own display?

He didn't seem to. He was mixing colors now, squinting at her, then at the paint. She knew from the night before that, to him, she nearly ceased to be a person as soon as he started work. His concentration fascinated her, and also soothed her nerves. How could one be embarrassed, after all, when one's breast or thigh was merely another object to depict?

"Wait!" she said, as he lifted his laden brush. His brows rose in inquiry but she couldn't let him do this. "You have to get a sidesaddle. Lady Godiva was a noblewoman. And a real horse wouldn't hurt, either."

"Stickler for accuracy, are we?" Nic's tone was droll. "Don't worry, Duchess. This is just a study. To see if my concept works. If it does, I'll buy you a sidesaddle. And a horse—though God knows where we'd pose you."

"A white horse," she insisted, her memory of the legend clear.

"Brat," he teased and tossed his beautiful hair back with a laugh.

COME MONDAY, NIC TOOK HER TO A DRESSMAKER ON Princes Street. To Merry's relief, it was no society haunt, not even a proper shop, but a private home in which the business was conducted. The proprietress was a shrunken old woman with a thick Parisian accent. Her hands were cold as she measured Merry and clucked. She reminded her so eerily of her mother's dresser she was afraid to open her mouth for fear the two women might be acquainted.

While this was going on, Nic waited in a tiny parlor by himself. Entirely a gentleman, he did not suggest he watch her being fitted, nor give instructions beyond a vague encouragement to "give her what she needs."

This presented a problem. Though Merry knew, despite her disinterest, precisely what the duke of Monmouth's daughter needed in her wardrobe, she had no idea what a maid turned artist's model might require.

Reduced to hazarding a guess, she ordered three plain warm dresses, an assortment of underthings, and two pairs of silk hose. These were not perhaps necessary, but even Merry could not bring herself to clothe her legs in scratchy wool.

Once she'd made her selections, everything was brought out for Nic's approval. The procedure made Merry feel peculiar, like a mistress instead of an employee. She didn't enjoy the feeling, but she supposed the old lady's assumption was understandable.

Nic showed no such discomfort. As if he vetted women's dresses every day, he examined the patterns and fabric. Merry tensed as his brows drew together above his nose. She wondered if, in her ignorance, she'd ordered too much, but he simply rubbed his jaw and nodded. Then he lifted his gaze to the bent old woman's. "Do you remember the royal purple you showed me last month?"

"Of course," she said with a businesswoman's smile. "A lovely silk velvet."

"We'd like something in that for evening. Off the shoulder and not too much bustle. But I leave the style to you. You know what I like."

"Indeed," agreed the seamstress, "and perhaps a matching cloak?"

Nic turned on his heel to look at Merry, a sharp, elegant motion that took her by surprise. His eyes were considering but soft. "A real coat, I think. Warmly lined. A dark tweed. Chocolate, if you have it. Or Chinese green. And velvet lapels. Black."

"Very good," said the seamstress. From her respectfully inclined head she obviously sensed that he was done.

Merry didn't speak until the assistant showed them out the door. "I need an evening gown?"

"You might," he said, his expression amused but uninformative. She fought a trickle of alarm. She hoped he wasn't planning to take her out in public. The last thing she wanted was to be spotted before her ruination was complete.

"And a coat?" she added as he whistled for a cab.

"Now that you need. The one you have is ragged."

He handed her up the steps of the old four-wheeled growler, his manners as impeccable as any son of noble blood. Merry had noticed this poise of his before. Had he been coached to do these things? Perhaps he'd hired a tutor. Perhaps, as an artist, the extra polish helped him attract a more affluent clientele.

He settled opposite her in the forward seat and stretched his long, lean legs to the other side. "If you feel awkward about accepting these garments, you could leave them behind when the job is through. Of course"—he grinned like a boy with his finger in the jampot— "you're so tiny no one else would ever fit them."

An unexpected warmth blossomed in Merry's chest. Why, he's worried about me, she thought. And doesn't want me to feel I'm taking charity. How sweet it was! And how comically unnecessary. Her father could buy a hundred velvet gowns and never miss a shilling.

She pressed her glove to her mouth to keep her laugh inside. "Thank you," she said, obliged to turn her twitching face to the window. "You're very kind."

It was beyond foolish, of course, but she found herself wondering just how long she could draw her employment out.

Chapter 5

THEIR DAYS SETTLED INTO A PATTERN THE RETURN OF THE servants did not break, since the staff never bothered Nic unless he called them. A motley lot, their presence spoke volumes about his openness of mind. Merry doubted her mother would have hired even one of them. The butler, whom she'd met, was too rough in appearance for so visible a position. The cook had the interesting habit of preparing what she thought Nic ought to eat rather than what he asked for. The maid was pert, the elderly gardener could barely hobble around, and the newest member of the staff, a gangly teenaged boy, hid his face with a succession of ugly scarves—like a monster from a tale by LeFanu.

Happily, Merry's room was swept and her linens washed without her having to ask. She'd surmised her position was similar to a governess, but hadn't known what protocol required. Either the servants knew or had gotten their instructions from Nic. He ruled them like a genial if absentminded king. She could tell they were proud to serve him, as if his standing in society enhanced their own. Certainly, they viewed the facilitation of his art as their foremost responsibility.

The center of this eccentric little empire, Nic would rap on her door each dawn to catch the light, grumpier than she, even after his morning coffee. She'd pose until darkness fell or his hand grew too stiff to hold the brush. He spent most of his time doing studies. *Esquisse,* he called them, after the French. She gathered they were a sort of practice painting in which he worked out color and composition for the real painting to follow. He did them either on canvas or heavy paper coated with white size, depending on how many canvasses he'd prepared the night before. His supply didn't last long, so quick was he to discard some in disgust, often scraping a painting down mere minutes after beginning it. Each time he did, the back of Merry's neck would tighten as if she'd done something wrong.

He didn't like to converse while he worked, but finally she couldn't keep silent anymore. "Why must you destroy these pictures?" she demanded. "Why not save them and choose the best when you're done?"

He raised his brows as if she were simple, but he answered. "I'm not like the old-style painters who start with a dark ground and work toward white. I begin with white and lay progressively darker shades on top. Because of this, I cannot rework as much as they do. My initial composition must be right."

That may have been true, but Merry knew a half-mad perfectionist when she saw one.

His mood turned increasingly inward as the days progressed, leaving her so stultified with boredom she barely noticed when he had her pose without her drawers. For an active young woman, the job was torture. The only advantage to the monotony was that sometimes she could trick him into answering her questions. Not often, though. Most of the time, his distraction made him curt.

"Where did you grow up?" she'd ask.

"North," would be his surly answer.

"Who sent you that letter this morning?"

"No one," he'd snap, then stride over to adjust her chin.

He kissed her sometimes when he did this, a brusque smack on her lips that left her humming from head to toe.

She was miffed to discover she could be silenced by a kiss, especially a kiss like that, but at least she knew she wasn't invisible.

"Must I entertain you?" he moaned, one unusually restless day. He was frowning at the canvas, an expression she'd learned might mean anything at all.

"I only wanted to know how old you were when you saw your first naked woman."

"Twelve," he said and drew a stroke that seemed to ease his glare.

Merry held her breath and struggled not to move. His answer, brief as it was, hinted at a story she wished to hear. She watched him nod in satisfaction at what he'd done. Now, she thought, ask him. "Who was she?"

"Housemaid. She was washing up in her room."

"Is that when you decided you wanted to be a painter?"

To her surprise, he lowered his brush and laughed. "You think I do this because I'm depraved."

"Of course I don't!"

"You do." His grin was utterly infectious. "Finally found a job where I could ogle naked females. But you're the one who gets hot and bothered when she takes off all her clothes."

"I am not!"

"Aren't you?" He set down his palette and walked around the folding easel. He was a messy painter, his shirt stiff with old stains, his arms and fingers every color of the rainbow. Without a care for mussing her, he lifted her off the posing saddle and slid her down his front.

Merry was too startled to struggle or perhaps, if she were honest, too interested in seeing what he would do.

His body was warm and hard, his thigh easing between her legs until she straddled its muscled length. If she'd ever forgotten she was naked, she remembered it when she felt that smooth black wool against her most private parts. The sensation of vulnerability was mysteriously appealing. His hand curved over her bottom, sticky with paint. He smelled of turps and linseed oil, a scent she knew she'd forever associate with him. As he pulled her closer, his sex began to stir.

"You're wet," he said softly.

The truth of the words brought a blaze of color to her face.

"You're hard," she shot back, rather than cede the point.

His head bowed toward her ear. "Not yet, Duchess. But I'm getting there."

The feel of him changing sent a shiver down her spine. He was stretching inside his trousers, against her hip, growing longer, growing thick. She heard him growl and then his teeth sank lightly into her neck. His hand, the one that wasn't wrapped around her bottom, skimmed her ribs and slipped beneath her hair. Her breasts were trembling with her heartbeat, with the intensity of all he made her feel. When he molded one in his palm, she couldn't suppress a whimper. His hand was larger than her breast, a stark reminder of his masculine advantage.

"You're hard, too," he whispered and feathered her nipple with his thumb.

Her back arched. His touch inspired more pleasure than she could bear—plucking her, playing her, stroking round and round while she struggled to be still. His thigh flexed between her legs and she went liquid deep inside. She hitched against him, once, but it did not help. She wanted his mouth on her, wanted him to lay her down and drive inside. In that moment, she wouldn't have had the strength to stop him.

But he was not a man to rush these matters. He brushed her hair aside with gentle fingers.

"How lovely you are," he mused. "Your nipples match your rosy-golden curls."

Without warning, tears stung the corners of her eyes. For years she'd been known as the plainest deb in London. She'd made a joke of it herself. But hard as she tried not to care, it wasn't easy knowing that no one, not even her parents, thought her pretty. "Ragamuffin" was the kindest term her father had ever used. And now this man, this artiste, spoke as if *she* were a work of art. The effect it had on her was extraordinary, as if he'd looked into her heart and fed it the meal it most desired, the meal it had been starving for all her life. She couldn't stifle a pang of regret when he set her on her feet and stroked her hair back down her breasts.

Smiling faintly, he lifted a sticky vermilion lock. "I've gotten paint on you," he said. "Perhaps you'd better wash."

Only pride enabled her to retreat. "Yes," she said, ignoring her body's protest. "I'd better."

Her earlier conversation with Isabel could not have been clearer in her mind. *Likes them panting after him, I'll bet,* she'd said. Merry hadn't met her employer then, but she'd guessed more truly than she'd known. Worse, if she didn't guard herself better, she'd end up panting as pathetically as the rest.

LAVINIA VANCE AND HER YOUNGEST SON WERE SHARING A silent breakfast, her sole attempt at conversation having met with a muffled grunt. For once, she wished she were more in the habit of talking with her children. At least then she'd have a distraction from her worries. But Peter seemed to have worries of his own. His mind plainly elsewhere, he glowered at the tablecloth while she pushed her eggs around her plate and wondered if the letter Merry had sent from Wales would suffice to keep the elder Althorp off her back. Her daughter's tone had been softer than she'd expected, expressing regret for harsh words and a certain nostalgia for times she'd spent with Ernest when they were young.

Surely Merry wouldn't mention him if she weren't rethinking her position.

Her second son wandered in as she tried to convince herself this was true.

"That's some frown," he said, loading a plate at the parlor sideboard. "You keep thinking that hard, you'll hurt your brain."

For one astonished moment, Lavinia thought James was addressing her, but then Peter shot a rude gesture at his brother from beneath the table, where he must have thought it would be concealed. Her pang of resentment took her by surprise. My children don't even see me, she thought.

But that was just as well, wasn't it, considering the secrets she had to hide?

"I didn't know you were in town," she said to James, tilting her cheek up for his kiss.

"Just for the day. Lissa's got a bee in her bonnet about this cradle she saw at a shop in Mayfair. Says it's been preying on her mind and I simply have to buy it." He grimaced. "You'd think the child was due to pop out tomorrow."

"Well, it is her first," Lavinia soothed and patted his hand. "I was just telling Peter we got a letter from Merry in the morning post."

Startled, Peter looked up from his plate. He hadn't heard a word. Again, she felt that tiny screw of hurt. She knew her children didn't share her interest in fashion or society, but she hadn't realized they blocked out everything she said. Or was she being too sensitive? Clearly, Peter had other things on his mind.

James set down his plate and took the seat next to his brother. "How is our little devil?"

"Fine," she said. "Apparently, Wales is rainy this time of year."

James grunted at this intelligence and tucked into his food.

"Are you going to write back?" Peter asked.

She strove to answer lightly. "I planned to this afternoon. Shall I send her your regards?"

"Better send her Ernest Althorp's," said James. "I saw him at the club yesterday. Looked all pale and stoic. Barely unclenched his jaw enough to say 'hello.' " He stuck half a biscuit in his mouth and chewed. "Damned if the fellow isn't in love with her after all."

"He couldn't be," Lavinia gasped, setting her coffee down with a clink.

Peter gaped at her. She realized she had not sounded very motherly.

"I only meant I'd be surprised," she said more mildly, "because Althorp is so sensible. Reining Merry in will be difficult enough without letting sentiment cloud his mind."

"Maybe he can't help himself," Peter said. "Merry's a good egg and not half as plain as you make her out to be. I don't see why he couldn't love her."

Lavinia's throat tightened at the challenge in his voice. Did he really think she regarded his sister as unlovable? And if so, was he right? Had she come to believe the lies she'd been whispering in people's ears?

If she had, she'd sunken further than she'd known.

"We all love her," she said firmly enough to make James glance up from his food. "I was simply pointing out that Ernest Althorp is not a man known for passion."

"Got that right." James chuckled around a bite of ham. "Not like Peter here with his danseuse." He switched his voice to falsetto. " 'Oh, James, she's a little doll!' "

At that, whatever disapproval Peter harbored toward his mother was forgotten in his attempt to shove his brother off his chair.

Their tussling brought back memories of other mornings. Once upon a time, they'd sat around this table every day: Merry, the boys, her husband. What a noise they could make, like a flock of starlings—especially Evelyn, who'd never lost his habit of speaking on top of everyone else.

One day soon only she would sit here. Or she and Geoffrey would, when he didn't leave early for his club.

Lavinia pressed her lips together. It wasn't like her to be maudlin. She spent time with her family, more than she cared to on occasion. Certainly, there was more to her life than a noisy breakfast—far more. At the moment, however, she could not think what that was.

NIC'S MOODS HAD TAKEN A TURN FOR THE WORSE. MERRY should have been grateful, she supposed. He hadn't so much as flirted with her in days. Unfortunately, the reprieve came at a price. He frowned more, snapped more, even threw his brushes across the room.

Their workday grew shorter and what work he did seemed listless. Nothing she said could cheer him.

One morning, she woke not to his impatient rap but to the sound of someone beating rugs off the balcony down the hall. She stumbled into the corridor, half fastened and panicked she'd overslept, to find only the maid and the eternally scarf-wrapped kitchen lad. Though he tended to scurry out of sight as shyly as a barncat, this morning his hands were too full of dusty carpet to escape. He did, however, hunch his presumably hideous head into the wool.

"What time is it?" she asked.

"Close on noon," said the sturdy maid. "We're sorry for waking you, but Mr. Farnham said we had to get this done."

"Noon!" Merry pressed her hand to her bosom. She never slept till noon. Nic mustn't have come by at all. "What happened to Mr. Craven?"

"One of his black fits," said the maid. "Likely sleep till dinner, then drink hisself back to bed."

Merry's throat tightened. "Is he ill?"

"Not ill, miss. Just ill-tempered from his work not going right. Makes him crawl into his hole like a prickly badger." The maid laughed. "Mr. Farnham says a whack on the rump'd do him more good than sleep."

Merry was accustomed to servants knowing their master's business. As a less than dutiful child, she'd often used their intelligence to her advantage. This maid's bluntness shocked her, but she supposed the staff considered her too close to their level to guard their tongues. Though the sensation of being taken for one of them was odd, it was not unwelcome. Clearly, her ruse was working.

"Maybe you could jolly him out of it," the maid suggested, slanting a smile at her. "The master likes his bit of skirt."

The kitchen boy released a muffled cough that did not sound amused. When Merry looked at him, the skin above his scarf had flushed the color of a plum. He was beating the carpet so hard the dust he raised threatened to engulf them all.

"I'll see if he's hungry," Merry said, tearing her gaze from the boy who so obviously didn't want to be seen. "Maybe Mrs. Choate will have something to tempt him."

But Merry didn't have to see the cook. Mr. Farnham shoved a tray at her as soon as she reached the landing on the stairs.

"Here," said the frazzled butler, "see if you can pry him out of bed."

Nonplussed by the order, Merry took the tray and headed toward Nic's door.

"Don't knock," Farnham advised. "He'll just ignore you."

With some trepidation, she took his advice. She wasn't at all sure she was ready to encounter her employer in his bed. Hand shaking, she reached for the knob.

Once it was open, she simply stood and looked around. His room was different from the rooms she had grown up in, simple and uncluttered. He'd hung no paintings here, not even his own. Her curious gaze found white walls and dark wood trim and on the ceiling a plaster rose from which descended a lovely blown-glass chandelier. The carpet was old but good, its colors so dark she could barely make out a pattern.

And then she took in the bed. Nic lay in it, a long, blanket-covered lump. His sleeping presence was enough to warm her face. More than that, though, the bed was huge. Japanese, she thought, from the pattern of squares and circles that formed the frame. No hangings draped it. Instead, six slim posts supported an elegant wooden roof. The structure resembled an open cage, as if Nic were a circus animal no one thought was very dangerous.

That, of course, was patently untrue.

Feeling very much as if she intruded, she noisily cleared her throat.

The lump in the coverlet moved. "Bloody hell," Nic swore. "Can't you keep your nose out of anything?"

Ignoring the sting this inspired, she set the tray on his bedside table and stood between him and a beam of sun. This was a trick she had learned from her occasionally hard-drinking brothers.

"Mr. Farnham is worried about you," she said.

He jerked at the sound of her voice, but did not emerge. "Just want a rest. Till my brain starts working again. Would have done it before, but then *you* came. Bloody Godiva."

Merry ignored this accusation just as she had the first. "One of the servants suggested a whack on the rump might do you good."

Nic's head surfaced from his cocoon. Though his eyes were clear, he gave every appearance of having been in his cups. His skin was pale and his hair hung over his face in a tangled mop. "You try it and you'll be sorry."

She smiled at the threat. She'd heard that from her brothers, too. "Perhaps if you shared what was troubling you, you'd feel better."

"No, no, no," he groaned, rolling onto his back with the pillow clutched to his face. "It's my picture and my problem, and I'll solve it my way."

"By hiding under the covers like a two year old?"

The pillow whumped her in the chest. Before she could catch her breath, Nic bolted up and the blankets slipped down. Her eyes widened. He wasn't wearing his Indian pyjamas. In fact, he wasn't wearing anything. She could see the halves of his bottom, smooth as cream, and between them the faintest down of black rising to lick his spine. A hollow shadowed the flesh behind his hip, evidence of a muscle as strong as it was spare. Merry swallowed hard before looking up. Nic pointed toward the door as if his arm were made of steel.

"Out," he rumbled, his voice as suited to anger as seduction, "before I give *you* a whack on the rump."

The words were comical but she sensed he meant them. Apparently, she could not dismiss his threats the way she did her brothers'. She goggled a moment, then backed away. Merry hadn't been spanked since she was ten and, given how hard Nic had thrown that pillow, she suspected she wouldn't enjoy it.

She sagged in relief as soon as she closed his door.

How peculiar he was, threatening to beat her just because she wished to help! And how different he seemed from the considerate man he'd been before. The change had to be more than artistic temperament. From what she'd seen, his work had been thoroughly acceptable. Perhaps this painting didn't have the depth of her father's portrait, but it hardly warranted him retreating to his bed.

Hard as she tried, she could not understand. Nic was successful, respected. His creations hung in the finest homes. Surely he couldn't doubt his talent. Why wasn't he satisfied? What drove him to seek perfection? Was that what genius was: a search for something no one else could see?

In spite of everything, she yearned to go back and ask. To soothe his brow perhaps, and reassure him he'd find his way.

Fear kept her from it, but not fear of failure. No, she was stopped by her all-too-vivid memory of his sleep-warmed body rising from those rumpled sheets. If she gave in to the urge, she feared his brow would not be all she soothed.

NIC PULLED THE BLANKET BACK OVER HIS FACE. HE TOLD himself he was glad Mary left. He'd only have been brutish if she stayed. The old fury had him in its claws: at himself, at life, at the stupid blobs of oil and pigment that could not catch the magic in his brain.

What had any of it been for if he couldn't paint? He didn't fool himself that his sacrifice had been the greatest. That honor belonged to the boy and Bess. Her life. Cristopher's happiness. All so Nic could learn to make his little daubs.

He had nothing to offer them. Not then. Not now. He was a mere pleasure seeker, a pitiful excuse for a human being. The only value he possessed was in his hands. If they failed him, he might as well rot in this bed forever.

Caught in the downward spiral, he let himself think of his boyhood friend. The way she hummed when she worked. The way the sun streaked her golden hair. By God, Bess had been young. Seventeen. Fresh from her parent's farm, the smell of hay still on her skin.

Coming to work at Northwick had been her grand adventure.

You're a marvel, Nic, she'd say as they lay together in the grove, her work-rough hand sliding down his shirtless chest. *I never knew a boy could be so nice.*

Her kisses had tasted of fruit, sweet and sharp and far more experienced than his. The first time she pressed her tongue between his lips, he'd trembled as if the earth had shuddered on its axis, overwhelmed by wonder and gratitude and a lust as sharp as whetted steel. For months, they'd played at the preludes of love: two strong, young bodies teasing each other hotter with a look, a kiss, a brush of skin on skin. He remembered backing her against a tree one day and thinking he'd die if he'd didn't come.

Do you want me to touch you? she'd whispered. *Do you want me to take you in my hand?*

He'd spilled the minute she slipped her fingers inside his linens. She hadn't even had to rub him. Despite the violent bliss of his release, he'd wanted to weep with embarrassment.

Don't worry, she'd cooed, kissing the shame away. *You'll learn to last and then I'll teach you what women like.*

The gift she gave him had no price. A precious thing. A thing no man should ever dare to steal. Not ever.

She'd soaked the bed in blood, they'd said. Had to burn it when she was gone. Hard to imagine the creature who gave those life-affirming kisses could ever die.

Moaning, Nic rolled onto his belly. Bess had been his Waterloo. The beginning of his fall. But when he ground his face into the pillow, the kisses he imagined were not hers.

NIC'S BLACK FIT, AS THE MAID CALLED IT, STRETCHED TO two days, then three. He slept the way other men drank, throwing himself into it as if he wished to drown. He had what meals he ate sent to his room, so Merry had no chance to speak to him at the table. She wondered how a body could stand that much sleep, and began to look back on the boredom of posing with nostalgia. Desperate for distraction, she played checkers with the cook, helped the maid clean a gasolier, and evaded the butler's suggestion that she "stretch her legs" in the neighboring park. Merry's peers were more likely to frequent Hyde Park than Regent's, but it wouldn't be impossible for her to encounter someone she knew.

Even if she was climbing the walls, she couldn't risk being seen in London, not while her scheme seemed so close to falling through.

"He *is* going to finish my painting, isn't he?" she asked Mrs. Choate from her perch on a counter in the kitchen.

The cook was stirring a pot of soup on the iron range, her hair steamed to wispy curls, her motherly face pink. " 'Course he is. Always does. Like my gran used to say, with every gift comes a curse. To my mind, these moods are the master's curse—never mind what Mr. Farnham says."

Merry rubbed her nose to hide her smile. The butler and Mrs. Choate had a more or less friendly rivalry: the one never agreed with the other if he could help it.

"Your picture will be special," the cook predicted. "The pictures he gets his fits over always end up the best. 'Course, like as not, he'll be down in the dumps again once it's finished, but far be it from me to tell an artist how to act."

"Maybe I'm not inspiring enough," she said, a worry that had been pricking her of late.

Mrs. Choate smiled at her through the steam. "Don't fret yourself over that. The master sees things other people don't, but that doesn't mean they aren't there. If he says you're Lady Godiva, I reckon you must be."

Merry's doubt expressed itself in a sigh.

"I think you're pretty," piped a voice from the scullery. It was the kitchen boy, who'd been in there scrubbing pots, so quiet they'd forgotten he was there.

"Well, bless me," said Mrs. Choate, laughing under her breath. "It speaks."

"Thank you," Merry called, but the boy might have sunk into the ground for all the response she got back.

Mrs. Choate rolled her eyes. "There's an odd duck," she murmured. "If freaks were fortunes, that one would own the world. Only thing he wants to talk about is Mr. Craven. Is he strict and do I think he's honest? Yesterday he asked old Max if he thought the horses liked the master!"

"Well, that is . . . I mean, people say that is the measure of a man: how he treats his animals and his servants."

"But why should a kitchen boy want to take his employer's measure? You'd think he'd be more concerned with what he's paid."

Merry had no answer but she did have another question. "*Does* he have a scar?" she whispered, remembering the omnipresent scarf.

"Spots is my theory," said Mrs. Choate. "But he works like the dickens, I'll give him that."

Merry wished she could say the same. Whatever the cook assured her, it was beginning to look as if her scandalous naked painting would never see the light of day.

Of course, if Nic continued to struggle, maybe she should take that as a sign her ruination wasn't meant to be. It wasn't too late to head it off. She could get herself to Wales; pretend she'd been with Isabel all along.

The prospect lured her. She could evade everything she dreaded: the embarrassment, the risk, her father's wrath. Not to mention Nic, who surely posed the greatest threat of all.

Social ignominy she could live down. Even a parent's fury would, in a decade or two, simmer back to its native affection. But to give one's innocence to a rake! Never mind hers was not a snowy innocence; the loss of one's virginity was still a matter of some moment. To give it to Nic—handsome, seductive, profligate Nic—seemed an invitation to despair. Three years had passed since her rejection by Edward Burbrooke, and she still cringed at the memory. She shuddered to think what Nic's rebuff would do.

Nic was so much more than Edward. He was heated oil and poppy smoke and damned nice when he put his mind to it. Nic said the words she'd always longed to hear. So what if she didn't believe them. He said them like they were true.

He was strange. She could not argue that. But Merry was strange herself. If she hadn't been, she would have married Ernest in a heartbeat. She wouldn't have been so drawn to risking everything she had. And for what? Adventure? Excitement? A taste of forbidden sins?

A sensible girl would have taken to her heels. A sensible girl would have said: to hell with independence I'm scampering home where I'll be safe.

Sighing, Merry kicked the old oak cabinet with her heels. She knew she wasn't sensible. Never had been. Never would be. The best she could manage was clever. Hopefully when it came to Nic, she hadn't been too clever for her own good.

Chapter 6

NIC FELT ODD WHEN HE AWOKE, AS IF HIS HEAD WERE FILLED with pulsing cotton instead of brains. The effect was not of brandy but of sleep and he knew that, heavy though his limbs might be, his body had no more slumber in it.

His refuge had kicked him out and barred the door behind him. He could lay here a few hours more but he would not recapture the oblivion he craved.

Rather than try, he swung his legs to the side of the bed and sat up, his elbows on his knees, his palms scrubbing slowly at his face. He had eaten and bathed during his periods of wakefulness, but his hair was nearly as bad a tangle as his model's.

He'd dreamed of kissing her, of her smooth, sleek limbs entwined with his. It had been a pleasant dream, sensual and slow, one whose memory buzzed along the surface of his skin. Perhaps she'd come into his room while he slept. He wasn't certain, but he thought he remembered someone light perched on the edge of the bed. He'd thought she was really there, but when he opened his eyes—or believed he opened them—he saw a ghost of himself as a boy, staring sadly toward the window as though he knew what tragedies lay ahead.

"You help other people," said his younger self, without turning his head. "Why won't you let them help you?"

"They deserve help," he responded, just as if the conversation made perfect sense.

The boy considered this. "Maybe you deserve help, too."

Everything faded after that, a dream lost in a dream. The encounter did not trouble him. Nothing much could when he was sleeping.

A soft tap brought his head out of his palms.

"Yes," he said, his voice croaking from disuse.

Mary peeped around the door. "You're up."

He quelled the sudden leaping of his heart. "Awake anyway."

She stepped in with a tray of coffee and fruit and toast. A flush crept over her freckles as she caught sight of his sex lying lax and unguarded between his thighs. Her eyes darted away and then back. The return flattered him, brief though it was. Flattered his manhood, too, for as soon as her gaze fell on it, it abruptly spurted longer. There was a wake-up call, he thought. Mouth curling with his first smile in days, Nic pulled the sheet fully over his legs. He'd forgotten what an innocent she could be, though not such an innocent that she'd shrieked.

Color recovering, she set the tray on the bedside table, then shifted both to his side. The ease with which she moved his furniture impressed him. What a little Amazon she was! With half an ear, he listened to her babble about Mrs. Choate putting chocolate in his coffee to get back at Farnham for ordering her not to cook anything fancier than toast.

"Don't care," he rasped, "as long as it's strong."

She poured a cup and handed it to him, her funny little face puckered with concern. She watched with great attention while he drank. Some small corner of his soul, a corner he was in no state to examine closely, decided it liked her care. The sense of well-being that suffused him owed as much to her furrowed brow as to the drink.

"I dreamed of you," he said, "that you sat on the bed and held my hand."

He watched her eyes, but she betrayed no sign of embarrassment, as she might have if it were true. Her brow puckered harder. "Would doing that have been wise?"

He laughed, this time at himself. His own snappishness had discouraged her from coddling him. "I'm sorry I was rude to you," he said. "And sorry that you worried. I can be a slug, I'm afraid, but I didn't mean to scare you."

"You didn't scare me. Only hurt me a bit because I wished to help."

He looked away from her expression, which was suddenly too sincere for comfort. Best not to encourage that.

"You're helping now," he said, putting a bit of carnal honey into his voice. He patted the mattress beside him. "And you could help even more if you wanted."

Instead, she stalked to the door.

"Huh," she said, with a spark that pleased him. "I know you're feeling better if you're on about that again."

"I'll have you yet, Duchess."

"Better go back to sleep then," she retorted, "so you can have me in your dreams."

He smiled. In *her* dreams, he suspected, she was nearly his.

IF MERRY HAD BEEN A MOUSE, NIC WOULD HAVE BEEN THE cat crouched in wait before her hole. They sat in the muraled French dining room, relaxing with coffee after their meal. Or Nic was relaxing; Merry merely strove to look as if she were. She watched him flick an envelope along his jaw. His gaze was considering, his pose a sprawling slouch. They'd returned to the studio today. Nic had thrown out just three studies, more in resignation than disgust.

She supposed this was cause for celebration, but she had the distinct impression his mind was more on her than on his work. For the first time since he'd had her bare her breasts, she'd felt self-conscious as she posed, as if the air were pressed too close to her naked skin. All day he'd stared at her not as a painter but as a man.

He'd touched her more often than he had to, adjusting her arm, her knee, the fall of a curl across her breast. Even now, fully clothed, she felt as if she were naked. His gaze was no leer but it seemed to strip her nonetheless. He knew what lay beneath her gown.

And he knew what his attention did to it.

She squirmed in her chair and turned her eyes to the trembling surface of her coffee. Pull yourself together, she thought. You're a toy to him: forgotten as soon as played with. This man couldn't possibly want her as much as she wanted him.

The fire hissed in the grate, the only accompaniment to the scrape of paper along his jaw. Merry could barely see his evening beard but she could hear it. The reminder of his maleness made her tighten deep inside.

"It seems," he said, his voice shockingly intimate in the quiet, "that I've been invited to a party."

He leaned across the table, one forearm stretched until his hand rested a tiny distance away from hers. She clutched her cup, but the warmth of this almost-touch was stronger than the warmth of the steaming drink. She told herself not to draw back. That would betray how strongly she was moved.

"A party?" she said, pretending to sip her coffee.

The tip of his finger brushed her hand. "Yes. And Farnham will box my ears if I don't get myself out of the house. I thought you might like to come."

"Me?" She was so startled she didn't notice when he took her hand, only that now he cradled it in his own.

"Yes." He stroked the delicate skin beneath her wrist. Sensation skittered outward from the touch. His gaze, both direct and intense, held her as much a prisoner as his hands. "I despise going alone. They're all couples. Old friends of mine."

"What sort of friends?"

His mouth twitched at her suspicion. "Let's see. Three artists, one former actress, a coatgirl and a Jewish banker—if that meets with your approval."

"No one else?" she said, thinking this sounded unlike anyone she might know. "Your friends will be the only ones who are there?"

"Not a soul besides," he assured her. "They're all perfectly agreeable. Well, maybe not perfectly, but they make up for it by being entertaining. Say yes, Mary. I want to show you off."

"Me."

He carried the back of her hand to his smiling lips. "Yes, you. You could wear the velvet gown."

"I could wear a hundred velvet gowns and I still wouldn't—"

His tongue wet the valley between two knuckles, silencing her skepticism. Her skin cooled, then tingled as he repealed the shameless lick. His tongue was sharp and agile, a bruised rose-pink that matched his mouth, that matched—she suddenly, vividly recalled—the head of his waking sex. She'd never thought of someone's tongue as being obscene but his most definitely was. Other stories overheard from the stable boys returned to haunt her: places they'd claimed experienced lovers liked to suck. She felt as if Nic's mouth were on them now. To make matters worse, his nails began scratching lightly across her palm. The caress had a singular effect, sending chills up her arm and down her breasts; forceful chills, like an electrical experiment. Heat gathered in her sex, its flesh beginning to contract and expand in synchrony with his strokes.

"What are you doing?" she gasped, trying to pull away.

"I'm taking liberties. And I'm going to take another each time I hear you speak as if you were not pretty." Looking up at her through his lashes, he licked her hand again.

"Stop it!" she ordered, her emotions too confused to tug very hard.

Rather than release her, he let her pull the back of his hand to her breast. He rubbed her lightly there, one finger swinging back and forth across the swell. "I'll stop," he said, "when you agree to come."

The final word jolted through her, a soft, hot spear. She knew he didn't mean come to the party. He meant "come" as in "climax" and no doubt not alone. The blood of arousal flushed his face and lips, which had parted for his breath. He looked so beautiful he made her heart clench. Next to him, she was a hideous, freckled troll.

"Say you'll come," he said, softer now, rougher. "Say you'll come and meet my friends."

"I don't see why you want me to."

"I told you." One hand rose to stroke her cheek. "I don't like to come alone."

"Do you ever?" she whispered, remembering the night he'd slammed into her smoke-filled room, the night he'd cupped his sex and rubbed it while she watched.

His eyes gleamed in the gaslight, soft, gray jewels; windows, perhaps, but only to more mystery. His pupils were black as jet.

"Sometimes I do. Sometimes my needs are too pressing to wait. But then I wish I had someone with me."

"Someone?"

His thumb smoothed her brow. "I should like the someone to be you, Mary. I think you know that by now."

Before she could gather her wits, he released her and rose, reminding her how tall he was, how slim and spare. Though he'd scrubbed, tiny flecks of paint clung to his nails. The imperfection did not matter. His hands were all the more beautiful for this evidence of their skill.

"Tomorrow night," he said. "We'll leave at seven. Cook used to be a lady's maid. I'm sure she'd be happy to help you dress."

She should have resented his command. More to the point, the risk of going out should have drained this creamy pleasure from her limbs. Instead, reeling in mind and body, she sagged in her chair and admired his retreating form.

His bottom was narrow and firm, the muscles moving with his strides. With far too much ease, she could picture it laboring over her.

I'm at his mercy, she thought.

If he decided to take her now, she would not have the will to stop him.

SHE'D RECOVERED FROM HER FATALISM BY THE TIME THE following evening rolled around, probably because she hadn't seen Nic all day and was able to rally her resistance. Rather than have her pose, he'd left her to bathe and primp and, as he put it, do whatever it is women do. Merry took this for the nonsense it was. She had no doubt he knew precisely what women did.

Mrs. Choate, the former lady's maid, was indeed a help, not only hooking her into the purple gown but also arranging her hair in a fashionable chignon. Her curls, for once useful, required no crimping to decorate her brow.

"I keep my skills up," said Mrs. Choate when Merry expressed her admiration at the effect. "In case they're needed."

She refrained from asking how many times they had been. She knew the answer would just depress her. Spirits dampened by the thought, she declined Mrs. Choate's offer to powder down her freckles.

"You'd have to powder everything," she said. "I'd rub off on whatever I touched.".

"S'pose you're right," sighed the cook. Together they surveyed her reflection in the rust-flecked mirror. Merry felt odd dressing up in this humble room, odd and precarious, as if she were more in danger of being marked an imposter now.

The velvet gown, while bold, was as flattering as anything her mother would have picked. The bodice was dangerously low, but it had to be in order to show off what decolletage she had. As was the fashion, the skirt was smooth in front, its luxurious fabric pulled into a fall of ruffles at the back. Having spent much of her recent life wearing nothing at all, Merry had never been so aware of the imprisoning nature of modern dress. Tiebacks beneath the skirt kept it from spreading and its narrow width made it difficult to walk, especially with the dragging fantail train. Even the weight of the dress was burdensome. Despite this, she could not regret being shown to her best advantage. She might not be the beauty Nic claimed but, by God, she was as fine as cloth could make her. She felt a different woman tonight: not who she'd been before, not who she'd pretended to be, but someone else entirely.

Someone who could seduce a man, she mused, then shivered prophetically at the thought.

Nic seemed happy with the results. "Bang up to the mark," he said as she descended his curving marble stairs.

Merry barely registered the praise. In his black tailed coat and trousers, he took her breath away. Now that he was dressed more like men she knew, she could better judge his figure. His shoulders were broad and straight, his hips as narrow as a dancer's. His waistcoat— almost as snug as her bodice—glowed in peacock blue embroidered with silver flowers. No man of her acquaintance would have been caught dead in such garish garb, but on Nic it seemed fitting. The color lent a hint of azure to his silver eyes. He'd combed his hair back from his brow, and the tempting, touchable waves spilled over his collar at the back. Their russet highlights gleamed as if they'd been oiled.

"You blind me," she said with a crooked smile.

He tucked his thumbs under his lapels and swelled his chest. "Can't let you outshine me."

"As if I could," she said, but there was no bitterness in her tone, only enjoyment at their banter and the pleasant shock of his splendor in evening dress. She couldn't recall having had so handsome an escort in her life.

They rode to the party in a small, closed carriage that was driven by the gardener and pulled by a nag so old and slow she could only have been hired out of pity. The night was misty and moonless and the foolish horse shied at everything that moved, including the swaying lanterns they'd hung on the carriage to light the way. Fortunately, they hadn't far to go, just a few streets north to a line of bijou cottages near the Eton and Middlesex cricket ground.

Nic sat next to her on the single seat, his scent mingling with hers in the tiny space. The effect was like a drug. With difficulty, she restrained the impulse to lean into his shoulder and close her eyes. When they drew to a halt, he put his arm on the sleeve of her new green coat. In spite of her vow to maintain a level head, her pulse began to skip.

She wondered if he meant to kiss her.

"I probably should warn you," he said, "that my friends can be a trifle wild. There's no malice in them, but if anyone says or does anything to discommode you, come to me and I'll see they stop."

Merry's eyes widened, wondering what he meant by "wild." Not debauched surely. Not licentious or depraved. Just how "discommoded" might she be? Would she be forced into the position of giving her unworldliness away?

I shall have to guard my reactions, she thought, and not let him see if I am shocked.

Sensing her nervousness, if not the cause for it, Nic pressed his lips to her furrowed brow. His voice was a velvet murmur in the dark. "I know you can take care of yourself, but I'd be honored if you'd rely on me."

His words simultaneously soothed her nerves and increased her caution. How alluring he was, and how unlike anyone she'd known. She felt dazed as he helped her from the carriage to the footpath, his kid-gloved fingers tight on hers even after she'd stepped down. "I shall make it clear," he warned, "that I intend to claim you for my own."

Thus saying, he led her down a short brick walk to a picturesque wooden door. Designed to resemble a country cottage, its planks had been painted the same vivid blue as Nic's waistcoat. The door opened before he could knock.

Light spilled out, outlining a woman's voluptuous form. She was garbed in a gauzy, flowing gown that was either a very informal tea dress or an elaborate negligee. Artistic, Merry supposed it would be called, in the style of the Pre-Raphaelites. The woman wearing it was taller than ordinary, but not towering, with soft brown hair and the loveliest oval face Merry had ever seen. Her eyes were so blue they were nearly purple. She could have modeled for a Madonna were it not for the lushness of her mouth, and the fact that her lips were painted poppy red.

Now this, Merry thought with as much awe as dismay, is how a temptress ought to look.

"Nic!" the vision cried, opening soft white arms. "We thought you'd never come."

The pair embraced like old friends, rather close old friends, pressing their cheeks together and smiling into each other's hair.

Though she tried to hide it, Merry's body tensed. She wondered at Nic bringing her to the home of an old lover when he obviously intended to seduce her. Were the manners of his set so different from hers? Or did the difference lay in who Nic thought she was: not the daughter of a duke, but a ruined maid?

At last, after what seemed like an eternity, he pushed back from their hostess. "Anna," he said, his voice warm, "as always, you steal my breath."

Anna palled his shoulder and turned to Merry. Her smile dazzled. "You must be this shameless flatterer's friend."

"Mary Colfax," she said. Anna seemed go expect neither bow nor curtsey, so Merry did not bend. Indeed, she wasn't sure she could have. Her spine had gone as rigid as a poker.

Anna dimpled as if her stiffness did not exist. "Come in," she said, her hand slipping gently behind her elbow. "Everyone will be so pleased to meet you."

Her coat was taken by a pretty parlormaid, her gloves by Anna herself. From this Merry knew the evening's manners would be informal. Indeed, the guests' behavior upheld her guess. Scattered about a comfortable, earth-toned parlor, they consisted of three couples besides Merry and Nic. The other women, one fair and one dark, sat on the arms of their partners' chairs and leaned familiarly into their sides.

That alone would have given her mother vapors.

Two of the men were painters like Nic. Sebastian Locke was a tall,

sardonic blond with a small goatee. His companion, introduced only as
"Lovey"—the coatgirl, Merry guessed—was plump and fair and given
to giggling for no cause. Gerald Hill, the second artist, was shorter and
more earnest. He had the flushed cheeks and defensive manner of a
man whose pride is easily bruised. To Merry, his partner was much
more interesting. Her name was Evangeline. She was slim but bosomy
and had an arresting, angular face, the left side of which was slightly
higher than the right. The anomaly made one want to stare at her,
though hardly in horror. She was striking but badly dressed in colors
that, even to Merry's eye, did not suit her at all. The style of her muddy
gown was mannish: high-collared, aggressively plain, as if she were
daring people to admire the way she looked. Though she sat with Gerald Hill, her gaze kept straying to Sebastian Locke.

Here is one, Merry thought, who hasn't learned to hide her infat-
uations.

The final gentleman, Leopold Vandenberg, was older than the others. The first sight of him allayed most of Merry's fears. He seemed
the essence of all that was conservative. Dressed soberly, he wore a full
beard, streaked with gray. No amount of expensive tailoring could
disguise the middle-aged thickening of his waist. Though his eyes
were kind and his face intelligent, he could not have been considered
handsome.

It did not take a genius to surmise he was the banker.

To Merry's surprise, he was also the lovely Anna's patron. But perhaps she should have expected the pairing. The lovely Anna struck
Merry as a practical woman.

Once the introductions were complete, Sebastian Locke ran his
gaze so boldly down her dress she felt like an object in a shop.

"Well, old boy," he said to Nic, "I see you've been holding out
on us."

"Of course, I've been holding out." Nic's voice was light but he
wrapped a protective arm around Merry's waist. "Your habits are too
dissipated for any sane man to do otherwise."

"Nonsense." Locke's eyes remained on Merry even as he caressed
his companion's flaxen curls. "You and I have supped from the same
dish before."

This was too much for Nic. He stiffened and drew a sharp breath
to speak.

"Stop it," Anna scolded, before he could respond. "I won't have
you two gnawing that bone in my house. Besides, you'll embarrass
Miss Colfax."

"That I should hate to do," said Locke with a mocking bow that took in her and Anna. "Please, Miss Colfax, say my thoughtless words have not offended you."

"Indeed not," Merry responded crisply. "I've no doubt you're only interested in me because I came with Nic."

Nic released a muffled laugh, which the dark Evangeline echoed without restraint. "She's got you there, Sebastian. To a T."

Sebastian glared at Evangeline from under golden brows, an attention that seemed to please her. Sensing the current, Gerald Hill pulled her hand onto his knee.

A skein of forbidden interest unfurled in Merry's breast. Was this what Sebastian meant by supping from the same dish? Gerald didn't seem eager to share, but she wondered what more she'd see before the evening closed. The possibility of witnessing genuine immorality both frightened and intrigued her. Caught up in her thoughts, she shivered as Nic drew his finger around her ear. His voice was intimately low.

"Don't dare him," he warned.

"I wasn't," she gasped, aghast that he could think she would.

Nic chuckled and tweaked her nose. "You should see your face, Duchess. Like the proverbial moth. But he and Evangeline would eat you alive."

She frowned but did not argue. The others were staring at them with interest, wondering perhaps if they were having a lovers' spat. The curly blonde sprawled lower on the couch. "I like her hair," she announced, as if someone had intimated they did not. "It's like a little lamb's."

Her declaration broke the tension in the room. Sebastian laughed, his sulky face transformed to dazzling boyishness. He pulled the glass from his partner's hand. "No more wine for you, Lovey. You're soused."

"Am not," she pouted, but snuggled against him as he kissed her hair.

Considering its prelude, dinner was more agreeable than Merry would have guessed. The food was fine French fare, served with equally fine French wine. Better than the meal, though, was the flattering care with which Nic treated her. Like a chivalrous knight, he fed her morsels from his plate, touched her cheek and hand, even fetched one of Anna's cloaks when she grew chilled.

Propriety did not matter. For once in her life, she felt a princess— with Nic her handsome prince. Perhaps it was the wine or the heat in his eyes or the sensual atmosphere of the night, but giving him what he wanted no longer seemed unwise.

"You devastate me," he murmured over the rim of his crystal glass. He had turned toward her in his chair, his knees bumping hers. When she looked down, her gaze found his hand resting on his thigh, his thumb touching the curve of an unmistakable erection. His mouth turned up at her involuntary gasp. He'd wanted her to see, to know he was aroused.

Merry felt as if something warm and plump had been slipped inside her sex. The others were talking amongst themselves, but if any glanced over they would guess what he was doing.

"All yours," he breathed as his thumb swept slowly up and down. "Every hot, hungry inch."

"*If* I want it," she said, then spoiled the effect by choking on too large a swallow of her wine.

He patted her back. "Little fraud," he teased close to her ear. "You know you're dying to cram me deep inside you."

His words were too true for comfort. That his behavior was outrageous did not matter to her body. By the time dessert had been cleared, she was lightheaded with arousal. The postprandial separation of the sexes would have offered a break, but Anna, apparently, did not observe that custom.

They adjourned together to the sitting room, where Nic pulled her crosswise into his lap and pressed the rigid evidence of his interest into her hip. She could feel it through all her petticoats, could almost hear it through her skin.

When Gerald Hill tried to light a cigar, the other women shouted him down.

"Even I," said Leo Vandenberg with his faint Austrian accent, "am not bold enough to smoke in Anna's house."

"And he paid for it," she said, patting his shoulder without shame.

Merry used the cover of the other's laughter to nuzzle her prince's neck. Nic's arms tightened. When she looked into his face, his eyes were molten. *Brat,* he mouthed, and pressed a kiss to her tingling lips. The tip of his tongue left a small wet mark behind.

"Aw," said the blond girl, "look at the lovebirds."

"Cockatoos," quipped Sebastian and Merry blushed.

He made what she'd done seem both sordid and exciting.

"Why don't I show the ladies the facilities?" Anna suggested. "And while we're gone, you gentlemen see if you can't elevate your minds."

"More profit to ask us to elevate something lower," Sebastian said to the amusement of the men.

Anna rolled her eyes at Merry as if they belonged to a common sisterhood. To Merry's surprise, she realized she wouldn't have minded if they did.

But that was before Anna drew her alone into the library. Like the sitting room, this was a place a man would feel at ease. At present it was cold, for the fire had burned down long ago. Merry pulled her borrowed cloak closer and looked around. Though small, the number of books the room held astounded. From floor to ceiling they were shelved, even sitting in crooked stacks beneath the windows. A man's black slippers lay before the smoldering grate. The stitching hoop that sat on a table nearby suggested Anna might have embroidered them herself. This struck Merry as a homely task for a mistress to undertake, but Anna was no ordinary mistress. From the clutter and wear of the decor, she concluded this was the couple's private sphere.

"I suppose you're wondering why I brought you here," said her hostess.

Merry was curious but waited for the other woman to explain. Anna fingered a fold on her gauzy overskirt. Her skin was cream-colored, her hair a glossy oak. Even her hands were feminine: plump and soft with perfect oval nails.

Merry tried not to picture them pricking Nic's naked back.

Finally, Anna spoke. "It's none of my business," she said. "But you're young and obviously impressionable. Decency compels me to offer you this advice." Again Merry said nothing. Anna released a breathy laugh. "All right, perhaps you're not as impressionable as I'd thought."

"You want to warn me about Nic," Merry said, "because you know him better than I do."

"For donkey's years." Anna's smile was wry. "And in all that time, he's never kept a woman more than a month."

"Not even you?"

The question was petty but Merry did not call it back. A hardness entered Anna's face that had not been there before.

"Not even me," she said blandly, and Merry knew she'd hurt her pride. She felt a twinge of shame. This was a woman who, had circumstances been different, she would have liked to befriend.

Unaware of her regret, Anna continued. "I know whereof I speak," she said. "And little as I imagine you want to hear it, you'd do well to heed my words. Nicolas Craven is a rake. I don't deny he's charm-

ing or that he can be kind, but he does not have it in him to give a
woman his heart. Not even for as long as it takes to fuck her."

With all her strength, Merry hid her blanch of shock.

"You're right about his charm," she said, in her chilliest, most
duchesslike voice. "And his kindness. More to the point, though,
since he fucks so very well, perhaps one shouldn't complain if he keeps
his heart."

Anna stared at her, then burst into startled laughter. "By God,
you're a cool one. If I hadn't seen the way you look at him, I'd believe
he'd met his match. But you're a girl, Mary, a warmhearted, starry-
eyed girl and all Nic's kindness will only break your heart the harder."

"That's not your concern," Merry said, wishing she could draw
herself as tall as the other woman.

"No," Anna sighed, "I suppose it's not. And who am I to warn
you against breaking your heart? If nothing else, it will make a
woman of you."

Was that what made a woman? Merry had never thought so, but
maybe . . .

She shook her head before the idea could form. No. Anna herself admitted Nic had failed to give his heart to her. Perhaps her
disappointment colored her opinion. In any case, Merry was not
going to let a warning from Nic's old lover spoil the nicest night
she'd ever had.

Just once, she wanted to be the princess she'd always dreamed of
being.

Chapter 7

EVEN IF MERRY WOULD RATHER HAVE GONE HOME, PRIDE
demanded she brazen the evening out. Her pulse still ragged, she returned to the sitting room and paused inside the door. She felt better
as soon as she spotted Nic, though his pose was strange for a man in
the midst of company. He sat on the floor in front of a large leather
chair, his legs stretched before him, his head resting back on the
empty cushion.

To Merry's eyes, he seemed more elegant than ever.

"You should come to Venice with us in March," Sebastian was say-ing. "I'm sure you could pick up a few commissions."

"I have my show at Tatling's in March."

"Well, la-di-da. A show at Tatling's."

From Sebastian's tone, Merry concluded he had not been invited to exhibit at the exclusive London gallery. Rumpled and vaguely feral, Sebastian sat across from Nic on the long brown sofa. His forearms rested on his knees with his hands clasped in between. He seemed restless and dissatisfied, but vulnerable as well. With a gentle smile, Nic stretched one boot to tap his fellow artist's shin.

"Give it a few years, old man. By then the galleries will be fight-ing to hang your work."

Sebastian wagged his head. "I wish I were as sure as you."

"Hah," barked Evangeline, "I wish I believed I had a chance in hell of ever being hung. But we know what people think of female artists."

"You're an artist, too?" Merry asked.

Everyone looked up at her in surprise, making her feel very much the outsider.

"Only according to my gran," said Evangeline, after a brief, un-comfortable pause.

"And me," Nic added in the same soft tone he'd used to reassure Sebastian.

"I always tell you you've got promise," Gerald put in, clearly ag-grieved to be ignored. Evangeline shot him a scornful look that said what she thought of his opinion. "Well, I do," he insisted.

The couple made faces at each other while Nic beckoned Merry closer. He patted the chair behind him. "Sit with me," he said in a hot, rough voice that made her forget to care whether she belonged. "I missed you while you were gone."

Restraining the impulse to look around and see if Anna was close enough to hear, Merry slid into the chair in her narrow purple gown, then coaxed Nic's head to rest back on her knees. He smiled up at her, fond and sleepy-eyed, and pretended to bite her leg. Merry took that, too, as a token of victory. Maybe she meant no more to him than other women, but she flattered herself at least she meant as much.

"Where's Anna?" Sebastian asked, with the air of one who wishes to liven up an evening. "I think we need a story."

Anna chose that moment to reappear. "Of all the nerve. First I make you supper. Then you expect me to sing for it."

"Leo's Frenchman made the supper," said Sebastian. "And as host-ess, you're obliged to entertain your guests."

Rather than contradict him, Anna turned to Leo. The older man had the armchair by the fire. Plainly, he was content with the comforts of his life. He seemed happy to indulge any manner of foolishness from his mistress's eccentric friends.

"Do as you wish, my dear," he said. "You know I always enjoy your tales."

His approval decided her. She crossed the Turkish carpet with its bold, dark shapes of red and brown, and perched her uncorseted form in the circle of the banker's arm. The fire gleamed on her loose chignon, a wood fire that smelled pleasantly of cedar and autumn leaves.

"Very well," she said, composing herself, "I shall tell the tale of the queen of the fey and the randy shepherd lad."

Despite Merry's jealousy of Anna's many charms, and the thought of how she'd once used them on Nic, the prospect of hearing something risqué pulled her forward in her chair. None of her brothers had shown a fondness for lewd books—for any books at all, truth be told—and Merry had long wanted to read one, if only to discover whether their authors knew more than stable boys. She held her breath as their hostess began.

"Queen Mab," said she, "was no puppet on a throne. She ruled the fey with an iron will and an eagle eye. No detail was too small for her royal notice, no task too humble for her delicate hand. Thus it was that when a shepherd and his flock wandered into forbidden lands, Mab immediately flew down from her pearl-encrusted palace to investigate.

"Now, as everyone knows, some faeries are as large as you and I, while some are as small as enchanted mushrooms. Mab was of the larger sort, and quite the most beautiful faerie who ever lived. Her hair was black, her eyes green, and her breast as snowy as a dove's. Her wings sparkled with dew-drop rainbows wherever they caught the light. Naturally, she could not allow a mere human to gaze upon her glory so, as she approached the intruder, she cast an invisibility spell to hide herself."

"Invisibility," leered Sebastian. "Imagine what a fellow could do with that!"

Evangeline snorted and rolled her eyes, but Anna ignored them both.

"The unsuspecting shepherd, no doubt bored by his duties, was napping beneath an apple tree. Mab was able to draw quite close without disturbing him."

"And he was handsome," Merry said, beginning to see where this was leading.

"Quite," Anna agreed, her eyes sliding coolly to Merry's face. "With wheaten curls and a scent like hay on a summer day. Mab didn't fall in love with him, of course. A faerie who gives her heart to a human must forfeit her powers. She did, however, immediately fall in lust. How could she not? The shepherd was as graceful as that statue by Michelangelo in the Louvre."

"Better equipped, I should hope," Nic said as he rubbed the back of his head against Merry's legs. Helpless to resist, she combed her fingers through his hair.

"Much better," Anna assured him. "I'm not implying Mab did anything so crude as disarrange the shepherd's clothes but, suffice to say, before she left the slumbering lad, she knew all of him to the inch—relaxed and at the ready. You see, she was so taken with him she sent him a dream of herself, posed in her diaphanous faerie gown, her nipples like cherries, her curves and dips a marvel no man could see without rising to the occasion. In the dream, she let him kiss one breast and herself drew one ivory hand up the tender inside of his thigh.

"This, however, was all the contact she permitted. He had not earned the right to more, not even in a dream."

"And when he woke?" Sebastian prompted.

Anna smiled. "When he woke, he thought he'd grown a hammer between his legs. No mortal man ever suffered such a cock-stand. It throbbed like the earth's own heart, long and thick and as glowingly red as a blacksmith's fire.

"Being a sociable sort, and not realizing his dream had been a true faerie visitation, the shepherd hobbled home as fast as he could, grabbed the first milkmaid he saw, and proceeded to churn her into a froth behind the village pub."

"I can guess what Mab thought of that," Nic said, prodding Merry's skirt again with his head. He'd drawn his knees up as Anna spoke and she suspected he was aroused. Feeling flushed herself, she stroked the cords along his neck. Her reward was a momentary closing of his eyes.

"Mab didn't like it at all," Anna said. "Here she, the queen of the fey, had deigned to let a mortal see her secret charms and what did he do but pour the lust she'd stirred into the first coarse vessel he found.

"Seething with fury, Mab cursed him. Even as the shepherd labored over the sighing maid, the queen took her revenge. From now on, she vowed, tup as he might, this scoundrel would not know completion's bliss until he turned his lust where it belonged."

"Ouch," said Gerald.

"Ouch, indeed," Anna agreed. "Cursed though he was, the hapless fellow's mighty instrument did not soften in the least. If anything, it grew in stature and demand. By this point, the well-sated maid was pushing him off her in disgust. Maddened by desire, the randy shepherd sought relief from every woman in the town. Young, old, handsome or hideous, he thrust his sword in every sheath. All to no avail. The faerie's curse had taken root. Give pleasure he could, even take it, but the ultimate joy was forever just out of reach.

"Finally, the women hid when they saw him coming. A truly tireless lover, these damsels discovered, was not a comfortable thing.

"Thrown back on his own devices, the shepherd tried to relieve the pain himself. For hours it seemed he wanked his monstrous prick until he feared both for it and his weary arm.

" 'I have been cursed,' he concluded, his mind clearing for a moment in exhaustion. 'That faerie I saw in my dream must have been real. Mayhap if I return to what I was doing when this began, I can find her again and beg her to release me.'

"Holding firm to this purpose, the shepherd—hobbling even worse than before—retraced his steps to the faerie mound. Again he lay under the apple tree and again, though without much hope, he composed himself to sleep. His effort was rewarded. As soon as he closed his eyes, the queen of the fey returned. Dazzled by her beauty, the dreaming shepherd fell to his knees. He knew he had found the source of his trouble. Between his trembling thighs, his organ buzzed as if it harbored a nest of maddened bees.

" 'Forgive me, queen of queens,' the shepherd pleaded. 'I am not worthy to kiss your wondrous toes. If only you'd tell me how I offended you, I'd do whatever is in my power to make amends.'

"Naturally, Mab was not pleased he could not guess what he had done, but knowing how men are, and impressed by his humility, she took pity on him. 'You must give me what you wasted on other women,' she said, 'and you must not cease until I say.'

"Scarcely able to believe his luck, the shepherd fell upon his beautiful tormentor. How his skin burned as he ripped aside her gauzy clothes! How his heart thundered as she clasped him to her breast! His need seemed to triple at the thought of finally achieving his culmination. As soon as his raging rod plunged into her tender grotto, the faerie said the words that dispelled her curse. At once the shepherd knew that he could come but, no longer the fool he'd been, he remembered Mab's admonition. He must not cease until she allowed it. He had no doubt that if he failed, the vengeful creature would curse him again, quite possibly with something worse. Gritting his teeth and shuddering with effort—for he was precious close to spilling as it was—the handsome young shepherd gave his all to the haughty queen.

"At last, after many painfully close calls, she sighed with pleasure and shivered delicately in his arms. 'Now,' she said, lifting her snowy hips against his own. 'Now you may claim your prize.'

"The shepherd could not wait a second longer. With a roar that shook the ground, he exploded in release, spewing his pent-up seed like so many gouts of fire. The bliss was unimaginable, for the faerie had enhanced it by magical means. The crisis left him boneless when it passed. He had not even strength to lift his eyes. Knowing he could not hold her, the faerie pulled free of his embrace.

" 'That will teach you,' she said, 'not to spend on a maid a passion fit for a queen.' "

Gerald was the first to recover from the silence that gripped the room. "Bravo," he said, clapping loudly. "Your best ever."

Anna inclined her head as everyone echoed his praise.

Merry clapped as well, though she hardly knew where to look now that the spell had broken. She didn't wish the others to see her face, but couldn't help wondering how the tale had affected them. She knew it affected Nic, for the hand he'd wrapped around hers was damply hot.

He's infected me, she thought. Soon she'd be as depraved as he was.

But her reaction held more than titillation. For all its silliness, Anna's story made her sad. Two people who could have touched hearts had wasted their chance: one out of pride, and the other out of lust. Was that to be Merry's fate when she ventured into the world of carnal pleasure?

She could not say "if" anymore, only "when." Right or wrong, Nic had won her over. Worse, he seemed to know it. Grinning up at her, he pulled her knuckles to his mouth. "Ready to go?" he whispered.

Merry hesitated, then nodded with a blush. As always, he knew the question she'd really answered. Triumph gleamed in his smoky eyes.

She hoped with all her heart it was a triumph they could share.

Chapter 8

NATURALLY, THEY COULD NOT LEAVE AT ONCE. NIC KNEW
Mary wouldn't be comfortable with everyone guessing why they
went. So he waited, itchingly impatient, through one last glass of
Madeira. To his immense gratification, Mary's flush had not faded by
the time he rose and stretched. He fancied he could hear her body
humming with awareness. She hadn't met his gaze since Anna finished and that, oddly enough, aroused him most of all.

He knew she wanted to hide the hunger in her eyes.

He made their good-byes and ushered her out the door with as
much haste as was seemly—perhaps a bit more. Anna lifted one brow
at him when they left, but he honestly couldn't care. For once, he
knew how his women felt.

He had to have her. Tonight. This minute. Sooner if they could
manage it.

He swung her into his arms outside the door, thanking God old
Max had brought the carriage round.

He practically tossed her onto the narrow seat.

"Nic!" she cried as she landed. He followed in an instant, pulling
her sideways onto his lap. The carriage was icy, her body warm. Her
startled hands flew to the breast of his winter coat. They belonged
there. On him. All over him.

"Kiss me," he said. "Oh, God—*God*—put your mouth on mine."

Too eager to wait for her compliance, he clasped her head and
forced his mouth to hers. She gasped but did not resist, and Nic
abruptly felt as desperate as that bloody shepherd. Her lips were soft,
yielding. He pushed inside and claimed her with his tongue. She
tasted of wine and lust, of carmine red and throbbing violins. His
throat closed on a moan. Deeper, he thought, and then: Damn, I could
devour her. The kiss was rough, but his usual restraint had fled. To his
relief, after her first stiff moment of surprise, she kissed him back, her
strong, lithe arms wrapping his head and ribs, her tongue both sweet
and greedy.

His heart pounded wildly in his chest. This kiss was so good. Too good. She pulled him into her mouth as if she could not wait for him to breach her. When he drew on her just as strongly, her sigh was a paean of agreement. She felt what he felt. She wanted what he wanted. Images swept through his mind, things he'd seen as her painter and now wished to see in bed. Her blush. Her breasts. The curve of her derriere. To touch her . . . To be given the right . . . He could not think. He wanted her until he hurt.

Her chignon began to fall. With a groan of pure sensual pleasure, he tore the pins away and buried his hands in the rippling mass of curls. Her hair was cool and thick. He found her scalp and rubbed, loving the way her breath caught in her throat, the way her neck seemed to lose its prideful starch.

"Mary," he said, his voice like gravel, "do you know what you do to me? Can you guess how mad I am to have you?"

He could not wait. He wrenched off his coat and opened his bursting trousers, drawing his erection from the tangle of sweaty cloth. He was heavy with arousal, leaden. The stiff, aching length fell against the purple velvet that draped her thigh. Merry gasped when she felt its living weight. Like magic, her cheek blazed with heat beneath his lips. Nic reached for her glove.

To his amazement, she pulled her hand away.

"Touch me," he said. "I want your fingers on my cock."

"But the coachman!"

"Fuck the coachman."

"But—"

He kissed her to silence. He was too near to getting what he craved to care who else might see. Max would not turn around in any case. Max was too well trained. Sinking deeper into desire, he nuzzled the bend of her neck and gloried in her sigh. She smelled wonderful, of vanilla and woman, of sweat and musk. His body wanted to absorb her through its pores. He slid his hand down her coat sleeve and tugged her wrist.

"Come on, Mary. I want those little calluses on my skin."

"Nic," she said, a laugh in it, "we haven't left Anna's yet. We're standing in the lane."

He cursed more creatively this time, and tried to steady his breath. Long before it calmed, he rapped on the window to rouse their dozing driver. "Max," he ordered, "take us home. And Lord help you if you stop for anything on the way."

Mary was still giggling when the carriage rumbled forward.

"You weren't supposed to notice that," he said, as disgruntled by her presence of mind as he was pleased by the yearning way she stroked his lapels.

She slid her hands behind his neck and laced them beneath his hair. "I take it I'm supposed to be overcome by passion."

"Yes," he huffed.

She tilted her head at him, her face in shadows, her eyes glinting with amusement. "Kiss me again, and we'll see if you overcome me."

His body leapt but he did not move. "If I kiss you again, I'll take you in the carriage. I admit, I'd be happy to do it, but it isn't what I'd planned for our first time."

"Oh, you've planned, have you?"

"Only since the moment I laid eyes on you."

Pleasure gurgled from her, a sound he'd never heard her make, one only the most confident woman could. The music warmed him deep inside. Wanting, needing to be closer, he pushed her skirts up her legs and turned her until she faced him on his lap. Her knees slid to either side of his hips, their progress stopped by the back of the leather seat. He scooted forward to bring her closer. Oh, that was better. Her gown was a tangle between them but beneath that only her drawers stopped the press of his raging flesh. Her warmth bled through the cloth, a humid warmth, perfumed by her arousal. He knew if he reached to touch it he would not stop.

Instead, he waited for her to touch him. Down her hands fell. From his shoulders. To his waist. Her thumbs rested on either side of his abdomen. She looked at his erection, rising thick and high between them, its thrumming surface lit by flickers of misty light. She bit her lip and then her hand was there, there on the upswung curve behind the head. Her thumb steadied him, then tightened. He tensed and fought a groan. The clasp felt shockingly good on his naked skin. She still wore her new kid gloves, their surface cool, their stitching a teasing rasp. Later, he thought. Later I'll strip her bare.

Her fingertips strafed the flare as if it were a harp string.

"If you won't kiss me," she murmured, "do you think I might kiss you?"

He had no power of speech to answer, just a groaning sigh.

She responded by brushing her lips across his own.

This was the kiss he'd dreamed of the day she'd showed up on his doorstep: a sweet kiss, a slow kiss. Her lips were a whisper over his, then a press, then a shy, wet exploration that ventured no further than the delicate skin above his teeth. He shivered under the silky tease as long as he could bear, breathing harder, twining tighter. He didn't want to scare her but his pulse was pounding so hard his skin was shaking. She wasn't touching his erection. She'd abandoned it to stroke his face with tender hands and even that sent sparks spangling down his nerves.

Finally, he couldn't stand it.

"More," he said, when her mouth began to wander down his jaw. He stroked her neck above the collar of her coat. "Open for me. Let me taste you."

Her pulse stuttered under his fingers as she lifted her face to his. Her eyes were huge, unsure, but she did not object. "Like this," he whispered and went deep, wanting to drown in her, wanting to drink her in. He sighed, long and low, and pulled an answering sigh from her. Her hands moved from his face to his back, wrapping him as he wrapped her. The pleasure of the simple embrace surprised him. Despite the urgency of his need, he felt suspended in the moment, happy to spend the hours till sunrise in her arms.

Then the carriage wheels ceased crunching on the gritty drive and a different sort of tension took hold of his partner's limbs.

"We're home," she whispered.

Nic did not move except to lick the peak of her upper lip. "Nervous?"

She nodded with shyly lowered lashes and the conflagration inside him rose. He didn't know which made him ache more: her schoolgirl blushes or her boldness. He was going to enjoy this, really, truly enjoy this. He slid his hands down her back until they filled the hollow above her bustle.

"I'm not letting you back out now," he warned, "but I'll make you happy you gave in."

She gaped at his effrontery. Then she laughed.

"Tuck yourself in," she ordered, more breathless than reproaching. "Unless you want your servants to see a good bit more of you than they should."

He grinned at that, did as she advised, and kicked open the carriage door.

HE CARRIED HER OVER THE THRESHOLD LIKE A PRINCESS IN a tale. The house was empty this time of night, the gas turned low, the shadows still.

"Light as a feather," he teased, bouncing her in his arms as he carried her up the stairs.

The action made her blood course faster through her veins. Light she might be, but to toss her like that meant he must be strong. The memory of his naked chest slid through her mind. She gripped his arm and felt his muscles through his sleeve. She wondered how he'd got them since he'd never done anything resembling exercise in front of her.

"At last," he said, shouldering through his door, "I have my sweet Godiva where I want her."

The light from the hall sconce lit the nearer objects of the room. Her eyes went to his huge Japanese bed, one corner of which stood out from the shadows. The door swung wider. Her body tightened. The bed loomed as big as a cricket ground, the posts like spears, the quilt a stark white field of snow. She pictured herself lying across it, impaled like a dying soldier, and shuddered involuntarily in his arms.

He laughed and kissed her temple. She thought he would toss her onto the bed and ravish her; she wanted him to, really, because she didn't wish to think too hard on what lay ahead. Instead, he carried her to the adjoining bath chamber and set her down. He lit a candle for her, then stroked her fallen hair.

"I know you've a shy streak," he said. "Do whatever you need to be comfortable. I'll wait. All night if you need me to."

She hoped the light was too dim to show the sudden moisture in her eyes. Anna was right. His kindness was a danger.

"I should hope I wouldn't take all night," she said as flippantly as she could. "Shyness is one thing, but insanity is quite another."

He laughed before backing away. "All night," he repeated.

His growl gave the promise an entirely different meaning.

Left to herself, she removed her clothes and washed up and tried to subdue the trembling of her hands. She wanted this, wanted him. Who better to introduce her to the secrets of the bed chamber? Most of all, she couldn't go back on her word once she'd implied she would give in. Female or no, that would have been dishonorable.

There's nothing to fear, she assured herself. After tonight, she couldn't doubt he wanted her. In that, at least, they were equal. She spared a moment to wonder if he'd notice her virginity. Perhaps she should pretend she hadn't actually been despoiled. Of course, if he knew she was a virgin, he might not want to take her. She screwed her eyes shut and shook her head. The last thing she needed was to complicate her lie. Besides, if her mother's exasperated warnings were reliable, she had nothing to worry about. She'd climbed too many trees and ridden too many horses astride to be left with anything more than a virgin's ignorance.

Inexperience, she corrected with a firm, outward breath. True ignorance hadn't been an issue since she was twelve.

I'll let him take the lead, she thought, and he'll never guess a
thing.

HE'D TOLD HER HE WOULD WAIT, BUT IT WASN'T EASY.
Hours seemed to pass since he'd set her trembling on the blue-and-
white Delft tile. His straining ears caught the rustle of silk and linen,
the splash of water in the sink.

He lit candles—not too many—and turned down the covers on
the bed. The sheets were fresh and smelled of Mrs. Choate's lavender
potpourri. He doffed his coat and shoes and waistcoat, smoothing
them over the back of an armchair as if they were a woman's skin. He
wore one of his poet's shirts tonight, with flat, box-pleated ruffles on
the cuffs. He unbuttoned the garment to his breastbone, then
stopped.

Still no Mary.

He pressed his hand to his diaphragm and willed himself to calm.
He'd done the right thing, letting her ready herself. She wouldn't
change her mind. And if she did, tonight wasn't the night he was
meant to have her. He could wait. He'd always been able to wait.

Oh, Lord, he prayed, casting his eyes to the ornately plastered ceiling. Please don't make me wait.

The door clicked open and he spun around.

She'd taken off her clothes. Every stitch. Even her hair was pushed
behind her shoulders, which she'd squared in the challenging way
he'd grown so fond of. Despite his amusement, the sight of her drove
the breath straight from his lungs. He sank to the edge of the bed. She
seemed magical standing there, an otherworldly sprite with the light
flickering over her slim, feminine curves and her high, rose-tipped
breasts. The triangle of curls between her legs glinted like antique
gold. He wanted to run his fingers through it, wanted to part it and
bare her treasure.

He gestured her towards him, coaxingly, reassuringly, and won
two forward steps.

"You don't have to stare at me like that," she said. "You've seen it
all before."

He smiled and shook his head. "Not like this. Not when I knew
I'd be inside you."

She bit her lip and stopped, but she was close enough that he could
catch her hands and pull her between his open thighs. She was shiv-

ering. He rubbed her from wrist to shoulder, hoping to warm more than her skin.

"Don't be afraid," he said, holding her worried gaze. "Making love to me won't be like it was with—" He stopped because he didn't want her to remember. "This will be pleasurable, Mary. For both of us."

"I hope so," she said, almost too soft to hear. "I'm not very experienced."

The confession touched him. That she could harbor any doubt as to his pleasure was quite ridiculous. At this point, shameful as it was to admit, he'd have enjoyed himself if she did no more than lay there and spread her legs. Laughing silently at the depth of his own lust, he hid his face between her breasts. They were silk against his evening beard, small and firm and kissable.

"Ah, Mary," he groaned, his hands slipping up her back as he reveled in the soft perfection of her skin, "the only experience you need is the kind we'll make together."

She gasped when he took her nipple in his mouth, then again when his hands slid down her back to squeeze her bottom. She was a feast for his touch, her skin like satin, her every muscle firm. He suckled her gently, teasingly, flicking the butter-smooth pebble with his tongue. The way she squirmed and shivered made him feel as if she'd never been touched this way before.

And maybe she hadn't. Maybe he was the first to take the time.

"Nic," she said as he found the hollow behind her knees and made them wobble. "Nic, I want you naked, too."

He stood so swiftly she almost lost her balance stepping back. "Don't do that," she scolded. "I need room."

He spread his arms, the picture of innocence, and won a grudging smile.

"Arms up," she ordered, and slid her hands beneath his shirt. "Why you didn't wear your American buttons tonight, I can't imagine."

He couldn't help laughing. God knew why, but her grumping made him happy. He bent forward so she could pull the shirt over his head. The cuffs caught on his wrists and she swore like a sailor as she struggled to undo them. The brush of her fingers, the way she bit her upper lip in concentration, made his breath huff like a train. He wanted to kiss her again, to penetrate every orifice she possessed. His chest was damp by the time she reached up to smooth his hair, a procedure that required her to go up on her toes. Nic was no giant, but she made him feel like one. Her breasts jiggled temptingly against his ribs before she stepped back to consider what she'd revealed.

"You're right," she said, one tapering finger to her jaw. "You do look different now that I know I'm going to have you."

His laugh burst out but the sound became a choke when she reached for the waistband of his trousers. "Careful, Duchess," he warned. "You wouldn't want to pinch anything valuable in those buttons."

She froze, then clucked when she realized he was teasing. She made short work of the placket, as if she were familiar—not to mention comfortable—with unfastening gentlemen's clothes. It was yet another contradiction in the puzzle that was Mary. Younger brothers? he wondered. Or perhaps her duties in the laundry? He didn't think she'd spent enough time with Monmouth to grow easy with this procedure. Nor could he doubt her claims of inexperience.

At least, he didn't think he could.

With the same unsettling efficiency, she shoved everything to his ankles and looked up at him from her crouch. Nic tensed. He didn't generally worry about his body; too many women had called it comely for him to waste time on that. Nonetheless, as Mary tilted her head and studied him, he found himself hoping she was pleased. He was certainly hard enough to flatter, whatever she thought of the individual configuration of his sex. He was high now, like a boy with his hand on his first breast. The head pulsed just beneath his navel, its foreskin drawn so eagerly back he felt as if he were stretching in two directions. When Mary's hand slipped up his thigh, his balls actually jumped in excitement. He thought she might touch them, hoped she might, but her fingers stopped at his hip and fanned across the bone. Again he felt that roughness that had piqued him. Hot tingles of sensation streaked down his legs.

"You should have lit more candles," she said. "I can hardly see you in this light."

His laughter shook his belly and his sex. He pulled her to her feet and kissed her. "I'll light them all," he said. "Every one I own."

Then he pulled her tight against him. She cried out as their bodies met, stretching up to hold him, to fit them more intimately together. Blood rushed to his skin in licks of fire. He groaned and lifted her and turned to lay her on the bed. She clutched him so closely he had to lower them both to the mattress together. He pressed her down beneath him, knowing he might be heavy but unable to resist. Her smallness drove him wild, but her strength made him fearless. He felt as if he could crush her, savage her, and she would only moan for more. She moaned now as he ran his hand down her curves, molding her, squeezing her, thrilling to the equal force with which she squeezed him back.

"Yes," he breathed as she gripped his buttocks. "Hold me as closely as you want."

Her mouth opened on his neck, hot, panting, and he knew she needed more.

He slipped his hand between them to find her wiry golden curls. Once past them, her sex was as soft as he'd dreamed, as warm and wet.

"Oh," she gasped as he slid his finger up the melting satin crease.

He swallowed the piping syllable in a kiss, easing his finger inside her, easing his thumb to the center of her joy. Her limbs went lax, then taut, and then she poured a moan of hunger down his throat. Her sheath was a clinging cushion against his finger, tight but very welcoming. The thought of how she'd clasp his shaft made him coil like piano wire on a peg.

Wait, damn you, he ordered his pounding prick. Let her come before you test how warm her welcome is.

He pulled back from the kiss. Her eyes opened wide, clearly wondering why he'd stopped. "I want to watch," he said. "I want to see you take your pleasure."

Her back arched—a trembling, involuntary stretch—and he knew his request had deepened her excitement. Her eyes were dark, her hair a glorious tangle on the sheets.

"You always . . . want to watch," she said, so aroused she couldn't get the words out on one breath.

"Everything," he agreed, and slipped a second finger inside her. She was so narrow it almost wouldn't fit. With another sighing squirm, she pushed against him, driving him in to the webbing of his hand.

She laughed at his sharp inhalation, but her laugh was no steadier than her limbs.

"Touch me," he said, his voice like a match rasping sun-warmed brick. "Put your hand on my cock."

She touched him. This time her hand was bare, her palm damp, her fingers hot where they wrapped the thudding skin. Who'd have dreamed such strong, work-hardened hands could be so delicate? He thought he'd burst as she held him. Her touch was that good, that necessary. He swelled impossibly beneath it, overcome by a gratitude as deep as it was unprecedented. He'd needed this more than he knew, needed *her* more than he knew. His hips rolled forward, moving him in her grip, subtly, just enough to shift the skin along his shaft. The effect nearly shattered him.

"Shall I rub it then?" she said, as tentative as a girl.

The offer sent a blaze of heat across his face. He gritted his teeth and shook his head. "I couldn't take that now. Just hold me. There, under the crown. I want you to feel what happens to me when you come. I want you to feel my veins swell. I want you to count my racing pulse."

Her fingers tightened almost painfully as she arched again at his words. "I'm sorry," she said, forced to release him. "No one's ever made me feel this way."

He could not doubt it. Her head rolled from side to side, rustling her hair against the sheet. He could see she was near her limit. "Don't fight it," he said. "Just let go."

"I have to—" she gasped and her hips began to rock.

He quickened the motion of his hand until her eyes squeezed shut with embarrassed bliss. "Yes," he urged. "Take it. Take what you want."

Her conflict was a pleasure for him to see: her need betraying her shyness, her cries tight and keening in her throat. She was flushed in the candlelight, her breasts trembling, her nipples blood-kissed stones. Her legs twitched as her crisis neared. Her hands fisted on his back. Leaning closer, he looked down to watch his hand, then up to watch her face. He would not miss this. Not for anything. Her sheath began to flutter, gripping, releasing, pulling his fingers deeper. He pressed up against the throat of her sex where she'd feel it most and she broke with a violent shudder, her actual climax silent but intense.

For long moments she shook, arched up like a bow with her veins showing blue and fine against her neck. She was lost to him, but locked to him as well. He would have painted her like this if he could. The image was one he would have prized. It ended, though, as all sweet things must.

As he petted her down, she brushed her fingers along his shaft. His skin tingled for a moment, then suddenly felt twice as hot.

"I forgot you," she confessed. Her eyes fluttered slowly open, her smile curling into her flushed and freckled cheeks.

He kissed the dint at the tip of her nose. "Forgive me if I consider that a compliment."

She laughed and flung her arms around him, a gesture of thanks so natural and exuberant it made his throat feel oddly tight. He cleared it and pulled back, then brushed his thumb across one rosy-golden nipple. His hand was wet, fragrant. He lowered his head to lick the shining mark it had left behind. Mary quivered in response.

"Now," he said, "let's see if you're ready for the second course."

*   *   *

MERRY WAS AFRAID SHE'D NEVER BE READY, NOT FOR THE
devastating intimacy of his touch, not for the sound of the bed creak-
ing as his weight moved over hers, not for the hot, wet press of Nic's
naked skin.

Nic, she thought, his name trapped in her throat. The happiness
he inspired was a kind of ache.

He'd been so generous, so knowing. She wanted to hold him tight
and never let him go. Knowing the urge was foolish did not dim it in
the least. The touch of his fingers parting his way for entry was
enough to melt her anew.

She wasn't ready for this. Couldn't be ready.

"Sweet Mary," he whispered, fitting himself against her most private flesh. "Say you want me. Say you need me inside you now."

She groaned. He was silky hot, his tension both threat and promise. He would fill her, ease her. And then he would leave her empty.

"Say it," he urged, half plea, half growl.

She closed her eyes and gripped the sweating muscles of his waist.
How could she deny him? She wanted everything he said. "I want
you," she whispered. "I want you inside me now."

He pushed at once and moaned, his thickness slipping inside her
like buttered steel. She felt the shape of him forcing her to give way,
making room for itself, jolting a little inside her as her body clung
and then relaxed. She could feel his pulse now, pattering against her
own. More, she thought, enchanted by the heat and movement, by the
astonishingly personal invasion. *Oh, more.* But then he stopped and
hung above her on his forearms. A bead of sweat ran down his neck.

"Okay?" he asked through gritted teeth, shuddering when her
body clenched in rising greed.

"I want more," she whispered, too shy to say it loudly.

"Jesus." He groaned, almost laughing but not quite. She feared
she'd done something wrong. To her surprise, he rolled onto his back
with her above him. "You'd better do it, Duchess. You're so damn tiny
I'm afraid I'll hurt you."

Too tiny? she wondered. She liked how he felt stretching up inside
her, but who knew how it felt to him? His grimace when she wriggled worried her. She braced on the straining tendons of his chest.
"I'm not hurting you, am I?"

He laughed in earnest then, until he shook inside her. "You really
don't know much about men, do you?"

Her cheeks burned with embarrassment. "Well, I—"

He silenced her with a gentle finger to her lips. She looked at him more closely. His face was flushed and his pupils nearly swallowed his smoky eyes. He might not have been panting but he was close. Of a certainty, he was not unhappy with his lot.

"It's all right," he said, still amused. "You're tight is all. Delectably so. Perfect, if you want to know the truth. I just want to make sure you're comfortable."

"I am," she said and worked herself down until she held him full and hot within her.

He swore and gripped her hips as if he didn't know whether to hold her off or yank her closer. Merry could have sworn herself; the shock of his presence was such a marvel. She'd thought what they'd done before was intimate, but this! They were joined now, flesh to flesh. A wave of strange sensation swelled inside her, part dizziness, part excitement, filling her body just as he filled her sex.

This was better than a moonlit gallop across a moor.

"Nic," she breathed, his name a prayer. Driven by a compulsion she couldn't resist, she dropped her hand. He shuddered when she touched the place where he pressed inside her.

"Don't move," he rasped, his sex flexing, stretching. A vein jumped wildly beneath her hand. "Do not for God's sake move."

But he was the one who pulled her down and wrapped her close, who rolled them to their sides and slowly began to stroke.

"Closer," he said. Crooking his arm under her knee, he pulled her calf over his ribs. When he had her as he wanted, he ran his hand down her thigh to cup her bottom. His smallest finger curled into the valley there, stroking, tickling, making her blush and heat. Then the finger came to rest against the pulsing place they joined.

So, she thought, with a secret inward shiver, he can't believe it either.

"There," he said, "that's where I want you. That's where I need you most."

When his hips cocked forward, pressing him even deeper, she realized he hadn't just opened her completely, he'd also made it impossible for her to interfere with what he did. His arm held not only her leg in place, but her bottom and hip as well. He was controlling her movements, bracing her for his thrusts, keeping her to his lazy push and pull.

She was helpless and could not even mind. Each thick, slow stroke seemed to drag her deeper under his spell. His rhythm, his breath, was hers. When he gripped her bottom, her nails scored his back.

When he coiled and thrust harder, so did she. In everything, they were together, bound by his will like solid ropes of gold. He shifted angles, going deeper, faster. The sense that he was losing control excited her. Need rose in a gathering wave. He felt it, too. His expression was harsh now, his motions wild.

"Fuck," he said, the word a soft explosion as his hips jolted hers. "Tighten, Mary. Pull me in."

It was what her body wanted most. She tightened, her very soul opening for the thrust. He swore at the strength of her pull, rigid, slamming into her with desperate force. "Mary," he cried. "Oh . . . God." She rode the edge, aching, needy, and then the storm crashed over them with a fury. She knew when he came because he stiffened and gasped in shock. The evidence of his climax threw her over. They shook in tandem, clinging like the last survivors of a wreck. The release was too sweet to bear. She buried her face in his neck and felt him do the same.

When the madness faded, a lull swept over her, but it was not a lull of peace.

She was sorry then. She wished she'd told him how special this night had been, that no other man had known what she'd given him. She wished the name he'd called her had truly been her own, wished she hadn't lied to and misled him. The deception seemed a betrayal not only of him but of her deepest self.

This little rite of passage, this loss of her virginity, had meant more than she'd expected. If she'd told him the truth, maybe, just maybe, she wouldn't have gone through it alone.

Neither of them spoke. Merry could feel herself shaking in his arms, hard, as if her body meant to rattle itself apart. No matter how little she knew about the act of love, she knew she wasn't supposed to react like this.

Finally, Nic stirred. "Good Lord," he said. "You must be freezing. Stay here. I'll build up the fire."

"No!" she cried, unthinking. "Don't leave me."

He stiffened at her plea, one brief, irretrievable moment. She knew she'd misstepped even as he chuckled and rolled her underneath him where she'd be warm.

"Mary," he said as she hugged his waist and hid her face against his chest. The word was a gentle scold she pretended not to hear. Alas, Nicolas Craven was not a man to let a woman live in a dream. He kissed the top of her lowered head.

"Be careful who you cling to," he said, soft and full of doom. "Men like me don't trade in hearts. In fact, men like me don't have them. Better save yours for someone who will cherish it as you deserve."

Well, Merry thought, if that condescending twaddle didn't cool her misplaced ardor, she didn't know what would. Blinking back what she told herself were tears of fury, she wriggled out from under him and sat up. Glaring, she shoved her curls back from her face.

"You should be so lucky," she huffed.

"No doubt," he agreed, and lazily scratched his chest. He lounged on his side like a sultan, his head propped on his hand, his still thick organ beginning to stretch and bob. With an effort, she wrenched her gaze away.

"I am not in love with you," she said. "Not even close."

"Good," he said. "See that you stay that way."

When she scowled at him, he merely cocked one brow. Infuriated, she climbed altogether out of the bed, the better to remove herself from temptation. "I'm going back to my room now."

His eyes narrowed. "Are you?"

"Yes, I am!" she snapped and turned to go.

She had the door halfway open when he slammed it shut before her. His hands caged her against the wood, his tall, lean body a wall of heat. His aggression excited her, though she tried to hide the sudden leaping of her blood. Instead, she tossed her hair in defiance, wishing she could whip him with its length. Nic blew a cloud of it from his face. When he spoke, he sounded angry.

"I'm not done with you."

"And when you are?"

"When I am, I'll let you know."

His arrogance made her sputter. He didn't seem to care how angry she was, didn't even seem to know. He lowered his head and sucked the tender skin of her nape against his teeth. She should have kicked him then, should have ducked under his arm and slipped away. She shouldn't have shivered, or wobbled on her knees, or turned to melted sugar between her legs.

"I don't want you to do this," she said, but he slid his hand down her belly to find the lie.

"Mary," he groaned, and somehow the sound of longing broke her will to hold him off. He knew it, too. His breathing quickened. She felt him at the small of her back, growing long again, growing thick.

"Spread your legs," he ordered, already nudging them with his own. "I want to take you from behind."

"Here?" she gasped. Was this a thing people did? Make love standing up, as if they were animals, as if a bed were miles away?

"Here," he said, probing for entry. *"Here."*

He slid into her as he said it, blunt and swift. Caught unprepared, she braced her arms against the door. He grunted, moving already. This time he was not lazy. This time he took her with single-minded haste. His hands were iron on her hips, his voice a honeyed rasp that spoke of things a lady should not hear. If Merry had ever doubted it, she knew she was no lady now.

Caught in the strangeness of the act, she watched her feet, planted wide, and his between them, the same long, naked feet that had unnerved her when they met. His tendons tightened as he thrust. His toes curled. He was working hard to get inside her, making the floor creak underneath. The boards where the carpet ended were dark and highly waxed. When she realized she could see their reflection in the shine, a gush of warmth slid down her leg. Nic groaned in appreciation. Their bodies sounded wet as they slapped together, not just outside, but in.

Wet, she thought, the word a tickling flutter in her sex. Wet with seed. Wet with cream. She pushed out with her bottom and silently begged for more.

He gave her what she needed, locking their hands in conjoined fists against the rattling door, shoving into her so hard he nearly lifted her off her feet.

"Yes," he crooned. "Oh, Mary, you're on fire."

Though she bowed her head and closed her eyes, she could not hide from this truth.

Chapter 9

NIC WAS ODD. THAT WAS THE ONLY EXPLANATION MERRY had. Perhaps other men did trap their lovers against the wall. Perhaps they, too, delighted in watching their women's pleasure. But when Nic stood her in his claw-footed tub to instruct her in the use of Dr. Allbutt's cleansing syringe, she knew a few of the bats in his belfry were unique.

Murmuring reassurances, he lifted her foot to the curving rim and helped her insert the perforated nozzle. Gentle and sure, he might have been a physician but for the subtle quickening of his breath.

"Sorry," he said, when she jumped at an unavoidably personal touch. "Should have remembered to lay in a supply of sheaths." He frowned. "Don't know what got into me. I always plan ahead."

The reminder that there was an "always" did not thrill her. Nor did the possibility this night might have consequences beyond abandoning her virtue.

"I want you to know," he said, his eyes on the careful motions of his hands, "if anything happens . . . well, I'll take care of you."

Bemused by his euphemistic language, she pondered what he meant by taking care of her. Not marriage, she didn't think. Not that she wanted marriage. No, indeed. If that were the case, she wouldn't have turned to Nic in the first place. Still, whatever he was offering—financial support most likely—it was more than many men would. His own brand of decency, she supposed.

Oddly touched, she stroked the shadowed hollow of his face. "I'm not completely alone in the world. I have friends."

His laugh was wry. "Not friends who'll come pounding on my door, I hope."

If only he knew, she thought, doing her best to push the guilt away. Given his history, Nic must have faced irate relatives in the past. Surely hers would be no worse. It was even possible that, with her to calm them, they would be better. Aside from which, she saw no point in leaving the job half done. Ruined though she was, the public portion of her undoing was incomplete.

"I haven't told them where I am," she said, the half confession uncomfortable on her tongue. "I'd only notify them if, as you said, something happened."

He sighed and kissed her brow. "Ah, Mary, I'm a beast to make you worry. I meant our first time to be perfect."

"It was," she assured him. "I've never known anything like it."

She held his gaze, willing him to read her secret. For a moment, it seemed he did. His brows pulled together as if he were perplexed. Then, shaking his head against some thought, he smiled and cupped her cheek, once again the pleasant, worldly rake.

"You won't mind my French letters," he promised. "I have them specially made by a firm in Kingsland. They're sheep's intestine, double-layered and superfine. When they're wet, you can hardly tell they're there."

In spite of herself, she began to laugh. What would her mother say if she could see her daughter now, standing naked in a tub discussing prophylactic sheaths with a man who'd just slipped an irrigator up her quim? Even her best friend, Isabel, would be horrified. One might employ such instruments, but one would never discuss them, much less involve a man so intimately in their use!

"Nothing embarrasses you, does it?" she said.

He bent to dry her with a towel. "Sensible people can't afford to be embarrassed. Protection is part of the business of love."

Her neck tightened. How easy it was to forget he did this all the time, to believe what they shared was rare. She firmed her jaw. "You're right," she said. The business of love might be pleasant, but it didn't necessarily touch the heart.

NIC LAY ON HIS BACK, ABRUPTLY WIDE AWAKE. SOMETHING had disturbed him.

If a sound had roused him, he did not hear it now. Mary slept quietly by his side, curled away from him with her head pillowed on his outflung arm. He knew some men wouldn't let a woman stay the night, but he'd never minded—as long as they didn't want to stay all the time. In any case, her presence was not what had woken him.

Something I forgot to do, he thought. Or something I did do but shouldn't have.

The answer elusive, he eased his arm out from under Mary's neck. She made a tiny whimpering noise as he caught a snarl of hair, then subsided with a fetching wriggle.

Nic smiled. Her little freckled arse, stuck up higher than the rest of her, a curve as profound as the hills of Rome. Helpless to resist, he ran his hand down the silken slope. The noise she made then was decidedly grumpy. He'd worked her hard this night, too hard no doubt, though she'd been with him sigh for sigh. Giving her shoulder a last caress, he let her be.

More than time you played the gentleman, he thought, but it was hard to regret a moment. She'd been like a child on Christmas morning, virginally tight, whorishly wet, delighted by each and every pleasure they unwrapped.

Maybe too delighted.

His mouth turned down as he remembered how she'd clung to him at the end. Of course, he'd held her rather tightly himself. Couldn't help it. That first climax had been a spine-wringer. For

Mary, who appeared not to have had a half-competent lover before himself, the effect must have been dramatic.

Chances were, that was why she'd become emotional. He needn't assume she was falling in love, no more than he was.

He'd been stupid, though. Unforgivably so. He, of all people, knew better than to endanger a woman's health. He never forgot to use his sheaths, never forgot to have them on hand when he thought he'd need them. And he had thought he'd need them. For weeks now.

He didn't really believe Mary was pregnant, but the forgetting, that troubled him.

An image slipped into his mind. A child. Fat and bowed of lip. Golden curled. Snub-nosed. *Freckled.*

Shuddering, he thrust the covers off his body. No children. No, no, no. One Craven bastard was enough. His skin abruptly tight, he used the nearest post to swing up and out of bed. Time to work. He'd avoided that painting long enough.

This decided, he padded barefoot down the stairs, one fraction of his mind dedicated to the foolishness of donning no more than a robe in the dead of winter. The lion's share of his awareness was in his studio already. He sensed he was close to the answer, that the pressure of almost knowing was what had shaken him from his rest.

The sconces flared bright as he lifted the glass and lit them. With light to see by, he stood the half-dozen canvasses that had survived his latest purge against the wall. Each showed Mary riding a large white horse through a small medieval town.

The angles and the pose changed in the pictures. Some showed more of the buildings, some less. The horse didn't look half bad, despite Mary's warning against working without a model. The perspective was fine, and the play of light and color. Overall, the compositions were unobjectionable. He did not doubt he could sell them.

And every one bored him to tears.

They had nothing beneath their technically perfect surface. No blood. No heart. No glimmer of the lively woman they portrayed.

"Blah, blah, blah," he grumbled and fought an urge to toss them in the fire.

He wouldn't find the answer by hiding from his mistakes. He had to face them down, to stare his own stupidity in the eye.

Mary was the key: her spirit, her strange, unfashionable allure.

He plunged his fingers into his hair and pulled until the ends tugged at his scalp. He remembered how she'd responded the night he'd said he wanted to show her off at Anna's party.

I could wear a hundred velvet gowns and I still wouldn't—

He hadn't let her finish because he'd known how the sentence ended in her mind.

I still wouldn't be pretty.

He could almost hear her say it, could almost read the half-challenging cry that lay beneath.

Who says I can't be pretty? Who says!

Mary was a fighter, God bless her. Whatever her insecurities, some part of her refused to accept the world's opinion of her looks. Some part rebelled like a child thumping its heels against the injustice of adults.

Adults who, in this case, were quite, quite wrong.

Beauty often hid where the common man could not see it.

Nic could see it, though. That was his gift: to see it and to show it.

His arms fell from his head, slapping his silk-robed sides. The pressure inside him grew. What had she said when he accused her of being too eager to give her heart?

You should be so lucky.

He nodded at the memory. He should be so lucky. That's how he wanted to make the people who saw her portrait feel. He wanted to rub their noses in her gorgeous, sunny self. Wanted to make them long to know her. Wanted to shove her peculiar beauty in their . . .

The hair at the back of his neck prickled, then stood up on his arms like grass in a sudden wind. He froze, blind to everything but the image crystallizing in his mind.

Yes. He had to shove her in their faces. Literally. He had to flatten the picture's depth. Brighten the colors. Sharpen the shadows.

A chill shivered down his spine as he grabbed a blank canvas and stood it on the easel. The chalk was in his hand almost before he knew he'd wanted it.

In three quick strokes he drew the tailor's window. This frame within a frame would make each viewer the Peeping Tom, the one resident of Coventry who could not resist a look. The tailor's room he'd leave in darkness, the better to blind them with the noonday light outside. Through this blaze would ride Godiva, close enough to touch. Her eyes would flash, her smile seduce. No lady, she, no slave to convention. She'd meet each gaze directly and dare the world to disapprove. One night with her, the men would think, and *I'd die a happy man.*

And the women . . . Well, maybe the women would cluck their tongues and maybe they would smile, inside, where they knew they shared Godiva's power.

Nic felt as if a god had seized his arm. The sketch seemed to draw itself, quick, sure streaks of umber brown. There the curve of Mary's cheek. Here the prancing lift of the horse's tail. All along it had been waiting for him to find it. And then it was done. His hand fell like a puppet with its strings cut. He was breathing as hard as if he'd run down the street he'd drawn. The picture seemed a miracle and yet he knew the source of every line. From each of his discarded efforts he'd saved a scrap of good. A turn of the head. A balance of light and dark. He might tinker yet, just to be sure, but for all intents and purposes, the portrait he would paint was sitting on this easel.

He smiled at it, ghost though it was, his eyes welling with the immensity of his relief. He had broken through the wall.

From this point on, the rest of the work was play.

MERRY SMOOTHED HER SKIRT FOR THE DOZENTH TIME AND cursed her trembling hands. She'd woken early to an empty bed and had crept, thankfully unseen, to the privacy of her room. There she'd washed and dressed and stared at herself in the rusty mirror.

Her reflection told her nothing beyond the fact that her hair was now completely hopeless. She looked no more a ruined woman than before. Her eyes did not sparkle with secrets, nor her cheeks burn with shame. If anything, she looked pale.

Despite which she was convinced the moment anyone saw her they would know.

He'd been inside her. He'd made her spend with pleasure until her breath whined out like tortured steel. He'd left his seed on her, his scent. The memory of his thrusting, eager shape had been imprinted between her legs.

Surely this was not an alteration one could hide.

Disgusted, she turned from the mirror. What did she care if Farnham guessed, or Mrs. Choate? They could not think the worse of her. This was only what they'd expected all along. She was plain Mary Colfax here, not Lady Merry Vance—neither one of whom should have been prey to such simpering fears.

She'd enjoyed herself and so had Nic. She would not be sorry. With one last lug on her bodice, she ordered herself downstairs.

Nic waited at the bottom where he bounced on his toes with unusual excitement. He wore one of his painting shirts, the ruined linen starched and ironed by the scrupulous Mrs. Choate. The collar lay open at his neck, baring a wedge of smooth brown skin she longed to touch.

She wondered when she'd feel she had the right to caress him as she pleased.

Oblivious to her desire, Nic kissed her briskly on the cheek. "Glad you're up," he said. "Come eat quickly. I want to work. Today is going to be a good day, Mary. Very, very good."

She let him pull her to the Chinese parlor where a breakfast of rolls and ham and coffee awaited on a lacquered tray.

As she ate, he chattered about short perspectives and frames within frames and the necessity of challenging the viewer to become a participant in the picture. Fortunately, he required no response, for little he said made sense to her. His gestures were sharp as he paced the crowded parlor. Watching him—his energy, his intensity—made her heart beat faster in her chest.

"Now everything will be easy," he said. "Now we'll get somewhere."

As happy as she was for his breakthrough, the suggestion that he'd soon finish the work dismayed her. Whether he realized it or not, she'd have no justification for staying once he was done. Her father might conceivably forgive a brief adventure, but not an ongoing liaison. Merry wasn't sure she'd forgive that herself, not with a man who did not—no—who could not love her.

"Nothing to it now," he declared, and snapped his lingers on a laugh.

She struggled to swallow a bite of roll.

He was too euphoric to notice her dampened mood. When she finished her meal, he pulled the tray aside and scooped her into his arms. His hold felt different from the night before: more possessive and yet more casual, as if he'd lost any fear she might object. He carried her through the house that way, merely winking when the maid tittered behind her hand.

"Nic!" Merry protested, wishing she were silly enough to hide her face against his neck.

He chuckled and kissed her nose. "Can't be shy. We've gone beyond that, you and I."

Apparently, he also thought they'd gone beyond letting her undress herself. His sole nod to modesty was closing the studio door before he attacked her buttons. The winter light, cool but clear, poured through the windows as he peeled each barrier in turn. He murmured praise to her, then laughed at the state of her hair.

"Now this," he said, "is going to slow me down."

He sat her on the fake Egyptian chaise and brushed her curls himself, working with surprising patience from tip to crown, one thick section at a time. When the tangles were gone, his strokes made a sound like a horse being curried, rhythmic and gentle, as if he meant to put her in a trance. In minutes, the waves of honey gold began to shine.

"Like that, don't you?" he said as she melted beneath his care. "Perhaps I should do this every morning."

His hand slid around to cup her breast. Merry bit back a moan. She sensed he wanted her arousal for the painting, rather than for himself. Nonetheless, his breath hissed through his teeth when he found her stiffened nipple.

"I'd like to mark you here," he whispered, one finger circling the swollen areola. "I'd like to suck you hard and paint the bruise."

She went liquid at his words, at the tiny tingling fireworks of his touch. He groaned, then kissed her shoulder with biting force.

"Don't tempt me," he said, rising to tug her hands. "I can't afford to waste the daylight."

"I wasn't tempting you."

He smiled with glowing eyes. "Trust me, Duchess, you tempt me just by being."

"You want me to believe that so I'll look sexy while you work."

He slid his palm down his paint-smeared shirt to the nascent ridge between his legs. Gently, shamelessly, his fingers rubbed it fuller. "I could prove how much you tempt me."

"Hah," was all she managed to get out, one glimpse of his "proof" having robbed her of her wits. She wanted him with a keenness the night before should have exhausted.

Fool, she thought.

But her traitorous body hummed as he helped her up to pose.

DAWN HAD BARELY BROKEN THE NEXT DAY WHEN NIC STUCK his head in Farnham's pantry, a room that contained not just shelves and the silver safe, but also his butler's sitting area.

"Sir!" said Farnham, clearly startled. With the faintest of blushes to darken his slashing scar, he slapped the paper he'd been reading closed. "I was just about to iron this."

Nic laughed at having discovered his starchy servant in a misdeed. "So. This explains the extra fingerprints on my *London News*." He cracked his knuckles, then took pity as Farnham began to sputter.

"I'm teasing, man. I don't care if you read my paper, not even if you do leave fingerprints—which you haven't. I'm hiring a hack for Mary to ride in Regent's Park. I want the new boy to hold his head."

The butler set the paper carefully aside. "I believe young Thomas is assisting with the laundry today. Mrs. Choate says he has a strong arm. I, however, could certainly help you hold a horse."

Nic considered this. "No. You're too big. You might block the view. Or the light. I need the boy. The laundry will have to wait."

" 'Wait'?" said Farnham in a tone that suggested waiting was not advisable.

Nic hadn't the faintest idea what washing clothes entailed, nor did he care, especially when he itched to sketch Mary on that horse. "Is that a problem?" he said, his brows lifting in full expectation of having his wishes met.

Though the butler winced, he did not disappoint. "No, no," he said. "I'll order dinner from the bakeshop and Mrs. Choate will be able to finish as she'd planned."

"Good," said Nic, the issue settled. "Have the boy meet us in the garden in half an hour."

He whistled as he strolled away, feeling sharper of mind and lighter of spirit than he had since the day he left his childhood home. Then he'd been starting his career. Now, if this picture lived up to his promise, he was about to enhance its luster.

Besides which, Mary would be thrilled with his surprise.

"THRILLED" WAS NOT THE WORD MERRY WOULD HAVE USED, especially when Nic borrowed a pair of the new boy's breeches for her to wear.

"I need to see your legs," he'd explained as she held them up in dismay. "I've decided you'll sit astride. But don't worry. We'll cover your top with an old reefer coal. No one who sees you will guess you're not a boy."

Merry was not so optimistic. She'd worn breeches in public on a number of notable occasions. Her appearance in them now was less than a good disguise.

"But my hair," she said weakly.

"Braid it up and slick it in a cap." He grinned as if he'd offered her a treat.

She hadn't the heart to spoil his fun.

When the new boy saw her in his knee breeches, he turned the color of a strawberry, the flush creeping over his omnipresent scarf, green today, with a crooked black stripe.

She didn't know if her appearance were the cause, but the lad seemed more turtlelike than ever, shrinking into the layers of wool as if he wished to disappear. When she realized he was there to lead the horse, she was tempted to fall off laughing. She hadn't needed anyone to lead her since she was four. Mary Colfax, of course, was another story. A city girl like her, and a poor one at that, had probably never been on a horse's back.

With that in mind, she tried to look as awkward as she could.

To her surprise—for she hadn't expected Nic to know one end of a horse from the other—he had hired a decent mount, a tall, gray mare with an elegant conformation. Though she wasn't as fine as Merry was used to, something inside her eased to feel a real horse underneath her.

The boy was easy with the mare as well, rubbing her muzzle and feeding her bits of carrot from his hand.

"You there," Nic called. "New boy. Take care you don't spook her with that scarf."

"Thomas," said the boy with a muffled sigh, then tucked the trailing end into his coat.

At a plodding pace better fit for a centenarian, Thomas led Merry and the horse through the gate to Regent's Park. From there they clumped past St. Dunstan's Chapel and around the boating lake. Finally, on a quiet stretch of lawn near the wintry remains of the botanical garden, Nic directed them to stop. Even now, with a frosting of snow on the ground, visitors strolled the park. Workmen hurried to jobs, servants walked dogs, and nannies from Cumberland Terrace guided their bundled charges toward the zoo. Two smartly gowned young ladies cantered past them but, to Merry's immense relief, they didn't give her or her companions a second glance.

She caught the tail end of their gossip as they swept by: something about purple gloves and an unfortunate yellow hat. She couldn't help wondering if their wearer were someone she knew.

For a moment she was split in two, yearning toward her old life yet dreading it as well. She might not know who she was in Nic's world, might indeed be falling on her face, but at least she was free to choose her way.

When Nic reached up to stroke the horse's neck, her gratitude warmed her smile.

"This spot will do," he said, his eyes crinkling back at her. He jerked his head at the bright, ice-skinned lake. "Plenty of ambient light."

By now, she was used to this being important. She watched as he set up his folding chair and propped his sketchbook on his knees. He grinned at her once before he started, then was lost to the world-swallowing distraction of his art. The most astonishing grimaces crossed his face, as if these contortions helped him draw. Like a cellist, she thought. Only by using his whole body could his passion infuse the work.

Young Tom, who had never seen this performance, was even more mesmerized than she.

"Hold her steady," Nic said, when the boy's fascination caused him to slacken his grip on the bridle. "I'll be at this for a bit."

A bit turned into a quarter hour, then a half. Apart from shifting her weight from one hock to the other and trying to nibble Tom's lumpy scarf, the mare didn't seem to mind the inactivity. Merry entertained herself by watching Tom. Cowed by his recent scold, he was sneaking looks at Nic whenever he thought the artist wouldn't catch him.

"He won't bite," she whispered from the corner of her mouth, "even if he did forget your name."

Her words startled the boy into looking at her and then she was startled, too. His gaze struck her like a curlew's cry, a piercing tangle of emotion. His eyes were a sweet spring blue, older than she expected and much, much sadder; adult somehow, though they were not a man's eyes yet. Lashed with starry, light-brown spikes, their clarity amazed. With eyes so lovely, few would mind whatever horror his scarf was hiding. Or maybe they would. Maybe the haunting beauty of his gaze would make the ruin seem even worse.

"Yes, miss," he said, and lowered his smooth young lids.

Color washed his forehead, pink as a country rose. She wondered if he were embarrassed that she'd addressed him. Would it embarrass a boy to speak to his employer's mistress? Assuming that's what she was. Merry wasn't sure there was a name for what she'd become to Nic.

At least, not a name she'd want to use.

"Do you ride, sir?" asked the boy.

Nic glanced at him in surprise. The boy—*Tom,* he reminded himself—hadn't said a dozen words since they'd left the house and none at all since they'd dropped Mary at the ostler's door. He supposed he asked because Nic had been running his hand down the mare's left foreleg. It was a habit from his youth, one his mother had insisted on.

You bring them back the way you take them out, she liked to say. *And if you find a problem, you tell the groom. A care for the creatures that count on you is the measure of a man.*

He'd only forgotten once. The horse came up lame and she'd made him muck out bedding for a month. He could still remember his humiliation. The stable lads had known they wouldn't be punished for taking advantage of the young master's fall from grace. They'd worked him like a navvy. At the time, Nic had hated every minute of the backbreaking work, but now the memory inspired a rueful smile.

The marchioness had known how to teach a lesson. Still did, he imagined.

"I used to ride," he said, smoothing the horse's windblown mane, "when I was a boy."

"Did you like it?" Tom asked.

Nic wondered at his boldness. The boy wasn't looking at Nic but the tension in his gangly frame led Nic to believe his answer was important. Why that should be, he couldn't guess, but who knew what crotchets boys that age got into their heads?

"I liked riding fine," he said, "but I liked drawing better."

"Guess you liked that better than anything."

Nic squinted. The boy's tone was oddly challenging. Did he think a real man ought to favor horseflesh over paint?

"Yes," he said, still confused, "I liked drawing better than anything. That's why I became a painter."

Tom nodded as if this were no more than he'd expected. His hand stroked the horse's neck. "Guess you've still got the eye, though," he said. "Best-looking horse in the stable. Must have cost you." His glance slid to Nic then back away. "The maid said you bought Miss Mary dresses, too."

Nic's temper pricked. "See here," he said, "if you're trying to cast aspersions on how Miss Mary earned those dresses, you can just—"

"No." The boy lifted one hand in denial. "I was merely noting that you're generous with your coin."

Merely noting! thought Nic, amusement outweighing his anger. Those national schools must be doing a better job than he'd suspected. "Angling for a rise then, are you?"

"No, sir. You've been generous with my salary, as well."

"That's Farnham's doing."

When the boy shrugged, his eyes disappeared into his scarf. The habit suddenly overwhelmed Nic's curiosity. What was Tom hiding that he thought no one but him could bear? Nic had believed him too shy to interact with people, but the way he'd spoken today revealed a considerable, if peculiar, self-possession. Maybe all Tom needed was a little encouragement to open up. Nic wouldn't have minded if he did. He'd never wanted a lot of starch among his staff.

He touched Tom's arm, about to press him, but the narrow shoulders twitched and the boy spun away. He spoke with his head hunched determinedly down.

"I'd better check on Miss Mary," he said, moving toward the cobbled yard. "She's been alone a bit. Might be a rough crowd out there."

Nic laughed softly through his nose. Far from casting aspersions on her character, it seemed young Tom had also seen what a prize "Miss Mary" was.

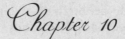

Chapter 10

MERRY COULDN'T BELIEVE NOW QUICKLY HER PORTRAIT HAD progressed. Nic worked like a man possessed, or at least like a man who didn't need food or sleep. At his insistence, she warmed his bed, but on many nights she was the only one doing so. When they did make love, he wasn't truly with her. Oh, his skill was as formidable as ever, and she couldn't deny she enjoyed herself, but somehow—without his full engagement—that enjoyment was not enough.

His distraction would have hurt if she hadn't been concerned for him. Where was the man who'd gone into raptures over a cup of coffee? Who made flirting an art form? Who considered the catnap a form a prayer? He seemed almost to be punishing himself with his current devotion to toil, though for what she could not guess.

She kept waiting for the real Nic to return. She didn't know how to be with this one and yet she could not bring herself to leave. He seemed to want her there, seemed to welcome, however distantly, her presence beside him in the night. He always pulled her close, always kissed her hair and sighed as he relaxed.

She worried that this small bond was enough to hold her. Her heart was too soft when it came to him, too soft by far.

One night, as he slept, he muttered a woman's name. *Bess,* she thought, or possibly *Beth.* It didn't even anger her. Instead, she wondered who the woman was and why her memory troubled her lover's sleep. She would have soothed him if she could, but his manner did not invite it. His Art was all to him now. Merry was merely a convenience.

NIC PAUSED AT THE DOOR TO THE LIBRARY. HIS NEWS forgotten in the image that met his eye.

Mary sat by the window, a book on her lap, her profile turned to watch the carriages pass outside. Her hair lay over her shoulders in sheaves of fiery gold, an extravagant contradiction to the primness of her pose. Despite being at leisure, her spine was as straight as a poker in the plain green gown, one of the few gowns she'd chosen at the dressmaker. High-necked and gently fitted, its sole adornment was a stiff white ruffle at throat and cuff. Her knees were pressed together, her hands folded neatly on the book. She reminded him of schoolgirls he'd known, well-bred schoolgirls, who do not forget their posture when they're alone.

His heart lightened unexpectedly at her beauty. He thought his brush had caught her but it hadn't. Nothing could. For all the time they'd spent together, for all the intimacy they'd shared, this spirited young woman remained a mystery.

"Mary," he said softly, not wanting to startle her.

She turned her head and the look on her face made the floor shift strangely beneath his feet. Her eyes were huge. In the firelight, they shone like amber washed in tears.

He moved swiftly to kneel beside her, his knuckles white as they closed on the worn leather arm of her chair. "What is it?" he said. "What's wrong?"

Wistfully, she touched his hair. "I was thinking how much I'll miss you when I'm gone."

"Gone! Why should you leave?"

"The picture is finished, isn't it?"

He shook his head to clear it. "How did you know I was going to tell you that?"

She smiled. "You have varnish on your shirt. And you're looking at me again, as if I were really here."

"Oh, Mary. I never meant . . ." Stricken by his own insensitivity, he had to stop and reform the words. "I never meant to neglect you."

"I know. You were simply caught up in your work." Her eyes shimmered as she cupped his cheek, a mixture of affection and regret. "You're happy with it, aren't you?"

"Yes," he said simply. "It's the best thing I've done."

"Good." She nodded. "I'm glad."

"I thought you might like to see it. Then we could go for a nice dinner at the Café Royal. Take in a show. Celebrate."

For the space of a breath she was silent. Thoughts crossed her face he could not begin to read.

"I can't go out," she said.

"Can't?"

She lowered her eyes. Her stillness frightened him. Suddenly, he didn't want her to explain, didn't want to know what had saddened her. He laid his hand on her sleeve, stroking her arm through the emerald wool.

"We could stay in." He cocked his head and smiled. "I could make up for my neglect."

Her lips curled into her freckled cheeks.

"Let me," he coaxed. "Let me make it up to you."

The growl was one he'd used a thousand times—suggestive, seductive—guaranteed to make a woman melt. For the first time in his life, the sound stuck in his throat.

"Let me," he whispered, and this time it was a plea.

Her eyes lifted to his, fathoms deep, a darkness into which a man could fall. Emotion trembled on their surface. He could barely swallow past the thickness of his throat. He ached to hold her, to cover that soft pink mouth and make it sigh. *Say yes,* he willed her. Say yes.

"Yes," she said, and leaned in for his kiss.

"WE CAN START ANOTHER PICTURE," HE SAID. "THERE'S NO reason this one has to be the last."

Mary snuggled closer but did not answer. They lay before the library fire, clothing scattered, sweat drying on glowing, rug-burned skin. Their coupling had been a quick, groaning thing, over too fast to fully recollect once it was done. Mary's lightly boned bodice lay like a carapace on the chair in which she'd sat. He couldn't remember taking it off, but his hands still seemed to bear the imprint of her thighs. He'd shoved them apart to take her, the tendons that led to her groin stretching beneath his hold. She'd moaned his name as he'd pressed inside, and once more when she came. Now her breasts shook in the dying firelight. The pulse was strong enough to follow both up her throat and down the sweep of her shallow belly. The triangle of curls at its base was sticky, matted in tiny caramel spears. He found the sight peculiarly arousing, though he had no doubt she'd have been self-conscious if she'd known.

Then again, she might have been furious. Nic had forgotten the blasted sheath again and hadn't pulled out quite soon enough at the end. At least one gush of seed was in her—which didn't bother him half as much as not having taken the time to savor her wet and bare.

The reaction was unprecedented and highly irresponsible. Worse, he'd have risked it again in a heartbeat.

He wasn't handling this well, wasn't handling her well. Long minutes had passed since his searing climax and his heart still thumped in his chest. It should have been slowing the way it always did at the end of an affair.

He told himself he simply wasn't ready to let her go. The picture had distracted him. Otherwise, he would have had his fill of her by now. Give him a few more weeks and he'd say good-bye without a qualm.

He'd be damned, however, if he'd beg for a few more weeks.

Beside him Mary stirred, her lips pressing his shoulder, her palm smoothing shyly across his chest. Simple though it was, her touch caused his shaft to thicken. Her head turned, her cheek petal-soft and cool. Her mouth found the rising itch of his left nipple. She'd never kissed him there before. The brush of lip and tongue was streaking fire. This was what he hadn't got enough of: this loss of her inhibitions, this victory over inexperience.

"When is your show?" she asked.

Nic fought a gasp as her teeth grazed skin. "Next Thursday."

Her hand trailed down his side to stop provokingly at his hip. When, he wondered, had these callused female fingers become the ultimate objects of his desire? Her thumb stretched to feather the edge of his pubic curls. He bit his lip, wanting her to take the leap herself. Just touch me, he thought. You don't have to ask permission. You don't have to worry you'll do it wrong. Just put your bloody fist around my cock. He held his breath in anticipation. Ridiculous, he thought, aghast at the depth his lust. Perfectly ridiculous.

"I'll stay till then," she said.

At first, he was too preoccupied with the position of her hand to comprehend. When he did, he opened his mouth to argue, then carefully shut it.

He had till Thursday. Four days to focus all his skill on her. Four days to wipe out his neglect. He rolled toward her, one hand sliding beneath her hair to knead her neck, the other stroking her silky back. She arched under his palm. She sighed.

He did not doubt he could change her mind.

*   *   *

SEBASTIAN LOCKE STOOD, STROKING HIS SMALL GOATEE, before the finished picture. He had a tall person's habit of slouching into his hips—though this, naturally, could have been his idea of acting Byronic.

Whatever his pose, and despite the sleepy narrowing of his eyes, his attention was keen. His lips were pursed with concentration.

"These glazes are very thin," he said.

"Yes," Nic agreed.

He'd used the sheer layers of color to create the vibrancy he desired. Though he knew the effect he'd achieved was good, he found himself biting the side of his thumb. Sebastian's eye was sharp. This was one of the reasons for his dissatisfaction with his own work: he could see what needed to be done better than he could do it.

"Left off her freckles, I see," he said, with a teasing lift of one fair brow. "Too much of a challenge?"

Nic shook his head. "They made the picture look too busy."

"Mm." Sebastian returned to his perusal. His eyes drifted from the crown of Mary's hair to the place where her breast peeped coyly through the waves. "Mm," he said again.

Nic lost his patience. "For God's sake, Seb, just tell me what you think."

Sebastian laughed. "You bloody well know it's good, old man. I thought I'd try to give you more response than that."

"Should have been a damned critic."

At the mutter, Sebastian's smile distorted the curve of his blond mustache. His face might have been designed for just such saturnine expressions. "Those who can't do, eh?"

"I didn't mean it that way. You can do. Very well."

"Nic, Nic, Nic," Sebastian tutted, "always the kind one." He tapped the side of his jaw. "You say you *just* finished this?"

"Last night. You want to touch it to prove it's wet?"

"No, no. I don't doubt your word. I'm simply surprised." He slanted Nic an ironic glance. "Usually, when you finish a big project, you don't send for me to take a look at it. You crawl into your bed and hibernate."

Nic juggled the handful of coins inside his pocket. "This painting is different."

"So I see."

Knowing his friend was waiting for him to prod again, Nic stubbornly held his tongue.

"Oh, very well." Sebastian surrendered with a husky laugh. "It's brilliant. You've broken new artistic ground—for yourself, certainly, and possibly for more than yourself. These colors make me drool, as does your scrumptious little Godiva. The fact that you made that scrawny creature look so fuckable is a miracle in itself. When Alma-Tadema finishes turning green, he's going to slap your bloody back."

Nic let his breath out in relief. Bubbling with the sudden release of tension, he rocked back on his heels. "Mary begged me to get a sidesaddle, but I just couldn't make myself do it. Ruskin will have a fit. Probably call me a menace to society."

"You've invited Ruskin to your show?"

"Of course." Nic grinned. "A man like me looks forward to being a menace."

Catching the grin, Sebastian squeezed the muscle of Nic's shoulder. "It's good," he said, his gaze for once warm and open. "It's very good. I'm wondering though . . ."

"Yes?"

Sebastian's eyes tilted at the corners as if he were holding back a laugh. "You're looking particularly hale and glowy. So I'm wondering if your mood isn't due more to your current light of love than to the successful finish of your work."

The back of Nic's neck prickled with alarm. If his friend took it into his head that Mary was important to him, he'd pursue her with every wile he had. He'd always been competitive and the steady rise of Nic's career just made it worse. Mary might not be important to Nic the way the other artist thought, but she didn't deserve to be embroiled in Sebastian's games.

"What do you mean?" he said, forcing a casual tone. "Why would Mary Colfax have anything to do with how I feel?"

"Oh, I don't know. Maybe the way you looked at her at Anna's, as if you were the starving wolf and she the tender sheep."

"We hadn't slept together then."

"Ah," said Sebastian. But he didn't seem convinced.

"I like her," Nic said, striving to sound reasonable. "I like women."

Sebastian pressed his thumb consideringly to his lips. "I know you do. It's the secret to your success."

"Quite. And there's no reason to think this is any different."

His friend studied him, one arm crossed beneath the other arm's elbow while his thumbnail tapped his teeth. His thoughts were hidden behind their customary veil of banked amusement, but Nic could guess what he was thinking. He fought an urge to squirm. Everything he'd said to Sebastian was true. He did like women. All women. If the sparks he and Mary struck were unusually bright, well, that was a happy coincidence of compatibility. It didn't mean his feelings were serious or that her presence had anything to do with the improvement of his usual post-painting disposition. The picture was a personal landmark. Any artist would have been ebullient.

Finally, Sebastian broke the silence. "You should ask her to join us in Venice after the show. The countess has invited us to stay in her palazzo."

"Us?"

The other man's grin was devilish. Nic knew at once what it must mean. "You're taking Evangeline, aren't you?"

Sebastian's mustache twitched. "Her affair with Gerald Hill seems to have run its course."

"Oh, Seb." Nic scrubbed his face in resignation. "You know you should leave her alone. Neither of you are good for each other."

"You have your poisons," said Sebastian, thoroughly unrepentant. He lifted a fan-ended scumbling brush and twirled it deftly around two fingers. "You could come without Mary if you prefer. I know Evangeline wouldn't mind. Be like old times."

"God forbid," he muttered, recalling how the pair liked to entangle him in their dramas.

"Now, now," Sebastian scolded, "it wasn't all Sturm und Drang."

"No," Nic admitted. It hadn't been all storm and stress. The trio—Sebastian, Anna, and Evangeline—had taken him under their wing when he first arrived in London. His schooling had led him all over Europe. He'd had passing acquaintances but not friends. After he lost Bess, he hadn't had the heart to make them. Sebastian's warmth, and that of the others, had brought him back to the human fold.

A love that generous, that lifesaving, should never cause regret.

Now Sebastian laughed. "Remember how we'd sneak into Anna's plays, then sit up all night talking in her dressing room? Idiots, all of us, thinking we knew the meaning of life and art, so poor we had to pool our money for a meal."

"I remember." Nic brushed his friend's jaw with the back of his fingers. Nic had been proud of his poverty, proud of never touching his father's tainted coin.

Sebastian sighed. "I miss those days."

"Well, I don't miss half starving," Nic said, though he did miss the lightness of all their demons. They'd been amusing then, more eccentricities than burdens. When one was that young, nothing seemed incapable of being healed by time. He was older now and not so optimistic. Sometimes he thought their knowledge of each other merely strengthened their power to hurt.

"I miss it," Sebastian said, his voice suddenly hoarse. "I miss when we all were equal."

The confession moved Nic to the burning brink of tears. Sebastian could be a sly, deceitful bastard but, by God, he could also strip the truth to its hardest bone.

"We are equal," he said just as roughly. "There's more to measuring a man than the opinion of the world."

His friend laughed through his nose. Recovered from the moment of sentiment, his eyes held their old, self-deprecating glint. "Just say you'll think about Venice. You and I haven't drunk ourselves stupid in ages."

"I'll think about it," Nic promised.

To his surprise, he knew he would.

NIC HAD GONE OUT—TO VISIT HIS TAILOR, HE SAID—LEAVING Merry free to sneak into his studio. He'd never forbidden her to come alone, but that wasn't why she had waited. She couldn't stand for anyone else to witness her first view of the painting. Not Farnham. Not Mrs. Choate. Certainly not Nic. So great was her anxiety she'd evaded all his invitations to look at it with him. Hadn't peeked at the thing in weeks.

Just in case.

He said he never lied. Not in words and not in paint. He would show her as he saw her.

She wasn't sure she could bear it if she were ugly.

Mouth dry, her gaze slid to the curving bank of windows. The sky was pale but clear, and the bedraggled pines dripped with the recent thaw. Spring was coming, though she wouldn't be here to see it. How melancholy that knowledge was. How it weighted her heart like lumps of stone. She'd been here six weeks. Six amazing weeks that felt like one.

Merry shook off her sadness. She hadn't come here to brood or to procrastinate. The sun was shining through the windows, warming the scent of drying paint, lighting the tall pine easel that stood like a gallows in the glare. That easel held her portrait. Unframed. Uncovered. Less than an arm's length on any side. A small thing, really, to inspire such fear.

The word made her square her shoulders. Her skirt swept the dusty floor as she strode past Nic's armless Venus, past the half-used roll of canvas and the jumble of period props. She closed her eyes and pressed her lips together. Then she stepped around the painting.

Her breath caught in her throat, a gasp of shocked surprise.

His sketches had not prepared her. The picture was gorgeous. So bright, so vivid, the color struck her like a blow. She had a childish urge to lick it, as if it were a dripping fruit. The picture glowed, and she glowed in it.

She glowed.

Godiva was her. Down to the dint on her nose and the kink of her horrid hair. Those were her knobby knees. Her wiry arms. Her naughty, laughing eyes. Apart from the omission of her freckles, he hadn't flattered her in the least.

Despite which, no mirror had ever made her look so radiant.

"My," she breathed, her hand to her throat, her eyes filling even as she broke into a laugh. For the rest of her life she'd remember this moment.

She was beautiful. The way he saw her, she was.

This was a gift she'd never expected to receive. Better than her purple dress. Better than the sensual indulgence he'd poured over her these past few days. Better even than her first ride on a pony.

Most of all, though, this was a gift that demanded one in return.

Chapter 11

THE SUN WAS STILL HIGH WHEN NIC RETURNED FROM shopping. He'd meant to seek Mary out, but hadn't expected to find her in his bedroom.

"I want to thank you," she said.

Since she sat on her heels in the middle of his mattress, wearing nothing but his favorite brown dressing gown, Nic had a sneaking suspicion what form her gratitude would take.

Smiling, he tossed all but the smallest of his parcels onto a chair. If she fell the need to thank him, his work of the past few days must be bearing fruit. His body tightened pleasurably, though he pretended to be confused. "Thank me?"

She nodded, her expression conveying both diffidence and determination. "For the painting. I looked at it this morning. It's very beautiful. No one has ever made me see myself that way."

"Ah." He lowered himself between the bed's two central posts—the doorway, as it were, to his magic cabinet. Thanks for his artistic skill he had not anticipated. He drew one finger up her paisley silk-clad thigh, then hooked it beneath the hastily knotted belt. Mary rewarded him with a squirm. In a mood to tease, he tugged at the tie but did not pull it free. "What if I think you're the one who should be thanked?"

"You've been thanking me. Ever since you finished."

Amusement slid through his chest like warm spiced wine. "I'm glad you noticed. But these past few days haven't been a thank-you. They've been a bribe."

"A bribe?" Her breath hitched as he mouthed her neck. He followed up the advantage by sliding his hand inside the robe to cup her breast. Her body jerked an instant before her nipple stiffened against his palm.

"My lovemaking is meant as an incentive, to make you want to stay."

"Because you're not done with me yet."

The words possessed a nagging familiarity. He pulled back from nuzzling her collarbone and peered into her face. "What do you mean?"

"The first night, when you"—her color heightened—"when you took me against the door to keep me from leaving, you said you weren't done with me."

His body heated at the memory, but he forced himself to match her serious tone. He drew his hand from the melting softness of her breast. "I never lied to you, Mary. I told you this would end."

"I know." Her red-gold lashes fanned down to veil her eyes, but she did not seem upset. She smoothed his robe more neatly down her thighs. For one irrational moment, the calmness with which she greeted his reminder vexed him. Most of the women he'd known had tried their best to hold him. Her gaze lifted again, steady and inscrutable. "I merely wondered: since you say you're not done with me, what is it you want that you haven't gotten? That's what I'd like to give you tonight. As my thanks."

"Your thanks," he repeated.

"For making me look so beautiful in the painting."

"I painted you as I saw you."

"I know." The grin that lit her face made his ribs feel strangely bruised. "That's why it's wonderful."

"Well," he said. For the life of him, he couldn't account for the extent to which she'd discomposed him. He glanced down at the paper-wrapped package he'd carried to the bed, the pièce de résistance of his campaign to change her mind. "I suppose this means you don't want your present."

"A present! For me?" She erased any doubts he might have had by snatching the bundle from his hand. The paper tore beneath eager fingers as she uncovered the object wrapped inside. "Oh," she said, holding it up to catch the light. The bottle was round and fat, the glass cobalt blue with a branch of almond flowers molded on its belly. "It's so pretty."

"It's oil," he said, pleased by her delight.

Her nose wrinkled in confusion. "Oil?"

"Not for cooking, Duchess. For massage."

"Oh," she said, then again, with a lascivious rise and dip. "Ohhh. For massage. I'm sure I can put this to good use."

"I'm going to use it on you," he clarified, reaching to take it back.

Eyes dancing with mischief, she hugged the bottle to her breast. "No, no, no. You gave this to me. That means I can do with it as I please and what I please is to please you."

Lust poured like hot, thick treacle through his veins. His trousers, normally well fitted, drew tight with the hard, tenting jab of his erection. He'd thought of oiling her, of smoothing his hands along each inch of satiny, freckled skin. He'd dreamed of it as he perused the apothecary's shelves, imagining how she'd sigh, growing heavy inside his clothes.

That arousal was a spark compared to the bonfire he felt now. He was hot all over, his skin fevered, his pulse drumming hard between his legs. A sense of alarm accompanied the heat. He could not recall wanting anyone this badly—certainly not so far into an affair.

Mary, naturally, took note of his condition. Her nipples pushed against the dressing gown, a response that fanned his need.

She eyed his prodigious bulge with a humor he wished he shared. "I see you like the idea of being oiled. Of course"—she put her head to the side, almost resting it on her shoulder—"you'll have to instruct me. So I know precisely what you like."

"Precisely?" he rasped.

"Precisely," she confirmed, then caught her upper lip in her lower teeth. No gesture could have conveyed her nervousness better, or her resolve to overcome it. A delicious pang speared upward through his cock, making the tip feel as if it were being pinched.

"I'll tell you what I wish," he said, a whisper as soft as it was rough.

"Would you—" She swallowed and began again. "Would you show me?"

His eyebrows rose before he could stop them. She wanted him to show her?

"I liked when you did that before," she said, the words falling over each other in embarrassment. "That night when I couldn't get my fire lit and you . . . touched yourself. I liked that and I thought maybe you wouldn't mind doing it again. You know, without your clothes on."

The smile he was fighting pressed his lips together. "You liked that."

She nodded earnestly. "I thought it was exciting."

He had to lower his head or give himself away. "I don't know, Mary. I'd have to be very relaxed to do something like that in front of you."

"Oh, I can manage relaxing you." She waved her hand in dismissal. "No harder than rubbing down a horse—or, er, so I've heard."

His laugh came out a snort. He felt like a horse, a randy, mare-sniffing stud who'd been locked in his stall for days. He rose from the bed and faced her. "Shall I undress then?"

"Oh, yes." She shifted around on her knees to get a better view. "That would be very helpful."

His eyes crinkled. "How flattering you are."

"Nothing of the sort! Only a nun wouldn't want to watch."

But she was flattering. His grin broadened as he disrobed. He could not have had a more attentive audience, or one more appreciative. Without hesitation, he offered her his enjoyment of his own body, his love of being watched. He knew she shared that love, no matter how reluctant she was to admit it. Tonight, for her, he would hold nothing back. Her eyes were like saucers when he touched himself through his clothes, squeezing the weight between his legs as he'd done for her once before. That he knew she liked, for she squirmed from side to side and clenched her hands atop her thighs. Watching her watch him was almost too arousing. He had to cut his fondling short for fear of slipping over the edge.

When he peeled his shirt slowly over his head, she blinked to clear her vision. Thumbing his nipples into prominence set her jaw agape. And she actually gasped when he pushed his trousers down his legs.

"Look at you." She spread her hands as if drawing attention to a wonder. "Who could tire of such a show?"

"Not you, I hope," he said and climbed into bed to kiss her.

Her body was warm and pliant, her mouth a clinging haven for his tongue. He rolled her beneath him and gloried in the press of flesh on flesh. As always, her firmness undid him. He slid his hand around the peach-ripe curve of her bottom, tickling her hair, seeking the tactile evidence of her lust. When he found it, a soft, feminine noise broke in her throat. That was a sound he would never tire of. Sighing with delight, he wriggled his finger deeper.

Before he could explore her fully, Mary put both palms on his chest and pushed.

"No," she said, "I'm supposed to be pleasing you."

Only those words could have stopped him. Amused and painfully aroused, he let her push him onto his back, let her spread his limbs out from his sides and tuck a pillow beneath his neck. She sat back on her heels between his legs. Currents of air brushed his groin, making him feel even more naked, even more sensitized. His shaft surged up and down as it were trying to reach her.

Mary seemed satisfied with her handiwork.

"That's better," she said, cradling the cobalt bottle between her breasts. "Now I can touch you as I please."

He could barely speak through the constriction of his throat. "That's what I've been waiting for. For you to do as you please. That's the thing I've wanted but haven't gotten."

"Oh," she said and laughed softly, "how fortuitous."

They smiled at each other, a hushed, hanging moment that felt— oddly enough—like friendship. For all his experience, Nic had not known this before. The feeling was good and warm, but it hurt a little, too, as if there could never quite be enough of it. Her eyes glittered briefly and then she grinned, full out, her face creasing with silent laughter. Her arm rose and tipped the bottle. The oil dribbled onto his breastbone. Warmed by her body, it rolled over his skin like cream.

She rubbed it toward his shoulders with her palms, sweeping around his pectorals, circling his jangled nipples with her thumbs. "I love your chest," she murmured, as if every tendon in his body had not gone taut. "Your muscles are so lean, and you don't have too much hair to see them."

"Pleased to oblige," he gasped with the ragged ghost of his voice.

Her strokes were long and strong. Once the first shock of contact faded, her hands seemed to stretch his muscles and pull them loose, easing tensions he hadn't known were there. She soothed the sides of his neck, then the back, then drew tight, oiled hands down the length of his tingling arms. When the pads of her fingers slid over his palms, his toes curled toward his feet.

"Good?" she whispered.

He groaned and closed his eyes. Her hands were magic: not too soft, not too hard. She seemed to have an instinct for his anatomy, knowing just where to dig to find a hidden knot. His erection eased but did not disappear, a pleasant throb now, a hunger that could wait. She shifted back to massage his legs, lifting them one at a time to work the muscles underneath. He shivered when she found the sweet spots on his feet, her thumb sliding firmly between each humming bone.

"Ah, Mary," he sighed, his spine arching uncontrollably, "this is heaven."

She kissed his instep, then laid down his leg and braced her hands on his thighs to scoot in closer. Roused from his stupor, Nic pushed himself upright. From heavy, pleasure-glazed eyes, he studied the architect of his bliss. Mary had tied her hair back with a ribbon, but her efforts on his behalf had inspired a predictable disarray. Tendrils curled wildly around her face. Her lips were soft, her freckles blurred by a wash of pink. She looked a wholly sensual creature, a woman awake to her sexual self. He'd wanted to see her like this since they met.

"Now," she said, "this is the part where you show me what you like."

Her fingertips feathered the bone at the top of his thighs, half tease, half nervous gesture. He knew he'd have to tread cautiously from now on.

"You want me to touch myself," he said, measuring the effect of every word. "You want me to put my hand on my cock and masturbate while you watch."

Her cheeks flamed scarlet but she did not deny his claim.

"Yes," she said firmly, "but *I* want to finish you."

"And you'll follow my instructions?"

She squared her shoulders. "To the letter."

Her pluck inspired both admiration and humor. "You needn't, you know." He touched her heated face. "Not if I ask for something you don't like."

She opened her mouth, then licked her upper lip in hesitation. "Could we pretend I had to? I think I'd feel more at ease."

Nic squinted in surprise. Mary's request was unexpected, to say the least. He'd seen more than a little evidence of her will. That she would want to take orders from him—even in play—stirred his interest deeply. He was careful, however, not to let his amazement show. A sexual wish was a fragile thing. It had to be treated with respect.

"I believe I would like that," he said and held his hand out for the oil.

MERRY WASN'T CERTAIN SHE COULD EXPLAIN HER OWN behavior. She only knew that, for their final time together, she wanted to surrender something more profound than her virginity. That had been a scrap of flesh. This was a piece of her soul. Offering it was reckless, perhaps, but she'd always regretted the things she hadn't done more than the things she had.

With a quiver of anticipation, she tipped a puddle of oil into his palm. He curled his fingers over it in protection.

"Look at me," he said, his voice darkening the way it did when he was aroused. "I want you to know what your eyes can do."

She looked at him: at the flush on his prominent cheekbones, at the pulse beating visibly in his neck. His chest rose and fell as she took in the whorls of sheer black hair, the coppery discs of his nipples, the small, sharp points within. His borrowed robe lay heavy on her breasts but she did not want to remove it. All these weeks she'd posed for him . . .

Let him be naked, she thought. Let him display himself for me.

His gaze locked on her face as he clenched the hand she'd filled with oil. His sex had relaxed while she massaged him, but now— within the space of breaths—it rose again, lengthening, thickening, until his fist hung over a pulsing crest. The marvel of his body's transformation made her hold her breath. He had not lied. All she had to do was look at him. He tilted his wrist. Oil ran out in a golden thread. It hit the stretched red skin, spilling over, spilling down. His second hand caught it at the bottom.

The scent of almonds perfumed the air.

"Watch," he said, as if she needed to be told. "Watch how I touch myself."

The fist he'd closed around the base pulled slowly, strongly upward, moving the loose outer skin onto the bulbous head. As soon as the tip slipped free of his hold, his second hand followed, oiling him even more. Again he did this, and again: the motion smooth, the pressure tight, until his erection shone like polished wood. Then he stopped and let Merry stare.

Her heart knocked in her chest. His shaft was fat and dark, flushed now along its length and vibrating with excitement. She could see every texture, every individual dip and swell. His penis could not be mistaken for anything but a part of the human body. Not marble. Not jade. This was living flesh, inextricably linked to the basest, most primitive functions of the male.

Its very meanness made her love it. She'd never seen anything more personal in her life.

"It's beautiful," she said, and the sack beneath his organ jumped.

"I'd like you to help me," he said, sounding as if his throat were filled with gravel. "Wrap your hand around the base. I want you to hold the skin taut while I rub."

He had read her unspoken desire, her unbearable urge to touch. She reached for the root of him, shaking now, almost afraid to do as he asked. He inhaled sharply when she wrapped him in her hand.

"Now push," he said, making it an order. "Stretch the skin back toward my balls."

She pushed until she bumped the swell of his testicles, using her strength to stretch his satiny outer skin, trying to match the force she'd seen him apply. He shuddered in her grip, but did not wince, and she knew she had not hurt him. She could not doubt he liked what she was doing. His brow and lip had beaded up with sweat. A thrill of power streaked up her arm. She was doing this to him: with her hand, with her eyes. Her sex pulsed, tight inside, as if a fist held her as well.

"Yes," he said, the praise a growl. "Now watch."

She could not help but watch; he was so close to her, pleasuring himself while she held his skin in opposition to his strokes. She didn't know why this increased his enjoyment, but it very clearly did. His body was tense, his respiration rigidly controlled. The music of his breath flowed through her like the act of love. In and out. Draw and blow. Old paint, green and yellow, clung beneath the nails of his graceful fingers. She watched where they rubbed, where they tightened until the tips grew white. The twisting rivers of his veins stood out from the flush of his phallic skin. She followed their rise up the thickened underridge, over the flaring neck to the smooth pink lip where they disappeared. His forefinger dug into a wrinkled fan of skin beneath the crown. His shaft quivered. His thighs twitched. There, she thought. That he really likes. Quivering herself, she pressed her lips between her teeth. His blind little eye was weeping a pearly tear.

She gasped for air. "I want to do it. I want to pleasure you."

He stopped, then released himself and put her second hand where his had been. Sensation jolted through her. He was hot. Pulsing. Slick from the scented oil. She pulled as he had pulled, not as smoothly perhaps, but with just as much concentration. Apparently, her technique was good enough. He sighed deeply and let his head roll on his neck. His shaft was like a hardened muscle, stiff inside but with a bit of give. Determined to do her best, she tightened the V of her thumb and forefinger when it crossed the sensitive spot beneath his crown. He responded to her touch the same as he had to his.

When she lifted her gaze, she found him watching her, his gray eyes quiet but intense. His skin was swarthy with arousal. His lips looked swollen, though they hadn't been kissing hard. When he licked them, she felt as if he licked her.

"You want something," she said, with an instinct as old as time. "Tell me, Nic. Tell me and I'll try to do it."

He hesitated.

"Tell me," she insisted, and swept her thumb across his crown. "Order me."

He laughed, a mere rush of breath. Then his face hardened.

"I want you to kiss it," he said. "I want you to take me in your mouth."

The words were gruff, not precisely an order but close. They created an image as stark as it was shocking. Surely she couldn't do this, couldn't draw that ferocious organ into her mouth. She wanted to, though. As soon as he said it, she grew wet.

Pretend, she thought. Pretend you must do what he says. Then whatever happens, however awkward you are, he has only himself to blame. Despite the injunction, she did not trust her voice. She nodded instead, a quick jerk with her teeth clenched tight together.

At her agreement, Nic's breath rushed out so swiftly his belly hollowed beneath his ribs. With the choppy motions of impatience, he shoved a pair of pillows behind his back.

"Do it," he said, more forcefully now. "I want to watch you suck me."

She did not close her eyes. Chin trembling, she lipped the flare, then slid the silky crown between her lips. The taste, the feel was indescribable. Softer than soft. Smoother than smooth. His fingers slipped between her knuckles, then covered the hand that held his shaft. His palm was warm and steadying. He'll tell me, she thought. He'll tell me if I do it wrong.

"Take a little more," he whispered, his thighs suddenly shaking. "I promise I won't . . . push too far."

When she did as he asked, he sighed as if she'd granted his dearest wish. He was hot in her mouth, alive. He tasted of almonds, of salt and skin. It seemed natural to lick him, to suckle this tender fullness to the limit of their hands' grip.

He gasped at the change of pressure, then stroked the tangle of her hair as if tempted to grab it. Even if this had not given him away, she would have sensed the rise of his excitement in the leaping of the flesh beneath their hands.

"Tighter," he said, compressing her sweaty fingers with his own. "Don't let me come."

She hadn't known she could stop him, but the thought that she could hold him on that edge seared her with aching fire.

"Here," he rasped, moving her hand to circle the top of his scrotum. "Squeeze and tug."

His testicles felt like two boiled eggs, odd and firm within the wrinkled skin. She had to pull them down, away from his body, to hold him as he asked. He grunted when she did it, then lifted his hips and pushed himself slowly into her mouth. His legs were drawn up, his heels providing leverage.

"Yes," he said, his own hand falling away. "That's good."

He drew back until her lips tightened around the flare. The tip of him was sleek and ripe. She licked it, circled it, gathering salt and shudders. When she dug into the little eye, he moaned and pushed again.

"Slow," he urged, though he was the one who moved. "Slow and easy."

But perhaps the advice was meant for him. He began to build a rhythm, gentle, careful, but with a tension behind it she could not miss.

He's making love to my mouth, she thought, amazed and aflame with the power he'd placed in her hands. He trembled like the victim of a fever, inside her, against her, fighting with all his strength to prolong the pleasure, to protect her from the violence of his need. She couldn't remember feeling anything so exciting.

"Don't swallow," he whispered. "Get me wet."

She let her saliva paint him, let it wrap him in liquid bliss.

"Yes-s," he said, a drawn-out hiss as his buttocks tightened on the sheets. "Oh, yes."

He was as lost as he'd ever been to his work, his eyes drifting shut, his fingers kneading and releasing in her hair. She was lost herself: to the pleasure of giving pleasure, to the lingering push and pull, to the smell and the taste and the stunning sense of trust. He'd surrendered himself completely. She could not disappoint him. With her free arm braced outside his hip, she let her head sink even lower. Her body began to sway.

"Can't," he gasped, pressing hard against her palate. "Can't last much longer. You—" He inhaled sharply and pulled back. "You can let go. You don't have to finish me in your mouth."

But she grasped his shaft, holding the crest against her lip.

"I want to," she said, letting the words buzz his most sensitive skin. His eyes fluttered open and searched her face. His fingertips touched her jaw.

"I want to," she repeated and eased him back inside.

He groaned at the slow engulfment and again at the tight withdrawal. He left it to her then: to move, to pull, to rub and tease the spots she'd seen him rub himself. His hands fisted in her hair and her name was a prayerful curse. The taste of him was heady. She did not hurry but soon he swelled against her tongue, as smooth and hard as heated glass.

"Ah," he said, a panicked cry that trembled in his throat. "Ah, Mary!"

She was glad she held his shaft because he could not restrain that final thrust. He stiffened and pushed and came in pulsing bursts. She felt each spasm, each surge and twitch. The experience was both peculiar and enthralling. Never had she been so close to his pleasure. Never had she felt it as if it were her own. His thighs pressed her shoulders, then fell away. As tired as if she'd come herself, she leaned her head against his hip.

"Mary," he said, the sound rich and low. He stroked a curl behind her ear. "Come here where I can hold you."

She groaned, then wriggled upward to the stack of pillows. His arms came around her, easing her head onto his shoulder, a spot that seemed fashioned just for her. The rise and fall of his chest was like the rocking of a cradle. When he rubbed her back, she thought she'd drift straight off to sleep.

"Thank you," he said, and she couldn't help but smile at his heartfelt tone. "I'll see to you," he added, somewhat drowsily. "Just give me a minute to get my strength."

Merry didn't mind a wait, or even a dismissal. Despite her own arousal, she was content. She knew a different kind of satisfaction, one that drowned out everything but the present. Any concern for her departure seemed a distant thing. Yes, she would have to leave. She'd gotten what she'd come for. Tomorrow's show would ensure her public ruin. She didn't expect her parents' reaction to be pleasant, but she knew they'd be far more understanding if she did not stay with Nic. He himself had reminded her of the limits of their affair. If she didn't end it, he would. Better she should leave before she found herself losing not just her reputation but her family. Being a pariah she thought she could manage. Being disowned she could not bear.

But these were worries for another day. Tonight she had pleased him, and pleased him well. Maybe in the weeks to come she'd regret having given herself so freely. Maybe she'd wish she'd kept a tighter rein on her heart. In time, however, she was sure this night with Nic would become a pleasant memory for her scrapbook: wistful, perhaps, but not repented.

She was strong, after all, resourceful and resilient. She had never known a pain too great to stand. For goodness sake, how long had it been since she'd spared a thought for Edward Burbrooke? Ages, it seemed.

She refused to believe losing Nic would be any different.

NIC DIDN'T MEAN TO FALL ASLEEP — CERTAINLY NOT BEFORE he'd seen to Mary—but his well-pleasured body did not consult him. When he stirred again, the light outside was a dusky rose. Mary lay across him, her hair a tangled blanket for them both. Her pubis warmed his hip while the curve of her thigh nestled beside his penis. It was a lovely, abandoned sprawl, made even more meaningful by the fact that she was awake. Her fingers played lightly in his chest hair, the gentle touch almost enough to soothe him back to sleep.

"Mm," he sighed, a moan so happy he barely knew it as his own.

She propped her chin on her forearms and kissed his jaw. "Hello, sleeping beauty."

"Hello, waking beauty."

Even now, she wrinkled her nose at the compliment, making the bump at the end turn up. He pushed her curls from her endearing little face. Just looking at her made him happy, at peace in a way he hadn't felt for quite some time. The knowledge forced a decision he didn't see any way to avoid. No matter his long-standing dread of romantic attachment, no matter his fears of letting his lovers down: this particular affair was too rewarding to let go. Sebastian was right. Mary was good for him. And maybe, at least for now, he was good for her.

"I know that look," she said, meeting his grin with a furrow of suspicion. "You're planning something."

He wrapped his arms behind her waist. "Not planning precisely. Hoping. I'm not ready to let you go, Mary. I want you to come with me to Venice."

"Oh," she said, scarcely the response he was looking for. She pushed away from him and sat up. "Venice. That's—that's very flattering, but—"

"I could paint you there." He dragged his hand slowly down her breast. "In a gondola. Drifting down the Grand Canal. You said you never got to travel. Venice isn't the Forbidden City, but it's very beautiful. And we could go to Rome. That was on your list, wasn't it?"

"Yes," she said and pressed her palm to her heart. "Nic." Shakily, she laughed. "You don't know how touched I am that you remembered. Or how honored I feel that you'd want to keep me longer than you usually keep your lovers. I wish I could accept. I really do."

"You could if you wanted to."

"It's not that simple."

Abruptly grumpy, Nic sat up and pounded a pillow behind his back. "Is it the expense? Because, as far as I'm concerned, you've earned it."

"No." She shook her head, her eyes shining with regret. "It's not the expense. My reasons are personal."

"And that means?"

"It means I don't want to discuss them."

"You're tired of me." He didn't believe it, but he had to say the words. Her speechless response was all his pride could wish.

"Of course I'm not," she said once she'd recovered. "How could I be? Good Lord, most women go a lifetime without meeting someone as skilled in bed as you." Her chin drew up with the stubbornness he'd grown to love. "Staying simply isn't possible for me and I don't want to spoil our last night by arguing about it. Please, Nic, let's not end what we've shared with a fight."

Only a cad could have refused her. He cupped her slender shoulders, his thumbs smoothing the muscle, his fingers drinking in her skin.

"Anytime you change your mind," he said, "I'd be happy to take you back."

The promise was one he'd never offered in his life. For him, once an affair was over, it was over. The lapse might have frightened him if he'd actually thought she would accept. Instead, she whispered his name and slid her arms around his back. Her lips found his ear, then his cheek, then the deep, drawing welcome of his mouth. The kiss was another plea to remember what they'd shared, to keep their last night sweet.

Nic could not resist it. Forcing his anger away, he lost himself in what was easy, in what he'd always known he was good at.

He might not be able to keep Mary Colfax, but he could damn well make her miss him.

Chapter 12

TATLING'S, THE PICTURE GALLERY, HAD ITS PREMISES ON Bond Street. It was an old brick building, five stories tall and extremely solid in appearance. Lighter blocks of stone encased the display window and formed a medieval-looking arch around the door. The effect was one of respectability and discretion, both of which were bound to be tried today.

Her stomach queasy, Merry let Nic hand her down from the carriage. His face was set in a glower, as it had been all morning. She supposed she should have been flattered that her refusal to stay with him had put him out of sorts. Maybe later when this was behind her she would be. For now, though, his mood merely added to her tension.

She wished she hadn't promised she would attend. She feared last night would make a far better parting memory.

Of course, letting him come alone would have been a disgraceful display of cowardice. She had walked into his studio—indeed, she had walked into his arms—with her eyes wide open. The least she could do was stand by him to face the public consequences of her acts.

If she secretly hoped there would not be any today, that was only because she was human.

She lifted her skirts to cross the pavement. "Oh, look," she said, feigning a lightness she did not feel, "they've put one of your pictures in the window."

It was a modern scene of couples strolling down the new Thames Embankment. Fog softened the figures' edges while a curving line of gaslights swirled like specters in the mist. It was an eerie picture, as different from his Godiva as it could be, though Nic's touch was apparent in the skillful handling of the light.

"It's almost menacing," she said, "the way that fog rolls off the river."

Nic grunted, then seemed to think better of his rudeness. "Won't sell," he said, "though the brushwork's good enough."

I'd buy it, she nearly said, then realized anew he wouldn't believe she could.

I ought to tell him who I am, she thought. Her face went cold at the idea, but her fear was worse than pointless. If she waited, the discovery would be worse and, really, she had no more excuses. He wouldn't stop the show now; he had to fulfill his obligations to the gallery. If she told him, before someone else could, at least he wouldn't feel so much a fool.

Resolved, she touched his sleeve with a shaking hand.

"Nic," she said.

When he turned to her, his face immediately softened.

"I'm being a beast, aren't I?" he said, misconstruing her tone completely. "And you've done nothing to deserve it." The corners of his mouth turned up as he covered her glove with his. "I'm sorry, Duchess. I'm going to miss you more than I expected and my temper's gone to hell."

Blast, Merry thought, assailed with guilt at the irony of him offering her an apology. She pulled a breath of courage into her lungs.

"Nic," she began again, "there's something I need to—"

The gallery door opened before she could get the confession out.

"There you are," said a dapper young man in a sober suit. "I was beginning to wonder if you'd arrive before the crowd."

Her pulse still unsteady, Merry pulled herself together as Nic introduced Mr. Tatling. He was the grandson of the gallery's founder and, from what she could tell, a sharp individual in his own right. His eyes didn't even flicker at being made acquainted with Nic's model— though it was obvious from Nic's manner that she was more. Whatever his private thoughts, Mr. Tatling's bow to Mary Colfax was as respectful as any she'd received as Merry Vance.

"Enchanted," he said with a pleasant smile. "So glad you were able to come."

He led them quickly through the exhibition, which was spread among three rooms. Capacious and high-ceilinged, they were furnished in the style of a nice, upper-middle-class home. Looking around, she found nothing pretentious, nothing in bad taste—and just enough comfort to make visitors relax. Small floral arrangements enlivened a few of the polished tables, their colors clearly chosen to match Nic's work. Merry thought it all looked very welcoming, especially the waiting samovars of tea.

"We can shift anything you like," Tatling said, "but I think you'll agree this arrangement allows the pieces to complement each other."

Nic nodded his approval, then returned to the largest parlor, where the Godiva stood on a separate, gilded easel. He stopped in front of her and stared, two fingers pressed pensively to his lips. Mr. Tatling moved quietly behind his shoulder.

"Makes a nice centerpiece," he said. "As you might expect, we were quite elated when we unwrapped her. We're asking seven thousand."

Even Merry's jaw dropped at that.

"You're mad!" Nic exclaimed. "The most Leighton ever got was six."

Tatling shrugged, his eyes dancing with the excitement of a salesman born. "Mr. Leighlon didn't paint your Godiva. Besides, wealthy people like to brag about what they spend."

"Maybe so," said Nic, "but that's a bloody fortune."

The gallery owner's response was cut short by the tinkling of a bell above the door.

"Bother," he said, suddenly discomposed. "I was hoping Ruskin wouldn't come till later."

Curious, Merry turned to see the famous critic. Though dressed like a parson, he was a handsome man, slim and well-formed with thick red hair lightly touched by gray. Beneath his shaggy brows, his eyes were pale and burning.

Nic gave him a casual glance, then turned away as if his presence could not have mattered less. He guided her into an alcove and pulled her a cup of tea. "You had something you wanted to tell me?"

No, no, no, thought Merry. They were not going to have this discussion with that critic in the room. She'd heard stories about Ruskin: that he was so obsessed with female purity he hadn't been able to consummate his marriage. Seemed the sight of his wife's pubic hair had thrown him into shock. He'd thought women were like statues: smooth and perfect and free of the slightest sordid taint.

She finished her tea in a scalding gulp and set it down. The last thing Nic needed was to be distracted by her confession when he had to confront a man like that.

"I'll tell you later," she said, "after that critic leaves."

This answer amused Nic, but, for Merry, waiting for Ruskin to go was torture. Every time the street door opened, her muscles tightened into knots, wondering if this visitor or the next would be the one she knew. She could scarcely bear to watch who wandered near the Go-diva. They'll know, she thought. Even if they don't know me, they'll know I'm the model when they see me next to Nic.

As if sensing her embarrassment, Nic did not introduce her to the people who stopped to chat. A few squinted at her, but no one said a word. She was glad she'd worn her plain green gown with the prissy collar. With luck, she might be mistaken for an employee of the gallery.

For his part, Nic was surprisingly at ease. He mingled here as gracefully as he had among Anna's friends. If Merry had not known, she'd never have guessed his living depended on the patronage of the people to whom he spoke. Whether well-born or simply well-heeled, he behaved as if he were their equal, with neither condescension nor undue pride.

It was a side of his character she'd caught glimpses of before, one light-years distant from the tortured soul who'd torn his hair out over flaws no one but he could see. He's earned this self-assurance, she thought, because the memory of those struggles tells him he's done his best.

She'd known titled men who did not approach his quiet poise.

Even Ruskin did not throw him. The critic wound back to them after touring all the rooms, his parson's brow marred by a tiny frown.

"You have a fine grasp of realism," he said, his voice judicious and low and just a trifle pompous. "You'd do well, however, to cultivate a bit more spiritual meaning. Perhaps you could take a leaf from Mr. Holman Hunt's book?"

"Or Mr. Millais's?" Nic suggested just as gravely. He'd inclined his head so that only Merry could see the devil in his eye. She remembered then that Millais was the artist who'd married Ruskin's rejected wife.

The critic cleared his throat. "Of course. John Millais is also a great talent."

As soon as Ruskin left, Merry punched Nic's shoulder.

"You're awful," she exclaimed. "That poor man!"

He didn't question that she knew the scandal, and why should he when it was so juicy? "Poor indeed," he chuckled. "Effie Ruskin was a treasure. In any case, I wouldn't have said it if he hadn't advised me to copy Hunt." He shuddered. "Lurid tripe is the kindest description I have for his work."

"Nonetheless," she said, even as a smile broke through her censure.

Catching the smile, Nic reached out to squeeze her hand. Whatever he'd meant to say was lost in an exclamation of concern.

"Good Lord, Mary! Your fingers are bits of ice." Oblivious to whoever might be watching, he stripped off her gloves and chafed her hands against his chest. "What is it, love? Are you worried you'll be recognized from the painting? You shouldn't be, you know. If people think anything at all, it will only be that I'm lucky."

If Merry hadn't been so overwrought, she would have laughed. She was here precisely to be recognized. A thousand times she'd imagined how she'd lift her chin to meet the first pair of knowing eyes, how she'd dare them to say anything, how she'd demonstrate with every line of her body that she wasn't the least ashamed.

The only thing she hadn't imagined was how hard it would be to do.

"I'm fine," she said, her jaw tightened to forestall a threatened chattering of her teeth.

Unconvinced, Nic brushed her cheek with the back of his hand. "I'm sure Tatling would let you rest in his office."

She shook her head so hard, her chignon wobbled. "No," she said. "I'm not a coward."

And then the bell above the door rang, as if to prove the lie. Merry jumped, then went cold from head to toe.

The duke and duchess of Monmouth were entering from the street.

She could not catch her breath. It stuck in her throat along with her heart, making it impossible to swallow. Of all the outcomes she'd imagined, facing her parents was the last. She'd thought someone else would carry the tale to them: one of her schoolmates, or one of her mother's gossipy friends. She'd thought she might have time to flee to Isabel in Wales, so as not to be home while their outrage was the fiercest.

How blind she'd been! How willfully, stupidly blind!

She should have guessed her father would be interested in the painter who had so recently—and so skillfully—done his portrait. As for her mother: what could be more natural than that she'd wish to come along? Nic was society's darling, his work as fashionable as Lavinia's sable-trimmed paletot.

Frozen in place, she watched the duchess hand that coat to the gallery's pretty maid. A cloud of panic filled her breast, one so alien to her experience she almost didn't recognize what it was. It felt like a heart spasm. In fact, she wished it were.

In a moment, her mother would turn, and her father, and— Lord!—there was Ernest behind them, her ever-hopeful, would-be fiancé.

Her nails were digging holes straight through her skin.

Oh, God, why hadn't she told Nic the truth when she had the chance?

Something snapped inside her that had never snapped before. She, whose courage had always been equal to any challenge, could not in the end face this, not now, not in front of Nic. Grabbing his arm, she dragged him bodily from the room, through the second gallery, and the third, to a door that led to a tiny scullery. Tea things waited in the dimness: dirty cups, tins of oolong and pekoe.

Nic rubbed his wrist when she let it go.

"All right," he said, his eyes worried, his mouth prepared to laugh, "why don't you tell me what's the matter?"

My parents are here, she meant to say. *I'm the daughter of a duke. I've been using you to ruin myself so they can't force me into marriage and I've probably embroiled you in a scandal people will talk about for years. If you're lucky, my brothers won't thrash you for it. If you're not, my father will try to run you out of town. I've been selfish, you see, and shortsighted and even though I thought I thought this through, it's painfully clear I didn't. You don't deserve this and I wouldn't blame you if you hated me forever.*

The thought of that, of him hating her, closed her throat around the words.

"I've changed my mind," she gasped. "I want to go to Venice."

She knew she was doing wrong, knew it in every fiber of her being. Running away was shameful, not to mention a mere postponement of the inevitable. In spite of which, as soon as she made the declaration, a terrible weight lifted off her shoulders. What matter if she'd have to face the same disaster later? Time was what she needed. To think. To plan. To be with Nic. Indeed, in that moment, delay seemed a gift from the Almighty.

Nic shook his head, his expression confused but tinged with dawning hope. Overwhelmed by a flood of conflicting emotions, Merry flung her arms around his neck.

"Please," she begged, "please let's go to Venice."

He slid his palms from the bend of her elbows up her arms. Merry bounced with impatience. "Goodness." He smiled. "You can't mean you want to leave this instant?"

"No," she said, her voice gone husky and suggestive, "this instant I want to go home."

She heard his breath catch, a small, flattering sound. His eyes darkened, and then his mouth took hers. It was a kiss so raw, so powerful, it literally made her forget everything but him. He crushed them together from chest to knee, his hands tight on her bottom, his arousal a burning ridge beneath his clothes. He rubbed it against her, groaning his pleasure into her mouth.

She could not doubt he was happy with her decision.

"Now?" he asked, a smoldering rasp against her cheek.

"Yes," she answered and tugged him toward the alley door.

He did not suggest they get their coats, nor say good-bye to Mr. Tatling. Nic was a creature of the flesh. When they emerged into the icy air, he simply laughed and began to run.

NIC CRAVEN'S PAINTING DISTURBED THE DUCHESS OF MONmouth more than she could express, like something soft and wet being dragged across her skin. It was too aggressively sexual to view without a wince, its very beauty an affront. Horrid, she thought, though one couldn't say that without having heard the judgment of one's peers. They might decide such a stance was unsophisticated, and where would that leave her? Realizing her hands were clutched together at her waist, Lavinia forced them to relax.

Whatever she did, she must not cause a scene.

Even then, she could not tear her gaze away. Dimly, she was aware of the chatter that surrounded them. This picture, slyly titled "Godiva's Ride," was causing a sensation. Well-dressed men and women chirped with titillation or disgust. Or both. It was "Ruskin said this" and "Craven said that" and "Did you hear what Tatling is asking? I doubt even the prince would pay seven thousand!"

Beside her, her husband jerked at the sum. "Seven thousand *pounds*?"

Lavinia barely heard him. A tide was rising inside her that took all her strength to contain, a fury that bubbled up from her very core.

How dare Mr. Craven suggest women could live like this hoyden, this Godiva, and be the better for it? Lavinia knew for a fact they couldn't. Her one fall from grace haunted her even now.

A woman's sins were never forgotten.

Only men escaped reprisal.

Behind her, Ernest Althorp shuffled closer. She'd asked him along in order to share the news from Merry's latest letter—in the expectation, of course, that he'd relay it to his father. Merry was softening. Anyone who read her words could see it. Lavinia had been grateful for the alacrity with which Ernest accepted her invitation, not to mention his willingness to see, as she did, much cause for hope.

Now, however, his blocky masculine presence made her want to scream.

Men were swine. This stupid, lascivious painting merely proved it.

"Hm," said Ernest, peering thoughtfully around her, "looks a bit like Merry."

Lavinia turned her head to gape at him while a sensation like a hundred icy spiders crawled up her spine.

Ernest flushed beneath her stare. "Er, I mean, around the hair a bit and maybe the, er, nose. But of course it isn't her." He stood straighter and filled his chest. "Merry would never pose for a thing like this."

"No, she wouldn't," said Lavinia, her tone chill. She wasn't even sorry when he flinched.

Merry wouldn't. More importantly, Merry couldn't. Merry was in Wales. With Isabel. They'd received a letter just this morning. So that couldn't be Merry's nose or Merry's hair or the mischievous glint in Merry's eye. Lavinia's daughter was no siren. She was a horse-mad tomboy. A *freckled,* horse-mad tomboy . . .

Who'd ridden astride as often as she had sidesaddle . . .

Who'd been more than angry enough at her parents to do something truly rash . . .

Who'd depended on Isabel to cover up pranks before.

Good Lord.

The spiders skittered back down Lavinia's spine. She was breathing too quickly but couldn't seem to stop. Some time had passed since she'd studied her daughter's knees but, unless she was very happily mistaken, Godiva's knobby joints were a shocking good match for Merry's.

She took but a second to decide what she had to do.

"I'm buying this painting," she announced, her voice too high but level.

When her husband widened his eyes at her, she lifted her head and spoke with even more authority. "It's a masterpiece. Worth every shilling."

"I agree it's good . . ." Geoffrey hedged, but she hadn't the patience to hear him out. If Ernest was right, if this was a naked portrait of her daughter, she couldn't afford to let it sit here another minute. Even if it *wasn't* Meredith, she couldn't afford to. Someone else might remark on the resemblance. The duchess's situation was too precarious to weather the slightest breath of scandal.

She had to buy it and she had to buy it now.

"I'll pay for it myself," she said, shocking Geoffrey to a blank and blinking silence, "out of the estate my mother left me."

With the air of supreme entitlement she'd known how to draw on all her life, she took the portrait by its carved and gilded frame and lifted it from its perch. She heard the seam under her sleeve rip as she did, but cared no more for that than for the buzz of exclamations spreading around the room.

"Let me help you," said Ernest. He reached for the frame but she ignored him.

"Where's Tatling?" she called above the noise. "Tell him I'm offering eight."

The painting banged against her ankle as she carried it through the crowd, heavier than she expected and quite unwieldy. Lavinia cursed the thing in her mind. It couldn't be Merry, simply couldn't.

But if it was, she'd make bloody damn sure no one ever found out but her.

"CARE TO EXPLAIN WHY YOU MADE SUCH A SPECTACLE OF yourself?" asked her husband, once their coachman dropped Ernest off.

His tone was calm but his arms were crossed over his chest and a muscle beat like a pulse beneath his beard.

Lavinia tugged her gloves farther up her hands. Her heart felt like a bird trapped in her throat. "I can't imagine what you mean."

"Can't you?"

"No, I cannot. I wanted that painting and I bought it. With my own funds, I might add."

"I'm not concerned about the money, Lavi. I think you know I'm happy to buy you what you wish. What I don't understand is your behavior. You haven't been yourself since Merry left."

"Don't be silly, darling. Who else would I be if not myself?"

Her airy laughter did not convince him. "Whatever is wrong, I wish you'd tell me."

"All I did was buy a *painting*."

He stared a moment longer, a shadow of worry behind his eyes. Before he could voice it, she turned away. She hated lying to him— truly, she did—but better a lie than seeing her world destroyed.

Too easily she remembered Althorp's grip around her neck.

Chapter 13

IT WAS NIC'S IDEA TO MAKE A SEA VOYAGE. TRAINS WERE dusty and cramped, he said, and unreliable on the Continent. According to him, a week on the Mediterranean, on a comfortable commercial yacht, could not fail to entertain her.

No doubt this would have been true if Merry hadn't proved an ill-starred sailor. To her supreme mortification, no sooner had she stepped on board than her stomach began to lurch. By the time the gleaming ship had steamed into the Channel, she was a miserable, retching heap.

She could hardly imagine anything less entertaining—not to mention less romantic—than holding one's lover's head over a chamberpot.

She half wished Nic would neglect her. Instead, he took her condition in surprisingly good-natured stride, even joking they ought to steam for Egypt instead of Venice, since he'd heard the streets of Cairo were very dry.

"I am so sorry," she said, during a jelly-boned lull on the second day. Too weak to stand and too nauseated to lie down, she sat on the floor of their small but elegant cabin with her back propped against the lower bunk. She wore only her chemise and drawers, since Nic had stripped her dress some time ago.

Now he opened the porthole to admit a blast of chilly air, then tucked a blanket around her shoulders. "No need to be sorry," he said. "It's not as if you're doing it on purpose."

"But I'm never sick. Never. I feel awful for making you take care of me."

"I can tell." With a faint smile, he wiped her brow with a cotton cloth. "You shouldn't worry. I've nursed my share of sick people."

Merry felt unaccountably better when he lowered himself to the floor beside her; she was comforted somehow, as if his presence alone was strengthening. The thought made her nervous. She knew she couldn't afford to become dependent on a man like Nic.

"Hard to imagine you as a nurse," she said.

"Oh, ye of little faith." He lifted her hair and spread it on the bed behind her. "I assure you, I'm a regular Florence Nightingale to my friends. When I first came to London and fell in with Sebastian and Evangeline, neither could hold their liquor, nor judge which glass should be their last. I can't count the number of hangover potions I've prepared, or the hours of moaning and whining they forced me to endure."

"I haven't whined, have I?"

He kissed her temple. "Not even once, love. You're the best-behaved sick person I've ever met."

Merry sighed in relief, then wrinkled her nose. "It's still disgusting."

"Well, yes," he admitted with a chuckle, then hugged her gently closer. "But look at it this way. I've seen you at your worst. From here on in it can only get better."

"One hopes," she said and succumbed to the urge to lean her head against his chest.

Most likely she shouldn't have let it happen, but the steady thump of his heart lulled her to sleep.

THE NEXT DAY MERRY FELT BETTER BUT COULDN'T BRING herself to eat for fear she would not keep it down. She hated being weak, especially in front of Nic. Even this he seemed to understand. He assured her he didn't think less of her and bullied her into drinking sips of peppermint tea. Merry loathed the stuff, but ever since their conversation of the day before, she'd been determined not to complain. That, at least, she could control.

On the fourth day, she tried to get out of bed and immediately lost her balance.

Nic turned almost as pale as she was. "That tears it," he said as he helped her back into bed. "I'm seeing if there's a doctor on this ship."

"Nic, I hardly think I need a doctor."

"You do, damn it." He huffed and pointed his finger at her chest. "I brought you onto this bloody tub. What happens to you is on my head."

"Fine," she said, too tired to argue, "but I promise not to blame you if I die."

"Don't even—" His voice was too choked to finish. She opened her eyes, touched by his concern even if it made her want to laugh.

"I'm just weak from too much lying around," she soothed. "I very much doubt I'll expire from mal de mer."

A sound broke in his throat that he immediately shook away. "Of

course you won't," he said heartily. "I simply think it would be pru-
dent to consult a doctor in your case. Perhaps you can be restored to
your former self a little sooner."

As it turned out, the yacht was too small to employ a doctor. Nic
did, however, beg a remedy from the cook, a drink composed of sugar,
lime juice, and some salt.

The captain himself came to see her, a courtesy that seemed unnecessary to her, though Nic pronounced himself very grateful. Indeed, his gratitude was fervent enough to be embarrassing, even if the
captain did take it with aplomb. He was an older, sun-bronzed man
in a crisp gray uniform who peered at her eyes and clucked like a
mother hen.

"I'm all right," she said faintly, struggling to sit up. "Haven't been
sick in days."

"She hasn't eaten, either," Nic put in, hovering worriedly behind.
"As you can see, she can't afford to lose the weight."

"Thanks so much," Merry snapped, which made the captain smile.

"I'll send down a bit of crystallized ginger," he said. "Nibbling
that should settle her stomach enough to eat. Then we can try some
soup and rice."

Merry bridled at being talked around like a child but managed to
hold her tongue.

After the captain left, Nic laughed at her expression. "You look so
fierce, Duchess. I suppose you aren't at death's door after all."

She scowled even harder, but his care had warmed her heart.

"TELL ME A STORY," SHE SAID AS THE RICE SETTLED UNEASILY
in her stomach. Nic smelled of fresh air and peppermint-lemon tea.
He'd squeezed next to her on the narrow bunk and sat with his arm
around her back and his long legs crossed at the ankle. When he spoke
his voice was guarded.

"A story about what?"

"Anything. You and Sebastian. What life was like when you were
young."

"I'm not that much older than you, Mary. I imagine it was similar
to what life was like for you. Knew the world was round and all."

"I didn't mean it that way. I meant where did you grow up? What
sort of games did you play? Did you get on with your parents? Are
they still alive?"

Nic squirmed perceptibly on the mattress. "That's a lot of
questions."

"Then just answer one. I need distraction from my digestion."

He smiled at that, though she could tell he was reluctant. No doubt it wasn't fair of her to push, considering her own lack of candor. All the same, she couldn't resist the chance to pry.

Nic intrigued her more than ever.

"Very well," he conceded, shifting her head to a more comfortable position on his chest. "I can tell you my mother is alive. My father, however, was killed in a hunting accident some years back."

Merry stroked his shirt where it lay above his heart. "How terrible for you both."

"Mm," said Nic, an odd, dry sound. "What's even more terrible is that it probably wasn't an accident."

That brought her head up. "You can't mean he was *murdered*?"

His mouth lifted crookedly as he stroked his finger down her cheek. His eyes didn't so much look at her as beyond her. Into the past, she imagined. She could tell he hadn't liked his father enough to mourn him. Good riddance, his attitude seemed to say, which to her—a papa's girl if ever there was one—was every bit as shocking as having one's parent killed.

But at least this explained why he had not wanted to share his past.

With a soft exhalation, he dropped his hand to his thigh. "The man who shot him said he mistook my father's hunting cap for a grouse. Possible—though there was talk that my father seduced his wife."

"Oh," she said, hardly knowing how to take this seamy tale. What sort of family did Nic come from? "Surely the matter was investigated?"

A flicker of amusement crossed his face. "I suspect the local constabulary didn't look into the matter as closely as they might. Neither my mother nor the purported adulteress were especially eager for the truth to come to light. Besides which, my father was hardly an innocent victim."

"Nonetheless," said Merry, aware she was treading on shaky ground, "a man does not deserve to die for an indiscretion."

"No," Nic agreed, his face drawing tight in a look as dark as she'd ever seen him wear. "Not for that."

Wanting to comfort him, she stroked the muscle ticking in his jaw. "It was the woman's responsibility as much as it was your father's. She wasn't helpless. She could have repulsed his advances."

"I believe her husband thought the same. He took his wife to Australia as soon as the inquest was over, as if they both were transported convicts. Of course"—he released a breath of laughter—"their hasty departure could have been my mother's doing."

"Your mother is that forceful?"

"Forceful doesn't begin to describe her. To be fair, she's almost always in the right. Has a keen sense of justice."

"I imagine that could be uncomfortable."

"Yes," he said wryly, then half drew breath as if a thought were just then occurring to him. "Uncomfortable for her as well, perhaps. Even with all her will she can't bring the world up to her standards. She must suspect, now and then, that she might be driving the people she loves away."

Mary opened her mouth to protest putting the blame for his father's choices on his mother. Then she realized he wasn't talking about his father. He was talking about himself. Nic was the one who'd run from his mother's judgment.

Before she could decide if this was a topic she ought to broach, he smiled warmly into her eyes. "You were thinking about your parents, weren't you, when you asked me about mine? That if they were alive they might disapprove of what you've done."

Since her parents *were* still alive and since there was no *might* about their disapproval, she hadn't been thinking anything of the kind. Rather than admit this, she looked down at her hands. "Maybe they'd be right to disapprove."

Nic made a soft, snorting noise. "You're thinking of society's rules, rules society itself does not follow unless they are convenient."

"But one must live by some code of conduct!" Amazed by her own words, Merry pressed her fingers to her lips. The objection was one she had not meant to make, one she would have thought more suited to her father.

Happily, Nic did not take offense. His gaze serious, he tucked a fallen curl behind her ear. "What does your conscience tell you is right? To me, it is not wrong to take pride in one's youth and beauty. Nor do I think it a sin to share the pleasures of the flesh with a willing partner. What is sinful is cruelty to one's lovers, cruelty and lack of care."

She could not answer. Her mind did not disagree but her heart was swiftly reaching the conclusion that the pleasures of the flesh, at least for her, were not a concern for flesh alone. Like it or not, her emotions were engaged.

"Can it really be that simple?" she asked, the question slightly rough. She lifted her head to gaze at him but he did not gaze at her.

Water-threaded light, pale as straw, danced across his skin, making his features seem by contrast very still. His eyes were soot-framed ash, his mouth a line of autumn rose. He looked both beautiful and sad.

"It can be that simple," he said, "if one remembers to be wise."

BY THE TIME THEY PASSED THE ISLAND OF CORSICA, MERRY was able to totter onto the deck and watch the stars rise from the sea. The water was calm, an inky glitter that swept unmeasured to the sky. A single line of portholes lit the ship while a net of foamy waves parted around the prow. Nic held her to his side by the forward rail, warming her, steadying her. Her enjoyment of his company should have disturbed her. Instead, she drank it in. This trip had changed her, perhaps as much as her experiences in his home. For the first time since childhood, she'd been completely reliant on another person. Nic had neither begrudged her his care nor abused her dependence, and that had shifted the axis on which she turned.

She was living in the moment now, weak yet serene, as if her past had been swept away like the wake behind the ship. Though she knew this was an illusion—the past was with her always—the effect was very real. She fell light and calm and, under that, a quivering sense of anticipation.

She didn't know what would happen next, didn't know who Merry Vance would turn out to be.

"I feel reborn," she said.

Nic chuckled, taking it as a joke. "Wait till you see Venice," he said. "Then you'll think you've gone to heaven."

Chapter 14

THE SHINING BLACK GONDOLA SLIPPED FROM THE DOCK AT St. Mark's Square into the shimmering mouth of the Grand Canal. The day was still, the water a luminous ruffled mirror. Watching the palazzos rise on either side, Nic felt the happiness only a surfeit of beauty could inspire. *La Serenissima.* He was in her arms again and she was as fascinating, as gorgeous, as crumbling and stained and change-able as ever.

No city had ever affected him like this one. Venice radiated a peace and a mystery time would never dim. He longed for his paints with an ache that was physical, but at the same time was content to have them packed away. Venice could not truly be recorded. Venice had to be experienced. One opened oneself, made oneself vulnerable, and then one soaked her in.

But perhaps he'd made himself too vulnerable, because when Mary's hand closed over his, heat burned unexpectedly behind his eyes.

"It's astonishing," she whispered as if they'd entered a holy place.

Blinking quickly, he turned on the narrow seat to smile at her. "Are you comfortable? Not too cold? I'm afraid the weather won't really warm up before next month."

"I'm fine," she said, her expression softly amused as she pushed an errant curl out of her eye.

Oh, that hair of hers. Titian gold, the perfect shade for Venice. In truth, all of her was perfect for Venice: her flaws and quirks the gilding for her charm. Nic brushed his thumb up the slope of her cheekbone and kissed her, really kissed her, for the first time in a week. The gondolier chuckled with a Venetian's tolerance for romance, but Nic wouldn't have cared if he'd disapproved. Mary's kiss felt as much like coming home as his first sight of the ancient city.

When he finally released her mouth, she was flatteringly breathless.

"You're too thin," he said, touching her kiss-reddened lips. "As soon as we get settled, I'm going to stuff you full of biscotti."

Mary dropped her lashes like a courtesan, her mouth curved and rosy, her hands folded primly in her lap. "Is that all you're going to stuff me full of?"

He hadn't realized he'd grown hard until she said it, but now he knew those demurely lowered eyes were measuring his lust. His erection pulsed at her attention, growing hotter and tighter at the thought of making up for its long neglect.

"No," he said, the answer a muted rumble. "As soon as I get you alone, I'm going to cram you full of every inch of me you can take."

"Good." Her grin went through him as potently as her kiss. "I'll be looking forward to that."

He could not contain his laugh, or the joy that bubbled up behind it. "Brat." He slung his arm around her neck. "Shall I introduce you to the city in the meantime?"

"Oh, yes." She sat straighter on the scarlet cushion, her eyes still glinting with carnal mischief. "I'm sure playing tour guide would help distract you from the rather formidable size of your discomfort."

So he pointed out the sights as the young Venetian rowed them up the *Canalazzo:* the domed white church of Santa Maria della Salute, the crooked Palazzo Dario with its colored marble front, the Accademia where he'd studied as a young man, and the narrow *rio* that wound through the Dorsoduro district to his favorite small café.

"We'll go there," he said, abruptly afire to show her his youthful haunts. "There's a place in the *campo,* the square, where the city's cats laze in the sun. You can't walk up the steps without tripping over them. I used to spend hours there as a student, trying to catch them in my sketchbook."

"I want to see it," she said with a blissful sigh. "I want to see everything."

He could not miss the adoration in her eyes, but for once he did not regret it. He was too happy to be here. The canal was quiet, the city drowsing in the quiet hour after lunch. A single gondola trailed behind them with another passenger from their ship, too well bundled for Nic to tell if the figure was man or woman.

He was thankful for the solitude. For this one magical hour he didn't want to share Venice, or Mary, with anyone. He found himself wishing he'd leased a palazzo himself, or even taken rooms in a hotel. He'd made his plans so quickly after Mary changed her mind he hadn't stopped to think whether he really wanted to stay with Sebastian and Evangeline.

He'd been too jubilant to think.

In fact, he'd been more jubilant than wisdom would advise.

Suddenly uneasy, Nic worried his thumb against his teeth while the oarsman adjusted their course to avoid a *traghetto* ferrying a pedestrian to the opposite bank of the canal. The gondolier's motions were smooth, almost hypnotic, the sun flashing off the water and the oar, the prow cutting smoothly through tiny waves.

No, Nic thought, his elation had been perfectly understandable. Mary was a charming bed partner and companion. As pleasure loving as he was, it would have been more surprising if he hadn't been glad. Plus, there had been her bout of illness on the ship. A stone could not have failed to admire the pluck with which she'd faced it. She'd seemed so fragile huddled in that bunk—a child, really—putting on her bravest face as he watched her getting weaker, as her skin thinned and paled and her veins stood out in threads of lapis blue.

She'd frightened him, not only for the echo of memories he'd been running from for years, but for herself. He didn't want to lose *her:* Mary Colfax. Her light was far too bright to leave the world. He had no intention of telling her now, but if she hadn't finally managed to drink and eat, she might have died on that stupid boat.

Haunted by the thought, he shuddered against a chill that came entirely from within.

"What is it?" Mary asked. "What's wrong?"

He could only shake his head. He knew what moved him wasn't love. He didn't have that in him. This emotion was no more than the primitive male urge to protect those weaker than themselves. Or maybe she called to the artist in him. She was original. Irreplaceable. But he would have felt the same for a crumbling villa or a snippet of ancient song. What he felt wasn't love. It was simply high regard.

Despite the logic of this argument, he could not explain his tenderness away. Giving in to it, he smoothed her curls around her beautiful little head. "We're taking the train home," he declared, "and Perdition take the dust."

THE PALAZZO GUARDI ROSE FROM THE FLICKERING WATERS in a fantastical Byzantine-Gothic heap. Its facade was painted the soft brick red Nic informed her was *pastel-lone,* against which peaked and balconied windows stood out in grimy white Istrian stone. Marking a berth for the gondola to slip into was a line of Venice's trademark spiral-striped mooring posts. On their brief journey up the canal, Merry had seen these listing poles in every color of the rainbow. The Guardis' were a striking green and gold.

Both Nic and the curly-haired gondolier helped her onto the landing where a shallow set of steps led straight out of the water. As a perch, it seemed precarious. The second tread from the top bore the mark of a recent tide.

"Goodness," she exclaimed, "what do they do when it floods?"

Nic laughed as he paid the boatman. "The same thing their great-grandfathers did. They nail a board over the door and move upstairs."

Still smiling, he lifted a golden lion's head doorknocker and let it fall. After a short wait, a portly man in a suit admitted them with a bow. "Ah. *Signor Craven e signorina Colfax. Buon giorno.* I believe signor Locke is out, but the other signora is working in the *portego.*"

Nic nodded and thanked him in fluent Italian. Assuring the man they could find their way, he led Merry down a broad hall toward some ancient marble stairs. "That's signor Vecchi," he explained, "the countess's man of business." He waved at the doors they were passing, one of which was open to reveal a number of straw-filled packing crates. "For five generations, the Guardis have exported

Venetian glass around the world. This floor serves as their warehouse and their office."

"They conduct their business from their home?"

"That's not unusual here, Duchess. Unlike the English peerage, Venetians are proud of being merchants. To them, the arrangement is practical."

Who would have thought it? she mused, then caught her breath as the musty, chilly stairwell widened into something quite extraordinary. Here, on a landing of colorful inlaid stone, four tall quatrefoil windows overlooked a sunny courtyard. Opposite this sudden flood of illumination, two flights of steps led grandly up from either side, their balusters carved in beautiful gray-white marble.

"One more flight," Nic said. "Then you'll really see a show."

The prediction was no exaggeration. Struck dumb, Merry panted to a halt when she reached the top. The central hall, or *portego,* was a vast, high corridor that extended from the front of the palazzo to the back. Rows of leaded windows lit either end. Between them lay an excess of ornament she'd never seen anything to equal. Garlands and festoons and gilt and more shiny patterned floors fought for attention from her confused and dazzled eyes. What surfaces weren't adorned with stuccowork had been skillfully painted to resemble it. Doors were embellished in this fashion, and lintels, and the frieze at the upper border of the walls. No less than six cut-glass chandeliers hung from the copiously frescoed ceiling, which itself was a maze of reality and trompe l'oeil.

The effect was both hideous and gorgeous, like a rose dipped in gold and hung with diamonds. Its sheer exuberance was all that kept her English aesthetic from revolt.

Dwarfed by this grandeur, but seeming at home in it, Evangeline knelt atop a tall wooden scaffold, obviously retouching the central fresco on the ceiling.

She cried out at seeing Nic and scrambled handily down, a process made easier by her simple white smock and loose brown trousers. Braided back, her straight dark hair framed the asymmetrical drama of her face.

Merry couldn't help thinking the outfit suited her a good deal better than the dowdy gown she'd worn to Anna's.

"Nic!" Evangeline exclaimed, pulling Merry's lover into a hug. "How glad I am to see you! Seb's been totally impossible. Maybe you can make him behave."

"I doubt that." Smiling wryly, Nic stroked the edge of Evangeline's paint-streaked hair. No image could have pointed up the interests they shared more clearly. To Merry's discomfort, Evangeline turned her head and pressed a lingering kiss into his palm.

"Nic," she said, her voice husky, "must you always be neutral territory?"

Nic pursed his mouth, but did not seem annoyed. "I've discovered neutrality is the safest position around you two." Turning back, he laid his hand behind Merry's shoulder. "You remember Mary, of course."

"Of course." Evangeline broke into a laugh. "Forgive me, Mary, but you should see your face! Like a little doe who's lost its mother." She pressed steepled fingers to her lips. "You mustn't mind me and Nic. We've known each other forever. Our flirtation doesn't mean a thing."

Merry's brows rose in response. Nic's flirtation might not mean a thing to him, but she harbored no illusions about Evangeline's.

"Mm," said Nic, his tone as skeptical as Merry's thoughts, "a bit less of that, Evie. We've come for a nice visit, not to play your games."

"*Mi dispiace,*" Evangeline murmured, probably under the impression that Merry would not understand. The limits of her finishing school Italian aside, the apology seemed spurious. Evangeline's eyes were glowing with enjoyment.

"Shall I show you to your rooms?" she asked.

"Room," Nic corrected, his temper beginning at last to show. "Mary and I will stay together."

Merry was surprised to find herself blushing at his insistence, especially in front of a woman who, the last time they'd met, had been with a different man.

Evangeline, however, was made of sterner stuff. She smiled as if Nic's anger were a compliment. "The countess suggested I give you the red suite. There's a bedroom and a parlor. Hence my use of the term 'rooms.' "

Rather than apologize, Nic hummed as he had before. Like Merry, he seemed to know Evangeline had been hoping to get a rise. Unlike Merry, though, his annoyance had disappeared. To her, this was surer evidence of their friendship than any kiss.

"Where is the countess?" Merry asked as they followed a slightly more modest flight of stairs to the floor above.

Evangeline answered with a shrug. "Morocco, last I heard. I doubt she'll return to Venice until the *Festa della Sparesca.*" She smiled, fey and feminine, over her shoulder. "*La Serenissima* will be too cold for her old bones until then."

Though Merry had no idea when the festival of asparagus might occur—if that was indeed what Evangeline said—she received this news with a sinking stomach. Without the presence of the older woman, however irregular a countess she might be, Evangeline's wildness would not suffer any check. Obviously, the woman intended to seduce Nic. Whether he would resist was beyond Merry's power to guess. He seemed to have grown more attached to her of late but, in Nic's moral view of the world, attachment might not imply exclusivity.

She fisted her hands in her skirts as Evangeline showed them around their quarters, barely taking in the faded crimson silk walls and the huge canopied bed. She hadn't a leg to stand on as far as objecting went. She'd presented herself to Nic as a free spirit, eager for adventure. She'd sworn her heart was in no danger of being lost.

It wasn't Nic's fault she'd been lying.

To herself, as well, she thought with a burning shiver of awareness. She'd been destined to fall the day they met.

In his canny way, Nic was sensitive to her mood. "All right," he said as the door shut behind Evangeline with a thunk, "let it out before you burst."

Merry gritted her teeth. The last thing she wanted was to rail at him like a fishwife. One little complaint, however, was more than she could restrain.

"Never in my life," she said, "have I stared at anyone like a doe!"

Nic laughed and embraced her from behind. "She was trying to make you angry."

"Well, she succeeded!" She turned in his arms, her fury abruptly spilling over. " 'Oh, you mustn't mind me and Nic. We've known each other forever.' As if I were some sort of interloper! As if she owned you!"

Nic cupped her cheeks between his palms. "She's probably jealous."

"Jealous! She's a bloody—" She swallowed the insult and tossed her head. "Anyway, why was Mr. Vecchi calling her signora? I bet she told him she and Sebastian were married."

"As to that," said Nic with a small, uncomfortable sigh, "they are married."

Merry's jaw dropped even as she drew breath for her next rant. For a moment, her lungs wouldn't work at all.

"I know," he said, lifting his hands, "they don't behave like man and wife. They consider what they have an 'open' marriage. In its way, for them, it works."

"But why even bother to marry?"

Nic pulled a rueful face. "They love each other. They simply love freedom more."

Merry began to speak, then found she couldn't. Freedom. Wasn't that what she'd claimed she wanted all along, how she'd pictured her later years: free to take lovers when she chose?

But not to *marry* them, she thought. Marriage was a promise to forsake all others. Or it ought to be. She hadn't realized she believed that but she did. Her brothers and her parents had taught her the value of commitment. For all its flaws, marriage was a matter of honor, of giving one's word and keeping it. Without being aware of it, she squared her shoulders.

It seemed the new Merry Vance wasn't quite what she'd expected.

Nic stroked her upper arms. "Do you want to leave? Find a hotel to stay in on our own?"

The offer startled her. Rather than give in to temptation, she shook her head. "I don't want to come between you and your friends."

"They'd understand. I want you to be comfortable."

"I am," she said, but her chin wobbled in spite of her efforts to keep it firm.

Seeing the telltale sign, Nic cursed under his breath and pulled her closer. She couldn't help curving into him; he was too warm, too caring—even if he didn't care as deeply as she did.

"I'm sorry," he said, his lips against her hair. "I didn't mean to expose you to the edge of Evie's wit. She fancied me once, years ago—at least, as much as she fancies anyone other than Sebastian. I think she hoped I'd save her from him: if I could make her fall in love with me, she could break her obsession with him. But those two are destined for each other, always circling, always taking little cuts. Whatever Evangeline thought she needed, it wasn't what I had."

"Were you sorry?" Merry dared to ask.

"Sorry?"

"That you couldn't be what she needed."

"Oh, Mary." His laugh was as arid as a desert. "In all my life, I've never been what anyone needed. But my heart wasn't broken, if that's what you mean. Even then, I knew better than to make promises I couldn't keep."

His arms tightened around her back, tense but possessive, as if his words stirred some conflict only her nearness could allay. You want me to need you, she thought, the knowledge as clear as the sun sparkling off the canal outside. You want me to need you because you need me, too.

She lifted her head and he met her gaze, his eyes troubled despite his smile. Don't say anything, she told herself. Just let this be and it might grow. Afraid to burst the fragile bubble, she dragged her hands down the slope of his back until their hips were snugged together. She forced herself to match his attempt at lightness. "You made me a promise, Nic. I trust you haven't forgotten it."

His expression turned sensual; practiced, the cynical side of her might have said, though his smile still warmed the blood coursing through her veins. "What promise would that be?"

"To stuff me full of every inch of you I could take."

"Ah. That promise." He bent and tugged her lower lip between his teeth. "Are you sure you want me to keep it now, when all of Venice lies before us?"

"Venice can wait," she said breathlessly. "I can't."

"Can't?" The word seemed to interest him as much as the mark his teeth had left on her mouth.

"Can't," she repeated, almost out of air. "I haven't held you in too long."

"Eight days," he supplied agreeably, his eyes heavy, his face beginning to darken, "and eight long, randy nights."

Her hands slipped over his bottom and squeezed his muscled cheeks. The crotch of his trousers grew measurably warmer. Inside them, his sex was hard and thick. "You've been a gentleman."

"More than you can imagine."

"If you'd stop being a gentleman now, I'd be very grateful."

"Would you?" His eyes danced as he gathered up the back of her skirts. A grind of his hips punctuated the question. "Would you cry with thanks while I pumped inside you? Would you quiver and sob and clutch me with your quim?"

She couldn't answer. He had found the parting in her drawers and, an instant later, the parting between her legs. She was wet for him, summer warm, as his touch skated over her sultry folds. The sound he made when he pressed two fingers inside her was like a lion's purr. His intrusion was just what she'd been craving. She squirmed over it, melted over it, and her voice broke on a sigh.

"So," he said, deep and rough, "my little Mary is no liar. She's weeping for me already."

He stroked her clutching walls, pressing the back of her passage, then the front. His knuckles nudged something sharply sensitive and she couldn't hold back a cry.

"Mm." He probed for the spot. "There's something good here, I see. Something worth exploring."

Merry gasped and tried to squirm away. "Don't, Nic. It's too much."

He chuckled but he stopped. "Maybe it's too much now," he said. "A bit later I'd wager you'll like it fine."

As if to prove he could make her like anything at all, his thumb slipped backward, oiled by the fluid of her lust. She jumped as it, too, probed her body, gathering a strange, tight tingle from a part she'd never thought to let anyone touch.

"Nic!" she gasped, a helpless protest. Or maybe it wasn't a protest. Maybe it was a plea for more.

Nic seemed equally aroused by the forbidden nature of his foray. His body was stiff, shaking palpably in desire. At her gasp of shock, he held her tighter, pushing deeper into her anus, setting his teeth to her neck and breathing hard. "Don't lie to me, Mary. And don't lie to yourself. Your body doesn't know what it's supposed to like. It only knows what it does."

She groaned as he rubbed her with all his hand. Heat surged through her, a deep, prickling ache that swelled beyond the regions he could touch.

"Imagine this as my cock," he said, the words coming hoarse and thick as he rotated slowly with his thumb. "Imagine I filled you front and back."

Try as she might, she couldn't deny her yearning for the experiment he described. Would it hurt? Or would it simply be a new surrender? Certainly, she was not hurting now. Her pearl of pleasure felt like a tiny sun, pulsing frantically against the pressure he was exerting. Her body was enjoying this. Her body was on fire.

Which didn't mean she was comfortable doing more.

"The window is open," she whispered, her voice too unsteady for sound. "There's a breeze blowing over my bum."

He laughed and kissed her, deeply, wetly, as if he meant to fuse their mouths. The kiss was wilder somehow, more excited—whether because of their recent abstinence or from his unusual play, she could not say. Before she could ask, he lifted her off her feet, his fingers slipping from her to leave a throbbing emptiness behind. With a swoosh of wool and cotton, her skirts fell down her legs. He was carrying her. The breeze grew stronger, the smell of brackish water, the cry of hungry birds. He set her down on the little balcony, steadying her when she tottered on her feet.

She wanted him so badly she was weak.

"Look," he said, turning her to face the balustrade of stone. "Here's something I know you'll like."

At first she thought he meant Venice, spread before them like a drunkard's happy dream: water and sky and palazzos bridging the gulf between. Then her skirts crept once more up her legs.

"Nic—" She started to turn, but he caught her head and gently, firmly pushed it back.

"No." Soft as it was, his voice held a ring of command. A snap of cloth and metal announced the opening of his trousers. His feet sidled between her own, spreading them, spreading her. She shivered as the length of him burned her through her drawers. He was so long, so deliciously thick and hard. His breath came heavily as he spoke. "Venice was built to show off beautiful things. Here, of all places, why shouldn't you do what you like best? Why shouldn't we both do what we need?"

The balustrade pressed her belly where he'd crowded her up against it. A crinkling sound told her he'd taken one of his sheaths out of his pocket. She bit her lip. She wanted him to take her, wanted it enough to cry. No one could see, not really; the front of her skirts covered everything below her waist. And Nic was behind her. They would look as if they were embracing, as any lovers might. The chance that someone might guess, though, set her limbs atremble. Sighing, she felt him breach her drawers. The skin of his crown was hot, both delicate and firm. He teased it over her lips, then between them, then around the tiny spear of her clitoris. Her sheath clenched down on itself, trying to grab what it wished were thrust within.

"I'm going to fuck you," he whispered. "I'm going to make up for every night I did without. In front of Venice and the world, I'm going to cram my hungry cock up to your womb. And you, Miss Mary, do not have the will to stop me."

"No," she admitted with the last of her breath, "I don't."

He growled in answer. His first deep thrust drove a cry from her startled throat. By luck or design he'd found the tender spot he'd pressed before. She whimpered at the sharpness of the pleasure, at the thrumming stretch of him inside. He steadied her, and perhaps himself, with a tighter grip around her hips.

"Sh," he said, drawing back until his rim was caught inside her clutching gate. "You mustn't let anyone hear."

His warning made it that much harder to be quiet, no doubt as he'd intended. He knew her too well, her Nic. She felt fevered, her fear of discovery the peg that tightened the wire of her desperate need. She wanted him to slam into her without restraint, to drive her beyond the bounds of sense, and yet this taut control was more exciting still. She trembled as he cupped her pubis and thrust again, his finger finding her swollen bud just as the tip of him crossed those fateful nerves. The stimulation was almost more than she could bear, the pleasure so deep it felt like pain.

Nic laughed at her tortured groan. "Better," he said, reversing the dragging glide. "But not quite quiet enough."

"I'll show you quiet," she swore, but it took all her strength to keep her reaction to a shudder.

When she licked her lip, she tasted blood.

He did not mean for it to be easy. With each slow thrust, he caught the place again, pushing the ache deeper, making her want it more. Nor was he immune to the charm of their position. He thickened with every pulse until he had to gasp for breath against her cheek. His whole body was rigid, coiled tight against the powerful lure of release. Even the arm that wrapped her waist seemed to harden into stone.

"Faster," she pleaded.

"Slower," he breathed.

She reached back to grasp his hip. "Harder, then. Do it harder."

He said her name on a laughing scold. "Look at the city. Look at this beautiful, decadent city."

She looked, but all she could feel was him. The thrust of his penis. The heat of his chest. The throb and quiver of his blood. "I can't," she said. "I can only think of you."

He put his mouth beside her ear. "There are people fucking all over Venice. Whores, Mary, and wives and hard young men with barely hair enough for a beard. They're making love in boats and in bedrooms. In gardens and in grottos. In tangles of limbs no sensible man can count. They're groaning, Mary. They're tugging cocks and suckling breasts. They're sweating and slippery. Hot. Desperate. Trying to spill or wishing they hadn't just. The sheets of Venice are stiff with come, the thighs of Venice sticky, the arms of Venice full. And now we're a part of it. We're fucking Venice until she screams."

She saw what he said. The men. The women. The body parts drenched with seed. She could not wait for him. She came from the magic of his voice, not with a scream but with a moan. He gritted out a curse as the ripples of her pleasure gripped his cock. The tension in him changed. Suddenly his thrusts came harder; not faster, but with more force. He was battering her sweetest spot with every drive, blunt, smooth, turning one release into a violent, blissful string.

"We're fucking her," he gasped, his arm a stranglehold, his fingers digging into her softest flesh. "Making love as if we never . . . had . . . before."

With that, he followed her into the maelstrom, shuddering, silent, with convulsively tightening muscles and bursts of seed only he could feel. Something swept through her—maybe Venice, maybe him— sweeter than sweet, softer than soft, deeper than any orgasm she'd known. The feeling was chocolate and velvet and kisses rolled into one; comfort, if comfort could shake one like the earth. She sighed from the pit of her belly, half sad, half happy, and heard him do the same. His hold on her eased but did not fall away.

He feels it, she thought. He feels the magic, too.

"Lord, Mary," he swore, curling round her like a cloak. "You are the sweetest thing."

She was ready to tell him then. That she loved him. That she had lied. That she sensed his heart was a good deal bigger than he believed.

But when she opened her eyes, the sight that met them drove the confession from her brain. Someone had been watching them. A man stood on the narrow landing beneath the balcony: a tall, slender man with a golden beard and the gleam of knowledge in his eyes. It was Sebastian. Evangeline's husband. Nicolas's friend. His smile curled upward, slowly, sardonically, changing her flush of sweetness to one of shame.

She couldn't pretend he did not guess what they'd been doing.

He brought his gathered fingers to his mouth, then opened them, an ironic Italian kiss. His lips moved. *"Bella,"* she thought they mouthed. *"Bella signorina."*

He looked as if he thought she'd do the same with him, as if he were imagining it even then. Her body tightened and heated, a response she could not control. She might hate herself for it but she could not reason it away.

Attraction doesn't matter, she thought. It doesn't dictate what I do.

Nic stirred behind her, pulling gently from her body. "Cold out here," he muttered, clearly unaware that they weren't alone.

"Yes," Merry agreed and turned to push him into the room.

If she had her way, he'd never know they had been seen.

Chapter 15

AS ALWAYS, NIC SLEPT LIKE THE DEAD. MERRY WISHED SHE could follow his example, but the day had left her with too many troubling thoughts. Instead, she lay in the dark staring up at the swagged baldachin canopy, listening to Nic breathe and wondering if she dared creep down the marble stairs to find a snack.

The cook would not be pleased. As they'd sat down to dinner, the countess's chef had burst into the dining room, bewailing the mysterious disappearance of a roast. Sebastian had laughed and told her Nic would buy another, but the servant had not been calmed.

"This means the death of trust," she had pronounced. "Someone in my *casa* is a thief!"

Unimpressed by her drama, Evangeline shooed her off. Sadly, the cook's departure didn't improve the evening's tone. Sebastian spent the meal grinning wickedly at his plate—most likely reveling in what he'd witnessed that afternoon—while Evangeline alternated between sniping at him and trying to get Nic to take her side.

"*You* understand the treatment a woman deserves," she said, which prompted a snort from her wandering spouse.

When she glared at him he answered with a smoky look, full of history and suggestion. "The treatment a woman deserves," he drawled, "isn't always the one she needs."

Evangeline pretended to be annoyed by this, but Merry had no trouble guessing why she was flushed. Chances were Sebastian knew what made her body tick as well as Nic knew Merry's. In fact, after all these years, Sebastian probably knew his wife's susceptibilities better.

The thought of staying with Nic long enough to develop that sort of rapport was dangerously appealing.

Not that any of this crossed Nic's mind. He spent the evening in a daze, very much as if he were planning another painting. To her surprise, when she asked if he wanted to see whether the valise with his sketching implements had arrived, he merely shrugged.

At dinner he seemed to hear no more than half of what anyone said.

Between his abstraction and the others' war of words, only Merry gave the clam-laden spaghetti *alle vongole* the attention it deserved. If she'd had any sense, she'd have eaten Nic's portion, too. To hell with being ladylike; Merry's stomach had catching up to do.

Because she'd ignored it earlier, it was making demands on her now. With a grimace of resignation, she pushed off the covers and swung out of bed. The terrazzo floor, a special surface of crushed and polished stone, felt like ice beneath her toes. Cursing, she grabbed Nic's robe from the end of the bed and groped her way through the elegant, moonlit suite.

Their rooms were shabby but impressive, filled with heavy chairs and ancient chests, just waiting to clap her knees. The aqueous light confused the shadows, as did the numerous gilt-framed mirrors. Twice the small Turkish carpets tried to trip her, causing her to gasp and flail her arms.

It was too much to hope that Nic would hear her and get up.

As luck would have it, she met Sebastian coming up the stairs as she was tiptoeing down. She saw him before he saw her, but didn't have time to back away. The landing windows, with their interlaced ogee peaks, cast circles of moonlight across his head and shoulders. In one hand he held a bottle, in the other a basket of bread. He was trudging up the treads as if he were weary—a sympathetic figure until he saw her, froze, and wolfishly flashed his teeth.

He closed the distance between them in two long strides.

"I'm going for a snack," she said rudely enough to discourage anyone but him.

Smile broadening, he braced his legs to block her way. "Work up an appetite, did you?"

"I was sick on the boat. Cast up my accounts all over the place."

His throaty chuckle was a pleasure she didn't care to acknowledge. "If you wish to disgust me, you'll have to do better than that."

"And if you wish to attract me, you'll have to do better than these childish games."

He threw back his head on a silent laugh, his throat bared, his eyes creased appealingly at the corners. He recovered abruptly, tucking the wine beneath his arm so he could cup her cheek in his lean, long-fingered hand. She shivered at his touch, but not completely in distaste. "Come with me," he said like a seducer in a novel. "I have something special to show you."

Merry crossed her arms. "I'm sure you do."

This time his chest was all that shook with his amusement. "Nothing of *that* sort, I assure you. I could hardly expect you to decide your sexual future this soon after meeting me. Unlike Nic, my personality takes a while to grow on one. No, I've something else to show you, something of artistic interest that may shed light on the tangled web that is Nic and Sebastian and Eve. Besides, which, I have prosciutto in this breadbasket, along with the most amiable sweet sparkling wine: Prosecco, Mary, the pride of the Veneto."

Her stomach betrayed her by rumbling loudly.

"You see?" Sebastian purred. "I *do* know what women need."

His beseeching smile, manipulative though it was, was too charming to resist. She did want to understand Nic better, which meant understanding his history with his friends. "No tricks," she insisted. "You'll show me whatever it is and let me go."

"Absolutely," he assured her. "I may not be as civilized as Nic, but I'd never take a lady against her will."

"SHE'S A GENIUS," HE SAID WISTFULLY, "A FUCKING BLOODY genius."

Sebastian had led her to a room in the palazzo's attic, one that had served for some time as an artist's garret: obviously Evangeline's. It was a cluttered, cozy space with exposed brick walls and dusty wooden flooring. A woman's shawl hung from a nail on one of the ceiling beams, and a volume of Browning's poems shared a rickety table with a paint-smeared palette. Not concerned with these homey details, Sebastian held a branch of candles before his wife's latest artistic effort. The flames wavered in what Merry guessed was inebriation.

The possibility did not frighten her as it might have with other men. Alcohol didn't seem to change Sebastian's personality to any discernible degree. She suspected he was too used to being foxed for it to matter.

"Nic doesn't hold a candle to her," he said, "and God knows a hack like me can't." Shaking his head, he swung the bottle at his side. "Fifty years from now the world will be ready to see her gift. Then they'll be sorry they ignored her."

Merry wasn't enough of an expert to dispute this. She only knew the painting was the strangest, most disturbing work of art she'd ever seen. It was a portrait of Nic and Sebastian and Eve—but just barely. Their figures looked like displaced shards of glass, the pieces shifted from one body to another so that breasts and eyes and hands jumbled all together. The colors screamed rage and sorrow and an odd, insinuating sensuality. "I'm ugly," the picture seemed to say, "but you know you can't look away."

The picture frightened her. It held a threat, or perhaps a warning, and even though Evangeline scarcely knew Merry, the message seemed to speak directly to her.

"It's powerful," she said, "uncomfortably so."

She could tell he was pleased with her answer. "Yes," he said, "I knew you'd understand."

His expression amazed her. Nic had claimed Sebastian loved his wife, but she hadn't believed it until she saw those tears of pride shimmering in his eyes.

She touched his arm before he could lift the Prosecco to his mouth. "Have you told her how you feel?"

The bottle descended with a slosh of sparkling wine. When he laughed, it sounded like a sob. "Too many times to count. She's afraid to believe me, afraid to admit she's better than either one of us. Oh, she pretends she hates how unfair the world is, that a woman is the equal of any man, but in truth, in secret truth, she wants Nic and me to be her heroes." He look a swig, long and thirsty, then saluted the extraordinary painting. "Ain't goin' t' happen, Evie. You've got more to say in your little finger than the two of us put together."

Nic has something to say, Merry thought. Maybe he says it more gently but he does.

She shut her mouth on the words. She suspected Sebastian knew this. And maybe, in secret truth, he needed his image of Evangeline to cut Nic down to size.

Fearing she'd learned more than she bargained for, she dried her hands on Nic's dressing gown and tried to frame her next comment with care. "Nic says Evangeline fancied him once."

"Hah!" Sebastian barked. "Not just once. She'd jump back in his bed the minute he invited her."

"You could stop her," she suggested.

Sebastian smiled, a lazy curl of mouth and mustache. "Maybe I could. But maybe I don't want to. Maybe I fancy Nic myself."

He wagged his fair, straight brows as if daring her to be shocked. Despite her best efforts, she could not hide the sudden hitching of her breath. Her heart had jolted as hard as when she'd tripped on the Turkish rug. Before she could gather her wits, he set down the candelabra and reached toward her with the wine bottle's neck. He wasn't offering her a drink. Instead, he drew the cool green glass down the hollow between her breasts. The tip of his fingers followed into the shadows. When he met her startled gaze, his eyes were amused but sympathetic.

"You could join us," he said, "square off our little triangle."

She shook her head, though the response wasn't as immediate as she liked. His offer held a dark attraction, one she knew better than to accept. "I couldn't do that to Nic."

"Who says Nic would mind?"

Oh, he was determined to shock her. Ignoring the implications behind his words, she firmed her jaw. "I couldn't do that to me, then. I won't watch Nic bedding someone else."

Sebastian's finger traced a path around the neckline of her robe, skimming the first slight swell of her breasts. Her nipples hardened beneath the silk but she refused to act ashamed. Sebastian wet his lips, then lifted his eyes to hers. "What if refusing to play meant you would lose him?"

Merry didn't believe Nic would stoop to this kind of blackmail but, in the end, it did not matter. "My answer would be the same," she said. "I was not born to share."

A grudging respect lurked behind the mockery of his smile. He didn't speak, merely turned back to the painting and took a drink.

She had the impression she'd been dismissed.

So much, she thought, for being fed.

"WHERE HAVE YOU BEEN?" NIC DEMANDED AS MARY DRAPED his robe on the bed's twisting bottom rail.

She was naked beneath the silk. The bedside lamp threw her slimness into relief, slanting the shadows of her breasts along her ribs. His throat ached at her blend of fragility and strength. She was a faerie in the moonlight: elusive, mysterious. He'd woke half an hour earlier to find her gone and had been sitting up ever since. Every creak of the old building had heightened his consternation, every watery slap of the canal.

Twice he'd gotten up to search for her and twice he'd stopped himself at the door. Nicolas Craven did not treat women like possessions. His lovers were free to go when and where they pleased.

But he hadn't liked wondering where she was, or the suspicions it invoked. Of course, he liked her failure to answer even less. Suspicions notwithstanding, he'd fully expected her to offer an innocent explanation. Her hesitation told him that would not be the case.

"Well?" he prompted.

She smoothed the paisley robe across the rail. "Sebastian took me to the attic to show me Evangeline's painting."

Her voice was uninflected, but he was too experienced not to realize she was testing him. He'd known women who lived to make their partners jealous. To them, this proved how highly they were prized— a ploy he had always scorned.

To his dismay, this time the ploy was working.

Rather than betray his weakness, he gritted his teeth and waited. As he'd expected, Mary gave in before he did.

"He tried to seduce me," she confessed, "but I declined."

A fury swept through him that had nothing to do with any game she might be playing and everything to do with the perfidy of his friend. Sebastian knew what Mary meant to him, better perhaps than he did. At that moment, Nic could cheerfully have smashed his teeth straight down his throat.

"Is that so?" he said tightly, and even he could hear the anger in it.

"Yes." She looked at him, pride in every line of her body: a funny-faced, pint-sized queen. "You can do what you like and I can't stop you, but I've decided for myself. For as long as we're together, I'll only sleep with you."

Her declaration disarmed him. He gaped in astonishment, but she was not finished yet. "I trust you'd give me the courtesy of a warning," she added stiffly. "I don't think I'd want to stay if you intended to be intimate with someone else."

"I assure you," he snapped, "I have no such intention!"

"You don't?" Her queenly mien had fallen away as if it had never been. What remained was a vulnerable and sweet young woman.

Nic grinned at the change, warmed in places no fire could reach. Knowledge burst inside him then—silently, brilliantly—like an unsuspected star. He didn't know how he'd managed to blind himself for so long. This afternoon, on the balcony, he'd felt the glow they made together and had fretted at what it meant. Now he knew. He loved Mary Colfax, loved her as he'd never thought to love another soul.

To his astonishment, the revelation was not as awful as he'd feared.

Then again, he would have to think carefully before deciding on a course of action. His relief that she'd turned Sebastian down might have made him giddy. What, after all, did loving Mary mean? Would it change him? Would it last? He knew very well she cared for him. Might he disappoint her despite the unexpected openness of his heart?

Until he could answer those questions, he had better keep the sentiment to himself.

He could not, however, keep her at a distance.

"Come here," he said, putting out his arms. "Let me prove how easily you entertain me all by yourself."

Though she clambered onto the bed with the agility of a stripling lad, the way she snuggled into his arms was purely female. He stroked her cloud of hair behind her back, the pleasure of touching her strangely new. When she slung her thigh across his legs—a possessive gesture, if ever there was one—he hardened as emphatically as if she'd taken him in her mouth.

She hummed at the feel of him stiffening, but did not move except to wriggle and hug his waist. Like him, she seemed content, at least for now, to hold and to be held. Her cheek moved like a cat's against his shoulder. When she spoke, her voice was still unsure.

"Tonight, in the attic, Sebastian implied that you . . . that the three of you . . ."

Ah, thought Nic as her query trailed away. Old Seb tried to set them at odds by disclosing that bit of history.

"Yes," he said, deciding truth was the best response.

Her head lifted slightly from his chest. "Yes?"

"Yes, we all were intimate together." He let out the sigh he'd been holding. "Looking back, the choice seems foolish. How could such a thing not complicate our friendship? Someone always feels hurt, or jealous, or simply less loved than someone else. For a while, after it ended, I wasn't certain we would stay friends. We should have guessed what we were risking. But we were young. Proud of our wildness. Proud of flouting society's rules. I don't think any of us realized that who you share your body with is more than a matter of the flesh."

Mary's hold tightened on his waist. He heard her draw a breath but she did not speak.

"I've shocked you, haven't I?"

"I—" She laughed, a soft exhalation. "Yes, a bit. When I first met you, that night you saved me in the street, when you touched my face and asked to paint me, I thought, 'Here's a man who has no limits. Here's a man who's done things.' It attracted me."

"And now?"

She feathered her hand across his shoulder. "It still does. I think you're very brave."

He smiled at that, then turned on his side to face her. "It had nothing to do with bravery. Just the ability to be open to something new. Sebastian was my friend as much as Eve. I'm not certain I can explain what they gave me. I was a stranger to London and more alone than you can imagine. They welcomed me back to the human fold."

She was quiet for a moment, her hand curled between them on the sheet. He sensed no judgment in her, simply an effort to understand. "Anna came after them, didn't she?"

"Yes," he said, remembering how she'd taken him in when he could no longer stand between Seb and Eve and their sharp, sharp knives. They'd made him feel again, but Anna had made him sane.

"They were the important ones, weren't they?"

"The important ones?"

"Of all the people you slept with."

"Yes," he said, surprised by her insight and by the fact that he'd never defined it that way himself. "They were the important ones."

"You'll be my important one." She said this with a hint of defiance, but also with satisfaction. She was proud he would change her life.

He went hot at the knowledge: his face, his eyes, the skin across his chest. "Mary," he said, his throat so tight the sound would scarcely come out. He was painfully aware of her youth, of the honor she did him and the responsibility it imposed. He had never said such a thing to anyone, never had the courage she was showing now.

"Don't worry," she said, "it's all right if you only like me."

He couldn't let her believe that, no matter if he ended up disappointing her, no matter how little he wished to bare his heart.

"I more than like you," he said, then silenced her—and himself—with a deep, distracting kiss. Sharing his secrets had grown too easy. It was time to return to safer ground.

Otherwise, he might tell her more than she could condone.

LAVINIA VANCE'S PRIVATE DRESSING ROOM WAS FILLED WITH gowns and gloves and all manner of feminine things. Here she stored her jewels and her cosmetics and sometimes, when she chanced to be indisposed, she spent the night on the soft, pink satin lounge. Only her maid entered this jasmine-scented sanctuary, and even she did not possess the key to the old armoire.

It was the perfect place to hide the painting: her enemy, as she'd come to think it; the squawking voice of all her fears. Staring at it tonight, by the light of a single beeswax taper, she felt so overwhelmed she had to set the candle down and sink onto the tufted chaise.

She knew Godiva was Merry, knew it without a doubt. Geoffrey had Craven's address, of course, from corresponding with the artist about his own portrait. Unfortunately, once she'd screwed up her nerve to go there, the closemouthed butler refused to say anything except that his master was not in England. Left with no choice, she'd returned to the gallery, to try her luck with Mr. Tatling.

"Charming young woman," he'd said when she asked him about the model. "Name of Mary Colfax. Quiet, but surprisingly well spoken for a girl of humble birth."

The gallery owner had no idea how surprising it really was, nor had he questioned Lavinia's urgent need to contact his client. Her claim that she wanted to commission another work was enough to earn her the intelligence that the artist, along with his female friend, had left on a jaunt to Venice. He had the address if she cared to write.

Lavinia didn't, but she took it all the same.

Venice. So far away. How tempting it was to simply leave everything be. But Merry would return. Eventually. No doubt trailing clouds of scandal like noxious fumes. Lavinia could have strangled her if she weren't so worried for her well-being. And she was worried. Truly, she was. She merely wished her impossible daughter had spared a second's thought for someone else.

Worst of all—or, rather, not worst but certainly very bad—the letters from Wales were starting to dry up, almost as if whoever was sending them was trying to make them last.

"Didn't think about Isabel, did you?" Lavinia accused her daughter's maddeningly happy likeness.

But the painting could not answer, no more than it could tell her how to put Althorp off.

He'd had the gall to drop by the house that morning during breakfast. Geoffrey had not yet left for his club and was still lingering over his paper. Althorp accounted for his presence at that highly improper hour by saying he'd come as a favor to Ernest, to see if some files he'd been missing had turned up.

When Geoffrey informed him—rather coolly, Lavinia thought—that he'd returned them the day before, Althorp simply laughed.

"So hard to keep track," he'd said with his butter-smooth bonhomie. "I wonder that you let your daughter out of your sight. One never knows, after all, what one's family is getting up to behind one's back."

"Trust is always a risk," replied her husband, "but so is mistrust. A man must weigh the cost of both."

That, too, inspired amusement. "Too true," Althorp had chuckled. He turned to go, squeezing her shoulder as he left. Casual as it was, the gesture was a clear, unspoken threat, a flaunting of his long-ago possession. I can unmask you, it said, in front of whoever I choose. Whether that meant the world or just her husband she did not know, no more than she knew if Geoffrey had noticed the impropriety.

He had taken his leave soon after, studying her from the door as coolly as he'd studied Althorp. He appeared to be waiting for her to speak, possibly to confess. At the very least, he'd begun to question her friendship with Ernest's father. Her pose of innocence would be harder than ever to maintain.

With a swallowed moan, she pressed her fists to her aching brow.

She had to act, had to get Merry back, as much for her daughter's sake as for her own.

Peter will help, she thought with a sudden burst of inspiration. Peter would do anything for his sister. She'd give him an edited version of the truth: that Craven had seduced Merry and that they had to bring her back before her father, and everyone else who mattered, caught wind of what she'd done. Lavinia was certain her son could manage one indolent artist. If not, well, she'd give him permission to tell his brothers. With luck—which, admittedly, had been in short supply—Lavinia wouldn't just rescue her daughter from that horrid Casanova, she'd return her to the arms of her future fiancé. They'd hush up everything, *everything,* and the world would go peacefully back to what it had been.

Fortified by decision, Lavinia stood. It was late, but Peter was a night owl. She'd go to him now, before she lost her nerve.

She gave the painting one last, hard look.

"I'll save you," she vowed through clenching teeth, "whether you want to be saved or not!"

Chapter 16

JUST BEFORE NOON, NIC WENT DOWN WITH MARY TO THE dining room. There they found Sebastian and Evangeline, bleary-eyed and eating a silent breakfast. A cerulean glass chandelier hung above their heads, one of the famous *chioche* of Murano. Neither of Nic's friends seemed to appreciate the way its twisting branches cast gossamer threads of light around the peacock blue walls. Sebastian, in particular, appeared to have lost his rakish spirits—either as a result of overindulgence or of having failed to seduce Nic's lover.

Nic suspected a bit of both.

" 'Morning," said Evangeline, her nose buried in the paper. For his part, Sebastian waved a hunk of toasted bread.

Since Mary seemed uncertain how to respond to their bad manners, Nic pulled out a chair for her at the opposite end of the oval table.

"Relax," he said as he headed for the sideboard. "I'll fetch you a plate of something nice."

"That's right," Sebastian muttered. "Treat the match girl like a queen."

Before Evangeline could add her tuppence to this topic, Nic covered her open mouth.

"Enough," he said, "from both of you. The way you've been acting, Mary will think I'm a few bricks short for being your friend."

"We were only—" said Evangeline, then stopped to glance helplessly at Sebastian.

"—only making trouble," Sebastian finished with a grin that said he expected to be forgiven, though beneath the confidence he did not seem quite sure. "Hell, Nic, we both think she's adorable. Far better than that puffed-up Lady Piggot."

Sighing, Nic let his hands rest on Evangeline's shoulders. Mary watched with widened eyes from the other end, clearly more intrigued than offended by this discussion.

"I am not your procurer," Nic said with a patience gained from a rewarding night in Mary's arms. "What's more, it's been some time since the three of us did anything like that together."

"But we can hope," said Eve, her expression a twin of Sebastian's.

"No, you can't," Nic corrected bluntly, "not with Mary and not with me." His grin broke out without his willing it. This joy was so sweet, so new he could not contain it. Seeing his smile, Mary turned her own down toward her lap. She *was* adorable in her snug sea-green gown with her tidy little figure and her upswept curls ablaze in the morning sun. She looked up, her cheeks pink with pleasure, and mouthed a "thank you" for his eyes.

"Lord save us," Sebastian burst out, "if I weren't queasy already, watching you two bill and coo would do the job."

"Drink your coffee," Eve scolded and lightly slapped his arm.

Obviously not sorry, Sebastian kissed the air at her.

Nic knew an end to their interference was the best he could expect from them for the present. Demanding they apologize to Mary would almost certainly be futile. Ignoring them both, he turned to fill his and Mary's plates.

No one spoke until he sat.

"Signer Vecchi came by this morning," Sebastian said, his eyes wary, his coffee cradled to his chest. "He said your servant arrived with your luggage and he put him in a room with the underfootman."

"My servant?"

"The boy who traveled with you."

"But Mary and I came alone."

Sebastian shrugged. "Perhaps it was an employee of the ship then, and signor Vecchi mistook his English. In any case, your luggage is here, waiting in the hall on the *mezzanino* until you tell the house-keeper what to do with it."

Nic rubbed the bridge of his nose. Should he bring his sketching things along when he and Mary went out, or simply be a sightseer? The latter, he decided. He suspected she'd had more than enough of watching him sit and scribble.

"You should take Mary to the Basilica San Marco and the Doge's Palace," Evangeline suggested. "I'm sure she'd enjoy the Tintoretto."

"Not to mention," Sebastian leeringly put in, "the cell where they imprisoned Casanova."

His tone was almost its former teasing self, but Nic regarded him with reserve. "I'll do what Mary wishes," he said.

He didn't care that his friends both rolled their eyes. He had a feeling the message that Mary came first had finally sunken in.

VENDORS CRAMMED THE PERIMETER OF THE PIAZZA OF San Marco: cafés, sellers of mementos, everything a tourist could desire—if only she dared to pick her way through the hordes of pigeons. Not for nothing was this square called the drawing room of the world. Merry heard greetings exchanged in more tongues than she could name.

Despite these distractions, she was suitably awed by the grandeur of church and state. Getting lost with Nic after their tour, however, was even better. Venice was a small city. By a straight path, one could cross her in an hour. Unfortunately, *La Serenissima* was not straight. She was a labyrinth of alleys and squares and narrow back canals that forced one to retrace one's steps or hire a boat. No matter how they tried, they couldn't find Nic's favorite café from his time at the Academy.

In the days that followed, the search became a game where the journey was the reward. This was a city of traders, of jewelers and weavers and sun-browned boatmen. She never knew what they'd find around each timeworn corner. A market filled with shining fish? An ancient well with a rim of gargoyles? Perhaps a goldsmith would appear to delight them, or a binder of leather books.

She enjoyed the artisans best because Nic would go in to meet them. Without being told who he was, the workers treated him as a member of their fraternity, a fellow maker of beautiful things. They could tell from his questions, and from the respect with which he listened, that he was a man of discernment. With Nic to help her, Merry's Italian improved by leaps and bounds. In all her time at finishing school, she hadn't learned half as much, nor been half as stimulated.

Her mind, it seemed, was coming awake as pleasurably as her body, not with effort but from their rambling exploration. *Gianduiotto,* a fabulous mix of chocolate and hazelnut ice cream, was her word from the Campo Santa Margherita, while history and commerce were the subjects at antique shops like Aladdin's caves. A spyglass from one was wrapped as a gift for Mr. Farnham and a pretty tea set for Mrs. Choate. Every afternoon a new *barcaro,* or wine bar, welcomed them for a rest. The churches were a revelation, the people a lesson in how to live every moment well. Sometimes, overwhelmed, they simply sat on a mossy wall and gazed about, their shoulders brushing, their hands linked companionably in enjoyment.

Sebastian and Evangeline might have ceased to exist for all the notice Nic and Merry took of what they did. The bubble that surrounded them was too perfect to be pierced.

Merry had never been this content, nor seen Nic so at ease within himself. She began to believe, tremblingly at first and then with greater faith, that they might live happily as man and wife. In spite of the obstacles between them—not the least of which being the difference in their stations—they rubbed along too well for her to doubt they could succeed.

Ironically, this hope was the only shadow on her horizon. Once admitted into her heart, the desire to bind herself to him grew to a passion she hadn't imagined she could feel. Even a child, which she hitherto had no urge to bear, became inordinately appealing. She wanted to cuddle a baby with Nic's eyes, to teach him to ride a pony, to give him brothers and sisters and a great big box of rainbow paints.

Seduced by the beauty of her daydreams, she would drift off even as the wonders of the city spread around them.

"Where has my Mary gone?" Nic would tease, and she'd have to invent a lie.

She told herself these longings were nonsensical. Love had softened her brain and she was turning not into her mother but into a mindless broodmare. She began to tense each time he brought out his French letters, even though, as he'd promised, they didn't diminish her pleasure in the least.

Despite his defense of her, despite his apparent—and probably temporary—commitment to fidelity, he had not said he loved her. No promises for the future had issued from his lips. In truth, all he'd done was give her cause for hope.

She had to wonder if this were not his cruelest kindness yet.

SWEARING HIS FRIENDS TO THEIR BEST BEHAVIOR, NIC allowed Sebastian and Eve to escort Mary to the opera. He would have gone along, except he desperately needed the time to think. He could no longer fool himself into believing his feelings for Mary would go away. If anything, they had grown stronger.

This week had proven how well they could get along. Her simple presence made him happy, her quick mind and quicker humor, her fearlessness in exploring. The proprietors adored her, sensing no doubt a spirit as independent as their own.

He was almost sure he should tell her he loved her. In fact, he was seriously wondering if he should ask her to be his wife.

It was a momentous step, one that sent chills of terror down his spine, though the urge to propose intensified each time he tried to reject it. He wanted her with him, through good times and through bad. He could fear neither with her beside him. She made him feel stronger, kinder, more connected to his better self. With her, he could be redeemed. With her, his role in Bess's death could truly become the past. Once she married him, she'd never want for anything again. He had the means to both cherish and protect.

But asking her was not without risk. If she said no, would that spell the end of what they had? He knew how he felt when a woman turned too serious: as if he couldn't run away fast enough.

If Mary ran from him, he didn't know how he'd stand it. If he said nothing, at least he could hold on to what he had.

Tangled in this dilemma, he wandered absently into the library. It was a large room, as long as the whole palazzo, its corners bristling with stucco cherubs, its painted ceiling a vision of the heaven he hoped to find. The gas was lit, though it could not hold back the weight of Venice's night. That loomed clear and black outside the windows, its velvet backdrop hung with pitiless diamond stars.

A muffled cough drew his attention to the center of the room. A boy of fifteen or sixteen, slim and straight, stood before a lectern on which a book of sailing ships lay open. His face was eerily familiar, though if Nic had met him, he could not remember where. He was staring at Nic with a seriousness beyond his years: a watchful, challenging stare.

"I'm sorry," said Nic, "are you a relative of the countess?"

The boy laughed, harshly, briefly, then stopped. "I'm your kitchen boy, Mr. Craven."

"My kitchen boy." Nic moved closer, squinting in confusion.

"I usually wear a scarf."

Nic's befuddlement cleared for a moment, then quickly closed in again. "Yes. Thomas, isn't it? We thought you had a scar."

When the boy spread his hands, Nic realized how unnaturally still he'd been before. "No scar," he said, his eyes never leaving Nic's. "At least, none that you can see."

"Then why—" Rather than get drawn further into things he didn't understand, Nic changed his question to one that seemed important. "What are you doing here? Surely Farnham didn't send you."

"I wanted to see Venice. But don't worry. I didn't stow away. I've been saving up. And I'll pay the cook back for that roast."

"That was you then. Sebastian was certain it was the cat." Nic's smile invited the boy to smile back, but his expression never changed. Closing the last few steps between them, Nic put his hand beside the boy's on the edge of the book of ships. This close, he could see a vein ticking at the boy's temple. Inexplicably, his own pulse felt as ragged. "Your parents don't work in the gasworks, do they?"

For some reason, Nic's guess called up a sheen of tears. Beneath it, Thomas's eyes were blue and clear. The flush that stained his cheeks made them glow even brighter.

"No," he conceded, "my parents don't work at the gasworks."

He seemed sadder than any boy his age had a right to be. Nic could only speculate what experiences had engraved that melancholy on his face.

"It doesn't matter," Nic said. "Whoever your parents are, whatever you did before you came to work for me, simply doesn't matter."

"I know it doesn't." The boy's mouth pressed together, then lifted wryly at the corners. "Because I know you don't give a damn."

Baffled, Nic pulled his hand back to his side. He did not understand this boy's manner and the mystery was making him uneasy. "Why did you follow us?" he demanded, his voice harder than he intended.

"I told you—"

"No, don't give me that Banbury tale about wanting to see Venice. Why did you follow me and Mary on the ship?"

The boy faced him, still flushed, though anger appeared to have the upper hand. "I came to see what the great Nicolas Craven is really like."

"Do you want to be an artist, then? Is that what this is about? Because you don't need my permission to be one. That's something that comes from inside."

"And you'll sacrifice anything for it, won't you?"

Nic rubbed his forehead. The boy's hostility rolled off him in trembling waves. Nic couldn't imagine what he was getting at, but he was losing patience fast. As if he knew this, the boy turned away. Both his hands were pressed to the book now, white around the nails and so tense the lectern shook.

"Look," Nic said more gently, but the boy cut him off.

"Why aren't you with your friends tonight? I hear the Teatro La Fenice is quite a wonder."

By now Nic was certain he'd never had a stranger conversation. Hell, he thought, mentally throwing up his hands. If the boy wanted to know the great Nic Craven, why not answer?

"I needed to think," he said, "to decide if I should ask the woman I love to marry me."

The boy's lips whitened to match his nails. "The woman you love."

"Can't recommend it," Nic added, trying to be jovial. "Turns a man inside out, love does. Not that I have much right to complain, since I've never fallen in love before."

The boy's head came up, his eyes gone wide with shock. "Never . . . you've never . . . ?"

"Well, damn," said Nic with an awkward laugh, "you'd think I'd told you I just escaped from an asylum."

Like a shade being pulled down a window, the boy's expression closed. "Forgive me," he said stiffly. "I shouldn't have intruded. I'll leave you to your decision."

Nic could only gape as he strode away.

Kitchen boys were not what they used to be.

Chapter 17

THE OPERA WAS MIRACULOUS. EXQUISITELY SUNG, GRANDLY staged, it portrayed a tragic romance that struck Merry's heart a little too close to home. Loathe to cry in front of her companions, she told herself what she'd seen wasn't truly love. True love, the sort that happened in real life, was rarely that dramatic and doomed.

Nonetheless, she could not go directly upstairs to Nic, not with her feelings stripped to the bone.

Bidding Eve and Sebastian good night, she crossed the canal floor hallway toward the door to the high-walled garden in the back. Her steps quickened in anticipation. The air had been crisp tonight but not chill, and the stars had hung like jewels on an ebony cloth. As amusing as Eve and Sebastian were, she was looking forward to enjoying the heavens on her own. The stars would calm her, she thought, and then she'd be ready to go to Nic.

The last thing she wanted was to show him how she felt before he could face it.

The heavy garden door resisted her efforts to heave it open. Only when she threw all her weight against it did it surrender. Fearing she might not get back in, she wedged a Guardi shipping crate between the wood and its pilastered marble frame.

To her disappointment, she did not have the courtyard to herself. Someone sat hunched on the bottom step beneath the door, someone young and male. She began to back away, then realized whoever it was was weeping. The sobs were choked but unmistakable, as was the resentment with which they wrenched from the youthful chest.

Merry could not walk away. Whatever their cause, she knew those feelings well herself. What's more, she thought she recognized the young man's coat, a battered corduroy sack that stretched across the growing shoulders it contained.

What on earth, she wondered, was Nic's kitchen boy doing here?

Questions could wait, however, until she found out what was wrong.

She lowered herself to the bottom step and slung her arm around the weeping boy, just as her older brothers had done for her. The boy covered his face but was too miserable to move away.

"There," she said, her breast warming with humor and pity. "Thomas, isn't it? Whatever it is can't be worth drowning Venice over."

"My name is Cristopher," he snapped with an anger she didn't understand until he lifted his face to catch the light shining through the open door.

The air rushed from Merry's lungs. Free now of its scarf, the face he revealed was a younger twin of Nic's. The color of his eyes and hair were different, but he had the same jaw, same nose, even the same ironic lift to his brows. "My God," she said, hardly able to take it in. "My God, you're his spitting image."

Cristopher's tears spilled down anew. "He didn't know me. He looked straight at me and didn't know me."

"Who didn't know you?" she asked, but in the pit of her stomach, she knew.

"My father. The bloody darling of the art world. Couldn't recognize his own son."

"Did he know he had a son?"

Cristopher laughed and wiped his nose on his sleeve. "Too right, he did. He's been sending me a tenner every quarter since I went away to school. That's how I ran away, how I paid for a berth on the ship with you."

The story he told came out garbled, but Merry managed to sort it out. Though not a legitimate son, Cris had been raised by Nic's mother who, according to Cris, was something of a tyrant. Nic hadn't been home since Cris was four and, naturally enough, the boy had developed a yen to know his father. In order to get around Nic's aversion to seeing him, he'd disguised himself as a servant.

"I just wanted to understand him," he said. "Why he left. Who he was. Grandmother never said anything precisely bad about him, but I could tell he'd disappointed her. I had to judge for myself. When I saw how good he was to the others, and that they weren't perfect either, I thought maybe if he got to know me, he might see that having me around wouldn't be so bad."

Her own eyes burning, Merry stroked his tear-wet cheek. "No," she said, "it wouldn't be bad at all. You're clever and resourceful and very brave. If you were my son, I think I'd burst with pride."

He couldn't have been much younger than she was, but when he flung his arms around her waist, she did feel like a mother. She sensed he hadn't heard this kind of praise before, maybe hadn't known how much he needed it. All thoughts of scolding him for running away flew from her head. After all, twenty years old or not, she was in no position to throw stones.

She patted his back until he settled, until he finally drew an easy breath. Then, with a dignity much like his father's, he pushed back and dried his tears.

"He good as told me he didn't love my mother," he said, enunciating each word as if to prove he could face the truth. "All this time, I thought that was why he'd never married: because he loved her too much to give his heart to someone else. I thought he couldn't bear to see me because I reminded him of what he'd lost. But he never loved her at all. He never loved anyone. I was telling myself a tale. He didn't come back because he never cared."

"You don't know that," Merry said, her voice husky with shock. "There may have been other reasons."

"What reasons?" he demanded. "Just tell me what other reasons could there be?"

He sounded as if, despite his disillusionment, he wanted her to supply them. Merry wished she could.

"I don't know," she said, hugging him again. "Maybe the reason is something neither of us understands."

She tried to believe the words but feared she, too, was telling herself a tale.

SHE FOUND NIC IN THE SITTING ROOM OF THEIR SUITE. HE stood by the window, staring out at the night as he swirled a glass of brandy around his palm. His red-and-gold waistcoat, which matched the silk-papered walls, hung open around a snowy shirt. His trousers were rumpled, his hair unkempt. An evening beard shadowed the elegant hollows of his cheeks. He was the picture of Bohemian élan except for the line of worry that creased his brow.

For once she did not care what lay behind it.

I'm as bad as Evangeline, she thought. Illogical as it was, she wanted the man she loved to be a hero.

He turned when her heel struck the shining terrazzo floor. "Mary," he said, his smile unusually hesitant, "I was hoping you'd come back soon."

She couldn't answer like a normal person, couldn't ease into the trouble or be kind.

"Your son is here," she said, so tired it wasn't even an accusation.

The blood drained visibly from his face. If she'd ever doubted Cristopher's tale of woe, she could not now.

"My son?"

"Yes," she said, "the one you hired to scrub your pots."

"The one I . . ." The brandy snifter slipped from his fingers. He tried to catch it, but it fell to a Persian rug and split in half. "My God." His eyes widened with rising horror. "No wonder he acted the way he did. I spoke to him. Tonight. In the library. I had no idea."

"I have to say, Nic, I really don't understand that. Even if you hadn't seen him since he was four, all you'd have to do is look in a mirror to know he's yours."

"It's not what you think."

"I scarcely have to think. The facts speak well enough by themselves."

"You don't know the facts." He left the window to take her hands. "Cristopher doesn't know the facts. Not that they're praiseworthy as it is." He must have felt her stiffness, because he loosed her hands and ran his own back through his hair. "I'll tell you everything—if you want to hear it."

She met his gaze as steadily as she could. She wanted to hear, she did, and yet part of her could not give a damn. This man had abandoned his son. How long before he abandoned her?

"I'm not certain you should tell me," she said. "Yes, we've enjoyed each other's company, but can you honestly say I need to know?"

He made a swallowed sound of protest, then cupped her cheeks between his palms as if he meant to press his sincerity through her skin. "Yes," he said, "you, of all people, need to know."

Against her better judgment, she was flattered. *She, of all people.* As if she were different from the rest. But this could be the fatal secret to Nic's charm: that he made every woman think she was the exception. Wary, she pulled free of his hold and sat on the edge of a scarlet loveseat. Nic did not join her. His chest lifted on a breath. He closed his eyes, then opened them and spoke.

"I'm not who you think I am. I'm not who anyone thinks I am."

"You're not Nicolas Craven."

"I'm Nicolas Herbert Aldwin Craven, the seventh marquis of Northwick."

This wasn't remotely what she'd expected, but the minute she heard the words, they made a terrible kind of sense. She'd always marveled at the way he carried himself, at his lack of awe for men she'd supposed to be above him. He was a marquis, a *marquis,* a single rank below a duke. Good Lord, if her parents caught wind of this, they'd be crying the banns within the hour. But that didn't matter, couldn't matter. Marquis or not, Nic was no better marriage prospect than he'd been before. Head aching, she squeezed her temples and tried to think.

"What," she said, "does being a marquis have to do with not knowing your own son?"

"I have to tell it all," he said, "or you'll never understand."

"By all means." She motioned dryly for him to go on. "Tell it all." Her sarcasm brought his head up. He hesitated, then forged ahead.

"My father was weak," he said, "though he didn't seem it. Outwardly, he was handsome and athletic. Most people saw him as a hale-fellow, well-met sort of man. I doubt they knew what a liar he was, or suspected how soulless he could be. Perhaps his arrogance seemed appropriate to his station. But my father's *droit du seigneur* ran deep. What he wanted, he thought he had a right to, no matter who he hurt to get it. No outrage was beneath him—not cheating, not theft, not rape—as long as he believed he would not get caught."

Nic's hand made a fist before his breastbone, the other wrapping around it as if he wished to hit someone. Fascinated in spite of herself, Merry waited for him to pull himself together.

"He feared my mother," he said with a quick, sardonic glance. "Of all the people in his sphere, only she knew what he was, and had known since she maneuvered him into making her his wife. She's a practical woman, my mother, a mere squire's daughter. She married him for his estate, then ran it better than any Craven ever had. For the most part, she let him go his way. Sometimes, though, she'd catch him in an act she couldn't stomach, usually an injury to someone too weak to stand against him. To her mind, my father could do what he liked to his peers. The servants, however, the tenants, or the young, she considered hers to protect. If he tried to take advantage of them, well, Hell knew no fury like Northwick's marchioness."

He laughed at that, but the memory did not cheer him. With a heavy exhalation, he sat next to her on the love seat. "I had a friend among the staff, a laundrymaid named Bess. She was like a lot of servants who work outside the house: sassy and independent. She was a little younger than you. Eighteen, I believe, and I was fifteen. Tall for my years. A man, I thought, though mostly I was just randy."

Smiling faintly, he drew his finger down Merry's nose. "We took a liking to each other, the way young people will. Played at kissing. Cuddled behind the barn. It was forbidden fruit, I guess, to treat each other as equals when the world would say we were anything but. Bess was the first to teach me what women liked. In fact, before Bess, I barely knew what *I* liked.

"But we never went beyond that bit of play. Bess wanted to save her maidenhead for her husband. She used to tease me, saying I could never be aught but a toy to her. She was going to marry a dairy man and raise a herd of cows."

His sigh came again, deeper this time and longer. He rested his forearms on his knees. "I don't know if my father discovered what we were up to, but whether he did or not, Bess took his fancy. She was a pretty girl, fair-haired and buxom, with a laugh that could make a man stiffen in his smalls. My father caught her alone one day and forced himself on her. Didn't even try to seduce her, just took what he pleased and left.

"For all her sass, he knew she wouldn't dare complain. She was a laundrymaid. He was a lord. With a word, he could ruin her chance of working anywhere again."

At that, he seemed unable to go on, his jaw bunching, his hands locked together between his knees. Merry touched his wrist, then gently wrapped her fingers around the bone.

"Didn't she tell you what your father had done?"

He shuddered and shook his head. "No. I think she was ashamed. And maybe she didn't want me to confront him. She must have known it would come to blows. The temper I had then, I'd have made sure it did. She might have feared for me, or not wanted to set her friend and his father at odds, no matter what had been done to her."

"She sounds like a special person."

"She was. Special and strong and brave. I doubt anyone would have known if she hadn't begun to show."

"Your father got her pregnant."

"Yes." He squeezed his knotted hands. "Naturally, my mother suspected him. She knew his habits. But he was ready for her accusations. He spun a story even he thought might be true. He claimed the child was mine. People knew Bess and I were close. An estate like Northwick is like a village. Gossip runs rampant from barn to ballroom. My mother kept abreast of goings on, so he knew she would have heard."

"Wouldn't your mother have believed you if you denied it?"

"Yes," Nic said, "but I didn't deny it." He met her startled gaze with the resignation of a man who knows the worst confession is yet to come. Tensing, Merry drew her hand back from his arm. Nic rubbed the place where she'd held his wrist.

"My father and I made a devil's bargain. He knew how much I wanted to travel to Europe to study painting. I was mad for it, like a knight with his holy grail. My mother hated the idea. She'd married my father so her sons could grow up to be lords. A painter worked for a living. A painter was in trade. To her, I might as well have wanted to be a butcher.

"My father swore he could bring her round, but only if I confirmed his lie.

"I knew I shouldn't have done it. Knew even as he swore up and down he'd take care of Bess and the baby. Give her money. Hire a midwife. Find them a good place to live."

"Did you think he was lying?"

Nic rasped out a laugh. "It didn't matter if he was lying. I knew my mother would do all he promised and more, whoever she thought the father of the child. Bess was my friend. I should have been there for her lying in. I should have stayed to make sure she was all right. I could have waited to leave until the child was born. But I was like him. I wanted what I wanted and I didn't care to wait.

"She said she understood. She told me to go, to be happy with her blessing. We'd never loved each other, either one. It was friendship between us, and a bit of fun. She told me to be the artist I was meant to be. And then she died giving birth to my father's son."

He covered his face, then dropped his hands as if he didn't deserve to hide. His eyes were red but dry.

"By the time I came home, Bess was gone and my mother had taken the baby in. No one had bothered to write me. I stayed at Northwick a month, until I couldn't bear the shame. I went to Paris that time and Rome and any place I could think of that was far. And then my father was killed in that hunting accident. My mother called me back for his funeral. Cristopher was four and hadn't the faintest notion who I was. Burst into tears the first time he saw me. My mother pressed me to take up the reins, but I couldn't be the marquis, couldn't assume the title my father had made a mark of shame." His hand clenched on his thigh. "It was my shame, too. I knew I'd never live up to their expectations. I'd already proven that."

"So you went to London."

He shook himself. "Yes, I went to London and began the career for which I'd left my friend to die."

"And you never told your mother the truth, not even after your father died?"

He snorted. "What would be the point? So Cristopher could have a dead bastard for a father instead of a living one?"

The simple bitterness of the statement broke through the guard around her heart. Nic had done wrong; she could not, would not deny that. To be sure, fifteen was young to expect a boy to carry the burdens of a man, but Nic hadn't come back later either, after he'd found his place in the world. No child should be abandoned by its parent, even if that parenthood was a lie. But, whatever his failings, Nic had not killed Cris's mother. Moreover, she knew he was far from heartless toward his father's child. He might think he was, might have acted as if he were, but no man suffered the kind of guilt she saw Nic suffering unless he very much regretted what he had done.

He's afraid, she thought. Afraid he *can't* be a father. Afraid he'll fail Cristopher the same way he failed Bess.

None of this excused his behavior but maybe, just maybe, it meant the wrongs could be redressed.

Of course, Merry had a reason or two to want to believe that. If Nic discovered he could love Crislopher, that he could fulfill a responsibility and didn't have to run from it, then maybe he'd discover a wife was no harder to keep beside him than a son.

"You hate me," he said, sounding as if he half wished she did. "You think I'm despicable."

She looked at him, her emotions strangely still, or maybe not still but simply waiting, like a storm that can't decide which way to blow. "I don't think you're despicable. I think you're a coward."

He flinched as if she'd struck him, his eyes welling with tears he struggled to blink away. Part of her was awed that she had the power to wound him. The rest was merely sorry. Helpless to stop herself, she cupped his cheek, stroking the bristled skin, wanting to soothe just a little of his pain.

"You don't have to stay a coward," she whispered, her vision breaking in watered stars. "You could change if you wanted. And maybe you wouldn't have to change as much as you think. I know you care about people. Look how you treat Farnham and Mrs. Choate. Look how you love Evangeline and Sebastian. You forgive them their flaws, Nic—and their flaws aren't exactly tiny. You're loyal. You're generous. No one else would have hired a boy like Cristopher. Him and his crazy scarf. They'd have kicked him out on his arse."

"Farnham hired him," Nic said as he wiped her dampened cheeks. His hands shook as much as if her tears were his own.

"You *let* Farnham hire him," she said, "as I'm sure he knew you would."

Without warning, he pulled her into an embrace so tight she could barely breathe. "Oh, God," he said. "I love you so much it hurts."

She clung to him, let him drop his desperate kisses across her face. They didn't take long to deepen, settling over her mouth and sinking in as his hands slid possessively up and down her back. "Forgive me," he said, the plea husky enough to sound like a seduction. "Forgive me, Mary. Please."

She moaned as he carried her to the bedroom, as he cradled her against his hardness and breathed her name. He laid her down like a treasure. His touch was gentle, reverent, as if he sensed how fragile the bond between them was. Her mind began to drift with pleasure, but even then she knew: hers was not the forgiveness he had to earn.

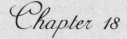

Chapter 18

WITH ONE LEG TUCKED BENEATH HER, MERRY SAT ON THE edge of the bed to watch Nic dress. One by one he pushed the buttons through his shirt, seemingly unaware of her attention or the comfort she took in watching him perform this simple task. This, too, was intimacy, as much as kisses or ardent words. It might not last, but it was sweet. She smiled as he smoothed his palm down the starched white cloth that molded so beautifully to his chest. The gesture spoke of satisfaction, both in the skill of his tailor and in the strength of his fine male form. He might not view his clothes as weapons the way her mother did, but his pleasure in them ran deep.

The reminder of home brought a tightness to her throat. Nic wasn't the only one who'd been running from things he feared to face.

But there was nothing she could do about that now. Not here in Venice, not with Nic so real and warm before her. Her gaze followed the hand that tucked his shirt into his trousers, picturing what lay beneath, remembering the way he'd taken her in the night.

After the first time, he'd been less gentle, his thickness forging strongly up inside her, his hands hard and sweaty on her wrists. "Lock your ankles," he'd gasped as the imminence of his finish forced him to fight for air. "Lock your ankles behind me and pull me in."

Now, catching her staring, he smiled lazily through his lashes. "Keep looking at me like that and we'll never leave the palazzo."

She smiled back but did not answer, not sure what she wanted; not sure what *he* wanted, despite the warmth he'd shown.

He'd said he loved her, but the words resisted sinking in. If he'd declared himself before she'd spoken to Cris, she would have leapt to say the same. Now she wondered if she should. She didn't doubt he had a heart, but having a heart wasn't the same as giving it to her, not truly, not fully, the way she'd given hers.

Whatever affection he might feel, he'd proved he wasn't a man who welcomed familial ties.

Troubled, and reluctant to show it, she pleated the folds of her sky-blue skirt between her hands. The dress was another gift from Nic, feminine as well as smart, with bands of black satin braid around the hems. She marveled that he could know her taste better than she did, and still not sense what was in her mind.

"We could take him with us," she said, not daring to look up.

Nic shrugged gracefully into his waistcoat. "Take who with us?"

"Cristopher," she said. "I'm sure he'd enjoy a chance to see the city."

He paused, clearly caught off guard, then finished fastening the navy silk. "He'll still be angry with me. I think I should give him time."

"He doesn't even know you know who he is. Do you want to make him wait, biting his nails and wondering if I've told you?"

"*I* need time, then. Time to decide what the hell I'm going to say. Christ, Mary." He raked his hair back. "What do I know about fifteen-year-old boys?"

"You know you were one."

"And a right young wreck I was, too."

"He needs you," she said. "He came all this way just to get to know you."

Nic's lips tightened, but a moment later his anger washed away on a pensive sigh. "You're right. I have to do something about him. And I will. Just not this minute."

"Soon," she insisted, pulling one of his hands between her own. His skin was surprisingly cold. She squeezed his chilly fingers. "Today."

He nodded curtly and bent to kiss her. His thumb stroked her temple while his fingertips speared the waves at the edge of her hair. His tongue slipped gently into her mouth, probing once, twice, before drawing wetly back. Merry's heart beat noticeably faster than before.

"Today," he agreed against her lips. "Today, but not right now."

TO NIC, THE DAY WAS A MOCKERY OF THE CONTENTMENT they'd shared before. Instead of embracing the city, they merely walked its streets. Sadness shadowed Merry's smiles. Meaning to make her a gift, he paid far too many lire for a pair of masks in the bustling alleys of the Mercerie. One was adorned with emerald feathers, the other painted in diamonds of red and gold. Hoping to make her laugh, he held the big-nosed, feathered half-mask before his eyes.

"We could return for next year's Carnival," he said. "See *La Serenissima* at her wildest."

She gazed at him from under gently lifted brows. A year is a long time, her expression seemed to say. Do you really think I'll still be with you?

Not wanting to hear the words out loud, Nic pointed out a coffee shop across the cobbled square. "There," he said, "let's warm up with an espresso."

Before she could answer, a group of schoolchildren tumbled into the *campo,* pushing and laughing, their voices like seabird's cries. They jostled her as they ran by and Nic had to brace her arm to keep her from stumbling.

"You're tired," he said, knowing he'd kept her out too long.

"A little," she conceded. "I wouldn't mind going back."

She didn't say what they both were thinking: that by dragging her around the city, he'd been putting off his promise to speak to Cris. He wondered if she knew her silence would scrape his conscience more roughly than any scold.

Chagrined, he led her to the nearest landing and hailed a gondolier. As they pulled away, clouds scudded over the red-tiled roofs, marking a change in the weather as surely as Mary's mood. All day he'd been seeing his actions through her eyes, not just what he'd done to Cris in Venice, but what he'd been doing all his life. Oh, he'd known he wasn't behaving honorably, but he'd never had such a vivid comprehension of the sin.

He'd wallowed in guilt, looking at Cristopher as the symbol of his shame, instead of as a person.

Now he realized his shame was worthless.

Only change mattered. Only fulfilling his obligations.

They poled from the Rio dei Fuseri to the Rio di San Moisè. Three boats could pass each other on these thoroughfares, and in places only two. The buildings' pale-gold brick closed in on either side, bridges sliding over their heads, flotsam bobbing around their upcurved prow. If he'd wanted, Nic could have reached out to touch the walls. This is my challenge, he thought, to push ahead no matter how cramped the way.

Despite his resolve, he wished Mary had said she loved him. If she'd believed in him, he knew he'd have found the strength to face his father's son.

But she didn't believe in him.

And if she didn't, why should Cristopher, who Nic had disappointed far worse than her?

With skin like ice, he helped her from the boat to the Guardi landing. The canal was low and brackish. He looked up at the windows of the palazzo. Glass winked in their ornate frames, the cloverleaf insets at the top throwing back the setting sun.

Maybe Cristopher wouldn't be here. Maybe he'd grown so disgusted he'd already left for home.

Mary touched his coat sleeve, her fingers fanning across the wool. "Don't worry, Nic. He wants to forgive you."

"But what if I let him down?"

Her laugh was a rush of air. "You'd have to work hard to do that. I suspect he'd be happy with crumbs."

A sudden rise of angry voices interrupted his response. They were English voices, loud and male and so aristocratic they sent a shudder down his spine.

"By God," one shouted, "there she is!"

Nic turned to see a wide, flat-bottomed boat lurch into the final slip. The three large men who rode in it immediately scrambled onto the tide-stained ledge. Behind him, Mary uttered a strangled whimper. He had just enough time to see her face turn white before one of the men barreled into him.

Mary screamed as they both went down at the impact. They would have rolled into the water if Nic hadn't stopped their slide by grabbing the nearest window's grill.

"Get her into the boat," ordered the man who lay atop him.

"Like hell!" said Nic, for which he was rewarded by a ham-sized fist smashing into his nose.

He heard his cartilage snap, blood spurting out in a quick, hot stream.

"Bastard," growled the man, and cocked his arm for another go.

Nic wouldn't have responded half as fiercely if he hadn't seen the others trying to shove Mary into their boat. She was struggling, but eventually they'd overpower her. Thanking Farnham with all his heart, he blocked the punch as he'd been trained, though the force of it ached straight through his forearm. The knee he drove into his attacker's crotch was more effective, and the uppercut to his jaw actually lifted him away.

Nic stumbled to his feet, bleeding like a pig, his mind such a boiling haze of fury he didn't hesitate an instant to take on the other two. The second man was dispatched into the canal by means of a well-placed boot to his arse. Then, as that one spluttered in the water, Nic grabbed the third by the collar and threw him face first against the front of the Guardi palace.

"No-o," Mary moaned, which he did not understand.

Ignoring her, he slammed her would-be kidnapper into the wall again. If Nic's nose was broken, he didn't see why someone else's shouldn't join it. "Who are you?" he demanded, sounding stupidly as if he had a cold. "And what the hell do you think you're doing?"

The man winced as Nic bent his arm up between his shoulders. Despite his discomfort, he did not seem afraid. "I could ask you the same," he snarled, his head twisted round so he could glare. "You must be mad taking her to Venice. Did you think no one would notice the missing daughter of a duke?"

"The missing what?" said Nic, beginning to be amused. "Good Lord, have you got the wrong girl!"

This, at last, surprised the man. He looked from Mary to Nic and back again. Something about the glance unnerved him. It was not a glance a person gave to someone he did not know.

Mary cleared her throat, her face as red as it had formerly been white. "This is my brother Peter," she said, "and the others are Evelyn and James."

"Charmed," said the one climbing out of the water, his tone much drier than his clothes. "Lord, Merry"—he peeled off his jacket and wrung it out—"you might have told him who you were."

A pressure was building inside Nic's head. He pushed back from the man she'd introduced as Peter. "What does he mean, you might have told me?"

Her neck bent as if a weight had pushed it down. If he hadn't known it was ridiculous, he'd have said she was ashamed.

"Mary?" he prodded, not liking this evasion.

Peter turned from the wall and lugged his crumpled coat. "Allow me," he said with a little bow. "Nicolas Craven, meet Lady Merry Vance—if you aren't beyond such formalities now."

"Peter," Merry whispered, a confession all by itself.

Nic stared at her, the pieces beginning to fit together, no matter how little he wished to read them. "Lady Merry," he repeated numbly, "the duke of Monmouth's daughter. But why would you pretend to be a maid?"

"Yes, why would you?" said the man who'd tackled him: Evelyn, Nic believed. He could see the family resemblance now that he wasn't being pummeled: in the brush of strawberry-gold curls, in the ginger-speckled skin.

Still suffering from the knee Nic had planted in his groin, Evelyn groaned as he pushed onto his feet. "Why don't you tell us all, Merry? I'm sure James would like to know why he had to leave his pregnant wife to rescue you from a man who's obviously as much in the dark as we are—a man Mother is fully convinced seduced you, I might add, as if any one could make you take one step against your will."

Merry pressed her lips together, but could not hide the way they shook. "Mother and Father were going to make me marry Ernest. I told them we wouldn't suit, but nobody believed me. Mother fired Ginny, *fired* her, Evelyn. An elderly woman, practically a member of our family, shuffled off to God knows where just because I wouldn't toe Mother's line. I'm sorry I worried you, I really am, but can't you see I had no choice?"

"No choice!" her brother exclaimed. "No choice but *this*?"

Nic barely heard him. The ground was rocking beneath his feet and he knew his encounter with Evelyn's fist was not the cause. All this time he'd thought she was the honest one, the good one, the one whose example he had to live up to. He'd wanted to be better for her. Hell, for the first time in his life he'd given a woman his blasted heart. But Merry had lied to him. She'd posed for him, and slept with him, just to avoid a suitor she didn't like. He suspected her plan had succeeded beyond her dreams. She was damaged goods, after all, publicly damaged goods. He doubled even the fortune hunters would chase her now.

"Well," he said, dizzied and sweating, but determined to reclaim his pride, "what a revelation. I must admit you had me fooled."

He had to steel himself against the entreaty in her eyes.

"I'm sorry," she said, her hand held out to empty air. "It was wrong of me to involve you."

"Nonsense." Nic shrugged the apology off. "Begging your brothers' pardon, but we both had a lot of fun."

Her eyebrows drew together in a little pleat. "Nic, you know it was more than fun. I care for you. I have from the very start."

He wanted to scream with wounded rage. How bloody nice of her to care for him.

"All the better," he said, his jaw like tempered steel. "No point having it off with a man you don't *care for*—unless, of course, it gets you out of a nasty marriage."

"As to that," Evelyn added darkly, "we'll have to see what happens when you get home."

Nic shook his head in spurious pity. "Too bad, Merry. Looks like your brothers have made up their minds to save you. None of my business, though. I'll just gather up your things, shall I? See you get smoothly on your way."

"Nic." Her voice seemed to thrum inside his chest, low, like a cello's deepest string. "Don't do this, Nic. Don't turn what we shared into something dirty."

"You're the one who turned it dirty," he said, "the minute you used me to get your way."

He climbed the steps and grabbed the handle of the door. His fingers slipped, with blood, with sweat, but he forced the wood in with his shoulder. When she called his name, he pretended he could not hear.

Just as he pretended he could not hear her begin to cry.

NIC SENT THE HOUSEKEEPER OUT WITH HER LUGGAGE. HARD as Merry tried to convince her brothers to let her at least send Nic a message, none were inclined to budge. "If I see that bastard again," Evelyn warned, "I'll smash his nose straight through his pretty head."

Her plea that Nic had never been at fault, that running to him had been her idea, did not soften them in the least.

"I swear," said James, who was still drying out, "if Mother hadn't made us promise not to tell Father, I'd look forward to him grinding that poncy rake into the ground."

With an effort, Merry refrained from pointing out "that poncy rake" had gotten the better of all three of them. "It wasn't his fault," she insisted for the dozenth time as they practically shoved her on the train at Mestre.

Through all this, Peter, her once trusty ally, had been silent. Now he spoke. "Yes," he agreed, "this wasn't Mr. Craven's fault."

She knew he meant that it was hers. Her eyes welled with burning tears. Peter's censure, mild as it was, hurt worse than the others' put together.

Blindly, she let him lead her into the private compartment, swallowing hard as he settled her into the seat beside the window. She touched his hand to keep him by her. "I know I've put you all to a great deal of trouble."

"Do you?" Peter's expression was unusually sober, as if her flight had aged him. "What you've done could affect us all. If word of this gets out—and it may, no matter how hard Mother tries to hush it up—Evelyn and James and their wives and, for all I know, their children will be breathing the dust from this scandal for years to come. You might not care for your honor, Merry, but you should have shown a care for your family's."

Her tears overran her control and she had to turn away. For some time she could not think, but only watch the mainland's factories slide into a haze of smoke behind the train. *Dirty,* she thought. I turned it all to ash. Nic's dismissive words echoed through her mind. "A lot of fun," he'd called what they'd shared, as if it were no more than a lark. She was almost certain he'd been trying to salve his pride. But even if he did still care, what hope could she hold out for their future? None that she could live with, not loving him as she did. If she couldn't settle for being his mistress, for a month or a year or however long it lasted, she didn't have a choice. She had to leave him.

She only wished she hadn't hurt him along the way.

Peter was right. Perhaps she'd had cause to rebel but, as always, she'd acted without thinking the consequences through. She'd treated the people she loved like obstacles to leap over or ignore. Worst of all, the minute she'd done enough to achieve her goal, she'd run like the coward she'd called Nic, compounding her sins for no better purpose than a few more days of pleasure.

Squaring her shoulders, she dried her cheeks with her gloves. What's done is done, she thought. Tears would avail her nothing now. She might have acted like a child but she'd face her punishment like a woman. Whatever choices she made from this point forward, she'd carry the weight of them on her own.

NIC STOPPED CLIMBING HALFWAY UP THE STAIRS.

Cristopher stood on the landing before the arch of the leaded windows. He was a shadow in the twilight, awkward, his arm extended behind him toward the corner, as if he'd been caught in the act of retreating into the dark.

Is this what I've done to him, Nic wondered, to this boy who was brave enough to leave everything he knew? Was the prospect of Nic's anger so awful he had to hide?

As he resumed his ascent, only the glitter of Cris's eyes tracked his approach. Blood throbbed in Nic's nose as if a steam engine had taken up residence in his head. He'd washed up in the kitchen and the unflappable signor Vecchi had snapped the cartilage back into place. All the same, he knew he looked like he'd been in a drunken brawl. The last thing he wanted was to talk about it; the first was to bury himself in bed.

With an inward groan, he forced himself not to trudge past Bess's son.

"Are you all right?" he asked, coming to a halt before him.

Cristopher nodded, white showing round his eyes.

Nic put his hand on his shoulder. "You should go home," he said softly, and the boy bowed his head. "I can give you money for a ticket if you need it."

"I don't need money." The words were a nearly inaudible whisper. "I only need you."

For the life of him, Nic could not respond. Why? he thought. Why do you need me when all I've done is let you down? Was his longing for a father so strong he'd forgive it all? Without meaning to, his grip tightened on the span of young muscle and bone. "I can't do this now. I'm sorry but I can't."

The boy swallowed and nodded and lifted the chin that was sharp just like his own. "Those men . . . ?"

"They were Mary's brothers. They took her back to her family."

"I'm sorry," said the boy.

Nic closed his eyes, but the pain didn't disappear. After a moment, he opened them and patted Cris's arm. "You can stay if you like. I won't send you away."

It was nothing, not even a crumb, but it was all Nic could manage. He felt the boy's gaze as he stepped past him to the next flight of stairs. Beneath his palm, the marble balustrade was as cool and smooth as glass.

He put his weight on it as his feet dragged up the treads, one step, two, each one a mountain in his mind.

Mary, he thought, then: *Merry.*

His hand made a fist, but his fingers would not hold it. They spread on the door to their suite and shoved at the inlaid wood.

Inside a decanter waited, an oasis of golden brandy. He poured a glass. Not too little. Not too much. Just enough to summon the gods of Lethe.

Chapter 19

NIC MEANT TO GET OUT OF BED, BUT INSTEAD SAT SLUMPED on its edge with his elbows on his thighs and his brow on the heels of his hands. Night pressed, moonless and dank, outside the windows. The day must have passed while he slept. All he wore were the same black silk-lined trousers he'd had on the evening Merry left. He wanted to take them off. He also wanted to eat, wash, then extinguish the lamp some interfering soul had set on the rosewood nightstand.

Of course, soon enough the flame would sputter out by itself. The wick was in need of trimming.

Trousers, he thought, his mind slowly ordering the tasks he wished to do. He'd pull on his robe, the robe that still smelled of Mary, then slip downstairs to the empty kitchen.

He had one arm through the sleeve when a shadow separated from the archway to the silting room.

The shadow was Sebastian. He carried a tray on which Nic made out a decanter and two glasses.

"Thought you'd have to wake up soon." He lowered the chased silver platter to the bottom corner of the bed. Nic saw that it held, along with the brandy, a plate of fruit and cheese. His stomach grumbled at the sight.

Sebastian straightened and half smiled at him, his eyes traveling slowly down Nic's front. Abruptly conscious of his undress, Nic stuck his arm through the second sleeve and pulled the brown paisley closed.

"What do you want?" he said, his voice like graveled fur.

Sebastian poured a glass and held it out until Nic took it. "Evie and I thought you might be in need of entertainment. We met a young tenor at the opera the other night. He came for dinner. An adventurous lad." He cocked his head. "Perhaps you'd like to help us make him sing."

The flush that moved through Nic's body was more reflex than desire. With a sense of detachment, he let himself remember how it was to tangle too many limbs to count, to be mindless flesh, to forget one-self in drunken laughter and faceless warmth.

Unfortunately, he also remembered how disconcerting it was to catch a stranger's eye in the throes of pleasure, and how empty one could feel when that pleasure drained away.

Sebastian seemed to read his reluctance. He covered Nic's fingers where they curled around the glass. "We could send him home if you'd rather. Keep it just the three of us."

But the thought of being alone with Sebastian and Eve was even worse, like willfully stepping into a pit of quicksand he'd just es-caped.

"Too old for those games," he said, not wanting to hurt his friend.

Sebastian's hand fell away. Folding his arms across his chest, he studied Nic like a boatman trying to gauge a stormy sky. "You have to forgive me eventually," he said. "After all, how many friends do you have in this world? Me, Evangeline, Anna. That's pretty much the sum. And don't add Farnham, old man. You pay him too much to know if he truly likes you."

But Nic hadn't been about to add Farnham. He'd been about to add Mary. She could have been a friend, once upon a time. At least, he thought she could have. But she'd left him. She'd used him. She'd seemed to love him but that had been a lie. The cruelest lie.

Hadn't it?

Pain beat dully between his brows but he didn't reach up to rub it. Nothing was clear to him, not even the anger he'd felt at her when she left. What if he'd been wrong? What if, in his hurt and humilia-tion, he'd made accusations that were not true?

But what did that matter now? She was gone. It was over. He couldn't have kept her even if she had loved him. A girl like Mary, like *Merry,* needed a man she could rely on. A husband. A hero. A re-liable father for her children. Nic had already demonstrated he could not handle that.

"Nic," said Sebastian, still watching him, "I'm sorry I tried to se-duce her. Sincerely sorry."

Nic shook his head. "Doesn't matter. You don't blame a cat for chasing mice."

"Maybe not, but you can blame a man. You had a right to expect better of me."

All Nic managed was a shrug. He was dead to everything tonight.

"You know," Sebastian said, with more gentleness than was his custom, "it wouldn't have worked between you and Mary, not in the long run. Women like that don't give their husbands the kind of freedom our sort need."

Nic said nothing, merely stared at the flickering depths of the lamplit brandy. The golden sparks were a match for Merry's eyes. His heart cramped in his chest. He didn't want the drink anymore, or the food. Come to that, he wasn't certain he could move.

STEAM ROSE FROM THE BATH, SHEER, SILVER CURLS THAT obscured his view of the brown-and-white tiled walls. The design was geometric. Greek, he thought, a squared rise and fall that lured him to close his eyes.

I could sleep right here, he thought, and let his lids sink down.

He woke to the feel of hands trying to haul him from the water.

"Idiot," said Evangeline. "Do you want to drown?"

Cris was helping her and Nic thought their presence must be a dream. If it was, it was a damned uncomfortable one. With Nic propped between them, they stumbled across the hall and dumped him in a chair.

Evangeline shook her head at him, her paint-splattered shirt plastered to her body by his bath water.

"You can go now," Cris said very firmly. "I'll take care of him from here."

To Nic's surprise, Evangeline nodded and withdrew.

He'd begun to doze when Cris threw a bath sheet across his lap.

"I don't know what you're still doing here," the boy snapped in exasperation. "Neither one of those lechers can keep their hands to themselves."

Nic slid lower in the soggy chair. "They're my friends."

"Could have fooled me."

"You don't understand them."

"Actually," said Cris, in a tone that reminded Nic of his mother, "I don't think *they* understand *you*. In fact, I'm not convinced you understand yourself. If you did, you wouldn't have let the one thing you wanted slip through your fingers."

Against Nic's will, anger began to clear the cobwebs from his brain. "I suppose you're going to tell me I should have fought to keep her."

"Nothing of the sort." Cris tossed his head. "She's far too good for the likes of you."

"I'm sure that explains why she lied to me."

"And you didn't lie to her?"

Cristopher's eyes were slits of hard blue steel. Annoyed by his defiance, Nic shoved himself upright in the chair. "She used me," he said, speaking as clearly as he could. "She never loved me at all."

"Huh," said Cris, "for a man who lives by his eyes, you're pretty blind."

"She was only trying to avoid a marriage she didn't—" Rather than continue the argument, which he wasn't certain of in the first place, Nic pushed to his feet and wrapped the sheet around his waist. With a grimace for the wobbly feeling that plagued his knees, he stalked past Cristopher toward the bedroom. "I don't have to explain this to you. You're fifteen years old. You couldn't know the first thing about it."

"Don't judge me by your own stupidity. I know more about love than you."

The voice was following him. Nic stopped and turned at the archway to head it off. "Oh, really."

Cristopher flushed but held his ground. "I know you don't give up just because the person you love turns out to be imperfect. I know you don't pretend not to love a person just because it would be easier if you didn't. I know you don't hide in bed and pull the covers over you just because fighting for what matters takes some work. Mary was right to go back to her family. You're a mess!"

"I wasn't a mess for her." Fully awake now, Nic jabbed his thumb against the center of his chest. "I changed. She made me change."

"Did a good job of it, too. Minute you face a challenge, you're back to your old ways."

Nic bit back a curse no fifteen-year-old should hear. "Leave me alone," he muttered and headed stubbornly for the bed.

Cris grabbed his arm before he could crawl in. "If I did what you deserved, I would leave you alone. You don't know what you're missing, you stupid bastard. There's plenty of people who'd be glad for a son like me."

Nic would have ignored him but for the tears he heard in his voice, the pride that wanted to believe but couldn't quite. Everything he said was true. Cris was bright and brave—good Lord, was he brave—not only to come here on his own but to speak his heart, and in full expectation of having it trampled! He wasn't responsible for their father's sins. He was a gift, a second chance that Nic had done his best to spit on.

Just as, in the end, he'd done his best to spit on Merry.

He blew his breath out through his nose, disgusted by the level to which he'd sunk. Cristopher obviously thought the sound was directed at him because he pulled away as if Nic's skin had burned.

"No." Nic caught him back. "You're right. I am a stupid bastard and you are a son a man should be proud of."

Cristopher's jaw dropped. For all his bravado, he seemed not to have expected Nic to concede. Nic found himself smiling, something lightening inside him, delicate but *there,* like a flicker of sun seen from the corner of the eye. He put his hand on Cris's shoulder, rubbing the ball of it with his thumb. The feeling in his heart intensified, not merely light but warmth. His knees steadied.

What if the thing he'd feared most was the very thing that could save him?

Cris started to speak but Nic lifted his hand to stop him. He had to get these thoughts out while they were clear. "There's something I need to tell you, something I think you're old enough to know."

"Yes?" said Cris, abruptly wary.

"I don't know if this will make you feel worse or better. Believe me, it doesn't change what I owe you."

"Just tell me."

"I'm not your father."

Cris stared at him. "Not . . . but you look just like me!"

"That's because I'm your brother."

Cris shuffled haltingly to the bed. Moving like an old man, he lowered himself to the mattress. Velvet covers heaped around him, red once, but now a dusty pink. How many dramas had this bed seen? How many broken hearts? "Then your father . . . your father was mine." He looked up, emotions sliding across his face. "Grandmother doesn't know, does she?"

"No, and I'm not certain I want to tell her."

Cristopher grimaced as if picturing how she'd react. Given her sterling standards of behavior, the dowager marchioness was not a woman one liked to admit one had deceived. "If you're not my father," he said, pausing to bite his lip, "then I was wrong to be angry at you for not treating me like a son."

Gingerly, Nic took a seat on the bed beside him. "You had every right to be angry. That's who you thought I was. Hell, I agreed to the lie myself. Some other time I'll tell you why. Right this minute all you need to know is that your mother was my best friend. For that alone, I should have been part of your life."

"Why weren't you then? If you knew that, why did you stay away?"

There it was. The heart of his failings. He had no justification. All he could offer was the truth.

"I was ashamed," he said, "for letting your mother down. I was young and scared and selfish and the longer I stayed away the harder it was to come back and face you. You didn't like me when you were little, you know. Just a big, scary stranger, I guess. It was easier to feel guilty than to do what I knew was right."

The boy mulled this over, quiet, serious, weighing everything all together. His thoughtfulness was a trait Nic could not trace. Bess had not had it. Nic certainly didn't, nor Nic's mother. Seeing it forced home the awareness that Cris was his own person, with his own unique feelings and experience. He was not a mistake, not a tragedy, not a burden, just a human being trying to find his way.

"What about now?" he said, once his deliberations were complete.

The fading daylight caught the golden peach fuzz on his cheek. For all his self-possession, Cris was still a lad. Nic must be careful not to imply promises he could not keep. Gathering his courage, he gripped his thighs through the bath sheet. "How would you like to go to Northwick? With me."

"Northwick?" Cris repeated, visibly struggling not to jump to conclusions. "With you?"

"Yes," said Nic. "It strikes me that I need to return to the place where I went wrong. See if my mother really does want me to assume my filial duties. I can't swear the attempt will work, but if I don't bollocks it up too badly, you and I can move forward from there. Unless you'd rather go back to school?"

Cris hesitated. For a moment Nic thought he would refuse, that too much damage had been done. Then his brother shook himself. "No, I'd rather be with you. I'd like to see if we can be family. If that's what you want."

"It is," Nic said. "At least I'd like to try."

Cris gnawed his lip again. "What about Mary? If you're set on fixing things, don't you want to fix that first?"

Nic considered this, not because he wanted to hurt his brother's feelings but because he knew only a careful answer would be believed. He wasn't sure what purpose running after Merry would serve, not as he was: all intention and no result. Now that he'd discovered whose daughter she was, he knew she needed neither his money nor his protection. Cris had implied she loved him, but love hadn't been enough to hold her, no more than pleasure. Until he had more to offer, he could not expect her to change her mind.

Aware that Cris was waiting, he squeezed his arm. "The situation with Merry is more complicated than it seems. In any case, yours is the prior debt. If I can't pay that, then what you said before is true: she's far too good for the likes of me."

"'Complicated,' eh?" said Cris with a skeptical, purse-lipped smile.

Nic pressed his hand to his heart at a sudden memory. "My God, you're the image of your mother with that expression. She used to smile at me just like that when she thought I was talking nonsense."

Cris looked at the floor and then back up. His eyes pierced Nic like shooting stars. "You *did* love her," he said as if expecting a contradiction. "I don't care what you say, I know you loved her at least a bit."

Nic smoothed his brother's hair back from his brow. "Maybe I did. And maybe I still do."

THE DUKE OF MONMOUTH WAITED ON THE PLATFORM AT Victoria Station, as tall and stern as a standing stone amid the flow of travelers. He wore a long black coat with a velvet collar, above which showed a silver-and-white cravat. His hat was high and straight, his walking stick clenched in the same broad hand that held his gloves. His expression was that of a general prepared for a battle he does not relish but can't avoid.

Merry hadn't known how much she loved him until she realized she couldn't run to his arms.

Naturally, her brothers were dismayed to see him, though he did not take them to task for trying to hide the truth. "You were doing as your mother asked," he said in response to Evelyn's stiff apology. "You aren't the ones who broke a trust."

"Yes, sir," said Evelyn, and they tactfully withdrew.

With her brothers gone, Merry had no choice but to meet her father's gaze. She could see beyond his sternness now: to confusion that his daughter would defy him, to hope that she could explain and, finally, to a love no amount of disappointment could destroy. He was as Nic had portrayed him long ago, the different sides of his nature like layers of vibrant paint: strong and weak, wise and foolish, prideful and forgiving.

She hadn't known it at the time, but Nic had given her a gift when he showed her how to see her father's heart, a gift she would need to get through the days ahead.

Fortified by a peculiar sort of pride, she put back her shoulders and stood straight. "Do you want me to explain myself here, Father?"

"Can you?" he demanded.

"Not as you would wish," she admitted. She smoothed the front of her coat, the coat Nic bought her, then forced herself to stillness. "May I ask how you found out where I was?"

"Hyde said you weren't with Isabel. Your mother filled in the rest. She recognized you from that painting. Bought it to protect you— much good as it did. Hyde told half the city before I could calm him down."

Merry bit her lip. The earl of Hyde was Isabel Beckett's husband. He must have discovered the truth about the letters. Merry hoped he had not punished her friend too badly as a result.

"I don't know what you were thinking, Merry, running off like that with a man you barely knew! The scandal's going to cost you dear enough. Hyde was livid at you for involving Isabel. Rightly so. He's convinced everyone will believe she's as wild as you are."

"I'll speak to him, Papa. Maybe I can—"

"You will not!" A porter turned his head at the furious denial. Her father lowered his voice and glared. "You'll not speak to anyone I don't approve beforehand. Honestly, that man might have done anything to you. You might have been killed and we'd never have known. Can't you imagine how desperate we would have been? We love you, Merry. We deserve more respect than this."

"I know," she said, tears spilling hotly down her face despite her resolve to hold them back. "I also know no amount of remorse can undo my actions. I only want you to understand one thing. Nicolas Craven never hurt me. He has his flaws, as do I, but he never forced me, never frightened me, never misled me about his intentions in any way." Her father's face twisted in protest but she would not let him interrupt. "He was a gentleman. Maybe not by your standards, but by mine."

"He is beneath you," spit her father. "Beneath any decent woman!"

"He is not," Merry said, her emotions calming with her words. "In his way, he's as good a man as you."

Her father didn't know what to say to this. Perhaps her quiet confidence had somehow unsteadied his. The crowd jostled them in the pause, porters pushing carts piled high with baggage, mothers herding children, men in dark suits striding swiftly with folded newspapers under their arms. The sheer Englishness of the scene assailed her. She was home again, though it would never be home quite like before.

Recovering, her father spoke. His words were gruff, reluctant, their brusqueness a mask for his concern. "I'm sorry to ask but I need to be clear on this. He did compromise you, didn't he?"

Merry met his eyes. Whatever the complexity of his emotions, her father's will was strong. If she wasn't careful, she'd put Nic even more in the way of harm. Only a fool—which, admittedly, she had been—would count on Nic's unsuspected title to stay her father's hand. In truth, she'd rather he didn't know who Nic was. A marquis was a person a duke could force into marriage, at least in her father's view of the world. She knew Nic would resist, but she'd brought enough ugliness into his life. If at all possible, she'd shield him from her father's wrath.

"In strictest truth," she said, "it would be fairer to say I compromised him."

Her father opened his mouth, then seemed to think better of asking a question whose answer he might not wish to know. Instead, he offered her his arm. His hold was stiff but steadying.

"Come," he said, "your mother will have more to say to you at home."

Merry's stomach lurched queasily toward her throat. As difficult as this confrontation had been, she knew the next would be even worse.

THE INTERVIEW WITH HER MOTHER WAS NOT PLEASANT, BUT she survived it. Unlike her father's quiet outrage, the duchess's hysteria struck no chord—not because Merry couldn't conceive of reasons for it, but because her mother's concerns seemed more alien than ever. Even before her time with Nic, Merry had cared more about people than position. The measure of a man, or woman, came not from titles or clothes or whether they knew which fork to use. It came from inside, from the soul. Merry knew her own soul was far from spotless, but what shame she felt was for being selfish. The experiences she'd shared with Nic, good and bad, she did not regret.

One regret, though, she could not shake: that she hadn't done more for Cris. As she lay in the bed of her childhood beneath her parents' roof, as she fought to feel like more than a daughter, she found herself dwelling on his dilemma. No doubt this turn of mind was illogical: their situations were more different than the same. Nonetheless, in the short time she'd known Cris, he'd touched her heart. In any case, it was less painful to think of him than of her and Nic.

So she wondered how he was and if he and Nic had come to an understanding. She thought about things she might have said to help: that just because Nic was afraid to care didn't mean that he did not, that even if Nic was indifferent, this didn't rob Cris of worth. Cris would have to work harder, was all, to think as well of himself as he should.

In this, she and Cris were matched; Nic had not been able to love either of them enough.

*   *   *

NIC'S MOTHER WAS IN THE GREENHOUSE STACKING TRAYS of seedlings. She wore a pair of soiled men's riding trousers and an equally soiled pair of boots. He'd forgotten how square her hands were, how strong and practical. Her waist was thicker than he recalled and her hair was definitely grayer. Other than that, she was precisely the same old warhorse.

To his surprise, he found the sight of her strangely dear.

She looked up when he made a quiet noise inside his throat. Her eyes were older, their blue more faded. The pain that flashed across them in that first unguarded instant took him aback. Up till then, he hadn't truly believed his absence hurt her. He knew how far short of her dreams for him he had fallen.

"Good Lord," she said, then hesitated as if she wasn't sure she was seeing true. "Nicolas, is it really you?"

"In the all-too-solid flesh." Though his voice was light, his hands were shaking. She'd always seen every meanness he'd slipped into. And she'd always demanded he try again. When he was young he'd resented her for it. Now he heartily wished he'd learned the lessons sooner.

She nodded, a curt dip of the chin that roused a thousand boyhood memories. "Finally decided to stop punishing me?"

He swallowed a surge of an old, old anger. This was not a rut he wanted to go down. "It was never my intent to punish you."

"Wasn't it? The boy's half convinced I drove you away. Least, that's what he tried to convince himself. I guess boys want to love their fathers no matter what."

Nic rubbed his hands over his face. He reminded himself he didn't come here to fight. He would not let her push him to it.

"Maybe I was angry," he admitted as calmly as he could. "Maybe I left in part to strike back at you. There was more to me than my failings, but that was all you seemed to see. It was hard for me to be around that."

"I only wanted you to live up to your potential."

"I know," he said, "and you're probably the reason I'm not completely pathetic now. But your ideas about my potential are not the same as mine. I'm proud of what I can do with these two hands. I've brought something into the world that wasn't there before. Something good, Mother, not just something that will sell.

"On the other hand"—he paused for a long, deep breath—"you're right about my not fulfilling my responsibilities. I'd like you to help me with that, if you would."

"You're asking me for help."

"Yes. I need to learn to be the marquis."

"Need to?" she repeated.

Nic shoved his hands into his pockets and struggled not to clench them. "You always could strike to the heart of things."

"And you could always evade it." Her knees creaked as she bent to retrieve a glove that lay on the rough slate floor.

"Not this time. I've come to stay, for a while anyway. I brought Cris with me. He's waiting up at the house."

She stared at him, measuring his use of Cris's name. "I imagined it was you he went to when he ran away."

"Oh," he said. He shifted to his second foot. "I hadn't thought . . . But of course the school must have notified you when he went missing. I suppose I should have written you, let you know he was all right."

"I knew better than to expect a letter," she said so blandly his temper rose. If she knew better than to expect a letter, why was she always haranguing him by the post? And what sort of guardian let a fifteen-year-old boy wander off without raising every possible alarm? She hadn't known for certain Cris was with him. He hadn't known himself. Anything might have happened!

But he swallowed all that back. No doubt she knew better than he how well Cris could take care of himself. Which of them had the right of it hardly mattered.

"I shall try to be a better correspondent in the future," he said. "What I'd like now is to take a share in running the estate."

"Just a share?" she said, judgment in the word.

"My share," he clarified. "And don't pretend you really want me to take over. You know damn well you like running this place as you please."

"I run it well," she said, her face going red with anger. "I've sweated myself to the bone to keep Northwick in fighting trim."

He smiled and she huffed at him, but they both knew he'd made his point.

"So." Eyes narrowed, she slapped the gardening glove against her thigh. "You still haven't told me why you 'need' to be the marquis."

Before he even spoke, the blush rolled hot and unstoppable up his face. "There's a woman," he mumbled.

For the first time since she'd seen him, his mother smiled. Her expression conveyed a mixture of gloating and affection. The gloating he expected. The affection he had not seen for quite some time.

Then again, maybe he'd been too defensive to see how much she cared.

"Not just 'a' woman," she crowed. "*A* woman couldn't get you to do all this."

Chapter 20

NO ONE CAME TO SEE HER, NOT EVEN HER BROTHERS' WIVES. Merry had been popular in her way; eccentric, yes, but a companion most people enjoyed. Now she'd become a social leper. Despite her father's efforts to quiet the earl of Hyde, whispers ran like wildfire through the upper strata of society. Merry Vance had run away with a painter and lived like a mistress in his home. She'd traveled with him and slept with him and laughed in the face of every rule that mattered—at least to them.

Merry didn't give a toss for the rules, but the rejection of people she'd thought her friends could not help but wound her.

Two notes arrived, one from Nic's friend Anna and another from Edward Burbrooke's wife. Both were kind but since both had had relationships with gentlemen who spurned her, she didn't much want to see either one. They were too manifestly what she was not: women who held their men.

I chose this, she told herself. *I might not have guessed how hard it would be, but I chose it.*

Crying over the milk she'd spilled would gain her nothing now.

Left to herself, she spent long hours in the family stables, riding the horses, grooming them, soaking up their simple animal code of right and wrong. All she needed there were two strong arms and a will to work. Once the grooms gave up their efforts to stop her, she could not fear she would fall short.

Finally, the second week after her return to London, Isabel Beckett paid her a call. She seemed nervous to be there, but hugged her tight and long. Merry cried a bit, as did her friend. When they saw each others' tears, they laughed and hugged again.

"I can't tell you how sorry I am," Isabel declared. "Andrew was so angry when he found that last letter, he couldn't keep his fury to himself. I don't even know how many people he told. Only your father's influence finally convinced him to stop." Annoyance twisted her pretty face. "He tried to forbid me to see you, but I told him he'd be sleeping in the guest room until he let me. I knew he'd give in. To tell the truth, though, I didn't expect him to hold out so long!"

"Oh, Isabel!" Merry exclaimed, seeing the glitter of pain beneath her friend's outward triumph. Despite Isabel's complaints, Merry knew she liked her stuffy husband. "I'm the one who's sorry. I never meant to come between you and the earl. I should have guessed I might, but I swear I never meant to. Believe me, if you felt you had to avoid me, I'd understand."

"Phooey," said Isabel, with a toss of her sleek blond head, "what sort of friend would I be if I did that?"

A wise one, Merry thought, much too grateful to say the words out loud.

When Ernest joined the trickle of visitors, Merry received her former suitor in the Corinthian-columned magnificence of the green salon—hardly a cozy venue but one that reminded her in no uncertain terms just where she was. Perched on the edge of a carved mahogany chair, poor Ernest looked as if he'd rather have met her in a dungeon. She couldn't help smiling at his chagrin. She was surprisingly happy to see him, almost as happy as she'd been when Isabel came to call.

Friends were worth the world, she thought, especially friends who stood by one when times were hard.

"You look different," he said.

"Do I?" Giving in to the urge to tease him, she smoothed her hair like a skilled coquette. "Perhaps the scandal has lent me an air of glamor."

Ernest wagged his head like a thoughtful bear. "No. You don't look glamorous, you look pretty."

"Pretty, eh?"

"Yes," he said staunchly, then pulled a rueful face. "I suppose whatever that blackguard did to you couldn't have been all bad. Unless"— he cleared his throat and drummed his fingers on his knees—"dare I impute your rosy glow to my presence?"

The words were so awkward, so un-Ernest-like, Merry had to bite her lip against a laugh. "You sound like a boy who's been coached to flatter his elderly maiden aunt."

Ernest flushed to the roots of his flaxen hair. "I meant every word. I'd like to think my being here makes you happy."

"It does," she assured him. "These days my friends are few and far between. If your gallantry didn't inspire my admiration, your bravery certainly would."

Ernest sighed as if her compliment filled him with gloom. He released the grip he'd taken on his knee to place his hand gently over hers. "I have to ask," he said. "Lord knows I've come to accept that you don't love me, but I'd be a heel if I turned away when you needed me most." He patted her fingers as if she were a frightened child. "Merry, won't you agree to be my wife?"

For the space of a breath, she was tempted. Here was the most reliable man she knew. His passion might not be grand but it was steady. She doubted he had the imagination to want a wife who'd offer him more than fondness. She'd have to rein in her spirits, but she'd be accepted again. Forgiven.

Marrying him would, however, be the most abominably selfish thing she'd ever done.

Taking a moment to gather herself, she covered the hand that had covered hers and met his sky-blue gaze.

"Someone will love you," she said, "with all her heart and soul. You're too good and too strong for that not to happen. God willing, you'll feel the same for her. I cannot marry you and rob you of the chance to know that."

"But you need me!"

"I need you to be my friend, not let me ruin your life to fix a mess I made. For heaven's sake, you could kiss your political career goodbye if you married me now."

"Maybe the kind of career my father has in mind, but I've never been one for shaking hands and making speeches. I enjoy the work I do for your father better. Behind the scenes. Hammering down the details."

"But I thought— It was my understanding that Papa would sponsor you for the Commons if we married."

"Yes, and I probably would have gone along if this hadn't happened. Gone along and been miserable. You aren't the only one who's had time to think lately about what kind of life you want to lead, about what kind of person you want to be. My father will simply have to get over his disappointment."

His face bore a harder expression than Merry had ever seen him wear.

"Your father didn't want you to come here today, did he?" she guessed. "He wants you to sever our connection."

Ernest shrugged, his evasion telling her more than words about the state of things with his father. Wistfully, he touched one curl that had slipped free of her coiffure. "Are you certain I can't change your mind?"

"Quite," she said with her fondest smile, "though I cannot express how much your asking means."

Her certainty must have sunken in. He rose, not so much upset as disconcerted. He had braced himself for the sacrifice, and now it was not required.

"Very well," he said, "I shall not ask again. I warn you, though, I take my responsibilities as friend very seriously. In the days to come, you may see more of me than you like."

"Impossible!" she declared, and rose on tiptoe to kiss his cheek.

True to his nature, Ernest bowed stiffly and took his leave. As he shut the wide door behind him, another sound, subtle but unmistakable, caught Merry's suspicious ear: the swoosh of a skirt on a polished parquet floor. Someone had been standing behind the drawing room's second door, the one that led to the shuttered ballroom.

No servant would be there now, not with so little prospect of its use. In any case, the identity of the eavesdropper could not be in doubt.

Apparently, Merry's mother had not given up on saving her from herself.

LAVINIA DIDN'T LET HERSELF THINK AS SHE CLIMBED THE curving stairs. She couldn't let herself think. If she did, she knew her nerve would desert her.

Althorp had lost everything. The match he'd counted on to raise his son's political stock was now a liability. To make matters worse, Ernest had defied him. She should have exulted to see her enemy brought low, but she knew how angry he would be, more than angry enough to lash out at her.

Her hand clenched against the pit of her stomach, sweaty, shaking, her tension a mix of fear and determination. When Althorp heard his son had been here, that he'd offered to save Merry, he would ruin her. He wouldn't care what he himself might pay by bringing the truth to light; he would simply want revenge.

Her arms still bore the bruises of their latest meeting, held before he—and everyone else—discovered what Merry had been up to with Mr. Craven. His anger had terrified her, for it seemed to have no limits. "This is your final chance!" he had roared, though the carriage in which they rode rolled through a public street.

"How can you do this?" she'd pleaded in desperation. "You yourself know the sting of society's censure. What did my daughter and I ever do to you that you would want us to suffer that same pain?"

His fury abruptly faded to cool amusement. "You left me, didn't you?"

"We were married, both of us. Besides, you cannot pretend you truly loved me."

She had never seen eyes so cold and dead. One gloved finger moved to stroke her cheek. "How skilled you are at lying to yourself. What you and I shared was nothing so mundane as love. But I see you've forgotten how you trembled with excitement when I made you crawl to me on your knees, how you moaned when I took you so forcefully you'd be tender inside for days. I could have refined you, Lavinia, could have taken you to heights your blockish husband cannot imagine. What's more, deep in your heart, you know it. You were made for me, though you haven't the courage to admit it." His voice sank to a growl that rasped her nerves. "Even now, if I touched you, I know I'd find you wet."

She gasped, unable to speak or move. It wasn't true. She would not let it be. He was sick and depraved and she was nothing like him!

He smiled as he read the panic in her eyes. "Yes, tell yourself I'm a madman. Then you can deny every thing I say. It does not matter anymore. You are useful, Lavinia, weak and useful. You can help my son to the future he deserves."

"Ernest wouldn't thank you," she dared to say, "if he knew what you'd done on his behalf."

Althorp's brows rose. Though he lounged against the squabs, Lavinia suddenly felt as if she were choking. "Is that a threat?" he said, his tone deceptively soft and casual. "If it is, I warn you, I'll crush you like a grape. Betray me to my son and these past few months will seem like child's play."

"N-no," she stammered. "Never. I wouldn't—"

He silenced her by drawing his hand down the front of her throat. The seat springs creaked as his shadow loomed closer, his mouth, his breath. She had frozen like a mouse before a snake. He nipped her lower lip, then her upper, the sensitive flesh left stinging in his wake. *Yes,* thought something inside her too primal to control. She whimpered as he kissed her roughly, crudely, and again as he tore away.

The kiss had not lasted more than seconds but her skin pulsed wildly from scalp to toe.

It's fear, she told herself. It's only fear.

"Fail me again," he said hoarsely, "and you'll wish you'd never been born."

But she wished that already. She couldn't live with this constant dread: couldn't eat, couldn't sleep. Her clothes, her pride and joy, hung on her like sacks. Her hands were constantly atremble. Worse than the fear, though, was the shame. Look what I've done, she thought. Look what I've done in the name of protecting my position.

She stopped in the upper hall, overcome by a revulsion that nearly made her ill.

She had betrayed a woman's most sacred charge: to love and protect her children. She could see now how wrong she'd been to try to force Merry and Ernest together. Merry's new dignity proved it.

Her daughter had come back from Venice changed. As stubborn as ever, but changed. Inside herself she was quiet, certain of her moorings, as if no matter what challenges lay ahead, she knew that she could face them, that she would be true to her personal sense of right and wrong.

Now Lavinia had to do the same. It was her only hope in all the world. She doubted it could save her reputation or her marriage, but perhaps it could save her soul.

Drawing a breath for courage, she knocked on the door to her husband's study and waited for him to call her in.

When she entered, he sat behind the broad oak desk with the shining red porphyry top. His smile, weary but welcoming, pierced her guilty heart. She'd forgotten how pleased she'd been to win him, not merely because he was a duke, but because he'd been so much a man. No beauty like Merry's painter, her husband's looks had been good and plain—a foil to her own, she'd thought, never dreaming how ugly she could become.

"Lavinia," he said, and pushed a stack of papers to the side: estate business, she imagined, or perhaps even business for the government. Geoffrey had always been good at cultivating alliances, not a subtle man, but respected. If he hadn't been, she doubted Althorp would have wanted their daughter for his son.

I should have gone to him at the start, she thought, newly horrified by her stupidity. He might have hated me, but he had the power to protect us all.

Now he tilted his head in inquiry at her silence.

"I must speak with you," she said.

"Yes?"

She swallowed. "Ernest offered for Merry again. Against his father's wishes."

Geoffrey's face tightened in what might have been disapproval. Whether it was directed at her she didn't know. "From your tone, I assume she refused."

"Yes. But that's not why I'm here." Though her hands were icy, runnels of sweat dripped down her rigid back. She bit her lip, then let the words out in a rush. "Ernest's father is blackmailing me. I—I had an affair with him. Years ago. He threatened to tell you if I didn't make certain Ernest succeeded in his suit. He thought if Merry wed Ernest, you'd throw your influence behind his son's career."

"But I already support his career. He's my secretary, for God's sake. I've given him loads of responsibility. As much as he can handle."

"Althorp wanted more than for Ernest to be someone's right hand. He thinks his son should be prime minister."

The expressions that crossed her husband's face were genuinely strange. Whatever his emotions were, outrage was not among them. He stood slowly, coming around the desk to lean against its front. If Lavinia hadn't known him so well, she'd have said he was stalling.

"Well." He rubbed the length of his bearded jaw. "There's an ambition—though if he expects to chivvy Ernest into it, he doesn't know his son as well as he thinks. May I ask why you decided to tell me now? Or is it because if you don't, you believe Althorp will?"

Lavinia fought the urge to drop her eyes. "Yes," she admitted, "partly. But it's also because I can't live like this anymore. I hurt her, Geoffrey. My own daughter. I spread rumors about her. Made sure everyone knew how difficult she was. I scared off her other suitors to ensure she'd have no one to choose from but Ernest." Her chin trembled at her husband's jerk of shock. "I know it was wrong of me. I can't tell you how dreadfully ashamed I am."

For a long moment, Geoffrey simply stared at her. Then he sighed. "Ah, Lavi, what a pair of fools we've been."

"What do you mean?"

He paused again, his eyes for some reason not just sad but bitterly amused. "I knew about you and Althorp."

Lavinia felt as if the floor had dropped a foot. "You knew?"

"I can even tell you when. It was the year I headed that committee to push funding for the underground through the House of Lords. I thought those tunnels would shape London's future, make her the strongest, fastest city in the world. Looking back, in my obsession to see the legislation pass, I neglected everything else. I took you for granted, love. I simply assumed you'd wait."

"Good Lord," she said, scarcely able to take it in. He'd known. All this time he'd known.

"Yes." He reached to smooth her hair. "When I saw what was happening, I realized I'd misjudged. I don't know what I'd planned to say to you, but you must have broken off the affair almost as soon as I stopped spending that time away. I decided it would be easier if I didn't confront you." He laughed without sound. "I told myself I was doing it to spare your feelings. To be honest, though, my pride didn't want to admit you preferred another man."

"Never!" Lavinia said, catching his hands in hers. She hadn't preferred Althorp. Couldn't. "I was stupid, and perhaps a little lonely, but I never preferred him to you. He wasn't even kind except at first. As soon as he had what he wanted, he let his true nature show."

Her husband squeezed her hands. "I'm sorry, love. You shouldn't have had to go through that alone. In truth, I'd begun to think, lately, the affair might have started up again. I confess I'm relieved to hear it was only blackmail."

Lavinia shuddered. Only blackmail! "I'm afraid he may make good on his threats. Now that Ernest has stood against him, he may decide he has nothing left to lose. He could tell everyone what we did."

"Oh, Lavi, I'm sure he was only bluffing. Say what you like about Althorp, his sense of self-preservation is finely honed."

"But you didn't see how angry he was!"

Geoffrey cupped her face. "He wouldn't want Ernest to know. Me, yes. I think he's always resented the privileges people like us enjoy. But he wouldn't tell the world. He loves that boy. No doubt he's angry Ernest isn't avoiding Merry, but the thought of his son hating him would destroy him."

"I don't know." Lavinia shook her head, remembering Althorp's choler, remembering—despite every desire to forget—his brutal kiss. "Oh, I wish I'd never met him! Most of all, I wish I could undo what I've done to our daughter. If I hadn't pushed her so hard, she might not have run away."

"Hush." Geoffrey moved his fingers to her lips. "Merry made her own choices, but none of that matters now. If she's turned Ernest down, she's truly on her own. She needs us to be strong for her, not to waste energy on 'what if.' "

His gentleness overcame her and she hid her face against his chest. His body was solid, his arms more comforting than any arms she'd known. Whatever twisted feelings she did or did not have for Althorp, when Geoffrey's hold closed around her, she knew she loved the man she'd married with a strength that was almost pain.

"We have to tell Merry," he said, "in case Althorp is as irrational as you say. It wouldn't be fair to let her hear it from someone else. Besides, she deserves to know what you did to run off her suitors. If there's any chance of her finding someone else, she'll need some confidence in her charms."

Lavinia closed her eyes and held tight to the back of his coat, unable to suppress a surge of resentment. She'd said she was sorry. Was it really necessary that she abase herself so completely? It wasn't as if her daughter had been drowning in suitors to begin with. And what if she told her brothers? They'd all feel sorry for Merry then, and they all would hate Lavinia.

"I'm not certain I can face her," she said. "She's going to be very angry."

"I'll help you," he said with a tenderness that shamed her. "Together we'll get through this."

Lavinia didn't see how telling the truth could be anything but awful. For the moment, though, in the soothing shelter of his arms, she let herself believe she would survive.

Chapter 21

THE CARRIAGE SET NIC DOWN AT THE CORNER OF PALL Mall and St. James Square. From there, he strode swiftly through a misty summer rain. Men hurried by him on the pavement, their uniformly black umbrellas bobbing like crows' wings above their heads: clerks and bankers, he suspected, eager to reach their homes. Exhaling softly in relief, he slipped from the bustling stream and up the steps to the duke of Monmouth's club.

His was the largest on the street, two long floors of arched windows with a heavy, garlanded frieze to top them off. Given the grandeur of the place, he wasn't surprised that the Cerberus at the door—a mournful undertaker of a man—was not happy to see Nic's sun-browned, canary-waistcoated, slightly dampened self.

"The duke will see me," he said and handed the man his card.

Nic's tension over the coming meeting was so great he couldn't enjoy the celerity with which he was admitted once the man returned. He buttoned his coat as they climbed the marble stairs. Merry's father didn't need to see his eccentric dress.

Monmouth himself met him at the door to a lofty, book-lined room. Other gentlemen sat inside, reading, smoking, or quietly playing cards. As if to forestall Nic's entry into this sanctum sanctorum, the duke immediately gestured down the hall. "We can speak in the visitor's room," he said, both his voice and manner stiff.

Though he was sorry to see the reaction, Nic couldn't blame him for it. He had, after all, despoiled the man's daughter.

As they entered a dingy parlor, a waiter wheeled in a drinks trolley, then withdrew and closed the door behind him. The furniture, an assortment of chairs and knickknack tables, was clearly cast off from the rest of the club, its cushions worn, its wood marred with cracks and stains. With deliberate rudeness, Monmouth poured himself—and only himself—half a tumbler of whiskey. He carried the drink to the single window and gazed down at the carriage traffic in the street. Sensing he ought to let his host collect his temper, Nic waited for him to speak.

Monmouth swallowed a mouthful of liquor, then turned his head to face his guest. His expression was hard, his eyes keen but unreadable. "I marvel that you have the nerve to come here."

"I would not have," Nic answered, "were it not for the urging of my heart."

"Your heart," Monmouth repeated, his gaze sharpening even more. His glass hung halfway to his mouth, the subtle vibration of the fluid all that showed he was not as calm as he appeared.

That, at least, Nic and he had in common.

"I am in love with your daughter," Nic said. "I would like to ask you for her hand."

Monmouth set his drink on the sill with a quiet click. He was breathing hard, head down, both hands clenched in fists. Nic knew what was coming as soon as he saw the duke inhale.

He did not, however, do anything to evade the explosive punch.

The force with which it connected staggered him. His vision blurred, the pain seeming to spike straight through his brain. Almost immediately, his nose began to bleed.

"Well," he said, handkerchief pressed to the flow, "I see where your sons get their gift for scrapping."

Monmouth seemed shocked by his own behavior, though he did his best to hide it. "I will not apologize for that," he said. "My daughter may be . . . in difficulties at present, but she need not stoop to marrying a painter, no matter if he has claimed the privileges of a spouse."

"No apology required, I assure you. I earned this broken nose, as I'm sure I earned the one I got from your son. What I have not earned is your scorn for the way I make my living. I have not been honest in every aspect of my life but in my art I've always given full measure, as you yourself have cause to know."

"You ruined her!" Monmouth insisted, red springing fresh into his face. "I don't care what she said about it being her idea. You took advantage of my daughter. You're older than she is and should have had more sense. And if you think offering to marry her makes it better, you are mistaken. I'll not have my daughter leg-shackled to some commoner, to a filthy rake with paint under his nails!"

Monmouth's anger filled the air like burning ice but Nic did not shrink from it. He had earned the right to stand as this man's equal, not because of his birth, but because he'd finally proved—to himself if no one else—that he was ready to pick up the mantle the former marquis had dropped. Thanks to his mother's idea of training, Nic's muscles were hardened from manual labor, his fingers stained with ink from hours of slaving over Northwick's books. His heart felt stronger, too, in ways he had not expected. After all these years apart, he and his mother had been strangers, much like he and Cris. Now he thought—with work and patience—they all might end up as friends.

He was richer for that, and more confident. When he answered Monmouth's accusation, he did so with as much dignity as he could, considering he had a square of blood-sopped linen squashed to his nose.

"Most of what you say is true, and promises of reform mean nothing until I prove them. But I believe I can convince your daughter I am in earnest. What's more, I believe she would be happy to let me try."

"People will laugh at her," Monmouth said, though less heatedly than before. "They will say she is desperate if she marries you."

"Most likely," Nic agreed, "though I do not think her a slave to pride. Still, she is a rare woman. She deserves the best, including a titled husband if she cares to have one. That is why I'm going to tell you something I haven't told anyone but Merry in fifteen years. I am not a commoner. I am the seventh marquis of Northwick. For personal reasons, I did not claim the title until now. Sharing it with Merry cannot erase what I have done, but I trust no one will say she has married beneath her."

Monmouth stared at him, every bit as stunned as Nic expected. "She did not tell me," he said once he'd found his voice. "I cannot believe she did not tell me."

Nic could believe it, but having his guess confirmed filled his heart with admiration. "When your daughter and I parted," he said, "she remained in some doubt as to my feelings. I imagine she did not want to see me forced into a marriage she wasn't certain I would welcome."

"Are you saying she loves you, too?"

"I believe that to be the case."

Monmouth blinked. "Well," he said, patently at a loss.

Turning back to the rain-spotted window, he stroked the neatly groomed edges of his beard. He was once again the man Nic had painted: proud but human, wanting to do right but uncertain what that was. After a seemingly endless pause, he offered Nic the drink trolley's bucket of shaved ice.

"Grab a handful," he said gruffly. "That nose is going to swell."

"Thank you," said Nic, relieved to finally be able to tilt his head back.

"She did defend you," Monmouth grudgingly admitted. "Practically swore she held you down and had her way. S'pose it's time we let her make her own decisions, since that's what she's likely to do in any case." He sighed with a resignation only a parent could express. "You may call on us tomorrow. If my daughter wishes to see you, I will not prevent it, but neither will I argue on your behalf."

Nic lowered the ice to thank him, but Monmouth forestalled him with a look, half warning, half amused. "My daughter can be extremely stubborn, Mr. Craven. Convincing her to give you a chance will be up to you."

"A chance is all I ask," said Nic, and left the duke with a formal bow.

Too restless to sleep, Merry tossed in her lightly sheeted bed. Tonight her sisters-in-law had thrown a dinner party at Evelyn's town house, and she'd been the honored guest: an apology, Lissa confessed, for being so slow to show support.

Merry had been touched but also troubled, because they'd invited Ernest, too.

His estrangement from his father was taking an obvious toll. He had circles beneath his eyes and his hair was almost unkempt. Rumor had it Althorp was furious over his son's continued loyalty to Merry—over other disappointments as well, though Ernest could not know that.

The duchess's confession had shocked Merry but, in a sad way, did not surprise her. Maybe her mother did love her. Maybe the tears she'd shed so copiously were a sign of remorse and not just regret that she'd been caught. Whatever the case, Merry suspected she'd always guard her heart against her. Forgiveness might come with time but probably never trust.

At Merry's insistence, her brothers were made privy to the truth on the grounds that they, too, might need to brace themselves for more scandal. Though their mother's tears seemed to weigh more persuasively with them, even they were regarding her with reserve.

Knowing one's mother had had an affair was bound to change a son's opinion.

This was part of the reason she hesitated to share the whole story with Ernest. Despite her mother's pleas not to risk enraging Althorp, her father had left the choice to Merry. "You're the closest to him," he'd said, "and perhaps we've all kept too many secrets. If you think he'll be better off, then he should know." But would Ernest be better off? Would knowing free him from dancing to his father's tune? Althorp probably didn't deserve a son like Ernest, but did Ernest deserve to hate his father? He'd shown some spine already. Maybe that was enough.

Still undecided, she'd found him alone in Evelyn's parlor.

With a grimace for being caught brooding, he set a miniature of Evelyn's wife back on the mantel. "I've never seen my father like this," he said without preamble. "Why can't he respect my choice to support a friend? He flies into a fury one moment, then shuts himself up to drink the next. I swear he's aged ten years in the last two weeks. I've tried to talk to him but he refuses. If I didn't know better, I'd swear he was afraid of me."

Merry stroked his sleeve. "Maybe he is."

Ernest stared at her. "What do you know, Merry? What does everyone know that they aren't telling? Your brothers have been strange to me all night, your mother won't meet my eye, and your father asked if I needed a vacation."

Merry sighed. "I want you to think before you answer. If your father had done something awful, would you truly want to know?"

"Something awful to you?"

"Only indirectly. And what he did, he did for you."

Frowning, he pulled her to sit on the couch. "Tell me," he said, and so she did. The white-lipped self-control with which he listened cut straight to her heart. She apologized for being the one to tell him but he thanked her.

"If I have to hear it," he said, "I'd rather it come from my best friend."

That cut her, too, that he considered her his best friend. She stared at her knotted hands. "What will you do?"

"I don't know. If I tell him I know, he may take it out on your family."

"But you shouldn't have to pretend!"

"My father and I spend a lot of time pretending. This wouldn't be anything new."

A history lay behind those words that she, his supposed best friend, had never guessed was there. This is wrong, she thought. Someone should know and love the whole of who Ernest is. Of course, if by chance he had feelings for her, that someone should not be Merry.

"Talk to Peter," she said in her firmest voice. "He could use some cheering since that opera dancer threw him over. Besides which, he's developed a bit of sense lately. It wouldn't hurt for him to practice it on you."

Ernest smiled. "I shall keep that in mind," he said with a touch of his old resilience.

It wasn't a cure, she thought later as she punched a stubborn pillow beneath her head. It was, however, a sign they'd both stepped onto the long road back.

MERRY HAD FINALLY DROPPED OFF TO SLEEP WHEN A muffled clatter startled her from her doze. Someone was in the sitting room, apparently breaking in. Could Althorp have decided to take a new revenge? Heart in her throat, she rolled out of bed and grabbed a poker from the fireplace, then crept silently to the door. She was just drawing breath to scream when she recognized the figure stumbling up from the broken flowerpots.

Heat flashed between her legs, a searing wave that spread quickly up her breasts. Their tips hardened so swiftly she couldn't restrain a blush.

Absence seemed to have made more than her heart grow fonder.

"Nic!" she gasped as he brushed the remains of a begonia from his thigh.

With a rueful laugh, he helped her light a lamp. "This isn't how I intended to make my reappearance."

He was dressed like a working man in baggy trousers and a sack-like coat. Despite his damp and rumpled state, he looked twice as elegant as any person of her acquaintance.

"What are you doing here?" she asked, her voice husky from more than sleep. "And what happened to your nose?"

He touched the sticking plaster that wrapped the bridge. "Present from your father, who—once he'd vented his displeasure—gave me leave to call on you tomorrow. I, however, discovered I couldn't wait." Before she could ask him what that meant, he kissed her, hard and quick at first, then slanting his mouth to sink hungrily in. After a moment, he broke for air. "Oh, I missed you," he said. "I can't even tell you how much." Again he kissed her and again he cut the foray short. "Tell me you forgive me for not returning sooner."

"Well, since I didn't expect you back at all, I—"

He silenced her with a deep, seductive penetration of his tongue.

"Since I—" she tried again, then lost her train of thought. His fingers had spread around her bottom to lift her against the startling bulge of his erection. Heat alone seemed to have dried the cloth that stretched across it. By contrast, the cover of her nightdress did little to hide her dampness from him.

With a smoky growl, he rotated his hips into the thin foulard. "Missed me, too, I see."

"Yes, but—"

"Sh. Tell me later." His lips opened on her throat and her head dropped back without her will. She couldn't have spoken if she wanted. All she could do was cling. "I know you had to leave me," he said, the words a heated whisper near her ear. "You couldn't have stayed, not the way I was. Not to mention your family must have been mad with worry. Just try to understand I couldn't come back until I was sure I had something to offer."

"What?" she said, breathless and shivering. "What are you offering?"

His next kiss was the sweetest yet, deep but soft, his lips gentling, his hands gentling, his body folding around her like a blanket of love and care. Long before she'd had enough, he released her with a deep, sighing moan that shot straight from her ear to the pulsing tissues between her thighs. Cradling her face in his hands, he gazed at her with concern. "Tell me this first, love. How are you getting on?"

She laughed with what remained of her breath. "Better than I was when I thought a marauder was breaking in."

"I mean, has it been very bad for you?"

"Because I came home a fallen woman?" She smoothed his wet hair back with her fingers, the feel of the silky strands a restorative to her soul. He was here and, for now, everything was well. "I won't deny having shed a few self-pitying tears, but there have been bright spots as well as dark. Isabel has been a rock and Ernest, bless him, actually proposed again."

"Tell me you didn't say yes."

His horror warmed her woman's pride. "Of course I didn't. How could I? Ernest deserves better than a woman who cannot love him with all her heart." Colored by the memory of the talk they'd shared in Evelyn's parlor, this declaration was possibly a bit too passionate. Nic was peering at her, his eyes narrow, as if *he* wanted to be loved with all her heart. She lowered her chin to hide her budding smile, then looked at him through her lashes. "I should warn you that in visiting me you risk your own reputation. I don't know if you've heard, but I'm a terrible influence on everyone I meet."

Nic grinned. "I could have told people that. But you're serious. Oh, Merry, tell me everything."

Suddenly able to see the humor in her predicament, she explained about Althorp's ambitions for Ernest and the lengths to which her mother had gone in order to satisfy his blackmail. Unlike her, Nic was not amused.

"Good Lord," he said. "Your own mother. You must have been devastated."

"Not as much as you might think. I always knew she didn't care for me very deeply. Awful as it sounds, discovering what she'd done freed me not to care for her. Papa has rallied the family round, united front and all, but I have to admit I'm rather enjoying how much my disgrace has embarrassed Mother. Her so-called friends are a bunch of cats. They're reveling in the chance to revenge themselves on her for all the times she lorded it over them. Childish of me, I suppose, but there it is."

"Surely you want to see her punished more than that?"

She pulled up her shoulders in a shrug. "Maybe being who she is is punishment enough. She was fighting to protect things I don't think truly matter. In the process, she lost much of her family's trust. And, to be fair, when I ran away that day at Tatling's, I was just as cowardly. Unfortunately, I'm not convinced she's changed in any lasting way. Perhaps she's incapable. So we smooth out the surface and go on. I can't regret what's happened. If she hadn't done what she did, I'd never have turned to you. I'd have missed out on memories I'll always treasure."

Nic was silent then, his fingers fanning the skin beneath the ruffled sleeves of her thin silk gown. As absent as it was, the caress sent tingles down her arms. She'd forgotten how much he could make her want him.

"I took Cristopher back to Northwick," he said. "We spent the summer learning how to run the estate. Actually, that was for me more than for Cris, but my mother bullied him, too, when she got the chance." He pulled a breath into his lungs and raised his eyes. "I've taken back the title, Merry. I told your father this afternoon. He gave me leave to court you."

Emotions washed through her: awe, happiness, followed by a sober-

ing twinge of doubt. If guilt were his only motivation, she didn't want
this gift. She put up her chin. "I won't be another responsibility."

His expression softened. "You're not a responsibility. You're a
blessing. I changed because I wanted to be worthy of you, but if you
refuse me, I won't go back to what I was. I'm ready for this, love. I
want to give you what I've learned to be."

"You truly want to marry me?"

She could not keep the disbelief from creeping into her tone. He
smiled, the understanding in his eyes threatening to make her cry. He
pressed his hand over his heart. "I'd be deeply honored if you'd marry
me. I love you, Merry, and I admire you. If you agree to have me, I'll
spend my life showing you how much."

"I want to run a stud," she blurted out.

A smile tugged the corners of his mouth. "So long as you mean
with horses, I have no objection."

"I don't believe a woman should sit at home looking pretty. At
least, not a woman like me."

"Have you noticed I'm not objecting?"

She bit her upper lip, then laid her palm across the hand he'd
pressed to his heart. His skin was warm, his fingers long and hard. She
remembered how they could pluck and soothe and feather like angels'
wings. Did she dare believe they could also support her dreams?

Burning with too many wants to name, she leaned toward him,
letting her breasts brush the rain-dampened linen of his coat. Color
washed his cheeks as he felt the subtle rasp of her hardened nipples,
their darkening visible even in the lamplight. Beneath their hands,
his chest began to rise and fall.

"Why don't you show me how much you admire me now?" she
said.

He moaned deep in his chest, then tore off his coat and pulled her
to him. "Oh, God, Merry." He kissed her hair, her cheek, the pulsing
hollow of her throat. "Oh, God, will I show you!"

They fought to remove his clothes, jousling over buttons and peeling chilly, sodden cloth from warm, hair-roughened skin. Her hands
were as greedy as his kiss, skimming over chest and belly, gripping
knotted shoulders and squeezing his clenched behind. The hair that
led silkily from his navel was an arrow whose compulsion she obeyed.
Down to his abdomen, into the cloud of curls. Combing through
them, she found the base of his rigidly swollen sex. His kiss broke on
a gasp.

She smiled up at him, fey and bold. Up she drew her fingers, inch by inch, vein by vein, then down again to wrap him firmly in her hold. She lightened her grip just to feel his flesh resist. He was magnificent: hot and thick, a pulsing, animal thing. Wrapping one finger beneath the rim, she tugged him gently into the air. His shaft seemed to stretch to match her pull. When she swept her thumb across the slippery crown, he jerked as if she'd struck him.

"Do you like that?" she crooned. Her second hand found the fullness of his balls. Carefully, her eyes never leaving his, she compressed them between her fingers and her palm. His breath hissed like a kettle left too long on the fire.

Teasing him was simply too entertaining. She started to sink to her knees to tease him more, but he caught her beneath the arms and pulled her up.

"Bed," he panted, "quick!"

Hardly waiting for her to point, he scooped her up and carried her to her room, peeling off her nightdress as soon as he set her down. He knelt then, his mouth pulling strongly at her breasts, his hands painting beauty into her skin. Her limbs began to tremble as if he'd drugged her. If he had, he'd used a substance that magnified her sensations. She felt every expulsion of ragged breath, every flicker of lash and tongue. When he twisted the tip of her second breast between two knuckles, the resulting spear of feeling was so intense, she had to speak.

"Nic," she whispered, "my legs won't hold me."

He chuckled and lifted her onto the tangled covers of her bed. Climbing up himself, he stretched his muscled length against her side. His erection burned its shape into her hip while his hands poured fire over her curves.

"Let's see," he said, "if I remember how to do this."

Two agile fingers slid between her curls, parting silky, lust-oiled folds. Their pads dipped inside her, leasing, tickling, before finally curling in.

She pressed a fist to her mouth to mute her tortured groan. Centuries seemed to have passed since he'd touched her, millennia of aching need. Her spine arched strongly as he stroked, deeply, slowly, bowing her body off the bed.

"Yes," he said, beginning to shift lower, "I think my memory is coming back."

She felt his smile as he nuzzled her trembling flesh, then his teeth in a teasing nip. He laved her with the tip of his tongue, then settled in to suck the swollen bud. Any worry for his injury was forgotten as feeling rolled through her in rich, intoxicating waves. With one broad hand beneath her bottom, he tilted her hips to press her close.

The pleasure was almost too much to stand. Her body ached and tightened as his fingers worked magically inside her, heightening the effect of his mouth, of the rush of his breath and the cool, wet tickle of his rain-spiked hair. The muscles of his shoulders bunched beneath her hands. His breathing hitched and rasped. He seemed to want this climax as much as she.

"Wait," she said, the longing too huge to keep inside, "let me taste you, too."

He stopped. A shudder swept through him, betraying how much he wanted to comply.

"Turn," she insisted, urging with her hands. "I want us to share this."

He turned until she had him in her reach. With a moan of welcome, she pulled him into her mouth: his heat, his fullness, his musky, throbbing silk. This was what she needed. This was what she'd dreamed of in the night.

They strained together, the position awkward but exciting, a challenge to concentration and control. Sweat rolled down their bodies, and fingers gripped harder than they should. Even that small pinch of pain was arousing. They couldn't control themselves, not completely.

Still fighting the lure of full abandon, Nic gasped out instructions. "Not so far. You'll . . . oh, God, don't make me come, love. Easy now. Slow."

She barely registered what he said. His groans were music, his involuntary twitches of response as stimulating as anything he did to her. She kneaded the muscles of his bottom, then pressed the puckered entry that hid within. He stiffened, violently, inside her mouth and out.

"Merry," he said, a hiss of smoldering sound, "you don't have to—"

But she knew what he wanted. She remembered what he'd done to her in Venice. She pushed, gaining a small but obviously pleasurable insertion. His warning changed to a groan. His spine rolled as if her touch had turned it liquid. She wriggled her finger and he thrust as if he could not restrain his reaction, filling her mouth, filling her being with nothing but the knowledge of his body's joy.

Even with that, with his erection stretched to bursting and his back bowed with desire, he still sent her over the edge before she could drag him with her.

She cried out. The climax was too sharply sweet to hold it in. Nic swore like a sailor, then pulled from her mouth and turned around. The bed creaked at the suddenness of his movement. She heard him curse again with impatience, felt him yank her thighs apart and fumble for his home. As soon as he found it, he thrust, one long, smooth stroke, before her quivers had a chance to fade.

He grunted, feeling her clench, and thrust again even harder.

He was bare inside her, his flesh to hers.

"Feel that?" he said, his nostrils flaring as his hips worked tighter still. "That's you and me, Merry. Nothing but you and me."

But even this failed to satisfy his need. He pushed his torso upward, his arms roped with muscle as he rose. His knees dug into the mattress. His thighs were so hard they might have been made of stone. He was big, his blood drumming against the stretch of her tender sheath. His crown seemed ready to breach her womb.

The sensation was utterly, meltingly delicious, as if his very life were held within her sex. Purring with pleasure, she dragged her palms down his back to press the sweaty dip at the base of his spine. He groaned as if she'd hurt him. She didn't know how to help except to let her legs relax even further to the side.

"Oh, Lord," he said as he slipped a fraction deeper. "That feels so good. I think I'll never move again."

He appeared to mean it. Still dazed from her orgasm, but coiling tighter by the second, she slid her hands around and up his ribs. His heart was thundering, the points of his nipples like little stones beneath her touch. She circled them, then pulled them gently by the lips. He inhaled sharply and breathed her name.

Lit by more than love or lust, his eyes burned in the dimness. She knew what he felt because she felt it, too. His need was raw, deeper than his body, deeper even than his heart, a desperation no one but she could fill. And she would fill it. She'd give him back the trust he was giving her.

"Nic," she said, her voice like brandy in her throat, "everything I am I share with you."

His face twisted with emotion. He didn't even try to hide the glitter of his tears. Her sex tightened in a spasm of pre-orgasmic bliss. He grit his teeth and swelled inside her. His shiver was a thrill that skittered sumptuously down her spine. Slowly, as if they both would shatter at a breath, he drew back through her body's hold.

"You," he said hoarsely, "make me whole."

He slammed into her then with wonderfully brutal force, hitting her high and hard. Two drives, three, his cock a velvet hammer. She thought he'd burst but on he went, working her, working himself inside her. He was completely beyond control, no polished rake but a creature of pure instinct. The cries he uttered were rough and rhythmic. Hungry. Sweat flew between them. Her sex felt deliciously bruised by his naked, pumping shaft. Her heart simply felt beloved.

She would fly, she thought, ready to weep with exhilaration. She would soar into the sun. Helpless to stop, she gripped his arms and came at the bottom blow of a stroke. A heartbeat later he unraveled with a groan, his hips shimmying against hers in quick, deep beats that locked and held as his ecstasy met hers.

He strained there, gushing, shaking, then let his weight sink slowly down.

She scarcely had the strength to wrap him in her arms.

"Very well," she said, panting out the words, "I will marry you."

His laugh rumbled against her breast. "Convinced you, did I?" He rose on his elbow to gaze at her, his cheeks flushed, his eyes shining with love and humor. With a musing smile, he wound one golden curl around his finger.

"I want to ask you something," he said, "and you needn't tell me unless you wish. That night, after Anna's party, that was your first time, wasn't it? You gave me your virginity."

Her fiery blush was all the answer he required.

"Lord," he said, "I'm a cur to be glad but I can't help it."

"You are a cur. Not to mention a dangerous seducer."

His dear, battered face grew serious. "From this day forward, Merry, I'm only seducing you. You gave me a gift that night, and I didn't even know."

She fought not to squirm with embarrassment and delight. "Well," she huffed, "I trust you know it now."

"Yes." He tweaked the turned-up end of her nose. "Now I'm lucky enough to know."

Chapter 22

THE SKIRT TO MERRY'S GOWN WAS ALMOST TOO FULL TO FIT through her dressing room door. She managed it, though, squeezing into the sitting room while the mothers argued over what sort of flowers should decorate her headpiece. Like ghosts of weddings past, their voices trailed into her refuge.

"Orange blossoms," insisted Merry's mother.

"Nothing at all!" boomed the dowager marchioness. "My son isn't marrying some French tart!"

"Don't catch those pearls on the furniture," Ginny called, the only one to notice Merry's escape. The old nurse had been called back for the wedding, though she'd refused Merry's offer of a position in her new home.

In the months since her dismissal, Ginny had enjoyed helping her sister in her Devon tea shop so much she'd decided she really was ready to retire.

Merry smiled at the irony. It seemed even Ginny had profited from this mess.

Careful not to snag her skirt, she lowered herself to the settee by the window. She'd never have guessed a wedding could be this tiring—especially when everyone else was fighting to do the work. The gown itself had proved a challenge to her less-than-stellar tact. In the end, the duchess agreed to let Nic choose the design, but only if Madame sewed it.

The result was lavish beyond her wildest dreams. The overdress was a rich summer green, and the underdress a froth of Venetian lace. The snug, sleeveless bodice was so heavily encrusted with tiny pearls, she felt as if she were wearing armor. More pearls spilled over the skirt in delicate fronds and curls. A princess could have worn this gown or, for that matter, an empress! Instead, it was gracing plain old Merry Vance.

She felt both ridiculous and gorgeous, more of a spectacle than she'd been since posing naked as Godiva. Interestingly enough, her mother had given her Nic's painting—after extracting a promise they'd hang it "privately." Now, arrayed in a dress that nearly outdid that undress, she didn't know whether to laugh hysterically or burst into happy tears at the thought of dragging this beautiful monstrosity down the aisle.

When her mother saw the final fitting, she'd nodded and tapped her chin. "I'll give Craven this," she said. "He knows how to make a woman look her best."

"You should call him Northwick," Merry corrected gently, "or Nic if that feels more natural."

Her mother sniffed. "I'll call him Northwick after he's kept you happy for a year. And I'll call him Nic when he hands me my next grandchild."

She seemed not to realize how surreal such comments were, as if—after all that had happened—Merry should now believe her well-being was her mother's dearest concern. She let the pretense stand for her father's sake but found herself thinking less of her mother's sense with every day.

Nic could not warm to her at all.

Oh, he was polite, even charming, and Lavinia professed to like him, but he saved his true self, his honest self, for the people who really loved her.

To Merry's surprise, Nic proved more than just a ladies' man. After an initial bristly meeting, with various veiled references to his healing nose, all three of her brothers had succumbed to his worldly glamor. When they discovered he was also a good sport, their last resistance gave up the ghost. The possibility of a male-only fishing tramp to Scotland had been thrown out for discussion—after the honeymoon, of course.

"Bah!" Nic's mother had exclaimed. "As if men have the patience to fish well."

Merry had been leery of the dowager marchioness until she saw how determined the woman was to like her. Rough around the edges she might be, and certainly used to running things her own way. All the same, her candor won Merry's respect, along with her still awkward love for her son.

When Merry realized how easily the marchioness would fit in among the rowdy Vances, she did feel a little sorry for her mother.

Not sorry enough, however, to get between the mothers now. That was Isabel's job. Finally forgiven by her husband, thanks to some bargain that made her giggle whenever Merry asked what it was, she was doing diplomatic duty as Merry's matron of honor.

"Wouldn't miss it," she'd declared. "This is absolutely, without question, the most romantic and gossip-worthy match anyone's seen in years. Imagine that Lothario turning out to be a marquis! Half the females in London are kicking themselves with envy."

Merry had to admit to liking that, even if a fair number of those females knew precisely what there was to be envious of. But that was a knowledge she could adjust to. Nic's past was Nic's past. His future was what mattered and he'd entrusted that to her.

Pressing a fist to her burgeoning laugh, Merry tipped her head back and closed her eyes. Thank God her family didn't know the truth about all their guests, Sebastian and Evangeline in particular. They thought this marriage was irregular as it was!

The sound of a hesitant knock brought her neck upright again. Cristopher hovered in the doorway, achingly adult in his formal white tie and tails.

"Hello, love," she said, the endearment easy. "Come keep me company until the madwomen track me down."

He shot a wary look at the dressing room, from which sounds of debate still issued out, then crossed hastily to the cushion she'd cleared her skirt from to make room. Perching on its edge, he pressed his knees together like a nervous debutante. "I need to ask your advice."

"Ask away," she said, airily waving her hand. "Right about now, I'd like to feel old and wise."

He gave her a boyish, quicksilver grin, but quickly sobered. "It's about Nic. I know you and I get on, so I was wondering . . . I don't want to presume, but I was wondering if you think he'd mind if I spent my next holiday from school with you two."

Merry put a hand to her tightening throat. Before she could speak, Nic entered from the hall.

"Why don't you ask me yourself?" he said, his eyes so bright and his voice so rough Merry knew at once what his answer would be.

"You can say no," Cris said quickly. "I know I haven't—well, we haven't lived like family for very long, and you'd only just be married. I'd understand if you thought it an imposition."

By the time he finished stammering, Nic had crossed the room. He cupped the side of his brother's face, then bent and pressed his lips softly to his temple.

"My home is your home," he said, "as much as if you were my son. You don't need to ask. You only need to show up."

"Yes," Merry seconded, holding out her hand. "Visit as often as you like."

"If I visit as often as I like," Cris said, with a grin to match his brother's, "the marchioness might get lonely."

Nic pulled Cris into a bruising hug. "We'll have her visit, too. We'll make room for everyone."

Merry felt as if she were watching him slay the last of his demons. She was so proud she feared she'd burst her stays. Then her eyes welled over and she remembered where she was.

"Oh, look what you've done!" she cried as her sniffles fought with her laughs. Already, she could feel her nose turning pink. "I'm going to walk into that church looking like a rabbit!"

"My," Nic teased, "what a vain, vain creature you've become."

But when he pulled her into his arms and kissed her, she found her looks didn't worry her in the least.